ENDLESS WINTER

Part One

Part Two

Part Three

This is a work of fiction. Names, characters, places and incidents either are the product of imagination or are used fictitiously. Any resemblance to actual persons, living or dead, events or locales, is entirely coincidental.

RELAY PUBLISHING EDITION, NOVEMBER 2021
Copyright © 2021 Relay Publishing Ltd.

All rights reserved. Published in the United Kingdom by Relay Publishing. This book or any portion thereof may not be reproduced or used in any manner whatsoever without the express written permission of the publisher except for the use of brief quotations in a book review.

Riley Miller is a pen name created by Relay Publishing for co-authored Post Apocalyptic projects. Relay Publishing works with incredible teams of writers and editors to collaboratively create the very best stories for our readers.

www.relaypub.com

ABC# ENDLESS WINTER

BLURB

A brutal new Ice Age covers the Earth…

When an experiment to reverse climate change goes disastrously wrong, Jarred and his daughter Hope are forced to head south in search of warmth. This man-made eternal winter shows no signs of stopping, and with temperatures continuing to plummet, fears of a new ice age drive survivors into a panic.

Jarred and Hope don't have the wilderness skills needed to survive this disaster. But when their car spins out of control, they're forced to fend for themselves in the ruthless and unforgiving forest surrounding them. And as they journey through the snow-swept wilderness, they slowly discover they are not alone…

Survivalist Fiona knows how to deal with a harsh winter on her own, but this new world is deadly. She's got a cabin stockpiled, and is all alone until she runs across Benjy, a forest ranger who's ready to help, but has his own reasons for staying with her.

Civilization is crumbling. There's no electricity. The cold is getting worse, and resources are scarce. To survive, Jarred and Hope will have to find allies they can trust, and push themselves harder than they ever imagined.

Because even a moment's weakness in this harsh icy wasteland can mean only one thing.

Freezing to death in the merciless cold…

Exciting news! Endless Winter is better than ever – it was expanded & republished in September 2023!

CONTENTS

PART I

Chapter 1	3
Chapter 2	8
Chapter 3	16
Chapter 4	20
Chapter 5	27
Chapter 6	32
Chapter 7	39
Chapter 8	44
Chapter 9	50
Chapter 10	54
Chapter 11	63
Chapter 12	73
Chapter 13	80
Chapter 14	85
Chapter 15	91
Chapter 16	98
Chapter 17	107
Chapter 18	112
Chapter 19	117
Chapter 20	121
Chapter 21	127
Chapter 22	132
Chapter 23	139
Chapter 24	145
Chapter 25	152
Chapter 26	159
Chapter 27	165
Chapter 28	173
Chapter 29	180
Chapter 30	187
Chapter 31	194
Chapter 32	201
Chapter 33	209
Chapter 34	213
Chapter 35	218

Chapter 36	223
Chapter 37	230
Chapter 38	235
Chapter 39	240
Chapter 40	244
Chapter 41	248
Chapter 42	251
Chapter 43	255

PART II

Chapter 44	261
Chapter 45	267
Chapter 46	272
Chapter 47	280
Chapter 48	289
Chapter 49	300
Chapter 50	306
Chapter 51	314
Chapter 52	326
Chapter 53	335
Chapter 54	349
Chapter 55	360
Chapter 56	367
Chapter 57	374
Chapter 58	382
Chapter 59	393
Chapter 60	397
Chapter 61	410
Chapter 62	416
Chapter 63	422
Chapter 64	434
Chapter 65	443
Chapter 66	447
Chapter 67	452
Chapter 68	457
Chapter 69	468
Chapter 70	475
Chapter 71	481
Chapter 72	486
Chapter 73	491
Chapter 74	494
Chapter 75	498

Chapter 76	502
Chapter 77	506
Chapter 78	509

PART III

Chapter 79	515
Chapter 80	520
Chapter 81	527
Chapter 82	533
Chapter 83	540
Chapter 84	548
Chapter 85	559
Chapter 86	569
Chapter 87	575
Chapter 88	585
Chapter 89	601
Chapter 90	608
Chapter 91	615
Chapter 92	624
Chapter 93	638
Chapter 94	650
Chapter 95	660
Chapter 96	668
Chapter 97	674
Chapter 98	682
Chapter 99	689
Chapter 100	698
Chapter 101	703
Chapter 102	711
Chapter 103	716
Chapter 104	724
Chapter 105	736
Chapter 106	740
Chapter 107	747
Chapter 108	753
Chapter 109	763
Chapter 110	767
Chapter 111	770

End of Endless Winter	773
Thank you!	775
About Riley	777
About Grace Hamilton	779
Sneak Peek: Escaping Anarchy	781
Also by Riley	789

PART I

PART I

1

"If you keep harassing the ladies, I'm going to make a big pot of mutton curry out of you," Fiona said, glaring at the big Saanen ram, who was poised for another charge.

Ramses was an enormous and rascally creature, a creamy white color with an impressive long beard dangling from his chin. Over two hundred pounds, he used his weight to his advantage. He was, in a word, a bully, and Fiona Scarborough had had just about enough of him. She was currently squatting in a corner of the paddock fence, a box of tools beside her, but she didn't dare take her eyes off the goat.

The goat paddock was a crude affair, made with her own hands, but a particularly fierce wind, bitterly cold, had swept through early in the morning and pulled three boards off. The crossbeam was still intact, so nailing them back in place should have been an easy job. All she needed to do was drive a few nails in, but she didn't dare turn her back on the bully. At that very moment, Ramses had his big yellow eyes fixed on her, and he kept raising and lowering his head, as if daring her to look away.

"Okay, if you want to pick on me, that's fine," Fiona said, waving her hammer at him. "Just leave the ladies alone. Better yet, don't bother anyone."

The female milking goats were mostly clustered together in the far corner, protecting each other from the unpredictable male. Ramses finally turned away and wandered off, snorting and shaking his head, as if he'd grown bored of Fiona.

Now's my chance, she thought, pulling a nail out of the front pocket of her overalls. She'd leaned one of the fallen boards back in place, but she pressed it against the crossbeam now and set the tip of the nail in place.

And then she heard it. The *clank* and *clack* of goat horns banging together. With a sigh, she lowered the nail and looked over her shoulder. Ramses had made his way to the ladies in the corner, and he was currently locking horns with Delilah, the oldest of the females. She didn't really want to engage with him and kept trying to back away, but the other goats were in the way.

Finally, Ramses backed up, lowered his head, and butted her. Fiona tossed the hammer down, rose, and went to him. As she approached, he gave her an ornery look over his shoulder, as if daring her to get in the way.

"Leave the ladies alone, I said." Fiona grabbed his collar and pulled him away. "Just stand in your corner and behave."

She walked him toward the feed trough, where a small bit of food remained.

"Look at all that food. Clean your plate," she said, petting him on the neck.

He bent down, as if to do just that, and Fiona went back to her corner. Still, she could hear him banging the edge of the trough with his horns. He was definitely in a mood, worse than usual, and the timing was especially annoying. As Fiona returned to the broken section of the paddock, another blast of cold air swept through the paddock and knocked the loose boards over. It pulled some of Fiona's long auburn hair out of her loose ponytail, and she angrily swept it back into place as she knelt beside the broken fence.

The paddock was in almost constant need of repairs, like the rest of her homestead, which kept her busy most days. With fifteen acres of old buildings that she'd patched numerous times, she was proud of what she'd achieved. She had a home, a barn, a garage, a workshop, a small greenhouse, and additional storage buildings, and somehow she'd kept them all together.

She set one of the fallen boards back in place, securing it with a few nails. By the time she picked up the second board, the chill began to bite the exposed skin of her face.

Ramses had ceased messing with the trough and was tromping about again, looking for trouble. Soon enough, he was back in the corner messing with the milking goats. Fiona finished nailing the second board in place before turning to him. She'd been thinking about butchering him for a while now, though at his size, it would be a lot of meat to deal with. Still, she wondered if he was more trouble than he was worth. Technically, he was a cart-puller, but he hadn't pulled a cart in years.

He locked horns with one of the females again.

"Ramses, get away from there, you creep," she shouted, reaching for the third and final board. "They don't like you."

Ramses bleated.

"Yeah, I know you heard me," Fiona said, positioning a nail.

She had just started to swing the hammer when she heard him coming. Hooves clawing the ground. With less than a second to react, she tried to rise, but Ramses slammed into her. He drove his curled horns into her back and shoved her against the fence, instantly knocking the wind out of her. She fell to one side, sprawling on the ground as she dropped the hammer and nail in the process. She rolled onto her side and planted her hand against the ground, but Ramses was already backing up, lowering his head for a second charge. Though she tried to pick herself up, she could tell she wasn't going to make it. This time, Ramses would hit her in the side, and she was already struggling to catch her breath.

"Mutton curry..." she managed to say.

And then she heard sharp, furious barking as Smoke came racing toward the paddock. Smoke was an Australian Cattle Dog, his fur mostly black with flecks of white. A stocky dog, he had boundless energy. Fiona couldn't keep him contained. She'd let him run wild around the fifteen-acre property while she worked on the paddock, but apparently, he'd finally sensed Ramses's orneriness.

The dog leapt over the low paddock fence. Ramses paused mid-charge and hastily backed away, as Smoke proceeded to herd him into a corner all by himself, dashing from side to side to cut off any escape.

With a groan, Fiona picked herself up, using the fence for support. She could feel a big spot on her lower back that would no doubt turn into a giant bruise in another day or two. Satisfied, Smoke finally padded over to her side, and she petted his head. Ramses stayed in his corner for the time being, clearly intimidated.

"Thanks, good boy," Fiona said. She bent down to retrieve the hammer and felt a twinge of pain. It was enough to turn annoyance into full-blown anger. She tossed the hammer into the toolbox, then kicked the side of the toolbox for good measure. Smoke was giving her an eager look, and she scratched him behind the ears.

"I sure wish you had opposable thumbs," she said. "I could really use the help. You have no idea."

She made her way over to Ramses and grabbed his collar, dragging him out of the corner. He came only reluctantly, keeping his eyes on Smoke, who circled around behind him. She led the goat across the paddock and into the side door on the barn.

"I've had quite enough of you for one day," she muttered, pulling him toward one of the box stalls inside the dim, dusty building. She got him into the stall and closed and latched the gate. As she backed away, Ramses strode toward the gate and gave her his weird-eyed look, as if to say, *What did I do?*

Yes, there were moments when Fiona found herself close to despair. It didn't take much, really. Getting headbutted by Ramses was quite enough. She'd worked so hard, day after day, for so long, yet it felt like she was just barely keeping the homestead together. Smoke was a great dog, and a good companion, but it wasn't the same as having other people around.

I don't want other people around, she reminded herself. *I don't need them.*

As she made her way back out of the barn, she stuck her hands under the front flap of her overalls. She was wearing leather work gloves, but they weren't made for warmth. Already, her fingers ached from the cold. Still, she made her way back to the fence and forced herself to finish the repairs, even as the cold sank deeper and deeper into her flesh.

When the final board was in place, she shut and latched the toolbox. Then she took her gloves off and vigorously rubbed her hands together. When that didn't help, she cupped her hands around her mouth and blew on them. Through all of this, Smoke kept watch, as if he thought Ramses might somehow sneak up behind them.

God, I hate the cold so much, she thought, grabbing the handle of the big toolbox and picking it up. *What is the deal with this awful weather? It's not even close to winter yet.*

She had just stood up again when she saw the first snowflakes falling. They were fat and heavy, falling from a pure white sky. It shocked her. She looked out beyond the gate and saw her house sitting on its low hilltop, with the tall trees at the edge of the property providing a dark green backdrop.

She had created a path of crude steps leading from the barn to the porch, which made for easy passage as she began her early morning chores. Now she was envisioning it all covered in snow.

"It's September," she muttered. "How can it already be snowing?"

No sense thinking about it now. If she'd learned anything during her time on the homestead, it was to deal first with the known before worrying about the unknown. This was the only way to keep from being overwhelmed. As she started toward the house, lugging the toolbox with her, Smoke pawed at her side. She bent to scratch his ears.

"We'll be okay, boy," she said. "We made it this far, didn't we? No matter what the season throws at us, we'll deal with it, you and me."

Smoke barked, ran a circle around her, and headed up the hill.

2

The cold took a few seconds to register. By the time Jarred had opened the mailbox on his porch and fished out a thick stack of coupons and junk mail, he'd started to shiver. He was flipping through the stack of mail, trying to find a single thing worth keeping, when he realized just how deep the cold went. He blew his breath out and saw it puff out in great, white billows.

"What is the deal with the weather?" he mumbled, leaning out from under the porch roof to gaze at the sky.

He lived on an unremarkable street in Bloomfield, a neighborhood right in the heart of Pittsburgh, where the houses were built extremely close together and most of them looked identical: two stories, red-brown brick, covered porches facing the street, phone and power lines strung all over the place. The slate-gray sky overhead made it seem especially bleak this afternoon, muting all color and perfectly complementing the unusual cold.

Jarred's cell phone began to shudder and dance in the pocket of his jacket, drawing his attention away from the cloudy sky. He took the stack of junk mail to the trash can in a corner of the porch and dumped it all inside, then drew the cell phone out of his pocket to answer it as he headed back inside the house.

"Hey there, man, how's life treating you?" a familiar voice said. "It's not a bad time to chat, is it? I know you're busy these days."

"Don't worry about it, Atul," he replied. He stepped into the small foyer and pulled the door shut behind him. "How's life treating you?"

Despite being two stories, the house was cramped: it had three bedrooms upstairs and a kitchen, living room, and den downstairs. It was a narrow building with narrow doors and small windows. Paula was scrubbing the countertops in the kitchen, and he waved a hello to her. Paying for a maid was an indulgence, an extra expense he couldn't really afford, but he had little choice. Either he hired someone to keep the place clean, or the mess would soon get out of hand. Even a modest house was more than he and his daughter could handle by themselves, especially with their busy schedules.

"Life is treating me okay," Atul said, on the other end of the line. "For now. Hey, you build any sentient robots in the shed out back lately?"

"No, I leave that sort of thing to my daughter," he replied. "She's working on a project right now, in fact."

He could hear Hope in the den now, and he made his way through the living room to check on her.

"So there's nothing unusual going on in your life?" Atul asked. "At work?"

"Hey, man, you're the one who works for NOAA," Jarred said. "You're the one with all of the interesting stories."

"You've got me there," Atul said. "And actually, I've got the story to end all stories today."

"Oh, yeah?"

Jarred poked his head into the den. Hope was sitting at a folding worktable, a circuit board propped at an angle in front of her. A few larger pieces of her robot, including the treads for its wheeled feet, were set nearby. However, Hope wasn't paying the least attention to them at the moment. Instead, she was flipping through pages on her cell phone. Jarred snapped his fingers to get her attention.

"Hope, what are you doing?" he said. "Get back to work on your project. Your submission is due on Monday."

"Well, you were talking so loud on the phone, I kind of got distracted," she said.

"I'll keep it down," he said. "Just get back to work. It looks like you have a long way to go."

"I know what I'm doing." She sighed and set her phone on the table, then reached to the laptop in the corner that had her project blueprint. Adjusting the screen, she said, "It's hard to focus. That's all."

As Jarred raised his phone again, he realized his friend on the other end was already speaking. "Sorry about that, Atul," he said, walking back across the living room. "I have to lower the volume here. My daughter is currently building a robot to take over the world."

"Oh, nice," Atul said. "A mad scientist in the making."

"That's right."

Jarred intended to step back onto the porch, but as soon as he opened the front door, frigid air blasted into the house. Shivering, he shut the door again and took a seat on an old wicker chair in the foyer.

"Boy, what is going on with this early winter?" he said. "It's never been this cold in September before, not that I can remember."

"That's a question a whole lot of people are asking right now," Atul replied. "I don't suppose you've been keeping an eye on these weather patterns lately, have you?"

"No, not really," he said, pinching the collar of his jacket shut. "That's *your* area of study, my friend. Unless I've got snow piling up in the driveway, I don't often think about the weather. Why? Is there a problem?"

Atul grunted softly, as he did when he was weighing his words. Jarred perked up. Honestly, he hadn't given the unusual cold much thought. He knew global warming contributed to more extreme weather patterns, but that wasn't news to anyone.

"Jarred, I know you're really busy these days with the kid and house and work, but this is something you need to be keeping an eye on," Atul said. "We're not just talking about a bit of cold weather in September, okay? The northern states and Canada are already seeing record snowfall. Some small town up in the northeast corner of British Columbia was literally buried in snow two days ago."

"Literally?" Jarred said with a laugh. That word was one of his pet peeves. It was almost never used appropriately.

"Yes, literally. A hundred residents had to be rescued," Atul continued. "They were trapped in their homes. They've evacuated the entire town."

"Yeah, that would suck," Jarred agreed, "but surely that's not outside of the realm of possibility when you live in northeast British Columbia. It's like living on the flood plains of the Mississippi River, right? You should expect that hundred-year flood to wash through town eventually."

The maid came into the foyer then. She started to say something, then realized he was on the phone and used hand signals instead: a spin of the finger to mean she was done, rubbing thumb and forefinger together to mean she wanted to get paid, and pointing toward the door to mean she wanted to go home. Jarred rose from the chair and dug his wallet out of his back pocket. As Atul began to speak, he fished a wad of bills out of the big pocket one-handed and passed them to her.

As she took the money, she glanced at his upper lip. It was a quick dart of her eye but he didn't fail to notice. It happened often enough that he was sensitive to it. Most people probably didn't even realize they did it. His cleft palate scar was mild, in his opinion, but it still drew people's eyes anyway, even people who had known him for years.

"*Me voy*," Paula said, making a little sweeping gesture. "I go."

"Yes, yes, thank you, Paula," Jarred replied, cutting off his friend again. "Be careful out there this weekend. We may be in for some snow. See you next week."

"Snow? *En septiembre*? No, no." Paula wagged her finger at him, grabbed her purse from the coat rack, and headed outside.

Just opening the door for a few seconds was enough to chill his bones, as the bitter wind blew into the foyer, stirred the coats on the coat rack, and whistled through the kitchen.

"It's so *cold*," Hope shouted from the den. "Why do people keep opening the door?"

"I'll get a fire going," Jarred called back, pushing the front door shut. "Just get to work!"

"I'm trying, Dad. It's hard to concentrate."

"If you stop texting, it'll help," he said.

To this, she made a little *bleh* sound.

"Boy, you really have to juggle it all, don't you?" Atul said, chuckling on the other end of the line. "Paying the maid, making your kid do her homework, and entertaining your old college buddy all at the same time. Ah, the life of a single dad!"

Clearly, he meant it as a lighthearted comment, even a compliment, but it made Jarred uncomfortable. He didn't exactly like being reminded that he was a single parent.

"Level with me, Atul," he replied, changing the subject. "How bad is this weather going to be? What do you know?"

"I know an early winter, especially a bad one, will wreak havoc on those parts of the country that don't have the infrastructure to deal with it," Atul said. "Especially areas with a lot of food production."

"Okay, but even areas that produce food have occasional early winters, don't they?" he asked.

"Right now, there is real concern that this early winter might also be a very long-lasting winter," he continued. "Jarred, I'm trying not to freak you out here, but I want you to hear what I'm saying. This is the real reason I called. Imagine months and months of harsh winter and blizzard-like conditions hitting areas so far south that they've never experienced a real snowfall before. Imagine the beginning of an irrevocable change in the weather pattern."

That did it. Jarred felt a rush of deep anxiety. He wasn't even sure how to respond to this. *Irrevocable?* Did Atul really mean that? As the word sank in, he felt his phone vibrate against his ear, and he pulled it away for a second. In an act of exquisite timing, a weather alert had popped up on his phone.

"Urgent – Winter Weather Message," it read. "Winter storm warning in effect from 4 pm today until Sunday or longer. Significant amounts of snow are expected or occurring. Total accumulations of six to twelve inches or more and ice accumulation of half an inch or more across the Northeast. Travel very dangerous. Reduced visibility. Strong winds are likely."

Jarred swiped it away and put the phone back against his ear, where Atul had paused, as if waiting for his reaction. From the den, his daughter had grown quiet again, and he wondered if she had overheard him. Maybe that was a bad thing. Best not to worry her, especially when she had a big school project to complete. To put a bit more distance between them, he made his way into the kitchen and headed to the utility room at the back of the house.

"This seems like it came completely out of nowhere," Jarred said. "Blizzard conditions in places that have never seen snow before? What is the cause of this? Did anyone see it coming?"

"I'm—" Atul stopped speaking abruptly. Jarred heard footsteps on a hard floor, then a door being shut. When Atul spoke again, he was quiet, hard to hear. "Okay, I'm about to tell you some things I'm not supposed to tell you."

It was such a strange, unexpected turn in the conversation that Jarred wasn't sure how to respond. Things he wasn't supposed to say about the weather? "Atul, hey, don't get yourself in trouble here."

"No, it's fine. It'll all come out sooner or later," Atul replied. "They're trying to keep a lid on it, but this is too big. The weather…" He paused again, and Jarred heard a door on the other end open and close again. "My friend, this weather is a man-made event. This isn't simply some hundred-year winter. We caused this."

"We caused it? Is it a global warming thing?" Jarred asked.

"Yes and no," Atul replied. "More intentional. What I'm about to say is top secret, so…"

"Maybe you shouldn't tell me then," Jarred said.

"It doesn't matter now," Atul said. "You need to know, so you can make the right decisions for you and your daughter. There was an experiment, okay? They were trying to rebuild the glaciers to stop the oceans from rising. It was a long shot, and kind of a crazy idea that some wealthy benefactors decided to fund. A desperation move because of erosion on the coastlines. A brilliant team of climate experts from different countries came up with a way to generate clouds."

"Generate clouds?"

"That's right. The process is a bit too complicated to go into, but the goal was to create a low-lying carbon dioxide cloud by pumping CO_2 into a large area to generate localized conditions for the glaciers to re-form. It was meant to be contained, but it spiraled out of control. What they intended as a small-scale trial quickly became a cascade of changing weather patterns, and now they can't stop it."

Atul had been speaking at a feverish pace, and he paused for a moment to catch his breath. As Jarred wrapped his head around what his friend was saying, he began to tremble—both from the cold and from fear. Atul had a few very high-level connections, especially among government scientists, so if such an experiment had indeed been conducted, he was one who would know about it.

"Where are you at right now?" Jarred asked. "Is it safe for you to talk?"

"I'm…it doesn't matter," Atul replied. "Don't worry about that. Listen to me. We set this thing in motion, and we have no idea how to stop it. There are too many clouds and no way to dissolve them effectively. It looks like we've rebuilt the glaciers, but at the cost of creating an artificial super-long winter."

"What am I supposed to do?" Jarred asked. "Where do we go?"

"Make some plans, man, because it's going to be *real* bad in your area. Real bad. Honestly, if it were me, I'd head way down south for a while and wait to see how things develop. Rent a hotel room on the Gulf Coast, where you'll have clear roads and access to food and water, but that's..." Atul paused again, then said, "Hey, I gotta go, my friend. Be safe."

And with that, the call ended abruptly. Jarred pulled the phone away from his ear and stared at the screen. His old college buddy was sometimes quirky, but he'd never been a liar. He was one of the smartest guys Jarred had ever known, and level-headed too. Not much got to him.

Jarred briefly considered calling him back, then he thought better of it. If he'd had to leave abruptly, he had his reasons. Jarred slid the phone back into his jacket pocket and began to pace from the utility room through the kitchen to the foyer and back, avoiding the den. Finally, after the fifth pass through the house, he went into the living room and picked up his tablet from the end table. He unlocked it and opened a weather app, scrolling to the live radar. Clouds, clouds, and more clouds covered half of the United States and all of Canada. The same winter weather warning was bolded in red along the top of the screen. He set the tablet down again.

Make some plans. Head way down south for a while.

"How's it going in there?" he asked his daughter.

"Fine. I'm working on it," she replied.

He went to the den door. Hope was currently wiring the control board to the robotic wheels, a soldering iron heating on its stand beside her. She glanced up, gave him a confused look, and returned to her work.

"Is everything okay?" she asked.

"What do you mean?"

"That seemed like a weird phone call," she said. "You sounded nervous."

"I think we're going to take a little trip," he said. "We'll load up the car, head down south, and find a nice, warm place to spend a few days."

"What? Now? But I have to work..." She trailed off, her gaze going to the window across from her table. Jarred followed her gaze and saw it: fat snowflakes falling in the backyard, already coming down hard.

It's started.

3

As Fiona stood at the top of the hill, watching the enormous snowflakes fall, she felt a moment of near panic. *No.* It was the wrong time of year. She had so many growing crops that needed to be harvested. As if sensing her anxiety, Smoke began to run circles around her, then he darted toward the front door and paused to wait for her.

"I know what you want," Fiona said. "You want to curl up beside me on the couch in front of a warm fire. Not today, boy. We're in real trouble today."

As soon as she opened the door, he ran inside, dashed across the living room, and hopped up onto the couch. But Fiona stepped past him. It wouldn't take long for the snow to accumulate. There was so much food at stake! Zucchini, squash, potatoes, melons, tomatoes, beans, carrots, and more. She needed to cover all of it.

Moving fast, she emptied her linen closet of blankets, leaving only the blankets on the beds. She stacked them all up on a handcart, added some nylon rope and wooden tent stakes. Then she pushed the cart out of the house, bumping and thumping down the porch steps, and hurried toward the half acre beyond the paddock where she grew her food.

She was halfway down the hill when Smoke came running after her again, barking in obvious confusion.

"It's a good thing I don't throw anything away," she said to the dog. "All of these filthy old blankets will come in useful."

The snow was falling in great billowing gusts so that she could scarcely see the far side of her property. In that moment, her general annoyance began to deepen into something more serious. Maybe this winter storm was going to be far worse than she'd expected. Just a few days of freezing temperatures and blanketing snowfall could prove catastrophic.

"No, no, Fiona," she muttered. "You're getting carried away. You can survive a single snowfall. Come on."

Still, as she went to work covering her crops, taking it row by row, she couldn't help but worry about what this single snowstorm would mean for the rest of the season.

"No way I'll be able to plant the fall garlic," she muttered.

Smoke had followed her into the garden, but he was standing at the end of the row. She had messed up his routine, and he was clearly not pleased. Fiona managed to cover the zucchini, squash, and potatoes before she ran out of blankets. Half the rows were still uncovered. Rather than trudging back up to the house to loot her linen closet again, she scrounged up a few filthy old horse blankets from the barn, a large plastic tarp from the main storage building, and even an ancient bit of sailcloth left by the former landowner.

Using these, she was able to cover the melons and tomatoes, but the beans and carrots were still uncovered. Even so, as she stepped back and analyzed her handiwork, she saw blankets with holes, frayed edges, wind blowing underneath. She'd spent the better part of an hour on this little project, and now she realized it may have been futile.

Smoke padded up to her then and hopped up, putting his paws against her leg, as if to say, *Can we please go back to the house now?* Fiona was sorely tempted to throw in the towel, but she couldn't do it. If she lost her crops, she'd be ruined.

"What do I do? What do I do?" she whispered. She knew the answer to the question, but she was dreading it.

With a deep sigh, she went to the storage building and grabbed a large crate, a trowel, and a pair of gardening gloves, setting them on the handcart. Then, starting with the carrots and beans in the farthest row of the garden, she began to harvest her crops. She'd hoped to get a few more weeks of the growing season. A lot of stuff was underdeveloped, but it couldn't be helped. Smoke finally whimpered and padded off alone.

"Sorry, boy, I know I'm breaking routine here," she called after him. He looked back briefly but kept going past the barn and up the hill.

Harvesting her garden would normally have taken a full weekend, but she worked at a furious pace now. No easy task. Still, if she'd learned anything during her years alone on the homestead, she knew how to push past discomfort and pain when work needed to be done.

After another hour or so, she took the crate, filled to overflowing with beans, tomatoes, and carrots, into the greenhouse. The greenhouse was where she started her seeds in the winter to prepare for spring planting. At the moment, there were a number of pepper plants growing there, set in small pots on a table in the middle of the room. She'd splurged on an expensive gas-powered heating system, which she could run on low and at least keep the indoor plants from freezing.

She set the crate in the middle of the room and covered it with one of the blankets. As she turned to leave, she looked at the whiteness all around her beyond the greenhouse windows. What was this freakish weather? A few flakes wouldn't have been a big deal, but where had this snowstorm come from? Such a thing was unprecedented.

You're not going to save the crops.

"Well, if you just stand here and mope, it's only going to get worse," she told herself, grabbing the handles of the handcart and pushing it back to the door.

Even if it was futile, she had to try. That's how she'd always operated. So she went back to the storage building, found another empty crate, and returned to the garden.

The crate was only about halfway full when she headed back to the greenhouse. By then, she was shivering violently, and her fingers were going numb. She took a moment to rub some warmth back into her hands before unloading the crate. She looked down at the two crates full of harvested vegetables and saw the harsh winter ahead of her. It wasn't enough. She wouldn't make it through the next six months, nor would the animals, with this small amount of food.

Something must have caused this weather, she thought, as she tucked the second crate beside the first. *A freakish cold front. Global warming. Something.*

She would survive. What other choice did she have? Grabbing the handcart, she started out of the greenhouse again. Across the way, she saw the milking goats all clustered together by the closed barn door, desperately trying to get some warmth from each other. Delilah, Ramses's number one target, had a little pile of snow right on top of her head, stuck between her ears.

When the goats noticed Fiona looking, a few of them bleated at her pitifully.

"I'm sorry, ladies," she called back, pushing the handcart toward the storage building. "You'll just have to wait a little longer. Crops come first. If we don't save the food, we don't eat."

4

As it turned out, a lot of people had the same idea as Jarred: get out of town before the worst of the winter weather hit the area. He found I-79 jam-packed all the way out of town, a situation that only became worse as the heavy snowfall created near whiteout conditions. He'd loaded up his little Toyota RAV4 as hastily as possible, tossing together some clothes, toiletries, and a few snacks. Hope had also brought the pieces of her robotics projects in a cardboard box, along with some school books. She'd made it very clear that she wasn't happy about the sudden trip, especially with a looming project deadline.

As Jarred drove through heavy traffic, trying to follow the tire tracks of the vehicle directly ahead of him, she spent the first few minutes sulking in silence in the back seat, her cell phone clutched in her hand but neglected for the time being.

"Yeah, this is definitely weird," she said suddenly, as if she'd been having a long conversation in her head. "I don't know why we're running away from a snowstorm. We live in Pittsburgh. We get snowstorms. So there's a freak early storm. What's the big deal?"

"We're just heading down south for a little while," Jarred replied. "Consider it an impromptu vacation. We'll enjoy the sun and wait for the worst of the storm to pass. No big deal."

"Well, if we're heading south, we might as well go all the way to Florida," Hope said. "Since I probably won't finish my project now, we might as well go to Disney World and waste time properly. Can we afford that?"

"We'll find a nice hotel somewhere warm," he replied. "You can work on your project there."

"You sound afraid."

Jarred considered his response. "I'm just concerned about the weather report," he said, finally.

"And whatever your friend on the phone told you."

"Well…yes, Atul works for the National Oceanic and Atmospheric Administration," Jarred said, "so he knows about the weather. That's how I know it's going to be a bad storm. Don't worry, you'll get your project finished."

Hope looked at him intently in the rearview mirror, eyes narrowed. "I'm supposed to get my work done in a hotel room? It's going to be so cramped. I won't have room for all of my stuff, and the Wi-Fi will probably be super slow. This doesn't add up, Dad, this whole *impromptu* vacation. It's just snow!"

At thirteen years old, she was at a particularly willful age. Jarred knew her surliness was a veneer, though he wasn't quite sure how to get her to talk about her real feelings. Perhaps the grief was closer to the surface than she let on.

"I'm sorry, sweetheart," he said. "This blizzard is supposed to be really bad and last a long time. I'd rather not get stuck at the house. Don't worry. We'll find a nice hotel with a great restaurant, and we'll make the most of it."

"Can we afford that?" she asked again.

Not really, he thought. That was the true answer. They lived practically from paycheck to paycheck. His professor's salary wasn't enough, and the meager sum they'd gotten from the life insurance policy was mostly gone now. Still, for now, he could make it work. He had enough on his credit cards to last for a while.

"We're fine," he said, after a moment.

His delay made her suspicious, and her eyes narrowed further, becoming slits. She clearly knew there was more he wasn't telling her, but she didn't ask. Indeed, many things went unsaid between them these days. Jarred felt responsible for that, but he also had no idea how to change it.

"Hey, if you really want to go to Disney World, I'll see what I can do," he said. "Maybe we can work our way down there eventually. It's a long drive."

"I was kidding," she said.

Ahead, he spotted a sign for the exit ramp onto I-70, and he started trying to change lanes. He tried to give plenty of room for the other vehicles on the road, but a big Chevy Caprice still honked at him. Once he turned onto I-70, the traffic opened up a bit, and he was able to pick up some speed.

Hope fell into a sullen silence for a long time, leaning against her door and staring out the window. In moments like these, she looked a lot like her mother—same brown eyes, same slightly frizzy hair, same prominent cheekbones. Somehow, that made the loss even worse, but he tried to put this out of his mind as he focused on the road ahead.

In truth, he had no idea where he was going. Atul had recommended the Gulf Coast, but Jarred didn't want to drive that far. Maybe he would drive until he saw sunshine again, until the unyielding white sky was no longer visible on the horizon.

"Do I really have to sit in the back seat the entire trip?" Hope said, after a while.

"I told you, you're not quite big enough for the front seat," he replied. "You're safer back there. Trust me."

"I read the airbag safety rules on the visor, Dad," she replied. "It says twelve and under can't ride up front, but I'm thirteen. Riding in the back makes me car sick."

"You're still kind of small for your age," he said. "I'm sorry, Hope. I just think it's safer if you ride in the back. Give it another year and then we'll see."

She unleashed a record-breaking long sigh and pressed her cheek to the window, but she said no more about it. Hope hated being treated like a child. He knew that. She wanted so desperately to be grown up, and sometimes he bent the rules to accommodate her. But when her safety was involved, he couldn't help being a stickler.

His cell phone was lying on the passenger seat beside him, and he was sorely tempted to pick it up and check the weather again. The snowfall seemed to be getting more intense. He was headed toward the West Virginia panhandle. Was it possible they were headed *into* the storm instead of away from it? He could see it accumulating on the highway ahead of them, and he was growing more and more concerned.

As they entered the hilly countryside near the West Virginia border, the road only got worse. At one point, he saw a nice black Audi fishtailing wildly about a quarter of a mile ahead of him. The driver finally managed to get it under control, but then he slowed down and pulled onto the shoulder. Jarred was tempted to do the same, if only so he could check his phone, but he didn't want Hope to realize what he was doing and worry.

"Whoa, look at that guy," Hope said, a bit later.

She'd turned around in her seat to look at something through the rear window. When Jarred checked his mirror, he saw a Silverado about a hundred yards back that had lost traction. It was slowly turning clockwise, still headed in the same direction. Suddenly, it veered off the road, regained traction, swung wildly to the other side, then hit a guardrail.

"Tell me you've got your seat belt on," he said.

"Of course, I do," she replied.

The Silverado driver finally brought the vehicle to a stop on the shoulder, but the damage was done. Jarred could see that the front right corner was crushed, shattered plastic from the front cowling all over the road.

We should have left the house sooner, he thought. *Spent too much time packing. We can buy clothes on the road somewhere.*

Atul's words kept playing in his mind. Jarred still didn't want to believe it. Maybe it was just the worst-case scenario, and the current storm was just a fluke, a brief consequence of a failed experiment that would soon blow itself out. Years from now, they would call each other and laugh about it. "Hey, Atul, remember that time you told me weather patterns had been changed forever, and we were going to have a winter that lasted for years? Ha ha! That was a good one."

Snow was blowing in at an angle now, stirred up by occasional fierce gusts. Each time the wind picked up, he felt it push the car, trying to force him into the left lane. The snow was beginning to pile up fast between the lanes and on the shoulder. Some cars had pulled over, as if to wait it out. He saw their brake lights shining through the white haze.

"Where are all the snowplows?" Hope said, rubbing the condensation off her window with the sleeve of her puffy coat.

"Probably on their way right now," he replied. "The snow hit with little warning, so I'm sure they're scrambling."

Ahead, he saw brake lights shining at an angle, and as they got closer he realized it was a Subaru that had gone into a ditch. He could see their tracks fishtailing for a bit before veering off to the right.

Poor guy, he thought.

He was through the West Virginia panhandle and into Ohio, somewhere between Bridgeport and St. Clairsville, when he felt his back tires slip. The snow itself wasn't the biggest problem, but the initial precipitation had laid down a layer of ice beneath it. He'd lost traction a few times along the way, but this felt worse. It was as if the road beneath him turned to liquid. It began as a wobble, and he managed not to overreact. He let off the gas just a little bit and held the steering wheel steady.

"Dad?" Hope said.

"It's okay. I've got it."

The front wheels lost traction then. Suddenly, the rumbling of the road was gone, and they seemed to be gliding. He turned the steering wheel just a little bit to the left, but the wheels ignored him. Then he turned to the right, but it seemed like the steering column had just entirely disconnected from the wheels. Suddenly, he had no control over the direction of the vehicle, and it was slowly drifting into the left lane. He tapped the brakes, hoping that if they slowed down, he might regain traction, but it only made things worse. The back end of the car swung to the left, redirecting them toward the shoulder.

"Dad, what are you doing?" Hope cried. "You're making it worse!"

He couldn't answer her. He was making constant small corrections with the steering wheel, but it was futile. Finally, he let his foot off the gas. When he did this, the front right tire somehow regained traction. He felt it catch, a vibration moving up through the vehicle. And then they were spinning, the car turning a complete circle while still flying down the road. Hope whimpered in the back seat. When he glanced in the rearview mirror, he saw her hunkered down with her hands over her head.

In a last desperate bid to gain control, he hit the accelerator just as they turned back around to face west. In doing so, the car stopped spinning, but the back end swung the other way, and the car slid sideways. They went across the shoulder, the rumble strip giving a brief bark.

Helpless! Can't stop it, he thought, a white-hot panic filling his mind.

And then the RAV4 went into the ditch, bouncing on rough ground, plowing through a snow drift, and finally coming to a jarring stop against the steep slope on the other side of the ditch. The airbag went off with a pop, slamming into Jarred's face. It was a bit like getting punched, and he saw stars and felt a burst of pain in his nose. Hope screamed, bouncing against the side impact bags.

The engine died then, and suddenly a dreadful stillness and quiet descended. In that moment, slumped against the steering wheel, the deflated airbag lying across his lap like a blanket, Jarred felt like he was dreaming. It wasn't real. His whole face throbbed, the pain centered around his nose.

Rubbing his eyes, he leaned back in his seat. The windshield in front of him was cracked a thousand times in an intricate spiderweb pattern, and steam poured out from under the folded hood. He saw the ground right in front of him, a slope that had pushed the whole front end of the vehicle about four inches into itself.

And still the relentless snow continued to fall, fat flakes landing on the cracked windshield as if to mock them.

5

Rubbing her frigid hands together, Fiona felt defeated. The last two rows of her garden were now covered in half an inch of snow, and she'd had to give up harvesting the crops. It was just too cold and the snow too relentless. The squash was too undergrown, so they were mostly a loss, some of the potatoes and tomatoes as well. That was a lot of food killed by the cold.

She peered through a narrow gap in the barn door, endlessly rubbing her hands together in a vain effort to warm them up, and watched as her homestead slowly disappeared under a layer of fallen snow.

"All my hard work," she muttered. "What was it for?"

All the blankets she'd spent an hour spreading over the crops and staking down, only to uncover them and then re-stake them, had been turned into humps of snow. Months of work planting and tending the crops only to have a freak snowstorm ruin it all. She could scarcely wrap her head around all of the wasted time and effort.

Shaking her head, she turned away. The goats, at least, were all safely penned now. She saw many of them staring at her from the shadows of the barn. She went to the nearest stall, where Delilah, the oldest milking goat, was lazily chewing and staring at her. Fiona petted her, though the goat quickly turned her head away. She didn't enjoy a lot of attention unless she was being fed or milked.

The animals can't stay in here for long, she thought. *It's too cold. If the snow doesn't end soon, I'll have to figure out some way to keep them warm. Could I move them into the greenhouse like I've done in the past? I'm afraid Ramses would tear the place apart. His behavior has gotten worse lately. Where else then? The house?*

She didn't have an easy answer, but she was going to have to figure it out soon. Fiona left the barn and began calling for Smoke. She'd lost track of him at some point, and the dog had given up on her. As she called for him, she felt a rare pang of loneliness, like a sudden heaviness catching right between her heart and stomach.

Maybe if I'd taken the time to develop a few casual acquaintances in town, I could ring them up now and ask for help, she thought.

Well, no sense whining about things she didn't really want to change. Smoke appeared through the white haze then, racing between the storage building and the greenhouse to reach her.

Having people in your life just causes a whole set of other problems, she reminded herself. *You know that all too well, Fiona. You came out here to live alone, and you've enjoyed it. Don't let one bad season take that from you.*

Smoke raced to the barn door, circled Fiona, and barked.

"Okay, I know. I know," she said. "We're finally going back to the house. Come on."

She trudged back to the house, circling around the paddock and heading up the snow-covered hill. Impatient, Smoke kept running ahead to the porch, then coming back to her, as if encouraging her to pick up the pace. She finally made it to the porch, and she stomped off her boots before heading inside.

"The zucchini is hardy," she said, thinking out loud. "It can survive, as long as the storm passes quickly." She stripped off her coat and slung it onto the coat rack. "We can live off zucchini all season if we have to, can't we, Smoke?"

She couldn't settle her racing mind. Fiona was a problem-solver by nature, and this was the biggest problem she'd encountered since coming to the homestead. A blizzard in September. Impossible. She forced herself to go to the fireplace and sit down on the hearth.

"It'll be gone in the morning," she said, stacking logs. "We'll wake up, and the sun will be shining through the windows, and all the snow will be melted. Right?"

She turned and looked at her dog, but he was staring at her impatiently. Fiona found herself sinking into a dark place, and she wasn't sure how to pull herself out of it. Everything had been so carefully planned and prepared. She'd made repairs to buildings, to the fence, planted plenty of crops, tended them carefully, day after day, week after week, and Mother Nature had decided to just sweep in with her giant frozen paw and smash all of those preparations to bits. It didn't seem fair.

Still, Fiona wasn't one to roll over and admit defeat, even in the face of historic bad weather. She got the fire going, stoked it until it was burning steady, then rose.

"You sit here and melt," she told Smoke.

He didn't need to be told. The dog was curled up on the end of the couch close to the fireplace, his head resting on his paws. Fiona headed into the kitchen at the back of the house. It was a quaint space, rustic, with pots and pans hanging from a row of hooks over the sink, an old wood-burning stove in the corner, and an antique cherrywood table beside the back window. She had a small icebox rather than a refrigerator—a deliberate choice to live a more rustic life.

She opened a cupboard near the icebox and reached onto the top shelf, fishing around until she found her big planner book in the back. Taking it down, she grabbed a pencil from a drawer, and sat down at the kitchen table. She flipped through pages, heading back through time until she reached the previous year's harvest. According to her notes, she'd sold ten sacks of potatoes then, along with a selection of other crops.

"Ten sacks of potatoes," she said with a sigh, thinking of the paltry selection of undeveloped potatoes sitting in the crate in the greenhouse. "I'll be lucky to fill an old sock with what I've got this year."

According to her records, she'd also sold quite a bit of goat milk soap and a few dozen eggs. Unfortunately, Delilah hadn't dropped a kid this summer. Apparently, Ramses had been a complete failure in the goat romance department. That meant the milk reserves were much smaller than Fiona had hoped they'd be. She flipped back another page. She'd also hauled some furniture into town and sold five items for good money. That had paid to replenish her stores of grains, spices, and water filters.

And would she have anything to sell this year? Anything at all? She slammed the planner shut and pushed it away from her angrily.

"No, I'm not going to let a snowstorm defeat me," she said, smacking her hands on the tabletop. "Even if the whole season is awful, I'm not going to sit here and let everything waste away."

She rose and headed into the nearest guest room. Despite its designation, she hadn't had an actual guest stay there in years. The full-size bed in the corner, with its nice blue quilt, was mostly used for laundry storage. At that very moment, big stacks of clothes covered most of the bed: dirties on the left, clean on the right. She'd gotten to the point where she rarely bothered to fold and put them away. She just worked her way through the clean pile until she was forced to wash them.

The largest furniture in the room, however, was the bureau and matching wardrobe set against the far wall. She'd worked hard on them, and they were mostly finished. She hadn't intended to sell them. Their absence would make the room look empty. Still, if it came down to it, she could fetch some good money for them. She made a mental note of it and headed to the next room.

Between the master bedroom and guest room, she had a third smaller room that was mostly used for storage. Shelves were crowded with tools and scrap parts. A sagging twin mattress and box spring, left by the previous homeowners, were propped against the wall, but they were so dusty and dirty, she didn't think she could get anything for them. However, she did have three handmade piano benches stacked neatly in the center of the room. Surely someone was in the market for a nice new piano bench.

"Make more furniture," she told herself. "Even if you have to freeze out there in the workshop in that mountain of snow, make more. You can't count on the crops *or* the animals."

Indeed, she'd relied on them too much over the years, and now she was paying the price for it. Maybe Mother Nature was just trying to teach her a lesson. *Diversify your income streams, or I'll bury you alive.* Is that what she was saying?

"Point taken, ma'am," Fiona muttered.

6

For the first couple of minutes, Jarred just sat there, watching steam rising from beneath the folded hood. The moment he'd gone sliding off the road, his brain had switched into a fuguelike state, everything happening as if in a dream beyond his control. Nothing felt real except for the dull, throbbing pain in his face.

The world beyond their little car seemed inordinately quiet and muffled. It had all happened so quickly that he could scarcely comprehend how he'd managed to lose control. Finally, he heard some soft animal noise, and he looked over his shoulder. It was Hope. In the dreamlike aftermath of the wreck, he'd forgotten about almost everything, even his daughter. Seeing her now dragged him back to reality. She was leaning back in her seat, holding her forehead in her hands, teeth bared.

"Are you okay?" he asked, feeling the sting of guilt. If she'd been injured by his own failed driving, he would never forgive himself.

"I'm fine," she replied, her voice strained. "I hit the side air bag and then I hit the headrest in front of me."

"You're not bleeding, are you?"

"I don't think so."

She lowered her hand to show him her forehead. She had a small red mark that he thought might eventually turn into a bruise, but otherwise, she was uninjured. She brushed tears out of her eyes and shook her frizzy hair off her face.

As the strange sense of detachment passed, he realized his whole body was trembling, his nerves raw and electric. From somewhere outside, he heard another vehicle slipping and sliding on the slick highway. Suddenly, it occurred to him that they were still in danger. What if a vehicle ran off the road and hit them? He turned to look through the rear window, but it was angled upward just enough that he couldn't see cars on the road.

"Stay in here," he said. "Keep your seatbelt on."

"What are you going to do?" Hope asked, rubbing the red spot on her forehead. "You can't go out there, Dad. You'll get hit! Cars are sliding all over the place! Let's call a tow truck or something."

"I'm not sure if a tow truck will be able to get to us," he replied. "Anyway, I need to check things out first. Hang on."

He opened his door, and a strong wind blasted into the vehicle, carrying fat snowflakes with it. Jarred was wearing his best winter coat, a padded, down jacket with a faux-fur-lined hood. He pulled the hood up now, then grabbed his sunglasses off the visor and slipped them over his eyes. Then he stepped outside into the bitter cold, bracing himself against the door. The wind immediately swept his hood back, and he had to grab it and pull it over his head again.

The back end of the RAV4 was a few feet from the shoulder. Visibility was quickly diminishing, and he could only see maybe a quarter of a mile down the road, where a pair of headlights shone diagonally across the southbound lanes, as if another vehicle had slid off the road.

"Dad, that wind is super *cold*," Hope called up from the back seat.

"Sorry about that." He stepped to one side and shouldered the door shut.

This is bad, he thought. *How long would I have to walk to reach a gas station?*

He pulled out his phone and opened the map. It took a few seconds for the map to appear, and he had to tilt the phone to one side to keep the screen clear. Finally, he saw the little arrow representing their vehicle, long stretches of interstate to the east and west. As luck would have it, they were between towns, with a couple miles of nothing in either direction.

"Damn," he muttered, shoving the phone in his jacket pocket. "I should have crashed back in town."

As he turned to examine the vehicle, he saw the front left tire. It was flat. The headlights were smashed, the bumper pushed in, the grill smashed, but he thought it was possible that the engine was still intact, despite the steam pouring from the radiator. However, as he walked around the vehicle, he saw that the front right wheel was bent outward, not just flat but pushed out of position.

It's done, he realized. *We're not going anywhere in this.*

He heard a door opening and closing, and when he turned back, he realized Hope was standing there, zipping up her pink padded coat all the way to the top to cover her mouth. Then she pulled the hood up and turned so she wasn't facing into the wind.

"I told you to stay in the car," he said.

"I don't want to just sit there by myself," she replied. "It's kind of creepy."

He considered fighting her on this issue. She was just a little too close to the shoulder of the road. Plus, the wind was brutal.

"Okay, well," he said with a sigh. "Don't get too close to the road. Remember what you said about cars sliding all over the place?"

As Hope stepped away from the shoulder, she turned and looked back the way they'd come, clutching the bottom of her hood shut to keep the wind out.

"Dad, what about that other car back there?" she said, pointing at the headlights in the distance.

He stooped down to inspect the right tire, but it looked even worse up close. Towing it out of the ditch was going to be a trick.

"Dad?"

Glancing over his shoulder, he saw his daughter gazing back toward the other car.

"Shouldn't we go and check on those people?" she said, pointing. "They're stuck like us. What if they're hurt?"

"I'm not sure we can do much to help them," he said. Indeed, the hazy beams filtering through the snow-thick wind made him even more anxious.

"It looks like their car is still running," she said. "The lights are on. Maybe it's warm inside. We can sit with them while we wait for a tow truck."

Her last argument finally got to him. At least Hope would be able to sit inside a warm car, assuming these strangers were somewhat friendly. Jarred knew that approaching strangers was a bit like tossing dice: sometimes you rolled snake eyes and wound up approaching a weirdo.

"Okay, fine," he said. "Let's go check on them. Stay behind me, but stick close. If another car comes spinning out of control down the interstate, be ready to jump out of the way."

"I will," she replied.

He went to the back hatch. Popping it open, he saw their suitcase pressed up against the back of the seats, along with Hope's robotics parts in a cardboard box. The box was smashed, and some of the parts had spilled out. He reached past these to a mesh pouch to one side and dug out a small plastic first aid kit, tucking it under his arm.

When he turned to leave, he saw Hope staring at the smashed box.

"Well, there goes my project," she said with a scowl. "I can't start over."

"Somehow, I don't think that's going to matter," he replied, shutting the back hatch. "The chances of you having school on Monday are pretty close to zero." When her scowl turned to a sad frown, he added, "I'm sorry, Hope. After the snow lets up, we'll tow the car out and get your robot parts. I'm sure they're still mostly in decent shape."

Judging by the look on her face, she didn't believe it. Jarred waved her on and started back down the highway, walking on the far side of the ditch along the tree line. He'd gone maybe ten yards when a large "dualie" pickup truck emerged from the haze, kicking up a wave of snow and slush with its back tires. Jarred turned and hunkered down as the wave sloshed over him, then he resumed his march.

"Why don't people drive safer?" Hope said from behind him. "They can see other cars off in the ditch. Why doesn't that make them slow down and be more cautious?"

Jarred couldn't help but take it as a bit of an indictment. Indeed, he now wished he'd been creeping along at about twenty miles an hour. His beloved RAV4 wouldn't be stuck in a ditch if he'd gone a lot slower. He trudged on and slowly approached the other car. It turned out to be the large black Subaru—a Forester, he thought—but it was in worse shape than Jarred's vehicle. As best he could tell, it had spun off into the ditch and hit the far slope on its back right panel. That whole side of the car was smashed in, the windows shattered, but the windshield had cracked as well, and despite the headlights being on, the engine didn't sound like it was running.

And then he realized the driver's door was wide open, and no one was inside the vehicle. He drew close just to be sure, looking in through the broken passenger window. The keys were still in the ignition, but no one was there.

"Did they get flung out of the car in the wreck?" Hope said, coming up beside him.

"I doubt it," he replied. "I think they left. Hopefully they got a ride and didn't try to walk."

As he looked along the side of the car, he realized both tires on the right were flat.

"What do we do now?" Hope asked.

He slid in behind the steering wheel and grabbed the ignition.

"If the engine still works, we might at least get some heat," he said. However, when he turned the ignition, the vehicle did nothing. It was dead.

"Okay, forget about that idea," he muttered, climbing back out of the car.

He briefly considered their options, even as the bitter wind sank deeper into his body. The Subaru's shattered windows were facing into the wind, which meant snow was quickly being blown onto the seat.

"I'm afraid we'll have to go back to our own car and try to call for help," he said.

He looked at his daughter. Her face was mostly hidden deep inside her hood, but he saw the glint of anxious brown eyes peering back at him.

"This sucks," she said, after a second. "We should've just stayed home. I'd be done with my project by now, and we'd be warm."

"Maybe you're right," he replied, gesturing for her to start back toward the RAV4.

I've always trusted Atul. I trust his advice. But I'm not sure why I didn't tell Hope the whole story. I guess the panic in his voice got to me. I just want her to feel safe.

She shook her head, turned, and trudged back down the shoulder, following their footprints. As Jarred went after her, he dug his cell phone out of his pocket, dialed 911, and thrust the phone deep into his hood. As soon as it started to ring, he had the notion that it would just continue, unanswered, as all the stranded drivers flooded the system. However, on the third ring, he heard a click and then a woman's voice.

"911. What is your emergency?" Under the circumstances, she had a soothing voice.

"Ah, thank God you picked up," he replied, shouting to be heard over the wind. "We're on Interstate 70, a few miles west of Bridgeport. We went off the road, and our car's in a ditch. Can you send help?"

"Sir, how many people were in the vehicle?" she asked.

"Just me and my daughter," he replied.

"Are either of you injured?"

Jarred reached up with his free hand and touched his nose. It was still somewhat tender to the touch. "Not seriously, no," he said, "but the car is totaled."

"Okay, sir," she replied. "We're dealing with a lot of stranded people right now because of the storm, so we've had to prioritize calls. There are a lot of badly hurt people out there. Give me your license plate number and the nearest mile marker, and we'll get to you when we can."

As he approached the RAV4, he read the license plate to her. However, he didn't see a mile marker in their vicinity.

"Ma'am, we're between towns, not yet to St. Clairsville," he said. "It's just trees on either side of the highway here. I don't see a mile marker or any other street signs."

"I understand that, sir," she said. "Someone will be there eventually, but it's going to take quite a while. Please remain in your vehicle and try to stay warm. What is your name?"

"Jarred," he said. "Jarred White. My daughter's name is Hope."

"Okay, Mr. White," the operator said. "Stay safe. Someone will be along eventually."

"Got it."

The call ended, and he shoved the phone back into his pocket. Hope was already back at their vehicle, fumbling at the front passenger door handle. She finally got it open and flopped inside, dragging herself onto the seat. Jarred shut the door in passing and went around to the driver's door.

"They're never going to send help," Hope said, as he slid in behind the steering wheel. "Because we're not injured. You should've lied and told them I was bleeding to death."

"It's fine," he said, trying to sound like he meant it. All residual warmth from the car's heater was gone now, and as he shut the door, he felt only the deep, aching cold. Still, he didn't want Hope to know how troubled he was by their situation, so he said, "We just have to wait a little while. They'll get to us in due time. Maybe we can just chat."

She was sitting with her arms crossed and her head down, and he tried to pretend like he didn't notice her rolling her eyes at his suggestion.

7

His every attempt at conversation failed. Clearly, Hope wasn't in the mood to have a nice chat. She was huddled in her seat, her hands shoved deep in the pockets of her jacket, brooding in the shadows of her hood. Jarred stared through the cracked windshield. Snow was quickly piling up in the folds of the bent hood, creating a drift that crept up the windshield as minutes turned into an hour, then crept toward a second hour.

The distant headlights were still winking through the white haze behind them, but otherwise, he didn't see any other vehicles. Perhaps they'd shut down the highway. If so, it would be a historic event.

"This is taking forever," Hope said. "No one's coming, Dad. They probably forgot about us."

"There are a lot of other stranded drivers to deal with," he said, "but they'll get to us eventually."

He pulled the phone out of his pocket again. At least he had almost a full battery. Jarred wasn't the best at keeping his phone charged, so that was a stroke of luck. He opened the map to take another look at his location. As he'd told the operator, they were smack dab in the middle of nowhere, stuck almost equidistant between the two nearest towns.

"Do you suppose the guy back there in that Subaru got out of his car and tried to walk to town?" Hope asked.

"If so, he's probably sitting in a warm diner by now, sipping hot coffee," Jarred replied.

Hope turned and glared at him. He laughed uncomfortably. Atul's words were ringing in his head. *Imagine the beginning of an irrevocable change in the weather pattern.* Irrevocable. What did he have to use that word? Watching snow pile up on the hood, that word carried a terrible gravity now. Jarred felt a deep, sinking dread and turned his attention to the GPS app on his phone.

"I'm sorry," he said to his daughter. "I got panicky and tried to beat the snow. Maybe we should've stayed put."

"I don't know why you got scared of snow," she said. "We've been through snow and ice storms and all kinds of stuff, and we never tried to run away from them like this. All the kids on our block are probably laughing at us."

"I didn't tell anyone we were leaving," he said. "Just Atul. Not even Paula knows we're gone."

"So she's going to show up tomorrow to clean and no one will be home," Hope said.

"We'll be home by tomorrow," Jarred said. "One way or another. Trust me."

Zooming in on the map, he realized there was a small town maybe a mile to the southwest on a side road.

"Glencole," he said.

Hope just looked at him, a flat and unhappy expression on her face. Boy, his daughter's gaze could cut through glass when she was in a bad mood.

"It's the nearest town," he said. "Not too far from here. Looks like they've got a nice convenience store. Glencole Stop."

"Is there a café or something there?" Hope asked. "I'm hungry."

"Possibly," he said. He looked through the side window and saw the snowy highway fading into the whiteness. Even in these conditions, a mile wasn't that far. Was it? "Is it the craziest thing in the world to suggest we walk there?"

"We're just going to leave all of our stuff?" she said, giving him an incredulous look.

"No, we'll take the stuff with us," he said. "The suitcase, at least. What do you say?"

"Aren't we supposed to wait here for someone to rescue us?" she said.

"Wouldn't you rather wait inside a nice, warm convenience store?" he said. "It's only about a mile. We can hike a mile through the snow." When she continued to stare at him, eyes narrowed in a way that suggested she didn't trust his judgment, he added, "Hey, if there's a café, I'll buy you a cheeseburger and fries. How does that sound?"

"Cheeseburger and fries sound pretty good," she said. "Walking there down the highway doesn't."

"It's only a mile," he said. "One measly mile. We can do it. I'll pull the big suitcase with our clothes."

Hope pulled out her cell phone. "What was this town called again?"

"Glencole," he replied.

She opened the map and scrolled south on the interstate. "Dad, Glencole is not actually on the highway, you know. It's down on some kind of country road." She held up the phone to show him.

"Yeah, I know," he said. "It's down a side road."

"Well, the point is, we don't have to walk down the highway. If we cut through the woods, it'll be safer, and it looks like we'd get there a lot faster." She pointed at the tree line on the other side of the highway.

"I don't think that would be safer," he said. "We could easily get lost. Plus, if rescue finally does come along, they'll spot us walking on the side of the highway, at least until we turn off. Maybe they'll give us a ride. In the woods, we'd be all alone."

Hope sighed and jammed the phone back in her pocket. "Fine. Whatever you think. But you owe me a cheeseburger and fries. Don't forget it."

"I won't. Come on. We can do this. One mile."

He opened his door again, pushing it against the wind, and climbed out of the car. As he trudged toward the back of the vehicle, he had a moment of paralyzing self-doubt. He opened the back hatch and opened their big suitcase. Rooting through the pockets, he found a pair of gloves and handed them to Hope, who quickly pulled them on. Then he found scarves, knit caps, and a pair of gloves for himself.

"I hope the gas station has hot chocolate, too," Hope said. "That sounds really good right now."

"Yes, it does," he replied, stuffing the first aid kit into the suitcase. "Personally, I'd prefer a big cup of black coffee, but I'll get you a hot chocolate. Come on. We can do this, Hope. It's not that far."

She gave him another one of her skeptical scowls. Jarred gave her a double thumbs-up that had absolutely no effect, then he pulled the suitcase out of the back of the RAV4.

"See, it's a good thing you signed up for cross-country this year," he said. "After training to run that 5K, a little winter stroll should be no big deal."

"We ran in warm weather," she reminded him, "not in a blizzard."

"Yeah, but you've built up your endurance," he said. "You can handle this. We both can. And, hey, it'll be worth it."

"If you say so." She shrugged.

It was the best he was going to get out of her. Extending the handle of the suitcase, he attempted to drag it behind him as he stepped away from the vehicle. The small plastic wheels on the bottom did little to help. Hope fell in beside him, her arms crossed so that her hands were stuck into her armpits.

Even with all the clouds and snow cover, he could tell by the changing light that the sun was going down. It was edging toward evening. The last thing he wanted to do was walk in the darkness. Still, it was only a mile. Only a mile! He told himself this over and over as he dragged the suitcase behind him.

8

When it was snowing like this, Benjy Hartman's little ranger station seemed more cramped than ever. At the moment, it felt like the walls were closing in on him, and he began walking aimless circles. A single room, little bigger than a studio apartment, it contained a kitchen, dining room, bed, and work area all in the same unwalled space. It was also stuffy and old and smelled bad. Benjy had mostly gotten used to the smell of the decades-old cabin, but sometimes, especially when he was walking aimlessly around the place, he would catch an odd whiff of it.

His work area was little more than a slab table with a single folding chair, most of the space on top consumed by stacks of books and reports, with an outdated computer in the corner beside the radio. However, the window above the work area offered a broad view overlooking the river. Normally, even on a cloudy day, he could see the river and numerous islands, as well as the far bank. In fact, the view from that window was just about the only perk of the job.

At the moment, the snowstorm was coming in so strong, blowing in practically sideways, that he could barely see the water's edge. A pot of coffee was percolating on the counter beside the stove, and he heard the occasional hiss breaking through the ceaseless howling wind. Finally, he stopped, grabbed his big ceramic cup with the Ohio Burgee on it, and poured himself a cup of coffee. He added his usual ridiculous amount of sugar and stirred it, but in his restlessness, he splashed quite a bit onto the counter. He wiped it with a filthy rag, tossed the rag back onto the counter, and turned.

"Oh, God, am I going to have to call in?" he muttered. "I don't want to have to call in. Come on, man. What's the deal with this snow?"

Sipping his coffee—it was lip-blisteringly hot, but he didn't mind—he strolled back across the small space, stepping around the kitchen table to approach the big window above his computer. Being closer to the window didn't really improve the view.

At first, he thought to check the weather on his computer, so he rifled through some papers on his makeshift desk. He cast aside a report book, folded maps, and a photograph of his favorite person—a woman in her early forties with auburn hair, hazel eyes, freckles across her cheeks and the bridge of her nose—with the initials *FS* written in Sharpie. He kept going until he found the laminated sheet that had the radio frequencies on it.

"I can't believe I have to call for help," he muttered. If there was anything he despised, it was radioing his station manager for advice. In fact, he hated it so much that he'd never memorized the appropriate numbers. "He's going to be so smug about this."

He flipped on the radio, sat down at the desk, and set the receiver close to him. Static crackled from the single speaker.

Don't let him know you're stressed out, he thought. *Don't give him the satisfaction.*

He pressed the talk button and leaned in close to the receiver. "Control Station, this is Station Five. Boss, are you out there? Come back." He released the talk button.

After a moment, the voice came back, half-buried under crackling static. "Hartman, this is Mohler. What's going on out there? Are you snowed in yet?"

Benjy tried to laugh casually. "Not yet, but it's coming down hard. What's the deal here, boss? Have you seen the weather radar lately? Visibility is about one mile."

"Yeah, it's real bad," his boss replied. "The whole state is getting slammed with this snowstorm. The radar on my screen here is all purple and red. Snow, more snow, and even a little more snow. That's all I'm seeing."

"Well...great." Benjy briefly released the talk button so his boss wouldn't hear him unleash a record-length sigh. "How long can I expect this to last? I don't know how I'm supposed to go outside and do my patrols when I can't see my hand in front of my face."

"I don't know what to tell you, Hartman," the station manager replied. "This storm came out of nowhere—they're saying it might be a bomb cyclone. It's caught us all by surprise. I've been watching this young meteorologist out of Cincinnati, and he's losing his mind. He never saw it coming."

Benjy released the talk button again and uttered a string of profanities.

"It's not going away anytime soon," his boss added. "On the radar here, it looks like it's just swirling in place. On top of that, there's a bigger system up in Canada."

"What the hell?" Benjy muttered. Till now, he'd mostly just been annoyed at the prospect of waiting out a snowstorm so he could do his job, but now, he started to feel a strange sinking feeling.

This is something way out of the ordinary, he thought. Even realizing that, however, he couldn't piece it together. He realized he'd just been sitting there not saying anything for almost a full minute, trying to wrap his head around this situation. Finally, he shook his head and pressed the talk button again. He'd wanted to sound like he had everything under control, but he couldn't help himself.

"Well, what am I supposed to do here?" he asked. "Is someone going to come dig me out of this place if I get snowed under? I don't have unlimited supplies for a blizzard that never ends."

"Keep it together, Hartman," his boss replied. "I didn't say it'll never end. No storm lasts forever. You should have enough to last for a couple of weeks, unless you've been going through food and water like crazy."

Benjy fought the urge to respond in anger. Mohler had no business making snide comments about his weight. Yes, Benjy was a bit thick, but he had plenty of muscle under the fat. Anyway, Mohler wasn't so thin himself.

"So, we're just supposed to stay put," Benjy said. "Sit here and twiddle our thumbs."

"That's what we're telling all field rangers," the boss replied. "You're safer in your cabin. We don't want anyone out there trying to get back to civilization. Roads are terrible. Okay?"

Benjy groaned and said, "Yeah, got it. Thanks. Station Five out."

He reached up and angrily twisted off the radio, shoving the mic back against the wall beneath the window. Stranded in his tiny ranger station. He didn't care for the place in the best of circumstances. He thought of his nice apartment back in the city. His nice apartment with central heating, plus the fireplace, plus space heaters.

I can't stay here, he thought. *Not under these conditions.*

And the truth was, he *had* gone through his food stores a bit faster than he should have. Boss was right about that, as much as Benjy hated to admit it.

He briefly entertained the idea of trying to drive out of the wildlife refuge in his Jeep. He had four-wheel drive. Could he make it? The roads were rough, even when they were clear. Gazing out the window, he saw drifts of snow piling up. Thirty or forty miles to the nearest highway, then another forty to get home. It was a long way to go while dodging a bunch of incompetent drivers. He could picture some idiot sliding into his lane, forcing him off the road into a ditch.

He raised his coffee cup to take another sip, then turned and flung the cup as hard as he could across the cabin. It hit the wall above the kitchen counter, breaking into pieces, and splashing hot coffee all over the wall and floor. Benjy stared at the big stain, grinding his teeth.

"Great," he muttered. "Now I gotta clean that up."

Pushing his chair back, he rose. As he did, however, his gaze landed upon the small photograph on the desk. Her face was smiling back at him, a hint of teeth between parted lips, bright hazel eyes full of hope. She always looked so positive, so upbeat, in her pictures. Benjy reached down and picked up the photograph.

"Fiona Scarborough," he said, whispering her name. "My angel in the storm."

Yes, there was another option, wasn't there? He didn't have to stay in the cramped little ranger cabin, but he didn't have to make the dangerous trek into town either. Fiona's homestead was just outside of the wildlife refuge on a piece of private property. And she had so much. Practically an entire farm. Heck, she'd probably stored *years* of food in her various buildings. On top of that, she had animals, a greenhouse, a big comfortable house on a hill.

I could make it there, he told himself. *Not in the Jeep, though. The snowmobile.*

She wouldn't be happy to see him, of course. He still recalled their last bitter conversation, when she'd finally, fully turned against him. And why? Benjy had never figured that out. All he'd ever done was try to get their friendship to evolve to the next level. Was that so wrong?

She exaggerates all of my faults, he thought. *Anything I say or do, she takes in the worst possible way. It's misdirected anger from a previous toxic relationship. That's what it is. I bear the brunt of her anger for some other man's sins.*

He didn't know that for a fact, but he had his suspicions. But maybe, just maybe, the bad storm had given her a change of heart. She was a single woman living all alone on five acres of wilderness property with only some farm animals to keep her company. Surely, she could use the help.

She might appreciate having a good strong man at her side in a time like this, he thought. As he grabbed a towel off the table and made his way to the big puddle of coffee, he began to imagine doing all sorts of manly tasks around her homestead. Shoveling snow from the steps, chopping logs for the fireplace, hunting for game in the nearby woods, as Fiona watched from a distance, beaming.

How could she not appreciate it? He stooped and began wiping up the coffee, the towel quickly becoming soaked, and he began to entertain old notions once again. Maybe if he helped out, maybe if he saved the day, she would come to her senses. That's all he'd ever wanted from her. For her to come to her senses and realize how she truly felt about him.

Maybe Mother Nature did me a favor with this freak blizzard, he thought. *All I've ever needed was some circumstance to force Fiona to stop seeing me as a bad guy.*

He picked up the broken pieces of the cup and tossed them into the nearby trash can. Confidence growing, he went to the small closet near the front door and pulled on his winter gear: heavy coat, padded cap with ear flaps, scarf, ski gloves, ski pants, winter boots, even a pair of snow goggles. Then he jammed a few more personal items into a small backpack and slung it over his shoulder.

As soon as he opened the front door, a fierce wind blasted into the cabin, but he pushed his way outside, shutting the door behind him. The snowmobile was parked in a small storage building close to the cabin, and he kept it fueled up during the off-season.

"I'm coming to save the day, Fiona," he said.

9

On brutally cold nights, when a fire in the fireplace wasn't enough, she used the generator to power the electric furnace. The rumble of the furnace took on a soothing white-noise quality that helped Fiona sleep. Of course, it was a luxury, because of limited fuel.

Her bed was set against the wall across from her bedroom's single window. The curtains were parted slightly, and just before she fell asleep, she saw snow melting on the windowsill as warm air filled the room. Technology battling nature's ruthlessness, keeping it at bay. Somehow, that was a comforting thought, and it helped her drift off into a comfortable sleep. Smoke was curled up at the foot of the bed, perfectly content that all was well.

She awoke suddenly in the middle of the night, a moonlight haze shining through the window, and she felt a strange anxiety. At first, she couldn't identify the source, so she sat there staring at the ceiling. Suddenly, it occurred to her. No comforting rumble from the furnace. Smoke must have sensed her waking, even though she hadn't moved, for he suddenly lifted his head, looked at her, then looked toward the window.

Still half-asleep, Fiona lingered for a few minutes, hoping somehow the generator would kick in again, but the silence persisted. Finally, she flung her multiple layers of blankets back and, groaning, sat up. Smoke rose and hopped down from the bed.

"You have to be kidding me," Fiona muttered. She reached down and grabbed her fuzzy slippers off the floor, pulling them on. Then she stood up, bracing herself against the headboard, and approached the window. Parting the curtains, she saw unbroken whiteness down the hill and across the entire homestead, blanketing everything. The residual heat from the furnace was already fading, and she felt a shiver run down her spine.

She headed to the bedroom door and opened it. Smoke slipped through the gap and padded down the hall. As she reached the living room, she saw him move to the front door.

"No, not that way," she said. "Not yet. Come on, boy."

She patted her thigh, and Smoke followed her into the kitchen. The basement door was in a corner past the stove. The stairs led down into utter blackness, but she kept a row of flashlights on a shelf just beyond the door. Grabbing one of them, she clicked on the light, and headed down the creaking steps. The basement was a cluttered concrete room that ran the length of about half the house. The electric furnace was set on a concrete plinth in an alcove near the exterior basement door. She maintained a clear path to reach it, but much of the rest of the space was used to store the extra supplies and partially built sections of furniture that wouldn't fit in the small workshop.

As she shone the light along the path toward the generator, something else caught her eye. Puddles everywhere. Water had started to seep in through the foundation.

"Oh, what the heck?" she muttered, approaching the bottom step.

She tried to find the source of the seepage. Unfortunately, the foundation hadn't been weatherproofed yet. She'd intended to have it resealed, but she'd assumed she had plenty of time to get it done. Now, it looked like the window of opportunity had passed.

If it keeps up, eventually you're going to have to lug everything out of the basement, she realized. As she looked at her many, many neat stacks of shelves, prepared wood, unfinished pieces of tables and benches, and more, she felt overwhelmed by the prospect.

She made her way across the basement, stepping over the puddles. When she reached the furnace, she gave it a quick look to make sure nothing was wrong. It seemed to be fine. The power was just off. That meant a brief foray outside. She braced herself, opened the exterior door, and rushed up the steps. This led to the back porch and the tiny aluminum shed that housed the gas-powered generator.

She headed inside and found that, indeed, the generator was dead. She knelt down and aimed the light at the fuel tank. Unscrewing the cap, she peered inside. The pungent smell of fuel wafted out. She flipped the generator switch off and on again, then hit the restart button. Nothing happened.

It made not the least sound or even the faintest attempt to turn over. The damn thing had just completely died for some reason. She smacked the side of it a few times, and gave it another attempt, jamming the starter button. Nothing.

"Great timing, damn you," she muttered, rising. "You ran fine last winter. What's the deal?"

Living alone off the homestead, Fiona had developed a wide range of skills. After all, she only had herself to depend on. She could fix many things, but the generator was beyond her skill level. She lacked the mechanical or electrical expertise to diagnose the problem, and if a part needed replacing, she didn't have access to new parts.

Fiona knelt there for a few minutes, looking for obvious signs of wear and tear, but everything appeared fine. She hit the starter one more time and still got no response, so finally she rose and headed back into the basement, stepping over the puddles. When she got upstairs, she found Smoke pacing anxiously from the kitchen table to the stove. She set the flashlight on its shelf and shut the basement door.

When Fiona sat down at the kitchen table with a huff, the dog padded over and rested his head on her leg. She petted him, gazing out the dark kitchen window, which had fogged over and become an opaque screen.

"Looks like we'll have to make the trek into town in the morning," she said to Smoke. He was staring at her intently, clearly still confused about why they were up so early. "I'm either going to have to buy a new generator, or get someone to come out here and fix the broken one. I can't imagine who that's going to be."

Neither option was great. The first would seriously deplete the remainder of her limited funds, and the second would force her to depend on the kindness of townies that she barely knew. More than that, she didn't like bringing people out to the homestead to root around in her things. It felt like an invasion of her privacy. It messed with her whole mission here on the homestead.

Well, learn how to repair complex machines, then, she told herself. *This is your fault. Freak snow storm or not, there are skills you lack, and you're paying a price for it.*

Scolding herself didn't make her feel better about it, of course.

Though she was now frustrated to the point of distraction, she felt sleep drifting over her again. She gently moved Smoke aside and got up from her chair. The road into town was fairly well-maintained, but she doubted they'd had time to clear it yet. With so much snow, they would probably prioritize plowing the major highways. With a sigh, Fiona headed back to her bedroom. As she flopped onto her bed, Smoke hopped up and resumed his position near the footboard. The freak snowstorm had been falling for less than twenty-four hours and already it was wreaking havoc on her life.

10

Jarred didn't think any rescuers were coming. Dragging the suitcase was next to impossible, as snow built up on the wheels, so he finally just carried it. Visibility was low, and as the afternoon wore on toward evening, it only got worse.

"Are you sure we're even on the road anymore?" Hope asked. "I can't tell what anything is."

"I believe so," he replied, shouting to be heard over the wind.

"We should have cut through the woods like I suggested," she said. "At least then the snow wouldn't be as deep."

As she said it, he gazed in the direction of the trees. They grew close, the branches practically interwoven above in a makeshift canopy that trapped the snow and seemed rather inviting. Although some of the branches seemed to have cracked and broken, it still seemed preferable to walking out in the open. Furthermore, if they cut through the woods, heading southwest, they might reach the town faster, though he was concerned about getting lost.

"Let's stick to the road for now," he said finally. "There's still a chance someone will come along and rescue us."

But as he said it, he spotted another car off the road ahead. A little compact car, it had somehow ended up on its side in the center island.

"I don't think anyone's coming, Dad," Hope said. "All the cars have crashed."

Indeed, at this point, they would have to send the snowplows first just to make the highway passable for emergency vehicles, and he'd seen no sign of them. He was tempted to call 911 again, but he doubted that would do any good. He glanced back at his daughter, who was walking hunched over, her arms wrapped tightly around herself, her head down and her hood dusted with snow.

Jarred felt another moment of crushing self-doubt. What had he done? Why had he tried to flee the storm and put his only child in this awful situation?

He'd always been one to set a course and follow through. It was how he'd managed to earn his PhD in mechanical engineering, how he'd managed to gain tenure as a professor while raising his daughter all by himself. But now? Now, at last, that famous Jarred White tenacity might have put them both in real peril.

Well, there was no going back now.

"We can do this, Hope," he said. "Just think about a big steaming cup of hot chocolate and a nice greasy cheeseburger."

"Believe me, Dad, I am," she replied. "I'm thinking about it every second."

"We'll be there before you know it," he said.

Just then, however, he stumbled on something. He'd been following the lump of a guardrail, but his right foot struck a large object hidden by the snow. He went down on his knees and lost his grip on the suitcase handle. He felt his right knee drive into the soft side of some big thing. He was pretty sure it was a carcass, and for a disturbing moment, he imagined it was human. A stranded driver who'd perhaps tried to make the same reckless trek to Glencole.

However, as he picked himself up, he looked down and saw the furry side of what was almost certainly a deer.

"Watch out," he said to Hope. "Step around this thing."

"Gross," she replied. "Did it die from the cold?"

"I doubt it," he said, noting flecks of blood in its fur. "Probably an out-of-control car hit it."

In fact, he saw the most likely culprit just ahead—an old pickup truck resting sideways across the inside shoulder, its front headlight shattered. The driver's door was wide open, the driver missing.

He bent down and grabbed the suitcase handle, stepping around the carcass as he resumed walking.

"I just wish I was still sitting in the den working on my science project," Hope said. "It was so warm in there."

"Not much farther now," he said. "Maybe the snow will let up by the time we get to Glencole."

But he wasn't feeling the truth of his own words. He was just saying whatever he thought might appease her, but he'd put them in this situation. It was entirely his fault.

This is why you need someone else to give your decisions a little perspective, he thought. *It was better when Janie could provide a bit of constructive criticism.*

But thinking that would only hasten his despair, he knew. Grief had been ever-present in his life after the death of his wife, Hope's mother. When she'd been diagnosed with stage IV breast cancer, the doctor had given her a year. Jarred, doing his own research, had pushed that to a year and a half in his own mind and planned accordingly. And then Janie had only lasted three months. The shock of the cancer's progression had never really worn off. He carried it even now. It was the seed of his self-doubt at every moment.

You idiot, you abandoned your vehicle in a blizzard, he thought. *What were you thinking? Are you out of your mind? Walking a mile in this weather to try to reach a gas station that might not even be open. You really are stupid.*

How had it ever made sense to him? He looked back at his daughter again, snow dusting her shoulders.

No, it was the right decision, he told himself. *You'll get to town, and it will all have been worth it. Don't be so quick to give up. Hope needs some assurance.*

"I know it's a big pain in the butt," he said to her, "but we're making progress. Just hang in there."

"It's one degree, and I'm already freezing solid," she said. "Plus, the snow keeps getting deeper. Can't we cut through the woods? There'll be less snow on the ground." As she spoke, she lifted her head and gazed off toward the trees. He noted the wistful expression in her face.

"I'm afraid we might get turned around in there," he said.

But she raised her hand suddenly and began pointing wildly toward the trees. "Dad! Dad, look! There!"

He looked where she was pointing. Through a small gap in the trees, he saw a dark shape tucked back in the woods. It took a moment of staring at it to determine what he was seeing. The gap was perhaps a dirt road, a driveway, and the dark shape appeared to be a small house tucked back off the highway about twenty or thirty yards. It was rustic, scarcely more than a cabin. He didn't see any vehicles parked in front of it, and the windows were dark.

"I see it," he replied. "Don't you want to keep walking to Glencole?"

"No, I want to go inside that house and wait for the snow to stop," she replied. "It'll be warmer in there. Maybe there's someone inside."

"I don't think so," he said. "It doesn't look like anyone is home."

"Can we check, please? You can call 911 again and tell them to find us there," she said. "I'm so *cold*."

"The cheeseburger—" he started to say.

"I don't care about the cheeseburger anymore," she said. "There's probably food in that cabin. I can't feel my feet anymore. Come on, Dad. Let's go." She pointed frantically toward the house.

His instinct was to refuse, to keep walking, even if he had to keep comforting her with hopeful lies. They'd already set their destination. Why turn aside now? But in his moment of self-doubt, her strong opinion held sway. Maybe it was better to wait out the worst of the storm somewhere safe. He came to a stop and turned to face the gap in the trees, considering the alternative.

"I'm going, Dad," Hope said suddenly. "This is awful. I can't be out here any longer."

"Now, just wait a second," he replied.

But she didn't wait. Even as he was still speaking, she stepped down into the ditch, sinking to mid-calf in the snow there, and made her way to the other side.

"Hang on," he said, starting after her. "Maybe you're right. We can at least check and see if someone's there."

As he climbed up the far side of the ditch, he could see that the snow wasn't as deep beneath the trees. There were even a few clear patches still, here and there among the roots. The small cabin's roof hung far out over the porch, which had kept the snow off. This made it doubly inviting. Hope was already trudging down the path, and he hurried to catch up, dragging the suitcase out of the ditch.

"Let me go to the door," he said. "They might not want to let strangers inside. I may have to bribe them."

"Pay them whatever they want," Hope shouted over her shoulder. "Just get us inside, please!"

As they drew close to the porch, he spotted a sign mounted near a corner of the handrail. "Sycamore Cabin Rentals," it said, and had a local phone number. Well, that explained why the place looked uninhabited. It was a seasonal cabin.

"I don't think anyone is home," he said.

"Even better," she replied. "Can we still go inside, please? You can call that number later and pay the rental fee."

"Let's get on the porch, and I'll try to call," he said.

As they reached the porch, Jarred saw through the parted curtains in the big picture window. A living room with a few rustic pieces of furniture. It all looked a little dusty, but it wasn't a cluttered space. Besides the furniture, there was nothing that would have indicated a long-term resident, no little knickknacks or anything.

They mounted the steps. Jarred went to the porch swing and sat down, leaning the suitcase against the handrail, but Hope walked over to the window, peering inside.

"Oh, man, it looks so nice in there," she said. "They've got a fireplace, too. I'll bet we could start a fire. Can you imagine how nice that would be?"

"There's no one home," he said, "but we can sit on the porch for a little while and catch our breath, if you want. I'm still dreaming about a cup of hot coffee."

But Hope wrapped her arms around herself and shivered, her teeth chattering. When she turned to him, he could see snowflakes stuck to the tips of her eyelashes. How could he ask her to march back out there into the snow and keep going in this weather?

"Okay, look," he said, beckoning her. "Maybe you've got the right idea."

When she approached, he rose from the porch swing and hugged her. It was a bit like wrapping his arms around a giant icicle.

"It would be better if it was an occupied cabin," he said, "A nice family might take pity on us and let us inside to warm up. As it is, we're better off heading into town."

She broke out of his embrace and turned, making a big sweep with her hand at the landscape around them. "Dad, I can't do it. I can't go back out there on the highway and keep walking. We're never going to make it to town. Not in this awful weather. We have to get inside the cabin."

"I really don't think it'll take that much longer," he said, lamely.

Hope harrumphed loudly and went to the suitcase, kneeling down in front of it.

"What are you doing?" he asked.

She unzipped the front pocket and pulled out the big flashlight they'd taken from the trunk. She rose and approached the living room window. As she did, she raised her arm, drawing the metal end of the flashlight back behind her head.

"Whoa, whoa, wait a second," he said. "That's breaking and entering—a felony. We could get arrested for this."

"If they come to arrest us, at least they'll have to take us somewhere warm," she said.

And with that, she swung the flashlight, striking one of the window panes with the heavy end. The first blow only cracked the glass, and the flashlight bounced off. She swung the flashlight again. This time, the end of the flashlight broke through the glass. It didn't break clean like a car window. Instead, the flashlight created a long, jagged hole that went from the windowsill about halfway up the pane, three sides surrounded by sharp edges.

"There, the damage is done," she said. "We might as well see it through now, Dad."

The damage is done, indeed, he thought. And would it really be so bad if they got inside the cabin? He was going to have to reimburse the owner at some point anyway.

"Let me at least take care of the rest," he said. He went to her and took the flashlight from her hands. "I don't want you to cut yourself."

He used the flashlight to carefully break the jagged edges of the glass, attempting to create a smooth enough hole to get his arm through safely. Hope had chosen the window pane closest to the front door, and it looked like the lock was within reach. Once the hole seemed large enough, he handed her the flashlight and moved his arm through, moving slowly to avoid the edges.

"Bust out the whole window, Dad," Hope said. "Then we can just step through."

"I'd rather not," he replied. "It'll be harder to cover the hole, and we'll have all that cold air blowing into the house."

He reached toward the door, fumbling blindly past the frame, feeling for the deadbolt. It took a few seconds to get ahold of it, and then he struggled to turn it. In the process, his arm pressed against the broken edge of the glass. Even though he'd knocked off the jagged shards, he felt the sharp edge cut through his coat.

Finally, the deadbolt turned with a satisfying click, and he drew his arm back out. Stuffing was poking out of a four-inch slash on the inside arm of his coat. He showed it to Hope.

"That's why I didn't want you messing with the window," he said.

"Well...I would've just knocked the whole thing out," she replied.

With a shake of his head, he opened the front door and ushered her through. She stepped inside the dim living room, stomping her feet on the threshold to knock off some of the snow. Jarred went back and grabbed the suitcase and dragged it inside after her. As soon as he was through the door, he pulled it shut behind him.

"Anyone home?" he called.

He waited a second but heard no response.

"Anyone?" he called again. "Sorry, we didn't mean to break in, but we were desperate."

Still no response.

"Dad, no one's here," Hope said. She crossed the living room and sat down on the stone hearth, setting the flashlight beside her. Jarred noted that it wasn't much warmer inside the house than outside. He could still see his breath puffing out in front of him. He felt a sinking feeling in the pit of his stomach. They'd broken into someone's private property, committed a criminal act. How had it come so easily? Hope had scarcely hesitated to shatter the window, and she certainly didn't seem to feel bad about it.

What sort of example have I set for my daughter? he thought, pulling the suitcase across the room and setting it down beside the couch.

It was done now, and he couldn't take it back. Under the circumstances, it was probably the right choice to get inside. Still, he didn't have to feel okay with it, even if it had been an act of desperation.

All it took was an early snowstorm to turn us into criminals, he thought, sitting down on the edge of the couch.

11

Fiona's pickup truck, a trusty Toyota Tundra, was half-buried at the top of the driveway near the barn. She saw the lump of it there, eight inches of snow piled up on top, the bed quickly filling. Clearly, driving into town was going to be an ordeal, but it didn't matter. The generator had to be fixed no matter what.

Still, she spent a few minutes just standing on the back porch, gazing beyond the generator's shed and down the back of the hill to the pickup truck—procrastinating. Smoke was sniffing around in the snow in front of her. Fiona had no reason to put this off any longer, but she was dreading the trip.

Finally, bundled up in her winter coat, her big snow boots, and her thickest gloves, she marched down the hill to inspect the truck. Smoke got there first, and he ran toward the back of the truck, as if he intended to hop up into the bed as usual. However, when he saw the snow piled on top of the rear bumper, he whimpered and ran back to Fiona instead.

"Yeah, you're not riding in the back today," she said, reaching down to pet his head.

She tried brushing the snow off the windshield, but the real problem, she discovered, was a crust of ice at the bottom of the snow. Then she tried to open the driver's door and found that it was frozen shut. She sighed and stepped back, considering the situation. The driveway completely blanketed, the windshield iced over—this was going to take some real work.

Is it worth it?

She considered giving up, but she couldn't survive without the furnace. The wood stove in the kitchen wouldn't provide nearly enough heat. There was another older wood-burning stove in an alcove at the back of the basement, but she rarely used it. Using it now would just burn through her stack of firewood much faster, and then what?

As Smoke ran circles around the truck, clearly trying to figure out how to get inside, Fiona considered her options. Digging the truck out of the snow with a shovel seemed like a daunting prospect. Fortunately, there was another option. She whistled at Smoke, so he followed her as she trudged to the barn door.

A low sense of dread was constantly threatening to overwhelm her. She could sense it at the edge of every thought.

A single freak storm is going to destroy everything I've worked so hard to build.

She quickly pushed it down, shoved it into the deep places where such things belonged. The only way to keep the feeling at bay, she knew, was to stay busy—to keep doing whatever was right before her. At the moment, that meant getting the generator repaired.

Inside the barn, the animals were stirred by her presence. She saw their little faces peering from the shadows of their pens, hoping perhaps that she'd brought an end to the cold. They couldn't stay here in the cold much longer. It was too much.

Another problem to deal with eventually. They should be fine for a little while, however. Long enough for her to make a trip into town. She hadn't come into the barn for the animals, though for a moment, she had an amusing picture in her mind of an ornery Ramses being tethered to the truck, dragging it out of the deep snow as Fiona used one of the females as bait.

What she was after was the large tarp-draped object parked against the wall at the back of the barn. She grabbed the tarp and whipped it off, revealing her Kawasaki Mule 4-wheeler. It was a strange little vehicle, like some deformed hybrid of a mini-pickup truck and a Jeep Wrangler. However, it was incredibly useful on the homestead. The sight of the Mule got Smoke excited again, and he raced toward it, leaping up onto the passenger seat.

The Mule had a snowplow attachment for the front, though she'd only used it a handful of times over the years. It took a moment to get it bolted in place, then she turned the ignition. To her relief, the vehicle started right up, and she puttered out of the barn, past the confused gazes on the goat. Ramses gave an annoyed bleat as she passed by, rattling the door of his pen.

The Mule was set up for off-roading, with extra-large tires and deep tread, but it still struggled to plow through a foot of snow. Fiona avoided the deeper drifts and worked her way around the barn to the truck, but occasionally, the tires slipped, spinning for a second before catching hold again. When she got to the driveway, she cleared the area behind the pickup truck using the snowplow. Then she cleared space on either side of the truck. What would have taken her an hour by hand took about ten minutes with the Mule.

"See there, little guy," she said to the dog, who sat dutifully on the passenger seat through all of this. "Always be prepared for all kinds of problems."

She hopped out of the Mule and tried the passenger-side door of the truck, which opened, thankfully. She slid over to the driver's seat to start the engine. It would need some time to warm up and unfreeze the driver-side door. She felt a slight flutter of worry as, unlike the Mule, it didn't start right away. The engine struggled to turn over, and she wondered if the cold might have sapped the battery. Finally, she got it going, and she left it running as she drove the Mule up the hill to the shed to retrieve the generator.

Moving the generator was another giant pain in the butt. She had to unchain it and use the handcart to carry it off its concrete plinth. Then she dragged it through the snow to the back of the Mule. The generator was over two hundred pounds, so she had a ramp that she used to get it into the back of the vehicle.

Even then, the work was only half done, because she had to drive the Mule down to the truck and transfer the generator from one vehicle to the other using the ramp. After that, she drove the Mule back to the barn, following the path she'd already dug. Then she parked it in the back, covered it, and returned to the truck. Smoke was more than ready. The second she opened the driver's door, he leapt past her, landing on the seat in an explosion of snow, and bounded over the armrest to his usual spot.

By now, the truck was warm, and the ice on the windshield seemed like it had softened along the edges. Fiona dug the big plastic ice scraper out from under the seat to finish the job. Clearing the windshield still took longer than clearing the driveway, and by the end, chipping away all of that ice in the cold made her out of breath. She flung the ice scraper into the back seat and climbed into the truck. By the time she sat down, her shoulders were aching, and she was worn out.

"Well, that sucked," she said, pulling the door shut. She looked at Smoke and shook her head. "All of that, and we haven't even started the drive into town."

As she headed down the driveway, she repeated a mantra in her head, one that had served her well during the early, difficult days on the homestead.

I won't fail at this. I won't fail at this. I won't. I won't.

The town of Glencole, Ohio, was a small community of about two hundred people set in a vast area of farming and ranching properties. It was five miles into town. Fortunately, it looked like some locals, perhaps using their own four-wheel-drive vehicles, had dug grooves into the lanes. This, at least, made the road usable. Still, Fiona took her time, creeping along and sticking to the grooves. The last thing she needed now was to slide off the road, where deep ditches on either side just waited to swallow the truck and hold it fast. The weight of the generator in the back of the truck helped with traction on the road, at least.

On either side, open land and low hills showed endless, unbroken snow stretching out seemingly forever, as if the entire world had been covered in a burial shroud. Normally, seeing the land covered in snow had a quaint holiday loveliness to it, but now, it just looked like ruin. Fiona fixed her eyes on the road immediately ahead of her and tried not to think about it.

She'd gone perhaps two miles when she spotted a large sedan lying on its side in the ditch, half-buried in the snow. She slowed down further as she passed by and tried to see into the windows, but they were iced over.

Because she was staring at the sedan, she was ill-prepared when the wind suddenly changed direction, blowing in from the left. Unable to compensate in time, it blew her truck to the edge of the road. She felt the right tires dip down, and Smoke, sensing the danger, rose from his seat and looked out the passenger window.

"Careful," Fiona muttered, trying not to oversteer as she eased back into her lane.

She felt the tires hit the grooves again, traction locking into place, like the teeth of two gears coming together. Snow had begun to fall hard again, and was blowing in sideways with the wind. A disheartening sight, for sure, and for some reason, it was the last straw. At last, Fiona sank into a foul mood. The anger and despair seemed to go hand in hand, folding in around her. She felt the sting of tears, and she blinked them away, gnawing at the inside of her cheek until she tasted blood.

More snow. Sure, why not, Mother Nature? Why not? Rub it in. Make it worse.

She slowed down even more, which made it easier to resist the wind. Still, it howled, blowing snow over the hood of the truck in massive shimmering clouds. Again, she might have thought it beautiful, but a darkness had taken her that she couldn't seem to claw her way out of. The whole world, nature, and reality itself had turned against her. Everything wanted her to fail.

When she finally spotted the small town in the distance, it did little to lift her spirits. Glencole had a lovely downtown area that occasionally attracted tourists visiting the nearby national forest. Local officials had leaned into the tourist trade as a last gasp, fixing up the downtown area and encouraging quirky little shops that sold antiques and collectibles.

Fiona saw it as she came over a slight rise, a row of antique shops running perpendicular to the road she was on. A renovated gas station stood at the intersection of the two roads, but she could tell even from a distance that it was closed for the day. No vehicles in the parking lot, no one moving through the big windows, no lights. Normally, there would be some traffic moving in the streets, maybe a few people walking between the shops. But there was no one, not a single person visible anywhere. She turned onto Main Street, heading for the hardware store, which was about halfway down.

She saw a lamp flickering on the counter of Cooper's General Store, someone grabbing items off a shelf inside. That was promising. And then she reached the hardware store—Moseley's Tools—and saw the dark windows. She came to a stop in front of the door and rolled her window down to get a better view.

A closed sign hung in the door. She'd never seen the hardware store closed, not even for holidays. Old Tate Moseley practically lived in his store and could be found behind the counter on New Year's Day and Christmas and every day in between. But not today. She was already in such a foul mood that she sat there for at least a full minute, glaring hatefully at the closed sign.

Her best chance at getting the generator fixed had been Moseley's full-time repairman, Charles Arnold. He was always in the back fiddling with something. Maybe he was still back there. Was it possible?

"You think old Moseley would forgive me if I broke into his store and checked on Charlie?" she said. She directed the question at Smoke, but really, she was thinking out loud. So when a real, live human answered her, it caused her heart to leap into her throat.

"Don't bother," the crackly voice said. "Moseley's gone. Charlie's gone, too."

She turned to see the man shuffling across the street. He had a weathered face, bushy eyebrows, a bulbous nose, and he wore a padded leather coat lined with white faux-fur that seemed like a relic of a previous decade.

"Duke," she said. He ran the general store, which included a small section with handmade furniture. That made him practically a business partner for her since he carried some of her pieces. Despite this, she'd had very few actual conversations with the man. "Are you open today?"

"Thought about it," he replied. "Don't see much point now. Nobody's coming in...unless you're here to buy something."

"I'm afraid not," she said. "Not today, anyway. So Mr. Moseley isn't around? I really need someone to take a look at my generator."

He came up beside her window, reeking of menthol cigarettes. "Tate and Charlie both headed out yesterday with most of the rest of the town, heading south for warmer climates."

"Most of the town?" she said. "They left town because of a freak snowstorm? That seems a bit extreme. Whose idea was that?"

Duke looked up into the sky, the wind blowing the few strands of white hair that stuck out from under his knit cap. "You know this is more than a freak storm, don't you? Haven't you listened to the radio or read the news on your phone?"

"No, I spent most of yesterday trying to save my crops," she said. Her voice was dropping into a lower register, despite her best effort. She felt a terrible heaviness inside of her. "And then I spent a couple of hours digging my truck out so I could get to town."

"Well, the so-called experts are calling this a seasonal storm," Duke said. "You know what that means? Means it could last all season. Maybe longer. Can you imagine that? Snow every day for the entire season?"

"You've got to be *kidding* me?" she snapped. She covered her mouth and leaned back against her seat until she'd regained control of herself, then she lowered her hands. "Sorry, I didn't mean to yell. I'm just...I can't believe this."

If her raised voice had bothered him, he didn't show it. He kept right on talking as if it hadn't happened. "City council issued an evacuation order for the whole town, and I know a lot of other towns have done the same. Everyone is supposed to head south and get ahead of the storm. I guess they're afraid of residents getting stuck in their homes and starving to death. Personally, I'd go to Pensacola, if I had any intention of leaving. Which I don't. I'll ride it out from the comfort of my own couch, thank you very much."

"A storm can't last a whole season," Fiona said. Needing comfort, she reached over and laid a hand on Smoke's side. He reached back and licked her hand. "That's not how weather works. I'm not abandoning my home, my farm, my animals just because of a heavy snowfall! I can handle unpredictable weather. I can handle it!" She was mostly talking to herself, trying to drag herself out of the darkness. She almost forgot all about Duke until she heard him laugh.

"Hey, I'm with you," he said. "You don't see *me* running away."

She turned to him, embarrassed by her outburst. Interactions with people were always awkward for her anyway. Current circumstances just made it worse. "Even if there's an evacuation order, they can't force us to leave, can they?"

"I'd like to see them try," he said with a laugh. "Most people left willingly, but the roads are pretty bad now. Only a handful of us are sticking it out."

Fiona bowed forward, pressing her forehead against the steering wheel. "I don't suppose you know anything about fixing a busted generator?"

"That thing in the back of the truck?" he asked.

"Yeah."

"I don't know the least thing about it," he said. "I can change a flat tire and balance a checkbook. That's about it for me."

"What other stores are open?" she asked.

"Not sure," he said. "I know Glencole Stop is closed—I drove by there earlier. I'm pretty sure the other gas station in town is open. Speedy's Superfast over by the high school. At least, they *were* this morning."

Fiona groaned. "Okay, well, maybe I'll fill up the tank before I head home. Thanks for the info, Duke. Good luck with everything."

"Same to you," he replied. He tapped the side of her truck and stepped back. "Be careful out on that farm."

"Of course."

She rolled up the window and set off again, heading down the street beyond the tourist area. Speedy's gas station was tiny, two pumps and a convenience store the size of a postage stamp. She saw it as she reached the end of downtown, a little red building and a small white rain cover.

A wasted trip, she thought. *A complete waste. I could have spent this time working on the homestead.*

"I have to pull myself out of this," she muttered, petting Smoke. "I can't be in this funk. It won't solve anything."

As she approached the gas station, she saw lights through the window. A full-size van was parked in front of one of the pumps. She recognized it by the big pink logo of a rose on the size. The local florist, whose business bore his name—Mr. Bishop—was screwing the cap back on his gas tank as she pulled into the parking lot. A tall, gaunt man, he had a neatly trimmed mustache, rosy cheeks, and tired eyes. His well-combed hair was currently hidden beneath a thick red cap.

As Fiona pulled up to the second pump, he stared at her. He wasn't the friendliest man in Glencole, and she'd done very little business with him over the years. As she put her truck in park, she saw him shrug at her out of the corner of his eye.

"Can you believe this weather?" he asked, as soon as she opened the door.

"It's pretty bad," she replied.

He grunted and shook his head, as if the snow offended him to the core of his being. "We're supposed to be heading south, but what's the point? Where would we go?"

"I'm not going," Fiona said.

"You're Fiona Scarborough, right?" he asked. "The woman who lives out on that farm?"

She nodded.

"I'm Larry Bishop," he said. She was afraid he was going to extend his hand for a handshake, but thankfully, he didn't.

"I know who you are," she replied. "You run the flower shop."

"That I do," he replied, with a brief, proud smile. "You're okay out there all by yourself? It can't be easy in this weather."

She almost didn't answer. As she reached for the gas pump, she realized she couldn't answer honestly, because she didn't know. "I'll make it work," she said. "Don't worry about me."

I won't fail at this. I won't fail at this. I won't. I won't.

"I feel the same way," Mr. Bishop said. "I'm not afraid of a storm. It can interrupt my business for a day or two, but it won't interrupt my life."

And that settled it in her mind. Somehow, Larry's defiance broke through the gloom. If the local florist could shake his fist at the storm, if the local general store owner could do it, then so could the rugged homesteader. Despair would not win out. She would adjust her plans to live without the generator and deal with this damned storm no matter how long it lasted.

12

Upon walking through the cabin, Jarred came to the conclusion that it was primarily intended for hunters. There was a large, empty gun case in one room, the door wide open and the keys dangling from the lock. A deer's head glared down with glassy eyes above the master bed, and a second bedroom had a couple of large oil paintings: one of Native American men hunting bison, the other of some wild mountain man stalking an elk. Hope seemed particularly taken with the paintings, and she spent a few minutes quietly staring at them. Dust coated almost everything.

"Well, the rental company decorated it nicely, at least," Jarred said, running his fingers along the bedpost of the full-sized bed in the second bedroom. "But it could use a thorough dusting."

"Yeah, and it's super cold," Hope said. "I don't think these walls are insulated at all. Can we get a fire going please, Dad?"

"Sure thing," he replied. "There's some firewood stacked on the hearth, so we're good to go. Give me a minute."

"Thanks."

As he made his way back to the living room, he had the strange sense that something was off about the house. He looked in the kitchen, the living room, the two bedrooms, the hall closet—what was missing? And then it occurred to him, and it seemed so bizarre that he made another pass through the house to double-check. When he passed by the bedroom door, he saw Hope staring at him, one eyebrow raised.

"Something wrong?" she said.

"No bathroom," he replied. "Actually, I don't think there's any indoor plumbing at all."

"Oh, no, you've got to be kidding me," Hope said, shoulders slumping. "We have to go to the bathroom. What are we supposed to do? Squat in the snow?"

He returned to the kitchen, where a back door opened on a small porch. When he peered through the small window set into the door, he spotted an outhouse just beyond the porch. He was still staring at it, when he heard Hope enter the kitchen.

"Well, I found the bathroom," he said.

"I'm not walking out there to pee," she replied, in a whiny voice. "Are you serious? Nobody uses outhouses anymore except the Amish, and even then, I'm not sure. What's wrong with these people?"

"If it's meant to be a hunting cabin, then it might be intentionally rustic," he said. "A chance to live like it's the nineteenth century all over again. Some people enjoy that sort of thing."

"What a terrible idea," Hope said with a groan. "Why erase more than a hundred years of technological advancement? What's fun about that?"

He turned from the door and motioned her toward the living room. "I'll get a nice fire going, and it won't seem so bad."

He followed his daughter into the living room. She glared at the kitchen sink in passing.

"There's not even a faucet in the sink," she noted. "Just a big basin. Where are people supposed to get water from?"

"I don't know," he said. "Maybe there's a pump somewhere outside, or at least a well with a bucket."

"Who pays money to stay in a place like this?" Hope dropped onto the living room couch with a huff. "I honestly don't get it."

Jarred knelt before the fireplace. Being stuck here with no running water and no bathroom was going to be rough, especially if they wound up stranded for a while. He tried not to think about it as he stacked wood in the fireplace. The owners had at least left a nice big box of long matches. He proceeded to get a fire going. Behind him, the blanket he'd secured over the broken window flapped ceaselessly in the wind, a sound that already irritated him.

"Dad, something's wrong with the fire," Hope said.

He was bent over the fireplace, so he didn't notice at first. However, when she said it, he leaned back and saw the problem. The logs had just begun to burn, a small flame licking at one end, but smoke was already gathering in the fireplace and seeping out into the living room.

"Dang, I forgot to make sure the flue is open," he said, bending even lower.

However, when he looked up into the chimney, he didn't see a flue, just the charred bricks. It seemed to be open, but for some reason, smoke wasn't passing through the chimney, as if it were blocked. As a result, smoke had begun to pour into the living room. Jarred tried to blow the fire out, but it was too late for that. Instead, he had to run outside and grab a big armful of snow, dumping it into the fireplace. The flames extinguished with a hiss, but it produced a big gust of thick smoke that rolled across the living room. He turned away, covering his mouth and nose.

"Chimney's blocked," he said, then fell into a coughing fit.

"Maybe it's ice," Hope said. "If we let the fire burn, it'll melt, right?"

"No, we can't risk smoke inhalation. We could asphyxiate." He went back to the front door and opened it wide, letting the chilly wind from outside stir and scatter the smoke from the fire. It took a few minutes before the worst of it was gone. By then, his eyes were stinging, and the whole room was hazy.

Hope had rolled face-down on the couch to avoid the smoke, and when she spoke her voice was muffled. "You mean, we can't even have a fire?"

"I'm afraid not," he said. Finally, the cold air was just too much, and he shut the door again. It was getting dark outside now, evening becoming night, and the temperature seemed to be dropping even further, though the snowfall had let up for the time being. "I'll try to figure out what's wrong with it in the morning when the sun is out."

"Ugh, what are we supposed to do now?" she said.

He considered their options. Honestly, he couldn't do much at the moment. "Maybe it'll be better if we just get some sleep."

"Those beds are going to be so cold," Hope said.

"We'll see what we can do about that. Come on."

In the end, they found some ratty old sleeping bags in the hall closet, and they wound up sleeping in individual sleeping bags side by side on top of the queen-size bed in the master bedroom. Even burrowed deep inside his sleeping bag, still fully dressed, Jarred could still feel the cold, and he heard Hope's teeth chattering.

"I just wish we'd stayed home" Hope said sleepily. "I want to be in my own room so bad right now."

Jarred bit back the urge to defend his actions. She was right, after all.

Morning seemed to come in record time. He shut his eyes, felt sleep coming on, and then the next instant, it seemed he was opening his eyes to a hazy morning light shining through the bedroom window. He felt stiff and sore, and only about half of his brain was functioning, but he crawled out of the sleeping bag and stumbled his way to the living room. He intended to get some stuff done before his daughter woke up—maybe clear the chimney and bring in some water—but she came shuffling into the living room right after him. Like him, she'd slept without even taking her coat off.

"Let's see if we can't get the chimney open today," he said, trying his best to sound optimistic. "Maybe we'll fix that broken window, as well. A nice piece of plywood will do a better job keeping that wind out than a blanket. We'll look for food, bring in some water…"

"I don't know why we left the car in the first place," she croaked, rubbing her face with her hands. "It was a really bad idea. Emergency guys won't see us now."

Jarred sighed, willing himself patience. He turned to face the big living room window. Their footprints from the previous day had completely disappeared. Snow was blowing in at a severe angle. It looked truly inhospitable out there.

"Is someone going to come and rescue us?" Hope said, taking a seat on the hearth. "We can't stay in this cabin. I need to pee, but I'm not going outside."

"I'm afraid we're stuck here for now," he said. "At least until there's a lull in the storm. Then we can press on to Glencole."

At this, Hope groaned. Her irritation was understandable, but he was trying his best.

"It'll help if we maintain a positive attitude," he said.

"What if the storm lasts for days?" she said. The slight quaver in her voice suggested she was scared, not just annoyed.

"Then at least we have a roof over our heads," he said. "Our situation could be a whole lot worse."

At this, she went quiet, bent forward, her face hidden in the deep well of her hood. Jarred decided to leave her alone for the time being, as he began making plans for the day ahead. However, after a moment, she cleared her throat and said, "Okay, fine, what can I do to help?"

He turned to her and saw her eyes glinting from deep in her hood. In reality, there wasn't much she could do, but he wanted to seize on her sudden change of heart.

"I'll tell you what you can do," he said. "While I work on the chimney, why don't you fully search the house. Look through all of the closets and cabinets, and make a list of what we've got. That'll be a big help."

"I can do that," she said, grunting as she stood up. "It's better than just sitting around."

"Exactly."

As she headed off toward the back hallway and the bedroom, Jarred knelt in front of the fireplace. Getting the chimney open was the priority. He bent down low and tried to get a better view up inside, but he couldn't see anything blocking it from this angle. Ice seemed the most likely culprit. Still, he grabbed a fire poker and got all the way down on the hearth, pressing his cheek to cold stone.

"Don't hurt yourself," Hope said. He glanced back to see her entering the living room again, clutching something in her hand. "That looks uncomfortable."

"I'm fine," he replied.

The object in her hand turned out to be a dusty old cap with big earflaps. Hope brought it to the living room window, lifted the blanket they'd tacked in place, and carefully pushed the hat into the hole. She worked it in until it was firmly in place, then let the blanket fall back in place.

"Good idea," he said. Already, he could tell the difference. Wind was no longer blowing into the room, shaking the blanket.

Hope turned to him and gave him a small curtsey, clearly sarcastic, then headed off to the bedrooms again. Despite this, he was proud of her for coming up with a solution. At least she was applying herself to the situation and not just moping. That was a hopeful sign. He decided to ignore the curtsey—much of raising a teenager as a single parent seemed to consist of deciding how much to ignore. He thrust the fire poker up into the chimney. About a foot in, he heard the clank of metal and felt a solid edge.

The flue. It was higher in the chimney than he'd anticipated. As he probed it with the fire poker, he finally figured out that it was hinged in the middle. By pressing on one end, he managed to slowly open it. While doing that, he felt what seemed to be a handle, but it was very short. Perhaps it was broken? Maybe the handle had been removed? Whatever the case, getting the flue open felt like such a moment of triumph that it brought tears to his eyes.

A warm fire will change everything, he thought. *As long as we're not stuck here too long.*

The small pile of wood on the hearth looked like enough for maybe three good fires—four, if he kept them small. How long would that last them? A day or two, maybe?

Don't think about that now, he chided himself. *All you need is a break in the weather, and you can hit the road again.*

13

A crackling fire did make all the difference. Within minutes, it had warmed up the entire living room. Outside, the world seemed harsh and hateful, but the fire kept it at bay. Jarred even dared to unzip his coat and push his hood back. It felt like a monumental accomplishment somehow, a victory over the hostile forces of nature.

"Okay, done," Hope said, after a while. She came into the living room lugging a bunch of stuff in her arms. She carried it to the couch and dumped it all: hats, socks, a canteen, some blankets, a tarp, and some other bits of junk and tools.

She walked over to the fire, unzipping her coat and shrugging it onto the floor. Jarred stooped down, picked it up, and tossed it onto the couch. Under the coat, she was wearing a long-sleeve t-shirt and a pair of sweatpants, and she had large sweat stains around her armpits and the small of her back.

"Want to know what we've got?" she said.

"Give me the good news," he replied.

She gave him a brief look, eyes narrowed. He could tell she was fighting the urge to say something sarcastic. "Fine," she said, at last. "Here's the rundown. A kitchen with no appliances, none whatsoever, except for a small stove. No toaster, no microwave, nothing. We've got the smelly old beds, but the foam mattresses are filthy and full of holes. The twin bed in the second bedroom is flimsy, with a thin mattress that's hardly suitable for a human being. Oh...the good news..." She glanced at him again. "There's a metal bedpan in the master bedroom. I guess that's our bathroom from now on, because I'm not peeing outside. Well, but I can't number two in a bedpan. No way. Never going to happen. I'll hold it for as long as I can."

"That's not good for you," he said.

"Neither is a blizzard in September, Dad," she countered. "Also, the cabin is really drafty. I can feel cold air seeping in from a whole bunch of places. I even saw gaps in the wall in the bedroom. But, anyway..." She gestured at the pile of stuff on the couch. "I found all of this amazing stuff, so there you go. That's it."

Again, he decided to ignore the undertone of sarcasm, giving her a brief hug instead. "Good job. Thanks for doing that."

At first, she resisted, stiff in his embrace, but then she hugged him back briefly. "So, you can figure out what we do next."

He considered the many things they needed to do to survive long-term in the cabin. The bathroom situation was bad. The water situation was bad. The food situation was also potentially bad. However, heat was the priority.

"I'll tell you what," he said. "Go drag the mattress off the big bed and bring it in here."

She gave him a funny look. "I don't think we can burn a foam mattress, Dad. Won't the fumes be toxic?"

"Not for that," he said. "We're going to keep in as much heat as possible. I think that's the most important thing."

She seemed to get it and nodded before heading to the bedroom again. Hope was a bright kid. He just wished she was quicker to lower her defenses.

While she wrestled with the mattress, he went to the tiny, appliance-free kitchen and rooted through all of the drawers and cabinets. He found a few utensils, including a decent steak knife, which he grabbed and set on the counter. One of the cabinets had a small collection of dented and dusty canned goods. He set these beside the knife. He even found a small, rusty hatchet and a half-used roll of duct tape in a junk drawer. He lined all of this up on the counter, then grabbed the steak knife and returned to the living room.

By then, Hope was dragging the big foam mattress across the room. She dumped it beside the couch, then made a sweep of her arm, as if she were showing off a prize on a game show. As she'd said, the mattress was filthy. It looked decades old, was stained, and had small missing chunks, as if it had been chewed on by rodents.

"I feel like I might've got a disease just touching it," she said.

"I'm sure you're fine," he replied, squatting beside the mattress.

"So…you're using it for insulation, I assume," she said. "Otherwise, I have no idea what you're doing what that knife."

"You're exactly right," he replied. As he said it, he proceeded to cut the mattress into small pieces with the steak knife. "This is why you're a straight-A student."

"Are you complimenting me or making fun of me?" she asked.

"Complimenting, of course," he replied. The foam resisted the blade, so he had to saw back and forth while twisting and pulling the mattress with his other hand to work it through. "When have I ever made fun of you?"

"I guess never. Do you want me to help you cut it up?"

"No, I've got it," he said. He cut the mattress all the way down the middle lengthwise, though it was a very slow process, then he began cutting it into quarters. Because it was so old, when he cut it, the foam seemed to produce a cloud of dust. He turned his head to avoid breathing it.

Hope was standing near the fireplace, and she shuffled her feet. It was a gesture he recognized—guilt. But where had it come from? She shifted from mood to mood so rapidly, he often struggled to keep up.

"What's wrong?" he said.

"I don't know," she replied, tapping the toe of her boot on the hardwood floor. "I broke the window in the first place, and then I kind of complained a lot. I'm just stressed out, Dad, but I want to help."

So that's what it was. He paused and looked at her, trying to give her a reassuring smile. "Hope, sweetheart, a little grumpiness is perfectly understandable under the circumstances. Hey, everything is going to be just fine. There will be a break in the storm, and then we'll get out of here. Until then, we just have to stay as warm and comfortable as we can, okay?"

She nodded. "I know. I'll try not to be so whiny from now on."

He felt bad lying to her. A break in the storm? *Not according to Atul.* He hadn't told his daughter the full extent of what he knew. As far as she knew, it was a freak snowstorm that might last a while. All of that stuff about seeding clouds to rebuild the glaciers...no, he intended to keep that close to the vest for the time being. Still, it made him feel guilty. He was filling her with false hope.

I'll tell her the truth soon, he told himself. *Once we've set things up a little better, and we can hunker down in comfort for a while. She'll be more ready to receive it then.*

He went back to work cutting the mattress into little pieces.

"Are those cans in the kitchen any good?" she asked. "I'm kind of hungry."

"They might be palatable," he replied. "We'll take a look when we get done with this. Sealed cans like that can last a long time, even past their expiration date."

"Well, I don't want to end up like the guys on the Franklin Expedition," she said. "Have you read about them? Two ships got stuck in the Arctic ice trying to reach the Pacific, and most of their canned food was rancid. Do you know what they had to do?"

"I promise you we won't have to resort to cannibalism," he said. He'd read about the Franklin Expedition of 1845, and he remembered all too well how the men had slowly starved to death in the bone-cracking cold of a relentless winter, their ships trapped in the ice. "Our situation is nothing like theirs. They were stuck in the ice for months in the Arctic and slowly ran out of food. We're just riding out a snowstorm a mile from town."

And if it's like this forever? he wondered. *If Atul is right and the weather patterns have changed irrevocably, what will the long-term consequences be?*

Afraid this line of thought might show on his face, he quickly pushed it aside and rose. The foam mattress was now reduced to a pile of fist-sized chunks. The dust was still settling, and cutting the old foam had filled the living room with an awful musty smell. But it was done.

When he turned to his daughter, she was staring hard at him.

Keep her busy for now, he told himself. *That'll give her less time to worry about what I'm not telling her. Eventually, I'll give her the whole truth, when the time seems right.*

"If you want to help, here's your chance," he said, beckoning her as he went back to the kitchen. He set the steak knife on the counter and picked up the roll of duct tape. "Anywhere you see gaps, cracks, or holes in the outer walls, I want you to tape a piece of that foam mattress over it. Anywhere a draft is coming in, cover it."

She took the duct tape from his hand and headed toward the back bedrooms. As Hope worked on covering the gaps, he dared to take a break for a few minutes, sitting on the couch and listening to the crackle of the fire.

Under different circumstances, this might be kind of nice, he thought. *If I didn't know what was waiting for us just beyond the walls.*

14

The little burst of determination induced by Larry the Florist lasted all the way home. Yes, she was going to hang in there, tough it out, and make this work somehow. No fleeing, no giving up, no moping around like a hopeless nobody. Fiona was tough, and she'd proven it to herself numerous times over the last few years. On her own, with little help, she'd carved out a homestead from the crumbling remains of old buildings. She had her own herd, her own crops and greenhouse, and she'd made plenty of modifications and improvements. She'd built a whole new life for herself just the way she wanted it.

Her confidence wavered slightly when she passed the cars still stuck in the ditches, but she managed to hold on. And then she pulled into her own driveway and saw the tracks from earlier that morning already getting soft on the edges as new snow filled them, and her confidence wavered.

"I have to put up with this stupid storm with no generator," she fumed, fighting fresh tears. "I'll run out of firewood, and then what? Chopping down trees in a blizzard!" She shouted this last part and slammed her hand into the roof of the truck.

It caused Smoke to whimper and stand up.

"Sorry, boy," she said, scratching him behind the ear. "You're not in trouble. I'm just ranting a little bit."

The generator's not getting fixed, and I can't buy a new one, and that's it.

She wanted so badly to hit the roof again, but she restrained herself for the dog's sake. No sense scaring him. She finally pulled the truck to the top of the driveway, parking it in the little divot where it had begun the day.

There was so much to be done. So much. She couldn't wrap her head around it, so she left the engine running, held fast to the steering wheel, and stared into the void for a few minutes. Seething.

"No, I can do this," she told herself. "I can survive without electrical power. It's not a big deal. You wasted a morning on a trip to town. So what? Come on, Fiona. Come on. Come on. It'll be more difficult than usual, that's all."

Smoke, as if trying to comfort her, stepped over the armrest and laid his head on her lap. She petted him for a while, and it helped. She felt better. A tiny bit calmer.

"I just have to take some steps to ease the strain around here," she said. "I can do it. Forget about the wasted trip today. Just don't think about it."

She managed to find her way back to something like boldness, and she seized the opportunity. Shutting off the engine, she opened the door, and stepped out into the wind and snow. She trudged back to the barn. Smoke followed, but he lagged behind a little—as if her previous outburst had unsettled him. When Fiona got to the barn, she was shocked at just how cold it was inside. Of course, the barn wasn't insulated, and there were gaps between some of the beams. Snow had even managed to seep through in a few places. The milking goats were huddled together, desperate for warmth. They scarcely responded to her presence.

"Poor girls," Fiona said. "Don't worry. I'm not going to leave you out here to freeze. Let's go somewhere a little warmer, shall we? We're going to make do until this stupid storm passes, even if it does last all season, and then we'll deal with whatever damage it leaves behind and get on with our lives. How does that sound?"

As she approached the nearest pen, she heard a long creaking groan coming from above her. She glanced up warily. Too much snow on the roof, it seemed. The weight was stressing the old barn. Not a good sign. At some point, she might have to climb up there on a ladder and sweep it clean, though she didn't relish the thought.

If I fall and break a bone out here, I'm done for, she thought.

She led the milking goats out of their pens, gathering them around the door. Smoke immediately went to work, dashing back and forth to keep them clustered close together. Once all the females were out, she saw Ramses glaring at her from his pen near the back, those weird yellow eyes with their horizontal pupils fixed on her.

"You'll have to wait, buddy," she said, wagging a finger at him. "We can't have you pushing the girls around."

As if he'd understood, he bleated loudly and aggressively, a truly ear-straining, ugly sound.

"Don't use that kind of language with me," Fiona said. "I feed you, remember?"

With all the milking goats together, she set off toward the house. Smoke kept the goats moving, following her dutifully up to the house and toward the basement door. Snow had piled up against the door and it took some effort to get it opened. Once open, she waved the goats down the steps into the basement. It wasn't ideal. They were liable to gnaw on her stuff, but at least they would be a few degrees warmer down there. Her gaze happened upon a glint of water at the bottom of the steps. The puddles on the floor had gotten bigger. And if it got worse? She couldn't have the goats standing in inches of cold water.

She decided not to worry about it for the time being. The foundation was cracked and probably sinking, but it was a slow leak. She had time. Meanwhile, keeping them down there might just keep them alive. Some of the goats were reluctant to go down into the darkness, but Smoke didn't put up with any hesitation. He barked and zigzagged and forced them all through the door.

"You're such a good boy," Fiona said, taking a moment to pet him. "Even on a day when your mommy keeps throwing fits. Come on. Let's go get the troublemaker."

She shut the basement door and latched it. Then she went back down to the barn for Ramses. Under the circumstances, she wasn't sure that Smoke alone would be enough to get the ornery male up the hill and into the basement, so she got a lead line and hitched it to his collar. He tolerated this, but when she opened his pen, he resisted leaving. Smoke tried to get around behind him, but he moved to block the dog.

"You can't stay in here," Fiona said, pulling on the rope. "Come on! You'll freeze to death. I've got a nice dark basement waiting for you. Let's go."

She kept pulling and finally he gave in, stepping out of his pen and looking around. At last, Smoke was able to get behind him, and that helped to keep Ramses moving. Still, he was a big pain in the butt all the way up the hill and around the house, constantly trying to veer off in the wrong direction, bleating for no reason.

"Stop fighting me, you big dummy," Fiona said. "I'm doing this for your own good!"

Finally, she opened the door, and Smoke barked to usher him inside. He tromped down the steps with a final bleat. Fiona followed him down, clicking on a flashlight as she went. Putting the animals in the basement was far from ideal. She knew it was asking for trouble. They would defecate and urinate all over the place, chew up the furniture and supplies she had down there, and generally make a big mess of the place. Still, it was better than bunch of frozen animals in the barn.

When she got to the bottom of the steps, she saw the animals all crowded together around some of her furniture, as if they were utterly fascinated by all of these strange new objects. Only Ramses was off by himself, sniffing and rooting around her worktable. They would need food and water, of course, and that probably meant dragging one of the troughs from the paddock. Her work was never done. She sighed and turned to head back up the stairs, where Smoke was waiting, pacing back and forth.

"We're far from done," she said, kicking the door shut behind her. "Let's go get the chickens."

She trudged back down the hill again. At least by now she'd cleared a nice path for herself, so she wasn't dragging her feet through the snow. She kept a dozen chickens in a small coop between the greenhouse and storage building, along with a single guard goose. The coop was built of old scrap lumber from house renovations. She'd built it like a tiny house of its own, covering it in white siding and fencing in a small area where the chickens normally fed.

As she approached, the goose saw her coming through a little window beside the door and began honking like mad. Fiona considered the predicament. How to get all of the chickens into the basement? Obviously, they couldn't be herded like the goats, though she didn't doubt Smoke would try. Finally, she went and got the Mule, driving it back to the coop and loading up the animals in the back. Smoke tried to help, running alongside her and barking at the chickens, as if they needed to be reminded who the boss was. Only the goose showed any resistance, honking and flapping his wings when she picked him up. Still, he took his place with the chickens without trying to jump out of the back of the Mule.

Putting the chickens and goats into the basement together proved a challenge. She had to move furniture around to create a makeshift wall, sectioning off an area for the chickens. The goats were already nibbling at the edges of tables, so her next task was hauling a bunch of hay and feed from the barn into the house so she could store it closer to the animals and keep it dry.

It turned into hours and hours of work—an endless back and forth of hauling things in and out of the Mule until she was absolutely soaked with sweat under her heavy coat, and her shoulders and back were crying out in agony. She paused only to feed Smoke, but otherwise, the dog stayed right beside her throughout, pretending to help even when there was nothing he could do.

Finally, she drove the Mule back down to the barn, parked it, and covered it with the tarp. She took a moment to catch her breath, as Smoke waited for her near the door. She might have stood there a while, but another prolonged groan from the ceiling beams overhead got her moving again.

At least if it collapses, it won't kill the goats, she thought, *but I really don't want to have to rebuild this barn once the snowstorm passes.*

She crossed the barn and pulled the big door shut behind her. Fiona trudged up the now well-worn path to the basement door to check on the animals one more time. As soon as she pulled open the door, the stench of the animals wafted out, and she heard Ramses bleating down there.

Smoke, sensing trouble, immediately raced down the basement steps, barking like mad. Fiona stomped as much of the snow off her boots as she could and headed down into the stinking darkness after him.

I've got this. I can handle it. The storm won't win.

15

Any time the fire started to die down, Jarred felt the presence of the brutal cold as it seeped in around them. It lingered along the walls, despite their best attempt to insulate all of the gaps. After hours of this, it felt like a furious battle against some unseen enemy force that had consumed the whole world outside of the cabin.

They stayed close to the fire at all times. Eventually, Jarred and Hope even dragged the couch closer to the hearth so they could soak up as much of the warmth as possible. Even then, he could feel the cold. Hope had been sitting on her end of the couch in silence, still bundled up in her coat, for hours, her hands tucked under her thighs. When the fire got low, she turned to him, silently willing him to add wood to the fire.

"We're going to run out of firewood fast at this rate," he noted, pointing to the remaining pieces at the end of the hearth.

"Well, we can chop down trees or something," she replied. "The fire is running low again, Dad."

"Just give it a little longer," he said, staring at the meager flames in the fireplace. Another thirty minutes or so and the fire would be gone.

"Dad," Hope said, "what if no one ever comes for us? They don't even know where we are. Shouldn't we call 911 again?"

"I tried to call," he replied, pulling out his cell phone and holding it up. "I couldn't get through. I'll try again when the storm dies down."

"Can't you try again *now*? Just keep dialing over and over. Eventually, you'll get through."

"I don't want to waste the battery," he said. "I'm at twenty-six percent, and there's no way to recharge it."

Hope sighed and leaned to one side, flopping over the arm of the couch. "Sorry, I'm not trying to complain so much. It's just stressful. It feels like we're stuck here, and I just want to go home. There's got to be a way out of here."

"I know how you feel," he replied, reaching over and patting her on the back. "I'm sure they'll clear the roads soon enough. It's going to take time. The storm hit so fast, no one was ready for it, so it's taking longer than usual. Maybe by tomorrow."

"Okay," she said. "If you say so."

In the silence that followed, he heard the faint rumble of her stomach. She wrapped her arms around her belly.

"Hungry?" he asked.

She didn't answer right away, her gaze fixed upon the guttering flames. Finally, she said, "Yeah, maybe we should've gone for the gas station cheeseburgers after all."

Jarred rose and headed toward the kitchen. "We've got food here. Let's pry open one of those cans and see what's inside."

"The Franklin Expedition begins," Hope muttered. "If you pry the lid off and see something moving around in there, don't eat it."

"I'm sure it'll be fine," he said. "Canned goods last for years."

He'd lined up the cans on the counter. The labels were old and faded. Some had no label at all, and a few of them were dented. Out of curiosity, he grabbed one of the unlabeled cans. He shook it, hoping to somehow determine what was inside, but he heard only sloshing. With no can opener, he had to use the big steak knife to punch a series of holes around the lid of the can, then use the tip of the knife to pry the lid back. In the dim, flickering firelight, he saw what appeared to be yellowish fruit in syrup.

"Let me guess," Hope said. "A fermented horse nose in tomato gravy?"

"Sorry to disappoint you but it's sliced peaches," he said, grabbing a spoon. He brought the can and spoon back into the living room. "Nothing is moving around in there, and it's not discolored. I think it's safe to eat." He angled the can so she could see inside.

"No way," she replied. "There's no mold, but it looks ancient. I'm not eating it. Help yourself."

"Are you sure?" He scooped up a piece of fruit and ate it. Though it didn't taste rotten, there was definitely something wrong with it. It was so mushy that it just dissolved on his tongue, and the taste was strangely muted, almost cardboard. He tried a second bite, and it was worse. "Yeah, maybe you're right. These might be a little older than I thought."

He took the can back into the kitchen and set it beside the sink. By now, the heat was notably diminishing in the cabin, so he finally set the last two logs into the fireplace. It pushed back the bitter cold, filling the living room with a bright, orange glow, but he stared at the bare hearth with a sense of trepidation. Hope had suggested chopping down a tree, but he dreaded the prospect of marching out there and attempting it.

"Dad," Hope said. He realized then that he'd been staring at the bare hearth for quite some time. "The bed frame in the master bedroom is made of wood. Why don't we chop it up for firewood? That'll last for a while." When he hesitated, she added, "You already ripped up one of the mattresses. What's the difference? We need fire."

It was certainly better than marching outside, so he retrieved the hatchet and headed into the master bedroom. The bed frame looked like it had been handmade—maple wood, he thought. It had the roughness, the slight irregularity, of a garage project. Fortunately, it didn't seem to have a lot of varnish on it. Maybe it would be safe to burn. Jarred dragged the box springs off the frame and went to work. First, he dismantled it. Then he began hacking the boards into reasonably sized chunks. It took a good half hour, but when he was done, they had a nice stack of wood on the hearth, enough to last quite a few hours, he thought.

He tossed one of the smaller pieces into the fire to see how it would burn. It smoked a bit more than the firewood, but otherwise seemed okay. When he turned around, he saw Hope wandering aimlessly around the living room and kitchen, as if she'd become restless.

"That was a great idea," he told her. "I'll have to see what other furniture we can use for firewood." When she kept wandering, he asked, "Are you okay?"

She stopped near the back door and slowly turned to him, her hands on her hips. "I don't want to go outside. I really don't want to go out there…but…"

"You need to use the restroom?"

She nodded. "I needed to hours ago, and I've held it as long as I could. It's getting painful now. I really think I have to go."

"I told you, there's a bedpan," he said.

"And I told you, I'm not using a bedpan," she said tightly. "That's gross."

"Well, look, you're not going to freeze to death in a couple of minutes," he said. "Just run out there to the outhouse, get it done, and run back inside. The fire is going really good now. You'll thaw out in no time."

She pursed her lips and scowled at him. "Fine. I'm going to do it." She grabbed the doorknob and held it for a few seconds. "Even the doorknob is like ice. I can feel it through my gloves."

"Count to three and go for it," he said. "Like jumping into a cold swimming pool. You just have to go for it."

That only intensified her scowl, but then he noticed her lips were moving, like she was counting under her breath. Suddenly, she shoved the back door outward. Frigid wind roared into the kitchen. It blew Hope's hood back, exposing her face and whipping her medium-length hair wildly. She shrieked and turned her face, struggling with one hand to get her hood up. Then she lunged through the open door and sank into the deep snow.

The outhouse sat no more than ten yards from the back door, but a large mound of snow stood between the house and the outhouse door. Hope had to hunch down and battle her way through the wind, and as soon as she stepped away from the house, the wind blew the door shut. It slammed hard enough to rattle the whole house.

I'll have to go soon, too, Jarred thought, *but I'm using the bedpan. I don't care if it's gross. It's a Plutonian landscape out there.*

He went to the room and retrieved the small stainless-steel bedpan and took it into the hallway closet, setting it on the shelf. The closet was just big enough to serve as a makeshift restroom. After that, he started gathering up anything they could use for firewood. Empty drawers from a dresser, unused shelves from the bedroom closet, a small night table. He even removed the wooden doors from the cupboards. All of them were suitable sources of wood, so he dragged them all into the living room and set them beside the hearth.

It seemed like a lot, but as he considered it, he realized that even all of this wood might last a day or two at most if he intended to keep the fire going. And then what? Despite his encouragement to Hope, he didn't expect anyone to come for them by then, even if they could reach someone to let them know where they were. City services would be overwhelmed as the storm continued unabated.

We can't stay here indefinitely, he realized. *We'll have to set out again at some point and try to reach Glencole.*

It was a terrifying prospect, and he was thankful that he could put it off for at least another day. They could melt snow for water, so they were okay on that front. If they had to eat the canned food, they would survive, he thought, but they could fast for a day, if need be. Yes, he could put off the worst for at least a day.

Just then, the back door flew open again, and another roaring wind blasted through the kitchen and into the living room, casting snow across the countertop and the floor. Hope trudged through the door, pressing her hood to her head. She appeared to be dragging something behind her, but he couldn't see what it was. As soon as she was in the kitchen, the wind blew the door shut behind her. It startled her, and she stumbled forward and fell to her knees.

"How was it?" he asked.

"Awful," she replied, flinging her hood back and running her gloved fingers over her frizzy hair. Her cheeks and the tip of her nose were bright red from the cold. "I didn't even make it into the outhouse, okay? It was too far, and the snow was too deep there."

"So where did you…?"

She swiped her hand at him. "On the ground by the wall. Don't worry about it. It was terrible. I should have used the bedpan."

"Next time," he said.

"There's not going to be a next time," she replied, picking herself up and brushing the snow off her shoulders. "I'll hold it for however long it takes until we get out of here." And then, clearly trying to change the subject, she stepped to one side and said, "Also, I found this. It was sitting by the back wall of the house. It's all wood."

Now he saw what she'd been dragging. An old wooden wheelbarrow, half-broken and filled with snow. It was small, a broken flowerpot still sitting in the back.

"We'll have to dry it out," Hope said, walking back into the living room and dropping onto the couch, "but it'll burn."

He retrieved the wheelbarrow and dragged it over to the rest of the pile, positioning it close to the fireplace so it would dry out.

"Wow, that was good thinking," he said. "It was your idea to use the furniture in the first place. Good job, Hope. Your smart thinking is going to keep us going."

He turned to look at her. She had a small embarrassed smile on her face. Clearly, she was proud of herself, and he thought her red cheeks and nose had turned a shade darker, as if she were blushing from his praise. She never handled compliments well, and she quickly sighed and changed the subject.

"I just wish the stupid storm would end," she said.

"I know," he replied.

16

Bringing the goats into the basement proved as problematic as Fiona had feared. They didn't know the environment, so their curiosity, and perhaps anxiety, made them trample and nibble at everything, and generally make a giant mess. She did her best to rearrange the basement to keep them away from her best furniture and supplies, creating makeshift walls that penned them into specific corners.

Fiona had laid down a bed of hay, but the animals were already urinating and defecating all over the floor, which mingled with the seepage from the subsiding basement to make a disgusting, foul-smelling stew. The chickens smelled even worse. It was warm down there, at least. Bringing all of the animals together in a small, insulated space had done the trick. She wasn't worried about them freezing to death.

She spent some time with them even after the work was done just to reassure them that all was well. As she petted and spoke to the animals, Ramses and the goose tried to outdo each other for sheer noise. It was in the lull between their ear-straining sounds that she caught another sound. At first, it was so faint that it was little more than a subconscious feeling. However, the second time, she caught it clearly. A distinctive banging sound. Smoke perked up, staring toward the open basement door.

The barn. That was her first thought. All of that snow on the barn roof had finally brought the building down, and she was hearing the walls collapse. But then she heard it again. The sound was muffled in the basement, but she was now sure it was coming from the house. Someone knocking on the door? Was that possible? People so rarely came to the homestead uninvited that she just stood there in amazement for a few seconds. Smoke whimpered, started to move into the kitchen, then looked down at Fiona.

Someone from town, she thought. *They sent someone to fix the generator!*

Duke might have done so since he knew of her need. Excited at the possibility, she rushed up the stairs. At the top, she had placed a welcome mat so she could wipe her shoes. As she did so, the knocking on the door intensified. She rushed through the kitchen and past the crackling fire in the fireplace. On the way, out of sheer instinct, she grabbed the fire poker from the hearth. She scarcely realized she'd done it until she reached the front door. When she saw it in her hand, she briefly considered returning it, but an abundance of caution stayed her hand.

Smoke went to the door and began pacing back and forth, whimpering.

Someone in trouble? Fiona wondered. *Someone injured, desperate? Dangerous?*

She peered through the peephole. The person on the other side was standing so close to the door that she saw only a black shadow shape against the harsh white background of snow. It seemed like a man, though, someone not particularly tall but somewhat stocky.

Just answer it, she told herself. *He's not too big. If it's a problem, you can take him.*

Drawing the fire poker back, she unlocked the door with her free hand and eased it open. The man immediately stopped knocking and took a couple steps back. He wore a heavy green coat and thick snow pants, snow clinging to every crease in his clothing. But she knew him then. He had a small black patch on his right shoulder that was mostly covered, but she knew what it was. Though a fur-lined hood put his face in shadow, she didn't have to see him. A park ranger's coat, a familiar stocky build. Behind him, parked near the porch steps, was a blue Yamaha Sidewinder snowmobile, its tracks trailing down the hill and off to the southeast along the edge of the woods.

Before he could say anything, Smoke leapt up and put his front paws on the man's hips. Well, now she understood why the dog hadn't started barking.

"Benjy. What the heck are you doing here?" Fiona asked. "Where did you come from? Tell me you didn't drive all the way from your ranger station on the river."

"Ha," he said, in his annoying little fake laugh. Now, he pushed his hood back, and she saw that face. Bushy eyebrows, a little pug nose, unshaved cheeks and chin. He had nice brown eyes. That was his one redeeming feature, but she hated the perpetual half-smile that always played over his generous lips. "I won't say it if you don't want me to, Fiona. It's good to see you, though. You seem to be doing well despite all this crazy weather. Do you mind if I come in for a second?"

She almost refused him entry. Indeed, it was right on the tip of her tongue, prepared and set in place just for Benjy Hartman long, long ago. But she looked at the harsh conditions outside, the snow still coming in sideways on the fierce wind, creating a kind of white haze in the distance. Benjy's face was already bright red from the cold, his lips chapped, and he was shivering. Though she wasn't at all happy to see him, she wasn't entirely heartless. Nor did she find Benjy dangerous—just annoying.

"Okay, you can come in long enough to warm up a little," she said, stepping back and pulling the door open. As she did, she lowered the fire poker.

He noticed. "Whoa, were you going to clock me with that thing? I thought we ended on better terms than that."

"Just get inside," she replied. Already, he had found more than one way to irritate her. Of course, he had to find the first opportunity to talk about their non-relationship. They'd never dated. Did he think they had? She had turned him down many, many times and finally booted him out of her life completely.

He stomped his boots on the threshold and came inside. He had a scarf, but he'd already pushed it down beneath his chin, where it rested in a groove of whiskery fat. As he stepped inside and the firelight caught his face, she realized that he was far more windburned and red than she'd realized. Smoke circled around him once, still excited, then ran over and hopped up on the couch. The dog knew him and liked him. Benjy had gone out of his way in the past to earn the dog's affection.

"It must be really bad at your ranger cabin out there in the woods," she said, heading back over to the hearth and setting down the fire poker.

"Oh, it's pretty bad," he replied, tugging his gloves off one by one and banging the excess snow off on the doorframe. "I kind of thought it might be worse here. I notice you cleared a path down the hill, but otherwise you're pretty much snowed in."

He hung his gloves on the coat rack. The front door was still wide open, and he was standing just inside, with the cold wind blowing past him. Fiona sighed and motioned for him to close the door. It was amazing how someone could feel both comfortably familiar and like a splinter under her thumbnail at the same time. Of course, he'd been hitting on her nonstop since the day they met, in overt and subtle ways. She'd made it clear that she wasn't interested in him, that she would *never* be interested in him under any circumstance, yet here he was. Tromping into her living room in his big ugly boots.

"I smell critters," he said, tipping his head back and taking a big sniff. "Oh, man, it's stinky in here. Do you live with farm animals or something. Because *that* is pungent."

"I'm keeping a few animals in the basement for the time being," she said, struggling not to sound annoyed. He finally pushed the front door shut. "Did you come all the way here just to make fun of the way my house smells? Because I don't need that."

He unleashed his forced laugh again, unzipping his coat to reveal his brown ranger shirt underneath. Yes, he'd clearly been on the job when he'd decided to pay her a visit.

"Hey, no offense intended," he said, taking his coat off and tossing it toward the coat rack. It failed to catch on a hook and fell to the ground, forcing him to walk over and pick it up. "Geez, Fiona, you take everything I say in the worst possible way. I'd thought you'd have mellowed out a little by now. I just noticed the smell and wondered what it was. Bringing the animals into the basement was a good idea. They'd turn to ice out there in the barn. Is that what you normally do when it's cold outside?"

"There have been a few winters where it was so bad that I moved animals into the greenhouse," she said, "but the goats aren't getting along. The big male is a bully. I was afraid they'd tear the place apart."

He gave her a big crap-eating grin, then gestured toward the couch. "Why don't we sit down and have a nice chat. It's been way too long. We should catch up." If he'd come all the way here just to try to wear her down again, she really was going to kick him right in the butt. She shook her head at his suggestion and headed to the kitchen door, as if she had work to do. When she got there, she turned to face him.

Why did I let Benjy Hartman into my house? You're too nice, Fiona. The guy's a pest, and you damn well know it.

"So did you come here for some specific reason?" she asked. "I'm not in the mood for small talk. Surely, you're not either. What's up?"

He pushed his cap back and furiously scratched at his thick blond hair. "I hate to admit it, but I was forced to abandon the ranger station. Nobody saw this storm coming—not in time to prepare for it, anyway—so I have no long-term supplies there. I could last a little while, I suppose, but they're saying this storm is here to stay. It's just swirling over us."

Fiona grunted unhappily. So, he wasn't here just to check on her. "Benjy, I don't know what to tell you. If you need long-term supplies, you might as well head into town. I don't even have power here. The generator's broke."

He walked over and sat down on the couch, leaning back and tucking his hands behind his head. Settling right in like he owned the place.

"There's not even a motel in Glencole," he said. Smoke snuggled up beside him.

"Maybe not," she replied, still standing in the kitchen doorway. "But there are people in town, and they will have access to a lot more supplies than I do. Duke Cooper is always willing to help people. It's going to take everything I've got just to make it by myself here on the homestead."

"Duke Cooper?" he said. "The guy who runs the general store? Yeah, he's fine, but the snowmobile is almost out of gas. It took most of the tank just to get here."

"You should have gone to town first," she said. "I can't do anything to help you."

"Well..." He rocked his head from side to side. "I thought...you know...maybe I could help *you* out here on the homestead."

Oh, God, how do I get rid of this guy?

"I didn't ask for help," she replied. "I handle myself just fine. You should know that."

"Look, I'll tell you what," he said. "If you've got a little gas to spare, I'll head on into town and see if Duke is around. How does that sound?"

"Just..." She sighed again and bowed her head. She did have enough gas to send him on his way. She had a full ten-gallon plastic jug of gasoline in the greenhouse that she'd stored specifically for the heater and as backup for the Mule.

"A couple of gallons is all it would take," he said.

It was like the world's worst game of "Would You Rather?" Give up some of her precious gasoline reserve just to get him out of her hair, or save the gas and potentially be stuck with him for a while. Either choice made her angry. To buy herself time, she went into the kitchen and opened the cupboard pretending to busy herself with a task.

"A couple of gallons, huh?" she said, moving plates and bowls around aimlessly. "Sounds like you don't get good mileage on that snowmobile."

"I normally get about nine miles to the gallon," he replied. "Not great, I know."

"One gallon will get you to town, then," she said.

"Maybe. It's rough out there, so the Yamaha will eat up more gas than usual. I wouldn't want to get stranded because I cut it too close. Anyway, I need enough for a round trip, you know?"

As she continued rooting around in the cupboard, she heard the creak and whoosh of the couch as he rose. Then his heavy footfalls as he came into the kitchen. She shut the cupboard and looked over her shoulder at him. He was standing there in the doorway with his red face and a big, dumb grin.

"Can I help with something in here?" he asked. "I'm not here to mooch gasoline from you. I'll be of some use, if I can."

Just give him the gas and get him out of your house, she told herself. But something in her resisted fiercely. Why should she give him anything? Especially something that she'd saved for herself.

"I'm fine," she said. "I'm handling everything just fine, Benjy. You didn't have to come all the way here, okay?"

She would have said more. She really wanted to rant at him. This was, after all, just another form of not taking "no" for an answer. He was always pushing his way into her life. The fact that he'd used all the fuel in his tank just to drive his snowmobile through the woods to her house felt like some awkward power trip.

She intended to say all of this and more, but she was startled by a sudden loud sound from behind her. It sounded like someone hammering on the basement steps. She spun to face the door, which was still wide open. Suddenly, a familiar strange face lunged out of the darkness: yellow eyes with wide pupils, long white beard dangling from his chin. As he passed through the basement door, Ramses's horns slammed into either side of the doorframe. He bleated at her and charged.

"How did you…?"

He was coming fast, as if seeking revenge for all she'd done to prevent his harassments. Hooves clacking on the wood floor, Ramses charged across the kitchen. Smoke immediately began to bark and rushed toward her from the living room, but Ramses was determined and moving fast.

Benjy moved with surprising speed, racing past both Fiona and Smoke, stepping right in front of the big charging goat. He grabbed the animal by the horns and leaned forward, absorbing the impact with his weight. Ramses bleated angrily and pushed at him, hooves losing purchase on the floor and scrabbling wildly. They wrestled back and forth for a bit, but Benjy slowly got the upper hand, forcing the goat back toward the stairs.

"You get back down where you belong, you ornery thing," he shouted.

Ramses finally surrendered and ceased pushing. He turned, and Benjy planted his hands on the animal's flank, forcing him through the door. As soon as he was through, Benjy grabbed the door and swung it shut. Ramses gave a final, frustrated bleat—as if admitting his defeat—and then Fiona heard him clacking his way back down the stairs.

And she couldn't deny that she was impressed. Benjy had handled Ramses like an old pro. He turned to her, hands on hips, beaming proudly.

"You just have to show the old boy who's boss," Benjy said. "Well, anyway, at least I was useful for a second. I may have just saved your life. Think about that! Wow! Now, about that gasoline…"

Fiona turned away, leaning against the counter. She did want to be rid of him, but seeing him manhandle Ramses had given her an idea. Was it wrong to get some use out of him before she sent him on his way?

It would be a fair trade for the gasoline, she told herself. *If he works for it, then he won't feel obligated to return someday and pay me back.*

"Okay, look…" She almost stopped herself then, but the magnitude of the problem finally decided her. "If you really want to be useful, there is something you could help me with."

"Hey, anything," he replied, giving her a totally unnecessary thumbs-up. "Just name it."

"The basement is leaking pretty bad," she said. Too late to take it back now. "I think the foundation is subsiding. I don't expect you to be able to fix that, but if you could seal the leaks, it will at least delay the inevitable. Animal droppings, urine, and a leaky basement don't make for a good combination."

Benjy gave her a little cocky smile. Oh, yeah, he loved that she needed his help. "Hey, no problem. You know how handy I am. But it might be a pretty big job. Might take me a few days to do it right."

Fiona nodded, suppressing an urge to sigh loudly. "Look, if you'll work on the problem, you can stay for the time being. Use the guest room. It's messy, but I'll clear off the bed."

"Awesome," he said. "Let me go get my stuff."

"Your stuff?"

"Yeah, I have a bag with some extra clothes, toiletries, and tools hooked on the snowmobile," he said, heading back into the living room. "Don't worry. I won't be any trouble." He paused at the front door and looked at her. For once, the smile was gone, and he had a serious look on his face. "I mean it, Fiona. I won't be any trouble. You won't regret this."

She didn't know what to say to this, so she just stood awkwardly while he headed back out into the snow. Smoke waited dutifully for him at the door.

Well, if he becomes a problem, I can always change my mind later, she said. *He's a pest, but I know how to handle him.*

17

They tried sleeping in the small bedroom closer to the living room. Jarred left the door open and gathered up plenty of blankets. Still, it wasn't enough. The cold was slowly taking over the edges of the house. When they lay down to sleep, he could feel its sharp needling, even through his sleeping bag and the layers of blankets. They'd burned through the firewood completely and started using more of the wooden furniture, but for some reason, the furniture wood didn't seem to burn as hot.

He lay there quietly for a couple hours, staring at the dark ceiling, knowing he might not fall asleep. He thought at least Hope might get some rest, but suddenly she stirred, flopping over under the pile of covers and uttering a loud harrumph.

"It just gets colder and colder," she said, voice muffled under the blankets. "Did the fire already burn itself out or what?"

"I'll go check," he said.

He worked his way out of his sleeping bag like a moth crawling out of its cocoon, pulling himself toward the door. When he got to the living room, he saw that the fire had indeed almost burned itself out. The furniture wood didn't last as long as the firewood either, it seemed. He added a couple of the cupboard shelves.

"We can't sleep in the bedroom," Hope said from the hallway. "It's too far from the fire."

"I think you're right," he replied, eyeing the stack of wood. "Let's drag the mattress into the living room. We'll have to push the couch back against the wall to make room. Come on."

They scooted the couch back against the wall, then dragged the twin bed mattress into the living room and set it between the window and the couch. After that, Jarred shut the bedroom door and stuffed one of the blankets into the crack along the bottom of the door. It would be easier to keep a smaller space warm. Maybe he could burn less wood. He sealed off the crack to the other bedroom, then the hallway closet as well.

Once that was done, he turned and surveyed the room, looking for anything else he might do to preserve heat. Hope was sitting on the mattress, blankets draped over her shoulders.

"It's a shame the fireplace is so open," he noted. "It's not the best design for heat insulation. I wish it kept more of the heat inside."

She didn't respond, and he thought maybe she'd dozed off again, still somehow sitting up. However, when he moved to the hearth, he realized she was frowning deeply and staring into the flames. He sat down on the hearth, and she glanced at him.

"Dad, you haven't told me everything you're thinking," she said. "Have you?"

He assumed she was referring to the rate they were going through the wood. It was true, he hadn't yet expressed his concern with how fast it was burning, but there was more that he'd kept to himself. For example, he hadn't told her that the battery in his cell phone was now dead, which meant they couldn't call for help again. Had she sensed this somehow?

"I guess we'll chop down some tree branches, if it comes to that," he said.

But Hope shook her head vigorously. "About the storm, Dad. I'm talking about the snowstorm. You've said a few times now that it might last a while, but I think you know more than you're telling me. I think your friend

Atul told you something more on the phone. If you're keeping it a secret from me then it must be really bad. When I look out the window, the snow and wind are blowing as hard as ever. It's not letting up. So, what's going on? You have to tell me everything."

Jarred had indeed held back the worst, but what was the use of telling her? What possible benefit could there be in taking away the last shred of hope that they might be rescued soon? Still, he could see by the look on her face that she did not want to be protected from the truth. Maybe she deserved to know.

He bowed his head and sighed. "I didn't want you to worry."

"I'm already worried," she replied, "so I might as well worry about the truth rather than my imagination. What do you know about this snowstorm?"

"Atul told me the storm is man-made," he said. "A side effect of an effort to stop the glaciers from melting and the seas from rising. A team of scientists created a low-lying carbon dioxide cloud in an attempt to re-form glaciers, but the experiment spiraled out of control and messed up weather patterns. This snowstorm is the result."

Hope's scowl slowly faded, eyes widening. "Who thought *that* was a good idea?"

"Multiple governments, apparently," Jarred said.

"Well, I guess there are a lot of stupid people in government," she muttered. "So what does it all mean? What's going to happen?"

It was a question that he'd tried not to think about too deeply himself. "Well, it means the change in weather is probably more of a long-term thing. A *long, long*-term thing."

"That explains a lot," she said. "There's no way I could have known about the experiment, but something told me this storm might be a long-term kind of thing. You should have just told me right away. Dad, there's no reason to treat me like a baby. I'm a little more perceptive than you realize."

Jarred felt chastised. She was a smart kid. A straight-A student who made robots in her spare time. Why was he trying to protect her from the truth, as if she wouldn't figure it out on her own?

"My friend Atul said the change to the weather pattern might be… irrevocable," Jarred said, "but I don't think he knows that for certain. Nobody knows."

"So they were able to start this thing, but they don't know how to stop it," she said.

"That seems to be the case."

She rose then, drawing the blankets all the way around her and holding them shut like a robe. Then she walked over to the living room window and peeled back the curtain. It was too dark outside to see anything, but she stared for a few seconds anyway.

Maybe I shouldn't have told her, he thought. Too late now. She knew the truth, and he couldn't protect her from it.

He stood up and went to her side, putting his arm around her shoulders. Through the dark window, he could see close to four inches of snow piled up on the windowsill. He felt Hope trembling, not from the cold, but there wasn't much he could say to blunt the impact of the truth.

"Look, we're in this together," he said. "As long as we're careful, as long as we make smart choices, we'll be fine. Hey, our ancient ancestors survived thousands of years of ice age, didn't they? Surely we can survive a few weeks of snow."

"I guess so," she replied. But then she broke out of his embrace and went back to the mattress. "I'm going to sleep now." And with that, she lay down, rolled up tightly in her blanket.

Jarred pulled the curtains shut and went to the mattress. It was eerily quiet out there at the moment, the silence broken only occasionally by the crack of a tree branch falling. He kept hoping to hear sirens from the nearby highway, but he never did. It seemed like the little hunting cabin was an island in an endless silent sea, but the island was slowly sinking into the snow.

A few minutes passed before Hope rolled onto her back and said, "So...do you have a plan? We can't just stay here in this cabin with rotten old food and a bedpan. I know you said we would walk to Glencole, but that's not really going to happen, is it? There's no way the gas station will be open, and I doubt there's a restaurant in town serving hamburgers to shivering customers. What's the plan, Dad?"

Walking to Glencole had been his only other plan, but maybe she was right.

"I'll level with you," he said. "I don't know what we're going to do next."

18

Fiona rooted through the pantry, making a careful inventory of the food she had stored in there. As she did, she heard Benjy tromping around in the basement. At least he was keeping himself busy and out of her hair for the time being. Still, she was distracted and felt silly for having given in to him.

He'll stop the leaking in the basement. It's worth it. She kept telling herself this, if only to keep from feeling like a fool.

After making a careful inventory of the food inside the house, she decided to check on the greenhouse. Anything to keep her busy under the circumstances, and suddenly a long walk away from the house didn't seem like such a bad idea. She'd left the heater running on its lowest setting, just enough to keep her gathered crops from turning to ice. Now seemed like a good time to see how fast she was going through the fuel, and maybe she would feel better about giving Benjy a couple of gallons.

Smoke was sitting patiently in front of the fireplace, but when Fiona put her coat on, he instantly bounded up and headed for the door. He was always ready at a moment's notice, night or day, to go to work at the slightest hint. Fiona pulled on a knit cap, wrapped a scarf around her neck, and pulled on her big winter boots. Then she zipped up the coat, raised the hood, and grabbed a pair of insulated gloves. It kind of felt like she was getting ready for an Antarctic expedition. Even more so when she opened the front door and the wind roared into the living room.

"Brace yourself, boy," she said to Smoke. "This is going to be intense."

And with that, she plunged headlong into the wind and stepped out onto the porch. Smoke came with her, though he seemed somewhat daunted by the wind. As Fiona pulled the door shut behind them, she eyed Benjy's snowmobile with irritation. It was just sitting there like it belonged in front of her house.

Fiona started down the steps and trudged past the blue Yamaha, cutting at an angle to meet up with the trail she'd cleared earlier. Of course, it was already starting to fill up with snow again. Still, it was easier than dragging her feet through the deep drifts. For once, Smoke didn't forge ahead. The snow had gotten deep enough now that he found it intimidating, so he hopped in her footsteps.

The barn, at least, hadn't collapsed yet, but the snow continued to pile up on top. It was only a matter of time. Fiona skirted well clear of it and headed to the greenhouse. The heater seemed to be working, judging by the smaller pile of snow on top of the greenhouse. When she opened the door, she felt the change in temperature. The heater was puttering away softly in the far corner. Smoke leapt past her and began tearing around the greenhouse, racing back and forth along the rows.

"Feels nice not to have two feet of snow on the ground, huh?" Fiona said, shutting the door behind her.

If there was any decision she'd made in the building of her homestead that now seemed prescient, it was splurging on a nice gasoline-powered heater for the greenhouse. She'd done it to protect her crops from the occasional cold front, but she'd never anticipated how important it would become. The heater was mounted on a concrete platform in the back corner of the greenhouse, vents running up to the roof and down the central apex.

She bent over the control panel. The lowest setting was fifty-degrees Fahrenheit. She made sure the dial was turned down all the way. Then she checked the fuel tank. Half full, so it would still last for a while. The extra gasoline was sitting in a large plastic container nearby. She checked this as well. It was full, of course. Everything down here seemed to be chugging along just fine. She looked up at the snow on the roof. The heat was helping to reduce the amount building up on the roof, but it couldn't keep up with the storm. Still, she figured the layer of snow on the roof might actually help to insulate the building.

Smoke had finally settled down, and had curled up beside the heater. Fiona stooped down and petted him, then filled up the heater's tank. It would need to run for a while now. Better to keep as much gasoline as possible. If anything, seeing how well things were going here made her less willing to share with Benjy, but maybe it was too late for that.

Next, she checked on the pepper plants in the greenhouse. They weren't exactly thriving. Fiona was staring at one of the plants, at the limp leaves, and she shook her head. She understood how the little plants felt.

"We're all just hanging in there, aren't we?" she said.

Finally, she grabbed a cloth bag and loaded up some of the produce she'd gathered: zucchini, carrots, and undersized potatoes. It would all be edible, even if some of it wasn't quite ripe. She would need to transfer them to the root cellar, so she had access to them once the pantry went bare. When the sack was full, she hoisted it over her shoulder and whistled for Smoke. He rose from beside the heater and came trotting over to her.

"Okay, buddy, back up the hill we go," Fiona said. "If we're lucky, maybe our visitor is just about done. What do you think?"

As if in reply, Smoke barked at her. But, then again, the dog liked Benjy for some reason that Fiona couldn't fathom. Fiona was looking in the direction of the heater, listening to the soft sound of the blower, when she felt a cold wind swirl around and touch her face. Thinking the greenhouse door had somehow come open on its own, she took it as a sign that it was time to leave. But when she turned, she saw Benjy standing in the open doorway.

As he stepped into the greenhouse, he gave a loud whoop, squinting against the cold wind. He shut the door and leaned against it, rubbing his gloved hands together.

"My goodness, that is just about the coldest wind I ever felt in my life," he said. "It cuts right through you like a machete, doesn't it?"

The little whoop had been meant to surprise her. She knew him well enough to know that. Even as he spoke, he kept chuckling to himself, as if it amused him. She stared at him flatly for a few seconds to make sure he got the point.

"So what are you doing in here?" he asked. "I came upstairs, and you'd just disappeared on me. I thought maybe old Jack Frost had snatched you away." This amused him far too much, and he laughed loudly. "Then I saw the fresh tracks going down the hill, and I thought, 'Uh-oh, she fled and left me here all alone.'"

Oh, just stop talking, she thought. *Please.*

"I'm gathering some of my produce to bring inside the house," she said, holding up the big cloth bag. "I'll need to can and preserve it all if it's going to last long-term."

"That looks heavy," he said. He approached, taking broad steps over the rows, and reached out. "Let me carry that for you."

She spun to one side, moving the bag out of his reach. As he tried to follow her, his hand brushed against hers, fingers sliding over her knuckles and along the back of her hand toward her wrist in a way that seemed deliberate. Fiona stepped back out of reach, narrowing her eyes at him, and he responded with a tooth-baring grin that seemed guilty.

"I've got this," she said. But he was still standing between her and the door, his hand poised in the air. "Would you mind, please, stepping aside, so I can get past you?"

The smile never left his face as he slowly, too slowly, moved to one side. Then his reaching hand swooped around, gesturing toward the greenhouse door as if showing her the way. Instead of walking past him, she continued to stare at him with narrowed eyes, her lips pressed tightly together, and gradually, his smile faded. She watched it die at the corners, collapsing into a frown.

As she stepped past him, he was still close enough that she bumped into him with her shoulder. He grunted, but she didn't bother to look back. Instead, she kept going to the door and yanked it open. Smoke came padding after her then, though he wasn't bothered by Benjy's behavior.

She started back toward the hill, resisting the urge to run and put as much distance between them as possible.

As soon as the basement leaks are patched, he's out of here, she told herself. *He won't stay one second longer, I swear to God.*

19

Moving into the living room proved to be a smart decision, and Jarred finally managed to sink into deep sleep, embraced by the warmth of burning furniture. Unfortunately, the sleep didn't last nearly as long as he'd hoped. He had a strange, unpleasant dream where the house was breathing, walls bowing in and out, and it dragged him back into the light. He opened his eyes, his head pounding, his whole body sore from lying on the uncomfortable mattress.

As he stared at the ceiling, where faint orange light danced along the beams, he realized he could still hear the house breathing. He turned toward Hope, but she was curled up deep inside her sleeping bag. For a second, he thought perhaps he was imagining it, so he sat up, flinging his blankets back. It wasn't quite a breathing sound. This was more like snuffling, the kind of a sound a dog might make when rooting around on the ground, only deeper.

It was loud, and seemed to be coming from somewhere in the room. Alarmed, the last vestige of sleep fell away, and Jarred rose, suddenly alert. He looked around, but there was no one else in the room with them. Hope definitely wasn't making the sound. As he turned around, he realized it was coming from the front door.

Early morning light burned through the curtains. As he approached, he realized there was a shadow at the lower right corner. He grabbed the curtain and slowly eased it back, revealing the frost-tinged window. Something was definitely moving on the porch, something big, but he couldn't see it through the frost.

"Dad, what is that?" Hope asked, her sleepy voice creaking. "That sounds like some kind of animal."

He leaned closer to the window, trying to make it out, as Hope appeared at his side. A big shadowy shape was hunkered down on the porch by the front door. Hope reached out and wiped the window with the sleeve of her coat. This removed enough of the frost that the massive shape suddenly became clear. Jarred saw huge furry shoulders, an arched back, a broad head with a long snout sniffing along the bottom of the door.

"Looks like a black bear," he said. "A big one, too."

"A bear?" Hope said in a little squeak, covering her mouth with her hands.

"I guess I knew there were bears in the wilderness areas around here," he said, speaking just above a whisper, "but I've never actually seen one. It must be desperate for food."

"It smelled us," Hope said, speaking through her fingers. "It smelled us in here, and now it wants to eat us."

"Well, they don't normally hunt humans," Jarred said.

"They hunt anything if they're desperate," Hope said, backing away from the window. "We're meat and blood just like any other animal, Dad. What difference does it make to a hungry bear?"

Jarred glanced over his shoulder toward the kitchen. A couple of open cans of food were sitting on the counter. They'd only taken a few bites of fruit. The other cans were lined up behind it. He rather preferred the possibility that the bear had smelled the canned food.

"We should toss the open cans outside," he said. "Maybe out the back door."

But before either of them could move to do that, he heard—and felt—a tremendous *thud* against the front door. Glancing through the window, he realized that the bear had reared up, placing its front paws against the door. He felt a shudder go through the door, and he heard the door creak and crack.

"Dad, he's coming through," Hope cried in a shrill voice. She covered her mouth again.

Jarred looked around, desperate for some way to scare the beast away. He didn't think tossing the cans out the back door would do much good now. They should have done it before the bear showed up, because the animal was determined to get inside now.

"I really wish we had a gun," he said. "I don't want to kill the bear, but maybe a loud shot would scare it away."

Hope was looking about frantically. Suddenly, she ran toward the fireplace. The door creaked again, and Jarred thought he saw it buckle in slightly. The deadbolt thudded against the strike plate. As he cast about for a weapon, Hope stooped down and grabbed a large piece of wood off their woodpile and shoved it into the fire.

"What are you doing?" Jarred asked.

"Maybe bright light will scare the bear away," Hope said. The fire flared up as the large piece of scrap wood caught, but it also created a big gush of dark smoke.

"We don't have enough firewood to spare," Jarred said. When his daughter reached for another piece of wood, he rushed forward and thrust an arm in front of her. "Hope, we can't waste wood. It's not going to scare him away."

"We have to do something," she said.

He glanced back at the door. It sounded like the bear was either scratching or biting at the door now. It was incredibly loud.

"Let's…" He wracked his brain, trying to think of something. "Let's try to scare him away by making a lot of noise. If he thinks there are aggressive animals in here, he might decide we're not worth the risk."

Eyes wide, she nodded. Together, they turned toward the door. Jarred started yelling, making loud guttural noises as he moved toward the front of the house. Hope opted for an ear-piercing shriek, and she rushed at the door. When she got there, she began to pound on the door with her fists, screaming and cursing loudly—clearly letting her terror feed into the noise. Jarred joined her at the door, slamming his fists into the wood wall around the door and shouting until his voice hurt.

After a couple of minutes, he realized he no longer heard the bear scratching on the door. He stopped yelling and signaled for Hope to do the same. Her screams wound down like a strange machine running out of power. In the silence that followed, Jarred held his breath and strained to listen. The wind was still howling outside, but he no longer heard the bear.

"Did we do it?" Hope said, her voice hoarse from screaming.

Jarred crept toward the window, grabbed a corner of the curtain, and eased it back. He leaned into the gap, but the window glass had already started to fog over again. Leaning in close, he gazed toward the door. He no longer saw the large, dark shape of the bear. He studied the porch for a minute, but it seemed the creature was gone.

I can't believe that worked, he thought.

"We did it," he said, turning to his daughter. "Or, more likely, *you* did it. You've got quite a scream there. The bear is gone."

He expected her to be proud of herself, or at least relieved. Instead, she shuffled back over to the fireplace, wiping tears from her eyes, and sat down beside their dwindling stack of makeshift firewood. Jarred went to her side, knelt down, and put an arm around her shoulders.

"I don't want to be here anymore," she said softly.

"I know," he replied.

His gaze was on the pile of wood. It burned too fast, way too fast.

There won't be enough to last the night, he thought. Even as he thought it, he heard his stomach growl.

20

He was always conveniently right in the way, always anticipating her path and inserting himself into it. Just now, she was lugging a crate of vegetables from the dining table to the sink and had to stop beside the counter as he suddenly sidestepped into her path. She was sorely tempted to keep going, barreling into him crate-first, but she feared he might somehow enjoy that.

"Can I help you with that?" he asked.

"No, I've got it," she replied. "Excuse me."

He nodded and stepped to one side, making that same completely unnecessary sweeping gesture with his arm. She moved past him and set the crate into the sink, dumping it rather loudly just to make her irritation known.

"How's it coming along down in the basement?" she said, her back to him.

"Oh, it's coming along," he replied. "I'm almost done."

"Great," she said. "It'd be nice if you could finish up. I can't have the animals stepping in cold water all day long."

"You got it."

And with that, she heard him tromp back across the kitchen and into the basement. Glorious relief. After a moment, he was thumping around down there, occasionally shouting at the goats. All of his little annoyances were building inside of her so that she felt a constant almost electrical tension. It took tremendous effort to concentrate on what she was doing. She'd intended to can all of the produce she brought back from the greenhouse, but she fumbled about for a bit before finally regaining focus.

She lined up some empty cans and lids, set down her cutting board, and got a pot of water for washing the vegetables. Normally, this was a task she enjoyed, but at the moment, it was just an exercise in frustration. She started with the carrots, washing and cutting them up, then placing them in cans.

As soon as the basement is done, she reminded herself. *Give him a couple gallons of gas and send him on his way. That's it. Don't let him talk you out of it.*

She'd filled an entire row of jars when she heard footsteps on the basement again, then Benjy yelling at Ramses.

"Nope, you stay down there where you belong! I'm not playing with you, boy!"

The basement door opened, and he came into the kitchen, stomping his wet boots on the welcome mat she'd placed there. He cleared his throat loudly and smacked his hands on his pants. Fiona glanced at him, and he seemed to take this as his cue to approach closely, giving her a broad smile.

"Well, do you want the good news or the better news?" he said.

"Both at the same time," she replied, screwing a lid onto a can.

"The basement is no longer leaking," he said, drumming his hands against the countertop in a way that caused the jars to rattle. "It was mostly coming from a spot in the corner, but I sealed it up. You might get a little bit of a trickle still, but it won't be much. You're good to go."

"Great. Thanks for that," she said, screwing a lid onto a second can. "I appreciate it a lot. I really do."

But that only made him inch closer to her, until he was preventing her from doing her work. She stepped to one side, abandoning a can to grab some more vegetables from the crate. However, he only shifted closer.

"What's the better news, then?" she asked.

"Just that I don't think the leak will get worse any time soon," he said.

"Great."

Finally, she turned to face him, giving him a flat, unhappy look. When he just stood there, she finally waved him aside. He moved back, but not nearly enough. She elbowed past him and resumed preparing the cans.

"You can go relax for now," she said. "I've got a lot of work to do here."

"Need any help?"

"I already said no," she replied.

He took another step back, but then he just stood there in the middle of the kitchen, arms crossed. Benjy had a loud presence. Even when he was out of her eyeline, she could hear his breathing, sense his big, fidgety movements, and smell him.

"You know, I think your homestead here likes having a man around to help out," he said. "I can handle the big jobs that need muscle, while you take care of the stuff like this."

She chose to ignore the comment as she continued to work, but as usual, he didn't take the hint. After a moment, he chuckled, as if he'd somehow amused himself and said, "Home is always better with a man and a woman working together."

That was it. She couldn't listen to this any longer. Making a loud grunt of disgust, she grabbed the pot of water and headed into the living room. Fortunately, for once, he didn't immediately follow her. Instead, he lingered in the kitchen for a few seconds before eventually wandering in and sitting down on the couch. A small mercy, but she would take it.

It was easy to keep putting it off because she dreaded the confrontation. Finally, she found herself lying wide awake in her bed, staring at the deepest shadows in a high corner of the ceiling. Despite long days of constant work, she couldn't get her mind to settle down, so she tossed and turned for hours before finally giving up.

If I knew he would go quietly, I would kick him out right now, she thought.

There was, of course, that smaller voice of doubt that kept nagging at her. Was she overreacting? He hadn't done anything worse than hitting on her a few times, and even then, it had been mild enough that she'd been able to quickly rebuff him. But, no, she knew Benjy well enough to know that he could throw a massive fit if he didn't get his way.

And it's just the two of us out here, she realized. *Smoke won't attack him, so what if he decides to push things further than before?*

The thought made her queasy, and she sat up in bed. When she did, she heard the dog stir at the foot of the bed. She reached down and petted him to reassure him. Then she reached over and felt along the edge of the nightstand beside her bed until she found the flashlight she kept there. Clicking it on, she shone the light up the wall to the wooden gun rack above the dresser. She kept a Mossberg shotgun and a bolt-action Weatherby rifle there, always within easy reach. Fiona was not naïve about the dangers of being a woman living alone on a large piece of property. She let the light linger on the guns.

So what? she told herself. *Are you planning to pull a gun on him? Now you're definitely overreacting.*

She clicked off the flashlight and set it back on the nightstand, then she lay down again, settling the covers around her. There was a part of her that didn't understand why she had such a visceral reaction to Benjy Hartman. He was a bit of a neckbeard, as the old saying went. Whiny, manipulative, unwilling to take a hint, and awkward, but did that warrant this fierce disgust?

Yet she could hear him snoring in the next room, and it just crawled over her flesh.

"This is my home," she whispered into the dark. "I built it with my own hands. I get to decide who stays here. If I want him to leave, I have the right to ask him to go."

That made her feel better about things, so she rolled onto her side and dared to close her eyes. No, she didn't have to let an interloper like Benjy, or anyone really, take up space in her own home. She had a right to her privacy, and if he couldn't accept that, then it was his problem to deal with.

At the moment, the storm had calmed down a bit. It seemed to follow a fairly regular pattern. The wind would howl, the snow would fall heavily for a few hours, then it would become calm, almost serene, for a while. Fiona decided that the next time the storm calmed during daylight hours, she would ask Benjy to leave. That would give him one less excuse. Two gallons of gasoline. That was going to be her offer, and he would simply have to accept it. She didn't intend to give him a choice. If he needed a place to stay, he could ask someone in town to take him in.

As she lay there, she felt closer to sleep than she had all night. She'd made up her mind, and that was it. No more debates. As she slowly drifted off to sleep, she heard a faint but familiar sound, and she perked up. *Floorboards creaking.* She thought it was coming from the kitchen. Someone walking but trying to be quiet. The house was small enough, the floorboards creaky enough, that she could track his movement throughout the house.

He walked into the kitchen, but she didn't hear the basement door or a cupboard opening. A minute later, his footsteps moved back into the living room, toward the fireplace, and then seemed to walk a circle for a bit. Finally, he headed back toward the hallway, only now he was stepping even lighter, as if he were on tiptoe.

The moment she realized he'd move past the guest bedroom, all possibility of sleep dropped away, and she became wide awake. She listened with mounting alarm as he crept down the hall and finally came to a stop outside of her bedroom. And then he was completely quiet. No breathing, no movements. He just seemed to be standing there on the other side of the door.

She felt Smoke rise. He sat up on the bed and whimpered, then he barked once toward the door. Fiona reached down and petted him, and he settled down again. In the silence that followed, she heard creaking floorboards again. They moved back down the hall into the guest room, and the guest room door clicked shut.

Oh yeah, he's out of here in the morning, she thought. *I don't know what that was all about, but he's done. I'm showing him the door the second the sun comes up, and I'll have a gun with me when I do it.*

21

It was early in the morning, still dark, when Jarred finally crawled off the mattress and approached the fireplace. The last of the makeshift firewood sat there: two measly crossbeams from the bed. He grabbed them and fed them into the dying fire, stoking the glowing embers to restart the flames. Once it was done, he turned to head back and saw Hope staring at him from deep within the nest of her blankets.

"Our last fire," she said, in a sleepy voice. "I guess we'll have to chop down some other part of the cabin. Maybe we can remove pieces of the walls or something. Heck, maybe we can break the couch apart. There's probably some wood inside, right?"

Jarred lay down on the mattress and drew his blanket over him. "The interior walls seem pretty thin and might be coated with fireproofing stuff," he said. "The couch feels like a wire frame with a single piece of plywood and some springs and cushions. It won't burn much."

"Well, what are we going to do, then?" she asked. "We have to keep the fire going, but we can't go outside and chop down a tree. That bear might be lurking around the house somewhere."

Jarred hesitated to tell her what he'd been thinking. She wouldn't like it. He tried to think of the gentlest way to break the news to her, but his silence caused her to push her blanket back and prop herself up on her elbow.

"Why are you not speaking?" she asked. "What are you not telling me?"

In the end, he decided to be direct with her. Hope would resent him for trying to sugarcoat it anyway. "I don't think we can stay in this cabin. It's a constant battle just to keep the cold at bay. We have no food, and nobody's ever going to find us here. I've tried to call out, and phone service is down."

Hope sat up then, flinging her blanket back. "Are you talking about walking to that gas station again?"

"Not the gas station necessarily," he replied, "but the town."

"We couldn't make it there before, and it's going to be so much worse now. Unless they've plowed the highway, which is unlikely, the snow will be deeper."

"Sooner or later, we're going to be forced to leave the cabin from lack of heat, food, water, whatever," he said, "and it's not going to get any easier. We can cut through the woods to the southwest, head down the hill, and get to the town a little faster than following the highway."

"It's still going to be a long walk," Hope said.

"True, but we won't go unprepared, and we'll wait for a lull in the storm," he said. "Every few hours, things seem to calm down out there a little bit. That's when we'll head out."

Hope dragged her hands over her hair and flopped back down onto the mattress, pulling the blanket over her. "And what about that bear? It might be waiting for us outside."

"I doubt it," he replied. "We scared it off, and there hasn't been any sign of it since then. I think it wandered off somewhere else to find food. If the bear is really hungry, it can't afford to just squat outside and stare at the house."

"You're not an expert in bear behavior," she said, from deep within her blankets.

"True." He couldn't argue with that, of course, but he could tell Hope was losing steam. Clearly, she knew he was right. They had to leave the cabin before things got really desperate, and heading into town was the only viable solution.

She was quiet for a while, though he could tell by her breathing that she wasn't asleep yet. Finally, she sighed and rolled onto her side. "Okay, if we have to leave the cabin, I guess I can handle it."

He almost said more, to explain his reasoning more thoroughly, but she didn't seem to need it. He lay there for a minute and soon heard her breathing get louder and slower, evidence that she'd fallen back asleep. He was impressed with how quickly she had accepted his plan once he'd addressed her concerns. Maybe she was a lot stronger than he gave her credit for.

Hope had always had trouble dealing with her emotions. So much so that he'd occasionally wondered if she might fall somewhere on the autism spectrum, though she'd never been diagnosed. Still, she seemed to be getting by just fine.

Don't forget, she's still just a kid, he told himself.

It was his last thought before he fell asleep. The room was very warm at the moment, the fire burning brightly, but he knew it wouldn't last. Indeed, he eventually woke from sleep due entirely to the cold invading his dreams. When he opened his eyes, early morning sunlight was shining through the edges of the curtains, and the fire in the fireplace had been reduced to a few smoldering embers. At first, Jarred tried to tuck his blanket in a little better so he might get more sleep, but the cold was relentless. At last, it had won the fight, and it was taking over the house.

When Jarred sat up, he realized Hope was already awake. She was sitting on the couch, blankets wrapped around her.

"Wind's not blowing as hard," she said in a sleepy croak.

She was right. He could hear the wind, but it was considerably quieter than it had been the night before. He pulled the curtain back and wiped off one of the panes of glass. This only helped a little bit, giving him a foggy view of the porch and the trees beyond. Still, it seemed like very little snow was falling, and it wasn't blowing in sideways like before. The storm had calmed for the time being.

To be sure, he went to the front door. As he did, he let his blanket fall off his shoulders, and he was shocked at how quickly the heat had left the house. Though he was still wearing his coat, the chill went right through him. He pressed his ear to the door and listened. Nothing but the wind. No indication of the bear. He undid the deadbolt and pulled on the door. It resisted slightly, as if the bear had knocked it slightly out of shape.

Indeed, he could still see where the bear had been on the porch. There were scuff marks along the threshold, huge footprints on the steps, and one of the support posts of the porch handrail was cracked. He saw other tracks moving back and forth across the clearing in front of the house, but the constant snowfall had half-buried them. It seemed to him that the bear had headed off into the woods toward the highway.

Some poor stranded soul sitting in a car might have a close encounter soon, he thought.

"How does it look out there, Dad?" Hope asked.

He shut the door and turned to her. "I think it's time to go."

Instead of arguing or asking questions, this time she merely nodded.

"We're on borrowed time here," he said. "We have no idea how long the lull in the storm will last, so we need to get to town before the wind picks up again. Let's load up anything and everything we can carry, okay? Clothes, cans, tools, anything that might prove useful. You found those backpacks in the hall closet. Are they in decent shape?"

"They're old and dusty," she said, "but we can use them." She shed her blanket then and rose from the couch.

As she headed for the hallway, presumably to retrieve the backpacks, Jarred began rounding up supplies. He grabbed the unopened cans of food from the kitchen. The food didn't taste quite right, but they could eat it if they were starving. Then he grabbed the water bottles, which they'd filled with melted snow. Finally, he rounded up any and all tools in the house that he thought they might need: the hatchet, screwdrivers, a hammer, a couple of folding knives, a steak knife, a roll of duct tape. He brought all of this into the living room, where Hope was currently dusting off the backpacks.

After setting all of the stuff down on the couch, he began to roll the sleeping bags up as tightly as he could. Hope was already loading up the tools, food, and water. She seemed to carefully consider each item before placing it, occasionally shifting them around. When she realized her father was watching, she said, "You want to put the heavy stuff on the bottom."

They looped the sleeping bags on top of the backpacks as a final touch, and then they were done. They were loaded up and ready to go. Outside, the lull in the storm lingered, and Jarred knew it was time. He slid the straps of the heavier backpack over his shoulders and went to the front door. By now, every hint of fire from the fireplace was gone, and the house was like an industrial freezer. He zipped his coat all the way up, pulled the hood forward. Then he tugged on his gloves. Hope appeared at his side, already bundled up tight.

"This is it," he said, reaching for the front door. "We can do this, Hope. We'll be in town in just a couple hours."

"A couple hours is maybe too optimistic, Dad," she said. "As long as we get there before sunset, we'll be fine."

"We will," he said, pulling open the front door.

"And if we encounter the bear?"

He patted the side pocket of his coat, where the handle of the hammer protruded. "We'll try to scare it off. If that doesn't work, we dump the packs as a distraction and let it have the food."

She nodded and muttered, "I guess that might work."

Jarred looked at the sheer whiteness of the landscape before them. It had piled up so heavily on the tree branches that they were bowed downward, giving the woods a resigned look, as if the whole world had slumped under the weight of the storm. Jarred felt the stinging cold on his cheeks and bowed his head.

"Time to go," he said, trying to work himself up to it. Finally, gripping the straps of his backpack, he stepped through the door and headed across the porch.

22

The snow in the front yard had piled up to mid-calf, which forced Jarred to drag each leg forward with each step. Fortunately, once he got under the tree canopy, it became easier. Here, the snow was just above his ankles, but the ground was littered with hidden debris and roots. Consequently, he was constantly tripping and stumbling along, catching himself against the tree trunks. Hope followed in his wake, using his footprints, which were considerably larger than her feet, to make her passage easier.

Their path circled around the cabin to the southwest, took them across the highway, then headed down a long downward slope into the dense woods in the direction of town. Though the sky was a wall of gray, Jarred could just make out the position of the sun—a brighter gray circle low on the eastern sky—so he used that keep them moving in the general direction of Glencole.

After about thirty minutes of slowly weaving through the trees, they left the woods and crossed some open terrain that was rugged and treacherous. This slowed them down even further, and the depth of the snow now approached his knees. Soon, he found himself fighting just to keep moving forward. In short order, he was out of breath, sweating profusely under his coat. Ahead of him, an expanse of snow stretched for a few hundred yards until the next line of trees.

He stopped for a bit to catch his breath. When he flung his hood back to cool off, the cold air soon began to turn his wet hair into ice. Glancing over his shoulder, he saw Hope a few feet behind him, massaging her thighs with her gloved hands.

"It's so deep," she said. "Another week of this, and the snow will be over our heads. We should've tried to make some snowshoes or something."

"I wish we had a nice set of cross-country skis," Jarred said, wiping the sweat off his forehead and cheeks. "That would make this a bit easier."

"We could have made some," Hope said. "Removed a few boards from the walls of the cabin, maybe created straps for our shoes with upholstery from the couch."

"That sounds like it would have taken a long time," he replied. "I wanted to set out while there's a lull in the storm. Although, under the circumstances, maybe the time saved in the long run would've been worth it." He pulled his hood back up. "That's the beauty of hindsight, I guess. How are you holding up?"

"I'm fine," she replied. "We better keep going, Dad. I don't want to be stuck out here at night."

"Don't worry. It's still morning. We've got plenty of time."

She grunted and gave him a look narrow-eyed look, as if to say, *Plenty of time? Are you sure?*

Jarred resumed trudging through the snow, heading across the open ground toward the nearest trees. In some places, he hit low spots where the snow was up to his knees, and he started to worry that he might step into a ravine and sink out of sight. The ground before him seemed practically featureless, and he had to feel his way along one footstep at a time. At least there were no visible bear tracks. The big creature seemed to have moved off in a different direction. When he looked behind, however, he was dispirited to see how little distance they'd covered.

Well, at least this is keeping me warm, he thought, as the frost in his hair quickly melted into sweat again. *It might be ten degrees out here, but I'm sweating like I've been working in a steel mill all morning.*

Of course, he knew that might change if the storm returned in full strength. That freezing wind cut like a knife. He tried to pick up the pace. After trying a few different approaches, he found that walking in deep snow was a little easier if he lifted his knees higher than usual and stomped a little farther forward. This helped him cut through the snow faster than simply dragging his legs forward. In this way, he was able to move faster.

Ahead, the slope appeared to get slightly steeper for a few yards, so he tried to check his speed. No sense tripping and losing himself beneath the snow.

"At least we're getting plenty of exercise," he said.

"Is there a point where you're getting *too much* exercise?" Hope asked.

"Maybe so," he said.

And then he brought his left foot down, stomping through the snow, and it just kept going. It was as if there were no ground beneath the snow, but soft white cold going down forever. Apparently, the slope was steeper than it looked, and he pivoted forward. He swung his arms, trying to grab something, but there was nothing around him. With a cry, he sank into the snow and kept going, the whiteness rising up around him, swallowing him.

He left foot finally found the ground, but it was steep, and his heel slipped out from under him. For a couple of seconds, he had the strange sensation of tumbling through snow, trying to grab it and feeling it part around him. Briefly, he felt the ground against the palms of his hands, but then he tumbled head over heels. Somewhere, distantly, Hope was shouting at him, as he picked up speed.

And then he came to a jarring stop, his left foot slamming into a large solid object. The weight of his body kept going, as he continued to claw fruitlessly at the snow. And then he heard a distinct *snap* coming from his leg, and he felt a kind of electrical jolt just above his foot. It wasn't pain at first, just a strange, intense tingling sensation that went all the way up his leg and seemed to crawl up his back.

Only then did he finally come to a complete stop, folded awkwardly against the side of a large rock. The sound of his leg snapping filled him with such dread that he began to shout in alarm, and then the tingling gave way to a sharp burning sensation. He didn't want to yell, knowing that would scare

Hope, but he couldn't help it. The sound came from somewhere deep inside of him, forcing its way out in a throat-scratching hoarse cry, as pain became excruciating agony.

He was on his side, facing back up the hill, his left foot bent to one side. Reaching out, he managed to claw at the ground, but when he tried to pull himself away from the rock, the pain became a sickening wave. For a second, his vision blurred, and he went limp, snow towering above him on both sides like great walls. Through the haze, he saw Hope scrambling down the hill, and he clamped his mouth shut to stop the screaming. The pain was so bad now, he could scarcely think straight.

Hope reached him and dropped to her knees, crawling on her hands and knees until she reached him. He tried to speak, but she was so out of breath, it took a moment for her to get the words out.

"Dad, are you hurt?" she asked.

"It's…it's my ankle," he managed to say, blinking back tears of pain. "I think it's broken."

She grabbed his wrists, pulling his arms. His vision went black for a second, but she kept pulling, dragging him away from the rock. Once his leg was no longer folded at an awkward angle, the agony diminished just a little. Finally, she lost her grip on him and fell backward, sitting down with a huff on the slope.

"It was a lot steeper than it looked," he said. "Oh, God, what have I done. Hope, I can't walk on it. It's broken." He tried to roll onto his back, but even that made the pain flare up. Finally, he managed to cross his arms and rest his cheek on his sleeve. "One bad step. I can't believe it. I should have been able to catch myself, I should have done…something."

"We can't just stop here," Hope said, her voice cracking. "Is there a way I can carry you, drag you, or something?"

He entertained the possibility, if only for a moment. Of course she couldn't carry him, and there was no reasonable way to drag him either. Maybe if they had some kind of cart or wagon, but there'd been nothing like that at the cabin. He realized there was only actually one possibility, but he hesitated to say it. He knew Hope wouldn't like it.

"You'll have to go on without me," he said. She immediately began shaking her head. "I know, I know, it's not what you want to hear, but you have to do it, Hope. Look, it's not that far to town, and you'll be able to move faster on your own."

She covered her face with her hands. "No, I'm not going to leave you here." She began crying, her shoulders shaking. "You can't just lie here on the ground by yourself. What if something happens? What if that bear comes along?"

"Then I'll defend myself," he said. "This is the only way, okay? You have to make it to town and try to find help for me. I'm sorry. This is my fault—I took a bad step—but this is what we have to do."

For a while, she just sat there covering her face. But suddenly, she sniffed, rubbed at her eyes, and sat up. Her face was red and blotchy, but she quickly pulled her hood forward and hid it.

"Okay, fine," she said. "If that's what I have to do…whatever." She sniffed again. "But first, I'm getting you out of the wind somehow. You can't just lie here in the cold. What if it takes a long time for me to get back?"

"Don't worry about me," he said, but another wave of nauseating pain swept over him. He pressed his face against his sleeve and waited for it to pass.

"Of course I'm worried about you," she said.

He heard her moving around. First, she took the backpack off his shoulders. Then he heard her rooting around inside, getting some tools. When he looked up again, he saw her clearing some of the snow around the rock, picking up sticks from the ground. She planted the sticks in a row, then unfolded one of the sleeping bags, and hung it from the sticks. She worked fast and deftly. He was impressed. When she finished, he realized she'd built a windbreak. She then pushed the snow around to stabilize it and fill the gaps along the bottom. In the end, it was quite effective, and he could no longer feel the cold wind blowing.

"Where did you learn to do something like that?" he asked.

"Don't you remember when you put me in Girl Scouts a few years ago?" she asked. "I didn't last long and never made any friends, but I did earn my wilderness survival badge."

He'd forgotten about her brief foray in scouting, but then again, he'd put her in so many classes and clubs and extracurricular activities that they'd all run together in his mind. Cross-country was only the latest of them. He'd always tried to help her find a place where she felt like she belonged, but she'd never flourished in any of them. Hope excelled at many activities, but she didn't make friends easily, so she rarely felt like she fit in.

"I guess I do remember Girl Scouts," he said. "You didn't care for it."

"Nope," she said.

"It didn't quite click like cross-country."

"Meetings were silly and pointless," Hope said. "The other girls didn't like me. But I did learn a few practical things."

His backpack was lying on the ground nearby, and he grabbed it, pulling it toward him. The big pocket was open, and a few tools spilled out onto the ground. One of them was the kitchen knife, and he grabbed it. He held it for a second, then thought better of it. Letting go of the knife, he grabbed his car key. It was like a relic from another lifetime, another age, a single large key with a gleaming silver key fob with the Toyota logo on it.

"Take this," he said, holding the key up. "If you hold it so the key is sticking out between your fingers, it'll serve as a crude weapon. Just in case you run into any weird people, you know?"

She nodded and took the key from his hand. "Yeah, I get it," she said. "I think I can handle myself, Dad. I'll head straight into town and find someone trustworthy, like a cop or something."

"Good idea," he replied.

She knelt beside him and gave him an awkward hug. He tried to return the hug, but he couldn't turn around to face her. "Be strong," she said. "Protect yourself. I'll hurry back as fast as I can, and I'll bring help."

"Okay," he replied, fighting another wave of sickening pain. "Don't worry about me. Just take care of yourself…and hurry."

"I will."

His vision dimmed again, and when it returned, she was gone. He heard her tromping through the snow somewhere behind him, but he didn't bother to look. He listened for a few minutes as the sound of her faded into the distance, moving southwest across the clearing. From the sound of it, she was moving very fast, almost running. Soon, even the sound of her was gone, and he found himself lying alone in the silence.

Jarred rested his cheek on his sleeve again and closed his eyes.

God, I really messed up, he thought. *I wonder how long it will take me to die out here.*

23

Fiona woke up early, energized and ready to deal with the problem dressed in the ranger's uniform. Kicking back her covers, she rose and crossed the room to her dresser. She changed clothes, considering carefully what she would wear when she confronted him. She settled on a red flannel button-up shirt and a pair of padded snow pants. Her hair was a mess, so she covered it in a red kerchief—red for determination, for power and control. Once dressed, she stared at herself in the mirror above the dresser. She looked bleary-eyed and greasy, and desperately in need of a bath, though heating up water would take a long time.

I'll treat myself to a nice, long bath once this is dealt with, she told herself.

Finally, she reached up to the gun rack and grabbed the Mossberg 12-gauge. She kept shells in a dresser drawer, and she opened it now. Grabbing a few, she loaded the gun and racked the slide.

Do you really need the gun?

She almost put it back on the rack, but then she remembered the footsteps moving down the hall, stopping just outside of her bedroom. Benjy lurking beside her door for long minutes, as if he'd been debating with himself whether or not to barge in. It made Fiona furious all over again, so she held the shotgun in her left hand as she went to the door and stepped through into the hall. Smoke didn't seem to realize something was wrong and followed along beside her, doing a little dance as if excited to get started on the day's chores.

Don't point the gun at him, she told herself, as she moved down the hall to the guest bedroom door. *Just keep it in hand for emphasis. That's all. Let him see it and draw his own conclusion.*

The guest bedroom door was still closed, so she stopped there, lurking much as he had done the night before. She leaned in close, but she didn't hear anything from the other side. No breathing, no creaking of the bed as he shifted around. Briefly, she entertained the possibility that he'd already left. Maybe he'd woken up at the crack of dawn and decided, contrary to his own character, that it was time to move on. Of course, she knew better.

She reached for the doorknob, prepared to barge in and rouse him, but then she heard the sound of the basement door opening in the kitchen. This was followed by footsteps on the kitchen floor and the sound of Benjy muttering. Smoke padded down the hall into the kitchen to greet him.

Fiona turned and headed into the living room. As she did, she saw him crossing the kitchen, wiping his hands on a rag. Their eyes met then, and they both came to a stop. Smoke had stopped in front of him. Only when Benjy reached down and petted him did he return to Fiona's side.

"Hopefully, I didn't make a bunch of noise down there and wake you up," he said, tossing the rag onto the counter. "I tried to be really quiet. I was in the basement moving furniture around, trying to pen in Ramses a little better. He keeps getting into the supplies and messing with other animals. We can't have that!"

He had a big grin on his face, as if he were incredibly proud of his own initiative. No doubt, he thought he'd earned his permanent residency. Fiona froze, unsure of how to respond, how to switch the subject from his work to her ultimatum. But then his eyes flitted down to the shotgun in her left hand, and the smile left his face, disappearing instantly, as if someone had wiped it off with a towel. His gaze went from the gun back to her face, and he must have seen the hard determination there. She saw a brief look of concern, though he quickly settled his face.

"I've decided to give you a couple gallons of gas for your snowmobile," she said. "It's waiting for you down at the greenhouse. You can fill up and be on your way this morning. Right away. Now."

"Wait…what?" He sounded genuinely shocked, and his eyebrows rose, as if he'd never seen it coming. "You're kicking me out? After all I've done for you?"

The tone of his voice seemed to bother Smoke, and the dog retreated to the living room, hopping up onto the couch.

"Yeah, you've overstayed your welcome," Fiona said. Even now, she felt the old, familiar urge to be nice, to soften the blow by perhaps giving him more time, but she pressed on. "I want you gone, Benjy. I'm grateful for your help, but I've repaid you with food and shelter. Now, it's time to go."

At first, he just stood there, gaping at her, his mouth hanging open. Then he shook his head, as if clearing his thoughts, and said, "What the heck, Fiona? I've been nice to you this whole time, and now you're just tossing me out? It's snowing out there."

"It's always snowing," she said, "and it doesn't show any sign of letting up. Since it's only going to get worse, you might as well leave now. Get whatever you brought with you and go." She stepped to one side, motioning him through the kitchen door.

Strangely, he grabbed the dirty rag off the counter and started to turn around, as if to head back to the basement. However, he froze mid-turn, twisting the rag in his hands. "Why now? What did I do?"

"I don't need a particular reason," she said. "The snow is only going to keep getting deeper, and eventually we may be trapped inside this house. You need to go while you still can."

But he just stood there, only now he was staring out the small kitchen window. His look of shock had faded, replaced by a deep frown. Benjy was looking rough, with untrimmed whiskers covering his cheeks and chin, crawling down his neck, and his blond hair all in disarray. If she'd encountered him on a city street somewhere, she might have quickened her pace to get away.

"You need me," he said, after a moment. He turned to face her again, planting his hands on his hips, the rag still crumpled in his right fist. "You won't survive this freak winter storm without me. Your homestead is being buried alive, and you've got all of your animals huddled down in the basement. It's too much for one person to handle, especially a girl. Look, if you don't want to talk to me, if you just want to ignore me, so be it, but let me stay here and help you shore things up."

He had a plaintive sound in his voice, almost childlike. Fiona could have handled anger a little better, but he was going for sympathy instead.

"I'll never make it back to the ranger station," he added. "Not in this weather. Heck, I barely made it here in the first place, and that was a couple days ago. What if there's nobody in town? What if nobody wants to take me in? Come on, Fiona. Aren't we old friends, at least? Let me stay until the bad weather stops. I'll help around the place, and I'll keep out of your way. I promise."

Despite this plaintive tone, he was crushing the life out of that rag, and she sensed a growing tension in his body posture. Without thinking about it, Fiona adjusted her grip on the shotgun. He heard it and looked at the gun again, but she pointed the barrel at the ground.

"I came to this homestead to live alone," she said. "That was my intention from the beginning, and you know that. I like it here. I like taking care of things by myself. While I appreciate your help, especially with the leak in the basement, the truth is I've never needed anyone else to help me *shore things up*. Please go gather your things and leave." She motioned him through the doorway again, this time more insistently.

Clearly seething, he held his ground for a few seconds. Then he unleashed an expulsive breath and tossed the rag back onto the counter. "I don't know what your problem is, honestly," he said tightly. "Your damned emotions are like a pendulum, just swinging back and forth. You've been like this as long as I've known you. I wish you'd pick a lane and stay in it, Fiona. I really do. Okay, fine, if you want me to go, I'll go. Let me go get my stuff."

As he headed for the doorway, she stayed well clear of him. His gaze went to the shotgun again, but he didn't mention it. Instead, breathing loudly, stepping angrily, he went down the hall and flung open the door of the guest bedroom. She heard him rooting around in there, making as much noise as possible.

"I just can't believe you," he said. "I came all the way here. I did all that work down in the basement. Nothing happened, and you just turned on me. It doesn't make any sense. *You* don't make any sense, Fiona. You never did."

"I can live with that," she replied, still standing in the kitchen. She realized she was shaking, the shotgun rattling against her hip. She tightened her grip on it, taking it in both hands. "You don't have to be weird about this, Benjy. You know damn well I came to this place to live alone. I don't know why you're acting offended. I never wanted a roommate in the first place."

He stomped back into the living room, his backpack slung over his shoulder. "I wasn't trying to be your roommate. I was just trying to help out. Okay, yeah, you came here to live alone, but you didn't know there was going to be some kind of nuclear winter burying the whole world. Extraordinary times demand extraordinary help, right?"

"Thanks for fixing the leak," she said. "Take some gasoline as pay, and let's part in peace. That's possible, you know? This doesn't have to get worse."

He stared hard at her, and in that moment, she thought she saw the mask removed completely. Angry little eyes, lips pressed tightly together, the tendons in his neck popping out. Finally, not wanting to soak in that face any longer, she dropped her gaze, and he made a little grunt, as if he'd won some kind of contest.

"Well, goodbye then," he said. "Hopefully, I don't freeze to death out there. Not that you'd shed a tear for me if I did. I'm not sure you care about anyone but yourself."

"You'll be fine," she replied. "You're a park ranger for the State of Ohio. Wilderness survival is kind of your thing."

"I know you think you're tough, but you're such a *girl*." And at that, he adjusted the backpack on his shoulder and headed for the door. "You and your emotions. No wonder you wound up by yourself."

She didn't take the bait. He wanted an argument, so he had a reason to linger. Instead, she stood her ground and stared at the far wall, settling her face so that her emotions didn't show. Benjy went to the front door and grabbed the knob, but he lingered again for a few seconds, as if giving her a final chance to change her mind. When that didn't happen, he finally turned the knob and swung the door open so hard that it banged off the wall.

"Don't break my door, please," she said.

"It's fine," he replied.

A fierce gust of wind and snow blew through the open door, rustling papers on the kitchen table. Fiona shivered. Through all of this, Smoke remained on the couch, and even now, he didn't rush to bid Benjy farewell. He seemed to know something bad was happening, but he didn't know how to react.

"Good luck with everything," Benjy said. "Don't come crying to me the next time your goat tries to kill you."

She left this comment unanswered. Benjy took a single step through the door and stopped suddenly. Then with a grunt, he stumbled backward into the living room, as if giving way to something.

What is this weird trick? Fiona wondered. *Is he going to feign a medical emergency?*

It wasn't entirely out of the realm of possibility, of course. However, as Benjy moved to one side, she realized there was another person standing on the porch. She was small, dressed in a pink coat with the hood up, her hand poised in the air as if she'd just been about to knock. Though her face was hidden in the shadows of a deep hood, her small size and slight frame suggested that she was very young, possibly a teenager, even a child.

She stumbled through the door, her arm dropping to her side, then dropped to one knee. "Please…help me!"

24

Fiona and Benjy both rushed to the girl's side. As they did, she reached up and pushed her hood back, revealing her face. She was quite young. Fiona would have guessed thirteen or fourteen. Her brown hair was frizzy, her face round with a hint of baby fat, especially in the cheeks. She had dark brown eyes, a button nose that was slightly upturned, and she was bright pink, as if she'd been out in the cold quite a while.

As Fiona approached her, she gazed through the open door, expecting to see other people following the girl. Surely, she hadn't come alone! However, Fiona saw only a single set of tracks dragging through the deep snow all the way down the hill to the northeast. It looked like the girl had emerged from the woods.

Fiona shut the front door, as Benjy knelt in front of the girl.

"Hey there, kiddo, are you okay?" he asked. All tension had left his voice, and he now sounded genuinely concerned. "Don't tell me you walked all the way to this house from town."

"No...not from town." The girl was out of breath, and her hair was absolutely soaked with sweat.

Fiona went to her side and laid a hand on her back. "It looks like you came out of the woods. How far have you walked?"

"I think I got turned around," she said. "I was trying to reach a town called Glencole, but…" She gasped for breath and unzipped her coat. "Somehow, I got lost. There were no landmarks or anything, and then I spotted this house. I'm sorry."

"You've got nothing to apologize for, young lady," Benjy said. His whole demeanor had changed. The petulance and anger were instantly gone, and he'd adopted the professional, public-friendly tone of an Ohio park ranger dealing with a scared kid. "What's your name?"

"Hope," the girl said. "Hope White."

"That's a great name," Benjy replied. As he spoke to her, he made sure to squat down so he was on her eye level. "Now, Hope, where did you come from, and how did you wind up here?"

"Please, you have to help us," she said. "My dad and I were stranded…on the highway, and we went to this old cabin with no running water. A bear tried to get inside the house, but we scared it off…And then we tried to walk to Glencole, but…but he fell." The girl had an awkward way of speaking, too quiet, constantly stopping and starting. Fiona recognized the evidence of social anxiety all too well.

"Did he get hurt?" Benjy asked.

"Yeah, I think he broke his ankle," she said. "It's really bad. He can't even sit up without screaming. I didn't know…I didn't know what to do, so I just left him there. He told me to get help, but I couldn't tell if I was going the right direction. It was snow and trees everywhere, but finally I saw this house, and I didn't know where else to go…I hope he's okay. I hope the bear didn't come back." She started crying.

"Hey, it's okay," Benjy replied, patting her on the shoulder. "Did you see my nice snowmobile sitting outside? I'll tell you what we're going to do. We're all three going to hop on that snowmobile, and we're going to head right out there and find your dad. We'll get to him before that bear, okay?"

He looked past the girl's shoulder to meet Fiona's gaze. And what could she do? This poor girl. There was no way Fiona was going to refuse to help her. The timing couldn't have been worse. If only she'd kicked Benjy out a few minutes earlier.

"You two go and get him," Fiona said. "Bring him back here. We'll get him warmed up, give him some medicine, and treat any injuries."

"Great," Benjy said. "You see there, Hope? Just like your name. There's hope! Did you know I'm a park ranger? You're in good hands, and everything's going to be okay. Let's go rescue your dad."

The girl looked up at Benjy and nodded. Then she looked over her shoulder at Fiona, brushing the dampness off her cheeks.

"Thanks," she said.

Benjy was proud of himself for how well he had bottled up his feelings. In a way, he was grateful to Fiona for her constant unreasonable shenanigans, because it tested him in surprising and relentless ways. He was strong. He'd proven that to himself plenty of times in the last couple of days alone.

No matter what she says or does to me, I'm going to prove to her that I'm a better man than she will admit, he thought. Fixing her leaky basement, dealing with her ornery goat, and helping this strange child—was she paying attention? He hoped so.

He'd been close to some kind of breaking point, so the kid had come along at the exact right moment. Now, Benjy was back in ranger mode, and his old professionalism had smoothed over the mounting frustration. He'd often found escape in work, especially when things were hectic. He was far more confident like this.

As the snowmobile roared down the hill and out across the open field, he dug a pair of snow goggles out of his coat pocket and pulled them on with one hand. Then he lifted the scarf up over his mouth. The girl was seated behind him. He felt her clutching at his coat. It was remarkable that she had walked all this way by herself, dragging herself through the deep snow and wind. He was impressed.

Benjy reached down and rubbed frost off the gas gauge. Fiona had kept her word about the gasoline at least. That was a good sign. Maybe she wasn't as annoyed by him as she pretended to be.

She wasn't really going to kick me out, he told himself. *She was just letting off some steam. The situation is stressful.*

No way would Fiona just toss him out into bad weather like that. And for what? What had he done to deserve it except to help her around the house and work hard for her benefit? No, she would have changed her mind before he drove away. It would have been essentially tossing him to his death. Fiona would never do that. Would she?

The longer he thought about it, the worse he felt.

She meant it. The nagging voice began to pester him. *She meant to toss you out into the storm all alone, even if you died. Fiona doesn't care about you or anyone else. She just wants to hoard all of her supplies and her safe home and keep it all for herself. You've been nothing but a friend to her for years, and she doesn't have an ounce of sympathy for you.*

By the time he drew close to the trees, he was fending off the rage with every ounce of willpower. Too much time to think. To distract himself, he shouted at Hope over his shoulder, trying to be heard over the wind.

"I might not be able to follow your tracks through the woods," he said. "The trees are packed pretty tightly in there. Do you think you could direct me to your father if I circle around?"

"Yes, I think so," the girl replied. She pointed over his shoulder, directing him to the northeast. "If you go that way, it'll be faster."

"Okay, you got it," he said, revving the engine to blast through a particularly deep snow drift. "Keep me headed in the right direction, kiddo. Got it?"

"Okay," Hope said.

Fiona doesn't realize how much she needs me, that's the thing. The thought came to him unbidden, and uninvited. *With the storm this bad, and this persistent, she won't survive on her own. She's built up a fantasy in her own mind about how strong and capable she is, but without strong arms to do real man's work around the homestead, she's going to get snowed under.*

He turned the snowmobile to the northeast, following the line of trees as it curved around toward some more open ground in the distance.

It's not just about my survival. It's about hers, too. I have to make her see that. She doesn't have to like me right now. That'll come along later.

Once he settled his mind on what he was going to do, it calmed him down. His course was set. He was going to save Fiona—from the weather and from herself. He'd talked his way into the house to begin with, so he knew he could reason with her if he did it just right. Now he could focus on the task at hand and stop wrestling over it in his head.

As he circled the woods, Hope redirected him toward some hills, so he turned in that direction.

"Once you go over those hills, there are some more trees," Hope said, yelling at his shoulder to be heard. "He's just on the other side of those, but he'll be hard to see from a distance."

"All right, kid," he replied. "We'll be there real soon. Don't worry, we're going to save your dad."

Strangely, though the kid was clearly scared, she remained focused, able to redirect him. He was impressed.

"So, how you'd guys wind up way out here in the middle of nowhere?" he asked. He had to shout over his shoulder to be heard.

"We left Pittsburgh to get ahead of the storm," she shouted back. "We were driving west on the interstate when we lost control and spun off into a ditch. Then we walked to this gross old cabin."

"Did either of you get injured in the crash?"

"I got a little bump on my head, that's all," she shouted. "Anyway, we couldn't stay in the cabin, so we tried to walk to the nearest town."

"Glencole. I know that town," he said. "Fiona goes there occasionally for supplies and stuff. It's a small place."

"Do they have a gas station or a restaurant that serves cheeseburgers?" she asked.

It was such a random question that he laughed. "I don't know. Probably. Most small towns do."

"Well, that's why Dad fell and broke his leg," she said.

"And then you walked all the way to Fiona's house by yourself," he said. "Wow, you're a tough kid," he said. He glanced over his shoulder at her again. She was tiny, and she had the big eyes of a very young girl. By the looks of it, she couldn't be more than fourteen, but she had a clear head on her shoulders for sure.

Fiona could learn a thing or two from this kid, he thought. *She's smart and capable, but she also knows when she needs help.*

They rounded a hill and passed another small stand of trees. Beyond, there was a large clearing, but Hope began tapping frantically on his shoulder.

"There! There," she said, pointing off to the right. It took a moment to spot it, an odd mound of snow near the bottom of a slope. Footsteps led away from the mound toward the nearest trees. Benjy turned in that direction, and now he spotted a bit of cloth rising up from behind the mound. There was no sign of the man, though the snowmobile was making plenty of noise to draw his attention.

He slowed down. Benjy had found his share of dead and gravely wounded people over the years. He'd dealt with weeping, wailing family members. There were plenty of ways to get killed out in the wild. What if this guy had died while his daughter was trudging into town? A broken leg probably wouldn't kill him, but exposure might. A hungry animal might.

Benjy came to a stop about five yards from the mound of snow and put the vehicle in park. As he stepped off the seat and sank up to his knees in the deep snow, he raised a finger.

"You stay right here, okay?" he said. "I'll go check on your dad."

She understood. He saw that in her eyes. She gave him a little nod and crossed her arms. Benjy dragged his way through the snow. As he did, he realized that a sleeping bag had been propped up on some tree branches. It was crude but clever, positioned to block the wind from the space on the other side.

As he neared the mound, he spotted what seemed to be deep drag marks on the other side. It was clear now that the mound was actually snow that had been piled up by some object sliding down the slope and sinking deeper into the snow. And at last, he saw the man lying there. He was on his back, his hands folded on his chest, a man dressed in a thick winter coat, his head propped on a backpack. His eyes were closed, his mouth open.

"Hey there, buddy, you alive?" Benjy said.

The man's breath came out in a big puff of white, like steam from an antique machine. Still alive. One eye opened.

"Who are you?" the man asked.

Benjy cleared a space beside the man and knelt down. "I'm an Ohio park ranger, and I'm getting you out of here. Come on."

He took the man's arm and started to lift him. As soon as he did, the man cried out, but Benjy kept going. He rose, turning, and dragged the man onto his back.

"Careful," the man said tightly. "My left leg is busted pretty bad."

"Yeah, your daughter told us all about it," Benjy replied. "She's a smart kid, you know? She saved your life. Now, come on. Let's take you someplace warm where we can set that broken leg."

As he hoisted the man onto his back, he started back toward the snowmobile, where Hope watched with wide eyes and a big smile on her face.

"This wind is awful," Benjy said. "It's a good thing your kid built a windbreak. You owe her your life, my friend. Never forget it."

"Yeah…I know," the man replied, his voice tight with pain. "Believe me, I know."

25

Fiona spent some time clearing a large space in front of the porch, driving back and forth with the Mule to push the snow to either side. For all of Benjy's frustrating behavior, she trusted him to do the right thing and try to rescue the girl's father. He wasn't the best park ranger ever, but he was a professional. He did have at least a few good qualities. It was a shame they were so overshadowed by his personality and choices.

That thought made her chuckle, despite herself, though the situation wasn't really amusing at all. After about half an hour, she'd cleared a space roughly twenty feet by fifteen in front of the porch all the way down to the dead grass. She was admiring her handiwork when she heard the distant growl of the snowmobile. Looking off to the north, she saw the blue Yamaha coming around the trees, following its own tracks as it returned to the house.

She could see that Benjy had a third person on the seat. It was a tight fit, but Benjy and Hope had tucked a strange man between them. He was leaning to one side, his head down, as if he were unconscious. However, as they drew close, she saw the twisted look of agony on the man's face. His left leg was wrapped in a crude splint made of two tree branches and strips of cloth. Fiona moved the Mule out of the way of the steps to give them easy access.

As the snowmobile pulled into the clearing and came to a stop, she climbed out of the Mule and rushed to their side.

"We got him," Benjy said, killing the engine. "Dude's got a broken leg. He's in a lot of pain. He passed out on the ride back."

Fiona went to the man's side. He seemed delirious, moaning and taking deep, gulping breaths. When she grabbed his shoulder, the moan became a grunt of pain.

"Dad, we're here," Hope said, hopping off the back of the snowmobile seat. "We made it! You're safe now."

Fiona had her arm around the man's shoulders when he opened both eyes and looked at her.

"Are you…my rescuer?" he asked.

"Well, Benjy did most of the work," she replied, "but I'm here to help."

At this, Benjy beamed proudly, as if she'd paid him the highest compliment in the world. Unfortunately, the injured man was tall and lanky, so getting him off the snowmobile proved a challenge. Fiona held him around the shoulders, and Benjy grabbed him around the torso. They lifted him to one side, carrying him at an awkward angle. He cried out in pain.

"We'll lay him on the couch for now," Fiona said. "It'll be warmer in the living room. He needs to thaw out. Hope, run and get the front door."

As they lugged the man up the steps, Hope slipped past them and opened the front door wide. Smoke was waiting on the other side, but he gave way as they entered.

"What's his name?" Fiona asked.

"Jarred," Hope replied.

"Okay. Jarred, hang in there. This is my home. You're safe here."

They lugged him across the living room and laid him down on the couch. He was clearly in a lot of pain, but he put up no resistance as they positioned him on his back. Fiona tucked a pillow under his head. He was covered in snow and mud, and it was getting all over the couch. Under the circumstances, Fiona didn't much care. She could always clean it later, or build herself a new one.

"Okay, buddy, I better take a look at this busted leg," Benjy said, taking a seat at the end of the couch. "Getting your boot off might be a problem."

"Just do what you have to do," Jarred replied through clenched teeth. "I'll deal with it."

As Jarred removed the boot, Fiona went and hung the Mule key on a peg near the door. Hope had shut the door, and she was now leaning against it, arms crossed over her belly as she watched her father. Fiona gave the girl a reassuring pat on the shoulder.

"Well, it looks like the ankle is broken in more than one place," Benjy said. "That's the bad news. The good news is that it doesn't appear to be dislocated, so you got lucky."

Jarred laughed at this. It surprised Fiona. How could he laugh under the circumstances? Actually, he had quite a nice laugh, and now that she saw him, she realized that he was quite handsome. His hair was sweat-soaked, of course, and he had a couple days' worth of whiskers on his cheeks and chin. Still, he was rugged, in good shape, and had really nice cheekbones. He also had a pleasant smile.

And then Benjy laughed with him, and it spoiled the moment. The difference was stark. Jarred had a genuine, deep-seated belly laugh, while Benjy had a nasally laugh that seemed half-forced. It crawled up her spine and settled at the base of her skull.

"It's a relief to run into a real park ranger," Jarred said, then flinched in pain. "After everything we've been through, having an expert around is refreshing, especially one who knows first aid."

"Yeah, I can set these bones for you," Benjy said. "Hey, Fiona, do we have any strong painkillers in the house? I don't want to go shifting any broken bones around until we can take the edge off the pain."

"I've got ibuprofen," Fiona said. "That's about it. Nothing stronger."

"That'll do," Benjy said.

As Fiona went to the kitchen to get the medicine, it occurred to her that she was now outnumbered. Her house was overrun with strangers. Dealing with Benjy was one thing, but now she had three people, and Benjy was a hero to Jarred and Hope. She grabbed a bottle of ibuprofen and the first aid kit. When she returned to the living room, she saw Hope watching Benjy carefully as he tended to her father. Fiona shook several pills out of the bottle and handed them to Jarred, and he swallowed them dry. Then she set the first aid kit on the arm of the couch.

"Okay, we'll wait half an hour or so for the medicine to take effect, and then I'm setting these bones," Benjy said. "Don't worry, I know what I'm doing. You'd be surprised at how many people break bones while tromping around in the woods. I've set broken arms, legs, dislocated knees, all sorts of stuff. The wilderness is a dangerous place for civilized people."

"I trust you," Jarred said.

At this, Benjy gave the man his biggest, toothiest crap-eating grin. Fiona fought an urge to sigh loudly.

Stop worrying about yourself, she thought. *We just rescued this guy, and you're irritated that they like Benjy. Get over it.* And yet she couldn't help it. She kept remembering his footsteps moving down the hall, stopping just outside her door in the middle of the night.

At the moment, Hope was squatting near the couch, watching Benjy gingerly examine her father's ankle and lower leg. However, she reared up suddenly and tipped her head back, staring at the ceiling. Then she sniffed loudly.

"Why is the room so smoky?" she asked.

Fiona was so lost in her own self-argument that the girl's words didn't initially sink in. Then she glanced up and saw the gray haze hovering near the arched ceiling of the living room. At first, she assumed it was coming from the fireplace. Maybe snow and ice had covered the chimney hole somehow, but when she looked toward the fireplace, smoke didn't appear to be backing up into the room. That left one other option. She had the wood-burning furnace going at low heat to keep the animals down the basement warm.

"The external vents for the furnace must be blocked," Fiona said. "I don't use it very often, and it's pretty old. Came with the house. I'd better get out there and clear the vents."

"This is a good way to get suffocated," Benjy said. "I'll fix it." He hopped up from the couch so fast that Jarred grunted in pain. "Don't worry, I'll have the vents cleared in minutes." He rushed toward the door, then paused, and turned back to the couch. "Just hang in there for a little bit, pal. I'll come back and splint that leg when I'm done, but, you know, we must prioritize the carbon monoxide poisoning."

"Oh, sure, I understand," Jarred said. "Honestly, the pain's not as bad as it was. I think maybe the ibuprofen is kicking in."

Fiona almost protested. She didn't want to owe any more to Benjy than she already did. But he was pulling on his gloves and zipping up his coat, and she didn't want to seem like a jerk. And then, to cement the deal, Benjy gestured at Hope.

"Hey, kid, would you like to help me out? Dad, do you mind?"

It was full-on professional mode. Benjy was practically a different person when he wanted to be. Hope had just been standing there staring at the smoke, but when Benjy recruited her, she gave him a big grin.

"It's fine with me," Jarred said. "Just be careful out there."

Hope clapped and rushed over to the coat rack, pulling on her gloves and flipping up her hood.

"Don't worry, Dad," Benjy said, opening the front door. "You've got a smart kid here. That's clear. You've raised her well."

He gave Jarred a thumbs-up and headed outside, Hope trotting along excitedly at his feet. Fiona kept a snow shovel on the porch, and he grabbed it in passing. It was heart attack weather, and she almost warned them. But she bit her lip instead. As soon as Benjy and Hope were heading down the porch steps, she walked over and closed the front door.

I'm stuck with him, she thought. *He'll use this situation as his opportunity to settle in for good, and what can I do about it without becoming the villain?*

Yet this line of thinking made her feel so selfish, and that only compounded her misery.

"Hey, I'm really grateful," Jarred said from the couch. "You two are really kind to let us into your home like this."

Fiona whipped around. "It's not 'you two,'" she said sharply. "This is my home, and mine alone!"

Jarred seemed taken aback by her response, and he just stared at her, before nodding slowly. Embarrassed, she cleared her throat and almost backed off what she'd said, but she couldn't do it. Her tone of voice had been honest, and she didn't want to lie about the situation. As a result, the two of them spent a few awkward seconds just looking at each other.

He was sweating a lot, and his face was still really flushed. Fiona seized the opportunity to change the subject.

"I'm a little concerned that you might have a fever," she said. "The ibuprofen should help, but if it doesn't, I've got flu medicine."

Mortified at her own outburst, she wandered over to the living room window. Pulling back the curtain, she looked through the frosty window. Benjy and Hope were off to the left, working at a corner of the house. He'd given the girl a trenching tool. Fiona assumed he'd taken it from the snowmobile. Together, they were digging out the snow around one of the furnace vents. Fiona watched them for a minute, waiting for her foul mood to diminish.

"Hey, is something wrong?" Jarred asked.

She realized she'd been standing at the window in silence for a while. "No, I'm okay," she said. The lie came easy, and she resented it, so she added, "Well, anyway, it's nothing for you to worry about. Just relax and try to take it easy. You need the rest."

"If I said something wrong…"

"Don't worry about it," Fiona said.

"I shouldn't make assumptions," he said.

"I said don't worry about it." She turned and forced herself to give him a smile. "It's okay. I overreacted. Just rest."

He got quiet after that, for which she was grateful. Fiona stood at the window, watching Benjy and Hope, and she felt caught in a vortex. No escape.

26

Benjy came bounding back into the house with a whoop, clapping his hands and stomping his boots. Fiona had noticed the diminishing smoke, but she'd turned her back on the window. When he entered with his shrill cry, she winced and covered her ears. That voice. That damned voice. Not wanting to offend the girl, she lowered her hands and turned to face them. Hope was grinning and rubbing her gloved hands together.

"Well, that takes care of that," Benjy said, ripping off his gloves and tossing them onto the coat rack. "Dad, you've got a good little helper here. She's a hard worker."

"Yeah, you're right about that," Jarred said. He sounded worse, and he kept dabbing his face with the long sleeve of his shirt. "I owe her my life."

"Twice over, actually," Benjy said, flinging his hood back. "She's the one who noticed the smoke." He turned and looked straight at Fiona, all traces of his smile gone. "Can you imagine if you'd been alone here? You might have gone to bed without noticing that smoke, and then you never would have woken up. See why it's better to have helpful people around?"

He was at least partially right, and she knew it. If she'd been sleeping when the vents had gotten blocked, she probably would have asphyxiated from carbon monoxide poisoning. And not just her but all the goats and chickens

—and the lone goose—down in the basement. It would have been the end for all of them, and when would anyone have found their bodies? She was so shaken by the thought that she didn't bother trying to dispute Benjy.

"Anyway, let's get this leg splinted," Benjy said, and the smile returned full force. He went over to the couch and popped open the lid on the first aid kit. "Hope, why don't you help me out here."

"Of course," Hope replied, rushing over.

Fiona initially went and sat on the hearth. There had never been so much noise and commotion in the living room. She'd gotten so used to living by herself that all of this movement and talking gave her intense anxiety, and she didn't know how to respond. For the first time in a long time, she began to suspect that there was really something wrong with her.

I just want to be alone, she thought sadly.

Benjy was seated on the end of the couch, unloading the first aid kit onto the arm of the couch. He gestured for Hope to stand beside him. "You hand me stuff when I ask for it, okay?" he said. "You get to be the surgical assistant. You're smart, so you'll know what I'm asking for."

"You got it," she replied, taking up a position beside the couch.

"Fiona, I could really use your help as well," Benjy said. "We need something to splint the leg. The sticks I used out in the field aren't exactly straight. They won't do. What we need are some kind of small wood boards. I take it you've got some among your furniture-making supplies."

"Yes, of course," Fiona replied. She pushed herself off the hearth. At least if she was busy, she wouldn't be lost in her own inner turmoil. "I'll go get a few. How many do you need?"

"Two or three," he replied. "Small boards. Narrow but thick enough that they're not going to bend. We don't want to leave this ankle just hanging around, unsupported."

"Got it." Fiona trudged across the living room. She walked to the third bedroom, the one that was mostly filled with her junk, including stacks of wood of varying sizes, already shaped and sanded and ready for work. It was yet another space in the house filled with her furniture-making supplies. A few more years, and her entire homestead might be a hoarder's house, but limited specifically to partially completed handmade furniture. As she picked through the stacks, looking for pieces of just the right size, she heard Jarred, Hope, and Benjy chatting in the living room. The father and daughter seemed so nice. They were good people, but it made the whole house feel unsteady.

Finally, she grabbed a few pieces that seemed suitable—one inch thick, one inch wide, and about a foot long. She bundled them under her right arm and went back into the living room. Benjy was already wrapping the man's foot and ankle.

"Come over here and help me," Benjy said to her, beckoning her over with a twist of his head. "Put a splint on either side of the leg, right where I'm pointing." He lightly tapped a spot about an inch above Jarred's ankle. "You doing okay, Jarred? We're not moving your leg around too much, are we?"

"I'm hanging in there," Jarred replied, though he had his arm laid over his eyes.

Benjy had great bedside manner. Fiona had to give him that. She knelt beside him and put the boards on the floor. Then she grabbed two of them and placed them where Benjy was pointing. As she held them in place, he continued wrapping the leg, winding the bandage over the wood. In the process, he kept brushing her hands with his own, and she couldn't help but think it was intentional.

Finally, she started moving her hands away from his, and it became a strange kind of dance. She was annoyed, but he just smiled through it all.

"Hey, Hope, hand me the medical tape there, would you?" he asked.

Hope grabbed the small role of white surgical tape and passed it over his shoulder. "This is it, right?" she asked.

"Exactly." He took the tape and ripped off a bit using his teeth. Then he taped the bandage in place.

Once it was secure, Fiona let go and moved away from him. He applied a bit more tape, then gave Jarred an OK sign. "There you go, buddy. It's not as secure as a real cast, so don't go hopping around, but it'll at least keep the bones in place while they heal."

"I'll be real careful, Doc," Jarred replied. "Thanks for all the help. Both of you." He gestured at Fiona then with a little flick his hand. "Fiona, is it?"

"That's right."

"Thanks for letting us into your home," he said. "I know I'm messing up your couch here, and I'm sure you didn't plan on having a couple of strangers invade your space today, but I don't know what we would have done if you hadn't opened your door to us."

"Well…" Fiona felt intensely awkward in that moment. She wasn't used to being thanked. Benjy certainly hadn't thanked her for letting him stay in her house. If anything, he'd acted like he was doing her a favor. "I'm glad we could help," she managed, finally.

Really, Jarred had such a great attitude considering everything he'd been through. He looked miserable, all flushed and sweating, and he only had a couple of over-the-counter pain pills to help with the pain, but he seemed to handle everything well. Fiona didn't think she would be nearly as upbeat and friendly if she were in his shoes.

Benjy turned and held up his hand with Hope. She seemed confused by the gesture, but he took her hand and raised it. Then he gave her a high five.

"Thanks for being such an awesome assistant," he said.

"You're welcome," she replied.

"Help me pack this stuff away, okay?" He began putting stuff back into the first aid kit. As she helped, Benjy kept grinning at the girl. He'd been super friendly with her from the beginning, but for some reason, in that moment, as he watched her putting stuff back into the first aid kit, Fiona felt uneasy. Once the kit was packed up again, he gave her another high five. "Dad, did I tell you what a great kid you've got here?"

"You might've mentioned it," Jarred said.

She knew Benjy too well. That was the problem. A stranger watching him interact with the kid wouldn't have suspected anything—just a friendly park ranger interacting with the public—but Fiona didn't trust him.

Hope is just a kid, she reminded herself. *Benjy's a creep, but he's not that kind of creep.*

No, he'd never done anything that like. Still, as Fiona stood there watching them interact, she decided to keep an eye on him, just in case. He carried the first aid kit back into the kitchen, and Hope trotted after him. Hope definitely seemed to respect him, and he began to regale her with wild park ranger stories.

"Let me tell you about one of my close encounters with a bear," he said. "It was a young male, maybe a year old, and it started stalking me on a trail one day."

"They don't usually attack people," Hope said. "That's what I've read. Unless it's a mother bear with her cubs. We had a run-in with a bear, but it ran away when we scared it."

"Now, that's very true," Benjy said. Fiona heard him open and close the cupboard near the sink. "But this particular bear was definitely stalking me for food. I don't know if he was hungry or just testing his hunting skills, but I knew I had to either scare him away or lose him on the trail."

"Wow, what did you do?"

Fiona tuned him out and sat down on the hearth again.

He's just being friendly, she told herself. *Don't impute your personal problems with Benjy into every interaction he has with other people.*

She realized Jarred was staring at her, a questioning look on his face. Apparently, some of her internal struggle was evidence in her expression.

"You feeling any better?" she asked.

"Um, the leg hurts like hell, to be honest," he replied, dabbing his forehead with his sleeve, "but I can take it. It's a relief not to be lying out there in the cold. We're very fortunate that we met up with some friendly people. This could have gone really bad."

"Yeah..." And then she was at a loss for words. Jarred seemed reasonable. Maybe, just maybe, he would prove to be an ally when the time came to get Benjy out of the house.

Not if you keep being an awkward weirdo, she told herself.

"Do you need anything?" she asked Jarred. "A drink. Something to eat? Maybe...I don't know..."

"No, I don't think so," he replied. "Thanks anyway."

"No problem."

27

The throbbing pain in his leg never let up. It was a constant sharp ache, pounding like a drumbeat that went right up his leg from ankle to thigh. Beyond that, he was also burning up. It kind of felt like he was coming down with the flu, but he assumed it was just his body's reaction to being stuck out in the bitter cold for a few hours while Hope went for help. The medicine they'd given him didn't seem to do much, but he tried to stay positive as long as he possibly could for Hope's sake.

The whole situation here in this stranger's house was odd, but he couldn't quite work it out in his head. There was bad blood between Benjy and Fiona. Why were they living together?

Unfortunately, as time passed, he felt his thoughts becoming muddier. The fever got worse, and soon he was swimming in a delirious haze. People came and went like shadows, but he found himself staring at the faint shifting firelight reflected on the arched ceiling above him. At one point, he was aware of Hope dabbing his face with a cool cloth. Fiona spoke to him, but he couldn't quite make out the words. And then suddenly she was gone, as if time had skipped a few minutes for him.

And always, the park ranger's voice moved in the background, drifting from room to room. The guy sure laughed a lot. He was loud, always joking, always upbeat and friendly. Indeed, that voice was the last thing he heard before he finally fell into a restless, pain-saturated sleep. After that, he had hours of moving through strange fever dreams. In most of them, he was still trapped outside, trying to claw his way through walls of snow, while people, animals, and indistinct shapes appeared and disappeared. He kept seeing his daughter walking away, often disappearing into the whiteness, never to return.

Hope, where did you go? Where are you?

At times, he heard the sound of the bear clawing at the ground around him, digging through snow as it tried to find where he was buried. Throughout them all, he felt pain and more pain. It was unrelenting.

And then, after what felt like days, he opened his eyes suddenly and found himself staring at the flickering orange light on the ceiling. The residue of the terrible dreams still clung to him, but he knew he was out of them now. Despite being dressed only in his long-sleeve t-shirt and boxer shorts, with a sheet laid over him, he was soaked with sweat, but he didn't feel like he was burning up any longer.

When Jarred made the mistake then of trying to sit up, a sharp burst of pain from his broken leg put a stop to that right away. He looked around and tried to reorient himself. Lying on an old couch in a small wood-paneled living room. The embers of a fire were still glowing in the fireplace, but he was alone. The curtains over the room's single window were parted just enough that he could see darkness through the frosty glass. It was night. The room was rather sparsely decorated. No quaint paintings hanging from the wall, no family photos or kitsch decorations, no fake plant in the corner. Really, there wasn't much of anything besides a coat rack, the couch, and a few tools in the corner.

He recalled the woman who owned the place. Fiona. That was her name. Just who was she exactly? He had a vivid memory of her sitting on the hearth, her hands clasped to her knees, looking like she was about to break into pieces with anxiety.

What is this place? Who are these people?

And then he became aware of some kind of soft, rhythmic tapping, and he was sure he'd fallen back into the fever dream. However, a figure stepped into his line of sight. Fiona. It was as if he had summoned her by thinking about her. She walked over to the couch and stood there, gazing down at him.

"I heard you making some noise out here," she said quietly. "Are you okay?"

The house was very dark and still. Even a whispered voice seemed incredibly loud.

"I'm not sure," he replied. His voice was rough, crackling up from a scratchy throat. "I woke up all of a sudden, and here I was. How long was I out? Things are kind of jumbled up in my head."

"Not sure," she said. "A while."

Fiona squatted down beside the couch. He's noticed that she wasn't particularly talkative, and she didn't speak now. She just kept staring, eyes narrowed as if she were analyzing him. Since he'd met her, she had often seemed to be quietly observing her surroundings, saying little. In that way, she kind of reminded him of Hope.

She was an attractive woman, with big hazel eyes and a dash of freckles across her cheeks and the bridge of her nose. However, there was a roughness around the edges, as if she'd worked hard for many years. There were no frills to her. She wore no makeup, wore flannel and seemed to like overalls, and kept her hair in a sloppy ponytail. Jarred couldn't quite make sense of her, and as the seconds stretched into uncomfortable territory, he finally spoke again.

"Did you have trouble sleeping?" he asked.

She seemed to hesitate for a second, then nodded, but she offered no further information.

"Well, hopefully I wasn't being too loud out here," he said. "I was sort of lost in bad dreams. A bear hasn't tried to break into the house recently, has it?"

At this, he got a hint of a smile from her, but it didn't last long. She shook her head. "There's never been a bear attack here. The only animal you have to worry about is an ornery male goat named Ramses, but he's down in the basement."

"A goat in the basement," Jarred said. Was she being serious, or was it a strange joke? In his current state of mind, he couldn't tell, but he noted that the house did sort of smell like a barn. "I take it this is your place. How long have you lived here?"

"Yeah, it belongs to me," she said. She sat down on the floor cross-legged beside the couch. "I've lived here by myself for fifteen years. I take care of it all: the animals, the crops, the greenhouse. And I build furniture as well. That's how I make money."

The way she said it, he could tell she was clearly proud of her independence, but he found the thought of living all alone out in the wilderness like this for fifteen years kind of sad.

He looked around the room again. There was a light fixture hanging from the middle of the ceiling, but it wasn't on. In fact, he hadn't seen any electric lights working. "It looks like this place is wired for electricity. I take it the storm knocked out the power."

"I don't run the electricity often," she said. "I have a generator that I use sometimes, especially when I need it for the electric furnace, but it's broken."

"Well, you seem to be getting by just fine without it," he said.

This brought out another smile, though it lingered this time. However, she didn't say anything.

"So you don't mind living out here by yourself?" he asked.

She shrugged. "I enjoy being alone," she said. "It was an intentional choice. Left an old life, an unhappy life, found this place and settled down." She paused, clearly uncomfortable with the conversation. Then, as if to turn the discomfort back on him, she quickly followed up with, "What about you? Is there anyone worrying about you at home? You know…Hope's mom."

The question hit hard. The fever and pain had lowered his defenses, and what should have been a casual question instead pierced deeply. Jarred took a moment to compose himself before saying, "No. Nobody at home." He was tempted to leave it at that, but he pressed on. Better to get it out there and satisfy Fiona's curiosity, so it wasn't hanging over them. Still, he spoke very quietly, so his daughter wouldn't hear from wherever she happened to be at the moment. "Hope's mother passed away when Hope was still was very young. Breast cancer. It all happened so quickly. She got the diagnosis, and three months later, she was gone and I was a single father."

Fiona bowed her head, as if in respect, but she didn't say anything to this.

"Hope doesn't have many memories of her," Jarred said. "I worry that she's going to forget her mother, but more than that, I worry about how she's been affected growing up without having a female influence in her life. That can't be good for a teenage girl, you know? I've dated a little, tried to bring some motherly figures into her life, but nothing ever worked out. It's not easy raising a kid. You worry about how every little decision you make, or fail to make, will impact their future."

To this, Fiona shrugged. "I wouldn't know. I don't really know anything about kids, what they need or don't need. Never had a child of my own. There was a time when I wanted to, but that was a long time ago. Anyway, Hope seems like she's okay, so you must've done a decent job raising her."

"She's a good kid." And then it was his turn to change the subject. The last thing he wanted to do while lying here in his misery was to remember his dead wife, whose voice had almost entirely faded away in his mind. "That park ranger really helped her, I think. He brought Hope out of her shell and got her involved in things. I think she's taken a real shine to him."

The change to Fiona's demeanor was dramatic and sudden. She scowled darkly at the floor, and the light went out of her eyes. It was the second time she had reacted with surprising negativity to the mention of him.

"Is there a problem?" he asked, and when she didn't respond to this question, he got more specific. "Is there something I should know about the park ranger?"

For a few seconds, she said nothing. She wouldn't look at him. And he thought maybe she was just going to leave it at that, but then she sighed and finally lifted her gaze. Instead of looking at him, however, she stared off at some point near the ceiling.

"Benjy Hartman is not my friend," she said, barely above a whisper. "I met him years ago during a camping trip, and he made a pest out of himself for a long time after that. Actually, he's the last person I'd ever want in my home. When your daughter showed up at my door, I was in the middle of kicking him out."

This revelation put an uncomfortable spin on the whole situation, and Jarred felt a little flutter of anxiety. There was a lot of emotion behind what Fiona said. Clearly, there was a dark history here. "Do I need to ask Hope to stay away from him?"

Fiona opened her mouth, as if to reply, but hesitated a moment before saying, "I'm keeping an eye on them. Right now, I think his motives toward your daughter are pure, but still, I'll never fully trust him around women."

Oh, God, who is this guy? Jarred wondered. Suddenly, the endless friendly chatter of Benjy took on a dark edge.

"You need to know," Fiona said, "I will be kicking Benjy out again as soon as the opportunity feels right. He's not welcome in my home."

"I understand," Jarred replied.

"He knows he's not welcome here," Fiona continued, speaking right over him. "We already had a big confrontation about it, but he's taking advantage of your arrival to stick around as long as possible."

"That explains it," Jarred said. "He seemed like Mr. Friendly. I thought it was just his personality, but now I get it. He's playing us against you."

"That's exactly right," Fiona said. "I'm glad you can see that, Jarred. I do have my little moments of self-doubt."

"Well, no one should feel unsafe in their own home. Even if he's a park ranger, even if he has first aid skills, he has to respect your wishes. I'm a stranger, too, so you shouldn't feel obligated to keep him around just because I'm lying here with a busted leg. Do what you need to do."

Fiona was quiet for a while, her gaze drifting back and forth. Jarred couldn't tell if she was still upset. Her facial expression was unreadable. Maybe she was just lost in thought. However, as the quiet stretched on, he decided to leave her to her thoughts.

Should I tell Hope about him? he wondered.

He knew his daughter well enough. If she had some reason to suspect that her new friend was actually a creep, it might have long-term negative consequences on her emotional well-being. She held on to such things. Ideally, it would be best to keep her out of it until Benjy left.

Don't tell her, he thought. *Not yet. Not ever, if you can avoid it. She doesn't need another reason to worry about this situation.*

At least a full minute passed without Fiona saying anything. She just sat there beside the couch, her hands clamped to her knees as she stared up at the ceiling. It grew increasingly awkward. Did she intend to just sit there the rest of the night while he slept? That wasn't going to happen. Finally, he had to break the tension.

"This house seems well-insulated and heated," he said. "It's quite comfortable in here, despite the storm raging outside. You seemed to be well-stocked with supplies, but you said your generator is broken. You can't fix it?"

Finally, Fiona snapped out of whatever internal pit she'd fallen into. Blinking, she looked at him and said, "No, I have a lot of skills, but I'm not handy when it comes to machines. I should have spent more time learning how to repair my own equipment, but I never got around to it." She waved her hand dismissively. "Oh well. It doesn't matter. The house can be heated by the wood-burning furnace, as long as we keep the vents clear, and I've got enough firewood stacked up to last for a while. I can live without the generator if I have to. Honestly, the only thing I'm really missing at this point is access to the radio. It would be nice to get some news about the storm—like, for example, if it's ever going to end."

Jarred couldn't help but smile. "Fiona, you're in luck. Of all the dying strangers you could have invited into your home, it just so happens that you got a mechanical engineer. I'm actually a *professor* of mechanical engineering. If you want help getting your generator up and running, I'm sure I can figure something out."

Fiona received this information with a grunt and a nod. She clearly wasn't the most expressive person in the world. "That's a stroke of good luck, for sure," she said.

28

Benjy was determined to make the best of it, even though Fiona was clearly moping about the whole situation. It must have been driving her crazy to have even more people invading her precious home. He couldn't help but take perverse pleasure in it. After all, her isolationism was unhealthy. Maybe fate or destiny had conspired with him to help her overcome her worst tendencies.

Still, when he got up that morning, he found her sitting at the kitchen table, dully flipping through what appeared to be an account book. Hope was sitting across from her, nibbling at a biscuit with jelly. There were more biscuits stacked on a platter in the middle of the table, and he grabbed one in passing. As he took a big bite, he heard a familiar clatter coming from the basement.

"Sounds like old Ramses is down there making trouble again," he said. "You know, I've been thinking about building some kind of more permanent structure for him. He's a persistent little rascal. He'll bust through the stacks of furniture sooner or later."

Fiona just continued to page through her book, as if he weren't even speaking.

"Fiona, do you have any extra fencing material lying in storage somewhere?" he asked. "A bit of barbed wire would be nice, some sturdy fence posts, chain link, that sort of thing. What do you say?"

She didn't answer immediately, but Hope looked up. The girl seemed to find the moment of silence uncomfortable, and her gaze flitted from Benjy to Fiona and back to Benjy.

"There's a bunch of stuff like that in the big storage building down the hill," Fiona said, finally, shutting her account book. "If you want to build a permanent pen for Ramses down in the basement, go right ahead. Help yourself to whatever's in storage. Just know that…" Whatever else she was going to say, she left it hanging, unfinished.

Benjy decided not to take the bait. He poured himself some clean water from the water bucket and swallowed it. "All right then," he said. "That'll be today's project. Hey there, Hope, how would you like to help me out?"

She nodded, eyes widening in excitement. "Definitely. I'm really good at designing and building things. I was in a robotics class in school. I came up with my own design for a robot, and I was close to finishing it, but it got left in the trunk of our car."

"Ooh, robots," he said, clapping. "That's way out of my league. Make sure your dad is okay with you helping me today, okay?"

From the living room, Jarred stirred on the couch and said, "It's fine, I suppose. Just don't stay out there too long."

"We're just going down the hill to get supplies," Benjy said. "Don't worry about it, Dad. I won't let her freeze out there." He beckoned Hope and headed into the living room.

She was a smart and capable kid, and he liked having her around. At least she was friendly to him, unlike sour old Fiona. As Hope pushed her chair back and came toward him, he felt a warm, fatherly moment. He would have hugged her, if he didn't think it might weird out Jarred. He grabbed her coat off the rack and handed it to her. Then he pulled his own coat on. She seemed so happy and eager to help him out.

This is exactly the kind of kid I'd like to have in my life, he thought. *Someone who looks up to me. A little buddy who's eager to follow me around. If only she'd rub off on Fiona a bit.*

As he pulled on his coat and gloves, he had a sudden image in his head. Him and Fiona living together in the house with Hope as their adopted daughter. It was such a nice image that he lingered on it.

Of course, her father is doing okay now, he thought, *but if anything ever happened to him, I wouldn't mind raising this kid. Me and Fiona. That would be good. A good life.*

Jarred was tucked deep under his blanket on the couch, watching his daughter as she put on her coat. Did he seem a little bit concerned or worried? Benjy wasn't sure, but he decided to stave off any concerns for now.

"I promise we won't be down there more than twenty, thirty minutes, Dad," he said. "We'll load up what we need for the project and rush right back."

"That's fine," Jarred replied. "Hope, if you start feeling too cold, or uncomfortable, or anything at all, you come right back."

Hope scowled at her father. "I'm not a baby. I'm not going to stand out there until I freeze to death. Don't you remember how I walked all the way here by myself?"

"I remember," Jarred replied. "I trust you."

Benjy decided it was time to leave before Hope got in trouble. He opened the front door and pushed his way into the cold wind. Hope followed right at his feet. He pulled the door shut as soon as she was through, then headed down the porch step.

He hopped up on the snowmobile and patted the seat behind him. "Climb on board, kiddo. We're going to whip this homestead into shape, you and me. Clearly, we're the go-getters around here."

"Yeah, I think so," she said, sitting behind him.

He started the snowmobile and headed down the hill. More than ever, the collection of buildings that comprised most of Fiona's homestead seemed to be sinking into the ground. Only the greenhouse, with its internal heater, had kept the snow at bay. Fortunately, the storage building stood near the greenhouse, and it had benefitted from the residual heat just enough that the front door was still clear.

Benjy headed to the barn. Although he hadn't asked for permission, he didn't think Fiona would mind if he used the Mule to carry the materials back up the hill. He'd grabbed the key in passing, though he didn't think she'd noticed. He pulled the snowmobile into the barn and killed the engine.

"Is this the right building?" Hope said.

"Well, we're swapping vehicles. Come on." He hopped off the snowmobile and pulled the Mule key out of his pocket. He thrust the key at her. "Want to drive the Mule for me?"

Hope stared at the key in his hand, her eyebrows climbing her forehead like they were trying to escape. "I can't drive."

"Oh…well, maybe next time," he said, smiling at her. He'd only been half-joking.

Maybe I should actually let her drive, he thought. *Kids love that sort of thing. I'd be her buddy and pal forever.*

He started up the Mule, waiting for her to take a seat, then drove out of the barn to the storage building.

"Let's make sure we get plenty of stuff," he said, stepping out of the vehicle and approaching the door. "Better to have too much than not enough, so we don't have to come back down here later."

The truth, of course, was that Ramses was hardly worth all of this effort. Benjy was sorely tempted to tell Fiona to just butcher the obnoxious animal. At least then he could provide plenty of meat. As it was, he offered no utility except as an excuse for Benjy to seem like he was an invaluable contributor to the homestead. Maybe that was enough for now, at least until this current project was complete.

"Okay, Hope, let's just look around in here and see if we can find anything that might help," he said, crossing the gloomy interior. It was like a walk-in freezer, but instead of big slabs of meat, the walls were lined with stacks of junk. He began picking through the nearest pile.

"How about this stuff over here?" Hope asked. She'd pulled the tarp off a pile against the opposite wall. "This looks like old fencing material, wood boards and stuff."

He went and looked at the pile. He'd actually been thinking about something with chain link and barbed wire on top, but this would do. A sturdy wooden fence attached to the walls on either side—that should keep Ramses at bay until they were ready to carve him into gyro meat.

"This'll do," he said. "Let's take the whole pile." He thrust his hand toward her again, the Mule key dangling from his finger. "Here you go."

"What?" She looked at him with a little half-smile on her face.

"I parked the Mule facing the door," he said. "We need to turn it around, so we can load all of this stuff in the back. Why don't you turn it around for me?"

"I told you, I can't drive," she said.

"Eh, this isn't really driving," he said. "It's just maneuvering. Didn't your dad ever let you drive his car around in a parking lot, just so you could get a feel for it?"

Hope shook her head.

"Well, today's the day," he said. "I'll show you what to do. Don't worry. It's not a big deal. What do you think?"

She reached out, hesitated, then grabbed the key from him. With a big grin, she wrapped both of her hands around it and said, "Okay, sure, why not? Just don't tell my dad. He might not like it."

"I won't say anything if you won't," Benjy replied. "All you're doing is moving it in a circle. It's not like I'm sending you out onto the highway or anything. Plus, heck, plenty of kids on farms learn to drive tractors when they're barely out of diapers, and you're, like, fifteen or sixteen, right?"

"Thirteen," Hope replied.

"Close enough."

He headed to the Mule and beckoned her to follow. When he got there, he opened the driver's door and motioned for her to hop on board. The girl was practically dancing at this point. It was just about the most excitement she'd expressed since he'd met her, and it made him feel proud. He was making this kid's day. Oh, yeah, he was the cool adult now, for sure.

Hope pulled herself behind the steering wheel and looked around at the controls. She seemed lost. Clearly, her father hadn't yet started teaching her about operating a vehicle. She hunted around for a few seconds and finally found the ignition, sliding the key in. Instead of turning the ignition, however, she resumed hunting around, as if looking for something.

"My dad's car has a button to start the car," he said.

"This is an old-school ignition," he replied. "You have to turn the key." He held up his hand and pantomimed it for her. "Like this. Got it?"

She grabbed the key and copied him, and the Mule's engine turned over. Hope grinned and tapped her free hand on the steering wheel. Hunting around again, she found the gear shift and grabbed it, but she shifted into first gear instead of reverse. Benjy was standing close to her door, and he had to lurch backward as the vehicle rolled forward, his arm banging against the doorframe.

"Oops, sorry," Hope said, stomping on the brake.

"No big deal," he said, forcing a laugh. "Just put it in reverse and back away from the door. Then put it in drive and circle around until your behind is facing the door. Got it? You can do this, kiddo."

"I got it," she replied.

Hope took a deep breath, seemed to settle herself, then put it in reverse. From there, she drove a few feet and hit the brakes hard again.

"Easy on the brakes," he said. "You've got this."

Nodding, she backed up a little more, following the ruts they'd left before. When she was a few yards from the storage building, she stopped and messed with the gear shift again.

"You're doing awesome," Benjy said.

Perhaps, he'd spoken too soon, as she lurched forward again, stopped suddenly, then lurched forward away.

"Easy, easy," he said. "The pedals are touchy."

Hope blew her breath out and shook her hands, as if to work out the tension. Then she reversed again, put it in drive, and drove a big circle in front of the storage building and the greenhouse.

"Okay, once the back is pointed toward me, put it in reverse again," she said.

She stopped when she was turned around, though she was pointed at an angle. Then she backed toward the open door, moving slowly and adjusting her direction constantly. Benjy waved his hands over his head when she was close enough, and she put it in park. It wasn't lined up perfectly, but it was close enough.

"You did it," he said. "Look at that, Hope. You drove for the first time!"

She flung open the door and hopped out with a squeal of excitement. Benjy rushed to meet her, holding up his hand for a high five.

"That wasn't so hard," she said, giving him the high five.

"You're a natural," he replied. "I figured you would be. You seem like a pretty smart kid. Now, come on, let's load up these fencing boards and head up to the house."

She was practically radiant.

This poor kid is starved for compliments, Benjy thought, as he walked over to the stack of fence boards.

As he picked up a big bundle of boards, tucking them under his arms, she copied him, though she couldn't gather nearly as many. He carried the boards to the Mule and dumped them in the back, and Hope did the same.

Yeah, she's a good kid, he thought, *and she'd be an even greater kid if she had someone to teach her more useful skills around the homestead.*

29

Fiona was troubled to discover that the snow was now up to her knees in some places, including the short path from the house to the generator shed. The back of the house was positioned perfectly to catch the snowfall.

"We'll be tunneling under the snow like moles before much longer," Jarred said. He was leaning heavily on the makeshift crutch they'd made him, but at least he was able to get around. Fiona thought he was probably in a lot more pain that he was letting on.

Smoke started to run past them into the snow, but as soon as his front paws sank into the deep snow, he stopped. Rearing back, he uttered a bark of frustration then dashed back inside the house.

"Yeah, you better stay in here, boy," she said, and then to Jarred, she said, "I'll go get the snow shovel. No need for tunneling like moles. Hang on."

While Jarred and Smoke lingered at the door, Fiona went and retrieved the snow shovel from the front porch. Digging out a path to the generator was going to be a pain, but there was no avoiding it. When she returned to the back door, Jarred reached for the shovel.

"Want me to help?" he asked. "We get a good bit of snow in the winter in Pittsburgh. I'm an old pro at shoveling the walk."

"No, you have to take it easy and let your leg heal," she replied. "I'll do it."

To his credit, he immediately relented. Fiona appreciated it more than she could express. She stepped outside and began digging into the deep snow, slowly clearing a path toward the generator shed. Jarred took a seat at the kitchen table, Smoke at his feet, and waited patiently. The dog seemed to like him, at least. That was also a relief.

It took the better part of half an hour to carve the ten-foot path, and Jarred never once pestered her about trying to take over or help. When she looked back, he seemed concerned for her, but he let her work in peace. Finally, when she was done, she propped the snow shovel beside the door and beckoned him.

"Maybe I'm way off base here," he said, rising from the chair with some effort, "but it almost seemed like you enjoyed that."

"Like I told you before, I've been taking care of this homestead for fifteen years," Fiona said. "It was in wretched condition when I first moved in. The buildings were all dilapidated and falling apart, and the ground was unsuitable for growing. I would never have made it this long if I didn't enjoy hard work."

Fiona grabbed a flashlight, then they made their way down the deep snow trench to the generator door. Inside, they found the generator sitting on its concrete platform, frosted over and looking quite dead. Jarred eased himself onto an available corner of the platform, as Fiona opened the toolbox.

"Okay, hand me the flashlight and I'll take a look at this thing," he said.

Fiona passed the flashlight to him. The generator was covered with a kind of aluminum shell, so she opened the hatch to give him access to it. Clicking on the flashlight, he leaned through the hatch and began rooting around inside. Reaching in, he fiddled around with a few things. She couldn't see what he was doing, but for some reason she trusted him. There was something simple and sincere about him. Unlike Benjy, who always seemed to be scheming, Jarred was fairly straightforward.

"Okay, after taking a look, I'm pretty sure the carburetor is clogged," he said, after a few minutes. "You don't happen to have any carburetor cleaner around here, do you? It's the kind of thing they would have on hand at a mechanic's shop."

"I'm afraid not," Fiona said. "I probably should keep stuff like that for the Mule, but I don't."

He scratched his whiskered chin for a second and seemed to be deep in thought. In that moment, Fiona saw the resemblance to Hope. They made a similar face when they were trying to figure something out. "Okay, I might be able to unclog it anyway. I'm sure you have a toolbox."

"Of course," she said. "Do you need any tools in particular?"

"A little bit of everything," he replied. "I'll need to get in there and make sure my diagnosis is right first."

"Okay, I'll go and get the *big* toolbox, then."

She rose and headed back into the house. The biggest toolbox was the one she used when working on furniture. It was a red vintage toolbox, an antique that she'd found on the property after taking ownership of the place. It held an impressive array of tools, but it was as heavy as an anvil, and it took both hands to carry it. Unfortunately, it was also located in the guest bedroom, tucked into the corner along with the stacks of furniture parts. When she stepped into the room, she felt an immediate twisting unease in her guts.

The stink of Benjy lingered in the room—a mix of some kind of cheap cologne or deodorant with an undercurrent of his musty clothes. The curtains were shut, and the shade was pulled, which made the room dark. Still, the shapes of furniture before her were familiar. It felt tainted. Benjy's presence had made it seem like an alien place, and she didn't like it. She rushed across the room, weaving her way to the back corner. As quick as she could, she grabbed the toolbox in both hands and hoisted it off the floor, then she backed toward the door. She couldn't get out of there fast enough.

I wish there was a way to scrub the presence of specific people out of the air, she thought.

She lugged the toolbox back out to the generator shed. The walls of snow on either side of her, rising up to her knees, seemed ominous. How much longer could it reasonably continue to snow, she wondered? How much precipitation could nature drop on them before it just ran out? Surely, there was a limit.

There only so much moisture on the earth, after all, she thought.

Snowflakes were still falling, so whatever the limit was, they clearly hadn't reached it yet. When she stepped into the shed, she saw Smoke sitting patiently in the corner as Jarred continued to root around inside the generator. Smoke looked up as she entered, then panted and flopped back down. At least the dog was comfortable around a man other than Benjy. Fiona had always resented the way Benjy had won her dog over, but somehow this made it just a little bit better.

"Okay, here you go," Fiona said, lugging the huge toolbox over to the generator and setting it down with a loud thump. "If you're looking for a tool that's not in there, you probably don't need it."

"Wow, impressive," he said, reaching down to undo the latches on the toolbox lid. "This must be an antique. A family heirloom, perhaps?"

"Maybe, but not my family," she replied. "The previous owners left it here. They were an old couple who retired, let this place fall apart around them, then died. The heirs took most of the old furniture, but left everything else. I bought the whole place—buildings, land, and leftovers—for a good price from the estate."

"Sounds like a good deal," Jarred said. "These old tools are amazing."

He rooted through the toolbox, pulled out a wrench, and went to work inside the generator again. Fiona couldn't see what he was doing, so she stood and waited. Clearly, he had some idea of what needed to be done, and she trusted him not to make it worse.

After a few minutes, he dug through the toolbox again and grunted. "Actually, there is one tool missing from this box, and it might just be the most important tool of all."

"Oh? And what would that be?" she asked.

"WD-40, of course," he replied with a wry smile. "There's a screw in here that's stuck like glue. I need to grease it up."

"I might have some," she said. Actually, she didn't have much call for WD-40 in her furniture-making work. She was sure she had can somewhere (didn't everyone?), but at the moment, she couldn't recall where it would be. "Let me go take a look."

"Hang on. I might be able to get this screw unstuck without it," he said. "I'll keep trying."

"I'll look while you work," Fiona said.

She headed back inside the house and began rooting through drawers. She started in the kitchen, digging through the junk drawer to no avail. Then she moved to the cupboard, but that was no good either. She was just about to head back into the guest bedroom when she heard a familiar sound coming from outside. The generator engine rumbled to life, then revved a few times.

"Ta da!" Jarred shouted.

Fiona headed back outside, feeling a great swell of elation. Despite his broken leg, Jarred was sitting there on the platform, shaking a fist over his head and laughing as the generator puttered away.

"Yep, carburetor was clogged," he said. "Once I got the rusty screws out, it wasn't too hard to get in there and clean it out. It could use a good flushing with some carburetor cleaner, if you ever make it back into town."

"I'll make a note of it," she said.

In that moment, she felt a strange, almost overwhelming sense of normalcy, and suddenly, she was on the verge of tears.

Come on, Fiona, she scolded herself. *It's not that big of a deal. Contain yourself.*

When Jarred struggled to rise, she grabbed his hand and helped him up. His hands were filthy with grease, but she didn't mind. On the contrary, in that moment, she felt a strong urge to hug him out of sheer trembling gratitude. She didn't do this, of course. It was so far beyond her comfort zone that she couldn't even catch a glimpse of it on the horizon. Still, it caused a moment of awkwardness to pass between them.

"You could power the radio now," he said. "Maybe we can get some news and see what's happening in the rest of the world."

She handed him the crutch, helped him get it positioned under his arm, then walked with him back to the house. Smoke finally rose and trotted after them. She hadn't thanked him yet, and she knew it. Why did it feel so awkward? Finally, as he hobbled through the back door, she forced the words out.

"Jarred, thanks for your help," she said. "It seemed so easy for you, but I never would have been able to do it on my own."

"I'm glad I could pay you back in some way," he replied. "After the way I've dirtied up your couch and intruded into your life, this was the least I could do."

"I've just…" It wasn't easy to admit it, and she never would have done so with Benjy around. "I've been on my own for so long, sometimes I forget what it's like to need other people."

But it was so much more than that. This man had only been in her home for a couple of days, and he'd already solved a huge problem on her homestead—without demanding anything of her in return or making her feel uncomfortable. This made her feel a complex array of emotions that she couldn't even clearly identify. As he made his way back inside, he looked tired and cold, and he winced every time the heel of his bad leg brushed the ground.

"You need to lie down," she said. "I think you've done enough for one day. I'll bring you something to clean your hands. After that, I need to go down and put out the fire in the old furnace."

"What about that toolbox?" he said.

"I'll lug it back inside once you're settled," she said.

With a hand on his shoulder, she guided him to the couch, then helped him ease onto the cushions. She laid the crutch on the floor nearby and positioned a pillow under his leg.

"I really feel bad about the couch," he said. "I'm ruining it."

"I made this couch myself," she replied. "I can make another one. Don't worry about a thing."

30

Benjy was in a pretty good mood for once. He spent so much of his time faking it that it felt strange to feel exactly how he acted for once. The kid seemed to genuinely like him. Actually, it reminded him a bit of Smoke. Fiona's dog liked him too. He tiptoed up the porch steps, then turned to wait for Hope. She was lingering in the snow, still grinning from ear to eat. Letting her drive the Mule had been a master stroke.

The power of being nice, he thought. *Why doesn't it work on Fiona?*

"Hey, I won't breathe a word about your driving," he said, speaking in a hushed voice. "I don't want your dad to get upset. I'm not trying to cause trouble between you two."

"Good. I'm not going to say anything either," Hope replied. "It's not a lie if he doesn't ask."

"Smart thinking." He tapped the side of his head.

He turned and grabbed the doorknob. They'd approached the house quietly, speaking barely above a whisper and stepping lightly. Now, he turned the knob and flung the door open, stepping into the living room with a loud laugh, as if he'd just told a joke. He didn't even fully understand his own reason for doing so. It just came to him naturally.

"We're back," he announced, stomping the snow off his boots.

He took in the scene before him in a fraction of a second. Jarred was sprawled on the couch, as usual, but he had fresh snow on his pants, and he was wiping his hands on a greasy rag. Fiona was sitting cross-legged on the floor beside him, her own boots covered in melting snow, as if the two of them had gone tromping around together outside.

Worse, Fiona had a big, stupid smile on her face. As soon as Benjy loudly announced himself, she stopped smiling—shutting it off like she'd flipped a switch. Then she scrambled to her feet and turned to face him.

She's acting like a teenager who just got caught getting felt up by her boyfriend, he thought.

And was she blushing, for God's sake? He was sure her cheeks were redder than usual. It wasn't wind-burn, he didn't think. No, no, this was some giddy schoolgirl garbage, and he had to fight a sudden surge of anger. Benjy's good mood burst like a popped balloon, and he stared at them with narrowed eyes. Of course, Fiona couldn't let him be happy for a little while. Of course, she had to mess around and hurt his feelings for absolutely no good reason, and after he'd lugged a big load of wood up the hill for her stupid goat pen.

When Smoke got up from his place near the hearth and approached him, Benjy realized he was still blocking the door. Hope was standing behind him, waiting to get inside. Through sheer force of will, Benjy pushed down the anger and stepped to one side, rearranging his facial features to hide how he really felt, but his imagination was already running wild. He even managed to reach down and pat Smoke on the side, which seemed to appease the dog, who padded back over to the hearth and lay down.

What had Fiona and Jarred been doing while he was down the hill working?

I'll figure it out, he thought, *but in my own way*.

He settled on what felt like a normal expression, not smiling but not scowling, and pulled his hat off, smoothing his sweaty hair back.

"Hey there, buddy," he said, nodding at Jarred. "Are you feeling okay?"

"About the same," Jarred replied. "Leg hurts."

"Yeah, I'd better take a look at it."

Benjy ripped off his gloves one by one and set them on the hooks of the coat rack. As he did that, Hope came fully inside and pushed the front door shut. Fortunately, she still looked happy, so maybe she hadn't noticed the strangeness of the moment. Still, Fiona was acting like a fool. She started to go to the kitchen, then stopped and stood in the doorway, saying nothing.

Do you not realize how easily I can read you, Fiona? he thought. *You think you're such a mystery, but you're an open book to me.*

He approached the end of the couch and sat down. They'd left the first aid kit and other medical supplies on the end of the hearth nearby, and he pulled it toward himself.

"I'm going to replace the bandages," Benjy said. "That way I can take a look at the injured area and make sure everything's kosher, okay?"

"Sounds good to me," Jarred replied, as if they were pals.

Yeah, I'm sure it does sound good to you, Benjy thought. *I saved your damn life, and then you start horning in on my territory the second my back is turned.*

He hoped none of this showed on his face as he retrieved scissors from the kit and began cutting away the bandage. Hope was removing her coat and gloves in the corner, as Fiona stood awkwardly in the kitchen door. The whole room was charged with tension.

I can't be the only one who feels it, Benjy thought.

Fiona didn't offer to help remove the splints. She just stood there. And he didn't bother asking. Nor was he as gentle as he could have been, pulling the boards away from Jarred's leg and dumping them on the ground. Jarred gasped and bared his teeth.

"Sorry about that," Benjy said.

"No, it's fine," Jarred replied. "I can handle it."

"I'm sure you can." Benjy forced himself to smile at the guy.

As he pulled away the cut bandage, he realized the leg was in bad shape. The ankle was red and badly swollen. The splints had left deep depressions in the swollen flesh. For good measure, Benjy gently prodded his ankle, and Jarred gasped again.

"Okay, level with me," Benjy said. "Have you been hobbling around on this leg? It's looking pretty rough."

"Sorry, I have to confess," Jarred replied, "I went outside to fix the generator. It was against doctor's orders, I know, but at least I did it. The generator's working again, so maybe the pain was worth it."

Benjy couldn't help himself. He looked up and stared hard at Jarred. The man only met his gaze for a second before looking away. Who was this guy? From the beginning, he'd seemed like a pretty typical, slightly dorky suburban dad. He was in decent shape, but he had the personality of a schlub.

Maybe I misread him, Benjy thought.

He forced his attention away and began re-splinting the leg, grabbing another roll of bandages from the first aid kit. Benjy had plenty of experience working when his mind was in turmoil. He'd done it many times while on the job as a ranger. It was practically a way of life. He put the splints back in place and wound the bandage around them. He didn't need Fiona's help. He hadn't needed it the first time he'd splinted the leg. However, as he worked, he glanced at her. Would she offer to help again?

Apparently not. She was just standing there, her hands in the front pocket of her overalls.

Why did Jarred fix the generator? he wondered. *Does this guy just go around fixing things that don't belong to him?*

But, no, there was no way he hobbled out there on his own. Fiona must have been helping him. Maybe she invited him out there. Benjy dared another glance at Fiona, this time giving her a more pointed look. She wasn't looking at him, but she seemed to sense it. Suddenly, she turned and went into the kitchen, staring out the back window, as if to watch the snowfall.

She was laughing at me when I walked through the door, Benjy thought. *That's why she reacted so strongly. Guilt. Childish guilt.*

As soon as he thought it, he became convinced it was true. It tormented him that she'd been in here joking around with this strange suburban nobody when she was so stiff and unfriendly to Benjy. He realized his anger was affecting his work when he pulled the bandage too tightly and Jarred gasped in pain.

"Sorry about that," Benjy said. "You can't let your leg get so swollen, okay? No more running around fixing things. Just lie there and let your leg heal. Got it?"

"You got it, Doc," Jarred replied. "I won't do it again."

"There are plenty of other people in the house to fix stuff," Benjy added. "Your job is to take care of your leg. That's your job." He managed to smile again, and he was so impressed with himself. It was important that Jarred receive this as friendly advice. "You need a few days, at least."

Damn, I'm good, Benjy thought.

He taped off the end of the bandage and rose, rubbing his hands on the sides of his jacket.

"That means no more heading outside for any reason," Benjy added. "You don't want this leg to get broken even worse, or it might never heal. Got it?"

Jarred gave him an OK sign. Benjy decided he'd made his point, and it was getting harder not to let his true feelings show.

"Fine. I'm going to unload the wood we brought up the hill," he said, heading for the front door.

Hope had moved closer to the fireplace, and she was currently rubbing her hands together and blowing on them. Her hair was sticking up in a crazy way, and her cheeks were windburned. Still, she appeared untouched by the tension in the room.

"Hey there, kiddo," Benjy said in passing, beckoning her. "You want to come with me and unload the Mule? You'll need to put all your gear back on."

"Yeah, sure," Hope said, and she immediately fell in line behind him.

"Actually, you've probably been outside enough today," Jarred said. When his daughter kept following Benjy to the door, he snapped his fingers. "Hey, Hope, I want you to stay in here with me for a little while, so you can warm up. Let Benjy do his work alone, okay? He can handle it. Anyway, you don't want to make a pest out of yourself."

"Dad, I'm not a pest," Hope said. She made it as far as the coat rack before she froze, her hands halfway to grabbing her gloves. "I'm really useful."

"I know," Jarred replied, "but I want you to stay inside this time."

Benjy was at the front door, but he stopped and turned. Hope was right, of course. She wasn't a pest. Heck, she was easily the least annoying person in this house by a long shot. He could have corrected her father. He could have put the man in his place, but he decided to let it go for now.

Still, he looked back over his shoulder at the stranger on the couch. The interloper. Jarred was currently looking at his daughter, but for a second, just a second, his eyes flicked up to Benjy. And there it was. Benjy read the accusation there as clear as day, if only for a brief moment, but it was enough. He knew everything he needed to know about the situation.

Somehow, in the couple of hours he was down the hill getting wood, the whole dynamic in the house had shifted.

Once that guy's fever broke, he became a problem, Benjy thought. *He was in here filling Fiona's head with ideas, turning her against me, while I was working.*

No, he didn't like it. Not one bit. Still, Benjy wasn't going to let it break him. He cleared his throat loudly to draw Hope's attention. She was scowling like she was ready to have a real fight with her dad, but that wasn't going to help the situation.

"Hey there, Hope," Benjy said. "You should listen to your father. You've been out in the cold a lot today. We don't want you to get sick. Anyway, your dad's in a lot of pain. He could use the company."

Hope's scowl faltered, and she lowered her hands. "But…"

"No, it's fine," Benjy said, opening the front door. "I can handle this part of the project on my own. Take it easy, okay?"

And with that, he stepped outside and pulled the door shut behind him, so proud of how *sincere* he'd managed to sound that he practically cheered. Instead, he took a moment to settle himself and headed down the porch steps to the Mule.

"This outsider doesn't know who he's dealing with," Benjy muttered.

31

The simple act of plugging in the old radio and seeing the red power light come on made Fiona feel as giddy as a kid on Christmas Eve. She set the big, black radio on the kitchen table in front of her, as Jarred, Benjy, and Hope crowded around the table and leaned in close. Things were weird with Benjy. Even though he was mostly acting like his usual self, she felt an even worse vibe in the air. She chose to ignore it for the time being. She would deal with Benjy soon enough.

Even now, though he had an eager look on his face as he leaned in close to the radio, he couldn't completely hide the tension in his body posture and around his eyes. No, he wasn't as good at faking his emotions as he probably thought he was. Fiona tried to ignore it for the time being as she began turning the dial on the radio. A bit of static came through the speaker, but the first few stations proved to be off the air.

"So it's entirely possible that there are no radio stations on the air," Jarred said.

As she turned the dial, she occasionally picked up crackly bursts of something—possibly voices or music—but they were so faint, she couldn't be sure. Still, she kept going, heading toward the lower frequencies.

"A snowstorm, even a bad one, isn't going to knock radio stations off the air," she said. "There has to be at least one. That's all we need. One station up and running."

"I could always try to raise headquarters," Benjy said, tapping the Ohio park ranger patch on his jacket. "Do you happen to have a short-wave radio lying around here somewhere?"

"I'm afraid not," Fiona said. "It's FM, AM, or nothing."

"I'll remember to bring you a short-wave radio once the weather lets up a little bit," Benjy said. "I know where I can get one."

Don't do me any favors, she almost said, but she bit her lip. No reason to antagonize him further. Fortunately, she was rescued from the awkward silence when a voice suddenly cut through the station around the very bottom of the FM dial. At first, it was too distorted to make out the words, but she kept tweaking the dial back and forth until she finally found the one tiny spot where it came in clear enough to make out.

"Like I said, folks, I wish I had some good news for you." An old man's voice. He had the cadence of an old broadcaster, but he had the warble of a man approaching the end of his first century on the earth. "They're having trouble at the National Weather Service getting the word out, but I've got the latest report here, and it's looks just like the last one. I wish I had some good news for you, but we're in this for the long haul."

Fiona heard the rustling of papers, as if the broadcast were being done by a single solitary figure just reading his mail. He seemed to be looking for something and spent a few seconds in radio silence. Then Fiona heard what sounded like an envelope being ripped open.

"Sounds like production quality has gone down a little bit," Benjy noted.

"This guy might be broadcasting all by himself there," Jarred noted. "Holding down the fort. He sounds like he's pretty old, so it's quite an achievement."

Benjy was on the verge of responding, so Fiona shushed him. "Listen, guys. Let's hear what he has to say."

The broadcaster was crinkling a piece of paper, clearly holding it too close to the microphone. "Now, ladies and gentlemen, this is a copy of the evacuation order from the governor. I know many of you didn't make it out in time, and there's quite a few who are trying to come back in. Look, you're not going to make it. They're trying to clear the highway, folks, but it's just not safe. Stay away. That's the governor's orders. Head down south and get beneath the latitude of the snowstorm, because otherwise, you're going to be stranded for a very long time. We keep saying this, but based on reports, many of you just aren't listening. This storm is not going to end. It's *not* going to end. Not for months, at the very least. Do you hear me? Months, and that's the most optimistic view."

As he spoke, Fiona felt a growing sense of despair. Not going to end? Had she heard him correctly? She traded an anxious look with Jarred, who had put his arm around Hope and pulled her close.

"Duke Cooper in town said something about a local evacuation order," Fiona said, "but I didn't realize it was statewide now. This is crazy."

"I can't believe they'd evacuate the entire state of Ohio," Jarred said. "By now, most people won't be able to leave anyway. Heck, Hope and I left our home on a gut feeling after a friend told me about the weather. It seemed like a good idea to head south to a warmer climate, but even then, the highway was treacherous."

"The state government is late to the game, as usual," Benjy said, drumming his fingers on the tabletop. "They have to know it's too late for most people to evacuate. Unless they got a million snowplows just constantly going back and forth on the highways, people are going to have a hard time getting anywhere safer. This is just a way to cover their butts when people freeze to death in their homes. 'Hey, we told them to get,' they'll say. I deal with these state government goons in my line of work, and they're the biggest morons you'll ever meet."

Hope was nodding vigorously, and Benjy noticed, giving her a weird little smirk, as if to say, *Yeah, you get what I'm saying, kid.* Seemingly in response to this, Jarred hugged Hope just a little tighter. It was the smallest of gestures, but it made the air thick with tension.

Suddenly, Fiona wanted out of the kitchen and away from the situation.

This is why I live alone, she thought.

"Well, we know the ugly truth now, anyway," she said, flicking off the radio. "This is going to last months, at least. Months of blizzard-like conditions. So there you go. That's it. With that knowledge, let's all try to sleep. Jarred, are you parked on the couch again tonight, or do you want to share the other guest room with Hope? It's up to you two?"

"Maybe I'll try the bedroom tonight," he said. "That couch is fine and all, but…" He shrugged.

Fiona nodded and pushed back her chair. "I'll get the mattress ready for you."

Benjy was up in a flash, right at her side, as if he intended to follow her down the hall. There was a tightness in his shoulders, a stiffness in his neck. Yeah, he was losing his grip on the phony friendliness. That was clear.

"Hey, Benjy, if you don't mind," she said, "would you stoke the fire and add another log before heading to bed?"

He started to say something but stopped. His mouth opened, hung there like it had a broken hinge, then slammed shut again.

"Yeah, I can do that," he said.

It felt like a mistake. Giving him another task would just strengthen his conviction that he was essential to her survival. Still, she was tired and didn't want to deal with him hovering at her shoulder. It was getting to be too much.

As Benjy headed into the living room, Jarred grabbed his crutch and slowly lifted himself from his seat. Months. Months with Benjy in her house like a stale fart that wouldn't disperse. Fiona couldn't stand the thought, especially now. Still, she was tired and not going to do anything about it now.

As soon as Fiona was through her bedroom door, she kicked off her boots. One of them went spiraling off toward the dresser and landed in the opened top drawer. Fiona decided to leave it there as she nudged her door shut and sat down on the bed. Smoke hopped up beside her, and she laid a hand on his head.

"What am I going to do?" she said to him. "Things were going so well on the homestead before all of this. I was headed for an amazing harvest this season, and then this freak weather comes along and ruins everything." She sighed, and Smoke laid a paw on her leg, as if trying to reassure her. "And now I've got a house full of people. People are so messy and weird. Hard to deal with."

Still, the radio report had given her the stark realization that this problem was much bigger than her little homestead. Bigger than Glencole and bigger than Eastern Ohio. As she sat there, she tried to envision all of the big cities being buried by the storm, all of the suburban homes vanishing as the snow piled up for months, whole families shivering in dim rooms with nowhere to go. The problem was so much bigger than she could wrap her head around.

Fiona finally rose and changed into a t-shirt and sweatpants before climbing into bed. Smoke waited until she was settled, then curled up on top of the blanket at the foot of the bed. She heard others in the house, a soft voice that sounded like Hope. Gradually, the others settled down, and soon the house was quiet except for the constant whistle of wind against the windows.

What if it's the end? It was the first time she'd really considered the possibility. *What if this is how all of civilization comes crashing down? A blizzard that never stops. Instead of war or disease, we'll just be buried by an endless winter, and that'll be the end of us?*

It was such a disturbing thought that for a long time she couldn't settle her mind despite the weariness in her body. The wind against the window now sounded like the moan of a dying world. Still, somehow, she eventually managed to drift off into a light sleep, pushed beyond her troubled thoughts by sheer mental exhaustion.

Sleep didn't last long. Only a few minutes passed before Smoke shifted on the bed and roused her. Fiona was going to ignore him, assuming he was just trying to get comfortable, but then she realized he was standing up on the bed and panting. She knew what that meant, and she opened her eyes.

Turning, she saw the dog leaning over the footboard and gazing in the direction of the bedroom door. A faint orange light flickered on the walls. Firelight from the living room. That meant her door was open.

The sudden realization stripped away the veil of sleep, and she rolled onto her back. Indeed, the door was open, and she saw light in the hallway beyond. A silhouette stood in the opening, and she knew that shape. She knew it all too well.

"What are you doing?" she asked, her voice little more than a raspy croak.

For a few seconds, he just stood there, saying nothing. The stench of cheap cologne and dirty clothes wafted into the room. He started to enter the room, but to Fiona's amazement, Smoke growled at him. Had he ever growled at Benjy? Maybe he sensed the tension in the air as well. Or maybe he sensed imminent danger. Whatever the case, Fiona sat up in bed.

"Benjy, what are you doing?" she asked again.

He grunted, and there was such contempt in that simple sound. "You've really been getting chummy with the kid's dad, haven't you?" he said in a harsh whisper. "The guy is close to useless. You must know that. He can't even walk across a snowy field without breaking his leg. So he fixed the generator? Big deal! I could've done it, too. He's pathetic, has no practical skills for working on a homestead like this, and he's not particularly bright. All he'll do is eat up your food and take up space. He's not the kind of guy you need around here."

Was he sleepwalking? No, she didn't think so. He sounded wide awake. Fiona cleared her throat so she could speak more forcefully, but her heart was racing.

"Get out of my room, Benjy," she snapped. "Get out of here right now!"

He made a weird snorting sound, almost but not quite a laugh. Then he backed away from the door and turned, disappearing down the hallway. As soon as he was gone, Fiona leapt off the bed, took a few stumbling steps across the room, and caught herself against the bedpost. Reaching out, she swung her bedroom door shut. Then, for good measure, she reached over and locked it.

In the silence that followed, she waited, her breath sounding especially loud in her ears. Smoke was still standing at the end of the bed, making a kind of wheezing sound now. She'd never heard the dog get angry at Benjy before, and that change alone turned annoyance into fear. For long minutes, she stood there between the bed and the door, waiting for her heart to settle. The house was utterly quiet again, and she was conflicted.

Get your gun and drive him out of the house right now, she thought. *Make him leave. It doesn't matter if it's the middle of the night.*

But, no, something about sending him out in the darkness made the situation seem more dangerous. She wanted to be able to see him leave, to watch the snowmobile fading into the far distance. She needed to see Benjy Hartman get out of her life for good with her own eyes. Finally, she forced herself to return to the bed, though she just lay there, staring at the ceiling.

He leaves first thing in the morning, she thought. *No matter what.*

32

She tossed and turned the rest of the night. Even Smoke eventually settled down again, but Fiona couldn't. Her nerves were on edge, and it didn't matter how much her body cried out for sleep. When the first hint of pink light appeared through the frosted bedroom window, she finally kicked backed the covers and got up. Her anger had been growing as the hours passed. Indeed, as she got dressed, her hands were shaking with rage.

Getting chummy with the kid's dad.

The entitlement in the way he'd said it. As if she had no right to make other friends. As if she owed him an explanation for her choices. As if he owned her. Fiona had to pause a moment to collect herself.

"He's out of my life for good," she muttered, pulling on a warm flannel shirt. "I don't care what it takes."

She stepped into a clean pair of overalls and pulled a knit cap over her head. Then she pulled on some warm socks followed by her winter boots. By now, Smoke had hopped down and was pacing in front of the bedroom door, ready to go out. Finally, Fiona went to the gun rack above the dresser and grabbed the Mossberg shotgun. It was heavy in her hands, loaded and ready to go.

She almost racked the slide, if only to feel the satisfying *chunk* of a shell entering the chamber, but she didn't want him to hear it, not yet. Holding the shotgun against her belly, she opened the bedroom door and stepped into the hall. The house was quiet. Fiona went to the nearest guest room. It seemed wise to have an audience when she made her move against Benjy, so she knocked on the door. Someone stirred on the other side, and she thought she heard a sleepy, "Yes?"

She eased the door open. Jarred and Hope were sharing the ragged old mattress. She'd attempted to clear and clean it, but they were still roughing it. The room was musty and filled with her junk. It was like being housed in a supply closet. Neither of them had complained, of course.

Hope was sleeping, but Jarred was awake, struggling to sit up when she opened the door.

"What's happening?" he asked, rubbing his eyes. He had his splinted leg resting on a pillow, his crutch propped against the wall within reach. His gaze went to the shotgun.

Hope was still sleeping, curled up under her blanket.

"I'm kicking Benjy out of the house," she said. "For good. Right now. I could use a little support, just in case he refuses to go."

She expected an argument. Surely Jarred would want to defend the man who had come to his rescue. She was so sure he would oppose her that she felt a moment of self-doubt. Maybe it was wrong to kick Benjy out, after all. Maybe she was blowing this out of proportion.

After a moment of silence, Jarred nodded and said, "I understand."

"You do?" she replied.

"Yeah, I sort of sensed something weird was going on yesterday," he said. "Weirder than usual. It felt tense around him. Well, I've got your back." He pulled his blanket back, and Fiona had the sense that if he could have, he would have hopped up out of bed and rushed to join her. "I'll stand with you when you tell him."

The fact that he didn't question her at all, that he didn't tell her to calm down or reconsider, that he instead offered immediate support, caught her off guard. Surprise gave way to a sudden surge of affection, and she found herself speechless.

I'm not crazy. I'm not overreacting. My feelings are valid.

How long had it been since someone had offered her such unquestioning support? How long since there had been someone who didn't questions her thoughts and feelings, who didn't treat her like she was unreasonable or silly? Had there ever been *anyone* in her life like that? Certainly not in her life before the homestead. Her old life had been filled with gaslighting and verbal abuse.

John would have told me I'm being hysterical, she thought. *He would've made fun of me for grabbing the shotgun.* Even though her ex-husband was fifteen years in her past, she could still access the emotions of that relationship all too easily.

Hope was still sleeping. She gave a little snort and sank deeper into her blankets.

"Do I need to bring anything with me?" Jarred asked. "A weapon. Maybe a big piece of wood."

"No, just stay by my side when I do it, and that'll be enough," she replied. "I want him to see that I've got support. I'm not alone, and I'm not overreacting."

"You got it." He grabbed his crutch and rose from the bed. "Let's try to keep Hope out of this. Hopefully, she'll sleep through it. She's still pretty exhausted. I'd rather she didn't know what's happening."

"That makes sense," Fiona said. "I'll try to keep my voice down, if Benjy lets me."

As Jarred hobbled toward the door, she backed into the hall and turned. Benjy's room was only a few feet away, and she thought she heard him moving around in there. Was it possible he'd overheard their conversation, even though they'd spoken quietly? Maybe so.

He should be packing, then, she thought.

As Jarred stepped into the hall, Fiona approached Benjy's door and knocked insistently. He immediately opened the door, as if he'd been waiting on the other side. Benjy was looking rougher than ever, but he had that dumb, fake grin plastered on his face.

"Well, good morning, sunshine," he said. His gaze flicked down to the shotgun, but his expression didn't change. "I guess I'll get to work on building Ramses his new pen this morning. We've got to keep that ornery critter contained, after all. I have so many plans. So much work to do. We have to get ready for months of snowy conditions, right? Right."

"No," she replied. It was all she could say at first. She looked at Jarred, and he nodded at her, as if to say, *You can do this.* By the time she turned back around, Benjy's smile was completely gone, as if it had been a stain, and he'd wiped it off his face.

In the end, she didn't even have to say it. Clearly, he knew what this was about. "Look, you can't toss me out into the cold, Fiona," he said. "We've been over this before, okay? It'll be a death sentence if you send me away."

He advanced on her, and she stepped back. "No, it won't. You've got your ranger station, and if supplies are running low, you can always contact headquarters."

"You need me, Fiona," he shouted suddenly, smacking the doorframe with his open palm. "Don't you get it? You need my help to survive! You're not going to make it without me. Heck, you'd have been trampled by your own damned goat if I wasn't here. You need me, and Hope needs me!"

"Hope will be fine," Jarred said.

"Stay out of it, *pal*," Benjy said, with an angry swipe of both hands. "We don't need your input. Who are you? This is between me and Fiona, and you're just some guy who fell down in a field and broke his leg."

"I want you out of my house," Fiona said. "Today. Right now."

"I don't know why you insist on playing this game," Benjy said, shaking his head. "You've been doing this to me for *years*. You admit that you need me, act like my friend, almost admit how you *really* feel about me, and then suddenly it shuts off. Suddenly, you're cold to me, and here we are. It's been the same roller coaster of emotions year after year, and I'm sick of it. Do you remember how we met? You were camping, and you need help getting a campfire started. I helped you. From the first day we met, I helped you. And you've only ever repaid me with rude behavior. Can you stop it?"

She wanted to argue with him. So much of what he'd just said was flat-out stupid, but she didn't want to waste any more time. "I told you to get out of my house right now, and I won't say it again."

But he just stood there in the doorway, a fierce light in his eyes, as if challenging her to enforce her will. Just then, Fiona heard footsteps behind her, and a soft little voice said, "What's going on out here? Why is everyone yelling?"

She glanced back and saw a bleary-eyed Hope moving up behind her father.

"Yeah, see what you've done?" Benjy said. "You've scared the poor kid."

Jarred moved quickly, putting an arm around his daughter and guiding her into the living room. They sat down on the couch, and he grabbed her hand, holding it tightly. Smoke padded over and sat down on the hearth, watching everything warily. Hope seemed mostly confused. Her lingering sleepiness was to their advantage, because it prevented her from fully realizing what was going on. She yawned, rubbed her face with her free hand, and stared at Benjy.

"The kid doesn't want me to go," Benjy said. "She's the only sane one around here."

"It doesn't matter," Fiona replied. She stepped back so she was out of his reach. "Get out of my house. Right now. You're no longer welcome here. And don't come back."

And when he still didn't move, she raised the shotgun and leveled it at his chest. He glanced down at the barrel and bared his teeth at her.

"Are you going to explain to me why I'm being exiled?" he asked.

"You know why. Get out."

He stared at her a second longer, his expression openly hostile. Then he struck the doorframe again and said, "I'm so sick of your damned flighty nature, Fiona. I'm so sick of it. You want to toss me out into the never-ending blizzard, then fine. Toss me out!"

And with that, he turned and stomped back into the room. Hope was now fully aware of what was going on, and she began to pull against her father's grip.

"Why are we kicking him out?" she said. "Benjy didn't do anything wrong!"

Jarred tried to hug his daughter, but she pushed him away. "No, you have to let him stay. He can't go out there. Dad, he helped us. We can't throw him out in the snow!"

Benjy was quickly gathering up his belongings, shoving clothes into his backpack, cursing under his breath.

"Don't worry about it, Hope," he said. "They don't like me for some reason, despite all the help I've provided around here, but it's fine. I'll be just fine. Don't worry about me. I am a park ranger, after all."

"Don't speak to my daughter," Jarred said.

Benjy flung the strap of his backpack over his shoulder and stepped out into the hall. He gave Fiona another lingering hostile look. On her own, she might have wilted, as she had so often done in the past. But she wasn't alone now, and she knew it. She felt it. So she kept the shotgun leveled at him and stood her ground.

"Don't talk to your daughter?" Benjy said in disgust, as he headed into the living room. "Buddy, she's old enough to see what's really going on here. Tell her I'll be just fine out there on my own, would you? I've got enough training to walk across a field without breaking bones, that's for sure."

As Fiona followed him into the living room, she saw that Hope was crying, furiously rubbing at her face. She tried not to let it get to her. They could explain everything to the girl once Benjy was long gone. Benjy opened the front door, and bitterly cold air swept into the room. This seemed to make Hope cry even harder.

"Oh, I think maybe it's one or two degrees warmer this morning," Benjy said sarcastically, pulling on his coat and gloves. Without looking back, he zipped up the coat, stepped into his boots, and went outside. He left the door wide open, so Fiona followed him onto the porch. By now, Hope was sobbing loudly, as her father spoke softly to her, clearly trying to calm her down.

"He's going to die out there," Hope yelled. "He's going to die because of Fiona!"

"No, no, you heard what he said," Jarred replied. "He'll be fine."

Benjy stomped down the porch steps and climbed onto his snowmobile. As he did, Fiona caught a hint of a smile pass over his face. Yes, he loved that the kid was on his side. He loved that he was at least leaving a little chaos behind. Fiona could see that, and she kept the gun aimed at him as he started up the snowmobile.

"Sooner or later, you'll regret this decision," he said, glancing at Fiona. "You'll regret all of your decisions about me. Mark my words."

"Is that a threat?" Fiona asked.

"Nope." He revved the engine. "A prophecy."

And with that, he put the snowmobile in gear and drove away, cutting a broad arc as he sped down the hill and joined with the half-buried tracks he'd left in the field beyond. Fiona watched him slowly disappear into the distance, heading in the general direction of Glencole. She couldn't believe it was actually happening. Benjy was leaving, and he'd hardly put up a fight. Yet her elation was tempered by Hope's meltdown. She knew she had to say something to the kid.

Fiona stepped back inside and shut the front door, lowering the shotgun.

"Hope, he's heading into town," she said. "There are still people there who can take him in. He'll be absolutely fine, just like he said. Benjy is not in any danger, okay?"

She turned to face the kid, trying to give her a reassuring smile, but Hope was thrashing in her father's grip.

"What about *us*?" she cried. "We're in danger! We need Benjy to help keep us safe from the storm! It doesn't make any sense to kick him out. He didn't do anything wrong, and we *need* him!"

"No, we—" her father started to say.

But Hope broke free of his grip just then with a loud cry, first flopping onto the floor then picking herself up. "No one ever listens to me! I hate both of you!"

And with that, she fled the living room. She ran down the hallway into the guest room and slammed the door. In the aftermath, Fiona and Jarred just stared at each other.

"I didn't realize she would take it so hard," Fiona said. "I'm sorry."

"It's not your fault," Jarred said, with a deep sigh. He sank forward, gripping his forehead. "This has all been such a struggle for her, all of it. I think she latched onto Benjy because he acted so confident about everything. It made her feel safe."

"That's what Benjy does," Fiona said. "He gets people to latch onto him. He had to go, but I didn't mean to hurt her."

"She'll calm down," Jarred said. "Give her a little time. Hope doesn't always process emotions well, but her meltdowns never last long. She's smart, and she'll figure out what happened here soon enough."

Fiona sighed and turned to lock the front door. She hoped Jarred was right. She should have been reveling in her freedom from Benjy Hartman. Instead, she just felt bad for Hope.

"Still, he's gone," she said, if only to remind herself. "I finally kicked him out of my home, and he couldn't make me back down. And that is a very good thing."

33

Jarred was restless, hobbling from room to room, trying to find something to do but unable to fully concentrate on any task. Despite his reassurances, Hope's meltdown had him worried. It was the worst tantrum she'd had in a long time, especially her last angry words. How had she become so attached to the park ranger so quickly? They'd only know each other for a few days, but she was acting like Fiona had murdered a close family member.

Finally, Jarred's leg was hurting too much, so he had to resign himself to lying on the couch. Moving around was a mistake, and he was going to pay for it. The leg already felt swollen again, and he no longer had a medic to tend to him. As he lay there, he realized he needed to use the restroom, but he didn't want to get up again. He decided to hold it for a while, as he rested and stewed in his own troubled thoughts.

Fiona worked in the basement for a while. He could hear her moving around down there, and he assumed she'd taken up the job of building the new pen. After maybe an hour, Jarred began to feel alone in the house. There hadn't been a peep from Hope. Maybe she had finally worn herself out and gone back to sleep.

Eventually, he heard Fiona move from the basement to the kitchen. By now, his leg was in absolute agony.

At this rate, it's never going to heal properly, he thought. *I need to get to a hospital, and I probably need to see an orthopedic surgeon to get some plates and screws put in.*

He didn't see that happening anytime soon.

"Is it really bad?"

He looked up to see Fiona standing in the kitchen doorway. Apparently, the agony was evident on his face.

"Yeah, it's pretty bad," he replied. "All that moving around. I need to take it easy."

"Well, I can handle all of the chores today," she replied. "Don't worry about that. Actually, I think we're having one of the chickens for lunch. She's become a bad egg-layer, so she's going into the soup pot. I'll be, uh, preparing it, so if that sort of things bothers you, it's best for you to stay in here."

"That won't bother me," he replied. "I feel bad. I wish I could make myself useful."

"You stood with me today," Fiona said. "You've more than earned your keep, as far as I'm concerned. I'll be forever grateful."

"Benjy's been a thorn in your side for a long time, it sounds like," Jarred said.

"Pushing his way into my life from the first time we met," she replied, "and then insisting that he knows how I *really* feel about him. I got away from him a couple of years ago, but somehow, I knew he'd be back. I wish I was stronger. I want to be."

"You got him out," Jarred replied. "I didn't do much. You seem pretty strong to me."

"Well, Benjy wasn't my first rodeo," Fiona said. "Believe it or not, I dealt with worse, but...enough about that. I'm going back to work, and you're going to take it easy until lunchtime."

As the morning passed, Hope remained in her room. He heard strange noises coming from the kitchen, a kind of soft ripping sound, which he assumed was the chicken getting plucked. Jarred just lay there by himself in the living room, staring at the ceiling. Eventually, he smelled the pleasant aroma of chicken soup and heard the bubbling of a large pot on the kitchen stove.

"It needs to sit and simmer for quite a while," Fiona called. "If you're hungry, I can bring you something to tide you over."

"I'm fine," Jarred replied. He'd mostly lost his appetite.

Okay, Hope has been hiding long enough, he thought. *She can't mope in the room all day. This is ridiculous.*

He grabbed the crutch off the floor and started to leverage himself up into a sitting position. As he did, he heard a sudden rumble coming from outside of the house. He scarcely had time to register what he was hearing before Fiona came racing into the living room, followed by Smoke. The dog went to the front door and began barking like mad, as Fiona pulled back the curtain.

"What is that?" Jarred asked. But there was really only one option, wasn't there? And it occurred to him as soon as he asked the question.

The rumble grew louder, as Fiona rushed to the front door, turned the deadbolt, and flung it open. Smoke immediately dashed onto the porch and began running back and forth, barking frantically. Jarred managed to push himself upright, but the pain in his leg was so severe, it took every ounce of will to remain standing.

Through the open door, beyond Fiona, he saw the taillights on the Mule shining. Even though she didn't have her coat on, and her hands were wet from cooking, Fiona stepped outside, waving her arms over her head. Suddenly, the Mule lurched forward and went racing down the hill, following the tracks of the snowmobile. Jarred caught a glimpse of a familiar padded, puffy coat, and he felt a jolt of sheer panic. Despite the pain, he hobbled toward the door.

"No, stop, stop!" Fiona cried, to no avail. "What are you doing?"

The Mule was moving fast, heading in a broad arc down the hill in the direction of town. Jarred just made it to the door, falling against the doorframe, when Fiona turned to him.

"Hope took the Mule," she said. "She's headed toward Glencole. I think she's going after Benjy!"

34

In his panic, Jarred tried to rush outside and chase after her, but a single step through the door caused his broken ankle to bump against the frame. A surge of agony went up his leg, and for a second, he swooned, vision dimming. He started to fall, but then Fiona was there. She wrapped her arms around him and kept him from going down. Smoke continued to bark frantically from the porch.

She's gone! She's gone! My daughter is gone! It kept running through his mind like an incessant drumbeat.

He tried to break out of Fiona's embrace and rush outside again, but she kept him pinned against the doorframe.

"We have to go after her," he said. "She can't even drive yet!"

"Okay, but you can't go running out there in your current state," she replied. "If you try to walk on that leg now, you may never walk again. Listen to me, Jarred!"

He realized he was still trying to break out of her grasp, driven by panic, and he slumped back. Still, he was frantic. Hope could be difficult when she was stressed out, but she'd never done anything like this. How had it happened? How had Benjy so warped her mind that she would steal a vehicle and race off to see him?

I should have strangled him, he thought. *I should have told Fiona to shoot him.*

Fiona started pulling him back toward the couch, and he allowed himself to be moved. He'd dropped the crutch, so he was forced to hop along on his good leg.

"We have to go after her," he said, speaking through clenched teeth. He wanted to scream, to lash out, to do…something, anything! "She's out in there in the storm all by herself. She can't drive, Fiona!"

"Okay, but you need to sit down before you hurt yourself even worse," Fiona said. "We'll figure this out. I promise. Just stop fighting me."

She finally got him to the couch, and he practically fell onto the cushions. Another spike of pain caused his vision to go black for a second.

Why would she do it? Why is my daughter chasing after a grown man like he is her only lifeline in the world?

He was so desperate that he could barely sit still. Only the fierce, throbbing agony kept him on the couch.

"Stay right here," Fiona said, wagging a finger in his face. "We'll figure this out, okay?"

Jarred had little choice, as he sank back into the cushion, tears of pain and grief blurring his vision. Through the veil, he saw Fiona dash back out onto the porch and lead Smoke back inside the house. Then she shut the front door and ran down the hallway.

"Is there another vehicle?" he asked. "Tell me you've got another vehicle hidden around here somewhere. We have to go after her. We have to hurry!"

Fiona came back a few seconds later clutching a large piece of paper in her hand. With a grave look on her face, she handed it to him. Jarred brushed tears away and took it, unfolding it. The paper had been hastily ripped from an old ledger and had a ragged edge. Hope's distinctive looping scrawl covered one side, written in descending lines. He read it, and his heart sank.

"Benjy is the only one who tells me the truth. He is the only one who treats me like I'm smart and capable. He's the only one who knows how to survive in the snow. He is nice to everybody. And you threw him outside all alone for no reason. No reason at all! Benjy told me Fiona doesn't like people, and he was right. Even though he fixed a ton of stuff and saved our lives, Fiona pointed a gun at him, and you didn't do anything to stop it! You may not care what happens to him, but I'm not going to let him die out there all alone! I'm going after him and telling him to come back. If you won't stand up for him, Dad, I will!"

And then, at the bottom, almost as an afterthought, she'd added, "Also, I quit the cross-country team last year! See? You don't even know what's going on."

He read the note and let the words sink in, feeling something close to despair. How had he let Hope get like this? How had he not noticed? She'd been so quiet the last few days. She'd seemed content even.

"Did he force her to write it?" Fiona asked. "Benjy is pretty good at getting people to do what he wants."

Jarred considered the possibility. Some part of him wanted to believe it, but he knew his daughter too well. "I doubt it. I just...I didn't know it was this bad. She's been hiding her real feelings from me."

If she quit the cross-country team last year, then she's been lying to me for months. Openly lying, faking it. Why would she tell me now?

He opened the note, smoothed it out, and read it again. Then he read it a third time, as Fiona stood nearby tapping her feet impatiently. Smoke seemed to sense what was going on. He wouldn't relax, but kept moving from the couch to the front door and back, whimpering.

"I thought I knew her better than this," he said. "Maybe not. Maybe I've been oblivious to my daughter's real feelings this whole time. I'm a complete failure as a father. A complete failure."

Fiona squatted in front of him and took the note from his hands. "Hey, this isn't your fault," she said. "This is entirely Benjy's fault. He is a manipulator and a creep. I don't know what he told Hope, but he got into her head somehow. That's what he does. I should have thrown him out a long time ago. If I had, we wouldn't be dealing with this."

It was small comfort for Jarred. This wasn't just about Benjy. Clearly, Hope had been hiding her real feelings about many things for a long time. All this time, he'd thought he was doing a pretty good job as a single father, and now it was clear he'd failed. Hope didn't feel like she could be honest with him. She felt underappreciated and neglected. All of these feelings couldn't have come out of nowhere. She must have been struggling for a long time and keeping it all to herself.

"I should have known," he muttered, feeling as miserable as he'd ever felt. "I was oblivious to her real feelings, and she wants me to know it. That's why she told me about the cross-country team."

"How old is she? Thirteen?" Fiona said.

"Yeah."

"Okay, well, emotions run wild at that age. Don't be so hard on yourself. This is Benjy's work. Trust me. Blame him and no one else."

"I hid things from her," he said. "I didn't tell her the truth about the weather, not for a long time. I was only trying to keep her safe, to keep her from being scared, but maybe it made her feel worse when she found out. Now, look at what I've done."

He felt himself sinking into a very dark place, but Fiona shoved the note into the front pocket of her overalls and grabbed him by the shoulders. She shook him slightly until he looked up at her.

"Jarred White! Stop. Blaming. Yourself," she said, emphasizing each word. "Blame the creep who manipulated her. You said Hope can't drive. How much you want to bet Benjy taught her to drive the Mule while they were out running errands? It's exactly the kind of thing he would do. He does something nice for you, then he uses it against you. That's how he operates. Do you hear me? Do you get it?"

Jarred shook his head. He heard it, but he couldn't accept it.

"I'm her father," he said. "This is my responsibility. My daughter just ran away from home. If that's not failed parenting, I don't know what is. I'm sorry, Fiona. I should have been more attentive. I…should have known."

Fiona held onto his shoulders for a moment, then finally sighed and let go.

"Fine," she said. "Take all the blame, if you want. You can sit there and regret your whole damned life. Or we can go after her."

Slowly, he lifted his gaze to her and saw the steely look on her face.

"What do you say?" she asked. "Shall we go after your daughter?"

35

She lost the tracks of the snowmobile when she reached the woods. Apparently, he'd decided to take a more direct route, so he'd driven the snowmobile right in between the trees. She could see the tracks winding beneath the dense snow-covered canopy, but the Mule was just a bit too wide to fit in there.

Hope came to a stop beside the trees, revving the Mule's engine for good measure. It had all built up to this. The years of feeling misunderstood and overlooked, of her father stubbornly refusing to see how she was really feeling, of all the dumb decisions. She'd put up with him as long as she could, but letting Benjy get sent away was too much. Hope felt a furious, willful defiance within her now that burned so hot, she could scarcely think straight.

Finally, she backed up and headed along the tree line, trying to circle around to the other side. She felt fairly confident behind the wheel. The Mule was responsive and seemed to handle the deep snow fairly well. Actually, it made her wonder why her father hadn't gotten her behind the wheel sooner. She was good at this.

They're going to take Benjy back into the house, and they're going to apologize to him, she told herself. *That's all there is to it. I'm done just sitting around and letting them make all of the decisions.*

She'd gone perhaps two miles when she saw what appeared to be a road. Snow had so thoroughly covered it that it was mostly just a broad clearing cutting through the woods. Still, it seemed a safe bet that this would lead her to town, so she turned and followed it. The weather was fierce, blowing right in her face. She tugged her hood forward a bit more, then made sure her zipper was all the way up.

Fortunately, she'd been wearing her coat, gloves, and boots when she'd retired to the bedroom the night before. What would she have done otherwise? Well, she still would have left. It was as simple as that. She was setting things right, and that's all there was to it.

She followed the road for a good hour, moving a bit slower in the deep snow than she wanted. Fortunately, the fuel tank had been a little more than half full, so she thought she was okay. There was no sign of the snowmobile path, however, and she began to doubt herself. Was she headed the wrong way? What if she just drove and drove and never saw him again?

Maybe he went back on his own, she thought. *Maybe Benjy doubled back to the house.*

She almost convinced herself that this was the case—she even slowed down and started looking for the best place to turn around—when she saw a tall gas station sign in the distance. The name on the sign was obscured by ice and snow. As she got closer, the single sign became a row of buildings in the quaint downtown area of a small town. By now, she was almost frozen solid. Snot had run from her nostrils and turned to ice on her upper lip, and she was trembling like crazy.

What if this isn't the right town? she wondered.

The place looked deserted. She saw the dark windows and empty parking lots of numerous shops. It didn't look like anyone was here. She finally reached the intersection and saw a quaint sign that was still legible; it said, "Glencole Main Street." Turning onto this street, she gazed at the row of buildings before her. Not all of them were dark. Her gaze was drawn to a single building about halfway down, where an electric light seemed to be shining from inside. The sign above the door said, "Cooper's General Store."

She aimed for the store, but as she got closer, she saw more tracks, fresh tracks, coming from a cross street and curving up in front of the general store. Snowmobile tracks!

Hope eased the Mule toward where she thought the curb was, until she felt the tires thump against them. Pulling to a stop, she put the vehicle in park, and sat there a moment. Benjy's blue snowmobile was parked in a little recessed area beneath the big awning in front of Cooper's store, and one of the doors was ajar. Through the big display windows in front, she saw aisles and shelves, like a regular grocery store, but most of them were empty. It looked like they'd been picked over. A few cans and boxes remained.

See, Benjy is smart, she thought. *He knew exactly where to come so he would be okay.*

She killed the engine and climbed out of the Mule, heading past the snowmobile. As she slipped through the open door, she heard the distinct rumble of a generator. Her shoulder bumped the door in passing, and a bell at the top jingled. Movement off to the right startled her, and she spun around.

A single small lamp sat on top of a glass countertop, the plug and extension cord weaving off down an aisle to somewhere in the back of the store. However, what drew her attention were the people standing there around the counter. They had all turned to look at her, and they stared now with strange expressions on their faces. Were they nervous? Scared? What was the strange glint in their eyes?

Five of them. An older couple, gray-haired, dressed in leather coats lined with what appeared to be white fur. A middle-aged couple in red coats and caps. A teenage boy, maybe a year or two older than Hope, with acne on his cheeks and a hat with a floppy brim tipped back on his head. She didn't know any of these people. For a few tense seconds, they all just stared at her, and Hope couldn't think of anything to say. Was she in trouble?

And then she heard footsteps behind her, heavy boots coming down one of the aisles. Spinning, she saw another man coming around the corner.

"Hope?" he said. "Is that you?"

She almost ran to him and hugged him, but the presence of the strangers stopped her. Benjy looked okay, and she realized she'd expected to see him in terrible distress. He stood there in his park ranger coat, his hands in the pockets, his hair messy, and in that moment, her eyes filled with tears. She tried her hardest to stave them off, but she couldn't help it.

Don't act like a baby, she chided herself. *You're here on a mission.*

"Benjy, I came all the way here to bring you back to the house," she said. "Throwing you out was a mistake. I don't care what Dad and Fiona said. I don't care what they want. You need to come back. We need you at the house."

She quickly brushed the tears away with her sleeve. As she did, she realized the others were approaching, slowly moving to encircle her. At first, it made her nervous, and she started to back toward the door. But then she saw smiling faces. They all seemed so happy all of a sudden. Benjy held up his hand at them, a signal that she didn't really understand. Then he approached Hope and clapped her on the back like they were old pals.

"I'm so glad you're safe, Hope," he said. "I know Fiona and her new best friend really upset you this morning. Sorry I couldn't say anything before I drove off, but…well, there was a shotgun pointed at me, after all."

"Yeah, Fiona was stupid for doing that," Hope said. "I told them how I feel, too. I told them *exactly* how I feel. It'll be different when we go back."

"Yes," he said. "Yes, it will."

"She's going to have to apologize, of course," Hope said. "My dad, too. But if you'll forgive them, then maybe it will be different going forward. Maybe we can go back to how it was."

Benjy gave her his biggest, broadest grin. "You talked me into it, Hope. Very well, I'll go back to Fiona's with you, and we'll all be one big, happy family again. Is that what you want?"

"We were fixing things up," Hope said. "I was learning to drive. Everything seemed to be getting better. I want it to be like that again."

"It'll be like that," Benjy said. "Actually, it'll be even better. I'm going to bring all of my friends here along with us." He made a little spinning motion with his hand, taking in the group of people around them. "More hands, more help, right? Think about how we could whip that homestead into shape with so many people contributing to the effort. The trick will be getting Fiona to be reasonable about it, but you, my smart friend, you are going to help us with that. Now, how does that sound?"

Hope liked that idea. She liked it very much, and she smiled at Benjy and nodded.

36

Fiona was really worried about him. Jarred was flushed and sweating, his eyes rimmed in red, tears streaming down his face. The poor guy looked like he was on the verge of collapse, and she felt stomach-churning guilt. This was all her fault. She'd waited too damn long to get rid of Benjy, and the creep had sunk his claws into Jarred's daughter. And what were they going to do about it now?

Part of her—the biggest part, really—just wanted to withdraw. People had come into her life and brought problems. That's what people did. And isolation was the only effective solution. Not this time. She owed Jarred for helping to create this situation, so she ignored her natural tendencies, pushing back the wall of resistance in her own mind.

"We have to get her back right away," Jarred said. "I don't know what to do."

She'd spent years living alone precisely so she didn't have to get caught up in the complex nonsense of human behavior again, and now that she was stuck in it, it felt like alien territory. Still, she knew she had to reassure him, so she spoke anyway.

"We're going after her," she said. "Don't worry. As long as we leave fairly soon, we should be able to follow their tracks and catch up. The maximum speed of the Mule is about forty-five miles an hour, and it'll be going a lot slower in the snow."

Jarred rubbed his eyes and ran his hands through his hair. "Okay, fine. That's good to know. So what do we need to do to get going?"

Jarred and Hope didn't come here to upend your life, she told herself. *Get over yourself. They needed you then and they need you now.*

She considered their situation. "Okay, here's what we need to do. First, we'll fortify your leg and dump a bunch of painkillers in your system. You have to be able to get around. Benjy will head into town. That's what I think. That's where we'll find them, so you'll have to travel."

She went to the kitchen first, dumped a few ibuprofens into her hand, and brought them back to Jarred. As he swallowed the pills, she next went to the guestroom and rounded up some of the extra wood and cloth. When she carried them back into the living room, she found Jarred smacking his own cheeks and trying to rouse himself from whatever pain-soaked stupor he was in.

"I'm sorry. This is going to be really tough for you," Fiona said, kneeling beside him. "I'd go by myself, but I don't think Hope would trust me or listen to me. Benjy's probably got her convinced that I'm a complete lunatic. You need to be there."

"I'm going," he agreed. "No matter how tough it is."

She used the extra wood to splint his leg even more sturdily, wrapping the long cloth around it and tying it off. This, at least, would help prevent the break from getting worse, but it wouldn't do anything for the pain. In the end, the lower half of his leg was a huge mass of wood, cloth, and bandages. Too big for him to wear a boot, so she tripled up on socks and then pulled a plastic bag over his leg.

Through all of this, Smoke remained near the fireplace, but he watched Fiona carefully. Clearly, he knew something was up.

"You didn't tell me if you've got another vehicle on the property somewhere," he said. "Maybe a snowmobile of your own."

"Yeah, I've got my Toyota Tundra," she replied. "Let me go get it started, so it'll warm up. The drive into town is treacherous."

And with that, she pulled on her coat, gloves, and boots and headed outside. Smoke tried to come with her, but she gently pushed him back into the house. Moving as fast as she could in the deepening snow, she headed down the hill to the place where the truck was parked. The clearing she'd created with the snowplow attachment was mostly filled in, and the truck was covered in snow again.

It'll have to warm up for a while, she thought, as she yanked open the driver's door.

She slipped inside, put the key in the ignition, and turned it.

Nothing. The engine didn't respond. Was the battery dead? She tried again, but the starter gave not the least hint of life. Fiona sat there for a few minutes, staring at the utterly white windshield, and feeling a mounting sense of panic. If they couldn't use the truck, how would they get into town?

It'll take days to walk that far, she thought. *Jarred will never make it.*

And then she realized there was an alternative, and when she thought of it, when she saw it in her mind's eye, it seemed on the verge of being completely ridiculous.

"Oh, God, do I really have to?" she muttered. "Is it really better than walking?"

But it seemed like the only other option. No sense sitting there and moping about it. Fiona sighed and got out of the truck, heading back up the hill. When she stepped back inside, Jarred looked up at her with wide, hopeful eyes, but then he must've read something on her face and the expression collapsed.

"Dead battery, I'm afraid," she said. "The truck's not going anywhere any time soon. I have a trickle charger, but that will take far too long."

"So we're walking into town?"

She shook her head. "We're not walking," she said. "Stay right here. Give the pills a few minutes to take effect. I'll get everything ready."

She left him sitting on the couch and went to the bedroom. She grabbed both guns from the rack above the dresser and came back. Fortunately, both had straps. The shotgun strap went over her shoulder. The bolt-action Weatherby rifle she set on the couch beside Jarred.

"That's yours," she said. "Can you handle it?"

He ran his hand along the stock of the rifle and nodded. "Yeah, I think so."

"Have you ever fired a gun before?"

"No, but I understand how they work."

She sighed. "That'll have to be enough. Hopefully, we don't need the guns, but it's better to be safe than sorry. Now, for our ride. Give me a few minutes." She headed for the front door, paused, and looked back. "Jarred, this is going to be…incredibly weird, but it's our only option. Brace yourself."

Seeing the tracks of the Mule heading off down the hill made her furious, but not at the kid. Benjy had done this. It was his slimy manipulation that had gotten into the kid's head.

I knew there was something bad going on there, she thought. *I need to listen to myself more often.*

She walked down to the barn. As she stepped through the big door, she saw that a back corner of the roof had collapsed. Broken boards were hanging down, and a huge pile of snow had filled Ramses's old pen. The tarp for the Mule was crumpled on the floor, but she strode past it to a small space in the other corner. Here, another cloth covered a much smaller object. She grabbed the cloth and pulled it away, revealing the small wood toboggan hidden underneath. It was a traditional-style toboggan made of bound wood slats, with a high curved front end and ropes for steering. In the front, it also had hooks for a harness. She grabbed the harness, set it on the toboggan, and proceeded to drag the sled out of the barn.

Well, this should be interesting, she said, as she considered her plan.

The toboggan was old and worn, another relic left behind by the heirs of the previous property owners. She'd used it a couple of times for fun in past winters, but turning it into an actual vehicle for travel seemed a tad absurd, especially when she considered the personality of the animal that was going to pull the damn thing.

When she got back to the house, she dragged the toboggan up onto the porch so Jarred could see it. By then, she found him standing up, testing himself as he leaned on his crutch. He had the rifle slung over his shoulder, and his cheeks were bright red from being slapped repeatedly.

"A sled?" he said, as she grabbed the harness and stepped inside. "That's how we're getting into town? Have you got a horse to pull that thing?"

"Not a horse," she replied, heading into the kitchen. "Something a lot more annoying."

And it must have occurred to him then, for he groaned and said, "Oh no."

"Oh no is right," she said. "Meet me on the porch in a couple of minutes."

The pot of chicken stew was still bubbling on the stove, so she picked it up and set it aside. Then she opened the basement door, the foul smell immediately assaulting her nostrils. Pinching her nose, she headed down the steps. She heard the animals moving around in the dim light. Ramses bleated loudly at her, and she saw his yellow eyes gazing from beyond his makeshift pen. All of the wood Benjy had gathered for the pen was still stacked nearby.

"Get ready to do something you'll hate," Fiona told Ramses, raising the harness as she approached him. "We need your help right now, so please do me a favor and be on your best behavior."

The walls of his pen were comprised of tabletops set side by side, braced and reinforced with smaller pieces of wood. Benjy had done some basic work. Ramses bleated at her and flapped his tongue in her direction, but when she put the harness over his head, the big goat endured it better than usual. Maybe he was desperate enough to get out of the pen that he was willing to put up with it. It took some work to move one of the tabletops, pushing it back and to one side, so she could get him out. Then she grabbed the lead line and led him toward the outer stairs. Ramses bleated again and kicked the other pens in passing, as if taunting the she-goats.

Just before she reached the outer stairs, she heard him coming. Turning, she managed to deflect his head before he could hook her with one of his big horns.

"Behave or I'll go get Smoke," she said.

She headed up the steps, leading Ramses outside. He came willingly, though not quietly. Once they got back to the porch, she tied the lead line to a support post and retrieved the toboggan. However, when she tried to attach the toboggan to the harness, Ramses tried to hook her again. Finally, she grabbed his face in her hands and held him still, gazing deep into those wide pupils.

"Listen to me," she said. "I need your help right now. Jarred and I both need your help. If you don't do this one task for me, you're going into the soup pot, and it's not a bluff this time. You will be dinner, do you get it? This is your moment of decision, so what's it going to be?"

Though it was impossible, she got the strange sense that he understood. He stared back quietly for a second then seemed to settle down, allowing her to attach the toboggan to the harness. When she looked up, she saw Jarred and Smoke on the porch, watching her.

"You did warn me that this was going to be weird," he said.

"Can you make it down here?" she asked.

"I think so."

Using the crutch and the handrail, he carefully descended the porch steps, trying to avoid putting any weight on his broken leg. Smoke tried to follow him, so Fiona had to guide the dog back inside.

"Not this time, Smoke," she said. "You guard the house while we're gone."

And with that, she shut the door on him. He whimpered and scratched at the door. She felt sorry for him, but like Hope, he didn't fully understand who Benjy really was. To her surprise, Jarred was able to hobble all the way to the toboggan and lower himself down in the back. Fiona climbed onto the front of the toboggan and picked up the reins.

"He's a big old goat, but can he really pull us both?" Jarred asked. He looked incredibly uncomfortable back there. He had tried to sit cross-legged, but his giant splint was set off to one side, and he had the worst look on his face.

"Ramses could probably pull the whole damn house, if I let him," Fiona replied.

She gave the reins a shake, and the goat took off. At first, he found moving through the deep snow difficult, and he kept leaping, as if trying to get over it. This made the toboggan bounce, and each time Jarred grunted in pain. Then Ramses reached the ruts left behind by the Mule, and he followed them, moving fast. Indeed, he was strong, and the weight of the toboggan didn't seem to be a problem for him. As Fiona tried to guide him with the reins, he trotted down the hill, following Hope's trail toward the distant trees.

When they were halfway down the hill, she glanced back and saw Jarred desperately trying to hold on to the toboggan.

"Grab on to me," she said. "We can't afford to lose you."

He hesitated a second, then grabbed her by the waist. Strangely, despite her years of isolation, she didn't mind. Not at all.

37

For the first time ever, Ramses's boundless energy and ornery nature came in handy, as he kept up his speed over the long distance. They followed the tracks of the Mule along the edge of the woods and onto the highway, turning toward town, and the big goat just kept plowing ahead. Indeed, the challenge of the deep snow, the heavy weight behind him, and the uneven terrain seemed to make him even more willful. Fiona struggled to maintain her hold on the reins and keep him pointed in the right direction, but they were moving steadily through strong wind.

I think I found Ramses's calling in life, she thought. *He's as persistent pulling a toboggan as he is trying to harass the girls.*

Still, it seemed to take forever. Every minute that passed was excruciating. Thinking of that poor girl in the clutches of creepy Benjy was too much. Jarred was holding on to her waist for dear life, and when she glanced back at him periodically, she could tell he was struggling. His face was scrunched up, his eyes clamped shut. There wasn't much room for his broken leg or the oversized splint that now covered it, but he laid it to one side as best he could, his knee bent at an awkward angle.

"Hang in there," she said, speaking loudly to be heard over the wind. "It's not much farther now, and at least we have clear tracks to follow. At least we're not hunting for her on foot."

"Sorry, I don't know how long I can hold on like this," he said.

"Get your arms into it," she said.

He wrapped his arms around her waist more tightly, linking his hands in front of her, and she felt him press up against her back. By the time the gas station sign finally appeared in the distance, Ramses had begun to wear out. He was breathing heavily, and he slipped from time to time in the snow. Fiona expected him to stop, but he pressed on, driven by sheer stubbornness.

"Don't die on me," she muttered, tugging on the reins as Ramses drifted too far to the side of the road. "Give it every ounce of willful defiance you've got."

Soon, she saw the familiar shapes of the downtown buildings and light gleaming on brick and steel, glinting fiercely off the blanketing snow so that it was almost too bright to look at. Fiona squinted to make it bearable. It had taken them so long to reach town on the toboggan that it felt like most of the day had passed. Though she couldn't see the sun beyond the never-breaking ceiling of gray, it felt like afternoon. That meant Hope had spent most of the day with Benjy, and how else had he twisted her mind in all that time? What if she wasn't willing to come back with her father? How would they handle it? Fiona just didn't know.

I hope the kid is okay, she thought. *If she's been hurt in any way, I'll never forgive myself. I let Benjy through the door knowing who he is.*

The tracks of the Mule led them onto Main Street, past all of the empty storefronts. Jarred was leaning heavily against her now, and she heard him grunt in pain from time to time. Still, he didn't complain, and more importantly, he never fell off the back of the toboggan. Ahead, the Mule tracks led to the front of Cooper's General Store, and when she drew near, she saw that the vehicle had been moved to a narrow alleyway just on the other side of the building. The back bumper stuck out.

Instead of approaching, she reined in Ramses before they reached the windows of the store. He resisted at first, though he was breathing heavily. However, exhaustion seemed to finally be gaining an edge over his stubborn will. He stumbled to a stop with a final, defiant bleat.

"We're here," she said, over her shoulder.

She thought she might find him passed out, latched so tightly that she would have to disentangle herself from his arms. However, he was wide awake, eyes red but staring hard at the front of Cooper's. As soon as she spoke, he released his hold and slid off the back of the toboggan, taking the crutch off his lap. Despite their circumstances, she felt a strange little moment of regret when he let go of her.

Get ahold of yourself, Fiona, she told herself. *It's not time for such feelings.*

Jarred hoisted himself up on his crutch, as Fiona disconnected the toboggan from Ramses's harness. Though the town was dark, she spotted a single light burning inside the store. Clearly, they had a generator. What was Benjy doing in there? Stealing whatever groceries remained, perhaps? He'd never been an outright criminal, though, just a manipulator.

Jarred headed immediately for the front door, but he was having trouble. Every step caused him to grunt in pain, so Fiona came up beside him and put a supporting arm across his back. She didn't want to leave the poor goat out here to freeze to death. He was already frost-covered and trembling, so she grabbed his lead line in passing and pulled him along behind them. Ramses, having been worn out, was docile as he followed.

Maybe we finally worked the orneriness out of him, she thought.

"What's the plan here?" Jarred asked.

She glanced at him. He had a pleasant face, a strong jawline and nice cheekbones. However, this close, she noticed the tiniest scar cutting through the whiskers at an angle on his upper lip. A cleft palate scar, she thought.

"Well, we won't point our guns at him, if we don't have to," Fiona said. "I think that will upset Hope and turn her against us even more. Let's just go in there and try to be friendly, I guess, for her sake. Then we'll see what Benjy does and respond accordingly."

He nodded. "Yeah, okay. I can fake it if I have to."

The door was ajar, held open by a small rock. Fiona eased it open further and slipped inside, supporting Jarred and pulling Ramses along behind her. Seeing the inside—the bare aisles, the single lamp glowing on top of a glass counter, the scattered detritus of a looted store—she felt a moment of trepidation, and she almost turned back.

This isn't normal. What's going on in here? Where are they?

But then she heard the creak of a door from somewhere in the back of the building followed by hushed voices and footsteps. Instinctively, she stepped away from Jarred and reached for the shotgun. Ramses was caught in the doorway, and she heard him stamp on the threshold.

A group of people came around the corner then. She recognized the first one. An older gentleman with a weathered face, bushy eyebrows, and a bulbous nose. The woman walking beside him wore a similar leather coat and had a big shock of white hair. Duke and Myra Cooper. This was their store, so why were the shelves almost bare? Had they been robbed? Duke smiled at her as he came down the aisle.

Before Fiona could say anything to him, she noticed the others. Benjy was right behind Duke, striding with confidence in the midst of the people, as if they were all one big, happy family. A small girl with frizzy, shoulder-length hair walked beside him.

"Hope!" Jarred cried.

He wobbled on his feet, and Fiona let go of Ramses's line to grab his shoulder. When she did, she realized she had the shotgun in her other hand. Despite her father's cry, Hope remained at Benjy's side, and when the group stopped halfway down the aisle, she stopped with them.

She knew all of the people in the group, though not well. The middled-aged couple behind Benjy was Larry and Lana Bishop, local florists, along with their teenage son, Zane. They were smiling, too, but why did the smile seem so unfriendly?

"Hey there, Duke," she said. As far as she knew, he was the most reasonable of the group. "I'm surprised to see you here. Myra, hello. Larry, Lana. What's going on?"

The Coopers glanced at each other, and Duke cleared his throat. "Well, you see, Fiona, we're almost out of propane and people took so much of my stuff here that—"

Benjy cut him off almost immediately, pushing past Duke to the front of the group. "Okay, Fiona, let's just cut to the chase. I'm done with your ridiculous behavior. This is the second time you've threatened me with a shotgun, and I've never *ever* posed a danger to you. So let's play the game your way." He gave her a strange look, not quite a smile this time but trying to get there. "We want your homestead. You've got crops, livestock, woodburning heat, supplies, and gasoline—enough to last this group of people here for months in relative comfort. I'm commandeering it all for the sake of these people. Time to share, like it or not."

38

Bringing the guns had been a mistake. Jarred saw that immediately, even through the fog of pain and confusion. He was leaning so heavily against the crutch that his arm was going numb. Even so, he would have fallen if Fiona hadn't been supporting him.

Hope is standing in the midst of them. We're not going to use the guns. All we've done is make ourselves look dangerous and confirmed Hope's worst feelings about us.

But it was too late. The damage was done. He stared at his daughter, but she pointedly would not return his gaze. She had a fierce scowl on her face. It wasn't normal. Benjy's manipulations had been very effective, but whether Hope realized it or not, she was being held hostage. Jarred's instinct was to rush to her side, but of course, he couldn't. His whole leg was on fire, and the pain kept shooting up to his hip in waves that turned his stomach. It took every ounce of will just to stay conscious.

This is what it's like to be completely helpless, he thought.

If not for his broken leg, he would have marched right up to the group, taken Hope by the hand, and pulled her out of this place. Anyone who stood in his way would have paid dearly. As it was, he couldn't do a thing except call her name—and that just barely. No, he'd never been this helpless, not even when his wife was dying of cancer.

"Hope," he said again, this time much less forcefully. Actually, he thought he sounded quite pathetic. "What are you doing here? Why are you with these people? You know it's not right to steal someone's home and land."

Still not looking directly at him, she said, "Dad, Benjy is right. I wish you would listen to him. He's not talking about stealing anything. He's talking about using his park ranger authority to help all of these people who are stranded by the storm. We have to share with everyone. If we all work together, we'll do a lot better." And then she burst into tears and covered her face.

Jarred didn't quite understand the tears. Did she feel sorry for him? Did she regret running away? Was she asking for his help, unable to say what she really felt? Or perhaps she was just upset about the whole situation. Whatever the case, it made him feel as low as he'd ever felt. He might have wept as well if he'd had it in him, but he was swimming on the edge of reality at the moment.

As he stared hard at the group of people gathered before him, he noted that they all seemed like normal townsfolk. These didn't appear to be desperate, ragged bandits.

"Who are you people?" he asked. "You're talking about forcing your way into an innocent person's home. Is that really who you are? I don't know any of you except my daughter and the park ranger, but you're basically holding my daughter hostage and using her to get what you want. She doesn't understand the gravity of this situation."

The middle-aged couple in back squirmed at his words, glancing at each other with what he thought might be guilt. Perhaps they were thinking about their own teenaged son who was standing at their side. The older couple, Duke and Myra, dropped their gazes to the floor.

Duke finally spoke. "We're just trying to figure out where to go, what to do. The latest reports say this snowstorm might last a year or more. We have no heat, no running water because the pipes froze up, and my store aisles were almost picked clean by looters."

"Mr. Hartman here works for the state of Ohio," Myra said. "He's an officer of the law."

"No, he is not," Jarred replied. "He's a park ranger."

"He's the closest thing to a government representative we've got," Myra said, with what seemed like an apologetic shrug. "Why shouldn't we listen to him?"

Through all of this, Fiona simply stood quietly, but he felt her hand trembling against his shoulder. He heard the pace of her breathing quicken. She was fuming, maybe trying to maintain her temper. She still held the shotgun in the crook of her arm.

"I guess you're all in this together," Fiona said, in a low, hateful voice. "Benjy must have roped you into his ridiculous scheme. That's what he does. He preys on vulnerable people and pushes them until he gets what he wants. Well, you've been misled. Duke, Myra, you've been lied to by this creepy loser named Benjy Hartman. Just because he's wearing a jacket with a badge on it doesn't mean he knows what he's talking about. The truth is I don't have enough supplies on my homestead to share with all of you. We'd go through it in a couple of weeks, and then we'd all be in trouble."

Benjy made an angry sound and swiped his hands in the air. "Don't lie to them, Fiona. I've been living in your house for days. I know what you have. The greenhouse is stocked. You've got shelves and shelves of canned vegetables. You've got goats and chickens, a goose, plenty of firewood, a working generator, fuel. I've seen it all with my own eyes. You have more than enough, and way more than you need for yourself."

"Come on, Benjy, don't pretend like you care about these people," she said. "This is just your latest attempt to force your way back into my life and maybe get a little revenge in the process. You're mad that I kicked you out."

"Yeah, you kicked me out," Benjy shouted. He turned to face the group. "This is the woman who forced me out into the storm all alone, even after I'd spent days fixing her leaky basement, building pens for her animals, wrangling her ornery goats. I practically saved her life when that big male goat attacked her. When she sent me away, she didn't care if I lived or died as long as I was out of her hair. Can you believe it? I'm telling you fine folks, Fiona Scarborough is hoarding supplies while people are dying in the cold!"

"You were never in any danger of dying in the cold, Benjy," Fiona snapped, the shotgun rattling in her arm. "I sent you away, yeah, but look, here you are, safe and sound. We live in Ohio, not the Alaskan wilderness."

"I survived because these nice people took me in," he said, spinning to face her. "Otherwise, I'd be caught out there in the storm, thanks to you!"

"Well, if you don't want to get kicked out of a woman's house, next time don't sneak into her bedroom at night and stand there staring at her," Fiona said.

At this, all of the women in his group looked at him. Myra and Lana grimaced, and Hope seemed confused. Fiona had had enough. She wasn't going to endure another endless argument with Benjy, while he tried to twist everything to his advantage. Stepping forward, she released her hold on Jarred, and took the shotgun in both hands.

Behind her, she heard the rattle of the rifle, and she glanced back to see Jarred pulling it off his shoulder. His face was flushed, sweat running down in rivulets, but his eyes were fixed on Benjy. Something in his demeanor had hardened. Perhaps the revelation that Benjy had come into her room. She hadn't revealed that detail yet, and notably, Benjy hadn't denied it.

"Oh, so you're both going to point guns at me," Benjy said. "Well, I'm unarmed, just like I was the last time you pointed a gun at me, Fiona."

"That girl beside you is a minor," she said. "Thirteen years old. She belongs with her father. You can't hold her, even if she wants to stay with you. That's kidnapping, as you damn well know."

At this, Duke and Myra stepped to one side, opening the way for Hope to approach. They even raised their hands in what seemed like a gesture of surrender. Hope was still crying, brushing tears off her cheeks, but she took a step forward.

"No," Benjy said, moving in front of her. "She knows who's right in this situation. Don't pretend like you're actually going to open fire when she's standing in front of you. It's a weak bluff, Fiona. Look, we've all discussed the matter, and we're taking the homestead. The decision is final, and you'll have to kill us all to stop it."

39

Benjy had been smart to call her bluff. There was no way Fiona was going to discharge a weapon at this group of people. Most of them were innocent civilians who'd been manipulated by Benjy, and Hope might get hit. Nevertheless, Fiona continued aiming the shotgun vaguely in Benjy's direction, hating the confident look on his face.

"My daughter doesn't want to stay with you," Jarred said. "Let her go. Hope. Come on." He had the rifle in his hands, but the presence of the crutch made it awkward. Fiona noticed that, unlike her, he wouldn't point it anywhere close to the others. He had it firmly aimed at the floor between his feet.

But Benjy held his ground. Then again, it seemed like Hope could have slipped past him if she'd really wanted to. She wasn't, after all, being physically restrained.

"She *is* coming with you," Benjy said. "We all are. We're coming to the homestead. It's a matter of survival. You're not going to hoard a bunch of food and supplies while all of these people are freezing to death in their homes. I'm making an executive decision, and as the only person around here with any real authority, my decision goes."

Fiona took another step toward him, and he held up his hands in a gesture that said, "What are you going to do?" Yes, he was definitely calling her bluff. Behind her, like some strange comment on the situation, Ramses bleated loudly and slammed his horns into the doorframe.

"See?" Benjy said with a laugh. "The goat agrees with me. We're all in this together."

Fiona was shaking with anger now, struggling not to make an irrational decision. Her finger brushed the side of the shotgun trigger, and she had to force it away. As it turned out, having a gun didn't resolve all problems. Sometimes, it was entirely useless, especially when she was unwilling to use it. Then again, even if Benjy had been entirely alone, with no risk of collateral damage, she wouldn't have pulled the trigger. She didn't actually intend to shoot him unless he got violent. Fiona wasn't a killer, and you couldn't kill a man simply for being a creep.

Could you?

"It's my home," she said. "I won't live with you, Benjy. You're never going to step through the front door of my home ever again. Is that clear?"

The people around him seemed increasingly disturbed by the conversation. Duke and Myra kept looking back and forth from Benjy to Fiona, and they had fear in their eyes. Clearly, they were in over their heads, but then again, they weren't saying much. They weren't so troubled by the situation that they were willing to back out, apparently. Not yet.

"Fine," Benjy said, giving her a wounded look. He took another step toward her, his arms held wide, as if daring her to act. "For the record, I came to your bedroom door to *talk* to you, that's it. You've cooked up some idea in your mind that couldn't be further from the truth, but if you don't want to live in the same place with me, you don't have to. We'll move into the homestead and fix the place up, and you can go wherever else you want to go. How does that sound? Fair trade?"

It was such a bold and rude offer that she could scarcely bring herself to respond. As she stewed over it, she realized that she'd raised the shotgun and leveled it at Benjy's face. Hope couldn't see. She was hidden behind him. But Duke and Myra saw, and they clasped each other's hands.

"Fiona, there's no need for this. We can all…" Duke started to speak, but Myra held up a hand to shush him.

Jarred's crutch thumped against the hard floor as he moved up beside Fiona. "Just give me my daughter back. Step aside and let her come to me."

Benjy glanced at him, and a brief hateful look crossed his face. Then he reached back, snagged Hope by the wrist, and pulled her close. She stumbled forward, as he moved her in front of him and held her there. Hope was staring at the ground. Fiona shifted the position of the shotgun, aiming higher, but still not moving it away from him.

Let him have the homestead. The thought passed through her mind, but it was fleeting. *It's half-buried anyway. You can start over. Take the kid and go.*

But no, she couldn't do that. It was her home. Who was she without it? Losing the homestead would be practically a death sentence. Then again, maybe there was another way. Benjy's entire group was just standing there, watching this unfold with dumb, anxious looks on their faces. Fiona glanced at Jarred and realized he was swooning, struggling to remain standing. She moved closer to him, so he could lean against her shoulder.

Yes, there was a way out of this. She saw it now, so she went for it. With a sigh, Fiona lowered the shotgun.

"Okay, fine, Benjy," she said. "I'm tired of dealing with you. I'm tired of the back-and-forth. You win. You can have the homestead. It's all yours. I'll head south and find some warmer place."

Jarred reacted as if she'd suddenly slapped him. He stumbled to one side, nearly lost his crutch, and caught himself on a nearby shelf.

"Oh, really?" Benjy asked.

"Yeah, you and your new friends here can have it," she said, slinging the shotgun over her shoulder. "Take it. Enjoy it. Jarred and I will leave, and when all of you die because you go through the food and supplies in two or three weeks, then your blood will be on your own hands. Enjoy it while it lasts. Duke." She stared at him, but he wouldn't return her gaze. "I hope my home makes you happy, considering the fact that you and all of these others were willing to use a little girl as a bargaining chip to get it."

She knew using the term "little girl" might offend Hope, and indeed, the teenager scowled, pursing her lips.

"It's a deal," Benjy said. "I'm glad you've come to your senses at last, Fiona. I didn't think you had it in you."

Jarred was still just standing there, propping himself up on the shelf, clearly confused by Fiona's surrender, but Fiona turned as if to leave.

"Come on, Jarred. We'll go together."

"Wait," Hope said suddenly. "I don't want my dad to leave!"

She took a step toward them, and Jarred shouldered his rifle and beckoned her with his free hand. But Benjy had hold of her other wrist, and he yanked her back. She tried to twist of out of his grasp, but he grabbed her shoulder and moved her in front of him again.

"She's not going with you," Benjy said. "Stop trying to scare her. Nobody is making her dad leave. That's *you* talking, Fiona. As hysterical as ever."

"Come here, Hope," Jarred said, his voice creaking.

She tried to step away from Benjy again, but he held fast.

"She's *not* going with you," Benjy said again. "I accepted your deal. The homestead is mine. Now, both of you get out of here."

And then he stared at Fiona with a flat, cold expression, but she had played her hand and now it was up to someone else. She held her breath to see what would happen, resisting the urge to grab the shotgun again.

Come on. Don't let me down. For once in my life, I'm betting on a human being I barely know to do the decent thing.

40

The old guy that Fiona had called Duke lifted his gaze again and looked at Jarred. His lower lip was quivering, and he couldn't tell if it was because he was struggling to speak or about to cry. Jarred had just about reached his limit. The pain was unrelenting, but he felt a weakness taking over, moving up his limbs. His legs wouldn't hold him for much longer, and the sheer strain of staying on his feet made it difficult to tell what was going on.

Did Fiona say something about leaving? Surely not. We can't leave Hope with these people.

And then Duke Cooper cleared his throat loudly and turned slightly so the group behind could see him. His leather coat had a big faux-fur-lined collar, and he reached up and grabbed it with both hands. Jarred wasn't sure what the gesture meant.

"This isn't what I agreed to," he said, his deep voice quavering. "This whole situation has gotten way out of hand. Look, I don't want to take Fiona's home away from her. We just needed help. The storm hit, everyone left town, and we got stuck here. By the time we learned it was some kind of apocalyptic seasonal storm, it was too late to get out. And then my store was looted in the middle of the night, and I was left with very little."

Benjy turned and gave Duke a withering look of contempt. The park ranger spent most of his time smiling, but Jarred had noticed, even in his stupor, that whenever the smile left his face, what remained was dead-eyed and hateful.

"Yeah, I'm not real comfortable with any of this," the middle-aged man in the back of the group said. Was his name Larry? Lloyd? Something like that. "I thought we were talking about moving into the homestead to help out and share resources. Mr. Hartman never said anything about kicking out the homeowners."

Finally, Hope lifted her gaze, tears in her eyes, and looked at Jarred.

"Dad," she said, a single plaintive sound. He noted that her right hand slid down into the pocket of her coat, as if she were reaching for something.

Benjy blew his breath out and swiped a hand toward the ground behind him. "You're all pathetic. You want to starve to death here in this dead town? Is that what you want?"

"There have to be other options," Duke said. "If we pool our resources here in town, we might be able to make a place—"

"No, there is no other place," Benjy shouted. "It's about Fiona…about the homestead!"

Ah, but she'd called his bluff. Even in his stupor, Jarred saw it. This wasn't about the homestead. It had always been about Fiona, and maybe now the others saw it.

And then Fiona said, "You can take my homestead. You can take whatever you want. But you'll never have me. Deal with it."

He rounded on her, his face going bright red, his eyes filled with a furious light. Duke and Myra eased away from him. It looked like Benjy was going to say something. His jaw clenched, his mouth opened, but then it just died on his tongue. Slowly, his mouth closed again, and he glared at her.

"Okay, look," Fiona said. "How about this? The rest of you are welcome to come to my homestead. Myra, as I recall, you're a nursing assistant. We could use you. Larry, you're a florist. Maybe you can help me get some plants growing. All of you. We'll make it work somehow." And then, coldly, "Except you, Benjy. You're not welcome. The first time I met you, I knew you were a creep, but you've gone well beyond even my worst expectations of you."

His grip on Hope tightened, his knuckles turning white, and she cried out.

"Hope..." Jarred said, helplessly. "Don't hurt her."

And then Hope drew her hand out of her pocket, and he saw the glint of a silver key thrust between her fingers. The Mule's ignition key. She had her fist clenched, the key sticking out between her forefinger and middle finger like a little spike. Jarred realized what she intended, and he shook his head.

She mouthed something at him. It took a second to realize what it was. "Not a baby."

"You're always blowing everything out of proportion," Benjy said, stumbling on his own words. "I've only ever been a friend to you! Look at how you mistreat me? You're sick, Fiona. Sick in the head!"

But Duke and Myra strode forward then, brushing past Benjy to stand with Fiona. Larry and Lana, with their son, soon joined them, leaving Benjy and Hope standing alone in the aisle. Hope drew her fist back, the key catching the light from the room's single lamp. Jarred almost called out to her to stop her, but he caught himself.

No, she's not a baby. Trust her.

"I listened to him because of the uniform," Duke said. He was now standing with his wife just behind Fiona. Ramses gave him a little bleat to acknowledge his presence. "It was clearly a mistake. This man is unstable."

Benjy made a wordless sound, a kind of angry snarl, and pulled Hope against his chest. His left hand reached under the hem of his coat and pulled out a knife with a black blade. He held it up, pointing the tip at Hope.

"I've had just about enough of *you people*," he shouted, his voice cracking. "Irrational behavior! Nobody listens!"

"Stop that," Duke shouted. "You leave that girl alone."

Jarred tried to raise the rifle with one hand, but a wave of weakness washed over him. For a second, the world dimmed. As soon as he came to, he saw

Benjy backing down the aisle, dragging Hope with him. She didn't come willingly, the soles of her boots squealing against the floor, but Benjy kept her close.

Suddenly, Hope made her move. She unleashed an ear-piercing shriek that caused everyone in the room to flinch. At the same time, she twisted to one side, driving her right hand up and around. She hit Benjy's left arm just past the wrist, the force of the blow driving the pointed end of the Mule's ignition key deep into his flesh.

Benjy yelped and fell backward, shoving Hope back against the shelves. When she lost her grip on the key, it remaining dangling from his arm, blood running down the side of the key and dripping onto the floor.

"Stupid *girl*," Benjy said. "You're all the same! Can't trust any of you!"

He lunged at her, bringing the black blade forward. And in that moment, Jarred felt the trigger against his forefinger, and he had just enough strength to pull. The first shot caught Benjy in the hip, and he stopped in his tracks, his eyes going wide. Hope cowered in front of the bare shelves.

"Who did that?" Benjy shrieked, turning and looking at Jarred. He still had the knife in the air, blade poised. "How dare you! This whole affair is none of your business. I should have let you die in the snow!"

The second shot caught him in the chest. Jarred felt the butt of the rifle kick against his side, and then he lost his grip. As Benjy fell backward, sputtering, the stuffing of his coat swirled in the air, and the rifle fell away from Jarred grip. They both hit the ground at the same time, and then Jarred's legs went out.

He would have fallen, too, but Fiona was there. He felt her arms around him, hoisting him off the ground. And Hope calling for him, her footsteps growing louder as she ran toward him.

41

Fiona lowered him onto the floor as gently as possible, trying to keep the broken leg from hitting anything. It wasn't easy. Jarred was tall and had just enough muscle to be unwieldy. Still, she managed to get him in a seated position, placing his back against the wall. The smell of gunpowder was heavy in the air, stinging her nostrils. She sensed movement around her, people dashing about, but Jarred was her focus.

"Dad, are you okay?" Hope wailed and pushed past Fiona, dropping onto the floor beside her father and wrapping her arms around his neck.

When Fiona pulled back to give her room, she realized Jarred was sobbing. The naked expression of emotion shocked her. Fiona was always so guarded with people, and Jarred had been as well thus far. She couldn't remember the last time she'd seen a grown man weep like this. He hugged his daughter, patting her back and stroking her hair.

Instead of feeling embarrassed for him, as she might have expected, Fiona felt a tightness in her throat. Suddenly, she was close to tears, so she grabbed Jarred's fallen crutch and rose, backing away. Then she spotted the rifle and stooped down to grab that as well.

"I'm sorry, Dad. I didn't know what he was like," Hope said. "He seemed so friendly. I didn't think he would ever try to hurt me like that."

"No, no, *I'm* sorry," he replied. "I should have listened to you. I should have done better."

"Listened to me?" Hope said. "But I was wrong, Dad."

"And you were hurting more than I realized. I should have listened."

Fiona turned and saw the other people clustered together around the front door, Ramses standing nearby and staring in weird confusion. Larry, Lana, and their teenage son Zane were all holding each other, clearly disturbed by the afternoon's events. Duke Cooper approached Fiona. His wife reached out and grabbed at him, as if to restrain—as if he were trying to approach a dangerous wild animal—but Duke held up his hand to her and kept coming.

"Fiona, I'm so sorry," he said, speaking softly. "We never meant for any of this to happen. Benjy made sense at first. He was someone in authority, or the closest to it, and we were all relieved when he had a plan. Until you showed up, he behaved himself. But once you got here and confronted him, he went out of control, and none of us knew how to stop him."

She didn't know how to respond to this. It was an apology, but was it really full acceptance of their role in this stupidity? The fact was, they'd entertained the notion of taking over the homestead. Clearly, they'd considered it, and only the violence against Hope had finally turned them fully against Benjy.

Lana Bishop strode forward then. She wore red from head to toe, and she had a thin, pinched face. When she spoke, she had a reedy voice, and she sounded desperate. "You meant what you said, didn't you? You meant it? You said we can come with you to your homestead. We don't..." She glanced back at her husband and son. "We don't have anywhere else to go. We have no electricity, no running water, and we can't get south at this point. Some of the highways have been shut down, and a lot of back roads are impassable. Plus, the banks are closed, and we can't access any ATMs with the power off. We'd have no money."

Fiona met her gaze and exhaled slowly. Yes, she had offered to allow these people into her home, but she'd only done it to save Hope. Now that the danger had passed, she found the actual prospect of bringing all of these people into her home more than troubling.

"Snow just keeps falling and falling," Lana's husband, Larry, said. "And it's so cold. Between the ice and the snow, everything is shut down from here to Georgia. And if they're right, if the snow keeps falling for months or years…well, I just don't see how we'll survive. But maybe if we all worked together, if we pooled resources and effort, we might be okay."

Fiona was tempted to shrug off the request, to say she hadn't really meant it, but that didn't seem right. Then again, having Jarred and Hope in the house hadn't been unpleasant. Quite the contrary, in fact—at least until Hope's blow up. Jarred, in particular, was nice company. Still, in the few seconds of silence that passed, she felt an intense internal struggle. She was aware of the still, silent form of Benjy in her peripheral vision, and the horror of it only intensified the struggle. Meanwhile, she had all of these townsfolk just staring at her, waiting with hopeful faces for her answer. As she looked at them now, she thought they seemed underfed and unwell. Maybe she was imagining it.

Well, I guess there's no better time than an apocalyptic snowstorm to step way, way out of my comfort zone, she thought.

"Yeah…yeah, I guess I meant it." So hard to say, but once the words were out, she felt a rush of relief. She'd done the right thing, and she knew it. "Let's gather what supplies we can, and we'll head back to my place. If we leave soon, we might get back before the sun sets. And…" She gestured toward the still form in the aisle. Despite everything, there was something sad about the whole awful thing. She hadn't wanted it to come to this, Benjy gunned down, but he would have stabbed Hope. "I guess we need to deal with the body."

"Can't we leave him here?" Hope said, her voice still shaking. "I don't want to go near him again."

"You don't have to, dear," Duke Cooper said. "We'll take care of it. You stay close to your dad."

42

The storm continued to rage, the snowfall ebbing and flowing from hour to hour but never stopping. At the moment, the snow was coming down hard, drifting in at an angle on a strong wind. Fiona stood at the front door, feeling the cold against her face. Fortunately, the room behind her was very warm, and it staved off the terrible weather. The toboggan and snowmobile were both on the porch, covered in tarps and lashed against the support posts. Fiona didn't like taking Benjy's vehicle, but they hadn't had any choice.

From behind her, she heard noise, so much noise. People everywhere. Smoke's claws on the hardwood floor, laughter, people chatting in the kitchen. It was so strange, so strange it just swept over her then, and she marveled at it. The house had never had so many people in it. Never. This was an entirely new sound.

It's not the worst thing in the world, she thought. *They all sound so hopeful.*

When she finally turned and shut the front door, she saw Jarred sprawled on the couch, his head propped on a stack of pillows. Myra Cooper had replaced the crude splint with a more suitable cast made from supplies she'd brought in her suitcase. Jarred seemed to be resting comfortably despite the noise. Nearby, Hope and the other boy, Zane, were playing with

Smoke, getting him to chase a big knotted piece of rope. The dog was in heaven getting so much attention.

Fiona waited for a break in the traffic and headed over to the couch, taking a spot at the end, careful not to bump Jarred's foot. He was awake, wrapped in a blanket, with his hands tucked behind his head. He smiled at her.

"It feels normal around here," he said. "Like having a real family. You could almost forget that the world is still being smothered outside."

"Yeah, I guess so," she replied. "Normal. Whatever that means. How's your pain today?"

"One a scale of one to ten?" he said. "Maybe a seven. Although, it feels more like a six when we're chatting like this."

Any time the people and noise started to overwhelm her, she liked to sit on the couch with Jarred for a while. He had a calming presence. Somehow, his gentle demeanor put the whirlwind of chaos in perspective.

"Are you able to sleep?" she asked.

"Not so much," he said. "Bad dreams. Gun and violence, that sort of thing."

"Myra might have something to help you sleep," Fiona said. "I'll check with her after dinner and see."

Duke and Myra were preparing dinner. Something was bubbling on the pot, and they kept coordinating their cooking. Finally, Smoke tired of the game and curled up near the fireplace. The teens went into the kitchen to join all of the others. How could they all fit in there? Didn't it bother them to be pressed up against each other?

"You came here to live alone," Jarred said. "I hope we're not driving you crazy."

Fiona shook her head. "I'm adjusting. You know, it occurred to me, I've never lived in a house with this many people, never, not even when I was a child. I was an only child, and after my dad left, it was just my mom and me. Two people and a succession of dogs."

"You didn't live in a dorm when you were in college?" he asked.

"Nope, I had my own studio apartment just off campus," she said. "And then I was married to…a guy you don't want to know about. Living with him felt like living with about fifteen maniacs, though. I guess that's why I came here to be alone."

"And we've ruined it," Jarred said.

"Not ruined it," Fiona replied. "This is a new experience, but I guess new experiences can be good for you."

"Yes, they certainly can," he replied.

She leaned back and tried to relax. Everyone sounded happy, and they had already proved to be hard workers. The animals were being taken care of. Myra was working on trying to grow some potted plants on the back window. The guest rooms had both been cleaned, rearranged, and transformed into livable spaces. The house was bursting at the seams, but somehow, it had never looked better. More than that, there had been conversations about expanding the house, clearing the hilltop, creating more enclosed space. Yes, they were ambitious. Despite her discomfort, Fiona was curious to see what they could all achieve together.

Suddenly, Hope made an excited sound from the kitchen. Fiona heard what she thought was the back door tapping against the door stopper.

"Do you see that?" Hope cried. "Do you see it? Oh, my gosh! It's stopped snowing! It's stopped!"

Fiona sat up straight. She would have assumed Hope was joking, but it didn't sound like it. She traded a look with Jarred.

"Is that possible?" he asked.

"I just looked outside about five minutes ago, and it was almost a whiteout," she replied. "It couldn't have stopped that quickly, could it?"

But now others were talking excitedly in the kitchen.

"Well, would you look at that?" Duke said. "It's like someone hit a big off switch. Isn't that something?"

Jarred reached down to the floor and fumbled around. "Where's my crutch? I have to see this."

He grabbed the crutch, and Fiona helped him sit up. It took a while to get him to his feet, but once he was up, he managed to get around pretty well. They entered the kitchen, where they found the others gathered around the back door. As Fiona approached, they parted to make room for her.

Fiona gasped. Through the open door, she saw the stillness of the white world. The snow was deep, filling in the low places and settling between the trees. However, as Hope had said, there was no snow falling at the moment. The gray sky was still, and the shock of it went right through Fiona. She brushed past Hope and stepped outside onto the back porch. The whole world was snow all the way down the hill to the trees at the edge of the property but not a single snowflake fell, and the wind had died down. The world was utterly still.

"I can't believe it," she said.

She felt a hand on her shoulder as Jarred hobbled up behind her, gazing past her at the landscape.

"I've forgotten what it feels like to step outside and *not* feel painfully cold wind against my face," Fiona said.

And then some great well of light seemed to gather at the base of the hill. Fiona looked for the source and saw a small part in the ceiling of gray clouds. A hazy beam of sunlight shone through. The sight of it was breathtaking, and she staggered back into Jarred's arms.

"My God," she whispered. "The sun. Can it be?"

"It's beautiful," Jarred said, hugging her tight.

43

"All of that snow piling up was bound to be a problem," Fiona said. "We should have cleared off the roof a lot sooner. I'd sort of hoped the residual heat from the furnace would make it slide off on its own, but I guess that was a fool's hope."

"Seems like the residual heat just melted the bottom layers of snow enough to let layers of ice form—making it get progressively heavier," Larry Zane said.

She was impressed with how fast Larry and Zane could shovel snow when they worked together. They'd cleared a large space down to the grass around the southeast corner of the house, then set up a ladder to reach the roof. Fiona watched from below, perched beside the large toolbox. As father and son mounted the ladder, she heard a loud creak and pop from the roof.

"Another day or two, and it might have been the whole house," Larry said, mounting the ladder as his son braced it from below. "We have to stay on top of this from now on. With snow this deep, the roof must be kept clear."

"It's worse than the barn, isn't it?" Fiona asked. She could only see some of the damage from her angle below. A small section of the roof near the corner had finally cracked and broken from the weight of the snow, and snapped boards stuck out of the gap.

"The barn is not beyond repair," Larry said. "We'll get to it, but it's going to be a heck of a lot harder. It looks like it's about fifty years old, not in great shape to begin with. Anyway, let's worry about the house first. Hand me a crowbar, would you? I need to pry up some of the broken decking. It's bowed down between the rafters."

Fiona opened the antique toolbox and grabbed a small crowbar from the nest of tools. She passed it to Zane, who handed it up to his father. Having these guys around had certainly proved beneficial. Fiona couldn't imagine what a nightmare it would have been if she'd had to fix the roof herself. Only a small corner of the roof had actually collapsed, but that put the rest of the roof in danger. There was no telling how much stress had been put on the rafters.

Little glimpses of sunlight were not enough, it turned out, to melt the snow or make much of a difference. Nearby, they'd stacked up some of the fence boards from the basement.

"Is this old wood really going to keep the roof from collapsing?" Fiona asked, reaching out to run her glove over the pile. The wood was coarse and weathered, intact but dried out.

"It'll shore up the corner, at least," Larry replied, prying up the broken panels. "At least most of the snow on this corner of the roof fell off after the collapse, but the rest of the roof is still piled high. Clearing it all will be a challenge. We really need some two-by-fours for proper repairs."

"We could salvage some from the barn," Fiona said.

She heard the back door open and turned to see Jarred. She thought he would just stand there, but he limped outside. Duke Cooper had helped Fiona make improvements to the design of the crutch, cutting it down a bit, bulking up the crutch pad with some foam rubber from a pillow. He hobbled up beside Fiona and watched Larry for a minute. The roof beams gave another gentle groan.

"I'm going to do my best up here, Fiona," Larry said. "I can't make any promises."

"I understand," she replied. "Do what you can, and I'll be grateful. From now on, we'll try to keep the roof clear of snow, especially if it starts falling heavy again."

"It's an old, old house," Larry said. "Needs a lot of work. Not just the roof."

"Then I guess it's good you're all here now," Fiona said.

As they watched him work, Jarred reached over suddenly and grabbed her hand. These small acts of affection still caught her off guard. A hug, a pat on the back, an arm around the shoulders—she wasn't used to it, but she liked it. Somehow, it was both strange and comfortable at the same time, and she smiled at Jarred, despite their circumstances.

"How long do you think it will last?" he asked her quietly. He nodded in the direction of the house. Yes, he was talking about the damaged roof, but he meant more than that. The pause in the snow had been temporary, after all, and a few flakes were already falling again. Just a few for now.

"It'll last as long as it needs to," Fiona replied, and squeezed his hand gently.

PART II

44

Though Fiona rarely spoke about it openly, there were always at least a few times during the day when the sheer number of people in her house, in her *life*, still felt overwhelming. There wasn't anywhere to go to escape them. The outside world was deep with snow, cold and unrelenting, and the basement was full of stinky goats and chickens. But it was the constant company that got to her sometimes. Years of isolation simply couldn't be overcome that easily.

Her guests were all nice people, decent and helpful, and the more she got to know them, the clearer that became. Duke and Myra Cooper were like grandparents, Larry and Lana Bishop like a kindly aunt and uncle. Zane Bishop had become Hope's buddy, almost treating her like a kid sister. And, of course, there was Jarred, her favorite of the bunch.

But, by God, they were everywhere all the time. She couldn't go anywhere in the house without bumping into someone doing something. Even in her own bedroom, she couldn't escape the noises: chattering voices, snoring, coughing, creaking floors, doors opening and closing. It was just so many damned humans, more than she had ever had to deal with, and occasionally, it became too much.

The only thing that really helped was staying busy, and fortunately, there was plenty to do. Though she was seriously concerned about the long-term survival of her beloved old home, she relished the work. At the moment, she had long wooden beams balanced on her right shoulder, with Larry walking a few feet ahead of her bearing the front of the load. They'd salvaged the wood from the stinking, animal-saturated basement. Formerly, it had been wood set aside for her handmade furniture projects, but it had long-since soaked up the smells of animal waste. It was no longer any good for making quaint furniture. Now, it would hopefully shore up the damaged roof.

Fiona picked her way carefully up the basement stairs, trying to match Larry's pace. In the kitchen, Myra Cooper was currently preparing some kind of soup, stirring ingredients into a giant pot on the wood-burning stove. Her impressively white hair poked out of the back of a kerchief. She was still wearing a long nightshirt, sweatpants, and fuzzy slippers, though it was nearing lunchtime.

"Careful around the table," she said, as Larry led the way across the room to the back door.

Fiona appreciated that the newcomers had developed such a fondness for her home. Though they crowded the place and made it noisy, at least they cared about it. Getting the beams over the table to the back door without hitting anything was a bit tricky, but Larry took it slowly, constantly looking over his shoulder to gauge Fiona's position. Duke Cooper was waiting for them at the door, and he swung it open as they approached.

Duke had a knit cap pulled low, resting on top of his bushy eyebrows. The tip of his bulbous nose was bright red from the cold, even with the padded leather coat that he'd zipped all the way up. To get the wooden beams through the back door, Larry had to walk a straight path toward the generator shed, then cut through deep snow to his left. Fiona followed, but she was able to stick to the well-worn path they'd created along the back of the house.

"We're going to have to crawl inside the attic, I'm afraid," Duke said, leading them toward the southwest corner of the house. "I'd like to reframe the whole rooftop, if we could, but I don't think that's going to be feasible.

Instead, we'll just have to identify the broken beams and try to shore them up, but that means getting up in there."

"We've done a decent job of keeping the roof clear of snow," Larry said. "The ice has been harder to chip off, but this house is just so old. Fiona, do you have any idea when it was constructed?"

"I'd have to dig out the paperwork, but I believe it was built in the late fifties," Fiona said. "The couple who built it lived here for decades, through retirement until they died. I bought it from their estate, and I've done a ton of repair work over the years."

Fiona dumped her end of the boards into the snow beside the makeshift table they'd created across a couple of sawhorses. Numerous tools and smaller pieces of wood were scattered across the table. At the corner of the house, two ladders rose to the rooftop. Even from down below, Fiona could tell that it was an ugly mess up there. Previous repairs hadn't gone deep enough, as the creaking and groaning over the last few days had made all too clear.

Fiona climbed a couple of steps up the nearest ladder and peered over the edge of the roof. A section to her right was currently covered with a tarp, but she pulled back a corner to look at the opening beneath. The attic of the house was quite small, practically a crawl space even at the peak. As she leaned toward the opening, she heard the distinct sound of wood creaking softly.

"Okay, if someone has to crawl in there, it makes the most sense for me to do it," she said, whipping the tarp to one side. "You guys can stand on the ladder and pass me the new support beams."

"This is not going to be easy," Duke replied. "You'll have to lift the beams, angle them alongside the supports, and wedge them against the ridge beam. Then, you'll have to hold it there while nailing it into place. Think you can manage all that by yourself?"

"I'll have to because the work has to be done," she said.

She climbed a few more steps, leaned against the edge of the roof, and slowly pulled herself into the gap. Sliding into the attic, she could feel the instability around her. The weight of snow over the past several weeks had slowly worn and cracked the beams and decking. Short of replacing the entire roof, all they could do was try to add extra support for each of the beams.

"Too bad we can't rebuild the entire roof," she said, pulling herself into the low attic space. "It really needs to be redesigned and rebuilt completely, but I just don't have enough treated wood for that."

The house had a shallow attic. It was a tighter space than she expected, so it took a minute to reposition herself. Once she was under the crossbeam, at the highest spot in the attic, she was able to get up on her knees. When she looked back at the gap, she saw Duke and Larry both peeking over the edge of the roof.

"Okay, let's try this," Fiona said. She sat cross-legged beneath the crossbeam, the top of her head brushing the wood. She couldn't shake the thought of everything crashing down around her, and the feeling made her skin crawl.

Larry pushed a small toolbox through the gap. Fiona grabbed it and pulled it toward herself. As she did so, she heard a faint groan that seemed to come from all around her. She froze, waited until it passed, then positioned the toolbox beside her.

"Here it comes," Duke said. "Get ready."

He pushed the long end of one of the wood beams through the gap. Fiona had to reposition herself again in order to make room for it. Then she lay down on her back, grabbed the beam, and lifted it. The plan was to set these long beams beside the existing rafters, but it soon became clear that the task would be more difficult than it seemed. The beam was heavy and unwieldy, and once she'd raised it into place, she wasn't sure how to hold it there while she nailed it against the other beam.

As she tried, she heard the roof frame around her give another loud groan. Somewhere, something cracked.

"I'm not sure this is going to work," she said after a minute, lowering the beam onto the floor beside her. They'd laid plywood across the joists, so at least she had plenty of floor space to move around.

"Okay, I'm coming in," Duke said. "Make room for me. Larry, we might need you, too."

"Should we put the extra weight on the joists?" Fiona asked, as Duke wormed his way through the gap.

"It'll go faster this way," Duke replied, grunting from the effort of getting his bigger frame into the attic crawl space.

Fiona pushed the toolbox to make room for him, and he wriggled up beside her, smelling of Old Spice and leather, as he always did. Larry came next. Fortunately, he was fairly gaunt, so he had less trouble working his way to Duke's other side. Once they were all in place, lying on their backs on the plywood floor, Fiona lifted the wood beam again.

"Larry and I will hold it up," Duke said. "Fiona, you can nail it in place."

Duke got his gloved hands against the top edge of the beam and pushed it against the nearest roof support, as Larry helped him wedge it into place. As he did that, Fiona reached for the toolbox and fumbled around until she felt the handle of a hammer. She was pulling it out when she heard a kind of ripple going through the entire roof frame. It began as a series of soft cracks, followed by a deep groan that moved from one end to the other. Fiona tensed up, Duke gasped, and Larry cursed.

Suddenly, the support above them shifted, and they almost dropped the new beam.

"It's coming down," Larry cried. He let go of the beam and wrapped his arms over his face.

Duke managed to maintain his hold on the beam, but he turned his head to one side, as if expecting the whole thing to come crashing down on top of them. Only Fiona went still, utterly still, holding her breath until the creaking passed.

"We're good," she said, after a moment. "It's not coming down yet, but let's pick up the pace."

"Man, I don't want to get killed up here in this attic," Larry said. He moved his arms away from his face and grabbed the beam.

Duke and Larry held it back up, then pushed the original support back into place, and Fiona went to work nailing the two together. She added a few more nails to connect both beams to the ridge beam, then nailed it at places along the length of the beam. This required some difficult maneuvering in the tight space.

"Okay, that'll hold," Duke said. "Next beam."

"This roof is just so old," Larry said, "and the wood is in bad shape. All of it. I'm sure the constant freezing cold has weakened it considerably. We're fighting a losing battle here."

"We don't currently have enough wood to strengthen every support beam," Fiona said. "We need more, and we need it fast. I'll chop down trees if I have to."

"We need pressure treated lumber," Larry said. "We can't use untreated wood. All this moisture would make it deteriorate way too fast."

"I know," Fiona said. "It would be a temporary measure, but we have to do something. This roof isn't going to hold much longer, and if it comes down, the whole house might come down with it. I'm not going to lose my house." As she said it, the stress of the last few weeks welled up inside of her again, and she struggled for a moment to get hold of herself.

At least you've got competent people around to help you save the house, she told herself. *See, a full house is worth the anxiety. You'd have no hope of saving the roof on your own.*

"We'll do what we can," Duke said. "Let's get the second beam in place."

45

Jarred's leg still had a long way to go, but he was so sick of sitting on the damned couch all of the time. Sometimes, he just had to leverage himself up off the cushions and find something to do. At the moment, Hope and Zane were sitting by the fireplace having an idle conversation about random things, sharing stories of their respective pasts. The constant buzz of voices was just enough to finally get Jarred to move. He sat up, carefully swinging the splinted leg onto the ground, then he picked up his crutch.

"You're not supposed to just walk around, Dad," Hope said. "Fiona said so."

"I'll be real careful," he replied, hoisting himself off the couch, "but I can't lie around all day. I've got stuff to do, and I've been stuck like this for weeks and weeks."

Once he was up, he had a moment of indecision. Which way to go? Finally, he decided to head to the kitchen and see if he could help Myra with the cooking. As he hobbled toward the kitchen door, he heard the loud groaning of beams coming from above.

"What's happening up there?" Hope asked. "It sounds like the whole house is breaking."

"Don't worry about it, honey," Jarred replied. "They're just making some repairs. That's all you hear."

"It's a serious problem," Hope said, giving him that sharp tone of voice she got when she felt like he was patronizing her. "I can tell by the sound. This old house is falling apart."

"I know it sounds bad, but I think we'll be okay," he said, giving her a hug. "Don't worry. Duke, Larry, and Fiona are dealing with it."

"The foundation is cracked and leaking," Hope said. "The roof is falling down. The floor is super creaky. There are a lot of problems, Dad."

He knew her well enough not to dismiss her words out of hand. Hope was a smart, observant kid. Still, he didn't want her worrying constantly. "They have a plan for reinforcing the roof and walls. Some repair work was already done in the basement before we got here, I think. Not sure what they can do about a creaky floor. Still, I'm sure they'd be open to suggestions, if you have any good ideas. You usually do."

"I don't have any suggestions. I never built a house before," Hope said, working her way out of his embrace. Still, his compliment made her smile. "Mostly, I'd just suggest they hurry up because if this house falls down, I don't know where we'll go next."

As he stepped through the kitchen door, he spotted the dog curled up lazily on the floor right in front of him. A real tripping hazard. The last thing he needed to do was take a tumble. If he broke his ankle again, it might never heal. At this rate, he was concerned that it might never be the same again anyway. He whistled at the dog, but it didn't do any good.

"Myra, can you come and relocate this guy?" he asked.

She was bent over the stove, stirring a big pot of soup, while a smaller pot of black beans simmered beside it. Myra looked over her shoulder at him.

"If you want my professional advice, I don't think you should be putting any weight on that leg," she said. "Not just yet."

"Sorry, ma'am," he replied with a smile, "but I can't help myself. I'm going crazy just lying on the couch all day. Could you use an extra hand in the kitchen?"

Before she could answer, Fiona came in through the back door, a pair of snow shovels balanced over her shoulders. She saw Jarred standing in the kitchen and gave him a playful scowl, wagging a finger at him.

"Now, now, Jarred, I don't want you putting any weight on that bad leg," she said. "We've been through this before. Once you're good and healed, you'll have plenty of opportunity to help out around the house."

"Yeah, I know," Jarred said, bowing his head in exaggerated shame. "Nurse Cooper here already got onto me for it. I just get restless."

She rattled the shovels over her shoulder as she passed by. "I'd let you help shovel snow and scrape ice off the roof—I mean, it's going to be a heck of a lot of fun—but I don't want you climbing that ladder. I don't think Nurse Cooper here would approve either."

"Now, look, I was a nurse's *assistant*," Myra said with a smile, "but I do appreciate the promotion."

"Fiona, please," Jarred said. "I have to do *something*."

Fiona nodded. "Okay. Give me a minute, and I'll find something for you to do. In the meantime, please sit." She pointed at one of the kitchen chairs.

Jarred sighed and made his way toward the kitchen table, easing himself down on the chair. Fiona continued into the living room and held up the shovels as she turned toward the fireplace.

"Okay, kids, it's chore time," she said. "It's coming down again and accumulating on the rooftop. You know what that means!"

Under normal circumstances, two teens might have balked at having to do chores, but apparently the sheer need for some kind of activity caused Hope and Zane to bound up from the hearth and rush across the living room. Fiona handed them each a shovel.

"Try to fling the snow as far from the house as you can," she said. "Don't get it in our pathways."

"Got it," Hope said.

"I couldn't get this kid to clean her room," Jarred noted, massaging his aching leg just below the knee, "but she can't wait to shovel snow these days."

"Dad, don't embarrass me," Hope replied, giving him a sour look as she headed for the back door, the shovel thrust out before her. "We're trying to be helpful."

"I'm proud of you, honey. Thanks," he replied.

Hope and Zane headed outside. Jarred watched the snowfall out the window. It had been coming down fairly strong for the last hour or two. With the ever-changing wind and irregular pattern of snowfall, the blanket of snow was very uneven out there. In some places, the snow was only a foot or two deep, but in many places, the storm had created deep drifts, especially against walls, trees, and rooftops. The biggest snowdrifts looked like they were four or five feet deep, maybe more.

"I'm glad they're so willing to work hard," Jarred noted.

Fiona pulled back a chair on the other side of the table and sat down with a huff. She pulled the knit cap off her head and tossed it onto the table, then combed her auburn hair back with her fingers. She was slightly flushed from the cold, giving her face a rosy glow that was actually quite attractive.

"Quite frankly, we're running out of places to put the snow," she said. "Every time they shovel the roof, they fling it into the yard, but it's just turning our pathways into deeper and deeper tunnels. I don't know what else we can do with it, but we have to keep the roof clear at all costs."

"Can't we just start another pile beyond the current pile?" That was Lana Bishop, who had just come down the hall and apparently overheard the conversation on the way. She stepped into the kitchen doorway, bundled up in a plush robe over her regular clothes. Apparently, the fire in the fireplace wasn't enough for her.

"Well, the problem is people are going to have to keep traveling farther and farther from the house to dump the snow," Jarred noted. "They'll have to expend more and more energy just to keep the roof clear, which is going to make the task increasingly difficult."

"Is there something else we can do with the excess snow besides dumping it?" Lana asked.

"Couldn't we just melt it?" Myra offered from her place beside the stove.

"That's not faster than shoveling," Fiona said, "and it would take a lot of fuel. The snow is relentless. It ebbs and flows—we even got some sunlight through the clouds once upon a time—but the storm always comes back with a vengeance. We've done a good job of staying on top of it, but we can't let up."

Lana took a seat at the table, folding her hands on the tabletop. She had a thin, pinched face and watery eyes that made her seem perpetually on the verge of crying. At the moment, it seemed appropriate. They were fighting a losing battle against the snow, and everyone in the house knew it. If it didn't bring the whole house crashing down, it would eventually just bury them all. This was more than a possibility—it was inevitable. No one had to say it. The realization was reflected on every face.

"I wonder if we could build some kind of contraption to take the snow down the hill," Jarred said, desperate to offer something, anything. "Hope used to design robots for her robotics club at school. She might be able to come up with something."

"I doubt we have the raw materials," Fiona said. "Can you imagine how difficult it would be to build something that big? Still, if Hope can come up with a plan that's feasible, I'm open to it. I'm open to anything at this point." She gave him a sad smile. His hands were on the tabletop, and she reached over to briefly pat him. "But I just don't see how we can make it work."

"So we just have to keep shoveling, then," he replied.

"I'm afraid so," Fiona replied.

It feels like a battle we can't win, he thought, but he decided not to say it. *Hope is right to be concerned. This house is falling apart, and in the end, nature will win. It's just a question of how long we can hold out.*

46

Jarred was standing at the living room window, driven off the couch by another bout of sheer restlessness. His ankle was hurting badly. The pain seemed to come in unpredictable waves, and the ibuprofen only blunted the sharpest edges of it. At the moment, he was deep, deep in the valley of misery, but he couldn't really hobble around when he felt like this. Instead, he stood at the window and gazed dully at the featureless whiteness beyond the porch and down the hill.

They'd cleared an area in front of the porch, but the piles of snow along the edges were getting truly alarming. It was like a wall rising up and up, and even now, snow was falling heavily. It was late afternoon, and the house was particularly quiet, which he found odd. Maybe the others were resting, reading, and working quietly on their own projects. In fact, his only companion in the living room was Smoke, the dog, was who curled up in his usual spot beside the hearth.

The wind roared against the walls, but suddenly, in the midst of it, he heard a loud groan moving through the house. It started somewhere above the kitchen and spread through the living room and into the bedroom, and Jarred tensed, clutching his crutch just a little tighter. The sound passed after a moment, leaving only the wind.

"We braced as much of the roof frame as we could," Fiona said, entering the living room from the kitchen. She was wiping her hands on a towel. "The roof has been cleared again of snow and ice again, but it's not in great shape."

She joined him at the window. In her overalls and heavy boots, she had the lingering smell of the basement. Jarred had almost gotten used to it, but damn, those animals reeked.

"I don't think the original owners ever planned for this kind of weather when they designed this place," Jarred said, "but you at least bought a little more time."

"There's more wood down there in the basement," she said. "Even if we have to take apart the walls and let the animals mingle, we have to do something to keep the roof up. We have no contingency plan. There's nowhere else to go. We can't live in the greenhouse."

"I'm sorry I haven't done more to help," Jarred said. "I *want* to do more."

"If you'll quit pushing yourself and let your leg heal, you'll get your chance." Fiona sighed and tucked the rag into a pocket. "Anyway, I'll get everyone back to work. We can't afford to have a lazy afternoon, not when our survival is in question."

Jarred pulled the curtains shut. He'd seen enough of the endless snow. Meanwhile, Fiona stepped to the middle of the living room and clapped her hands loudly a few times. The woman sure had a loud clap!

"Hey, everyone," she called. She had a loud voice, too, when she needed it. "Everyone please come here!"

To their credit, people were quick to react. They still knew who was in charge. Bedroom doors opened down the hall. Duke and Myra came first. Then Larry, Lana, and Zane. Hope was last, rubbing her eyes like she'd just gotten up from a nap. They took up positions around the living room, forming a semicircle around Fiona.

"Tell me it's not an emergency, please," Duke said, scratching his white, wooly hair under his hat. "I heard that awful creaking a moment ago."

"Yeah, sorry, guys," Fiona said. "I know everyone was relaxing, but I'm afraid we have to get back to work."

Jarred saw the disappointment on their faces, so he tried to support Fiona's position by fixing a smile on his face and nodding at her words. It was a wholly fake smile laid on top of a lot of agony and discomfort, and he wasn't sure it was fooling anyone. Indeed, Hope gave her father a weird little half-smile, as if to say, *What's that look on your face, Dad?*

I wish my darn leg would hurry up and mend itself so I could get out there and work, he thought. *I'm sick of this.*

"Well, if we have to work, we have to work," Duke said, putting an arm around his wife, who seemed decidedly unhappy about it. "We can relax later when we know we're safe. What's your plan, Fiona?"

"The snow is not at its worst right now, so we need to make the most of the time." Fiona was still the tiniest bit socially awkward, but leadership seemed to come naturally for her. Jarred was impressed at how easily she'd stepped into the role. "Okay, here's what I'm thinking. Let's have one group get back to work on the roof. We can scavenge more wood from the basement, even if that means breaking apart some of our animal pens." She pointed at Hope. "Why don't you and Zane head down to the basement? You can feed the animals and while you're at it, grab some wood beams and bring them back up. We'll use them to shore up the roof a little more."

"Does it matter what kind of wood we get?" Hope asked. Her frizzy hair was frizzier than usual, probably from a lack of proper hair care. She pushed it away from her forehead with both hands.

"At this point, we can't be too choosy," Fiona said, "but I'd say avoid anything that has been soaked with a lot of animal waste or water. It's all going to smell bad though, so prepare yourselves."

Hope glanced at Zane, and he nodded. "Okay, got it," Hope said.

"And watch out for Ramses," Fiona said. "You know the big he-goat can be a pain in the butt. Don't turn your back on him."

"Oh, Ramses likes us," Hope replied. "He's no bother."

"Yeah, we made friends with him," Zane added. "All you have to do is be sweet to him and give him a little treat when he acts right."

"Then you've accomplished the impossible," Fiona said. "I've had to rely on threats and Smoke to keep Ramses in order."

At the mention of his name, Smoke looked up from his spot near the hearth.

"Get to it, you two," Jarred said, making a little spinning motion with his hand. It felt like a useful contribution, however small.

The two teens headed off together into the kitchen toward the basement. They seemed to enjoy spending time together, which made them quick to do tasks. Jarred was glad for that, but he could also tell by the sad shake of Fiona's head that she found it mind-boggling that anyone could make friends with that ornery goat.

"Larry and Lana," Fiona said, gesturing at the middle-aged couple. "Would you two mind heading down to the greenhouse to check on the plants? I would do it myself, but I think I have to be on the roof team."

Larry and Lana glanced at each other. It was clear that neither of them was particularly excited about the idea of heading down the hill to the greenhouse, but after a moment, they shrugged at each other.

"Oh, but it's going to be so cold down there," Lana said, rubbing her hands together.

"It'll be a lot less cold down there than it will be on the roof," Jarred said.

"That's a good point," Lana said. "Okay, we'll do it, but it'll take a minute to get dressed for the weather. What do we need to do down there, Fiona?"

"First, make sure the heater is still running and keeping the place above freezing," Fiona said. "Fifty degrees is ideal. Check our fuel level, though, because once the gas is gone it's gone."

"Got it," Larry replied. "We'll head out as soon as possible."

He nodded at his wife, and the two headed back to their bedroom. That left Duke, Myra, Jarred, and the dog. Fiona looked at each of them in turn, even Smoke. When Jarred met her gaze, he gave her a little smile and nod. It was the most he could muster up at the moment.

"Thanks for the back up," she said quietly.

Duke seemed like he was on the verge of saying something, his lips poised as if he were trying to come up with the best way to start. Myra stood beside him with her hands deep in the pockets of her coat. They both seemed worried, and Fiona didn't blame them. Duke knew better than just about anyone how dire the situation was. He'd been up there in the roof, seen the cracked and shifting rafters, and he knew all too well just how inadequate their repair work had been. She almost hated to tell him that she wanted him to climb back up in the attic again, but she couldn't see any other way forward.

She glanced to her left, where Jarred was still leaning on his crutch beside the living room window. He had a strange look on his face, his eyes slightly narrowed and his eyebrows knitted. It looked like he either wanted Fiona to say something specific or he too wanted to ask her something. She gave him a second, but he just stared. Finally, she turned back around to Duke.

"You know, I fought in the war," Duke said, arms crossed over his chest. "I know a thing or two about dealing with emergency situations." Fiona wasn't even sure what war he'd been involved in, but it wasn't the first time he'd brought up his war-time experiences, usually followed by his trying to wrest a little bit of decision-making control. She was trying really hard not to let it annoy her.

Fortunately, before he could continue, Jarred cleared his throat loudly. He still had that little look on his face, but this time, he said, "Fiona, could I talk to you in private for a minute?" He glanced at Duke and held up his free hand. "No offense. I'm not trying to hide anything. I just need a little one-on-one conversation before we go any further with this."

Duke gave him a big, exaggerated shrug, as if to say, *Whatever you want, buddy.* But Fiona shook her head and replied, "Can you just say it here, please, Jarred? I don't want to start leaving people out of conversations. Whatever happens, we're all in this together, aren't we?"

"Okay," he said, with a little wag of his head. "I just wanted to say out loud what we're all thinking."

"What's that?" Fiona replied, but she knew what was coming. She dreaded hearing it, the echo of the thought that had plagued her mind for days. Still, maybe Jarred was right. Maybe it was time to put it out there in the open.

"Sooner or later, we are going to lose the house," Jarred said. "If we had the means, we could build a whole new roof, but we don't. Then there's the subsiding foundation to worry about. I'm not saying we should give up, but maybe it's better if we confront the worst-case scenario. One of these days, this house is going to come down on top of our heads, and if that happens, we might lose some people."

Fiona sighed deeply. "I'm not denying that possibility, Jarred, but what are we supposed to do about it?"

"Don't you think we need to consider packing up and leaving?" he said.

"And go where?" Fiona said.

"There are other buildings out there," Jarred replied. "We could convert one of the storage buildings, or the barn. Then again, there are buildings in town, and we can make it that far if we have to. It'll be hard, but it'll be better than being caught in the collapse."

Hearing him say it somehow made the possibility seem more real, and Fiona's heart sank. Her house hadn't been that sturdy to begin with, even before the snow. It was old, renovated, yes, but still in rough shape. It certainly wasn't built for a historic snowstorm, with relentless sub-zero temperatures and snowfall trying to pile up on the roof.

Still, she hated to admit it out loud, so she wrestled with herself for a moment. "Okay, if we need a whole new roof, then maybe…" she said softly, but then she sighed. "There has to be a way to build a new one, right? As for the basement, Benjy did some temporary work on it. Maybe it'll hold a little longer."

"I'm sorry, Fiona," Jarred said. "I know this is your place. It can't be easy to think about leaving it, but I hear the roof groaning and the way the structure is creaking, and I can see what's coming. We all can."

Fiona bowed her head. "I know. I know. It's in bad shape up there. Heck, it was in bad shape before the storm even started, and I had a lot of plans for fixing things up. Now, time is pressing, and we no longer have access to supplies. I just hate it…but I'd hate it more if it anyone got hurt." Heartsick, she shut her eyes and forced herself to keep saying it. "Okay, let's just bring everyone back into the living room. I don't know where else we could possibly go, but I guess we can figure that out together. We need a backup plan."

When she opened her eyes, she saw Duke nodding at her, giving his approval with what she thought was a smug look on his face. Somehow, this annoyed her far more than it should have. Fortunately, he turned then and headed to Larry and Lana's room, presumably to fetch them. As he did that, Myra went into the kitchen, headed for the basement.

Fiona hated that they'd discussed it openly, the thing she had most deeply feared. It was out now, an inevitability that she could no longer push to the back of her mind. Soon, all of the residents were back in the living room, seeming mildly confused that they'd been asked to return again so soon. Duke made a sweeping gesture at Fiona, as if to give her the floor.

"We've been working so hard on that roof," she said. "I keep telling myself that we're going to get ahead of the damage, the decay, ahead of the ice, snow, and constant freezing temperatures." In that moment, like punctuation, she heard a little crackle come from somewhere above her. Every eye went briefly to the ceiling. "Jarred is right. I guess someone had to say it. We can't just work hard, cross our fingers, and hope the house doesn't collapse on us. We're sitting on top of a sinking foundation, with a weakened roof over our heads, and there's only so much we can do. I think we need to pack a few vital things in case we have to leave suddenly."

"We're giving up on the house?" Lana Bishop said in her reedy little voice.

"We're definitely *not* giving up," Fiona said. "We're still going to make more repairs on the roof, but we need to be ready if our work fails. Just pack a few essentials and place them near the doors."

Duke gave her another nod of approval, slow and, she thought, patronizing, and she pointedly turned away from him, looking at the kids, who seemed anxious.

"There's not a lot of usable wood left down there," Zane noted. "It's mostly soaking wet and warped. Do you still want us to take the pens apart?"

Fiona's gaze went beyond the people to the hallway and the bedrooms. Of course, there were other options. "Forget the wood in the basement. Duke, can you remove the closet doors in the bedroom?"

"Those doors are made of thin panels," he replied. "Hollow."

"But they'll help," she said. "We can brace the broken rafters with the doors and buy a little more time."

"Fair enough. Whatever we have to do, I suppose. Come on, Myra. You can help me with this."

He beckoned his wife and headed down the hall. She fell in behind him, but Fiona heard her mutter, "I just don't know where else we can go."

You and me both, Myra, Fiona thought.

"How much time do you think we have?" Lana Bishop said, clasping her hands in front of her.

"It's hard to say," Fiona replied. "If not for this stupid storm, I could hire a home inspector to come out and take a look. We've seen the damage to the roof and the basement foundation, but there might be additional problems we're not aware of."

"So what do we do?" Larry said.

Fiona turned to Jarred. "I don't know what we can do about the foundation—probably nothing—but we're going to make one more valiant attempt to keep the roof standing. Then we'll plan our next move. Right now, we have to…"

She trailed off as the roof groaned again, but the groan was followed by a series of distinct cracks. Fiona instinctively tensed, raising her arms above her head, as Jarred ducked down, and the kids backed into the kitchen doorway.

47

Dust rained down from the ceiling as the cracking continued. When Fiona looked up, she noted a large visible crack cutting across the ceiling from the corner near the fireplace. Smoke bounded up from the fireplace and began frantically looking for some place to go, dashing toward the kitchen, then the hallway, then finally settling on the front door. He crouched in front of the door, sniffing along the threshold, as if looking for some way to get through.

Fiona traded a horrified look with Jarred. The cracking sound was followed by another groan.

"My God, is it coming down on top of us right now?" Larry Bishop cried.

"This is it," Fiona said, in a whisper. She spun around, saw Hope and Zane huddled in the kitchen doorway, Larry and Lana standing in the hallway.

"Grab your coats and get out," she cried, making a broad sweep with both of her arms.

"All of you, get out of the house right now," Jarred added. "Run!"

Hope and Zane were already wearing their coats, hats, and boots, so they turned and dashed into the kitchen, heading for the back door. Larry and Lana were still zipping up their heavy coats, but they stumbled together toward the front door. As the groaning of the house continued, Fiona felt a deep vibration moving up through the floor, shaking the walls. The living room window suddenly cracked, as dust became a steady rain, filling the room with a choking haze.

Jarred limped away from the cracked window, a pained look on his face. Fiona grabbed him by the shoulders, turning him toward the front door, even as Larry Bishop grabbed the doorknob.

"Jarred, be careful with your foot," Fiona said.

"Not much I can do about it right now," he replied.

They were the last words spoken before the ceiling crashed down. It was an ear-splitting, tremendous boom followed by a screaming cascade of wood against wood. Fiona saw the big beams dropping down on either side of her, and in that panicked moment, she wrapped her arms around Jarred, wanting to protect and be protected at the same time. He wrapped his arms around her as well and pressed her face against his shoulder. Beneath the crash of the ceiling collapse, she heard people shouting and cursing and Smoke yelping.

Cold air swept down with the ceiling, and she felt snow against the exposed skin at the back of her neck. The living room windows exploded outward, and some falling object hit her between the shoulder blades and pushed her forward. This drove Jarred against the windowsill, and he cried out as he sat down roughly.

The enormous crash was followed by a few seconds of almost gentle crackling, as smaller pieces tumbled down, and then the chaos passed. Fiona remained frozen for a few seconds, trying to gauge whether she'd been wounded, waiting to see if pain would suddenly set in. Other than a sore spot on her back, however, she seemed to be okay.

She opened her eyes and looked at Jarred.

"Are you hurt?" she asked softly.

He was sitting on the windowsill, an arm wrapped around the crutch. Despite the grimace on his face, he said, "Not any worse than I was before. How about you?"

"I'm fine," Fiona said.

"What about the others?"

She released her hold on him and turned. Behind her, the living room was mostly hidden in a choking cloud of dust and snow, but she saw great beams hanging crisscrossed in an enormous pile before her, filling most of the room. Late afternoon sunlight filtered down from above, along with the steady snowfall.

At first, she heard nothing from the others, and she began looking for some way through the massive pile before her. Ducking down, she spotted a gap between the beams that gave her access to the kitchen.

"Jarred, go through the living room window," she said over her shoulder. "Get away from the house."

"Where are you going?" he replied.

"I'll meet you outside. Hurry!"

Without looking back, she crouched and made her way through the gap. The floor was a minefield of fallen beams, jagged edges, and exposed nails, and with reduced visibility, she had to pick her way carefully. Unfortunately, she couldn't tell how much of the house had come down. Was it just the living room? Was it the entire building?

Somewhere, faintly, she heard someone moaning. It sounded like Myra Cooper.

"Is anyone hurt?" she called, but that only made her choke on the dust. She began coughing violently as she continued to make her way toward the kitchen.

People were moving around elsewhere in the room and beyond. She heard beams shifting, as if they were being pushed or leaned on. She wanted to shout a warning, but she couldn't stop coughing now. Indeed, she coughed so hard that after a moment it became a struggle to breathe. Fortunately, she finally reached the kitchen, and here she had a bit more space to move around.

The ceiling had collapsed here as well, but it had taken down the dividing wall between the living room and kitchen, pushing it on top of the couch. This took the heaviest of the roof beams away from the kitchen, leaving enough space to stand up. Still, she could see through the dust and snow that the floor was littered with dangerous debris, including wall studs with exposed nails.

"Hope, Zane, are you in here?" she asked, struggling to get the words out.

They rose timidly from behind the icebox, clutching each other, wide-eyed and terrified.

"We're here," Hope said in a little squeak.

"Are either of you hurt?" Fiona asked.

"No, ma'am," Hope said.

"Okay, stay close to the outer wall, and watch where you step."

About half of the kitchen was still intact. The collapse had spared the counter, sink, stove, and icebox, and she still had access to the basement door. Fiona picked her way over to the counter and opened a drawer, fishing around until she found a flashlight. She clicked it on and shone it back in the direction of the living room.

The light mostly illuminated the dust cloud, but she saw a large gap beneath the beams. A body slowly emerged from one end, a generous coating of dust on his red cap, on his shoulders, stuck to his mustache.

"Larry, are you okay?" she asked.

He rose and stepped into the kitchen, rubbing his upper arms. Lana followed a moment later.

"Some bumps and bruises, I think," he replied. "I can't get the front door open now. It's shifted too much."

Lana had a small cut on her right temple, and a trickle of blood ran down her cheek, though she didn't seem to notice. It didn't look bad, so Fiona opted not to say anything, in case it made her panic.

"I didn't think it would come down so fast like that," Lana said in a breathy voice. "If I'd been two steps in any direction, I would've been crushed!"

"What about my dad?" Hope said.

"Hope, Zane, make your way outside and circle the house. Jarred should be in the front," Fiona said. "Be careful out there. There might be debris. We don't want you stepping on nails or shards of glass."

Hope nodded, and they picked their way toward the back door. Fortunately, unlike the front door, it was undamaged, and Hope managed to open it. They headed outside, following the clear path around the house.

"Maybe the repair work did help a little bit," Fiona said. "It's not a complete collapse. The kitchen is okay, and the basement is probably okay as well. Do you think maybe the bedrooms…?"

Before she could finish the question, she heard a pained cry coming from elsewhere in the house. Larry and Lana both turned toward the gap behind them.

"That's Duke, I believe," Larry said.

And then, as if to confirm it, Myra began to shout, "Help! Help us! We need help!"

"Myra, are you hurt?" Larry shouted back. "Tell us where you are!"

"It's Duke," Myra replied. "We're in the back guest room. Please, he's trapped. I can't lift this. You have to help him!"

Larry glanced at Lana then at Fiona, a desperate look on his face.

"I'll try to make my way to him," Fiona said. "You two wait beside the door for Jarred and the kids."

The Bishops nodded and moved out of her way. Fiona grabbed a hammer out of the drawer, in case she needed it, and slid the handle into a deep pocket of her overalls. Then, clutching the flashlight in one hand, she crouched and headed back into the tunnel-like gap in the living room debris pile.

"Be careful in there," Lana called after her. "We can't afford to have you getting hurt."

"I'll do what I can," Fiona replied. "Just don't follow me. It's not safe in here."

She shone the flashlight to her right, in the direction of the hallway. Finally, she spotted another narrow gap through the heavy roof beams. She could see the hallway at the end and what appeared to be an intact bedroom door.

"Myra, which room are you in?" Asking this question got her another lungful of dust, and she resumed coughing until she had a splitting headache. If Myra answered, she missed it, so she squeezed herself into the narrow gap and made her way toward the bedrooms.

By this point, she was practically duck-walking, and even then, her shoulders and the top of her head brushed the fallen beams. At one point, the edge of her shoe caught on a nail, and she stumbled. Reaching out to brace herself, she grabbed the nearest beam, and the whole pile above her shifted. A dangerous chain reaction of sounds passed through the hallway, and she froze, holding her breath. After a few seconds, when the whole thing hadn't collapsed on her, she resumed her forward momentum.

Somewhere, Smoke was now barking frantically. It sounded like it was coming from outside the house. He didn't sound injured, just upset.

"Please, hurry," Myra whimpered. "Duke is really hurt bad."

The second guest room where they'd been staying was straight ahead at the end of the hall. There seemed to be enough space to get through the door. That, at least, was a good thing.

"I'm coming," Fiona replied. "Hold tight, Myra."

"We're not going anywhere. Duke can't move!"

About halfway down the hall, the debris opened up a bit, and Fiona found she had room to stand up. She pushed the bedroom door open and was greeted with a fresh gush of dust and snow. Fiona turned her head to one side and shouldered her way into the room.

She shone the flashlight across the bedroom, and at first, she assumed she'd chosen the wrong room. She didn't see anyone. The ceiling had come down across the back half of the room, leaving a gap around the door and bed. Only when she'd moved past the bed did Fiona spot Myra, who was on her stomach, her legs still under the pile. Her hands were grasping the edge of the bed frame, as she slowly pulled herself out from under.

"Oh, gosh, Myra, let me help you," Fiona said.

Dumping the flashlight onto the mattress, she made her way toward the debris pile. Myra reached up, and Fiona grabbed her hands. She pulled, gradually dragging Myra's legs out from under the beams. Once her legs were free, Myra managed to get her knees under herself and rise, Fiona supporting her shoulders. She had bits of wood sticking out of her hair, and Fiona noted a few small scratches on her cheeks, her neck, the backs of her hands.

"Are you injured?" Fiona asked.

"It doesn't matter," Myra replied, pulling herself onto the bed and sitting down. "Duke is under there. I couldn't get him out. Please, he's hurt so bad."

"Okay, stay put. I'll try to get him out."

Fiona patted Myra on the back, then lowered herself to the floor. She reached back and grabbed the flashlight, shining it through the small openings in the big pile of debris. As the dust settled, her view became clearer, and she eventually found him. His head, left shoulder, and left arm were visible, but the rest of him was covered by a large sheet of plywood weighted down by some of the broken joists.

"Duke, can you hear me?" Fiona said. "Look at me."

Slowly, he raised his dust-covered face and scanned his surroundings with pain-filled eyes.

"Can you move?" she asked him.

"There's something heavy laid across his back," Myra said, answering for him. "I couldn't push it off."

Fiona could see this was going to be a tough job, and dangerous, but there was no way around it. She took a deep breath, steeled herself, and began picking her way into the pile.

"I'm coming in there after you," she said. "It'll take time. I have to move slow so it doesn't collapse on us again."

To this, Duke just groaned softly and laid his head down again. Using the back of the hammer, Fiona slowly eased the broken boards out of her way, opening up a path to Duke. She moved the smaller pieces, tossing them over her shoulder. In this manner, inch by inch, she made her way across the room, creating a path.

By the time she reached him, night had fallen. When she shone the flashlight above, she saw snow still falling where the roof of the house had once been. Shifting one more broken beam, she finally got beside Duke and paused a moment to catch her breath.

"I'm here," she said. "Just a little longer. I have to get the beams off your back."

"I think my arm is broken," he replied.

"We'll take care of it when we get you free," she said. "Lie still for me, okay?"

"I don't have much choice," he grumbled in reply.

Piece by piece, Fiona cleared the pile on top of him. As she removed the debris, Myra helped by dragging the pieces into a pile near the bed. The large section of plywood across his back had a length of the ridge beam lying across it, and pieces of a few rafters were still attached. This, it seemed, was the major source of the problem.

Fiona tried to lift it, but it was wedged into place. She couldn't shift it more than about half an inch. This forced her to use the hammer to break some of the rafters free. Then she was able to push the beam down past his legs. Once she'd managed that, despite her aching arms and shoulders, she dragged the plywood off his back and flipped it to one side.

"That got it," she said, sweat turning the dust to gunk on her face. She slipped the hammer back into her pocket and massaged her right shoulder.

Duke rolled onto his back and struggled to sit up. Fiona had to help him, but even then, it took a couple of minutes. He was able to move his legs—a good sign that he hadn't broken his back—but he cradled his right arm against his stomach.

"Thanks," Duke said, then coughed, retched, and spat a gob of muddy saliva-dust to one side.

"Can you walk?" she asked.

"I'll certainly try."

Fiona rose, hooked her arm under his shoulder, and pulled him to his feet. He winced, cursed, and gasped, but he eventually managed to stand. When they turned around, they saw Myra sitting on the bed, the big pile of debris near her feet. She was weeping in relief.

"Myra, Duke, we have to get out of this house," Fiona said. "To do that, we have to make it down the hall and through the living room."

"But where can we go?" Myra replied, brushing the tears off her cheeks. "We have no home, and it's so far back into town!"

"There are other buildings on my property. There's the greenhouse, the big storage building, the barn." Fiona shrugged. "And any of them will be better than here. Come on."

One arm around Duke's shoulders, she guided him toward the bedroom door and the narrow gap on the other side.

48

It was getting late by the time the entire group finally reconvened in the clearing just beyond the front porch. Duke's busted arm was resting in a crude sling made from a couple of t-shirts tied together. The poor guy seemed to be in a lot of pain, and he endlessly gnawed on his lower lip as Myra rubbed his back and tried to comfort him. Larry and Lana were dragging a canvas bag from around the corner, as Hope and Zane followed behind carrying a few more items.

Fiona would have helped, but she was in quite a bit of discomfort herself. She was sore all over, but she was particularly concerned that she'd wrenched her back somewhere along the way. At the moment, she stood at the bottom of the porch steps. Though she, like the others, had her winter coat, hat, and gloves, she could still feel the biting night wind on her exposed face. She had the flashlight balanced between her knees, illuminating the area.

"Well, it could have been a lot worse," Jarred said, leaning on his crutch. "At least everyone got out alive."

"I think our repair work on the roof might have reduced the severity of the collapse," Fiona said. "That probably saved some lives. So all that hard work wasn't in vain."

"We knew the house was in danger," Jarred said, "but no one expected it to come down that soon."

"I really hoped we could prevent it," Fiona said, feeling suddenly overwhelmed by the loss. Her home, her beautiful wilderness home, brought down by a stupid snowstorm. "You have no idea how much that place meant to me."

"I'm so sorry, Fiona."

Larry and Zane dumped the canvas bag in the middle of the clearing.

"Well, we managed to retrieve a few things from the kitchen," Larry said, brushing his gloved hands together. "It'll take a lot more work to get the rest of our stuff, though. Most of it is buried in the bedrooms."

Hope added a folded blanket to the pile, and Zane added a couple of pillows. Fiona looked inside the canvas bag: kitchenware, dried food, utensils, tools, another pair of gloves, boots—not much.

"You know, at least the collapse seems to have put out the fire in the fireplace," Jarred noted. "If it had spread the flames, things might have been a lot worse for us."

He was trying to be optimistic, and she appreciated the effort. Still, she wasn't feeling it. Nothing about this situation alleviated her misery. She stepped away from the porch steps.

"There are still hot ashes under there," Fiona replied. "And the part of the building that's still standing may not last long. We'll have to wait a while before we try to get the rest of our stuff. Leave it all here for now. We'll come back up the hill for it once we're settled in another building."

She aimed the flashlight down the hill toward the rest of her homestead. She could make out the unfrozen windows of the greenhouse, the tarp-covered roof of her barn, the storage sheds, the lumps that had once been her crops. Jarred hobbled up beside her, using a broken stick from the house as a walking stick, and rested his free hand on her shoulder.

"I'm sorry about your house, Fiona," he said. "I know it meant a lot to you. I wish I'd been able to help you with repairs, especially after all you've done for me."

"I'm just trying not to think about it right now," Fiona replied. Her voice caught at one point, and she felt the sting of tears. Needing to change the subject, she turned toward Duke and Myra. "Duke, can you walk?"

"Yeah," he replied, though he sounded quite weak. "It's my arm that's the problem. And my head and back, to a lesser degree."

"Okay, we'll take a closer look at your injury when we get out of this awful wind," Fiona said. She beckoned the group. "Follow me, everyone. We're going down the hill. Step carefully."

As soon as she headed for the slope, Smoke rose from his place near the pile of stuff, gave a frantic little bark, and bounded after her. He kept going, racing down the hill, as if he couldn't get away from the collapsed house fast enough. Fiona started after him, wincing from the discomfort. They had a path leading down the hill that Fiona periodically cleared with the Mule, but it had been a couple of days. That meant tromping through a few inches of slick snow. On top of that, a fierce frozen wind was blowing, cutting through layers of clothing like an icy blade. Fiona wrapped her arms around herself and went slowly to keep from falling.

"What building are we headed for?" Jarred asked, picking his way along with the crutch.

"I don't know," she replied. She glanced over her shoulder to make sure the others were following. Larry and Lana were right behind her, their breath puffing out in the backwash of the flashlight like great billowing smoke. Zane and Hope were behind them. That put Duke and Myra at the end, and she was helping him. The poor old guy seemed to be in agony with the way he was shuffling along, a grimace on his face.

"The greenhouse, at least, is heated," Jarred pointed out. "It might be the most comfortable."

"There's hardly any floor space in the greenhouse because of all the rows of empty planters, the buckets, and the tables," Fiona replied. "If we pushed everything movable against the walls, we could clear a little spot in the middle, but not enough for everyone to lie down."

"The big storage building then?"

"The storage building might have more room, but it also has a concrete floor. We'd need some padding to make it bearable for people to lie down, but I spread almost every blanket and tarp over the garden. They're all crusted with ice by now."

"What about the barn, then?" Jarred asked. "Seems like that might be our only real option."

"Well, a big part of the roof collapsed in one corner," she said. "It's not exactly in the best shape."

"Didn't you and Larry do some repair work up there a couple weeks ago?" he said.

"We couldn't spare the supplies to fully repair it," Fiona replied. "We needed the wood for the house. But we made some basic repairs and covered the hole with one of the frozen tarps from the garden. There are still gaps and cracks in the walls, but it's the biggest building down there."

"There's a hayloft, too, isn't there?" Jarred said. "That'll get everyone off the cold floor, at least. Plus, we can bring the animals back in there. Right now, they're stuck down in the basement under the pile of debris."

And what are the odds that the barn will collapse on us, as well? she wondered. Still, Jarred was right; it was the only building with enough room for the people, their stuff, and all of the animals.

"Okay, I guess it's the barn, then," she said. "It's not like we have much choice."

She reached the bottom of the slope and led them alongside the barn. She unlatched the big door in front and pulled it open. Inside, she saw a bit of snow still covering the ground. The collapsed portion of the roof had been along one corner above the goat pens. They'd spent a couple of days trying to fix it, but a small hole still remained. It was covered with a blue tarp, which flapped in the wind.

As she waved the others through the door, Smoke came running from the direction of the crop mounds, cut between Larry and Lana, and raced into the barn. Neither of the Bishops said anything about the choice of new home. They just walked into the room and headed toward the ladder to the hayloft in the back. Zane and Hope did the same. Finally, the Coopers came around the corner, Duke shuffling along one small step at a time.

As he approached the door, he glanced at Fiona and said, "The barn? Really? Like a herd of cattle?" That was it, but those simple words carried an obnoxious amount of weight.

"Yeah, the barn," Fiona replied. "Really! It's the only reasonable option, Duke. Sorry. Go find somewhere to sit down. We need to take a closer look at that arm."

Once they were inside, Fiona motioned Jarred through, then followed him, pulling the barn door shut behind her. Jarred gave her another gentle pat on the back. He'd apparently picked up the mild hostility in Duke's voice.

"He doesn't approve of our new shelter?" Jarred said.

"He's just a crotchety old man," Fiona replied quietly. "And with his busted arm, I'm sure he'll be a lot worse."

"I guess he can sleep outside, if he wants," Jarred muttered.

"Don't tempt me," Fiona replied.

Myra led Duke to a bench along the wall and eased him down. Larry and Lana were already heading up the ladder to the hayloft. Fiona really wanted to join them. Lying down on a bed of hay sounded nice at the moment, but she did need to take a good look at Duke's arm. If it was broken, it would need to be set. She made her way toward the bench, and thankfully, Jarred came with her.

"Okay, can you take your coat off for me, Duke?" Fiona said with a sigh, taking a knee in front of him. "We need to examine your arm to see if it's broken."

"It sure *feels* broken," he replied. "Hurts like the devil, and I can barely move it." Myra undid his zipper and began carefully pulling the coat off. They had to remove the crude sling, which took a minute. Finally, the arm was exposed.

Fiona handed the flashlight to Jarred, who shone it at the arm. Duke was scowling, but she tried to ignore his expression. He was in a bad mood, clearly, but he was also suffering. She could overlook it for now. She held his arm and lightly probed it from wrist to elbow. He had a big bruise forming about halfway up. Still, she could feel the forearm bones, and they seemed intact.

"Well, I'm not a doctor, of course," Fiona said. "It doesn't feel like the bones are broken to me. Myra, you're the only one with medical training of any kind. What's your professional opinion?"

Myra gently felt his arm, pressing lightly with her fingers, as he winced and grunted. Finally, she said, "I don't feel a break, but that doesn't mean there's not one. Could be a hairline fracture or something like that. Then again, it's possible the arm is just deeply bruised."

"Well, at least it's not a severe break," Fiona said. "I think you were lucky, Duke."

Duke grunted unhappily and said, "The only reason I was in that bedroom in the first place was because *you* wanted me to remove the closet doors. I told you a set of hollow doors wouldn't do hardly anything to prop up that roof. I told you."

"Now, now," Myra said, rubbing his back. "She was just trying to help."

"Well, we all heard the roof cracking," he said. "*I* didn't decide to go back there, did I?"

Larry and Lana were up in the hayloft, but Larry leaned over the edge and said, "Come on, now, Duke. We were trying to save the roof. We were all inside that house. Any of us could have been hurt in there, or worse."

"Ah, put a sock in it, Larry," Duke snapped. It was so loud that Fiona immediately rose and backed away from him. Myra began to rub his back more frantically, but it did no good. "All I wanted was to keep working peacefully in my store during my twilight years. That's all I wanted. And here I am exiled on this damned farm, crushed by the roof of some flimsy seventy-year-old house that wasn't even built to code, and now I'm hiding inside a half-repaired barn that smells like seven decades of animal waste. Hell, the roof could fall on us in here, too." He tipped his head back, looking up at the ceiling. "It's still got a hole in it. Who's to say it won't fall on us in the middle of the night and kill us in our dreams?"

Despite his annoying crankiness, he had a point. The barn was at least as old as the house, and it was in worse shape. A strong enough wind could push it over. Still, Fiona didn't need to sit and listen to the grumbling. She left Duke to his ranting and swept the flashlight around the barn, looking for anything they might be able to use to make the place a more livable.

"I just don't understand how it came to this," Duke continued. "That damned park ranger walked into my store, flashing his badge, and got us all riled up. Then there was that big fight, he bled out in the canned soup aisle, and suddenly here we are. This is sheer human misery, that's all I'm saying, and we're not out of the worst of it yet."

Yeah, tell me about it, Fiona thought, as she hunted around the barn. She found an absolutely filthy horse blanket hidden under loose hay near the back of the barn. Though it reeked, she gathered it up in her arms. *My homestead was my sanctuary for years, and now it seems to have turned against me. This place is no longer a haven.*

When she turned back around, the blanket laid over her arm, she saw Jarred standing awkwardly near the bench. Myra was drawing desperate circles on Duke's back with her hand.

"We're all in this together, Duke," Larry called down from the hayloft. "No sense acting like you're the only one's had a hard time. We've all been stuck in this blizzard for weeks now."

"I told you to put a sock in it, Larry," Duke replied. "I'm the guy who had to be dug out of the rubble. I'm the guy with the broken arm. It's not fair!" He practically roared this last.

Okay, Duke, give it a rest, Fiona thought, though she didn't dare say it. *Everyone's hurt, angry, and tired, but none of us are ranting like overgrown toddlers.*

"Oh, Duke, you're absolutely right," Myra said. She was rubbing his back so intensely that Fiona thought she might just wear a hole in his shirt. Her tone of voice made it sound like she was talking to her child, not her husband. "It's so unfair to you, honey. You tried so hard to help."

Somehow, her patronizing voice had the right effect. It was like magic. Duke stopped ranting, bent over, and got this pathetic little frown on his face. Fiona dared to approach, dumping the blanket on the end of the bench. As she did, Myra leaned in and spoke softly to Duke, and Fiona just made out what she said.

"Now, look, you're practically a grandpa to those two kids, Duke," she said. "Poor little Hope and Zane are going to need your help. You've got to be strong for those kids, especially Hope, after all she went through. We don't want them to get scared."

Duke's eyes flitted toward Zane and Hope, who were standing near the ladder, staring at him with obvious embarrassment. Whether or not Myra had meant what she said, it finally pulled Duke out of his foul mood.

"Yeah, that's right," he muttered. He sniffed and nodded. "I'll be all right. Just let me rest here a little bit." He noticed the blanket then. "Myra, would you help me wrap that around my shoulders? It sure looks warm. I don't care what it smells like."

As Myra grabbed the blanket, Fiona resisted an urge to sigh and turned to face the others. Jarred gave her a little shake of his head, clearly disgusted by Duke's outburst.

"Well, whatever," Fiona said, trying to get her mind back on track. "I need a few able-bodied people to come with me up the hill to get our stuff." When it looked like Hope might volunteer, Fiona quickly added, "Hope, why don't you stay in here? Maybe you can keep Mr. Cooper company. Tell him a few jokes or stories or something. Help keep his mind off the pain."

I guess I'm conspiring with Myra to use the kids as a buffer for cranky Duke Cooper, she thought. *Hopefully, the kids won't resent me for it.*

"We'd like to go with you," Larry Bishop said, crawling to the edge of the hayloft. "Lana and I. We'll be real careful in there."

"Okay, that's fine," Fiona said.

Jarred hobbled toward her, leaning heavily on his walking stick. "I'd like to go, too. I know what you're going to say, Hope, but I made it all the way down the hill. I've got my staff here to help me keep weight off the healing leg."

Fiona gave him a look of uncertainty. She was tempted to order Jarred to stay behind for the sake of his foot, but she enjoyed his company. More than that, she thought she might need his backup if she had some disagreement with the Bishops.

"Okay, but if the pain gets really bad, you have to take a break," Fiona said.

He gave her a playful salute. "You've got it."

As Larry, Lana, Fiona, and Jarred headed for the barn door, Zane joined them as well. That left Hope with the Coopers. She was sitting in the hayloft at the top of the ladder. She seemed shaken still by the collapse, and she didn't complain at staying behind. However, as Fiona led them to the door, Hope said, "Dad, be careful with your leg. Don't let adrenaline make you too confident."

"Don't worry, I can still feel the pain plenty," he replied. "I promise I'll take it easy."

They headed outside, back into the bitter cold wind and heavy snowfall.

"Just head back up to the porch and start grabbing whatever you can," Fiona said, shining the flashlight ahead of them.

"Can't we use the Mule?" Lana asked. "We'd putter right up that slope in no time."

"I'd rather not waste the fuel," Fiona replied. "Not on something we can do by hand. We need the gasoline for the greenhouse. But I have a wheelbarrow in a storage shed."

Lana seemed to accept this. Fiona led them across the way to the big storage shed, where she retrieved a wheelbarrow. Larry offered to push the wheelbarrow, and the Bishops headed back up the hill. As Fiona went after them, Jarred made a little motion with his hand, apparently asking her to slow down. She let the Bishops get a few yards ahead, and Jarred limped in close to her.

"Sorry, I didn't want them to overhear," he said. "I think we need to talk about Duke. Are you okay after his little outburst? It was uncalled for."

"I'm fine," she replied. "He was just venting. I mostly just disconnected from it, to be honest." She sighed again. "People are weird. I was married to a maniac who would rant about the smallest thing. Duke is a lot milder than him, but there's a similarity. I saved his life in that back bedroom, but he still found a way to blame me for his trouble. Whatever. This is why I lived alone for so long."

"Fiona, you've got enough to worry about," Jarred said. "I'll deal with Duke, if you want me to. I can have a little man-to-man talk about his attitude, maybe put him in his place. Even with a busted leg, I'm not afraid of the confrontation."

She swiped a hand in front of her face, as if shooing away a fly. "Thanks, Jarred, but no. Don't do that. I'd rather not talk about it. Let's give Duke a chance to be better."

"Well..." He hesitated a moment, and she knew he was about to say what was *really* on his mind. "If that's what you want, then I'll respect it."

"It is," she said. "Don't make it worse."

"You got it," he said. "So...what's next?"

"Next?" she replied. "I'm not sure I understand the question."

"I mean, we can't live in the barn forever," he said, "so what's next? Where do we go from here? The storm shows no sign of letting up, even after all these weeks, so we'll need a long-term solution. Should we head into town and try to find an empty apartment? Should we try to fix up the barn, maybe drag the furnace down the hill? What do you think?"

In that moment, tired and frustrated, Fiona decided to be brutally honest with him. "Look, I know the homestead. There's no way we're going to get that giant cast-iron furnace out of the basement and down the hill, and fixing up the barn will be an ordeal. Even so, I'm fairly confident I can keep these people safe as long as we're here on my land, even with our current crisis."

"For how long?" Jarred said. "Supplies are running out. There's not much left to feed the animals, and we'll run out of food to feed people in, what, a few weeks? Yes, the few trips we made into Glencole to scavenge supplies were fruitful, but that source of pretty much tapped out by now. We have to look elsewhere."

"Maybe I'm being stubborn," Fiona replied, "or too loyal to this place because it's meant so much to me, but I'm just not ready to head off to some other place. We don't even own a working vehicle that could carry everyone into town, and I'm not sure I could keep people safe on the road. I don't really know what the world is like out there right now. We haven't gotten any updates about how the storm has impacted other places, so we have no idea what we'd be heading into. Anyway, the world out there is not my place. I have no experience or habits to fall back on."

"You're the only person in this entire group who has built a homestead practically from the ground up and kept it running for years," Jarred said, giving her an encouraging smile. She marveled again at what a pleasant smile he had. It seemed genuine. "By yourself, you've taken care of all kinds of animals, crops, multiple buildings, vehicles, and whatever else. And if you can do it here, you could do it somewhere else. Hey, you kept me alive. You helped me get Hope back from Benjy. You've coordinated all of these people day after day, even that cranky old man down there. You're a natural leader, Fiona, whether you realize it or not, and I trust you. I fully trust you—here, on the road, wherever."

The combination of his smile, his encouraging words, and his sheer kindness filled her with such warmth that for a moment she was speechless.

"I just think if we're going to find some new place," Jarred continued, after a moment, "we should head for it while we're still able to make the trip. Let's not wait for *real* desperation to set in."

That put a damper on her warm feelings, as the reality of their situation sank in. "Maybe you're right," she said, miserably. "It's just hard to let go."

49

Larry, Lana, and Zane gathered around the pile in front of the house and began packing the items they'd retrieved from the house into the wheelbarrow as best they could. Fiona was tempted to spare them the effort and just start up the Mule anyway, but she couldn't bring herself to do it. Once the fuel was gone, it was gone, and they needed it to keep the greenhouse above freezing so their food wouldn't spoil. Now more than ever, they couldn't afford to waste anything.

"Larry, I'll leave you in charge of this stuff," she said. "You can start lugging it down the hill if you want. I'm going to try to rescue the animals down in the basement."

"Be careful down there," Larry said, shoving towels into a cloth bag. "The goats, in particular, are bound to be agitated." Larry, at least, was usually mild mannered, even when things were falling apart. Fiona didn't think she could've handled a second crotchety old man.

"Oh, yes, I expect the worst from Ramses," Fiona replied. "He'll think I dropped the house on him just to keep him from pestering the ladies."

Jarred came with her as she approached the corner of the house, hobbling along with his crude walking stick as they circled around to the basement door. Fiona shone the flashlight along the wall. Since most of the exterior walls had remained intact, the collapse didn't look as bad from outside, until she shone light through the shattered living room window and revealed the broken beams hanging down.

"How bad is your leg?" Fiona asked Jarred. "You haven't pushed yourself too much, have you?"

"For some reason, it doesn't hurt as much as it did before the collapse," he replied. "I don't know if it's adrenaline still surging through my system or just my mind having something more important to think about, but right now I feel little more than a dull ache."

"Good. Just don't let the adrenaline make you reckless. You can't do as much as you might think you can. Let me handle Ramses."

"Got it," he said. "I can at least carry a chicken or two for you. Maybe the goose."

"And that'll be enough."

Fiona approached the angled basement door, which was built into the ground just beyond the exterior wall on the north side of the house. As she turned the latch and pulled it open, she wondered if she was going to find a bunch of squished animals down there. But, no, the kitchen floor had remained intact. The animal stink of the basement wafted out so strongly, it burned her nostrils. She aimed the flashlight at the steps and made her way down.

The desperate bleating of a goat let her know that at least one of them was still alive. When she reached the bottom, she swung the flashlight to her right and illuminated the weird yellow eyes of Ramses, the male goat, staring at her from his pen in the back corner. He was making quite a bit of noise.

"Yeah, I hear you, boy," she said. "Sorry about the little scare tonight. We'll get you out of here in just a minute. It might take a few trips to get everyone, so be patient."

As if in reply, he kicked against the wall of his pen and bleated at her again. Fiona swept the flashlight to the left and saw all of the female goats clustered together near the middle of the room, as if to comfort each other. They seemed to be just fine. Then the light reached the other corner, and she saw a large support beam from the underside of the basement ceiling hanging down. It had landed right inside the chicken pen.

Cursing under her breath, she made her way through the basement to the corner. Gradually, the light revealed that, indeed, she'd lost most of the chickens and the single goose. They were caught beneath the beam, their legs and feathers poking out from under it. The survivors were trapped in a small space under the angle of the beam.

"Sorry, girls," she said. "I'm guessing you'd like to get out of here, huh?"

The basement ceiling—which also happened to be the kitchen floor—gave a soft little creak, and that got Fiona moving.

In the end, getting the animals down to the barn was mostly just a tedious series of trips. She had a long line for the goats. First, she brought the females, since they behaved well together. Jarred was as good as his word, carrying a couple of chickens in a basket as he accompanied her back down to the barn.

Once the female goats were in place, she went back for Ramses. Despite his desperate bleating, the big male goat seemed relieved to get out of the basement, and he trotted along dutifully as she led him to the barn. When she tried to put him in his old pen, he kicked and pulled against the line a bit, but she got him in place.

She made a final trip to get the last of the chickens. By then, the Bishops were done lugging all of their salvaged gear into the barn, and Hope was tending a small campfire that she'd started in a cleared space in the middle of the room. She'd surrounded the fire with a ring of bricks and rocks.

Duke and Myra were still sitting on the bench, quietly chatting. The Bishops were huddled together behind Hope, who had apparently taken the lead on getting the fire going. Jarred was resting against a wall, looking flushed and tired. He'd pushed himself too much. At least the hardest work was done for now, though there was still a lot to do.

Fiona took a moment to gather her thoughts. All of this would have been so much easier to deal with if there weren't so many people to worry about, so many personalities to juggle. For a moment, she daydreamed about being alone again on her homestead—maybe with Jarred and Hope. Then she scolded herself.

No sense living in fairy tales. Deal with the world as it is, not as it was.

She stepped toward the fire and cleared her throat to get everyone's attention.

"That's all of the surviving animals," she said. "Hope, good job on the fire. It already feels warmer in here."

"We don't have a chimney," Duke noted. His voice sounded rough. "Is that small hole in the ceiling enough to vent the smoke? I'd rather not get asphyxiated in here overnight."

"We'll push the tarp back a little," Fiona said. "That should be enough."

"You think so?" Duke grumbled.

Still in an excellent mood, I see, Fiona thought. She decided not to respond, but Jarred jumped in.

"That hole up there is at least as big as a chimney hole," he said. "And there are cracks between the boards all around us. We're not going to asphyxiate."

Duke glanced at Jarred and frowned. "I was just asking."

"Okay, guys, there's quite a bit of junk in the barn," Fiona continued. "We should go through it all and see what can be salvaged. There are plenty of scraps to feed the fire, at least."

"What do we use for a bathroom?" Zane said.

"For now, step outside," she replied. "I know that's going to be unpleasant, but it's all we've got for now. We'll figure out something better later. Come on, folks." She snapped her fingers and headed toward the nearest pile of junk. "Let's get to work."

It helped her to stay busy. Larry and Lana joined her without complaint or comment. Zane lingered for a minute. He was staring longingly at the fire, but when Hope rose, he came with her. Together, they began rooting through the junk. Most of it contained things like old pieces of gutters, scraps of what hadn't been taken to the dump yet, and filthy bits of cloth.

Duke didn't help, except to provide an ongoing stream of surly advice as they worked. "Don't pick through metal things without leather work gloves," he said. "Those gutters might be rusty. Tetanus. You've heard of tetanus, I assume?" And a minute later, "Those scraps of cloth could be infested with lice or carpet beetles. Burn them." And then, "Someone's going to get a spider bite just digging into a wood pile like that. Brown recluses love to hide under wood like that."

Finally, as Fiona was lugging an armful of broken and water-damaged wood shingles to the trash pile near the door, she overheard him muttering to his wife, "We should've just left Glencole when everyone else did. Why are we sitting here in this barn like homeless people?"

Despite her best efforts, it finally got to Fiona. Without really meaning to, she glanced in his direction and snapped, "Got something to say, Mr. Cooper? Want to share it with the whole class?"

A mistake. He gave her a poisonous look, his lip curled, and said, "I'm saying your house let us down when we needed it most."

And she could tell by the way he said it that "your house" really meant "Fiona." She felt such rage and embarrassment in that moment that she stopped in her tracks and dumped the wood shingles at her feet. Larry Bishop looked like he was about to say something, but she held up a hand to stop him. Jarred, fortunately, had fallen asleep against the wall, so he couldn't step in and defend her. That was fine because this time she didn't want any mediation. She'd had enough.

This is my house. He doesn't have the right to speak to me like that, she thought, as she turned to face him fully.

"Mr. Cooper...Duke, the whole reason you're here in the first place is because your own home wasn't good enough to keep you safe during the blizzard," she said. "You couldn't survive on your own. That's why you came here, and you *have* survived. I took you in, even though your original plan was to force your way onto my homestead with Benjy Hartman. Since then, you've had good food, clean water, heat, and a bed to lie down on.

You were incapable of surviving on your own, so maybe you shouldn't throw stones."

Duke met her gaze a moment longer, then finally grumbled under his breath and bowed his head, averting his gaze.

That's what I thought, you sour old fart.

"He didn't mean it," Myra said, after a moment. "He's hurting a lot."

"Don't take it out on me, Duke," Fiona said tightly. "I'm trying to help you. I'm trying to help all of you. Don't make me regret it."

Fiona gave him another few seconds of cold, hard stare-down, then stooped to pick up the wood shingles. When she glanced back, she saw Hope and the Bishops looking at her with anxious eyes.

"Everyone, get back to work," she said, stacking the shingles in her arms. "For the rest of the night, if any of you feel like snarking, just clamp your mouth shut and keep it to yourself. We're all alive, aren't we? We still have a roof over our heads, don't we? Okay, then. Good."

And with that, she rose and headed to the trash pile, still seething.

50

Sleep simply wasn't going to happen, not for Fiona. By the time they were done picking through absolutely everything in the barn, she was still restless. She couldn't even bring herself to sit down. Duke had finally gone to sleep lying on the horse blanket near the fire—clearly unconcerned about lice or carpet beetles, despite his earlier complaint. Smoke was sleeping beside Hope, who was tending the fire. Jarred was still out, but Fiona, Larry, and Zane remained wide awake. For a while, Fiona just paced the room, trying to wear herself out.

Eventually, she rearranged their supplies, trying to find better places for everything. Then she checked on the animals, but they were settled down for the night. Finally, she stoked the small fire a bit, just enough to make sure they had plenty of light. All the while, she kept thinking about the house, about all of her stuff still buried inside. Clothes, toiletries, weapons, furniture, canned food—so much that they still desperately needed.

Sometime around what must have been midnight, she turned to the others who were awake. Zane was edging toward sleep, still sitting up but staring glassy-eyed at the glowing embers in the firepit. Larry, however, remained wide awake, sitting cross-legged and fiddling with a small piece of salvaged wood, as Lana snored softly beside him. Fiona cleared her throat to draw his attention.

"I'm going back up to the house," she said, speaking softly.

"This late?" he replied.

"I just want to salvage whatever I can," she said. "I hate the idea of leaving so much stuff exposed to the weather all night. And, to be honest, I have a lot of restless energy."

"Because of Duke?" Larry said.

"Maybe. Yeah. When I'm frustrated, it helps to be productive."

"You shouldn't let him get to you like that," Larry said, casting the bit of wood into the fire.

"I didn't make it to my bedroom earlier," she said. "My guns are back there. We might end up needing them. I'd rather just get it over with, and then I'll be able to sleep."

"Is it safe up there?" he asked.

"I'll be careful. I can retrieve the old wheelbarrow again from the storage shed, grab some tools and flashlights. It shouldn't be a problem. Anyway, if the others wake up and ask where I am, feel free to let them know."

She started toward the door, then heard Larry make a little huffing sound. When she glanced back, she saw him coming toward her.

"I'll join you," he said.

"Are you sure?"

"Yeah, if you don't mind," he said. "I mean, if you'd rather work alone, I understand."

"It's fine. Come on."

And then, as if her assent had stirred interest, Zane suddenly roused himself, stifled a yawn, and stood up. "I want to help, too. I'm tired, but I can't sleep either." He zipped up his coat, adjusted his cap, and came toward her. "When I sit there, I worry about stuff, so I'd rather do something."

"Come along then, son," Larry said, clapping him on the back. "Just be careful up there. Lots of exposed nails and splinters."

"I know. I know."

Fiona grabbed a flashlight from a shelf, pulled the barn door open just enough to pass through, and stepped out into the bitterly cold night. She'd never removed her coat, gloves, hat, or boots, so she was ready to go. Larry came through the door after her, his tall, gaunt form bent against the snowy wind, his long fingers pressing his hat to his head. Zane came next, sniffing and rubbing his eyes.

Under normal circumstances, Fiona would have expected Smoke to wake up and bolt after her. The dog was usually highly attuned to her comings and goings. However, the day's events seemed to have freaked him out just enough that he never left his spot in the back corner of the barn. Something about that struck her as sad.

"Okay, be real careful walking around out here this late," she said. "It'll be hard to tell where the ice slicks are."

Fiona beckoned the little group and headed to the big storage shed. From the shed, she grabbed a toolbox, another flashlight, and the wheelbarrow. Then she led the group back along the well-worn path beside the barn and up the hill. Larry offered to push the wheelbarrow again, but she waved him off.

"I'd like to do it this time," she said.

"Very well."

Instead, Larry took the flashlight from her and shone it ahead, revealing the great glittering expanse of the snowy hill. Under normal circumstances, Fiona might have found the sight of it breathtakingly beautiful, with a constant, steady snowfall coming in at an angle from the dark sky.

However, as they approached the top of the hill, she saw it falling against the crumbled ruin of her beloved home's roof, and any awe went away. No, the house was a sad sight, and it looked like more of the roof had fallen since they'd left. So much was ruined, gone, unrepairable.

Save what you can, she told herself. *Save as much as you can. Don't let the storm take anything else from you, if you can help it.*

As she passed the front of the house, she asked Larry to shine his light through the master bedroom's window, thinking it might be a way in. However, she could see the fallen roof through the cracked glass, drywall and broken joists leaning against the windowsill.

I'm not getting in that way, she thought. *Maybe the hall door will be accessible.*

She led the group around to the back of the house, pushing the wheelbarrow down the cleared path along the exterior wall. The easiest way in now was the kitchen door, so she parked there and opened the toolbox. She grabbed a hammer, put it in the pocket of her coat, then grabbed a crowbar. When she turned, she saw Larry and Zane standing eagerly behind her. It seemed they were all restless and ready to do something useful.

"Okay, be very careful moving the beams," she said. "We don't want to bring anything down on top of us. Always look for exposed nails before you grab anything. I'm heading down the hallway to my bedroom. Where do you two want to start?"

"I'll head to the living room and see what else I can find there," Larry said. "I know there's a closet that we didn't get into last time. Zane, you stick close with me."

"Okay, grab whatever tools you think you'll need and let's get to work. Remember, anything you salvage may end up saving our lives in the days to come." And with that, Fiona picked up the other flashlight, opened the back door, and headed inside.

Snow was already coating the surfaces inside the house. Fiona moved past the table and ducked to enter the gap between the fallen beams in the kitchen doorway. Picking her way along, she turned toward the narrower gap that led down the hall. From there, she inched her way forward, her shoulders and head brushing against the beams as she went.

"I can't believe this is my house now," she muttered, feeling something akin to grief.

Behind her, she heard Larry and Zane talking quietly as they made their way into the living room. She kept going to the end of the hall until she reached her bedroom door. A beam had fallen at an angle to block her way, so she squatted there and pulled out the crowbar. She then proceeded to do exactly what she'd told the others *not* to do, working the crowbar between the doorframe and the fallen beam and pulling at it. Slowly, the beam shifted and moved toward her. She heard the great heap of wood above her creaking, but she was persistent.

Slowly, the beam shifted away from the door, until she had just enough room to reach up and grab the doorknob. She turned it and pushed the door. It opened about two feet before it hit something on the other side.

"No, no, don't push at that board with your hands," she heard Larry call to his son in warning in living room. "It'll bring that whole section down. We can reach the closet behind the coatrack if we go around this other way."

Fiona carefully pulled herself over the beam and through the bedroom door. In the process, she bumped a couple of fallen joists on the other side, and she heard a large object above her move. She stopped, held her breath, and waited a moment to make sure she wasn't about to get crushed.

You don't have to go in here, you know, she told herself.

Yes, I do, she replied. *I need my guns. I need them more than just about anything else in this house.*

She resumed moving forward, sliding carefully along the joists as she entered her bedroom. As she turned in the direction of the dresser, her shoulder bumped a beam and pushed it, and a big section of drywall fell down onto her back. It was more startling than painful, and she bit back a cry.

"No, no, Zane, you can't move that." Larry again.

"I have to, Dad! The closet door is right there!"

This might be a fool's errand, Fiona thought. *I'm going to get us all killed digging crap out of these unstable ruins.*

That thought wasn't enough to make her turn back. Her desperate need for *her stuff* compelled her to continue. The dresser was in front of her now, but more of the fallen roof stood in the way. Fiona went to work with hammer and crowbar to start moving it out of the way, bit by bit, trying to work slowly enough that nothing would suddenly fall on her.

She wasn't successful. More chunks of drywall collapsed onto her back and shoulders. The end of a small board hit her in the back of the head hard enough that she saw stars. She reached under her knit cap to make sure she hadn't split her scalp. No blood. She resumed working, and it took a good hour or more to clear enough space in front of the dresser that she could work her way next to it.

I should have slept on this, she thought. *Maybe I would've planned more carefully if I was rested and thinking clearly.*

She worked her arms up into a narrow gap above the dresser and felt the bottom edge of her gun rack. She grabbed it, lifted it off its nails, and slowly lowered it. The Mossberg shotgun and bolt-action Weatherby rifle were both still sitting on their pegs. It was like finding a pirate's buried treasure, and she was so elated that she practically shook with excitement.

Once she had both of the guns, she tried to get into the dresser drawer for additional ammo. However, she found a large pile of connected beams pressed against the drawer. When she gave it a little push, the whole broken pile around her groaned.

You're not getting in there, she told herself. *Not now. Not like this.*

She checked the guns. Both were loaded, at least. The Mossberg held five shells. The Weatherby's magazine held five rounds as well. It wasn't much, but it would do. Holding the guns in the crook of her arm, Fiona turned and started working her way back through the house. When she finally reached the back door, she found Larry and Zane standing at the wheelbarrow with armfuls of clothing—coats, shirts, pants, socks, and more.

"Well, we got in a couple of closets and grabbed a bunch of clothes," Larry said, dumping his pile in the wheelbarrow. "Zane got hurt a little bit, but nothing too bad."

Zane dumped his pile in the wheelbarrow and held up his right arm. He had a large tear in the sleeve of his coat. When he peeled the edges back, Fiona saw an ugly scrape on his arm.

"That felt really unsafe," Larry said. "I'm not sure we should go back in again."

Fiona sighed. "No, let's call it a night. I want to check on the generator, but then we'll head back. Come on."

She had the flashlight in her coat pocket next to the hammer, and she drew it out now. When she turned the light on, she swept it along the back of the house. And then she stopped, shining the light at the generator shed, and her heart sank. It seemed the house wasn't the only victim of the relentless snow. The generator shed had crumpled inward. What remained looked like a big pile of scrap metal.

"Well, I guess we're not going to retrieve the generator tonight," she said.

"We couldn't bring it back with us anyway," Larry noted. "Wouldn't fit in the wheelbarrow."

Guns and clothing. They'd risked their lives for these things. Fiona picked up the handles of the wheelbarrow and turned it around. As she started down the pathway, she felt embarrassed more than anything. Digging around in an unstable, collapsed house in the dead of night. And why? Because Duke had yelled at her? She was even more tired and sore, her head still hurt, and Zane had a fresh wound on his arm that needed treatment.

Just go back to the barn and sleep it off, she told herself. *You're not thinking clearly. Don't let petty things get to you.*

Larry, being his usual kindhearted self, tried to put a positive spin on things. As they were headed down the slope, he said, "Well, we've got food, clothing, plenty of scrap wood to burn for warmth, a roof over our heads, and the animals. It could be a whole lot worse. We should be okay for a while, right?"

"Yeah, for now," Fiona said.

"How long will we live in the barn?" Zane asked.

"I don't know," Fiona replied. "It doesn't feel like a long-term solution. Sorry, I wish it was, but we're not going to sit around until another roof collapses on us. We'll figure out something else."

"But what can we do?" Larry said. "Where else can we go?"

And Fiona had no answer to that, so she didn't try to provide one.

When they got back to the barn, she found Jarred sitting up and staring at the door, as if waiting for them. She pushed the wheelbarrow inside, and he came toward her.

"What risk did you take to get that stuff?" he asked.

"Perhaps a bit more than I should have," she replied, "But I got my guns. We got some clothes."

"Fiona, please don't hurt yourself," he said. "It's one thing for me to hobble around with my busted leg, but if you get seriously injured, we're going to be in real trouble. Plus, I sort of want you around—*need* you around."

It was the mildest scolding she'd ever received, and he had a look of genuine concern on his face. Fiona was too touched to be annoyed. "Okay, I won't do it again, not unilaterally. But the guns were worth the risk. They can't keep us warm, but we might need them for protection and maybe getting some extra food." She tried to give him a confident smile, but in truth, she felt a bit foolish about the whole endeavor.

51

The laminated map came from the storage shed. Ironically, it had once belonged to Benjy Hartman, Fiona's old stalker, and had the logo of Ohio State Parks & Watercraft in the corner (green hills and trees above a stylized boat riding a wave). Benjy had given the map to her years earlier, boasting that she wasn't supposed to have it because it was for Parks employees. That made her feel incredibly weird about using it. After digging it out of a pile and pulling it off a shelf, she made it about five steps before handing the map to Jarred.

"It covers the entire county in a lot of detail," she said. "If there's anywhere worth going in the county, it'll be on that map."

"This is a high-quality map," Jarred said. "And it's huge. Where do you get a thing like this?"

"You have to have inside connections with the Ohio state government," Fiona replied. "Really unfortunate inside connections."

He seemed to understand and gave her a knowing smile and nod.

They brought the map back to the barn, where the others were sitting around the fire. They'd eaten a late breakfast of canned vegetables and crackers. Hope seemed to have taken full responsibility for the fire. She kept an eye on it, stoking it from time to time, adding bits of wood now and then. Duke sat sullenly on his blanket with his arm in its sling. He'd rolled his sleeve back to reveal the nasty bruise that now went from his wrist almost all the way to his elbow. Myra tended to him, agreed with many of his grumpy comments, and generally tried to keep him calm.

The barn was smoky, but at least it was a few degrees warmer than the outside. The goats and chickens created a constant backdrop of noise and smells, and the wind howled against the walls. From time to time, Fiona heard the walls creak softly in a way that made her shudder

"Folks, we hit the map jackpot," Jarred said, holding up the map. "Fiona has the map to end all maps. Shall we take a look?"

Larry rose and came toward him, taking the map from Jarred as he eased himself down onto the ground beside the fire.

"Do you mind if I open it?" Larry asked Fiona.

"Be my guest," she replied.

Larry, Jarred, and Fiona sat in a circle as Larry unfolded the enormous county map on the floor between them. It was an incredibly detailed map, including topography, physical features, roads, cities, landmarks, and more. Looking at it in the dim firelight was a bit eye-straining, but Fiona bent in close as Larry tapped a small spot a couple of inches from Glencole.

"Aren't we right about here?" he asked.

"Yeah, close enough," Fiona said. "That winding little road there is at the end of my driveway."

"I don't suppose we could just go back to Glencole and find a building with an intact roof," Duke said. "They can't all be collapsing, can they? Heck, the back office and break room in my store would be better than this barn. It's a hard terrazzo floor, but we've got blankets and such."

"Running water? Heat?" Larry asked.

"No, the pipes froze up, and the walls aren't well insulated," Duke said.

"Has anyone been shoveling the snow off the roof?" Jarred asked.

Duke shook his head. "Of course not. But it'll be the same for most of the buildings in town—no water, no electricity, and snow piling up for a month and a half. What's the alternative?"

"Big cities might be dealing with the storm a little better," Jarred said. "We could try to make it to St. Clairsville and see if there are better options."

"St. Clairsville's not *that* big," Larry said. "And it's not that close, not with the highways shut down."

"Fiona, could the Mule make it that far?" Jarred asked.

Fiona considered his question for a moment, then shook her head. "If we used all of the remaining fuel in the greenhouse, we might—*might*—get as far as Blaine, though the engine would probably die a couple miles past Glencole. Anyway, the Mule is a two-seater, with a very small bed in the back. We have eight people and numerous bags and boxes of supplies."

Jarred grunted and pursed his lips. "So we need a place within walking distance."

Larry began tracing roads with his finger. Fiona watched and felt herself sinking into a dark place. The very real prospect of leaving her homestead was like a nightmare she couldn't escape from. Had it really come to this?

What if they left, and I stayed? The thought was fleeting. She pushed it away. Despite her fondness for isolation, there was a significant part of her that feared being alone in this weather. At the very least, she'd grown fond enough of Jarred that she didn't want to be away from him. Yet she was torn.

"Maybe there's some kind of a government shelter that's been set up," Duke said. "They're not going to let people freeze to death with no electricity and no heat, and if the government starts housing people, it'll be in an official building with a roof over it that isn't going to fall on top of us."

"If the government had set up a shelter, we would have heard about it on the radio," Jarred said. "All we've heard on those rare occasions when we get a radio station is that the storm shows no sign of letting up."

"What if there's another option besides running to the next town?" Larry said. His index finger had left the road and was heading across a large field toward some high hills south of Glencole. "Not a shelter or a house or the back office of a grocery store—not any kind of building at all?"

Yeah, there's another option, Fiona thought. *We stay right here and make it work somehow, by God.*

But even as she thought it, she heard the wind whistling through the walls, and a soft crackle went up the wood toward the ceiling. She kept the thought to herself.

"What did you have in mind, Larry?" Jarred asked. "What option could there possibly be that doesn't require a building of some sort?"

Larry stopped at a spot in the hills and tapped the map. "What about a place with a sturdy roof over our heads that will never collapse on us? A roof that can handle all the snow in the world? But also a safe place that's out of the wind, with plenty of room to store our stuff, move around, even have some privacy?"

"A vault in the bank, maybe?" Duke said, and attempted a laugh.

Zane leaned in close to the map, staring at the spot his dad was pointing at. "Snowbird Caverns," he read. "Is that what you're talking about, Dad?"

"That's right," Larry replied. "It's a natural cavern system that's mostly untouched. They do a few guided tours. I've been there myself. It was during a hunting trip a few years ago, and the place is really impressive. The temperature is a steady fifty-five degrees year-round. Not only that, but it has a water table inside."

The suggestion hung heavily in the room for a few seconds. Fiona could see that it didn't sit well with anyone.

"Living like literal cavemen," Lana said. She had a blanket around her shoulders, and she pulled it little tighter against her throat. "Is that what you're suggesting?"

"Well, in a sense, yes," Larry said. He looked up from the map, glanced at his wife, then fixed his gaze on Fiona. The others were looking at her as well, as if waiting to see what she would say. Even Ramses bleated in the background, as if asking the question.

"I've heard of Snowbird Caverns," she said. "It's fairly close to Glencole, but I've never been there."

"I've been there," Zane said. "We went on a middle school field trip for earth science. I don't think I'd want to live in there, but I do remember that it's pretty huge. The guide told us the cavern system is so large that they haven't even fully explored it."

"So, plenty of space to spread out and live the good life with the bats and the guano and the cave spiders," Duke Cooper said, with a snort of contempt. "I might prefer to have the roof collapse on us again."

"The steady temperature would be a plus," Jarred said. "Access to clean water would be another. But living in a damp, dark cave wouldn't be easy."

Larry tapped the map. "It doesn't look *that* far on the map here. There's a river in the way, but I see a bridge that goes over the river. We can make it. Anyway, that's my suggestion. I know it sounds crazy, but the snow's going to keep falling. Buildings aren't safe. The caverns will put a roof over our heads. I mean, there's a reason why our ancestors lived in caves, but…it's whatever you think, Fiona. I'll trust your judgment."

"Surely we could find a safe building in Glencole," Lana said. "That's better than living in a cave. Every roof in the world is not going to fall down."

All eyes were still on Fiona. *They want me to make the decision*, she realized. The weight of that responsibility was smothering. *They don't realize what leaving this place will mean to me.*

Well, maybe Jarred did. He reached over and gently laid his hand on her shoulder, as if to comfort her. Fiona glanced around the barn. The tarp overhead flapped in the wind, the haze of smoke struggled to escape the crude chimney hole they'd made in one corner, and she could hear the continual creaking of the wood walls as if they were trying to remind her of what had just happened to her home. And whether she liked it or not, she knew what the answer had to be.

Just say it and deal with the emotions later, she told herself.

"We can't live in the greenhouse. It's simply too small. We can't live in the storage buildings. They're even smaller," she said. "Plus, we're running out of fuel. The house is unsalvageable, and the barn is doomed. I hate the thought of leaving my homestead, but I guess living in a cavern makes more sense than staying here or just moving from building to building. So, fine, I say we go for it. Snowbird Caverns will be our destination. We can ride out the storm there, however long that takes. I'll understand if anyone decides not to go with us."

"Is it *going* to end?" Duke grumbled.

"Hopefully," Fiona replied. "Surely, it must. Anyway, I think that's the plan. Snowbird Caverns."

She heaved a great sigh and let her decision sink in for a few seconds. Duke made a soft clicking sound, as if he wanted to say something, but whatever it was, he held back for once. Hope was stoking the small fire, but she looked like she was on the verge of crying.

"I don't suppose we could take the Mule to this cave," Lana said. "I know you said it wouldn't reach Blaine, but…"

"It's almost as far as Blaine, but in a different direction," Fiona said. "Same problem. And, like I said, the Mule is tiny. We can't carry everyone, much less all of our supplies or our many animals. I think the Mule is out of the question. I'm sorry."

"So we just have to carry all of our stuff on our backs like a bunch of hobos?" Duke said.

"No, we'll rig up sleds with as much of our stuff as we can carry," Fiona said. "We'll have the goats pull them. Ramses is used to it. The females aren't, but they'll just have to learn. We'll need every goat to help pull the weight."

"We're going to lead a bunch of goats across the snowy wilderness to a cavern?" Lana said. "Is that really our plan?"

"I guess it is," Fiona said. "It shouldn't be a problem. Does anyone disagree with this idea? Speak now, because if we're doing it, we have a lot of prep work ahead of us."

Lana began chewing furiously on a thumbnail. Zane was rocking back and forth. Hope was endlessly stoking embers that didn't need to be stoked. Myra was rubbing her loud circles, and Duke was breathing a little louder than was necessary through his nostrils.

"I know it must be hard for you to leave this wonderful place you've built over the last fifteen years," Jarred said. "I wish we could pack it all up and bring it with us, but it'll be here waiting. Someday, when this damned storm finally ends, we'll come back and fix everything that broke. In the meantime, I say we head for the caverns. Steady temperatures year round will make it so much easier on us."

He'd managed to make her feel better about the whole horrible thing. A weight was lifted. Yes, someday they would come back. Someday, she would rebuild. There was hope. They were just trying to get through the present crisis. "Thanks, Jarred. What about the rest of you? Are you comfortable with this plan? I want everyone to have a voice about this."

"Not comfortable, no," Lana Bishop said, "but I'll go along with it."

"I guess I'm okay with it," Zane said. "At least the caverns look cool. You people just wait until you see the inside. It's all misty, and there are big rock formations and pools and bottomless pits."

"Bottomless pits?" Hope said. "That's not safe. But if it's warmer in the cave, then I want to go there."

That left the Coopers, and when they didn't give an answer, Larry finally reared up from the map and looked at them. Fiona was glad he did it, so she didn't have to.

"Duke? Myra?" he said.

Duke groaned. Fiona tensed, expecting a fight, but then he said, "Well, if that's the best option, then so be it. I'm tempted to head back to Glencole anyway, even if it's just me and Myra, but I remember what it was like before we came here. So cold. I'm so sick of feeling the cold air. So sick of it, my God. Until this damned storm ends, a cave is no worse than any other place."

Good for you, Duke, Fiona thought. *Back to your old less-crotchety self.*

"Well, if Duke says it's okay, then I guess I'm fine with it," Myra said. "Speaking as a medical professional, the warm, damp air down in that cavern may put us at risk of respiratory problems, so we'll need to take care of ourselves and look for symptoms."

"I'll trust your expertise about it, Myra," Fiona said. She bent over the map again. "Okay, it looks like the best and fastest route will take us across the field behind the barn, around this forested area here, and then pretty much due south until we reach this line of hills." She traced the path with her finger. "Because of the changing wind, there are a lot of deep snowdrifts out there, but in some places, the snow is actually pretty shallow. I think if we keep to the shallow places, the terrain shouldn't be too hard for the goats to navigate."

"I don't suppose anyone found the radio in the ruins of the house?" Jarred asked. "It would be good to try to get a weather report before we head out."

"I'm afraid not," Fiona replied. "It was on a shelf in the living room, in a corner that fully collapsed. Let's just assume the weather is going to be blizzard-like conditions and make our preparations accordingly."

"Sounds like a smart idea," Jarred said. "I think it's important to reiterate that our trek to Snowbird is a temporary measure, a warmer place to wait out the cold, but we can always come back here if it turns out to be inhospitable. And we certainly *will* return once the storm lets up."

Fiona nodded at him. "Exactly. Okay, let's get ready."

As Larry refolded the map, Fiona rose, brushing off the seat of her pants. She knew keeping busy would help her face the moment of abandonment. The emotion would catch up to her eventually, but she would worry about that later.

Just do what needs to be done. Get the sleds ready, and don't let any regret take root. Not yet, she told herself.

"Okay, we're going to construct a few sleds to pull our gear," she said. "We'll use the old toboggan, wood and sheet metal, whatever we can find. The more we take with us, the better, so let's get to work. Who wants to help me come up with a design for the sleds?"

Hope immediately dropped the stick she'd been using to stoke the fire, as if someone had flipped a switch in her mind. "I can help with that," she said. "Please? I love designing machines, even simple ones."

"I can vouch for her," Jarred said. "The kid takes after me in the engineering department."

"Okay, come on, Hope." Fiona beckoned her. "We'll go through the stacks of stuff we salvaged and see what we can come up with."

Hope bounded up from the fire to join her. Fortunately, Fiona had made sure to create orderly stacks from all of the bits and pieces they'd gathered in the barn. Metal in one pile, wood in another, cloth in a third. Hope approached the stacks, tapping her chin with one finger. She seemed deep in thought.

"You think it over," Fiona said. "I'll be right back."

As Hope went from stack to stack, Fiona walked to the back corner of the barn and retrieved the old toboggan that she'd once used to reach Glencole. It was in decent enough shape, not especially large but sturdy and already attached to ropes. She dragged it toward the front of the barn, then grabbed a couple of smaller snow sleds that hadn't seen action in years. By the time she'd lined these things up near the front door, Hope was ready. The teen clapped her hands and turned to Fiona.

"Okay, I've got a few ideas," she said. "We'll need screws, duct tape, glue, and some ropes."

"We have all of those," Fiona replied. "Let me get them."

In the end, Hope's design suggestions proved rather ingenious. Working together, Hope and Fiona were able to create one enormous sled using old rain gutters as runners, securing sheet metal between them, and strengthening the frame with old fence pickets. Then they used additional sheet metal and wood to enlarge the toboggan. Finally, they connected the smaller sleds together and added runners to the bottom. In the end, they had three sturdy sleds of varying sizes—small, medium, and large—attached to ropes and harnesses. The largest of the three was almost too wide to pull through the door.

Larry, Jarred, and Zane helped with the construction work, so it went pretty fast. Once they were done, Fiona and Hope stood back to admire their work.

"Well, what do you think?" Fiona said to Hope. "Our design looks pretty good. What do you think? Are you satisfied with the end result?"

"Yeah, I think so," Hope replied, grinning proudly. "We make a good team, I guess."

"Yes, we do." Fiona turned to the others. "Okay, it's time to load up. This part will require all hands on deck. We'll take as much as we can fit on the sleds, but everything needs to be packed well."

Duke was still sitting on his horse blanket and glowering into the fire. "Does that mean me, too?"

"I'm afraid so, Mr. Cooper," Fiona said. "You have one good arm, and we could use your help."

"We're all in this together," Jarred added, moving to stand beside Fiona. "Let's make it a group effort."

Duke glanced at Myra, grunted, then picked himself up.

"Just keep your bad arm in the sling," Myra said. "You'll be alright."

Fortunately, once he got moving, he didn't mope or hang back. He joined the others as they began the long, tedious process of packing and preparing their stuff. They loaded the smallest sled with tools, matches, as well as blankets, the last gallon of gasoline in a plastic jerry can, some scraps for possible repairs, and their meager medical supplies. The medium-sized sled got all of their clothes and toiletries, of which there were many, and the enlarged toboggan was reserved for food supplies, potable water, and a single jerry can of gasoline taken from the greenhouse heater's tank.

Fiona and Jarred spent a good hour carefully bundling seeds and seedlings, making room for them on the toboggan alongside dry goods, canned vegetables, the remaining crops from the greenhouse, and two large plastic jugs of clean water. In the end, they left just enough room for a couple of people to sit down on the large toboggan in case someone wound up being unable to walk. Otherwise, the sleds were as fully loaded as they safely could be.

"I can't believe we're going to *walk* all the way there," Duke said, as the group stood before the loaded sleds, afternoon sunlight streaming through the gaps in the barn ceiling. "Suddenly, this doesn't seem like such a good idea. This barn is drafty and falling apart, but maybe it's not so bad."

"We'll take it slow and steady," Fiona said. "We'll have to. We might need to clear the path in some places, even if we stick to the shallowest snow."

"And everyone still feels good about this?" Duke said. "Going to this cave, I mean."

"We all discussed it," Jarred said. "You said you were fine with it. Why did you wait until we're all packed and loaded to complain?"

"It seemed sort of theoretical before," Duke said. "I guess the reality is sinking in that we're really doing this."

"To answer your question, no, I don't feel good about it. I doubt anyone feels good about it," Fiona replied. She turned to him and gave him a hard look. He dropped his gaze to the floor. "But unless you have a better option, this is what we're doing. We'll set out tomorrow morning, so get plenty of rest. I expect it to take us a full day to get from here to the caverns. We can survive a one-day hike, if we're careful and cautious. Unless you decide you don't want to go. I'm not trying to force anybody to do something they're not comfortable with."

Duke turned to his wife, and Myra frowned at him. "Well, we have to go, Duke," Myra said. "We're not staying here by ourselves, and if someone gets hurt, they'll need my help."

"Okay, okay," Duke grumbled, swiping a hand in the air, as if batting at invisible flies. "I just wanted to double-check. No harm in that."

And with that, Fiona stepped past the Coopers and went to check on the goats. Jarred was standing to one side. She noticed that he was putting a bit of weight on his bad foot.

"Be careful," she said, pointing at the foot.

"It's not so bad," he said. "I think the bone is partially healed. It's been a month and a half. Anyway, I have to retrain it to bear my weight again. I don't want to hobble on a crutch all the way to the caverns."

"Just take it easy," she said. "Don't make me report you to our resident nursing assistant for a proper scolding."

"Anything but that," he said with a laugh.

After they finished packing and preparing the sleds, they settled down for a final meal in the barn. Fiona was in a bleak state of mind, trying desperately not to think about what the morning would bring. Her homestead was practically her identity. It was harder to leave than she realized, even if Jarred had reassured her repeatedly that it was a temporary abandonment. She didn't join much in the conversation that night, and as soon as they were done eating, she climbed into the hayloft to sleep.

Anxiety followed her into her dreams, even as the barn roof above her sang her a gentle lullaby of creaking and cracking wood, and she awoke in the early morning sunlight with a pounding headache.

This is it, she said, sitting up in the hayloft. Larry and Lana were lying together on a blanket across the way. Zane was curled up near the ladder, and Hope was on her stomach in the back. Fiona made her way to the ladder, stepped over Zane, and climbed down. Without Hope to tend it, the fire had gone out. Duke and Myra were on their blanket near the ashes, and Jarred was sleeping beside the toboggan, as if guarding it.

Smoke was still lying curled up in a shadowy corner of the barn. The poor dog had clearly been traumatized by the collapse of the house, and he wouldn't leave his spot in the corner, even when Fiona whistled and snapped her fingers at him.

"Okay, everyone," Fiona said loudly, clapping her hands to rouse them all. "It's time to go. Get up! We're leaving."

Let's get this over with, she thought. *So fast that I can't really feel it until I'm far down the road.*

52

Like Lot's wife, Fiona had a fierce desire to turn and look back longingly at her homestead as they trudged away. Unlike Lot's wife, however, she successfully resisted the urge. She had hold of Ramses's reins, guiding him as he pulled the toboggan, and that at least gave her something to fix her attention on. Four of the female goats, harnessed in pairs, pulled the medium-sized sled, with Larry holding their reins as he walked along beside them. Finally, the other females pulled the smallest sled, with Zane and Hope holding their reins. All of the humans walked, to spare the goats from having to pull them. Only Smoke got to ride. The anxious dog was curled up on blankets on the smallest sled, his muzzle tucked between his paws.

"This is going to be more challenging than I thought," Larry Bishop said, shouting into the wind to be heard.

It was a stark and haunting landscape, utterly alien. Fiona no longer recognized the field and forest that had once been the backdrop of her homestead. As she had expected, the depth of the snow varied tremendously. This seemed to be a product of the ever-changing strength and angle of the wind, coupled with an unnatural snowfall pattern. In many places, it was at least four feet deep, but in some places, it was only less than a foot and somewhat more compact from the constant pressure of the wind. The trick was finding and sticking to the shallow spots, but even the shallow snow was difficult to trudge through. After what seemed like forever, they'd only gone maybe a hundred yards.

"This just isn't going to work," Fiona said. "The snow hasn't been compacted enough for our weight. The goats can walk on top of the snow in the shallow parts, but we just sink in every couple of steps."

Fiona called them to a stop, and they huddled together in the hostile landscape.

"The snowy landscape is worse than it was when I broke my leg," Jarred noted. He had the additional challenge of using a crutch. "Speaking as a mechanical engineer, I think the problem here is that we need to distribute our weight more broadly."

"How do you propose we do that?" Larry said, brushing fresh snow off his shoulders.

"What we need are a good set of snowshoes," Jarred continued. "We have to adapt to the environment and climate, just like the indigenous peoples who lived in the Arctic for thousands of years."

"Do we have what we need to make snowshoes?" Fiona asked. Currently, she was standing in snow up to her mid-calves, huddled against a sharp wind blowing in from the northwest.

"I'll bet Hope and I could come up with a design," Jarred said, turning to his daughter. "Another father-daughter project. What do you say?"

"Oh, sure," Hope replied, pinching the hood of her coat tightly against her face. "We could use the extra wood and rope we brought. They won't look pretty, but they'll get the job done. You just have to expand the surface area of your shoes for better weight distribution."

"See? There you go," Jarred said. "I'll bet we could get it done right here, right now."

Fiona pulled on Ramses's reins to bring him to a stop. Despite his temperament, he didn't require much convincing. They brought all of the goats to a stop in the middle of the field south of the homestead, as Hope and Jarred trudged back to the smallest sled. Larry moved to join them. Smoke briefly raised his head from his nest of blankets and looked around, but then he quickly dropped back down again.

"We should have thought about this before we left the barn, damn it," Duke snarled, hugging his bruised arm like it was his very own infant son. "We spent hours building these damned sleds, and we never thought about snowshoes?"

"I thought about them," Hope said. "A while ago."

"You should have said something then," Duke replied. "We're ill-prepared for this journey, folks. We lack coordination. Problems are solved on the fly. It's going to get us in trouble sooner or later."

"Yes, problems are solved on the fly sometimes," Fiona said, tightly. "That's life, Duke. Some issues are bound to be overlooked in a chaotic situation. Fortunately, we've got really smart people with us, so we can handle it."

Hope, Jarred, and Larry rooted through their supplies and hastily cobbled together simple snowshoes using scrap wood and ropes. They then strapped a pair to each person's shoes. The end result was crude but effective. Fiona found that she could now stand on top of the snow without sinking more than a couple of inches.

"Good work, you guys," Fiona said, taking her position beside Ramses and grabbing his reins. "Jarred and Hope, you two make a fine engineering team, and Larry, you do good work, too."

Jarred traded a proud look with his daughter. Fiona tugged Ramses's reins and got the big goat moving again.

"Okay, let's go," she said. "We wasted a good hour or two trying to walk through the snow in boots, but at least the problem is now solved. Good engineering is the answer to most of life's inconveniences. I guess that's the lesson for today."

Hope gave her a big smile as she took her position next to Zane. The sleds were moving again, but they were going faster now. Just adding more surface area to the soles of their shoes had made a world of difference. The goats were still struggling a bit, but they handled it better than the humans.

They'd gone another hundred yards or so when Larry cleared his throat loudly and turned to Fiona. "I have an idea," he said. "If you don't want to do it, I understand, but what if we took a little detour toward Glencole. Not all the way into town, mind you. Lana and I own a flower and garden center on the outskirts. It's cold and dark, the pipes are frozen, and there's no furniture, so it's not a long-term solution by any means. But we've still got some supplies there, and we could rest for a bit out of the wind. Getting there will take us a little out of the way, but it shouldn't be too bad. What do you think?"

Fiona heard Duke grumbling, but she turned to Jarred. He shrugged at her and said, "I'm open to it if you are."

"Garden supplies might come in handy down the road," Fiona said, after a moment. "I guess we'd better do it."

"I'll show the way," Larry replied. "Follow me."

He pulled the medium-sized sled in front of the other sleds in order to guide them. As Fiona and Ramses fell in behind him, she felt a strange sense of déjà vu. She'd seen a lifeless icy landscape like this before. Yes, in a documentary about scientists living at the North Pole. How could this be Ohio? Everything was disappearing.

As slow hours passed, and they moved out beyond the forest to follow a path parallel to the old highway, she saw great lumps of snow in the distance that she thought were homes. Some of them had chimneys or roof peaks poking out of the snow. Others were completely buried. In the open fields, she saw snowdrifts that were so huge they looked like dunes in the Sahara.

It was cold, slow, and miserable, and for a long time, no one spoke as they trudged forward. The goats needed occasional coaxing, especially the girls, as they had little experience pulling sleds. In a strange twist of fate, Ramses wound up being the easiest to control. The ornery male goat knew this routine, and he surrendered to it.

At some point—she didn't see when—Duke gave up trying to walk and took the available space on the large toboggan. Myra kept walking for a while, then finally joined him. Fiona decided to let it go for now, though she was annoyed. If anyone deserved a spot on the large sled, it was Jarred.

If Ramses starts to slow down, I'm kicking Duke off, she told herself.

For most of the morning, they went in what felt like a southerly direction, but Larry gradually turned them more to the east. By now, they were across the road and moving through wild lands that Fiona didn't recognize. Indeed, the endless white was disorienting, and she couldn't gauge the position of the sun with the unbroken gray expanse overhead.

"Larry, how good is your sense of direction?" she asked. "Is this going to take us to the garden center near Glencole?"

"Well, I think so," he said, scanning from left to right. "Everything looks the same now. No landmarks to guide us. If I didn't know better, I'd think we were lost in Antarctica."

"I was thinking the North Pole," Fiona replied.

That, at least, got a chuckle out of Jarred, who was otherwise struggling with his crutch.

Larry pointed off to the left, at a broad field with a long dent in the middle. "I'm pretty sure that depression there is the old culvert that runs along the edge of the farmland just outside of town. If we follow it for a while, we'll find a few buildings on the southwest corner of Glencole. One of them is our flower and garden center."

"Okay, I'm trusting your judgment, sir," Fiona said.

They kept going, one slow step at a time, the landscape barely changing around them no matter how much time passed. Finally, more lumps appeared in the distance. Buildings. Larry waved his free hand over his head and pointed at them.

"There it is," he said. "We made it!"

They'd gone at least a few miles, and it felt like more than half the day was gone. The prospect of being able to stop for a while made Fiona's whole body cry out in desperation. She was cold, shivering, and still had a headache. Just getting out of the snow for a while seemed wonderful.

"Good job, Larry," Fiona shouted back.

"Larry the Trailblazer," Jarred added.

Larry raised a fist in exaggerated triumph.

As they drew near the buildings, the garden center became obvious. Because of its sharply angled roof, much of the snow had fallen off. Fiona could see large glass panels set into the roof at one end. The top edge of the business sign stuck out of a mound of snow as well. At least it had an intact roof and walls. That would provide some shelter. But as they pulled up alongside the building, Fiona felt terribly discouraged. Had this whole trip been a mistake, after all? They'd only traveled a few miles, and it had taken them more than half the day. Of course, she wasn't sure how much time had actually passed because the unbroken cloud cover hid the position of the sun.

Larry pulled the goats to a stop near a half-buried door. He handed the reins to Lana as he fished in the inner pocket of his long coat.

"I don't know why we don't just stay here," Duke Cooper said. "The building seems stable enough. You've got plants in there, right? We could make a go of it, couldn't we?"

Larry fished a key ring out of his pocket and used one of the keys to unlock the deadbolt on the door. "Well, let's see what sort of a state it's in." He unlocked the door itself, pushing it open into the dim carpeted room beyond. "Come on in, folks. Let's see what we can salvage. There'll be at least a few things we can use."

Fiona had pulled Ramses to a stop behind the other cart, and she tied the reins to a nearby mailbox post. Jarred hobbled over to join her, and they entered the building together. Smoke finally bounded up from his nest of blankets and rushed inside after them. The garden center had a small carpeted shop in front with shelves, display cases, and a glass counter. In the back was a greenhouse separated by a glass wall and doors.

Since the walls of the greenhouse were glass, they had a broad view of the interior. It wasn't good. The ceaseless, bitter cold combined with general neglect had killed most of the plants. Fiona saw withered leaves, brown and crumbling flowers, shriveled stalks. It was a shame, because it looked like

Larry and Lana had had a pretty good selection of plants at one time, with various kinds of trees, many kinds of flowers, decorative shrubs, and more. Smoke was running around the garden center, sniffing everything and panting.

"It's about what I expected," Larry said, slowly crossing the room toward the greenhouse doors. "Without us here to keep the plants watered, fed, and warm, they've all given up the ghost."

"I'll bet I know something that's still in good shape," Lana said, coming up behind him. She was patting the snow off her shoulders, sleeves, and hood. "Something that should come in handy. Wait for me." And with that, she pulled off her crude snowshoes and hurried down one of the aisles, disappearing through a side door.

Hope and Zane entered the building next, their snowshoes clopping loudly on the thin carpet and the concrete beneath. While looking around the room, Fiona noticed a particular shelf to her left. It was partway down one of the aisles, a display case containing numerous seed packets arranged alphabetically.

"We should save all of those seeds," she said. "We might find a way to grow some of them eventually."

"Good thinking," Jarred said. "Hope, Zane, you want to help me collect them?"

The three of them approached the careful rows of seed packets. Just then, Lana returned, pushing a small shopping cart piled high with bamboo cane. "Here we go," she said. "This bamboo is still good."

"What did you have in mind?" Fiona asked.

"Well, for one thing, now that we're out of the weather, we could build some better snowshoes with it," Lana replied. "I mean, all we've done is tie scrap wood to our shoes, but this bamboo would make something more comfortable and more durable. What do you think?"

"Sounds good to me," Fiona replied. "Anything we can do to make the rest of the trip faster, more comfortable, and safer will be worth it."

"Well, great then," Lana said, pushing the shopping cart toward the glass counter. "Hope, I could really use your input on the design of some sturdy bamboo snowshoes. You seem to excel at this sort of thing."

Hope had been gathering seed packets, but she came running at the opportunity to help with the snowshoe design. Just then, Duke and Myra came through the door. His mouth was moving when he entered the room, and Fiona caught the last of what she assumed was some complaining. As soon as he was inside, he began working his injured arm out from inside his coat.

"You should try to keep your arm warm," Fiona noted. "It'll heal faster that way, and it will certainly feel better."

"I think I know my body better than you do," Duke snapped. "The muscles have started to tighten up because I'm not moving it enough. I need to stretch it out regularly. Myra agrees."

He pulled the arm out of the sling, revealing the ugly bruise that ran along most of his forearm. As he slowly stretched it out, he gasped in pain.

"Now, maybe Fiona's right, Duke," Myra said, grabbing the strap of the sling. "You shouldn't be waving it around in the open like that."

"I'm doing nothing of the sort," he replied. For some reason, he was headed over to the shopping cart, gazing fixedly at the big stack of bamboo, as if something about it appealed to him. "All I'm doing is loosening up the elbow joint. Leave me alone."

His good hand went into his jacket pocket and produced a black folding knife. Fiona found his behavior odd enough that she kept an eye on him while the others went to work. When he reached the shopping cart, Duke grabbed one of the smallest stalks of bamboo. He propped it against his elbow, then began whittling the tip with his pocketknife.

Before she could ask him what he was making, he realized she was watching him and said, "If there's one thing I learned in Desert Storm, it's that a sharpened bamboo stake can always come in handy." Now it became clear that he was simply trimming the end of the stalk down to a long, sharp point.

Fiona found it odd, but he hadn't done anything too alarming. He was grumpy, not dangerous. "Just don't jab yourself with it," she said.

"Oh, I won't," he replied.

Once Jarred and Zane finished gathering seed packets, placing a generous number of them in a cloth bag, they joined Lana and Hope. Larry joined them as well, and they went to work making the snowshoes. It was actually a rather ingenious design, using bamboo to create a long teardrop-shaped framework, then stretching smaller strips of bamboo across the gap. It looked a little like the traditional snowshoes made by Inuit. They were maybe two feet long, half as wide.

Still, making them took forever, and Fiona was restless. After a while, she began to pace the small shop area, walking the aisles but looking at nothing in particular. Finally, as the quality of daylight began to change outside, she had to admit the truth to herself.

"I think we'll have to spend the night here," she said.

She turned to face the others. Everyone was working on the snowshoes now except Duke, who had seated himself on a stool behind the counter. His arm was still out of the sling but resting on his right knee, and he had that weird sharpened stake in his other hand. At her words, the others turned to look at her. Smoke had find a nice spot under a shelves of gardening books, but he stared at Fiona fixedly, as if waiting for her to make sense of it all.

"That's just as well," Jarred said. "Breaking up the trip over two days will make it easier on us, and on the animals."

"I do wish we could start a campfire in here for some warmth," Lana added, "but this place is just a bit too flammable. Still, I'm ready for sleep, so I don't mind."

"I can rest here as easily as I could rest in a cave," Duke said. "So it doesn't make a difference one way or the other to me."

"Fine. Let's settle in for the night," Fiona said. "We'll leave at first light."

53

They were well-rested, at least. That made the delay almost worth it. Fiona had certainly found sleeping in the garden center easier than trying to bed down in the uninsulated barn. Ultimately, they'd had to bring the animals inside, which had quickly stunk up the place. They penned them in the greenhouse area, where the mess they made was less of an issue.

"Not that it much matters," Larry noted, gazing at the animals through the glass, as Ramses tore apart a small Bradford pear tree in his attempt to see if it was edible. "I doubt this place will ever be a functioning business again. Everything's dead in the greenhouse. It might as well collapse once we leave."

"We can always collect insurance and rebuild," Lana said.

"We'll have to build from the ground up," Larry replied. "I'm exhausted thinking about it."

Fiona knew it would become a problem if people starting speaking and thinking pessimistically. Thus, right before they all turned in for the night, she made herself give what she intended to be an inspiring speech. She hoped no one picked up on the forced enthusiasm. Jarred, in particular, was seated on a box at the end of an aisle, giving her a funny little half-smile as she spoke. If anyone knew how much she was really struggling, he did.

"Tomorrow, we'll have better snowshoes, thanks to Lana and Hope," she said. How was one to stand when giving an inspiring speech? She tried pacing a little, but that felt odd. Then she tried standing still with her hands clasped behind her back. Finally, she chose to sit on a ledge near the greenhouse doors. "That'll make it easier for everyone to walk. The goats will be warmer and well-fed. What I'm trying to say is that we should have a much better day tomorrow. It might seem strange to work so hard just to reach a cavern, but we'll have greater protection from the weather down there. A stable temperature, no snow, places to store our supplies. It's going to be better. Life is going to be better for us. We'll have a safer, warmer place to wait out this storm, however long that takes. So don't despair." She ended somewhat lamely with, "Okay, let's get some sleep, if we can."

"Thanks, Fiona," Jarred replied, giving her a thumbs up. "We all needed to hear that, especially after our brutally cold walk today. Life is going to be better. We have to believe that."

Most people nodded at Fiona, all except for Duke. The old man had a scowl on his face, and he was rocking back and forth. Fiona expected a sarcastic response from him, but for once, he kept his mouth shut. After that, everyone turned in. They'd make pallets on the carpeted floor using any cloth they could find: blankets, tablecloths, tarps. It was good enough.

Fiona was the first to awaken in the morning, when the sun was just barely touching the sky beyond the windows. She heard the others snoring and shifting around her under their blankets. Duke Cooper's championship snore was on full display. Fiona gave them another half an hour to sleep, even as she rose and began gathering their supplies. Only when the sun was fully up, the light shining brightly through the windows, did she finally rouse them. She hated to do it, knowing they had a rough day ahead of them. She found Smoke wandering around the room, still sniffing at everything, clearly confused by this new location.

"I'm tempted to stay here," Duke said, one pain-filled eye glaring through a gap in the blanket that covered him. "The rest of you can journey on to the cave without me."

"Now, now," Myra said. For once, she didn't go along with him. Whipping his blanket aside, she began prodding him. "We decided we're all going to stick together. Remember? We're not going to back out now."

"You wouldn't last long here," Larry said, sitting up and rubbing his face. "There's little food. You'd have to hike into town and try to scrounge up enough to eat, and we all experienced the futility of that before we went to the homestead. Plus, it's at least as cold as the barn in here thanks to all the big windows."

"We're going, Duke," Myra said, "and that's final. Now, let me check your arm before we head out today."

He grumbled under his breath and turned his injured arm toward her.

Pairs of snowshoes were lined up on the glass counter. Fiona grabbed a pair, checked to make sure the straps were in good shape, then headed to the greenhouse door. "Don't forget your snowshoes, everyone. I'll round up the animals."

It took a while to get everyone moving. Fiona, Larry, and Jarred harnessed the animals to the sleds, while Lana helped everyone put on their snowshoes. Hope and Zane loaded up the sleds with additional supplies from the garden center: seed packets, blankets, a big bundle of bamboo. Then it was time to go. Fiona noted a few longing looks toward the garden center door—not just from Duke Cooper—as they headed out.

No, we're not stopping here, she thought. *They want it. I can see that, but we have a destination in mind, and we can make it.*

Larry and Lana led the way, guiding the she-goats in a broad arc, as they circled around the garden center and set off toward the south. Fiona had no trouble getting Ramses to follow this morning. He seemed full of restless energy, and she had to constantly keep him in check so he wouldn't move too fast for the walkers.

"How are the snowshoes?" Lana asked, after a few minutes. She seemed anxious to learn if the design was a hit with the others.

"Takes a bit of getting used to," Zane said. The teen was trudging alongside the small sled. "But they're better than the ones we used yesterday. They stay on top of the snow easier. You and Hope did pretty good."

"They work great," Jarred said. He seemed to be using the walking stick less this morning. Though he still held it in his hand, he rarely put his full weight on it. "You improved on our original design."

"We had access to better materials, that's all," Hope said. "The bamboo was Lana's idea, though, and that was really smart."

Lana grinned proudly, and Larry gave her an affectionate pat on the back.

After leaving the outskirts of Glencole, they headed across a broad field toward a line of distant hills. The wind was blowing harder this morning, which made things more unpleasant, but they pressed on.

At first, the snowshoes felt awkward to Fiona. She kept stepping on them, and even pulled them off her shoes a couple of times. Finally, she learned that she had to take wider steps than normal, and that solved the problem.

They traveled a few good hours throughout the morning, fighting the wind, until they eventually spotted an enormous snowdrift piled against a row of trees. It was so high that it towered over them, forming an effective windbreak, so Fiona called them to a stop on the leeward side. They circled the sleds for even better protection.

"We can't linger long," Fiona said, as she broke open a big container of feed for the goats. "Have something to eat, take a drink, and rest for a little bit, but don't get too comfortable."

"God forbid we should get comfortable," Duke Cooper said, sitting on the edge of the big sled. He laughed when he said it, as if he wanted to sound like he was joking. But Fiona heard the sharp edge beneath the laughter.

"We don't have a ton of travel food, you know," Larry said, breaking out some large bags of trail mix. "Not much that can be eaten on the road. It's mostly ingredients and raw materials that require cooking."

"The trail mix will do," Fiona said. "Half a cup to each person."

"Half a cup of trail mix?" Lana said, retightening the straps on her snowshoes. "That's not much."

"No, but it'll be enough for now," Fiona replied. "We'll have a nice big meal once we get settled in the cavern."

"We could build a small fire in the circle here," Hope said. The teen had already marked out a small circle in the snow. "It'll be good for us, and for the animals, to warm up a little. We'll last longer during the afternoon that way."

"Building a small fire on top of all of this snow?" Fiona replied, scooping feed into a feed bag and carrying it to Ramses. "Won't it just melt all the way down and make a hole in the snow?"

"We can make it work," Jarred said. "Hope, you'll have to lay something flat on top of the snow, something that won't burn, and build the fire on top of that. Use that noggin of yours. See what you can come up with.

Hope nodded brightly. "Okay, I'll figure it out."

"Just keep the fire small," Fiona said. "We won't be here long."

Hope nodded and dashed off toward the nearest trees. As Fiona fed the animals, Hope and Zane created the fire. They used a flat piece of metal from their scrap supplies, laying it on top of the snow as the foundation of the firepit. Then they built a small pyramid of sticks and stuffed some kindling inside. It took a minute or two to get the kindling to burn, but the windbreak helped protect it from the elements. Once the flame caught, they continually fed it until they had a small but comfortably warm fire burning.

Indeed, that small amount of heat made a world of difference. Soon, everyone had gathered around it, huddling together. The animals were brought closer as well so they could feel at least some of the warmth while they ate.

"You've got a smart kid over here," Larry said to Jarred. "You've taught her well, Dad." He gestured toward Hope while he munched on his serving of trail mix. "You two are just a font of good ideas."

"I've taught her well, but she's also taught herself quite a bit," Jarred said.

Hope grinned proudly, as her father gave her a hug. Unfortunately, it didn't take long for Fiona to see what a danger the fire was. The warmth made them all reluctant to move on. Smoke was curled up between Hope and Zane, snoozing comfortably with a belly full of trail mix. Even Fiona, who had intended to linger no more than an hour, found that she was unwilling to step out of this small circle of warmth and back into the brutal wind. Looking beyond the windbreak, she saw snowflakes falling at a sharp angle, heard the wind howling in the branches, and felt the reluctance growing within her.

Finally, after what might have been close to two hours, during which she'd mostly just stood before the fire with her hands thrust out in front of her, she took a step back and forced herself to take action.

"Okay, we'd better kill the flames and get going," she said, reaching back to grab a shovel off the nearest sled. "We've lingered a little too long by the fire."

"Already?" Larry said. "It's so nice here."

"Too nice," Fiona said. "If we don't get moving soon, we may never want to move again."

"Can't we let the fire burn itself out naturally?" Duke said, slumped over on the edge of the big sled.

"No, I'm sorry." Fiona scooped up a shovelful of snow from the drift. "It's time to go." And with that, she dumped the snow on the flames, killing them almost instantly.

"Fiona's right," Jarred said. He rose, brushed off the seat of his pants, and stepped up onto the sled. "We can't afford to get too comfortable out here."

A few accepted this with Zen-like calm. Larry took the rest of the trail mix and placed it back in their supplies. Others let their unhappiness be known. Hope was clearly disappointed at leaving her fire, but she grabbed a corner of the metal sheet with her gloved hand and dragged it back toward the sled. It hissed on the snow as it lost heat along the way.

The fire had melted a shallow crater in the snow where they were parked, so the sleds were now tilted at a slight angle. Water was pooled in the center of the crater, but Fiona saw that it was quickly turning to ice along the edges.

"Any longer, and we'd have been standing in a pond," she said.

Larry unhobbled the goats, while the others repacked their gear. Then it was time to leave. Fiona shook the reins to get Ramses moving. The big goat stomped his feet, clearly annoyed that he had to leave again so soon. But then he snorted and pulled.

Fiona saw the lines go taut, felt the sled shudder beneath her, but then there was a kind of grinding sound. The sled didn't move. The same thing happened to the others. The animals pulled, the harness lines went taut, but the sleds wouldn't move. It didn't take long to realize the problem.

"The runners are stuck in a layer of ice," Fiona said, looking across the shallow crater toward the bit sled. "The flames, and probably our own weight, melted the snow around the runners, and then it quickly refroze."

The goats were still trying to pull the sled, and the straps began to creak alarmingly.

"I don't think we can pull free," Larry said. "Not without breaking the ropes or the sleds."

Ramses was doing his best, pulling and pulling, stomping and snorting angrily, as if he thought someone were messing with him. Fiona felt the sled tremble beneath him and give a loud groan of stressed wood.

"Stop the animals," she cried, pulling back on the reins. "Larry, Zane, stop the goats now before we bust the sleds."

Ramses resisted a moment longer before finally giving in and settling down. The she-goats did the same. Still, Fiona was concerned that some damage had already been done. Then she turned to look at the others. Duke was glaring back at her, as if he thought this were all somehow her fault.

"If we can get the sleds moving again, we'll be fine," Fiona said. "They won't freeze in place while they're moving, so we just have to heat up the runners."

"We could build another fire," Jarred said.

"Oh, I can do it," Hope said. She was standing beside her father, but she started toward the back of the small sled. "Give me a few minutes."

"That's not necessary, Hope," Larry said. "Kindly avert your eyes, folks."

When he reached for the zipper on his pants, Fiona suddenly understood. Embarrassed, she quickly turned away.

"Jarred, Duke, want to help me out here?" Larry said. "Pick a sled and do what needs to be done."

"I've got nothing in my bladder," Duke growled.

"Zane, then?"

Jarred and Zane both moved to join him. Soon, Fiona heard the sound of them urinating. The ice crackled and popped. A startled Ramses pulled forward. At first, the sled resisted, but then it broke free and slid forward a few inches.

"That's it, guys," Fiona said. "You got it."

Fiona heard zippers beings raised. Then all of the sleds were moving again, heading out from behind the windbreak and across open ground.

"You just gotta use every resource at your disposal," Larry shouted into the wind, laughing. "Is that thinking like an engineer, Jarred?"

"Pretty much," Jarred replied, "but mechanical engineers don't usually resort to urine."

Despite herself, Fiona laughed, too. That got Jarred laughing, and then most of the others joined in. There was something invigorating about the sound. There hadn't been much to laugh about in the last few weeks, and the group hadn't shared many moments of levity, certainly not since the collapse of the house. Even Duke seemed to rally a bit. His back was a little less bent, his expression a little less surly. Fiona could almost see the kinder, gentler man that he had been before.

Just that brief, shared laugh made the afternoon easier, though their circumstances were little changed. They were crossing mostly wide-open spaces, across very deep snow, avoiding the towering drifts and skirting smaller clusters of trees. The trees were almost entirely buried by drifts in some places, which was disconcerting. However, as the afternoon wore on, Fiona spotted a grove of towering pine trees off to the east that rose well above the snow, like sentinels standing watch over the buried earth.

Though they were moving a bit faster today, it soon became clear that the group would not reach the caverns before nightfall. Fiona waited for a break in the howling wind to talk to the others about it.

"Guys, I think we'd better head for those tall trees over there," she said, shouting to be heard by everyone. She pointed off to the left.

"They seem really far," Duke replied.

"That's because of the haze," Jarred said. "They're not as far as they appear."

"We can reach them before dark," Fiona said. *Maybe*, she thought, but didn't say. "Snow will be shallower in there, anyway."

She expected more complaining from Duke, but he seemed to quietly accept his fate. She wanted to hope that maybe he was feeling better now and coming out of his foul mood. Then again, maybe he was simply sinking into despair. Fiona saw distant hills on the horizon and knew Snowbird Caverns lay somewhere among those hills, but the journey was taking them a lot longer than she had anticipated.

How many days can we survive out here? she wondered. They only had a few more days of food, and only if they really made it last. After that, they would be trying to eat raw ingredients out in the open.

As she was thinking about this, keeping her real worries to herself, she happened to glance to the right and make eye contact with Jarred. His eyebrows went up, as if he'd read something in her expression. He came toward her.

"You don't have to do all the worrying by yourself," he said, quietly enough that the others wouldn't hear. "We're in this together, and we'll make it to our destination together."

Fiona wanted to be reassuring. The group needed to keep their spirits up, and that included Jarred, so she resisted telling him about her fears at first.

"I'm not sure what you mean, Jarred. I was just thinking about the route ahead."

"*Worrying* about the route ahead, you mean," he said.

"Well…yes," she said, softly. "It seems so much farther now that we're out here, but I can't let these people sink into despair. I have to be positive and hopeful, if I can." Even as she said it, she realized she was trying to smile for him, to give him a reassuring look.

"You're doing just fine," he said. "If you don't want the others to despair, feel free to confide in me. I can take it, and it gives me something to think about other than this aching foot."

"Thanks," she said, and indeed, it helped. Knowing that someone else wanted to help carry the burden helped. "Well, the thing is, I'm worried about food. I don't think we have enough for the journey, quite frankly. Plus, we're going really slowly, and the weather might be getting worse. Things are going to get really bad for all of us after another day or two of this. Really bad. Anyway, keep this to yourself for now."

"You got it," he replied with a smile and a nod. "We'll go easy on the food. I can fast for a day or two, if need be."

"Let's hope it doesn't come to that," she said. "Anyway, let's keep this kind of talk just between us, okay? We'll encourage openly, and brood privately. Honestly, that might be a bit therapeutic for me."

He laughed briefly and nodded. "Good. As you wish, Fiona."

It took a long couple of hours to reach the grove of tall pine trees. Up close, they seemed even more massive than they had at a distance, enormous and towering trunks that must have been fifty or sixty feet tall. As Fiona had hoped, the snow sloped down beneath the dense canopy of branches here. They descended into a kind of bowl where the air was notably warmer, though still well below freezing. The wind was negligible as well, especially once they'd gone deep into the grove and descended a few yards beneath the rim of the snow.

As they went deeper, the trees got closer together, and finally the big sled could no longer pass. They reined in the goats in a place that had a bit of wiggle room and proceeded to set up camp. It was edging toward evening, so Fiona set Hope and Zane to start a small fire again. They used a piece of scrap metal as a base for the fire again, then a second piece to shield the flames from the closest tree. This time, however, they parked the sleds farther from the heat.

"Couldn't we risk a little cooking," Lana said, setting a load of branches onto the stack. "It wouldn't hurt anything."

"What did you have in mind?" Fiona asked.

Duke spoke up first, shuffling toward the fire and plopping down on the snow. "I don't suppose you'd let us slaughter one of the chickens, would you? A nice drumstick roasted over the fire would suit me just fine right now."

"No, let's save the chickens for later," Fiona replied. "We need them for eggs. You want to check and see if any of them are laying?" She gave Duke a pointed stare that he did not return.

"I think I'll leave that to someone else," he replied, unzipping his coat and working his bruised arm out of the sling. The arm was as purple as ever, and he laid it across his lap like it was a beloved dying pet.

"I'll check the hens," Jarred said, hoisting himself up on his walking stick.

"We'll do it together," Fiona said.

"To be honest," Lana said, "I was thinking about roasting some seeds and nuts. We could add a bit of the jerky. I think it would be enough to tide us over, at least for tonight."

"Sounds good to me," Fiona said. "Go right ahead, Lana."

As Lana gathered up supplies for dinner, Fiona went to join Jarred at the big sled, where the cage with the chickens was covered and nestled in among the supplies. They'd done as much as they could to shield the animals from the cold. Still, as she leaned over to grab the blanket that covered the cage, she half-expected to find them all frozen stiff.

Jarred leaned over to grab one of the other corners. "I think I hear them moving around in there."

"If I lose all of my chickens, I'm going to be majorly bummed out," Fiona said. "Half were already killed in the collapse, including the goose. I don't like losing my animals. Even Smoke has been different since the collapse. He's just so timid now. He won't leave the sled. I don't know what to do."

"We've kept the chickens well covered," Jarred said. "I'm sure they're fine, but let's make sure."

With his help, they dragged the blanket back, uncovering the front half of the cage.

"See there, they're all still alive and moving around," he said. "Fiona, you're doing a good job. The animals are fine, and the humans haven't revolted yet. Believe in yourself. You'll get us there. We're going to make it, all of us."

"Maybe you're just being nice, but I'll take it," she said.

She climbed over a large crate and leaned down to get a clear view inside the chicken cage. She saw them all huddled inside, clustered in individual beds on plush bedding. Jarred worked open the small front door, and Fiona reached inside, feeling under some of the chickens. She was surprised to find that a few of them had laid eggs. She worked the eggs out. The chickens were grumpy, and they pecked and flapped at the intrusion. However, she managed to remove three good eggs.

"Maybe Lana can do something with these," she said.

As she brought the eggs to Lana, Jarred covered the cage again. There was some brief debate about what to do with the eggs. Lana decided to scramble them with the roasted nuts and seeds. Everyone would get at least a couple of bites, though it might not be the most filling meal. Myra even dared to leave Duke's side to help her cook. Fiona found this encouraging, as well.

Duke, if you would just pull out of this funk you're in, Fiona thought, *we could really use your help. The old Duke was such a helpful guy.* She was tempted to say it out loud, but she feared a confrontation might undo the progress. Humans were complicated and weird, and it was so hard to predict how they might react, even to a well-intentioned plea.

As Lana and Myra prepared the food, Fiona and Jarred fed and watered the goats, then gathered them together in a nice spot to settle down for the night. The goats were tired, which made them more compliant—even Ramses. They seemed grateful for the food.

"You know, Ramses has been a pain in my butt since I first bought him," Fiona said to Jarred. "He was always picking on the other goats, and sometimes picking on me. But it turns out, the secret to making him calm down and behave is to work him hard. He's had a big personality change for the better since we left the homestead."

"The old boy just needed a job," Jarred said. "That's true of so many ornery young men."

Finally, they strung a tarp over part of the camp to block out the rest of the wind. Then everyone finally settled down around the fire. Smoke found his way to Fiona's lap as she rested with her back against one of the bigger pine trees. The fire was lovely, its orange light reflecting off the bowl of snow around them, flickering off the branches overhead. The heat was perfect, and she even had a mostly full belly of good food. It was amazing what a difference it made.

"In a moment like this, you almost forget what the world is like," Jarred said. He was sitting beside her, Hope on the other side. "You almost forget that everyone's buried under a freakish apocalyptic blizzard."

"Almost," she agreed.

If not for all of these strange people sitting with me around the fire, I would feel normal, she thought. It almost made her laugh.

There was an exception to the strangeness. Yes, one person that she felt almost entirely comfortable around, and he was sitting right beside her. Even after all they'd been through, she still felt awkward around the Coopers and the Bishops, even Hope to a certain extent. She couldn't fully relax around them, always very conscious of their presence, and she'd begun to fear that the feeling would never go away.

Jarred was a different story. Somehow, he'd broken through whatever wall was around her, whatever crust had built up on her skin. She didn't mind sitting close to him, chatting with him, working with him. She was sure that it was partly his personality. He worked hard, rarely complained—even about his busted leg—and never said anything to make her feel weird. But that didn't explain it fully. In reality, there was just some quality about him that she liked, something sincere and easy.

As she thought about this, she began to feel a strange, almost embarrassing heat in her belly. Then, as if he sensed her thought, he turned and smiled at her—a genuine smile that lit up his whole face—and the heat spread through her chest. It was so intense, she had no idea how to respond to it, so she quickly looked away, fixing her gaze on the dancing flames in the middle of their camp.

"I guess…I guess maybe we should set up places to sleep tonight," she said. If she had to sit there beside him any longer, she feared she might just melt. And then what?

"Sounds good," he replied. "I'll sleep really good tonight. It's nice here."

"It is nice," she agreed, then picked herself up. "Never thought I'd say that on our way to the caverns. I hope it stays this way…at least for a little while."

54

It was Hope's turn to take watch, and she was more than pleased to be up and moving around. They'd kept the fire going, and the heat was such a wonderful feeling, she hated to sleep through it. She wanted to soak up as much of this warmth as possible, so she could daydream about it later, when they were back out in the unforgiving cold wind.

Lana gently shook Hope awake, trading places with her. Wordlessly, rubbing her face, Hope rose from the pile of blankets where she'd been sleeping. Lana handed her the shotgun and a flashlight, then walked over to the place where her husband was sleeping. Hope slipped the strap of the shotgun over her shoulder and turned to face the fire. Lana had fed it a few more branches, clearly, and it was going strong.

Duke's snoring sounded like his ribs were breaking. The old man slept sprawled on his back. It seemed super uncomfortable to Hope. No wonder the cranky fart was in a bad mood most of the time these days. He needed a more comfortable sleeping position, and maybe some Ambien.

Hope picked her way through the sleepers and circled the fire. The goats were penned in their own area on the other wide. She moved past them, too, finding a fallen log where she could sit down, and fixed her gaze up the shallow slope of the snow bowl. After a minute, she heard the crunch of snow behind her and turned to see Smoke approaching. The dog hopped the log and settled at her feet, and she reached down to scratch him behind the ear. He was a nice little dog, sweet-natured and well-behaved.

These were strange days. Every once in a while, their harsh new circumstances hit her all over again, and it seemed to have a strange dreamy quality. Hope didn't always hate life now. In some ways it was better than her old day-to-day life full of dull teachers, uninteresting students, and boring classes. She'd never really been challenged enough.

Now, at least, there were constant problems that needed to be solved, and her ideas were usually appreciated by Fiona. Maybe the novelty of being useful would eventually wear off, but for now, she found it invigorating. She didn't even mind sitting like this in the dark, staring off at the hostile world and hoping nothing attacked them.

She'd sat for maybe thirty minutes—time was so hard to gauge these days—before Smoke suddenly bounded up, panting, and looked around. Then he hopped back over the fallen log, heading back toward the camp. Not warm enough out here on the fringes, perhaps.

"That's okay," Hope said softly. "I don't blame you. Go nestle in with the other people and stay warm."

But she realized that Smoke had stopped on the other side of the log. He was just standing there, his tail brushing against her back. When he started making a low sound in the back of his throat, she first thought maybe he was in pain. She'd never heard Smoke growl before, so it was a completely new sensation. Startled, Hope spun on the log to face him, fumbling at the gun strap over her shoulder. Had someone entered the camp? Some intruder?

She saw Smoke standing with his head low, staring off into the darkness, as he growled. He was pointed toward the area where the goats were penned. A predator, perhaps? Maybe a hungry black bear? Heart racing, Hope leapt to her feet and pulled the shotgun off her shoulder. She could see the goats all huddled together in the small space where they'd been penned. She strained to make out anything unusual in the vicinity. Just goats and more goats, like always.

And then, as suddenly as it started, Smoke stopped growling and returned to panting. For some reason, Hope found that just as alarming. It was like something was flipping a switch back and forth in the dog's brain. She squatted down beside him and patted his head.

"Are you just being silly or what?" she asked. "Maybe a bear walked by and kept on going. Is that it?"

But Smoke pulled away from her and bounded off toward the sleeping area near the fire. Hope soon saw why. Zane was awake. As he rose, the dog went to meet him. Rubbing his sleepy eyes, Zane came toward her. As usual, he was bundled up in his heavy coat, but he flipped up the hood now as he approached. He stooped down to pet Smoke in passing, stifling a yawn.

"What's going on?" he asked Hope, trudging up the shallow slope toward her log-seat. "Is something wrong? I was sleeping kind of shallow anyway, but then I heard Smoke growling."

"I don't know," Hope said. "Something disturbed him. He was staring at the goats over there, but then it must've passed. Never heard him growl like that, but it didn't last long."

"Maybe the growling scared it off, whatever it was," he replied. He yawned again, pressing both hands over his mouth. "Did you see anything?"

Hope shook her head. As she gazed off toward the goats, they all seemed to be resting comfortably. Even Ramses was calm. Nothing had spooked them. "I didn't go over there," she said. "It was a little bit spooky, to be honest."

"Let's go check it out," Zane said. "Hang on. I'll get a flashlight."

He trudged back toward the sleds and rooted through the tools for a moment. Finally, he produced a small flashlight and turned it on. Either the batteries were running out, or the cold had affected the electronics, because it produced only a faint, flickering light. Still, he shone it on the ground as he returned to her.

"Okay, let's go," he said.

He held out his gloved hand, and she took it. She still had the shotgun in her other hand, the barrel resting against her forearm. Having someone beside her, Zane especially, did make a difference. Suddenly, it seemed silly to be afraid of some passing animal, especially when they were armed. Still, she let him take the lead as they approached the goats.

The females had been placed together in a small roped-off area. They were huddled close together there, sitting on a pile of filthy blankets and resting their heads on each other's backs and necks. Ramses was in his own roped-off area nearby, but he moved as close to the others as he could get, pressing his body right up against the nylon ropes which marked his pen.

The goats were all light sleepers, Hope had learned, and a few of them woke up immediately when they got close. She saw their yellow eyes shining in the firelight, turning to regard the humans who had approached.

"It seems unlikely that a bear passed by," she said, speaking just above a whisper. Still, this caused a few other goats to wake up and look at her. "The goats were asleep when Smoke growled. Any sounds or smells from a predator would have roused them, don't you think?"

"Yeah, probably," he replied. "Does it seem like there are fewer of them than usual? Are we missing one?"

Hope did a quick count of the goats. There should have been eight females, but she only counted seven. Thinking perhaps one was hidden in the pile of resting bodies, she walked around to the other side of the penned area and counted again.

"One is missing," she said. Which one? She tried to account for each of them. She knew their names. Fiona had told her, and she had a good memory. "I think it's the doe named Maria," she said, after a moment. "She's speckled, white with brown spots."

"Maybe a predator dragged her off," Zane suggested, approaching the ropes.

"Wouldn't we have heard something?" Hope replied, coming with him. "There would've been a commotion. Blood on the snow. Something."

But once she stepped up to the nearest ropes, she did see something. She gestured for Zane to point the flashlight in that direction, and it became clear: hoofprints in the snow and a shallow depression that went under the rope. Maria had somehow squeezed herself through the gap at the bottom, and her hoofprints went winding off away from the pen and up the slope toward the darkness.

"Oh, no, she escaped," Hope said. "Somehow, I missed it."

"Why would she wander off?" Zane asked. "What could she possibly be looking for? They were all watered and well-fed."

"I don't know," Hope said. "Maybe she just didn't like being penned. Come on. We'd better go find her before she gets too far."

She pulled her hand out of Zane's grasp so she could hold the shotgun right. Then she bent over and followed the hoofprints through the trees. He kept the flashlight pointed at the ground right in front of her. One advantage of the snow was that every moving animal left clear tracks—at least until fresh snow covered them. It didn't seem like Maria was headed anywhere in particular. She'd just meandered her way through the trees, but her path led her gradually up the slope.

"Should we go back and get our snowshoes?" Hope asked. Already, the soles of her boots were sinking into the deep snow.

"I think we'll be fine, as long as we don't go too far," he replied. "Going back and putting on the snowshoes will give that goat more time to wander."

The grove was fairly large, so Maria had plenty of places to go. As they followed her, they got farther from the heat of the fire, and Hope felt that familiar biting cold settle into her bones again. Just a little bit of warmth made such a huge difference. Already, she felt her enthusiasm, her optimism, waning.

"Hey, can I ask you something?" Zane said, after a moment.

"Of course," she replied. "Just about anything."

He hesitated a second before saying, "Well, I overheard your father say something to you the other day, and I've been thinking about it ever since. I don't remember the exact words, but he said something about a 'code.' A code you're supposed to follow. I just wondered what he was referring to. Are you part of a cult that has weird rules or something?"

"No, no, nothing like that," Hope replied, chuckling. "The code just refers to a rule that Dad and I came up with for this new world after the incident at the general store. We said we'll do anything we have to do in order to survive except hurt people. That's the code."

"Oh." He grunted thoughtfully. "Did you come up with that rule because he killed Benjy Hartman and you don't want him to do something like that again?"

It was one subject Hope did not like to discuss. She didn't even want to think about Benjy Hartman or her weird little escapade with him. She'd done a fairly good job of forgetting about those strange days before the Bishops and Coopers moved into the house. Even now, she couldn't quite explain why she had felt so connected to the park ranger. He'd been nice to her, more appreciative of her intellect, and he'd flattered her a lot. At the time, she'd been particularly vulnerable because of lingering resentment toward her father. However, Benjy had turned out to be a creep through and through.

Zane's sudden mention of the man's name dragged her back into a dark place. She could still remember that last confrontation, when his demeanor had changed so suddenly. She could still see him falling to the floor as the blood poured and puddled around him. She sighed and tried to stuff the memories of that bad day back down into the furthest recesses of her mind where they belonged.

"I'm sorry," Zane said. "I shouldn't have brought him up. I was just curious."

"Well…you're right. Benjy's death was the reason my dad came up with the code," Hope said. "He doesn't want us to turn into the kind of people who find it easy to kill in order to survive, and I agreed with him."

"Oh. Yeah. I guess that's—"

A sudden shrill cry cut him off. Hope was already in a bad place, so the sound sent her scrambling. She brought the shotgun up, aiming into the dark as she stumbled to one side. They had moved far enough from the camp that the shadows were getting long and dark. Zane hunkered down, as if expecting something to charge at him.

The sound didn't last long. Two or three seconds, a quick panicked cry, and then it was gone. But Hope knew it wasn't human. She pushed away from the tree, shaking, and tried to steady the gun. She considered retreating, but Zane beckoned her onward and inched forward. Hope came with him. Eventually, she spotted a long, dark trail on the bright snow. He turned the flashlight toward it. Blood. There was a large puddle of it, then drag marks heading off around a large tree.

A few more steps, and they saw her. Maria was behind the tree, lying on her side and weakly kicking her legs. As they drew near, Hope realized one of the back legs was mangled, half-missing. Whatever had attacked her and tried to drag her off had left marks of its own, big ones that kicked through the deep snow. Hope aimed in the direction it had come from, but it had apparently already fled.

"Whatever it was, I think we scared it off," Zane said. "What do we do about her?" He nodded toward the goat. Maria was still breathing, but she'd lost a lot of blood. Still, the mangled leg seemed to be the only serious wound.

"Let's drag her back to camp," Hope said. "Maybe we can save her."

"I don't think a three-legged goat has much of a chance," Zane replied.

"Well, we have to try. Come on."

She shouldered the shotgun and dashed toward Maria. Zane came with her, though she could tell he wasn't all that enthusiastic about the effort. First, they tried to lift the goat, but she thrashed and became unwieldy. Finally, they each grabbed a foreleg and dragged her, lifting the front half of her body off the ground just enough to keep her head from hitting low objects in the snow. He had to pocket the flashlight to manage it, however, which cast the light straight up and made the shadows around them long and ominous.

As they drew near the camp, Smoke came running to meet them, prancing back and forth in front of them. He seemed both anxious and excited, and he unleashed a rare series of barks.

"What do you think it was that dragged her off?" Zane asked, straining to speak.

"Not sure," Hope replied. "It was big, so probably a bear. They scare pretty easy most of the time, too, from what I've read."

As they drew near camp, walking backwards to drag the goat, they heard other voices. She recognized the low growl of Duke Cooper, the higher voices of Myra and Lana, Jarred and Fiona chatting quietly. It seemed the commotion had awakened everyone else.

"There you are," Jarred said, when they backed into the firelight. "We were just about to come looking for you two."

"What was that awful noise?" Myra Cooper asked, her voice a soft sleep-croak.

They didn't have to answer, as the injured goat suddenly became visible to the others. Hope let go of the leg and stumbled backward, just as the adults began to gather around her. Maria snorted softly and looked up at them, and there seemed to be a kind of pleading expression on her face.

Save me, humans, it seemed to say.

"Did you see what got hold of her?" Fiona asked, squatting beside the goat and stroking her belly. The poor woman seemed almost distraught, frowning deeply like she'd lost a member of her family.

"No, but it was something big," Hope replied. She stooped down and used the snow to clean blood off her fingers.

"I think we scared it off," Zane replied. Unlike Hope, he wiped his hands on the sides of his pants.

Duke, Larry, Fiona, and Jarred circled the goat. Myra and Lana hung back —apparently, neither of them felt like they needed a closer look.

"What can we do for her?" Hope asked.

"Nothing," Duke Cooper replied. His wounded arm was out of the coat and sling again, and he was gently massaging a spot just beneath his elbow. "We'll have to put her down."

"But it's just her leg," Hope replied. The poor thing, with her desperate eyes, her labored breathing. "There must be something we can do to save her life. Bandage up the leg, put her on a sled, or even make her a prosthetic. I'm sure I could come up with something for her using the bamboo."

All of the adults were looking at her now. Was that pity on their faces?

"I'm sorry, Hope," Fiona said, in a soft, sympathetic voice. "Even if we had access to a vet, there's not much we could do for her. The leg wasn't removed cleanly. It was shredded, and the injury looks deep. I bet she's lost a lot of blood. It would be cruel to keep her alive like this. She would only suffer."

"So...what, we're just going to shoot her?" Hope asked.

Duke struggled to kneel down then. His good hand went inside his coat, fishing around. "We shouldn't waste ammunition when it's in limited supply anyway. There's a much easier way."

He drew his hand out, revealing a long knife. The wooden handle seemed ancient, worn soft around the edges, as if Duke had carried it around for many years. The four-inch blade was dark with age, but the edge had been honed to a silver sheen. Without hesitation or delay, he thrust the tip of the blade deep into the animal's throat.

Hope shuddered and turned away, but not before she saw the goat thrash. Maria managed a single gurgling gasp, but Duke dragged the knife through her throat quickly. Though Hope didn't see it, she heard the cutting, the splash of blood.

"Duke, for God's sake, you could've given her some warning," Fiona said sharply. "Let people avert their gaze first, if they want to. Anyway, Maria was *my* animal. You should've let me deal with it."

"Better to get it done right away," Duke replied. "What's the point of being sentimental about it? The longer you wait, the more the sounds of the dying animal will draw other predators. They hear that labored breathing, and to them it sounds like dinner bells ringing."

"It wasn't your decision to make," Fiona said.

"I didn't think we had to take a vote on it," Duke snarled. "I was trying to be helpful. God, woman, do you have to jump down my throat about everything, even when I'm trying to be helpful?"

Hope dared to turn back around then. Duke was wiping his blade on the dead animal's pink belly.

"He was only trying to get it done so Hope wouldn't have to keep worrying about it," Myra Cooper said, patting her husband on the back of the head. "Duke hasn't been feeling good since he busted his arm, but surely you can see that he's trying to do the right thing."

Duke went to put the knife back, but he fumbled it. It sank into the snow, and he spent a few seconds digging it out.

"Well, since we went ahead and killed the goat, I guess I'll have to stay up and butcher her," Fiona said with a sigh.

"Oh, gee, sorry to inconvenience you, *lady*," Duke replied bitterly. He finally dug the knife out of the snow and quickly pushed it back under his coat into whatever sheath awaited it. "You act like I'm the one responsible for its injury. Sorry you can't go back to sleep right away."

"Hey, it's fine," Jarred said, holding up his hands.. "Calm down, Duke. Your attitude isn't helping. None of us are likely going back to sleep anyway. It'll be morning soon enough. We might as well get ready. While Fiona butchers the goat, the rest of us can pack up and get ready to move again."

"I didn't start the argument," Duke said. "Why don't you scold Fiona?"

"It wasn't an argument until you made it one," Jarred said, heat in his voice. "You've had a bad attitude toward Fiona for long enough, and I don't appreciate it."

"Oh, you speak for her now?" Duke said.

"No, but I've got her back. Don't forget it."

At this, Duke merely grunted and turned away.

Hope had seen enough. She took the shotgun off her shoulder and propped it against the nearest tree. Someone else could figure out where it belonged.

She didn't particularly care. At the moment, she just wanted to get away from all of these people. The adults could be so insufferable sometimes. She trudged back to the sleeping area, intending to pack up. Still, one question nagged at her every thought: What in the world had attacked Maria? It might still be out there somewhere close, waiting to attack again.

55

By the time Fiona finished butchering the goat, the sun was up, and their campfire was dead. She had slabs of meat arrayed in the snow before her. She'd cut them small enough that they could be packed in bags or boxes and carried without too much trouble. Her irritation at Duke Cooper's latest surly episode had actually helped her get the work done faster. Fiona always found that anger motivated her to stay busy.

Finally, when the meat was prepared, Larry Bishop helped her drag what was left of the goat well away from the camp and bury it in the snow. Then Jarred joined them as they packed up the meat and found places to store it.

"Whatever attacked her did us a favor," Larry noted. "All of this protein will give us plenty of energy for whatever work lies ahead once we reach the cavern."

"But it also means one less goat to pull the sleds," Fiona noted, hoisting a rack of ribs wrapped in a tarp down in among the boxes. "At least with the cold the meat will keep for a lot longer."

After packing and storing the meat, she went to check on the chickens. She pulled the blanket back and peeked in through the top. She spotted the dead chicken immediately. One of the smaller hens. The cold had apparently been too much. Now, she lay on her side, one lifeless black eye staring upward.

"This day is not starting off well," she grumbled, unlatching the cage door. She grabbed the dead chicken by the feet and pulled it out. She turned and held it up, showing it to Jarred and Larry.

"It was a bad night for the animals," Jarred said. "I'm sorry about that, Fiona."

"Not your fault," she replied. "No need to apologize."

The others had mostly finished breaking camp and repacking all of their supplies. The coals from the fire had been buried under the snow, the tarps and blankets refolded. Zane, Hope, and Lana were currently harnessing the surviving goats to the sleds.

"I think the chicken can wait," Fiona said. "I'll butcher it later. For now, we'd better get going." She wrapped the dead chicken in a towel and shoved it in with some of the goat meat.

People were already taking up positions around the sleds, ready to set out. With fewer goats to pull the sleds, they were going to have trouble, so Fiona decided to dump one box of supplies. It was mostly scrap wood and metal, stuff they'd intended to use to repair the sleds in case of an accident. She hated to leave it. She hated to leave any of the stuff they'd brought. Who knew what they were going to wind up needing at some point? But she just couldn't see any alternative.

"It's a risk we'll have to take," she explained to the others. "We have to drop some weight for the sake of the goats. The most they can pull is about fifty pounds each."

She expected someone to disagree with her decision. Maybe Hope, since she was most likely to use the scraps for one of her projects, almost certainly Duke, but everyone went along with it. Jarred even nodded. Still, it was a glum group that finally set out that morning. Lana had the reins for the small sled, walking beside the lead goat, while Zane and Hope guided the large sled. Fiona took her place beside Ramses.

Though it was hard to gauge direction with the constant cloud cover, she pointed them in what felt like due south. Letting Ramses lead, she guided their small caravan of sleds through the trees. She spotted the large bloodstain off to the left and had a moment of disquiet. Some dangerous creature was out there. It knew now where to find fresh meat. She fully expected it to try to follow and attack again.

We'd better be ready next time, she thought. *We can't afford to lose another goat—or worse.*

As they approached the edge of the grove, Fiona could see that a gentle flurry was falling out in the open. The warmth of the camp was already long gone, and as she drove Ramses out of the trees and onto the broad field, the cold wind returned with a vengeance. It swept over her like a hateful reminder of all that awaiting them on the road ahead.

They drove the sleds in a line. Fiona tried to pick up the pace. She could see the great humps of hills in the distance. The caverns were there somewhere, according to the map, but the scale was deceptive. She couldn't tell how close they were, and the grove of pine trees where they'd spent the night wasn't on the map. She couldn't determine their location with any real precision.

The snow that had started out as a flurry grew in intensity throughout the morning, until it became a blinding force of wind and snowflakes that reduced visibility to no more than a few yards. Worse yet, the snow stuck to everything, so it quickly began to pile up on the sleds. By midday, it was so bad that Fiona called them to a halt so they could spend some time clearing it off. She would have used the opportunity to take a break and let the others rest for a while, but they were out in the open. With no shelter, the wind and snow would make resting impossible.

She assigned Zane and Hope the task of shoveling the snow off. They did so without complaining, but she could tell they weren't excited about it. As they went to work, Fiona made a visual check of everyone else. Their hoods were up against the wind. Most of them were huddled in the cold, but she caught Duke working at the zipper on his coat again. He thrust his bruised hand out of the sling and shook it, as if it had gone numb. At first, she wasn't going to say anything. He had proved to her that his commitment to being a pain in the butt was firm. Still, she figured it was best to stay on top of things.

"Is your hand bothering you?" she asked.

At the sound of her voice, he flinched, clearly startled, then turned to face her. He was scowling at first, but he quickly wiped the scowl off his face and gave her a blank look.

"I'm fine," he replied, pulling the hand back into his coat. He offered no more than that, so she let it go. He clearly wasn't fine, but she wasn't going to drag it out of him against his will.

After Zane and Hope finished clearing off the sleds, Fiona got them moving again. Unfortunately, the snow started to stick again right away. The hills seemed to be getting closer, but way too slowly. Fortunately, she saw a large building groaning under the weight of the snow piled on its roof. She beckoned Jarred close.

"Do you see that building there?" she said, when he limped up beside her. "Do you think it'll make a good shelter?"

He stared at it for a few seconds, then said, "Not sure how stable it is, especially with all the snow on top, but it'll give us shelter from the wind on the east side."

"That's good enough for me," Fiona said.

They reached the building after another slow hour of trudging across the open ground. Fiona aimed Ramses to the left, moving them out of the worst of the wind. It made a huge difference. Somehow, the cold felt more bearable when snow wasn't being blasted against them at a forty-five-degree angle. The red wood wall identified this as an old barn.

Larry guided the second sled up beside hers and reined in the goats. The small sled came last, led by Lana.

"We'll rest here for a little bit," Fiona said. "The goats need to be fed and watered."

"Sort of feels like we're on a long walk to nowhere," Duke Cooper remarked. "I don't suppose we could dig our way into this barn here and take shelter."

"There's a lot of snow on the roof," Jarred replied. "If it hasn't already collapsed, it soon will."

"I don't think that's a risk we want to take, not again," Fiona said.

"Well..." Duke gazed at the vast mound of snow on the rooftop for a second, then nodded and said, "I suppose that's true. Had enough houses dropped on top of me."

Just as he finished speaking, some faint but familiar sound came to them, rolling over the vast field of unbroken snow. Fiona felt a momentary shiver of unease, as Jarred turned and looked at her.

"Wolves," she noted.

"They're howling," Larry said, cupping a hand behind his right ear. "Does that mean something? Are they after us? Are we being pursued?"

"The howling is just their way of communicating across long distances," Fiona said. "Wolves don't normally attack people."

"These aren't normal conditions," Larry replied.

They waited in the silence that followed, but the wolves did not howl again. Still, the sound had been unsettling, and they had trouble resting. Fiona stood beside the big sled, holding Ramses's reins. Hope and Zane paced a bit. The others just stood around. The air was tense.

Wolves don't hunt people, she reminded herself. *Bears might, even desperate coyotes or feral dogs, but not wolves. I've never heard of such a thing.*

It was one situation where Benjy Hartman might have been able to offer some expert advice. Finally, as quiet minutes passed, the group started to relax. Fiona dared to sit down on her sled. Jarred took a seat beside her. Lana broke out the trail mix and passed it around. Duke sat on a box, his good hand clamped to his left knee. Myra brought him a canteen of water, but he had to spend time breaking ice off the lid before he could take a drink.

And then it came to them again. It started softly, rising like some singing voice, and rang out across the field. A second wolf responded, then a third. Duke was in mid-drink, and he almost dropped the canteen. Myra grabbed his hand to steady him.

"That was closer," Jarred said. "A lot closer."

Fiona couldn't deny it. She scanned the distance, but visibility was still limited. She saw only white sheets driven by the wind. No wolves were visible in any direction.

"Okay, it's possible we're being tracked," she said.

"You took too damn long butchering that goat last night," Duke Cooper snarled. "Plenty of time for the smell of all of that meat to waft on the air."

"They're not after the meat," Fiona said sharply. "They don't want a dead goat. They want the living animals. They want the goats and chickens. They probably would've attacked already if not for the presence of humans."

"You don't think a wolf will eat a person, if it has a chance?" Larry said.

"Not when its natural prey is right there," Fiona replied, pointing at the harnessed goats. "That's what they're after, guys. The goats and the chickens, but it doesn't make much difference. If they manage to kill our animals, we're just as dead as if they'd attacked us directly."

"Duke, this has nothing to do with how long Fiona took to butcher the goat," Jarred said. "That was a pointless thing to say."

"Freedom of speech," Duke said with a sneer. "Get off my back."

Fiona rose then, brushing off the seat of her pants, then glared down at Duke Cooper. His head was bowed, and he didn't look up.

"Jarred's right. Pointless, silly accusations don't help anything," Fiona added. Still, he wouldn't look at her. "I need everyone to move faster. We're increasing our speed. We're going to push ourselves harder. We have to."

"We'll never make it to the caverns before they catch up to us," Larry said.

Fiona went to the medium-sized sled and dug the folded map out of its box. She opened it, laying it across the top of the box, and studied it for a moment, as the others gathered behind her and peered over her shoulder. She pointed at the tiny speck of Glencole, then dragged her finger across the map to Snowbird Caverns. Finally, she tracked her finger north to a small gray square.

"Right here," she said.

"That's where we are?" Lana Bishop asked.

"No, no, this appears to be a large quarry," she replied, "but it's close. If we're as far along as I think, then we can reach this a lot faster than the caverns."

"Isn't a quarry just basically a big pit in the ground?" Larry said. "What good'll that do?"

"Well, for one thing, it'll be a big enough landmark that we should be able to find it easily, even with reduced visibility," Fiona said. "For another, we might be able to lose the wolves there."

"Seems like it could be a more defensible position," Jarred said. "There should be buildings there. Might be easier to protect the livestock and maybe even take out the wolves so we can continue in peace."

"Exactly," Fiona said. She appreciated that he was always on her side. The others, however, seemed less certain, judging by all the frowning and scowling.

Duke Cooper finally sniffed loudly and said, "A cavern, a quarry, what's the difference, as long as one's closer."

"Good," Fiona said, refolding the map. It was the closest thing to an endorsement that she was going to get out of him, it seemed, especially after she'd scolded him. She put the map back in place and rose.

"Let's get going."

56

The howling of the wolves chased them back out into the open, as Fiona turned Ramses in what she estimated was the direction of the quarry. It was a truly eerie sound that seemed to come from multiple directions, and she couldn't help but wonder if the wolves had them surrounded and were slowly closing in. Would they actually attack the livestock with humans so numerous and so close? Fiona didn't know, but she wasn't about to run the risk. Without the livestock, they were doomed.

She set a brisk pace, approaching a near jog. She had grown comfortable enough with the snowshoes that she could manage it without tripping over her own feet. When she glanced back, she saw the other walkers struggling to keep up. The female goats were struggling a bit as well.

"What if the quarry's not there?" Larry shouted at one point. "What if it's an old landmark on the map that's been replaced or filled in with snow?"

Fiona was moving fast enough that she couldn't comfortably answer. Fortunately, Jarred did it for her.

"Unlikely," he said, shaking the reins again to keep Ramses moving. "A quarry is rarely a good candidate for development, and even with all of this snow, I doubt it would be filled."

"Just thinking through possibilities," Larry replied. "Not trying to be a pessimist or anything. I'm sure it'll be there."

And then, as if to punctuate his words, they heard a single wolf howl carried on the wind, an almost plaintive sound this time, but close, too close. Fiona dared a glance over her shoulder, looking past all of the sleds and people to the wintery expanse behind them. She saw nothing moving in that direction except the fat snowflakes that endlessly fell.

She pressed on, moving even faster. Over the next hour or so, she sensed the ground sloping very gradually downward. Then, a great heap appeared in the distance. Though it was fully snow-covered, she thought by the lumpy shape that it might have been an old slag pile. Not long after spotting that, she saw the steep, sheer walls just off to the right, walls that had clearly been mechanically carved. The quarry.

"There it is," she cried over her shoulder, pointing to the right. "That's the quarry there. We made it."

She headed in that direction. With all of the snow, the quarry looked like an otherworldly place, a flat space surrounded on three sides by enormous stone walls with odd towers and turrets here and there produced by slag piles and tumbled stones. In the distance, she saw a few small buildings, their roofs heaped with snow. Even a few construction vehicles poked out of the snow like frosty relics.

The towering sides of the quarry shielded them from the wind. Fiona aimed for the nearest building. It was little more than a mobile home that had been pieced together near a corner of the quarry's outer wall, but it had a sloped roof, which had caused much of the snow to slide off. This had probably saved the building from collapse. Fiona gestured toward it as she turned in that direction.

Sound was muffled here in the quarry. She scarcely heard the blowing wind. Even their footsteps and the creaking of the sleds was dampened somehow. The loudest sounds were the occasional snort from the goats or the labored breathing of tired humans.

"That building is intact," Fiona said, out of breath. "There should be room for all of us, and all of our stuff, inside. Come on."

"Thank God for intact roofs," Duke said. "They've become rarer than diamonds."

They finally reached the building, which butted right up against one of the sheer walls of the quarry. It took a minute to clear the steps that led to the front door. Fiona put Zane and Hope on it, since they'd proved so efficient at clearing the sleds. Then she grabbed the shotgun and mounted the steps. There was a single narrow window set in the front door, but it was either dirty or misted over. She couldn't see anything inside the building.

"Be careful," Jarred said, moving up the steps behind her. Though he still had his crutch in his arm, he wasn't really using it at all at the moment. "If there are people inside, they might be hostile to an intrusion. You want me to go first? They might have pity on a limping man with a crutch."

"No, I'll handle it."

Fiona rapped on the hollow metal door and waited a minute. When no one answered, she tried to turn the L-shaped door handle. It proved to be unlocked, and the door swung open, revealing a dim interior that smelled of musty paper and old carpet. She saw a file cabinet in the near corner, then a small desk against the wall, a dark lamp that gave no light, a set of shelves high on another wall. She listened for a moment, but the interior was utterly silent.

Finally, she dared to step through the door. Looking back, she saw the sleds parked in front of the building, goats and people watching her carefully as she entered the building. She gestured for them to stay put then moved fully into the room. Only Jarred came with her, slipping through the front door just before it swung shut.

Fiona made her way across the room, straining to hear anything out of the ordinary. She led with the gun, but kept it pointed at the floor. Better not to risk accidentally shooting anyone if they startled each other. She approached a small open door on the far side of the room. Beyond, there was another room, smaller, with more filing cabinets and shelves lining the walls and a small dusty couch.

"Not much here," Fiona said. "Looks like they left in a hurry. It's messy."

"Tons of paperwork," Jarred said. He had slipped behind the desk and pulled open a drawer.

"Should be useful for starting fires," Fiona noted, coming back into the front room. "Or maybe insulation of some kind. Anyway, I don't see any significant supplies of food and water."

"Can we fit everyone in here?" Jarred said.

"Yeah, it'll be cozier than I'd like." Fiona went to the front door. "We'll need to at least spend the night. The animals can go in the back room. We'll take the front. Maybe a night in here will dissuade our pursuers."

"Well, at least we'll get better rest in here than we did last night," Jarred said, sitting on the edge of the desk.

"Don't relax just yet," Fiona said, beckoning him. "We've got to unharness the animals and bring our stuff inside."

To his credit, though he must've been exhausted, he hopped up and came toward her, limping only slightly. Fiona went back outside and told the others her plan. They seemed exhausted as well. Duke heaved a great sigh of relief and made his way up the stairs.

"We need to unload the animals and supplies," Fiona said, stepping in his way. "Especially the meat. We can't leave it out here in the open."

Duke gave her a sour look, then turned and went back down the stairs. The simple joy of having insulated walls and a sturdy roof over their heads was enough to energize the entire group, and they went to work right away unloading the sleds. The goats and chickens were brought into the back office. It was a tight fight, but they didn't seem to mind. She cracked the single window in the room to let some of the stench escape, then shut the door on them.

As for the people, they set up camp in the front office, lining the walls with their supplies. The wrapped meat, as well as the chicken, were stacked on a windowsill, where they would stay close to the cold. Though Fiona had suggested starting a fire, everyone was so tired, they decided to sleep a little bit first.

If we're lucky, the wolves will realize they can't get to us, she thought, *and they'll wander off in search of other prey. If not, then we might need to deal with them somehow.*

Their ultimate destination seemed farther than ever, and Fiona took a seat in the swiveling chair behind the office desk with a feeling akin to despair. She didn't feel the same excitement about having a building that the others did. It was just another unfortunate delay. Still, she let them have their sleep. They laid blankets down on the floor, picked their spots, and collapsed. As for Fiona, she rested her head on the desk. It was enough. She was too restless to sleep anyway.

Soon, the room was filled with snoring, grunting, farting, all of the regular sounds of human hibernation. Fiona considered the road ahead. It all seemed like a crazy plan now. Using goat-pulled sleds to cross miles of open land in the worst winter weather of her lifetime just to reach a natural cavern where they planned to live long-term. It sounded ridiculous.

We could have stayed in Glencole, she thought. *Would it have been worse than this?*

But there was no turning back now. They'd come too far and worked too hard to reach this place. She would get them there, one way or another. Unfortunately, pushing them faster just seemed to be wearing them out faster, and now they'd taken this crazy detour.

Eventually, she drifted off to sleep with her head resting on her arms. When she awoke, it felt like a few hours had passed, though the light through the window hadn't changed much. Others were awake now, moving around the room. Hope was gathering up some office papers, carefully placing them into a bag.

When she realized Fiona was looking at her, she said, "I thought I'd get the fire started. Everyone's gotta be hungry by now. I never ate goat before, so I hope it doesn't taste weird."

"It's not bad," Fiona said, pushing the chair back and rising. "A bit like mutton."

"I've never eaten that either," Hope said. "It's only been beef, chicken, turkey, and fish sticks for me, but we can't be picky now. I'll eat whatever."

Jarred and Zane helped her gather up papers. Larry and Lana were setting out what remained of their fresh water and the trail mix. Duke and Myra were sitting together in the far corner, chatting softly. The room was small enough that their body heat had begun to warm it up. Condensation covered the window.

Fiona started around the desk, intending to select a good cut of meat for the afternoon's meal when she heard the sound again. Wolves howling. Everyone in the room stopped what they were doing for a second. Fiona traded an anxious look with Jarred.

"Still tracking us," he said. "Being inside didn't deter them."

"If they're starving, they can't afford to abandon the chase," Larry said.

"We're not going to try to outrun them," Fiona said. She approached the window and peered through the steamy glass. She saw the steep wall of the quarry outside, the towering piles of slag. Though the wolves sounded close, she still didn't see them.

"So we just wait here and hope they eventually get bored enough to go away?" Larry asked.

"They'll wait until we leave this place, and then they'll attack in the dark," Duke said. "Wolves aren't stupid. They'll track us until we let our guard down, and that's when they'll make their move. Desperate, hungry predators do desperate things."

"It might be better to confront them while we have some kind of advantage," Jarred said, "rather than waiting for them to catch us off guard. We need to get them out into the open somehow where we can a clear shot at them."

Fiona considered their options. One tall pile of rocks drew her attention. It was steep but not sheer, with small protruding sections every few feet. "Jarred, I think you have the right idea,," she said. "Rather than letting them continue to harass us, we can bait them and draw them out into the open. I didn't lead us into this quarry to trap us with the wolves. I did it because I thought it would give us some terrain advantage for dealing with them."

"So you have a plan in mind?" Larry asked.

"I do." She pointed through the window. "See that tall slag pile there about forty yards from the building?"

People began to gather behind her to peer through the window.

"We'll never be able to climb up there," Lana said. "Larry and I did a bit of rock-climbing years ago, but I hardly remember the first thing about it."

"No one's climbing up there," Duke added. "That's a good way to break your neck. All it would take is one slip on the snow."

"We're not putting people up there," Fiona said. The people were pressed in just a little too closely for comfort, so she waved them back and turned around. "We're putting the goats up there. They can handle the climb. We put them up there, take up positions nearby, wait for the wolves to arrive, then…take care of them as best we can."

This got her some confused stares.

"It could work," Jarred said, "but it'll be tricky. We'll have to be really careful."

"We'll be careful," she said. "I've dealt with a few predators on the homestead over the years. Bold, decisive action combined with good bait and a reliable firearm usually does the trick. Let's get the goats."

She stepped past them and headed to the back-office door. If they were going to make her lead, then they would have to live with her decisions.

"I think it might work," Jarred said. The only positive feedback any of them offered.

"Jarred, I appreciate the almost vote of confidence," Fiona said with a sigh.

57

Despite the danger, Jarred saw the wisdom of Fiona's plan. Bold, decisive action to eliminate a impending threat rather than waiting for it to strike when their backs were turned. It made sense. Even so, he wasn't naïve about the danger of what they were doing. At the moment, they were leading the goats across the quarry toward the tall slag pile. The animals were roped together with Ramses in the lead, pulling the sleds behind them.

Fiona and Jarred discussed leaving the sleds behind until afterward, but Fiona made it clear that she didn't want to be separated from their stuff, not even for a little while.

"What if the wolves, sensing threat, went for the sleds instead of the goats and tore apart all of their food supplies while the humans stood dumbly on the slag pile?" she said. "That would be almost as certain a death as the wolves killing everyone."

Jarred had agreed, but bringing the sleds added to the difficulty.

The goats seemed somewhat reluctant to come. Was it possible they knew the humans were using them as bait? Fiona and Jarred had the lead line. Larry and Lana walked to the right, Zane and Hope to the left. The Coopers brought up the rear, volunteering to make sure all of the animals kept moving. The slag pile was little more than a steep hill comprised of rocks of numerous sizes. He couldn't tell exactly how tall it was because of the snow piled on top. It seemed deceptive. Still, the sides were steep, and he wondered if even the goats could be prodded to climb the thing.

"Once we get the goats on top, where do we put the humans?" he asked Fiona.

"I'm working on it," she said. "Somewhere nearby." She pointed to a smaller pile a short distance away. "Maybe over there. Somewhere we'll have a clear shot if they appear and start circling."

Of course, they'd brought the guns. Fiona had her favorite Mossberg shotgun, and Jarred carried the bolt-action Weatherby. More weapons and more shooters would have been nice, especially if they were dealing with a sizeable wolf pack. Still, they would have to make do.

"Won't they smell us?" Larry asked. "Even if we're hiding behind another pile, they'll catch our scent on the wind. Will that keep them away?"

"Maybe not," Fiona said. "If they're desperate, and if it looks like the goats are an easy target. Heck, one of them apparently came right up close to the camp to attack Maria."

The limited visibility made the whole world seem alien, hostile, creating a gray background so that objects seemed to emerge suddenly at about fifty yards. Even now, he couldn't see the far side of the quarry. It just faded behind the veil.

They drew near to the slag pile, picking their way through a field of loose, tumbled boulders that surrounded it. Suddenly, Jarred saw movement out of the corner of his eye, some small shape emerging from the veil, behind Hope and Zane. Startled, he spun toward it, struggling to keep the crutch under his right arm. He started to raise the rifle, but Hope was in the way, blocking the shot. The smallish shape revealed itself as a gray wolf, but he only got a good look at it for about a second or two before it disappeared behind a boulder. Still, he raised the rifle, holding it somewhat awkwardly because of the crutch, and took a shot at it. The crack of the rifle echoed long and loud in the quarry, bouncing back and forth against the high walls.

He saw a small puff of dust as the bullet hit near the top of the boulder, but the wolf did not reemerge.

"Did you hit it?" Fiona asked.

He shook his head. "It was moving fast. Maybe forty yards that way." He pointed with a nod of his head.

"That's deeper in the quarry," Fiona noted. "They've must've already circled around behind us."

"If there's one, there will be others," Larry said, looking left and right. "They've planned their attack."

That thought made a little shiver go down Jarred's spine. He gazed hard at the gray veil, trying to see shapes moving in the distance. Because of his jumpiness, he kept seeing shadows that weren't there, hints of movement that were only snow and wind. Fiona handed the lead line to Larry and took better hold of the shotgun.

"Get them to the slag pile as fast as you can," she said.

Larry nodded and tugged at the line, encouraging the goats to move faster. They seemed skittish, even Ramses, but they came willingly. Clearly, they sensed the danger that was closing in around them. Fiona took up a position beside Jarred, pointing the shotgun in the other direction.

"Don't waste ammo," she said. "Only take the shot if you're sure you'll hit something. You have four shots left."

"Got it," Jarred replied. It was a tall order. In this weather, he didn't think he could shoot his own foot if he'd wanted to. Still, he aimed the rifle into the gray and stared with unblinking eyes. From the back of the caravan, Duke gave a little growl of alarm.

"I saw one," he said, in his low, throaty voice. "I saw a wolf! They're circling us for sure!"

Smoke had been padding along between Hope and Lana, cowering and scared, but he began to alternate between whimpering and barking. Although, he'd been content to stay with the humans thus far, he suddenly

Jarred stooped down, leaning against the crutch, and grabbed for the rifle. As he did, he heard another wolf snarl. It came from the other direction, just to his left, and it sounded shockingly close. He managed to hook a finger around the rifle strap. Just then, Zane made a terrible deep sound, a cry of fear and pain. Hope shouted his name, and Ramses bleated again frantically.

It's all going to hell, Jarred thought. *What do we do?*

He picked up the rifle, pulled himself up on his crutch, and planted the butt against his shoulder. There was frantic movement in all directions. Duke and Myra were dealing with the other goats. Larry and Lana had been attempting to right the sled and pick up their gear, but the cry from their son sent them scrambling. Hope was dancing back and forth, as if fighting an urge to run after Zane. Fiona continued to call for Ramses, but she was also nursing rope burns.

"Hope, move aside," Jarred said.

She looked back with wide and terrified eyes, saw the gun, and dropped to the ground. Jarred aimed into the haze. He could hear some kind of desperate movement. He even thought he spotted vague shapes dashing about, but he couldn't identify the shape of the wolf.

"Damn," he muttered, gazing down the sightline of the rifle. "Show yourself. Show me that gray head just for one second."

As if in reply, he heard another angry bleat from Ramses, then a sharp yelp from a wolf. He tried to pinpoint the wolf, straining to see which shape it might be. Then he heard another cry from Zane. At that sound, Larry and Lana started forward, as if they were going to rush after him.

"Someone do something," Lana cried, waving her hands in the air.

Among the jumbled shapes in the haze, Jarred finally picked out what seemed to be a wolf—low and sleek. He took aim, steadying his right arm against the top of the crutch.

His finger had just brushed the trigger when a heavy weight slammed into him from behind. It knocked the wind out of him, and he fell forward. In the process, the crutch went flying to one side. Jarred hit the ground, his face sinking into the snow. Struggling to get a breath, he tried to roll to one side, but some enormous thing was on top of him.

He rolled the other way and managed to dislodge it. However, as soon as he turned his head to the side, the stench of wet canine filled his nostrils. He fumbled for the rifle, grabbed it, and brought it up. The wolf had stepped back, moving from side to side with his head down, teeth bared. There was something both dangerous and sad about the creature's appearance. The gray wolf was thin, its fur wet and ragged, and it had a crazed look in its eyes. Clearly, it had not eaten in a while.

Behind him, Jarred heard both people and animals shouting. Had the pack launched a coordinated attack? He couldn't tell. He dared not take his eyes off the animal in front of him. Suddenly, it snarled and lunged at him. Though he had the rifle in his hands, he was lying on his side, unable to aim properly. Instead, he swung the stock in front of him, using it as a crude shield. The wolf tried to bite, gnashing its teeth, but the butt of the rifle pressed against its throat, forcing it back.

It danced away, making a weird dog-like whimper, looking intently for an opening. Jarred used the opportunity to get his knee under him. As he did, he reseated the rifle and tried to take aim. Off to the right, he caught a glimpse of Zane, who had backed out of the haze. The kid was swinging something wildly back and forth. A flashlight, perhaps. A pair of wolves were trying to approach, doing a strange kind of dance where they lunged forward, backed away, then shifted to one side and tried again.

"Zane, you're too close." That was Fiona. She'd practically yelled herself hoarse. "Get away, so I can use the shotgun."

Jarred tried to take aim, but his attacker lunged forward again, coming in low. He was forced to rise and stumble backward, even putting weight on his healing leg. This caused a twinge of pain, and he collapsed backward through the snow and away from the others. The wolf kept coming, snarling and snapping.

Finally, Jarred swung the butt of the rifle again, but he only grazed the creature's head. It scarcely seemed to care. Stepping to one side, it came at him from the right. Unfortunately, backing away meant dragging his legs through deep snow, and it seemed like it was getting deeper the farther he went, as if he were moving into a snowdrift.

However, the deeper snow also slowed the wolf. Jarred finally got the rifle positioned correctly and took aim at the ever-shifting shape, aiming for the thickest part of its torso, the biggest target. His feet were close together, and his balance was precarious. He took one more step back with the bad leg, trying to brace himself for the kick of the rifle.

The right foot sank into snow and found nothing solid beneath. He'd stepped onto some kind of void, possibly a deeper pit, and he fell. As he did, there was a sudden fierce sense of déjà vu. Only this time he was tumbling backward instead of forward. As the snow rose up and enveloped him, he heard that snarling breath. The wolf was charging. He just managed to pull the trigger, the blast of the rifle dampened by the walls of snow sliding up around him. And then he sank out of the world completely.

58

Fiona tried to reposition herself in a way that would put Zane clear of the shotgun blast. However, the wolves kept lunging in close. She heard another commotion behind her. Jarred was dealing with at least one other wolf from the sound of it, but the fight had moved off a little bit. She didn't dare take her eyes off Zane's attackers, however.

"I just need a little more space between you and the wolves," she cried.

"I'm trying," Zane said, taking another swing with the long metal flashlight. "They're persistent. They won't stop coming at me."

His parents had mostly been standing around trying to figure out how to help. But Lana suddenly stooped down and grabbed something. Then she reared back and threw it. A wrench. It sailed end over end, arcing over Zane's head. Her aim wasn't good, and the wrench landed in the snow to the left of the wolves. But it startled them anyway. They whimpered and retreated, and Zane was able to put some space between himself and them.

As soon as he did, Fiona tracked them with the shotgun and fired. Most of the shot caught one of the wolves in the flank. It yelped loudly and took off running, limping, back into the hazy distance. She quickly fired again, aiming for the other one, but the shot went high. At best, she nicked its back, but that was enough to send it fleeing. Both wolves continued to yelp and whimper even after they'd disappeared.

Fiona turned quickly to see how the others were doing. To her surprise, she saw Duke and Myra leading the other goats. They'd kept the females together, pulling them along with the smaller sleds. Smoke was racing back and forth, as if he couldn't decide which way to go, barking at nothing specific. Hope ran to Zane, grabbed a fold of his coat, and pulled, as if encouraging him to hurry.

"Where's Jarred?" she asked.

She saw no sign of him. As if he had disappeared into thin air. Had he gone running off into the haze? Had he run back to the building to retrieve something? She had no idea, but she couldn't deal with it right now. She could still hear wolves moving around them just out of sight.

She motioned at the Coopers. "Get the goats up on that slag pile. Quick. Everyone, help them. Hurry."

Working together, the Coopers and the Bishops disconnected the sleds and guided the female goats up onto the nearest edge of the giant slag pile. Unlike Ramses, they went willingly. It seemed they understood the importance of getting to high ground. Some of them began picking their way up the bigger boulders. Fiona joined the others, so they were moving in a line behind the goats, pressing them forward, keeping them moving up the pile.

"That's it," she said. All of the goats were on the pile now, but a few tried to linger down low. Fiona heard the sound of paws on the snow, and she turned. The two wolves reappeared. Even the injured one, bleeding badly now from its left flank, came charging toward the slag pile, approaching from beyond the line of humans, trying to get past them to reach the goats.

Fiona motioned the others to keep moving forward as she ran down the line. As soon as she stepped past Larry, the last in line, she raised the shotgun and fired again. She mostly missed this time, aiming too high, but some of the shot seemed to graze the back of the already injured wolf. It yelped and tumbled to the ground. She'd hoped for a killing shot, but it still managed to rise and limp off again, followed by its companion. They disappeared again into the haze.

"They never stop," Lana cried, clinging to her husband's arm as she climbed the slag pile. "Even when we shoot them, they keep attacking."

"They're hungry," Fiona said. "Desperate for food. Probably starving. They're never going to stop trying to get something to eat unless they're physically unable to. That's why we're fighting them."

A third and fourth wolf appeared then, unharmed, rushing in from Fiona's left. They ran toward the slag pile in what seemed to be a coordinated effort. The goats had climbed, but they were still well within reach. Indeed, most of them seemed reluctant to go any higher.

"Throw rocks," Hope shouted.

She'd clambered up onto a shelf of loose rocks near the goats, and she stooped down, picking up a fist-sized rock. Fiona wasn't sure how many shells were left in the shotgun. Had she fired two times? Three? She swung the gun to the nearest wolves. It was difficult to stand still and aim with ravenous animals rushing at you. Her whole body screamed at her to flee, to climb with the others, but she gritted her teeth and planted her feet.

She pulled the trigger. The blast caught one of the wolves square in the face, removing almost everything from the neck up in a gruesome spray of blood and flesh. The body fell and flopped about before coming to a rest near her feet.

She fired at the other wolf, but it lunged suddenly to one side as she pulled the trigger, and the shot went into the snow. The wolf retreated only briefly, dashing back for a moment before rushing again. This time, fearing the gun was empty, Fiona turned and fled, scrambling up the rocks. The others had all managed to reach the flat top of a large boulder about ten feet up, with the goats arrayed on various ledges above them. Fiona made her way toward them, even as she heard the snarling and snapping of the wolves closing in behind her.

Where is Jarred? she thought. *Where did he go?*

Larry reached down and grasped her free hand. Even then, she had trouble scrambling up the boulder without losing the shotgun. Hope and Zane were throwing rocks down at the wolves. She heard them hitting, bouncing, but the wolves kept coming. Duke was kneeling to one side, fumbling around inside his coat.

Finally, Lana took her other hand, and the couple was able to drag Fiona up on top of the boulder. She heard one of the wolves' paws hit the side of the boulder just as she swung her legs up out of the way. Larry and Lana pulled her away from the edge. When she looked back, she saw three wolves right below. They'd reached the boulder, and they were leaping and snapping at the air.

"Relentless beasts," Lana said. "My God, won't they leave us alone?"

Fiona had managed to hold on to the shotgun, and she rose to her knees, aiming it down at them. Just then, one of the wolves, the larger and darker of the three, leapt, scrabbled against the side of the boulder with its back legs, and managed to hook its front paws over the top. It was just to Fiona's left, lunging up toward Duke and Myra. She pointed the shotgun and pulled the trigger. It clicked but did not fire. No more shells.

As if emboldened by this, the wolf pulled itself up onto the boulder, snarling and snapping at the Coopers. Duke was close. The first bite almost clamped down on the front of his right boot. But Duke brought his hand out of his coat then. Instead of freeing the bruised arm from the sling, he'd pulled something from an inner pocket. It took Fiona a second to realize it was the sharpened bamboo pole from the garden center.

"You get away from us, you mangy cur," Duke said in his gravelly voice.

The wolf pulled itself higher, swinging its head from side to side as it tried to get its rear paws up on the boulder. Duke drove the sharpened stake forward, jabbing the end under the wolf's jaw and stabbing it in the throat. The animal yelped and thrashed, then lost its grip. It fell off the boulder, crashed below, and went tumbling down the slope. Finally, it came to rest in the snow at the bottom of the slag pile, still visibly breathing but no longer moving.

That left two wolves at the base of the boulder, and they were stalking back and forth. Hope and Zane kept throwing rocks at them, but they mostly missed. Even when they hit, it didn't seem to have much effect. Fiona started to reach for a rock, intending to join their effort, but shapes in the distance drew her attention. From out of the haze, down by the abandoned sled, three more wolves appeared, loping along like stragglers who'd finally decided to join the fun. They seemed bigger. And then, from another direction, two more, dark gray, almost black, with ice-colored eyes.

"Every time we drive one away, we get three more to take its place," Fiona said. It was too much. She had never heard of wolves behaving like this. They were like monsters, bloodthirsty monsters.

"We can't hold them off with rocks and a sharp stick," Larry said, out of breath. He tossed a small rock down at one of the wolves beneath them. It hit the animal squarely between the eyes, but instead of turning away, the wolf snarled and leapt at him. His forepaws scrabbled at the top of the boulder for a second before he lost his grip and fell back down. Fiona marveled at how huge the head and jaws of these animals were up close. Much larger than most dog breeds, sleeker and more dangerous.

Duke thrust something at Fiona. She assumed it was the sharp stick, but when she grabbed at it, she felt cold metal. Looking down, she realized it was a rust-speckled Zippo lighter, with a flip top and the fading words "1st Sgt Duke Cooper 1991" etched into the side.

"There," Duke said, pointing at the sled. "See the puddle of gas? Aim for that. You're probably a better throw than me."

She saw the puddle, a thin liquid of a slight yellowish tint, it had pooled on the snow beside the red jerry can. And if that much had stayed on top of the snow, how much had soaked in beneath? Most of the approaching wolves were still beyond the sled and the puddle, but they were closing in fast.

"You can do it," Larry said. "Aim carefully."

She opened the lid and flicked the lighter. The old cloth wick caught fire, burning brightly. Fiona rose, spreading her feet apart to brace herself. It had been a hell of a long time since she'd played softball. Taking a deep breath, she tossed the lighter underhanded toward the fuel. She heard the others breathing loudly, anxiously, as the lighter spun, the flame dancing end over end. It flew over the nearest wolf and arced down toward the snow. Toward the puddle.

And then it landed just short, maybe six inches from the puddle, and instantly sank beneath the snow.

"Oh, for God's sake," she muttered, as Duke gave an expulsive breath. "I missed."

And then, after about a two-second delay, the large amount of fuel that had soaked into the snow caught fire. There was a fierce thud and whoosh that Fiona felt deep in her chest as a great wall of flame burst up in front of the slag pile. It spread to either side quickly, and one of the dark wolves failed to get out of the way in time. The fire swept over it, catching its fur alight. It yelped and took off running, but that only made the fire burn faster, until the animal was a torch racing through the snow, a torch shining in the haze. And then it was gone.

The wolves at the base of the boulder saw the flames and immediately retreated, running down the slag pile at an angle that would take them beyond the fire. As they fled, the other surviving wolves moved to meet them. The snow was steaming as it melted. In turn, this diminished the flames, but not much. Fiona heard the female goats bleating in terror behind her. But the wolves fled, moving together as they raced at full speed back into the haze, disappearing behind the veil of snow and mist. For a few seconds, she heard them, wheezing and whimpering, and then they were gone.

Though the fire continued to burn below, she rose and shouldered the shotgun.

"Is everyone okay?" she asked, turning to the others.

Zane and Hope were slumped back against the pile, sweating and out of breath despite the cold. Duke still clutched the sharpened spike, Myra leaning against his shoulder. Larry and Lana were huddled together near the boulder's edge, peering down into the bright orange flames.

"Jarred, Smoke, and Ramses," she said. "They're all missing. Did anyone see what happened to them?"

"I saw the dog when we were down there by the sled," Larry said. "He was just sort of running around frantically like he didn't know where to go. By the time we got up here, he was gone. No idea what happened."

"And Jarred?" she asked.

No one said anything. Larry shrugged.

"I think I heard him take a shot or two at some point," Duke said.

"Everything was just so crazy," Myra added. "We couldn't keep track of everyone."

"Damn it." Fiona climbed down the boulder. "There can't be much daylight left." As she considered their options, she hated every single one of them. "Do we search for him? Do we press on?"

She half-hoped one of the others would weigh in, but they just stared at her. She sighed.

"Okay, here's what we'll do," she said. "One group stays and look for him. The other group presses on to the cavern. We'll all meet there."

The others clambered down from the boulder. She got no pushback about her plan, but then again, no one expressed any opinion either way.

"I'll lead the search party," she said.

Duke shook his head. "No way. Not you. You're the leader of this group, like it or not, and the animals are yours. You have to stay with the sleds."

Larry and Lana both nodded.

"Let me look for my dad," Hope said. "I'm sure I can find him."

"I'll look too," Zane said.

Fiona didn't like this idea. She didn't like any of it. Everything had fallen apart. Their whole plan was in ruins, and the group was scattered.

Poor leadership, she thought, her heart sinking. *It's all my fault. I can't lead people.*

"An adult needs to go with you," she said, doing her best to hide the true depths of her despair and self-pity. "I'm not sending two teenagers off alone in this horrible weather."

"I'll stay with them," Larry said. Lana shook her head, but he held up a hand. "Lana, dear, we'll stick together. It'll be fine."

In the end, there was no better plan, so they all agreed to it. They climbed back down to retrieve the sleds. The big sled had taken extensive damage from the fire, which even now continued to smolder. Then they brought the goats back down and harnessed them to the remaining sleds, salvaging as much of their supplies as they could manage.

By then, they were quickly running out of daylight, and the snow had begun to fall much harder, reducing visibility even further. It was a bad situation all around, and she began to wonder if any of them would make it to the cavern. Suddenly, the whole journey seemed doomed. As Fiona and Duke took their places on the two surviving wagons, Larry, Zane, and Hope prepared to set off on foot, with Duke's sharpened bamboo pole as their only weapon. They'd called for Jarred for a while and gotten no response. Either he'd wandered off in the chaos, gotten turned around and lost, or else he was lying out there dead.

No Jarred. No Ramses. No Smoke, Fiona thought. *And who knows if we'll ever see Larry, Zane, and Hope again. This is bad. All bad.*

"Be careful out there," she said. Could they hear the absolute hopelessness in her voice? "Try to stick together. The weather is getting worse. Listen carefully for the wolves. They might come back."

"Try not to get bitten," Myra added. "There's a lot of bacteria in a wild animal bite."

"We'll be extra careful," Larry said. "As soon as we find Jarred, we'll rush to meet you. I believe I can find my way to the caverns."

"Oh, God," Fiona muttered. She couldn't help it. And as she watched the trio turn and march into the snow-void, her heart felt like it sank right out of her chest and went tumbling down to her feet. *And now I'm stuck with those godawful Coopers.*

She picked up the reins, but before she shook them, she glanced back at the other sled. Duke and Myra were standing in front. She made eye contact with Duke, and to her amazement, he gave her a thumbs-up.

"Let's just do what we have to do," he said.

Fiona nodded and shook the reins. The four goats pulling her sled started to move, straining at the weight. Duke and Myra soon followed. She moved alongside their own faint tracks, mostly buried now, back out of the quarry, moving much slower than before. Maybe that was a good thing. If Jarred came across the sled tracks, he might be able to catch up, even with his busted leg.

I meet one guy that I like, she thought, *and now he's dead or lost out there in this white hell. That's just my bad luck, isn't it?*

It was quiet now. She had no one to talk to, of course. Lana was walking behind the sled, but she wasn't an easy conversation even under the best of conditions. The goats seemed subdued, and they were struggling to keep moving anyway. The heavy snow had dampened sound even more. The world seemed to close in around her, and the light was waning.

Eventually, after what might have been an hour or so, Fiona became aware of some noise off to her right. A wolf? She wasn't sure. It was faint and vague. Still, she reached down behind her in the sled, fumbling around to find some kind of weapon. She came up with a rubberized mallet from their tools. Suddenly, Hope stumbled out of the heavy snow.

Fiona reined in her sled and went to meet her.

"I lost everyone," Hope said. She was crying hard, caked in snow. "Fiona, did you see Zane or Larry? We heard something out there, and it was real hazy, and then we sort of scattered, Suddenly, I couldn't find anyone. Did you see them?"

Fiona grabbed one of Hope's extended arms and led her back to the sled. "No, you're the first to return," she said. She helped Hope sit down on the edge of the sled.

"Didn't you call to each other?" Lana said.

"I thought the wolves might be close," Hope said. "I couldn't find my dad. I couldn't find anyone."

Fiona traded a look with Lana. The other woman was glaring back at her hard, as if she blamed Fiona for all this. But then Larry came stumbling out of the snow, and Lana's angry look instantly melted. Larry was bent over and hobbling.

"Is Zane with you?" Lana asked.

"I don't know," he said, grimacing as he dropped to his knees beside the sled. "We heard an animal out there. Something. It spooked us, and then I was alone."

Duke and Myra had left their sled and approached then. Duke's bruised arm was out of the sling again, exposed to the cold air, and he was gently massaging it with his other hand.

"We're all going to get lost out here," he said. His voice was tight and labored. "Shouldn't we turn back to that building?"

"We're an hour out, at least," Fiona replied. "The cavern's not that far, assuming we're not completely turned around." She smacked her forehead with her free hand. She'd never felt so lost, and it was becoming harder and harder to think clearly.

Larry pulled himself up onto the sled and fell against some of the boxes. Lana put her arms around him, trying to comfort him, as Hope continued to quietly cry. Duke and Myra were both staring at Fiona. Waiting for her to decide the next step, it seemed.

"If only this weather would clear, just for a minute," she muttered. But, no, she caught herself. No use in hoping for better circumstances.

"We have to find our son," Lana said, in the most pitiful voice. "He's out there somewhere! He can't have gone far."

Fiona bit her lip. Her mind was racing, but it was getting darker. Then her gaze happened upon Duke's hands. One hand was furiously massaging the other, but she noted some discoloration on his fingers. Reaching out, she gently grabbed the hand and turned it over. He didn't resist. The tips of three fingers had turned dark purple, almost black.

"Duke, have you seen this?" she said.

He glanced down at his hand. "They've sort of gone numb."

"Frostbite," she said. "It's because you keep sticking your arm out of your coat!"

"Why didn't you tell me?" Myra said to him, grabbing his shoulder. "Is that why you kept messing with it?"

"I've been trying to rub some feeling back into the fingers." He quickly tucked the hand and arm back under his coat. "Not much I can do about it. Not out here."

"Duke, you're going to lose those fingers," Myra said. "Maybe the whole arm! We can't undo the damage! What were you thinking?"

Fiona rocked her head back. *Everyone is going to die out here.*

"We're going to the cavern," she said. Lana started to say something, probably to protest, but Fiona pressed on, raising her voice. "If we don't, every single one of us is going to die out in this cold! Remember, Snowbird Cavern has a steady temperature of fifty-five degrees. If at least a few of us don't get down in there, we won't have any survivors to go looking for Zane and Jarred. Is that what you want? Is that what any of you want?"

"If I was lost, Dad would keep looking for me," Hope said, her voice quavering. "He wouldn't stop looking for anything."

"When your father fell and broke his foot, he told you to keep going," Fiona reminded her. "That's how you first arrived at my house. Do you remember? He was lying on the ground in pain, but he sent you on ahead because he knew you both had a better chance of survival that way."

At this, Hope bowed her head and said no more. Fiona clamped her eyes shut, tears burning behind her eyelids. A few seconds passed and no one responded. Finally, she heard Duke and Myra making their way back to the other sled. Hope moved up beside Larry and Lana. The decision was made, as much as Fiona utterly despised it. She picked up the reins and reluctantly shook them.

"As soon as we get to the cave, we'll send out a search party," she said. "I hate this, but I don't know what else to do."

God forgive me, she thought. *I have failed these people. Maybe I can at least keep most of them alive.*

59

The snowfall was getting heavier, and Fiona feared they would soon be dealing with a complete whiteout. Still, she hated to move ahead. Where the heck could Jarred and Zane have gone? They resumed moving forward, slowly creeping along. As they did, they shouted for the missing. The heavy snow muffled their voices, so it felt to Fiona like the words only made it a few inches from their mouths before dropping dead.

"It's like they just disappeared from the world," Larry said. He was walking just behind Fiona and gazing off into the snowstorm. "I don't understand it. Even if they were injured, they should be able to respond, cry out, make some kind of sound."

"Larry, what if they're dying?" Lana said. She was walking behind the sled. "What if they're dying right now?"

Fiona had the reins, but she found them hard to hold. Her whole body was trembling violently, and not just from the cold. Jarred and Zane were out there. Had the snow somehow swallowed them whole? Were they drowning in a deep drift somewhere? Had the wolves killed them? She didn't know, but she felt like the rest of them were getting close to the edge. Suddenly the deaths of each person in this whole group seemed all too possible. The cold had sunk in deep, and the warmth of the fire was long gone. The cold had overthrown the primal gods of fire, leaving scarcely any hint that only an hour earlier, a great wall of flame had been burning brightly.

"I'm sorry, guys," she said suddenly. As Fiona walked, Hope was seated on the sled now, hands in her lap. She'd cried for a while, but now she was in a traumatized silence. She didn't respond to Fiona's apology. "Maybe we shouldn't have detoured into the quarry. I wanted to deal with the wolves before we got to the cavern. I was afraid we would meet them out here in the open with no way to defend ourselves."

"And we *did* meet them out in the open," Larry replied. "To that end, your plan worked, and if we'd had time to set up and bait a proper trap on the slag pile, maybe it would have worked better. But we no longer have Ramses. That'll hurt us, even when we get where we're going."

"I know. I know," Fiona replied. Tears burned in her eyes, but they began to freeze as soon as they ran down her cheeks. "I'm sorry."

"I wasn't blaming you," Larry said with a sigh. "I was just considering our present condition. Truth be told, it could have been a whole lot worse."

"How can you say that?" Lana snapped. "Our son is out there somewhere!"

Even Hope stirred, though she didn't speak. Clearly, his comment had offended her as well. A whole lot worse?

"The wolves could have killed all of the goats," Larry said. "They could have killed all of us. They would have if not for the fire. Don't you think that would've been worse, Lana?"

She pointedly didn't respond.

"I'll set out and look for Zane again as soon as the weather permits," Larry said.

"It may never permit," Lana replied. "You see how bad it's gotten just in the last hour."

"It will let up eventually."

To this, she merely grunted in disgust. Fiona didn't blame her. Despite the reduced visibility, Fiona could see a hint of the hills off to their left. The shape was familiar to her. She turned them in that direction, knowing it would eventually lead them to their destination. When she looked back, she realized Duke and Myra had fallen behind a bit. The goats appeared to be okay, but Duke was bent over in some kind of struggle. Myra was trying to help him hold the reins.

"Duke's in trouble," she said.

"For all of his complaining, he doesn't take care of himself," Larry said. "I'll head back and help him. Otherwise, we're going to lose him, too."

Lana started to complain, but she only managed a small whimpering sound. He turned to her and leaned down, laying a hand on the side of her head. "Maybe they found each other," he said. "Zane and Jarred. Maybe they found each other out there in the cold. Maybe Smoke led them to each other."

"You really think so?" she replied.

"Absolutely," he replied. He sounded like he believed it. Even Fiona wanted to believe it, too. "That's why we haven't heard from either of them. They found each other out there, and they're taking care of each other. Jarred is hurt. Maybe Zane is treating his wounds. The boy is handy in a pinch. You know that."

"Yes," Lana replied. "Yes, he is. I think you're right. Do you hear that, Hope? They found each other out there in the snow. They're taking care of each other."

Hope seemed to perk up a little. She pushed her hood back and revealed her face, tears freezing on her prominent cheeks. "It *is* possible, when you really think about it," she said. "Maybe there's a cave or a crevice out there where Jarred took shelter, and Zane found it. That would explain the silence."

"They're both really smart," Lana said, reaching out and patting Hope gently on top of the head. "Working together, they'll survive. I'm sure of it. Once the snow lets up a little bit, they'll be able to find their way to the cavern. They may even get there before we send out a search party."

"The snow always lets up after a while," Hope said. "The storms come in waves, waxing and waning every few hours. That's what I've noticed."

"There you go," Larry said. "Stay hopeful, ladies. I'm going to help Duke." And with that, he trudged back to the smaller sled.

Fiona gave the reins another little shake, and they were able to pick up some more speed. She adjusted their course again to keep them pointed toward the distant hills. Still, she couldn't quite get to a hopeful place like Hope and Lana. Yes, she knew full well that Jarred and Zane were both smart and resourceful. They had an above average chance of survival, but the odds were stacked against them.

People don't disappear without a sound unless something is really wrong, she thought.

And the only reason she wasn't grieving their deaths already was because she thought there was also an above average chance she would be joining them before the day was through. The cold had sunk so deeply into her body that she felt strangely disconnected from it, almost like she was having an out of body experience.

"They're going to make it," Hope said softly from her place beside Fiona. "*We're* going to make it, too. The snow has to stop soon. It's almost time."

Keep telling yourself that, kid, Fiona thought. *Hold on to that hope as long as you possibly can.*

60

Jarred's descent had been surprisingly long, like some hellish playground slide. He was beneath the snow but definitely on a steep slope. He flailed his arms and legs, trying to arrest his descent, but then the injured ankle bumped into something hard and a burst of pain shot up his leg. The white snow all around him dimmed, as his vision went momentarily dark. After that, half-conscious, everything took on a surreal quality. And still he slid.

In a moment of clarity, he tried to make sense of what was happening. It must have been some deeper section of the quarry, hard to spot because of the optical illusion created by the nearly featureless snow. And perhaps the steep slope was a driveway for trucks leading down to the bottom.

As some point, he veered too far to the side of the driveway and felt himself slip over a steep edge. Again, he tried to grab something, anything, to arrest his fall, but nothing felt solid around him. It was all crumbling snow that broke into pieces when he tried to take hold of it. He felt himself dropping. And then he finally slammed into the ground below. It was solid enough that it knocked the wind out of him, and his vision dimmed again.

This time, the darkness lingered at the edges of his vision. Even after he'd come to a stop, the snow continued to fall down on top of him for a few seconds, burying him. When it finally stopped, he was completely buried in snow, struggling to stay conscious. He managed to raise his left arm and push through the loose mound of snow on top of him. Then he rolled to his right, breaking out of the mound. He felt the wind blowing into his hood. When he opened his eyes, he could tell that he was, indeed, at the bottom of a large pit. A sheer rock wall rose up in the distance.

He rolled onto his belly, but that only caused another twinge of pain in his leg. Jarred dragged himself forward, pulling his body out from under the snow. An enormous gray lump rose from the snow nearby. As he drew near, he saw blood-soaked fur, blood-speckled snow, a single paw sticking up. He swept some of the snow aside to reveal the body of the wolf, the large gunshot wound in its neck, the open mouth, lifeless eyes.

At least I killed it, so it can't go after the others, he thought.

He kept going past the wolf, and his hand found some hard, cold object beneath the snow. He pulled it up to reveal the barrel of the rifle. It slipped from his fingers and fell. When he tried to grab it again, he couldn't quite get a grip on it. The darkness was closing in before him. The throbbing pain was turning into a kind of aching numbness, dragging him deeper and deeper into the depths with every heartbeat.

I'm going to die out here, he thought.

Looking back over his shoulder, he saw the sheer rock side of the driveway leading up and out of this place. There were sounds above. Gunshots, shouting, violent sounds that he couldn't identify. After a while, he thought he saw a faint red light shining over the top of the pit. Then the darkness won out, and he went limp. He had a last vague sense of his face coming to rest on the back of his arm, feeling the soft material of his winter coat against his cheek.

It wasn't sleep. It wasn't even unconsciousness, really. Just some dazed state full of pain and cold that he couldn't pull himself out of. He was aware of shouting, a lot of shouting, monsters howling. It seemed to go on and on, and then a terrible quiet fell, and it was in a quiet moment that he finally rose from the depths. Jarred blinked and felt his eyelashes flutter against his sleeve.

Turning his head, he saw fat snowflakes falling into the pit all around him. Above him, the snow-covered path seemed a million miles away. In reality, he'd probably fallen about twenty or twenty-five feet. A distance that could have killed him if he'd landed differently, or in shallower snow.

He became aware of the other person only gradually. Another big lump, his mind had assumed it was the wolf. When he looked right at it, however, he realized it was the humped back of a person wearing a heavy winter coat. He was on his stomach, arms folded beneath his face. He recognized that coat. Zane Bishop. Somehow, he'd fallen into the pit and landed nearby.

"Zane." Jarred tried to say his name, but his throat was so scratchy, the sound was barely recognizable. He cleared his throat and tried again. "Zane!" He couldn't manage much volume.

He pushed himself onto his elbows. He had some of his strength back, at least. Despite the pain in his leg, he crawled toward Zane. When he got close, he reached out and shook him.

"Hey there, kid," he said. "Are you okay? Tell me you're okay."

Zane groaned and lifted his head. Slowly, he turned and looked at Jarred, blinking rapidly.

"How'd you wind up down here?" Jarred asked. "Where are the others?"

"We went looking for you," Zane said, his voice strained. He rose to his knees, brushing off his sleeves and the front of his coat. "It's getting really hard to see, but I thought I spotted some kind of tracks that might have been you. Then we heard a wolf, and I ran. I saw the slope there, but I didn't realize how steep it was. I couldn't really tell because of all the snow. Then I fell off the side and dropped straight down and landed here, pretty much knocked myself out."

It was snowing very heavily now. Jarred could barely see the far side of the pit. He pushed himself up and managed to get into a seated position.

"Where are the others?" he asked.

Zane looked unsure. "Hope and Larry were looking with me," Zane replied, pointing up the slope to the top of the pit. "I thought I heard them shouting for a while, but I couldn't respond. My head is all swimmy, you know?"

"Believe me, I know," Jarred said. "I guess we'd better try to climb back up there. Do you see my crutch anywhere?"

Zane rose and began searching the area. He found the dead wolf first and pushed it farther from them with the side of his boot. Then he found the rifle, shook as much snow off it as he could, and handed it to Jarred. As he continued hunting around, Jarred cleaned snow off the rifle and checked to make sure it still had some bullets in the magazine.

"Two shots left," he noted. "Better use them wisely."

"Here it is," Zane said. "Your crutch." He'd gone a few yards away, but he came rushing back now, Jarred's crude crutch tucked under his arm. "It went quite a way. You must've fallen hard."

"Felt like it," Jarred said, taking the crutch from him. "I suppose I'm lucky I didn't break my neck."

Using the crutch, he leveraged himself off the ground. He found he could still put weight on his leg, but it hurt more than before. It didn't seem to be broken, at least. He seated the crossbar of the crutch under his armpit, then turned to face the ramp behind them.

"I guess that's the way back up," he said. "Shall we try it?"

Zane shrugged. "With your leg and all, why don't I give it a try first and see how it goes?"

Indeed, looking up the steep slope, Jarred really didn't see how he would ever make it up there. He motioned for Zane to go ahead, and the teen approached the bottom of the slope. The snow had piled up especially high here, but he managed to kick his way through it, and he started up the slope, picking his way carefully. He made it about ten feet up before his feet slipped out from under him, and he fell. Landing on his hands and knees in the deep snow, he slid right back down to the bottom.

"Careful, Zane," Jarred said.

"Let me try another route," Zane replied.

This time, he stuck close to the sheer wall of the quarry as he picked his way up the slope. He hunched over, occasionally using his hands to clear the way or grab some snow-covered object as a handhold. Inch by inch, he ascended the slope, but he didn't get much higher. Maybe twelve feet up, his feet slipped out from under him, and he came tumbling down again.

A third attempt failed. So did a fourth and a fifth. By then, they'd wasted a lot of time, and the snowstorm was getting worse.

"I don't think it's going to happen," Jarred said. "If you keep it up, you're going to injure yourself."

"But we have to get out of this place," Zane said. He was at the bottom of the slope, bent over and gasping for breath. The front of his coat and pants were plastered with layers of crusted snow and ice. "The others are waiting for us up there somewhere."

"Let's see if there's another way," Jarred replied. "A safer way."

He turned and scanned the rest of the pit. While he could see some sections of the outer walls on the far side of the pit, the reduced visibility made it difficult to pick out every feature. However, he thought he saw some irregularities here and there, shadows and shapes, possibly gaps. As he was studying some of these distant features, Zane walked over to join him, still out of breath.

"Let's walk to the other side and see if there's an alternate route to the top," Jarred said, gesturing with his free hand.

"If you say so," Zane replied, angrily brushing off the front of his coat. "I wish we had, like, climbing spikes or something. Then we'd get up that ramp really quick."

"If we're wishing for things we don't have, I'll take spring or summer," Jarred said. "Come on. Let's see what we can find."

He beckoned Zane and started across the pit, stepping carefully. It was an exercise in constant frustration, because the snow was deep and hid numerous irregular formations. Jarred kept stumbling on things he could not see. This made it an excruciating slog. Zane was patient, walking slow enough to stay by his side, but he kept glancing back at the ramp, clearly frustrated that he hadn't tried again.

Suddenly, the ground seemed to change beneath Jarred's feet. It went from constant irregularities to a remarkable smoothness, as if the snow here had fallen on a big pane of glass. He took a few more steps to make sure.

"Hey, Zane, dig under the snow here, if you can, and see what lies beneath," he said.

Zane gave him a funny look, as if he thought Jarred had lost his mind. Then he squatted and used both gloved hands to sweep the snow aside. After a few feet, he uncovered a strange flat surface. He kept clearing it, revealing a layer of bluish ice, which he tapped with his knuckles.

"Feels like it must be thick," he said.

"Seems like we're standing on a pond," Jarred noted. "At least part of this quarry was filled with water. Maybe it has a way to flow out of here."

"Or maybe it was just rainwater that collected over a long time," Zane said.

"Maybe. Let's find out."

Jarred kept going, making sure to keep the smooth surface under his feet. Eventually, the far side of the pit emerged fully out of the gloom. He saw the rock walls rising up forty or fifty feet to the top. But as he scanned the distance, he realized that the wall was split in the far corner. It looked like a natural formation that had been deepened by the digging of the pit, winding off into a kind of narrow chasm.

"There really *is* another way out," Zane said. "I can't believe it! You were right."

"I was lucky," Jarred replied. "And desperate."

They picked their way along, entering the narrow chasm and following it out of the pit. Eventually, the high walls on either side dropped down, and the artificial drainage ditch merged with what appeared to be a natural creek or river with steep banks on either side. Jarred was so turned around, he couldn't tell which way they were facing. South? East?

"Are we still in the quarry?" Zane asked.

"I'm not sure," Jarred replied. "We should climb up out of this river and take a look."

The snow was falling so thick now that Jarred could scarcely see more than a few yards in any direction. The cold was working its way deep into his body, bringing with it an aching weariness. The pain in his leg kept him alert, however, counteracting the cold. He turned toward the nearest riverbank and considered climbing it. The sides were steep, though not nearly as steep or high as the walls in the pit. Still, it looked like a good way for one of them to get injured. Even if Zane made it, how would Jarred follow him?

"I guess we'd better follow the river for a while," he said. "It's frozen over, so we're not in any danger here. Maybe we'll find a way out somewhere downstream."

"I think we're in big trouble," Zane said softly. He had his arms wrapped tightly around his chest, and his teeth were chattering. "Hope and my dad probably found their way back to the group. They were going to keep going to the caves. But we have no idea if that's what happened. We don't know how to get back to that building, and no idea how to get to the cavern. Heck, we don't even know if we're heading in the right direction, and…it's just so cold."

"Hang in there, Zane," Jarred replied. He knew the kid was right, but he also knew that sinking into despair would reduce their chances of survival. And he was damn sure going to do his best to get back to Fiona and Hope. "Let's not assume the worst just yet, okay? We'll follow this river until we find a place where the banks are shallower, and then we'll climb back up. From there, we should be able to find our way to the others. They can't have gone far, not at this pace."

Zane groaned and hung his head. "Well, if you say so."

"I say so," Jarred said, even as he tripped on a buried rock and Zane had to catch his arm to steady him. "Listen, Zane, we can do this. We're stronger than this weather, and we can make it to the others."

"Is that really what you think?" Zane said.

"It is." Despite his answer, he wasn't sure. Finally, he decided that the best course of action was to stop thinking about it, so he changed the subject. "I'll tell you what, let's talk about something else, so we don't worry about it, okay? Tell me, Zane, are you a junior or senior in high school?"

Zane gave him a little frown, as if he were irritated at what Jarred was trying to do. But he replied anyway. "I'm a senior, but I skipped ninth grade. I'm only sixteen."

"Any idea what you want to study in college?"

Zane started to reply, then stopped and made a weird little face that Jarred couldn't quite read. Was he embarrassed? How could something as simple as a college major be a source of embarrassment?

"You don't have to tell me if you don't want to," Jarred said. "I was just curious."

"Actually, I really want to major in video game design," Zane said, after another moment's hesitation. "The thing is, my parents hate the idea. My dad said it's a bad industry. People are overworked and underpaid. 'It'll be a waste of a scholarship, if you get one,' he said. 'And if you don't get one, I don't want to pay for four years of college that only lead you to a miserable career.'"

"What does he want you to do instead?" Jarred asked.

It did indeed seem like the riverbanks were getting shallower the farther they went, if only gradually.

"He hasn't said," Zane replied. "He just told me to pick something else. And my mom agrees with him. But it's my life, after all." He swept an arm in the air, as if to swipe the snow away. "Anyway, whatever. I'll get a scholarship and do what I want. That's the only option for me."

"I'm sure you'll do just fine," Jarred said. "I don't know if she told you, but Hope really wanted to be a vet. At least, that's what she told me last year. I always thought she'd pursue something with technology since she's so good at it. She may have changed her mind by now. After helping us deal with all of the goats and chickens, she may have had her fill of animals."

Zane shook his head. "No, she still wants to be a vet. She feels really strongly about it, sir. I know because she confided in me. Actually, that's why she volunteered to help down in the basement so much. She likes the goats and chickens."

Jarred was impressed by how well this kid seemed to know his daughter. As her father, he hadn't spoken to her about her future plans for months, yet this kid that she'd only known for a few weeks seemed to know everything about her. In truth, it made Jarred a little sad, if only because he'd always struggled to get Hope to open up to him.

"Well, I'm glad to hear she still has some plan for the future," Jarred said, after a moment, swallowing the momentary sadness.

"Sure, but it's not like it matters now," Zane replied.

"Sure it does."

Zane shook his head dramatically. "Neither of us are ever going to college, and you know it. Even if we don't die out here. Heck, I'll probably never play another video game in my life. We're going to be living like cavemen now. All that's missing are a few mastodons to hunt."

Jarred knew damn well the kid was probably right. At best, he hoped they would somehow create a sustainable life that was somewhat safe, with protection from weather and access to food. More than that seemed like a pipe dream. Still, he wouldn't dare say this to the kid.

"There's still a chance that this winter storm will end soon," he said. Could Zane tell he didn't believe his own words?

They were moving very slowly. Jarred had to be careful of the obstacles hidden under the snow, so he stepped lightly. Still, the riverbanks were gradually dropping down, and he thought they might be able to climb out in another hundred yards or so.

"It probably sounds weird to an older guy like you, but losing video games is one of the worst aspects of all of this," Zane said. "I used to ditch gym class and sneak off to the computer lab so I could code. That's how much it means to me, and I think I was getting pretty good at it. I almost had a playable alpha of my game right before this snowstorm started. Now look where I am. Following goat-driven sleds through this North Pole-looking wasteland, fighting off wolves, and marching off in some random direction to nowhere. This is not the life I expected, and it's definitely not the life I would have chosen."

Jarred felt like he should say more to comfort the kid, but he just didn't have anything, not anything that wasn't a complete lie. Still, Fiona wasn't here, so it was up to him to show some leadership.

"I have to believe that we'll eventually get back to something like normal life," he said. "Not sure how long that will take."

"Generations," Zane grumbled. "Centuries."

"Well...you never know. Keep trying to hope, if you can."

Jarred hobbled along, slowing them way down. Zane didn't complain, but it was a struggle for him to match Jarred's speed. Eventually, they reached a spot where the riverbank on their left was relatively smooth and shallow, a long slope leading back up to high ground.

"Let's head up and see if we can tell where we are," Jarred said, pointing up the slope.

"We could be anywhere at this point," Zane replied. "Back in Glencole, for all we know."

Still, he did as Jarred suggested, turning and started up the slope. As Jarred followed him, he found the snow especially deep here. It was also loose enough that the snowshoes didn't entirely work. Still, he pressed on, despite pain, weariness, and an aching back. As they reached the high ground above the riverbank, he saw a stand of trees nearby and endless snowy ground extending beyond, quickly disappearing into the veil of heavy snow. Though he couldn't see the sun, the quality of light seemed to be changing, turning ever grayer.

"We're lost," Zane said. "You can't see anything out there, sir. It's all white and gray and nothing else. Just a few trees. Do you have any idea where we are?"

"I wish I could say I did," Jarred replied, pausing for a moment as he leaned on his crutch. "Zane, I don't want to scare you or anything, but I'm starting to wonder if our plan wasn't a mistake. Maybe we should have stayed put in the quarry. That's what you're supposed to do when you're lost. Stay put and wait for people to find you."

"I was afraid they would never see us down in that pit," Zane said, brushing the accumulation of snow off his shoulders and hood. "We should have just kept trying to get up that ramp. We could have done it. Surely, we could have found a way."

"I'm not sure about that," Jarred said. "We'd have been better off if we hadn't tried to do anything."

He strained to see something, anything, through the heavy snow, some natural feature beyond the trees, anything that might give him a hint about where they were in relation to the quarry. Even the river, with its constant winding had turned him around.

"So we really are lost, then?" Zane said softly.

"It's a distinct possibility," Jarred said.

"Does that mean we'll never find Hope and my parents and the other people?"

Jarred sighed. He glanced back over his shoulder toward the snowy river. They'd walked for hours. Nevertheless, he wondered if it wouldn't be better to head back the way they'd come. He might have done it, if not for the fact that the sun seemed to be setting.

"Kid, I don't know where the others are," Jarred said finally, "but we can't worry about that right now. Looks like we're going to be stuck out here at night, so let's head for that small stand of trees. We'll at least get some relief from the wind and snow in there."

Zane groaned and resumed trudging through the snow, adjusting his course for the trees. They stood in a little cluster, maybe two dozen, mostly silver maple and sycamore. The tree cover was at least fairly heavy thanks to the densely packed branches. Jarred thought that might at least give them some chance for surviving through the night. And at least he had the rifle over his shoulder to protect them if the wolves came.

"I don't suppose we'll be able to start a fire," Zane said, approaching the trees. "A little warmth would make a huge difference."

"We don't have the supplies for it," Jarred replied. "Almost everything was packed on the sleds. I've got a pocketknife, but I don't have a lighter. Do you?"

Zane shook his head. "No, but I've got a pocketknife, too. I guess that won't start a fire, will it?"

"I'm afraid it'll be close to impossible," he said.

They reached the small grove and passed through the first trees. Jarred struggled to get over some large roots without banging his bad foot. However, once he was among the trees, the wind diminished and that alone made a significant difference. The snow was less deep here, as well. He even saw a few bare patches. He couldn't remember the last time he had seen uncovered ground.

Zane approached one of the largest bare patches and came to a stop. "Do we just stop right here or what?" he asked.

"This'll do," Jarred replied. The gray light was edging toward true darkness now. "Without the wind or the snow falling on our heads, we'll have a better time just getting through the night."

"It's still so dang cold," Zane muttered, easing himself down at the base of a large sycamore tree. "And I'm really thirsty. We could melt snow if we had a fire."

"Yes. Yes, we could." There wasn't much more to say than that. Jarred leaned against a trunk and slowly slid down onto the ground, careful to keep his bad leg from hitting anything. Once he was down, he wondered if he would ever get up again. He took the rifle off his shoulder and laid it across his lap.

Zane was quiet for a minute before muttering, "I'll bet my parents are freaking out that they can't find me. Especially my mom. If I ever see them again, they're going to yell at me for running off."

"I doubt they'll yell at you," Jarred said. Indeed, he felt the distance between himself and Hope, between himself and Fiona, and he felt a pang of sadness. What if he never saw either of them again? What if this was it? A terrible thought, and he tried to drive it from his mind.

Suddenly, he heard the crunch of snow behind him, the shifting of some animal body. Heart racing, he picked up the rifle, and struggled to turn himself. Zane dropped to the ground and backed away from the tree, as Jarred braced the rifle against the trunk and aimed in the direction of the sound.

"Wolves found us," Zane said in a terrified whisper. "I figured they would."

Jarred motioned for him to keep his voice down, then gazed down the sight of the rifle. It was gloomy beneath the trees, but he heard another footfall. Then a shadow appeared between two trees. Jarred shifted the rifle toward it, his finger sliding down to the trigger.

Just hold still a second, he thought. His arms were trembling, making it difficult to hold the rifle still. *Just a second.*

And then the shadow shape made a strange sound, distinctly un-wolf-like. He did it once, then again. A plaintive bleating. And then the shadow bounded toward him. In disbelief, Jarred lowered the rifle.

"Are you kidding me?" he said.

"What?" Zane said. "What is it?"

The great creature stepped out of the shadows and resolved itself before them. An enormous cream-colored male goat, snow piled on his back and between his horns.

"Ramses, you old rascal, it's you," Jarred said. "How in the world did you find us?"

61

Jarred carefully rose, shouldering the rifle, as the big animal lumbered toward him. As Ramses drew near, he lowered his head, as if he were going to charge. Jarred realized suddenly that the goat might feel resentful rather than relieved to see his humans, and he tried to ease his body behind the tree to avoid the blow. However, Ramses didn't charge. Instead, he simply came close and raised his head again, bleating softly.

"If Ramses found us, then we can't be that far from the others," Zane said, daring to pick himself up from the ground.

"Maybe so," Jarred replied. Then again, he knew it was possible that the wolves had chased him quite a distance before giving up.

He slowly stretched his hand out and stroked the side of the goat's neck. Ramses seemed pleased, or at least tolerant of this, so Jarred swept some of the snow off his back. The goat came even closer to him, until his furry flank brushed up against Jarred's shoulder.

"Should we go back the way he came, just to the edge of the trees, so we can take a look?" Zane asked, coming up on the other side of Ramses and patting him on the shoulder. "His trail might lead us back to our people. You never know! It's worth a try, right?"

"I suppose so," Jarred replied. Ramses still had a harness around his neck and a broken length of rope hanging down. He grabbed the end of the rope and held it up. "Take this, Zane. I don't think I can lead him with my crutch."

Zane grabbed the rope and immediately headed back through the trees, following Ramses's hoofprints. Jarred adjusted the crutch, shouldered the rifle, and went after them.

"He came right to us when we thought we were doomed," Zane said. "That's gotta be a good omen."

"I don't usually believe in things like omens," Jarred replied, "but right now, I'll take it."

Ramses scarcely needed to be led. He followed close enough that the short bit of rope still had some slack. Apparently, his little escapade in the wolf-ridden snowstorm had taught him the value of humans. Zane and Ramses reached the edge of the grove and waited for Jarred. Once he limped up on the other side of Ramses, he leaned against a large, low branch for support and gazed out across the open snowy expanse, where the last vestiges of light burned shapelessly beyond the unbroken cloudy horizon. He could see Ramses's hoofprints winding off across the open ground, but they were quickly getting covered. However, it seemed the goat had headed right for the grove, as if he'd arranged to meet his humans there.

"Do you suppose goats can smell people at a distance like dogs?" Jarred wondered aloud. "It looks like he came right to us."

"I don't know much about goats," Zane replied. "Maybe Hope would know something. Or Fiona, for sure."

"Well, anyway, I don't see any sign of our people," Jarred said.

But Zane batted at him lightly with the back of his hand and pointed off to his right. "Hey, do you see that over there? That sort of bright spot there?"

Jarred turned in the direction he was pointing. Indeed, there seemed to be some brighter spot of light flickering deep within the heavy snowfall. At first, it almost seemed like an optical illusion, but the longer he looked at it, the more certain he became that it was firelight.

"There's someone out there," Zane said. "That's probably a campfire. Don't you think?"

"Certainly looks like it," Jarred replied. He didn't want to get his hopes up, but what else could it be?

"And if it's a campfire, it has to be our people," Zane continued. "Who else would set up camp out here? Maybe they ran out of daylight after fending off the wolves, and they had no choice but to settle in for the night."

"There's one way to find out," Jarred said, rising from the supporting branch. "Let's go."

Zane clapped his gloved hands. "Man, I thought we were dead meat, but it's all working out. See, it's good we left the quarry. I knew it." Then he stooped down and grabbed Ramses's rope again and immediately headed out into the open.

"Careful," Jarred said, limping after him. "Let's make sure to keep our bearings. Try to remember the direction of the river, in case we need to come back this way."

"Forget the river. That's a campfire up there," Zane said. He was moving just a bit too fast. Jarred struggled to keep up with him. "It'll be so warm!"

"Don't get too far ahead," Jarred said.

Zane looked back, saw the gap between them, and held back. But he frowned as he did so. Clearly, he was impatient and ready to get over there. Jarred, at least, had used the crutch enough that he was pretty good with it, even in snow like this. He considered handing the rifle to Zane, then thought better of it. He was a better shot than the teen, should any wolves come loping out of the storm.

The wind was brutal as night fell. It cut all the way through him and made the many layers of clothing feel as thin as a single layer of silk. Fortunately, the fire didn't seem to be as far as he'd feared. Soon, the vague glow took on the more distinctive shape of a flickering campfire. A hill emerged from the snow, and he realized the fire was on the other side. The camp appeared to have been established on the leeward side, out of the wind.

Zane stopped at the bottom of the hill and waited for Jarred, beckoning him impatiently. They were close enough now that Jarred could hear voices. Soft conversations barely audible beneath the howling wind. He listened to them for a moment and felt a flutter of anxiety.

"Those aren't our people," he said softly.

Zane gave him a confused look. "It has to be," he replied. "Who else could it be?"

"I don't know," Jarred said, "but those voices aren't familiar. Listen. Can't you tell?"

The teen cocked his head to one side and pulled back the edge of his hood. After a few seconds, his eyes widened. "Maybe…maybe our people encountered some strangers, and they're all camping together."

"Maybe," Jarred said. "Let's go take a look. But we're not going to approach openly until we get a good look at them, okay?"

Zane nodded, but said again, in a sad little whisper, "It just has to be our people. Who else could it be?"

They trudged up the hill. Jarred could hear one voice that was very deep, another that sounded high and sharp, a third who kept laughing. Something about the tenor and tone of the conversation reminded him of barroom talk. The conversation of drunk, unhappy men.

As they approached the top of the hill, he reached out and tapped Zane on the shoulder, waving him back. "Stay back with Ramses for a minute. Let me go up and take a look. They're more likely to see the goat."

"Okay, but even if we don't know them, we should still go down and introduce ourselves," Zane said. "We need people right now."

"I just don't want to spook anyone," Jarred replied.

He continued up the hill, leaving Zane and Ramses just below the peak. As he reached the top, he carefully lowered himself to the ground, which was no easy feat. Then he did a kind of Army crawl forward. He was aware of the constant throbbing pain shooting up his bad leg, but he was able to keep going.

The campfire came into view. It was robust, larger than he'd expected and burning well despite the snowfall. The firepit was ringed with large stones, and the ambient heat was forming a puddle from all the melting snow that hissed and popped. People were huddled around the fire, one of them constantly tending the fire with what appeared to be a length of rebar. They all appeared to be young adults. No families here. No children. No old people.

A few crates of supplies were stacked to one side, but he couldn't see what was contained inside. One of the people was larger than the others, a big man wearing a knit cap with ear flaps. He was also the loudest, with a deep voice, and he kept talking over others. Despite this, he still seemed quite young, early twenties perhaps.

"Do you suppose they would let us share the warmth just for one night?"

Zane had crawled up beside Jarred, and he spoke now in a whisper. Jarred turned to look for Ramses and found the goat just standing there near their feet, staring in strange directions with his yellow eyes.

"I told you to stay back," Jarred said.

"Sorry. I had to see for myself. Can we go down there now?"

"I don't want to approach until I know they're safe," Jarred replied, then tapped a finger to his lips.

He turned back to the camp. Just then, he saw one person, tall and lanky, emerge from the snowfall on the far side of the fire, a long rifle of some kind in his arms. As he approached, one of the other young people rose and headed toward him. They said something to each other as they passed. Then the new arrival passed the rifle to his fellow and sat down by the fire.

Scouts, Jarred thought. *Taking turns keeping an eye on things*.

And just then, he heard the metallic click of a rifle bolt being pulled. It was loud and close, too close. Jarred looked to his left and saw the figure standing there beside him. In a long coat and ski pants, sturdy rubberized boots, and a fur-lined hood, he seemed well-equipped for the brutal cold. His face was hidden behind a ski mask and goggles, the glow of firelight dancing on the lenses. In his arms, the broad-shouldered man bore an impressive rifle with a shiny silver barrel and a large scope. He was breathing loudly, steam puffing out of a small gap in the face mask, and when he spoke, his voice was sharp and unfriendly.

"Who are you and why are you watching our camp?" he said, pointing the barrel at Jarred's face.

62

Jarred briefly entertained the notion of trying to outgun the stranger. In his mind, he saw himself rolling onto his side, bringing his rifle up, and taking a shot before the other man could pull the trigger. Of course, Zane was partly in the way, so it wasn't safe, even if he was crazy enough to try it. Instead, he just lay there, staring up at the stranger and trying to think through the pain to figure out his next move before he got killed. Zane had pushed himself to his hands and knees, but he was stuck as well. As for Ramses, he was the only one who seemed unconcerned by the encounter.

"I said, 'Who are you and why are you watching our camp?'" the man growled.

"We're not hostile," Jarred said. Afraid of making any sudden move, he took his hands off his rifle and slowly, very slowly, sat up. "We got separated from our people, and we spotted the fire in the distance."

"We just wanted to share the heat," Zane said. "That's all. It's cold out here!"

"Yeah, just wanted to share the heat," the stranger said with a short, sharp laugh. "That's why you're watching us from the hilltop with a gun in your hands." The stranger took a step back and beckoned with the rifle. "Get up. You're coming with me."

"I have a gun, yes, but it wasn't pointed at anyone," Jarred said.

"Get up!" the man snapped.

Jarred glanced at Zane and nodded. A little paranoia was understandable under the circumstances, but Jarred didn't doubt that this stranger would kill them if he felt threatened.

"You don't have to shoot anyone, man," Zane said. "We're not bad guys."

Jarred rose, holding his hands up. Zane reached over and grabbed Ramses's rope, then raised his free hand above his head. The stranger motioned them down the hill with the rifle.

"Get going," he said. "Leave your rifle right there, and don't make any sudden moves."

"We're not a threat," Jarred said.

"That's not for you to decide," the stranger said.

Seeing no other choice, Jarred hopped over his rifle and limped down the hill. Zane followed, pulling Ramses with him. The goat seemed to have no reservations about being taken captive. Apparently, it was better than whatever he'd found out there on his own. The stranger picked up Jarred's rifle and slung it over his shoulder before accompanying them down the hill.

Try to make friends, Jarred thought. *Maybe he'll hesitate just a little bit to pull the trigger if he feels like he knows you.*

"So what's your name?" he asked the stranger. "I'm Jarred. This is Zane."

"You can call me Andy," the stranger said.

"What's your story?" Jarred asked.

"You don't need to know my story."

As they descended the hill and drew closer to the fire, Jarred saw some massive shape emerging out of the heavy snowfall. A building that had been beyond visibility from the top of the hill. The camp, it turned out, had been set up in front of it. He saw an overhanging roof piled high with snow, a series of narrow pillars, a front wall made almost entirely of large glass panels, double doors. It looked like the entrance to a shopping mall, but the building wasn't big enough for that. Then again, except for the front doors, which were under the overhanging roof, the rest of the building was almost completely buried. It could have been anything under there.

The other people around the fire began to notice them then, and one by one, they rose and turned to face them. Most of them had their faces uncovered, and Jarred saw hostility, fear, and a whole range of negative emotions etched into their features. Whoever they were, clearly they didn't care much for outsiders. However, he caught a few brief amused glances toward Ramses.

The biggest man in the group stepped forward. He had an ugly, patchy beard that covered most of his cheeks, chin, and neck. His cheeks were round and also quite chapped above the beard, and he had a prominent forehead. A woman walked by his side, her bronze complexion complementing gray eyes and a mouth that seemed to perpetually frown.

"Andy, who are these people?" the big man said. "Where did they come from?"

"I caught them spying on us from the hilltop, Sarge," he replied. "Said their names are Jarred and Zane, but who knows if they were telling the truth. Anyway, they brought you a couple of gifts. This rifle." He thrust the Weatherby at the one called "Sarge." "And also, this weird-looking goat over here."

Sarge took the rifle in his big hands and turned it over, examining it. Then he passed it to the woman at his side. "Here you go, Jessica. It's yours, if you want it. Otherwise, put it with the supplies."

Jessica brushed some of the snow off the rifle, then slung the strap over her shoulder. "I guess I'll hold on to it for now."

"Here's the goat," Andy said. He grabbed the rope and wrested it from Zane's hand. Zane resisted for a second and seemed like he was about to say something, but he clamped his mouth shut and bowed his head. "I don't know what you want to do with it. Eat it, maybe?"

He handed the rope to Sarge, who seemed reluctant to take it. Sarge gave the goat a sour look, then turned and motioned at someone by the fire. The young man who had been tending the fire dropped his rebar and came running. He was blond and pale, with a lean face and an angular nose.

"Sherman, take this goat inside the rest station, I guess," Sarge said, thrusting the rope in his hand. "We can probably find a use for it. Maybe it'll be good for trade or something. Who the hell knows?"

"You got it, Sarge." Sherman tugged at the rope, but Ramses resisted. "I don't think he wants to come with me."

Sarge reached out and smacked the goat on the flank. That got him moving. He bleated angrily but allowed himself to be led toward the building.

He called it a rest station, Jarred thought. His heart was pounding. They'd gotten themselves into a dangerous situation, but he was trying to pay attention and take in the details. As he looked at the building now, he could see it. A small rest stop, like the kind you might encounter by the side of the road on a state or national highway. That's what it looked like. If so, the highway was nowhere to be seen. It had been buried long ago.

Ramses continued to bleat angrily as he was led to the building and through the doors into the dim interior.

"Now, then," Sarge said. He stood facing Jarred and Zane, easing the flap of his coat open to reveal the holster at his hip. Jarred thought he was going for the gun and braced himself to fight or flee. However, Sarge tucked his thumbs under his belt instead. "Who are you, and where did you come from?"

Jarred glanced at Zane. The kid was breathing fast, arms wrapped tightly over his chest.

Just hold it together, kid, Jarred thought. *Don't spook them, or we're not getting out of this.*

He didn't dare say it, of course. As for Sarge's questions, he decided that a bit of truth might be the best way to go. "We were caught in the storm," he said. "Then we saw the light of your fire and decided to find out where it was coming from. We had no intention of bothering anyone. It was simply a matter of survival."

Sarge sniffed loudly and looked at Jessica, who gave him a brief bemused look. "What were you doing out there in the storm? Just hanging out? Building snowmen or what?" Other members of the group had begun to approach, gradually encircling Jarred and Zane.

Jarred thought about Hope and Fiona out there in the snow. Still perched on the slag pile, perhaps. Hopefully, they'd driven away the wolves and set up camp. He decided to keep this information to himself for now.

"We were traveling with a larger group," he said, "but we got separated in the storm. They continued on without us, and we've been wandering around for a while, trying to figure out which way they might've gone. It's a bit hard to find your way out here when nothing looks like it did before."

Zane was beginning to fidget. Clearly, he was getting restless. Jarred tried to make a subtle hand signal at him, motioning him to stay calm, but he didn't think the teen noticed.

"As for the rifle, everyone travels with protection these days," Jarred continued. "It doesn't mean we're hostile."

Jessica examined the rifle again, turning it this way and that. After a few seconds, she grunted and shrugged. "It's not in bad shape, but we don't really need it. I think I'll add it to the pile." And with that, she walked over to the stack of boxes, lifted a lid, and dumped the rifle rather roughly inside. Jarred caught a glimpse of a duffle bag inside, the pouch unzipped to reveal the barrels of many other rifles.

"But that's ours," Zane said suddenly. "We'll need it!"

Jessica gave him a contemptuous look, and Jarred held up a hand.

"It's fine, Zane," he said. "Don't worry about it."

"Listen to your friend," Jessica said. "We're going to look after your rifle now. You won't need it."

All of those rifles, and that was just one of the boxes. These people were clearly well-armed. They had enough rifles to supply a small army. As he realized it, his stomach sank. How in the world were they supposed to get Ramses and escape from this place? Because it felt very much like they'd just been taken prisoner.

63

They stood appraising each other for a few seconds. Jarred sensed Zane's tension. He was still fidgeting, clearly fighting an urge to act out. The confiscation of their stuff really seemed to bother him. Jarred, however, managed to keep his composure. Most of the group was now standing behind the one called Sarge, staring either at their leader or at the newcomers.

Suddenly, Sarge sniffed loudly again and nodded, as if he'd come to a decision. Jarred didn't know if that was a good thing or a bad thing.

"Okay, I think I believe your story," he said. "You understand why we might not like it when we find armed spies lurking outside the camp."

"Of course," Jarred replied.

Sarge raised a gloved hand to him. "My name is Tom. The woman over there is Jessica. She's my wife. We kind of run this show. Isn't that right, Andy?"

Jarred accepted his handshake, though it was rather rough and went on too long. The guard with the covered face, the one named Andy, lowered his rifle and said, "You're in charge. Sure."

"Come on. Join us at the fire," Tom said, finally releasing his grip on Jarred's hand. He turned and beckoned them as he went back to the fire. "Take a seat."

Jarred traded a disbelieving look with Zane, then did as he was told. Despite the danger, and the initial unfriendly welcome, the heat from the fire felt almost miraculous. Jarred felt the terrible deep cold in his bones melting away as he selected one of many small folding stools around the fire and sat down. Zane sat beside him, casting furtive glances at the strangers.

Andy wound up sitting on Jarred's other side. He pushed his hood back, removed his face mask, then lifted a pair of goggles to his forehead. The face underneath was young like all of the others, with a short black beard, broad nose, generous lips, small brown eyes. He had a notable scar bisecting his left eyebrow.

"We keep the fire going no matter what the weather's like," he said.

"I have to admit, it feels pretty amazing," Jarred replied, holding his hands up in front of the flames. "Especially after tromping around in this snowstorm for a few hours."

Zane followed Jarred's lead, raising his gloved hands to the fire. Still, he seemed anxious and jumpy. When Tom and Jessica, the camp leaders, took their seats on the far side of the fire, Zane hunkered down, as if cowed by their presence.

"You. Kid," Tom said, gesturing at Zane. "How old are you?"

Zane cleared his throat and looked at Jarred. Clearly, he didn't want to talk to these people. Maybe he feared what he might say, or how he might say it.

"He's nineteen," Jarred lied. Aging him up a few years seemed wise. It would make him appear less vulnerable. With all of his bulky clothing, it would be hard to accurately tell his exact age anyway. "Just out of high school."

Tom seemed to buy it. He nodded. Just then, the lean young man named Sherman returned from the building and took a seat near Tom. He grabbed his rebar out of a puddle of melting snow and resumed jabbing the fire with it.

"Nineteen," Tom said. "That's a good age. On the verge of becoming a full man."

Zane didn't react to this, so Jarred nodded for him.

"Well, if you'll notice, we're all in our prime here," Tom said, making a little spinning gesture with his hand to take in all of the people gathered around the fire. "And we're always looking for more. You're a little on the higher end, I guess, Jarred, but I won't hold it against you."

"But who are you people?" Jarred asked. "It's a very diverse group. How did you come together? What's the common bond?" A few seconds earlier, he wouldn't have dared such intrusive questions. Now, he thought he could risk it, and it was certainly information he needed to know.

Tom grinned and opened his coat to reveal a shiny metal object pinned to the breast pocket of the shirt underneath. A police officer's badge. Jessica did the same, pulling a police badge from a pocket inside her coat. Then Andy and the others one by one produced similarly styled police badges, until they were all holding them up in the firelight like some kind of cult symbol.

"Oh, we've got a common bond all right," Tom said. "We were all police officers. Not on the same force, mind you, but in the same line of work. I brought us together."

He tucked his badge away, and the others did the same, almost as if on cue. Jarred didn't know if this revelation should make him feel better or not. It didn't. Zane seemed to settle a bit, so maybe he'd received it as good news.

"You all seem roughly the same age," Jarred noted. Should he keep picking away? "Mid-twenties, I would guess."

"I promised my brothers and sisters here that I would find a way to survive," Tom replied. "That meant we had to make some difficult decisions, including who could be part of our group and who could not. Hate to say it, but the young and old are a real burden in this new world. They're not cut out for it, so they'll pull down any group that is trying to make it. No minors, no one over forty, those are the boundaries we set."

Jarred saw some of the others nod. Clearly, this decision had widespread support. Jessica cleared her throat then and spoke.

"Kids and old people are a waste of resources, honestly," she said. "It sounds cruel, but if you don't use the limited available resources wisely, no one's going to live long."

"We decided it would be better to use our resources to keep the strongest people healthy and fit," Tom said, zipping up his coat.

Whatever elation Zane had felt at learning they were police officers seemed to have left him. Jarred could see him become increasingly tense and anxious on his little camp chair. He couldn't stop fidgeting endlessly, and he picked at the hem of his coat. No teens or old people. So, lying about Zane's age had been the right thing to do, after all. And as Jarred was past forty, it seemed like he might want to keep his own age to himself as well.

Hopefully, I looked a few years younger than I am, he thought.

Feeling the precariousness of their situation, Jarred forced himself to nod and say, "Well, all of that makes sense to me."

Tom seemed pleased by his approval and gave him a big, ugly smile. The man had an impressively broad face, so his smile seemed half a mile wide. Clearly, he wasn't suffering from a lack of resources. "Well, buddy, I'm glad to know we're of the same mindset." He reached out and clapped Jarred on the shoulder. "Too damn many people are unwilling to face the reality of our present circumstances. If we don't—"

A loud thud interrupted him. Jarred saw one of the glass doors swing open, the glass wobbling as if some heavy thing had slammed into the other side. Tom and Jessica wheeled around immediately. Andy rose from the seat and turned, and Sherman leapt to his feet. Something slammed into the door again, shoving it open, and a familiar angry bleat came out.

"Oh, gosh, he must've broken loose," Sherman said. "I thought I tied that rope really good."

Ramses slammed the door a third time. The glass cracked dramatically, and he charged out of the building, bleating again. Sherman approached, reaching out as if to grab the dangling rope. However, as soon as he got close, Ramses lowered his head and charged at him, forcing him to leap out of the way. Andy approached next, and Ramses turned to charge at him. When Andy dodged the charge and tried to circle around, the goat swung his head to the side. A horn slammed into Andy's chest, pushed him off balance, and sent him sprawling onto the ground.

"Would someone please grab that animal?" Tom snarled, rising from his seat.

Sherman came around from behind, but Ramses sensed his approach. He spun, bleated loudly, and charged at him again. Sherman backed out of the way, but his feet slipped, and he went down on his rump.

"It's one goat, you idiots," Tom said. "You're embarrassing yourselves."

Andy rushed forward, dodged another swing of the horns, and managed to grab the rope. But that only caused Ramses to bolt forward directly at the supplies. Sherman rose and came toward him, wrapping his arms around the goat's back leg.

As all of this unfolded, Jarred felt sick to his stomach. Clearly, Ramses had been spooked being tied and left inside a strange building, but nothing good would come of this outburst. Zane watched the men struggling with Ramses with an anxious look on his head. Jarred laid a hand on his shoulder.

"He's stronger than he looks, Sarge," Sherman said.

Working together, the two men managed to slow Ramses to a crawl, but the big goat was still dragging them along. Tom sighed loudly and stepped away from the campfire, unzipping his coat again. He reached inside and drew his pistol.

"Okay, I'm just going to kill this creature before he damages our stuff or injures someone," he muttered. "He's probably good eating anyway."

Jarred's blood ran cold. Of course, eating one of the goats wasn't an entirely unreasonable idea, but the loss of the animal would be a huge blow. Andy and Sherman finally dragged Ramses to a stop mere inches from the stack of supplies, but the goat was still bleating and resisting. Tom approached cautiously, flicking the safety on his gun.

Jarred cleared his throat loudly. "Actually, he wouldn't be very good eating. That old goat was run ragged. He's mostly sinew at this point. I doubt there's any fat left on him. And besides, eating him would be kind of a waste, don't you think?"

Tom stopped his in tracks, but Jessica snorted and said, "A waste? Why would it be a waste? A good protein-rich diet is important."

"He's a cart goat," Jarred said. "He's trained to pull heavy things. He's actually a really useful beast of burden. You'd get a lot more use out of him that way than just reducing him to a single unsatisfying meal."

Ramses seemed to have finally given up the fight. Now, he was just standing there, giving Andy and Sherman his standard unreadable weird stare. They both had hold of the short rope, but they were panting, their breath steaming in the frigid air. Tom and Jessica looked at each other.

"A cart goat could be very useful," Jessica said.

"Useful and timely," Tom said, holstering his pistol.

Jessica turned to Jarred, a strange little smile on her face. "We could use some help with a project we've been working on." She flicked a finger at Jarred, at Zane, and said, "Come with me. Sherman, bring the goat."

Then she turned and headed toward the building. Jarred shrugged at Zane and went after her. Zane hesitated a second then came with him. At first, Ramses seemed more compliant, and he allowed himself to be led back. But then, out of the blue, he swung his head and slammed a horn into Andy's ribs. Andy cursed and stumbled to one side. As he did, he yanked the rope out of Sherman's hand.

"Forget it. Just forget it," Andy grumbled, rubbing his side. "Let these guys deal with it." He grabbed Zane by the arm, pulled him close, and pressed the short rope into his hand. "There. Lead your dumb idiot of a goat."

"He's ornery with people he thinks aren't trustworthy," Zane said, taking the rope. He patted Ramses on the side of the neck.

Jarred winced at the teen's comment. *Did you have to say it like that, kid?* It wasn't even true, precisely. Ramses was ornery when he wanted to be, and any person could be a target of his antics.

Jessica grabbed the handle of the door, sparing a disgusted glance at the cracked glass. She pulled it open and ushered the others inside. Jarred stepped through the door into a dim place, but the smell that wafted over him was both familiar and surreal, like something out of a buried memory. Concrete, bathroom tiles, wetness, a hint of cleaning supplies and mildew. The room was large and open, with benches lining the wall on the left and two large bathroom entrances on the right.

Ramses had apparently been tied to one of the benches, because the bench was tipped over and dragged toward the doors. The only light in the building came from the campfire shining through the glass wall at the front. However, it was enough to see that the very back of the building had collapsed. The ceiling had fallen down, the walls folding inward to create a big mound of debris.

"I haven't been in a highway rest stop like this in a long time," Jarred said, looking around. "This feels a little bit like walking through a museum exhibit."

Just then, Ramses unleashed an ear-straining bleat. Andy and Sherman both covered their ears, and Jessica winced. She was leading them straight across the room toward the crumbled back wall.

"It's not a museum," Jessica said. "It's a hidden pirate's cove."

She came to a stop before the big mound of debris and squatted down, beckoning Jarred closer. He moved up beside her and squatted down. The ceiling and walls had fallen in such a way that there were many gaps throughout the pile. Jessica pointed into one of the larger gaps.

"And there is the buried treasure," she said. "Look closely. Do you see it?"

She leaned to one side so light from the front windows would shine into the gap. Jarred had to bend down lower to see inside. When he did, the silver metal side of a large vending machine became visible. It was tipped at an angle, leaning on what appeared to be a broken table, a large amount of debris piled on top. Jarred could see numerous cuts and gouges in the surrounding material, as if they'd already tried on multiple occasions to get it out.

"A vending machine," Jarred said. "That is quite a find."

"Can the goat pull it out of there for us?" Jessica asked. "Because that would certainly be a good reason to keep him around. I think it would earn him a reprieve from the soup pot."

Since she put it that way, Jarred didn't see how else he could respond. "With some sturdy ropes and a bit of time, I'll bet he could drag it out of there."

Even as he said it, he felt a little flutter in his belly. In point of fact, he was not at all convinced that even Ramses could drag that heavy vending machine out from under such a huge pile of debris. Still, his life depended on it, so he was going to have to try.

"Well, you know him best," Jessica said. "You tell us how to get it done."

Jarred rose and stepped back, examining the collapsed section of the building.

I could really use Hope's input right now, he thought. *She would figure out the best way to do this.*

He considered their options. The heaviest weight on top of the machine appeared to be an enormous, intact section of the cinder block wall. However, some long support rods stuck out of the ends on either side.

"Instead of trying to drag the vending machine out of there," he said, "what if we got him to pull most of the weight off the top? We could tie some ropes to those support posts and slide it right off."

Jessica gave him a little half-smile and a nod. "Well, see, it's a good thing we didn't make that soup." She snapped her fingers at Andy and Sherman. "Hey, guys, go and get some sturdy rope from the supplies."

"Bring me that length of rebar as well," Jarred said, "the one he was using to poke the fire."

Andy and Sherman turned and trotted back across the building. Big Tom was standing with most of the other group members near the front doors, watching the proceedings unfold. All eyes were on Jarred, and he felt the pressure. Ramses's life depended on what he did next. As if recognizing this, the goat nuzzled up against him, and Jarred gave him a little pat on the back.

Just do your part, buddy, Jarred thought. *I'll try to keep you out of that soup pot.*

As they waited on the rope, Jarred hunted around the debris pile again. By then, Andy and Sherman had returned, the former bearing two lengths of rope, the latter carrying the rebar, which they presented to Jessica, as if they were offerings to a queen. She shook her head and waved them toward Jarred.

"He's the one with the plan," she said. "Do what he says."

Jarred grabbed both lengths of rope and handed one to Zane. Then he took the rebar. "Help me attach both of these to Ramses's harness, would you?"

Working together, they attached the ropes, tying multiple knots. Then they unwound the rest of the ropes and tied them to some of the protruding support poles on the fallen wall.

"Okay, Zane, you're going to get Ramses moving," he said. "While you do that, I'm going to use this rebar to help leverage the wall off the vending machine. That should help it start to slide. Make sense?"

"Sure," Zane said with a shrug. He was not fully invested in any of this, it seemed, but he took up a position beside Ramses and grabbed the harness.

As he did that, Jarred walked to one side of the fallen wall and wedged the end of the rebar in a narrow gap beneath, using another large piece of debris for leverage. He then grabbed the rebar near the end and leaned over it. His leg was still bothering him, but at least he could put weight on it. Still, he had to be careful now not to overdo it. He couldn't afford to rebreak the bone. A man with a broken leg would probably not be valued by this particular group of people.

"Okay, Zane, now," he said.

Zane tugged on the harness, smacked Ramses on the flank, and said, "Go, boy! Go!"

Ramses blew out his breath and lunged forward until the ropes went taut. The support posts creaked, and the section of wall shifted, but it didn't budge.

"I think it might be too much for him," Zane said.

"No, it's not," Jarred replied. "I'm going to help. Keep him pulling!"

Jarred pushed down on the rebar, using his weight to add to his strength. As he did, Ramses backed up and lunged forward again. The cinder blocks scraped against the rebar, but he didn't have enough force to lift them. Once again, Ramses was able to make the posts creak, but the wall wouldn't budge.

This isn't going to work, Jarred thought, leaning his full weight against the rebar. *Ramses, you're toast, pal.*

Suddenly, he became aware of another figure moving up behind him and large hands grabbing the rebar. It was Tom, and he had his coat and gloves removed. He nodded at Jarred, bared his teeth for a second, then put all of his enormous weight into the push. The rebar immediately began to bend dramatically, but the section of wall lifted maybe half an inch. And then Ramses pushed forward again, and the whole thing began to slide with a deafening groan.

Once it started moving, the big goat had no problem keeping it going, and the section slid off the vending machine and crashed down on the floor. As it did, it broke into pieces, the ropes came free, and Ramses bolted all the way to the doors. The other group members scrambled to get out of his way, as Zane ran after him.

Jarred let go of the bent rebar and stepped back. His palms hurt from the effort. He pulled his gloves off and rubbed his hands against the sides of his pants. As he did, Tom turned to him and gave him an OK sign. As if it were a signal, the others began to applaud.

"Well, it was a good plan, after all," Jessica said.

The vending machine was now revealed in all its glory, and the group began to gather around it. Working together, they slowly dragged it forward and set it upright. While they were doing that, Jarred's eyes went back to the length of rebar. It was too long, but he saw a smaller length that had been exposed nearby. As Tom's group was working on the vending machine, laughing and chatting excitedly, and Zane was still trying to calm Ramses, Jarred bent down and grabbed the smaller length of rebar. He slid it up his sleeve, folded the cuff back to help keep it in place, then put his gloves back on.

Once the vending machine was upright, Jessica waved everyone back. She took the rifle off her back, checked the safety, and raised it above her shoulder. She drove the butt of the rifle against the glass front of the vending machine. The first blow resisted, but with the second, the glass shattered and fell in a thousand tiny pieces. As Jarred backed up, he saw rows and rows of snacks. Candy bars, potato chips, crackers, gum, mints, and much more, all still tucked neatly in their little spiral spring holders.

The sight of all of that food made him practically swoon with hunger, but he stood off the one side. Zane walked over to him, pulling a panting Ramses.

"Oh, gosh, those cookies in 3E look amazing," Zane said, pressing a hand to his belly.

Jessica, with Andy and Sherman's help, began pulling snacks out of the vending machine and passing them out. And then she walked over to Jarred and shoved a Snickers bar and a bag of tortilla chips into his hand.

"You proved yourself to me," she said. "Enjoy the fruits of your labor." And then she shoved a packet of cookies and a bag of pretzels at Zane. "You, too, since you seem to be such a good goat wrangler. Enjoy. Consider this a reprieve."

And with that, she turned and went back to the vending machine. Jarred noted she hadn't asked Tom for permission to give snacks to the newcomers. It seemed she was just as much in charge as him. Of course, Jarred was tempted to decline the snacks so he wouldn't owe these people anything else. However, his desperate stomach won out. By the time he got the chips open, Zane was already devouring the cookies.

Once the vending machine had been thoroughly emptied, Tom and Jessica led the group back across the building and out to the fire. They had to step over the scattered chunks of cinder blocks. More than half of the snacks went into one of the supply crates. As Andy and Sherman were packing them away, Jarred caught a glimpse of the duffle bag in the middle box. The barrels of many rifles were just visible. He quickly looked away and followed the others toward the fire, Zane at his side.

No matter what happens, I'm not leaving here without Fiona's rifle, he thought. *And her goat, if I can help it.*

64

Sherman and Andy took the next watch, as the others prepared beds. Jarred noticed that they didn't sleep inside the building. Indeed, they wouldn't even sleep under the overhanging roof. Clearly, they didn't trust the instability of the building. Instead, they laid down multiple layers of canvas in the gap between the fire and the supplies, then created rows of beds using thick rubber mats and foil blankets. It wasn't the most comfortable-looking arrangement, but since Jarred had expected to sleep out in the open with no fire, it was a marked improvement.

As Sherman and Andy marched off into the storm with rifles in hand, the others began settling down on their beds. Tom pointed to a couple of mats in the row nearest the building, then flicked a hand in the direction of Jarred and Zane, who had been standing awkwardly to one side for a while.

"You two can bed down here," he said. "Now, look, I'm a very light sleeper, so don't be moving around in the night. Got it?" He gave them a stern look, nodded, and moved to his own bed mat near the fire.

Jarred sat down on one of the mats and began unfolding the foil blanket. Zane took the bed beside him, grumbling under his breath as he pulled his own blanket over his lap.

"I don't know if I'll be able to sleep at all," he muttered. "It's plenty warm, sure, but we've still got snow falling on our faces, and it all turning to slush beneath us."

"Just do what you can," Jarred said, glancing at the others around them. They were far too close for him to talk openly with Zane. "Close your eyes and rest, at least until *someone* wakes you up."

"Fine," Zane said, lying back on the mat and pulling the blanket up to his shoulders. It crinkled like paper as he moved it. And then, very quietly, he added, "I just hope *someone* wakes me up soon."

Maybe the kid is reading my mind, Jarred thought.

He turned on the mat to watch the others settle down. Andy and Sherman were gone, but he thought he could hear them crunching through the snow somewhere on top of the nearby hill. A group comprised only of people in their twenties. If they were all former police officers, then none of them had been on the force for long. There were no older people, no teens or kids. He found it all disconcerting.

Tom and Jessica lay next to each other. Their faces were turned toward each other, and they seemed to be quietly chatting. They were the only people in the group that acted like a couple. It wasn't the happiest or most loving group. Indeed, their joy at retrieving snacks from an old vending machine had been the closest thing to real excitement that he'd seen. Overall, they were fairly sullen and subdued, and most of the group, other than Tom and Jessica, rarely spoke.

Jarred finally lay down, rolling onto his side away from the group, and pulled the blanket around him. It was a strange thing to feel both the warmth of the fire and the bitter cold of the wind and snow at the same time. Before closing his eyes, he glanced at the open crate in the middle stack, the blue edge of a duffle bag sticking out. Then he glanced at the glass front of the building. Ramses had been tied to one of the metal handles of the door, and he was currently standing under the overhanging ceiling.

After gauging distances as best he could, Jarred shut his eyes and pretended to sleep. Though it had been a long exhausting day, and he had a belly full of snacks, his raw nerves meant that he was about as far from sleep as it was possible to be. Still, he kept his eyes shut, forced himself to stay still, and waited as long minutes passed. Soon, the camp was a symphony of unhealthy snoring and other unpleasant sleep sounds from the group. Still, Jarred waited, working through his escape plan over and over again.

Finally, after what felt like a couple of hours, he dared to open his eyes and roll over. When he did, he saw that Zane was wide awake, staring back at him from beneath the foil blanket. The campfire had burned down to mere embers, still casting a warm orange glow over everything. Slowly, Jarred worked a hand out from under the blanket and pressed it to his lips. Then he began lowering the blanket. He had to do this incredibly slowly to keep it from making a bunch of noise, and even then, it crinkled constantly.

This could get us killed, he thought. *The merit gained from retrieving the vending machine will only go so far.*

The snoring was incredibly loud, especially the deep throaty growl of Tom. The poor guy sounded like he had a very bad case of sleep apnea. In the old world, he might have used a C-pap. But in this dying world, he could only struggle for breath.

Once his blanket was off, Jarred signaled for Zane to follow him and rose to his hands and knees. He could see rows of sleeping faces. Bellies filled with junk food had helped them drift off, it seemed. Jarred crept off his bed mat and moved toward the front of the building. As he did, he heard the soft crinkle of Zane's foil blanket. He was less concerned about the crinkle of the blanket than he was the possible bleating of an excited Ramses, so he tried to approach swiftly enough that the animal wouldn't get confused about what was happening.

In fact, the animal turned and looked at him with his yellow eyes. Jarred reached out to him, and Ramses snorted. It was loud enough that Jarred flinched, but it was better than a bleat. Zane appeared at his side then, and he quickly reached out to pat the goat on the side of the neck. It seemed to settle him a bit. Jarred gave Zane a thumbs-up. As the teen kept Ramses calm, Jarred worked on undoing the knots holding his rope to the door handle. This took quite a bit of work. Sherman had tied the ropes, and he was apparently quite good at it. Finally, Jarred took his pocketknife out and just sawed the rope in two.

He had thought through the next few steps of his plan quite extensively. Of the two building doors, one opened quieter than the other, so he slowly pulled that one open and waved Zane through. Nodding, Zane grabbed Ramses's rope and led the goat inside. The hoofprints on the concrete floor were loud—like someone tapping a drumstick on the edge of a drum—but Tom's broken snoring was louder.

Just before following them inside, Jarred looked back at the sleeping group. He saw half a dozen bodies curled beneath foil blankets. He didn't see anyone who was obviously awake. His gaze flicked over to the crate with the guns, then he backed into the building. As the door swung shut, he cushioned it with his arm so that it closed gently.

Then he turned to Zane. "We're going out the back of the building," he said in a whisper. He pointed to the far corner of the building near the bathroom, where a sturdy metal door with a crash bar was located at the end of a short alcove. "First, we need to make sure that door there leads outside and has a clear path away from the building. Then, I'm going to try to sneak back and get Fiona's Weatherby rifle."

"Forget the gun," Zane said. "Fiona probably used up all the shots on the wolves. Let's just get out of here!"

"We need it," Jarred said. "The only other weapon the group possesses is the Mossberg shotgun. I'm not going to take anything from these people that doesn't already belong to us, so when they discover we're gone, they'll have less reason to be angry. But we need the rifle, and it belongs to Fiona."

"It's right beside where they're sleeping," Zane said.

"Yeah, but I'll approach from the other side, grab it quietly, and run," Jarred said. "Fortunately, unhealthy Tom is providing us some cover with all of that noise he's making."

Finally, Zane shrugged. Clearly, he didn't think the rifle was worth it, but Jarred knew otherwise. A functioning rifle was one of the most important tools in this broken world. Maybe he could even grab more ammo. He beckoned the teen and headed across the building, picking his way over the large pieces of scattered debris from the shattered wall. The broken and looted vending machine stood in the middle of the room like the bones of some picked-over carcass.

"What about the guys keeping watch?" Zane said, pulling Ramses across the room. "Andy and Sherman. If they see us out there, we're going to get shot."

"Then we'll make sure they don't see us," Jarred replied.

He leaned against the crash bar, pushing the door gently at first, not wanting to make any noise. It resisted, unmoving, so he pushed a little harder. Still, it didn't budge. Finally, he leaned against it hard, and it slammed forward. The door swung outward, and Jarred fell into the next room with a thud. It was all so loud that he froze, holding his breath.

And in the silence that followed, he still heard Tom snoring in the distance. He looked back and saw Zane standing with Ramses, his hands pressed to his ears as if he could stop all noise by blocking it out. With a sigh, Jarred rose and surveyed the room before him. It was a small utility room of some kind, with cleaning supplies stacked haphazardly on shelves, mops and brooms stacked in the corner, and a large sink near the floor. There were also some other bags and boxes dumped against the back wall, including blue duffle bags just like the one in the supply box. Fortunately, there was also another door in the opposite corner.

"That has to be the way out," Jarred said, pointing at the door. "Come on."

"We probably woke up half the people just now," Zane said, leading Ramses into the room.

"Maybe not," Jarred said. "Let's not stick around and find out. Come on. Prop that door open, so we have light from the fire."

He headed across the room. As he did, he could feel increasing cold coming from the next door. It, too, had a crash bar. He reached out to push it, but something caught his eye. The blue duffle bag on the floor near the door was unzipped, and a bright, colorful piece of cloth stuck out. Jarred stooped down and grabbed it, pulling it out of the bag.

As he did, it unrolled, and a shotgun that had been wrapped inside tumbled out onto the floor. It was an old double-barrel shotgun of a make and model he did not recognize. He lifted the blanket into the light. It was small, light blue, made of felt and generously stuffed with soft padding. A baby's blanket. However, the corner he was holding was dark, stained reddish-brown.

"Blood," he noted. "A lot of it."

Disgusted, he flung the blanket away.

"Oh, my God," Zane said, pointing at the duffle bag. "Do you see all of that?"

Jarred pulled the unzipped pouch open, revealing more cloth wadding up inside. Children's clothing. He pulled something out at random and unfolded it. A small t-shirt with a huge smiling cartoon cat on the front. It also had a few large bloodstains and an obvious bullet hole in the chest. He dropped it and dug into the bag again.

Get out of here, he thought, his mind screaming in horror. *You don't need to see anything else. You don't need to understand it. Just go!*

But his fingers brushed against some small, cold shape. He grabbed it and pulled it out. A small black can of pepper spray, the label declared, "5 Million SHU! Hottest Pepper Spray!" It felt full, so he tucked it into his coat pocket. He started to grab the shotgun as well, but he could see now that it was broken—the trigger and trigger guard were bent to one side, as if it had been used as a crude club.

"Please, please, let's go," Zane said. "I feel sick to my stomach. There's a bunch of bloody clothes in there."

"Yeah, I'm trying not to envision what happened," Jarred said. "Come on."

"You know what happened," Zane said. "No children, no teens, no old people. That's what Sarge said."

Jarred's mind was filled with white horror at what they'd found. He tried his best not to think about what it all meant. Instead, he leaned against the door until it popped open. The bitter cold swirled into the room, but under the circumstances, it was a relief. Anything to be away from here. He stepped outside and held the door for Zane and Ramses.

They were standing to one side of the building, a broad treeless expanse spreading out before them. He thought it might be an old parking lot, possibly even the highway itself. Some distance to the left, a dense stand of trees marked the wilderness. As soon as Zane and Ramses were outside, Jarred pointed in that direction.

"Head that way as fast as you can," he said. "Keep an eye out for Andy and Sherman. They're out there somewhere. Get under those trees into the darkness. I'll catch up to you."

"Dude, forget about the rifle, please," Zane said, pulling his hood forward against the driving storm. "They'll hear you."

"It's in a box right on top of their supplies," Jarred said. "I'll be quick. Go!"

He waved them on, and Zane set off with Ramses toward the highway and the trees beyond. Of Andy and Sherman, there was no obvious sign, but the shadows were deep and dark. They could have been out there anywhere. That thought, and the gruesome discovery, made Jarred's skin crawl. Zane gave him a final unhappy look and tugged at Ramses's lead line, drawing him away from the building and down a slight embankment toward the snow-covered highway.

Jarred turned and went the other way, sticking close to the wall as he approached the front corner of the building. Tom's snore was still ringing out over the hills and dales. At the corner, Jarred peeked around the cinder block wall and saw the overhanging ceiling, the careful stacks of supply crates nearby. The supplies acted as a wall blocking his view of the sleeping figures.

Move fast. Grab the gun. Then leave, he told himself.

And with that, he stepped around the corner, moving low, and rushed toward the supplies. As he drew near, the toe of his right shoe kicked some hard edge under the snow. It felt like a cement parking block. He stumbled and went down on his knees. As he did, Tom's snoring stopped, uncovering the sleeping sounds of the other people. Jarred froze, holding his breath, preparing to flee back the way he'd come.

Sorry, Fiona, he thought. *I couldn't get it back.*

And them Tom snorted, sniffed, and resumed snoring. Jarred rose again, achingly slow, and crept forward, staying beneath the level of the supply crates. The crate he wanted was on top in the center, the lid shifted to one side to reveal the edge of the duffle bag.

These people are loaded down with guns and supplies, he thought. *They've got bloody blankets and clothing hidden in a closet. The two are connected. They've been killing and stealing.*

He'd been nervous around these people from the beginning, even after sharing snacks with them, but now he felt the real danger he was in. These were monsters. Maybe they'd never really been cops in the first place. They hadn't shown Jarred photo IDs, after all, just metal badges. But badges could be stolen. Was it possible that they'd stolen the badges along with the guns and other supplies by looting a police station? Tom certainly didn't have the physique or the bearings of a former police officer. If anything, he seemed like a neckbeard driven out of his basement hovel by the new ice age.

He reached into the supply crate, easing the lid aside, but he felt the presence of the group on the other side. Sleeping devils. With his free hand, he pulled the pepper spray out of his jacket pocket and held it at the ready.

The barrel of Fiona's Weatherby rifle was right on top, but the rest of the gun had been shoved down among all the others. As he grabbed it and pulled it out, he felt and heard the shuffling of dozens of other rifles. Finally, to avoid making too much noise, he grabbed the handles of the duffle bag instead and slowly pulled it out. It seemed to take forever to get it free, and once it was, he hooked the straps around his shoulder.

"What the hell...?"

Tom's voice. He went from snoring to speaking in a second. It startled Jarred so badly that he hopped backward, winced at the twinge of pain in his foot, and almost fell down. He managed to maintain his balance by spinning his arms, but he heard Tom moving. It was like the rousing of some huge yeti. The huge man lumbered through the camp.

"Where the hell did they go?" he grumbled. "I swear to God, if they tried to leave..." And then he grunted and said, "They went inside the building." He sounded relieved.

Jarred ducked down to make sure he was hidden, listening as Tom tromped toward the building. But that would lead him to the back door and then Zane. Jarred couldn't allow that. Now, he heard others waking up, yawning, thrashing on their beds. The shadow of Tom appeared at the end of the supplies.

Distract him now, Jarred said. *Do it quick!*

He looked down at his left hand, at the can of pepper spray there. It was a crazy idea, and he wasn't sure it would work. But he couldn't think of anything else. He rose until he could just see over the top of the supply crates to the glowing campfire. He did his best to gauge the distance, then he chucked the pepper spray over his head, over the supplies, and right into the fire. It landed on the edge, bounced off the glowing coals, and went right into the hottest part of the ember pile.

65

The can exploded faster than he expected. Maybe four seconds. Tom was under the roof, snorting and grumbling under his breath, just reaching for the door when the heated can popped. The can itself went spinning off with a little whizzing sound into the storm, as a huge cloud erupted and swept through the camp. Startled, Tom cried out and slammed against the door.

The pepper spray began burning in Jarred's eyes almost instantly, so he clamped them shut, turned, and fled blindly back the way he'd come. People began to shout in the camp, and Jarred heard the crinkle of foil blankets as they rose. He dared a glance back just before he rounded the corner, and he saw the smoke filling the camp, swept by the wind against the building. That kept it in the area rather than blowing it out into the open.

Tom was hunched over, hacking and coughing, swiping his arms around his face. Others were crawling away from the camp, heading toward the building, perhaps falsely assuming they could escape the pepper spray that way. Some shouted or cursed. Most were coughing violently.

"Who did it? Who did it? How did it happen?" That was Jessica, her voice shrill and desperate, and then her voice cracked, she retched and began to cough.

"You know…you…know…" That was the most Tom could say in between violent deep-lung coughs.

And then Jarred ran around the corner and lost sight of them. Still, the coughing and cursing chased him. Ahead, he saw the back door of the building, the trail of goat and human tracks leading down the slope toward the highway. They hadn't gone far. Zane and Ramses were approximately where the shoulder of the nearest lanes might have been. It looked like they were trying to move fast, but the snow was deep and undisturbed.

They'll see our tracks, Jarred thought. *They'll be able to follow us easily. We have to get in the woods and lose them.*

Of course, Jarred was only able to limp along, especially since he'd left his crutch behind, but he went as fast as he could. As he reached the slope that led down to the buried lanes, he had to move even slower so he didn't lose his footing. Zane heard him coming and looked back. It seemed like he was going to stop, but Jarred waved him on.

Behind them, the group was still coughing and retching, flailing about, but Jarred heard a crash that sounded like the crate of supplies being knocked over. Were they arming themselves or simply flailing about in pain? He didn't know, but he kept expecting to hear, or feel, a gunshot. A tingling unease stuck somewhere between his shoulder blades.

He caught up to Zane and Ramses by the time he'd reached the far shoulder of the highway. As he did, Jarred tried to map out the area in his head. He remembered their path to the rest stop, so he had a pretty good idea of where the small grove and the frozen river were located.

"What did you do to them?" Zane asked.

"Gave them something to cry about," Jarred said. "Should keep them busy for a while." His eyes stung, and his throat burned. Fortunately, he'd only gotten a slight whiff of the pepper spray, so it was bearable.

They reached the far embankment, heading up toward the line of trees. But Jarred turned them to the right, veering back toward the river. The shouting and coughing echoed far and wide, creating a hideous ghost symphony. Just before entering the forest, Jarred looked back and saw the faint orange glow of the campfire shining from behind the building. Shadows were moving there.

"Dude, they must be in a lot of pain," Zane said. "Listen to that!"

"Yeah, I don't envy them," Jarred replied. "Then again, I guess it's better than what they deserve."

Once in the forest, they followed the general course of the highway. Jarred kept expecting to see the river, but they walked for a good hour or two and saw only trees. The duffle bag was getting heavy, so finally he came to a stop and signaled for Zane to do the same.

"It doesn't sound like they're coming after us," he said, panting. "Not yet, at least. I think we can risk a minute or two. Hang on."

"Are you in too much pain?" Zane asked. "Maybe you could ride on Ramses."

"I don't think he could easily bear a rider," Jarred said. He dumped the duffle bag on the ground. When it hit, it popped open, and a bunch of rifles poked out.

"Whoa, you stole a lot of guns," Zane said.

"I only meant to grab Fiona's rifle," Jarred said. He squatted beside the duffle bag and rooted through the guns. "Honestly, I had no intention of taking anything that didn't already belong to us, but it got really hectic there at the end. I just ran away."

Handguns. Rifles. All makes and models. In various conditions. Some battered and old, others pristine. He pulled Fiona's rifle out of the midst and slung the strap over his shoulder.

"I don't think you stole anything from those people," Zane said. "It looks like maybe they stole them from others."

"Yeah, I think you're right," he said, closing the duffle bag and zipping it. "Well, we can't take them back now. I guess they're ours."

"You don't have to lug the bag around." Zane reached down and grabbed the handles. "I bet we could tie it onto Ramses's back and let him carry it."

He took the rope and looped them back behind the harness, tying the duffle bag in place. Then he looped the other end of the rope under the animal and back through the harness. This left only a short length of it for him to hold, but it kept the bag of guns on the goat's back. Ramses accepted it with no complaint. Clearly, he was relieved to be away from the camp.

They had just resumed walking when gunshots rang out in the distance. They sounded close, too close.

"Is someone shooting at us?" Zane asked.

Jarred looked around. They were deep in the shadows beneath the trees. Had someone spotted them? Had someone taken a few shots at them? He couldn't be sure. He turned them deeper into the woods, toward darker shadows.

"I think the chase is on," Jarred said.

"It won't be hard to follow us," Zane replied. "Where do we go?"

Jarred pointed ahead. The ground sloped down here, and he saw a break in the trees. Beyond, a deep snow-filled riverbed cut across their path. It wound back toward the highway and passed beneath it.

"That'll take us back the way we came," Jarred said.

Now that he didn't have to lug the duffle bag, Jarred was able to move quite a bit faster. He got ahead of Zane and Ramses, picking his way down the slope into the river. The banks were shallow enough here to make it easy to enter. As soon as Zane and Ramses reached him, he turned back toward the highway overpass and began hobbling along. As he entered the darkness beneath the highway, he heard another gunshot—this time far too close. Instinctively, his hand went to the strap of the rifle around his shoulder.

We may have to fight, he thought.

66

They'd gone maybe a quarter of a mile down the river when he began to hear voices in the distance behind them. It was fully dark now, so he could barely see the ground in front of them, much less their pursuers. He could only tell they were getting close. When he looked back, he saw some kind of faint glow upstream. A flashlight, perhaps? A torch lit by the campfire? He couldn't quite tell.

"Where do we go?" Zane asked. "What do we do?"

Ramses was the brightest object in the immediate vicinity, an enormous pale shape in the midnight gloom. Jarred considered their predicament. The river was leading them back to the quarry, but this was no safe place for a gun battle. They had no cover, and Ramses was an easy target. Jarred looked around, straining to see in the dark.

The riverbanks were steep, but he spotted a possible path up. He pointed. It was steep but had a few curled roots that looked like they might serve as crude steps. "The high ground might give us some advantage in a fight. Let's get up that slope there."

"Are you sure about that?" Zane said. "Can Ramses make it?"

"Easier than us."

Zane guided the goat toward the path and gave him a little pat on the flank. Ramses bleated loudly and bounded up the slope, hopping from root to root and reaching the top in seconds, the duffle bag bouncing and rattling on his back. Jarred feared he might run off, but instead, he turned and looked down at them, bleating again as if to taunt them.

"Well, if they didn't know where we were before, they definitely know now," Zane said. "Thanks to that stupid goat."

He reached up and grabbed the lowest handhold, pulling himself up. Zane had far more trouble than Ramses. First, he struggled to maintain his grip, then he kicked his feet against the slope for a few seconds in vain. Finally, he seemed to get purchase, and he climbed up to the second handhold.

Jarred waited below, but he felt a kind of trembling desperation. Everything within him cried out for him to flee. It took a monumental act of will to stand still. He pressed Fiona's rifle against his belly and hunkered down, listening to the haunting sounds of their pursuers closing in.

"Hurry, kid. Just hurry," Jarred said.

Zane was on the second handhold, pulling himself to the third, but again he found it hard to maintain his hold. Ramses bent down to sniff at him. The goat seemed confused by his struggle. Ramses was also in the way, so once Zane reached the third handhold, he had to gently swat the goat on the front leg to encourage him to step aside. He eventually did it. Then the teen climbed to the top of the slope.

"I'm up," he said, breathless. "Your turn."

Jarred approached the slope and reached up to the first handhold. With his foot in such pain, it was going to be a real challenge, but he felt the desperation driving him. Zane leaned over the edge and beckoned him frantically. Suddenly, the teen stopped beckoning and cried out.

Jarred sensed a shadow moving in from the right, but he scarcely had time to react. Some huge thing slammed into his side and shoved him away from the slope. As he fell, his ankle crying out in pain, he heard a rumbling breath right in his ear. And then he landed hard, that massive shape slamming down on top of him. Tom. The vast mountain of Tom. Somehow, he had managed to sneak up on Jarred. It was a feat that seemed nearly impossible.

As soon as they were both down, Tom began pawing at him with his big hands. Jarred felt a hand grab the strap of the rifle. Going for the gun. Trying to get it away from him. Jarred rolled to one side and managed to get out from under him, but Tom had the gun strap and pulled at it. To keep from being dragged back onto the ground, Jarred twisted around and shoved his forearm at the massive figure.

"You thought I didn't see you running away," Tom said. "You thought the forest would hide you, but you made no effort to cover your tracks. You're out of your league."

Jarred managed to get his forearm under the man's chin, pressing into the prodigious neck fat beneath.

"I followed you while my people were still recovering," Tom snarled. "You heard them a mile back, but you didn't hear me! I'd chase you to hell before I let you take our weapons."

Jarred didn't see the punch in time. That huge, meaty fist slammed into his cheek, and he saw stars spinning in the void before him. Jarred swung his other hand blindly, punching in the general direction of Tom. The first punch missed. The second was a glancing blow. The third hit Tom's whiskered chin, and Tom grunted in pain. But he let go of the rifle strap, and Jarred rolled away, pulling the rifle out of reach. As he did, he grabbed the strap and yanked the gun free.

He sat up, the rifle in his hands, but Tom rose up before him. He reeked of the pepper spray, and he was snorting like a bison.

"You're not police officers," Jarred said, fumbling with the rifle to try to get it positioned correctly. "I don't buy it. I don't know where you got those badges, but I think you stole them. Maybe killed for them. You've killed a lot of people. Families. Children. We saw the evidence. What the hell is wrong with you people?"

"You haven't accepted what kind of world it is now," Tom said. "We have."

He lunged at Jarred. At the last second, without even knowing if the Weatherby rifle was aimed in the right direction, Jarred pulled the trigger. There was a brief, bright flash from the muzzle, and in that momentary light, he saw the broad black coat, massive gloved hands, Tom's big whiskered face closing in. The fierce crack of the bullet seemed to rise up and up forever.

Tom came to a stop, making a weird gurgling sound. Then he stumbled backward, grasping at his chest. Suddenly, they were bathed in light, as if the clouds had parted to reveal some secret sun. Tom had his gloved hands pressed to a spot slightly to the right on his heart, and blood was running over the glove and pouring down. It had stained the snow between them. Tom's eyes were wide, confused, his mouth hanging open.

And then the great mountain of a man fell backward and landed in the snow, sending up a billowing plume. Behind Jarred, a woman wailed. When he looked back, he saw the rest of the group. They were maybe thirty yards away, cautiously making their way down the river. Jessica was in the lead, and she had a shaded brass lantern in her hand—the source of the light.

"What did you do to him?" she cried. "What did you do?"

Jarred could scarcely think. The pain in his foot was a fierce agony that drowned out everything else. Still, he managed to push himself off the ground. As he did, he swung around and aimed the rifle at the rest of the group. Jessica stumbled to a stop and thrust an arm out to stop the others. Jarred saw tears glistening on her cheeks in the lamplight, though she had a fierce twist to her lips.

Andy was behind her. He stepped forward now and raised his rifle at Jarred.

"I guess this is a standoff," Jarred said, speaking through clenched teeth.

"I'll kill you for what you've done," Jessica said in a hateful hiss.

"No, you won't," Zane said from atop the slope. Jarred looked up and saw the teen crouched there, mostly hidden by a tree. He had a long rifle aimed down at the group. "Because I'll kill you next, lady. Lower *your* gun."

They all stood there for a few seconds. Then Jessica nodded at Andy, and he lowered his rifle. Jarred backed toward the slope, unwilling to take his eyes off of the group.

"You don't realize what we are," Jessica said.

"I have a pretty good idea," Jarred said. "Murderers. Child killers. Brute beasts. Not cops."

He dared to sling the rifle over his shoulder and reached up to the nearest handhold. Turning his back to the others made his flesh crawl even stronger than before, until he could scarcely think straight. As he pulled himself up, he heard Jessica crying quietly, angrily. He heard other members of the group muttering to each other. It was a dangerous and troubling sound.

"Just stay right there until we're gone," Zane said. "I've got a bead on you, lady, and I'm a pretty good shot."

"We spared you," Jessica said. "Fed you. Shared our fire with you. We won't forget this."

Jarred finally dragged himself onto the snowy ground above the slope. Ramses leaned down and sniffed at him, then bleated softly as if in greeting. Jarred picked himself up, fighting through the gut-wrenching pain to stand on both feet. Zane slowly rose beside him, still aiming down at the river.

"Don't let us see you again," Zane said. "I mean it, lady!"

And with that, he shuffled backward and turned. He grabbed Ramses's rope and set off into the woods above the river. Jarred hobbled after them. As he did, he heard Jessica wail in grief and fury. The sound chased him as he hurried away, tears of pain blinding him.

67

The river was entirely frozen, and the ice seemed quite thick. It was at least fifty feet from bank to bank, and under the circumstances, it seemed really far. The sleds were parked side by side, the goats looking restless and tired at the same time. They'd been fed and watered, but they clearly wanted to press on.

The long night was over, thank God, and the snowstorm had let up a bit. Still, they had suffered through long hours, stopping from time to time whenever they could find any shelter at all from the wind. Fiona didn't know how much longer the goats would last. They seemed lethargic, unable to fully recover. The humans weren't doing much better.

Larry and Hope stood on a rocky shelf, gazing down at the river, while Lana and Myra sat together on one of the sleds. Fiona went down to the river's edge and stepped onto the ice, testing its strength. It felt sturdy beneath her. Finally, she turned and walked back up to where Larry and Hope were. Currently, Larry had the big laminated map open in his hands. "I'm pretty sure we're right around here," he said, tapping a curve on a blue line. "It's an actual river, not a creek, as you can see."

"I intended to approach the cavern from farther south," Fiona said, "where the road crosses the river. I figured there would be a bridge over the water there."

Duke grumbled. His free hand was endlessly massaging the other arm through his coat. Fortunately, he was no longer pulling the injured arm out and exposing it to the cold. Not that it mattered. His fingers were already frostbitten and dying.

"If there's a bridge," he said, "then that's where we have to go."

"Unfortunately, it looks like that bridge is a few miles away," Fiona replied, "and the way the river curves, we'd be backtracking to get there."

"Well, what's the alternative?" Larry said. "You want to try crossing the river right here and just hope the ice holds?"

"I'm fairly confident it will hold," Fiona said. "I tested it just now. And it'll save us at least a day of travel to cross here."

Duke made a kind of outraged sputtering sound. "Have you lost your mind? You want us to pull these sleds over that river just to save another day of travel? If that ice breaks, we're all going into the water!"

"We can't afford another day out here," Fiona said. "It could make the difference between life and death. You said yourself practically your entire hand is numb now. You're almost certainly going to lose your fingers. I don't want you to lose the whole arm."

"Let me worry about that," he replied, though his voice was thick with pain. "We have to head to the bridge. It's the only sure path. Come on, Fiona. Think clearly! Be reasonable."

Fiona sighed. How could she get Duke Cooper to the same frame of mind? She wasn't sure.

"We have to get you down into the warmer air of the cavern as soon as possible," she said. "It's the only way to stop your frostbite from spreading even further. Myra agrees with me, and I think we can trust her professional judgment on this."

"It's my hand, my arm, my problem," Duke said.

"It's not just about your frostbitten hand, Mr. Cooper," she said. "We might find Jarred and Zane at the cavern. It's where they'll head, if they can. And even if they aren't there yet, we need to hurry and get settled, so we can send out a search party."

Duke looked at Larry with a kind of wide-eyed desperation, as if silently pleading for his friend to talk sense into her. Larry refolded the map and said, "Adding a whole other day of travel could prove catastrophic, but then again, if we all drown in an icy cold river, it'll have been for nothing. Ice cover can be uneven. You can't always tell where the thin spots are."

"Then you agree with me," Duke said, and before Larry could assent or dissent, he added, "Fiona is asking us to trust that the ice will hold, and I don't. I don't trust it. There's no way to know how strong the current is under there, and the ice might be thin and dangerous in some spots. One more day for a safe crossing sounds reasonable to me."

"The goats won't survive. Your arm won't survive. Hell, *you* might not survive," Fiona said, handing the folded map to Larry. He walked back to put it with their supplies. "Anyway, we have no idea if the bridge is any safer at this point. We don't know its condition. All of this cold, and the constant snowfall, might have compromised its superstructure."

"Superstructure," Duke said, spitting out the word as if it tasted bad. "You act like you're some kind of bridge expert."

Hope had been quiet through most of the discussion, staring quietly down at the icy river, but she piped up now. "Superstructure is the correct word. It refers to the girders, bearings, and deck, basically the parts above the piers and abutments."

"Well, that's good to know," Duke growled. "I guess we should let the kid here decide which way we go."

At this, Hope pulled a face and shook her head vigorously.

"Duke, here's the thing," Fiona said, as Larry returned to her side, "I say we're crossing the river, and that's my decision. Time saved *is* safer. Our very survival, and the survival of our animals, might depend on it. Every additional hour we spend out in this cold is another hour closer to death."

Duke shook his head in disgust, but Larry grunted and said, "That's the decision then. You won't get any resistance from me, Fiona. Duke, do I need to drive your sled for you?"

"No, no," he replied, waving a hand at him. "I want to make my disgust at this course of action known. If we had some process for filing a complaint, you can be damn sure I would file."

Fiona sighed. She really wanted to snap at him, to tell him that it didn't matter what he thought. He'd spent most of this trip complaining, and she was tempted to say, *We're crossing here whether you like it or not.* Instead, she decided to try a more diplomatic approach, if only so it would save her more trouble down the road.

She motioned for Larry to stay put, then beckoned Duke, and backed away. He shrugged and gave her a confused look, but as she moved a short distance away from the sleds, he eventually followed. She kept going until she thought they were far enough that the others wouldn't overhear. Nevertheless, Myra, Lana, and Larry were all watching carefully.

"Oh, what now?" Duke grumbled, furiously rubbing at the bulge of his arm against his coat. "Did you take me aside to scold me? I'm not a child. I'm just a concerned man who doesn't want everyone to die."

"Duke, you've been difficult from the moment we left the homestead," she said. "Actually, before that. When the house collapsed. You've been a rude pain in the butt, as if I dropped the house on top of you on purpose. What's your deal?"

"I don't know what you're talking about," he said, pulling his hood farther forward, as if he wanted to hide from her. "All I've done is express my concern when it was appropriate."

"You've been rude to me every step of the way," she said. "You complain constantly. You're always angry. Your whole personality changed as soon as you hurt your arm. What's going on? What's *really* going on? I have to get to the bottom of it, because you make it ten times harder for me to lead."

He bowed his head and scowled at the ground, shifting one of his snowshoes from side to side and digging a groove into the snow in the process.

He grunted, shook his head as if he were having an internal debate, then finally lifted his gaze to her.

"Okay, fine, fair enough," he said softly. Then he sniffed and said, louder, "Truth be told, this new world is horrible, and I guess I realized at some point just how old I am now, how less capable I am. If this had happened ten years ago, it would be a very different experience, I can tell you that. I'd almost certainly be in charge, or at least in the front lines, but as it is, I'm just a frail old man."

"So you're mad at me because you realized you're old?" Fiona replied.

"No, no, not that," he grumbled. "I'm upset because…because, damn it, I never realized how much of a liability I am now that I'm old. I'm not mad at *you*. I'm angry because I screwed up. At the house, when it collapsed, and now again, out here." He patted his arm. "I'm the only one who got frostbite out here. It was a dumb mistake. A really dumb mistake."

"As I recall, I tried to stop you from sticking your arm out of the coat," Fiona said. "I wanted to save your hand. Partly so you would still be useful to the group."

"I know, damnit," he snarled. "I'm not mad at you. I'm just mad. Don't you get it?"

Fiona shook her head. "No, Duke, I don't get it, but then again, there's a lot of things about human behavior that don't make sense to me. Look, if you still want to be useful to the group then stop complaining all the time, stop butting heads with me, stop being so angry at me. We can debate and discuss plans, but in the end, I need you to trust me, trust the group, and help us get where we're going. I'm trying to keep you safe. I'm trying my best. Can't you trust me?"

Duke made a long, low sound and bowed his head again. For a few seconds, he stopped massaging his arm and just stood there, the wind blowing the fur lining of his hood.

Finally, he nodded, as if to himself, raised his head and said, "Okay. I trust you."

68

They'd lost most of their sturdiest rope in the fire, but one length of yellow nylon rope remained. It was rolled up into a ball and tucked deep in a crate on the small sled. As Larry and Lana readjusted the supplies on the sleds to distribute the weight more evenly, Fiona unwound the rope and wrapped it around her waist. Duke, clearly wanting to prove his usefulness, checked the ropes and harnesses on one set of goats, making sure everything was sturdy, while Hope checked on the others.

"It wouldn't be a bad idea to leave some more stuff behind," Larry said. "A little less weight might give us a better chance of getting across safely."

As Fiona tied a knot, she considered their remaining supplies. They'd lost an entire sled's worth of stuff. She hated to lose anything else, but she could see Larry's point.

"We could afford to lose some more of our scrap wood and metal," she said. "I'd hope to use that stuff for sled repairs and maybe even building a shelter when we get where we're going, but it's a lot of weight."

Larry nodded. "Okay, then, I won't dump all of it, just in case we need something. Just the heavier stuff."

As he went to the back of the big sled, Fiona grabbed the loose end of the nylon rope and brought it to the small sled. Myra was sitting there, her gloved hands on her lap.

"Hey there, Myra, would you hold the end of this rope for me?" Fiona said.

Myra reached up and took the end of the rope from her. "I'm not sure I'm strong enough to pull you back if you fall. I'll do my best."

"No, I don't need that," Fiona said. "Just hold the rope for me. I'm going to crawl across first and make sure it's solid. Then I'll tie the rope to something. That should make it easier for everyone else to get across."

"I accept that this the right thing to do," Myra said. "We need to get Duke inside that cavern, to warmer air, as fast as possible, because the frostbite is spreading. He's running out of time. But it's so dangerous. Please, be careful. If the ice gives way…well, I don't need to tell you what will happen."

"That's why I'm going first," Fiona said. "Hold the rope for me."

At this, Myra stood up and grabbed the rope with both hands. "Okay, I'll hold on tight." She seemed to have diminished a lot during their trip from the farmstead. She was stooped, her face thinner, and she had tufts of ice-white hair sticking out of her hood. Her eyes were tired, her face sagging.

"Once I'm across, Larry can tie it to something on this end," Fiona said, and then, because she wanted to offer some comfort or encouragement, she added, "It'll be okay. Before you know it, we'll all be on the other side."

At this, Myra nodded and pulled the rope against her belly, as if it were suddenly precious to her. Fiona turned and gazed toward the river. Larry had dumped a small pile of scrap metal. And now Lana was working to redistribute the weight on the sled again. Duke had made his way through all of the goats, and he was trudging back toward the sleds.

"Okay, let's get this done," Fiona said.

She took a step, but Myra reached out suddenly and grabbed her shoulder. When Fiona looked back, Myra leaned in close and said, "He might have a temper, but he's not a bad man. When he's hurting or upset, he says and does things that he doesn't really mean."

Fiona met her anguished gaze and said, "I understand. We kind of worked things out. I think we're okay now."

At this, Myra almost smiled. Fiona saw the attempt. Larry and Duke approached at this point.

"I think we're ready," Larry said. "The sleds are as light as we can get them without losing anything we absolutely need."

"The goats are harnessed," Duke said. "Ropes are strong. They're not going anywhere."

Fiona checked the rope around her waist again and nodded. "Okay, let's do this. I'll go across by myself first. If it seems safe, then you guys can follow. I think in terms of the order, we'll send the goats first, since they're the heaviest weight. Larry you can make sure they get across. Then Lana and Hope will go next. Then Duke and Myra. Is everyone good with that?"

She looked at each of them in turn. They seemed nervous, all of them, but they each nodded. Duke even gave her a thumbs-up.

He's trying, Fiona thought.

"This is going to work," Larry said, after a few awkward seconds passed. "I really think so, Fiona. Just find the sturdiest path for us across the river."

"I will," she said. "Wait for me. Wait until I tell you it's safe."

And with that, she turned and headed toward the river's edge, shifting the knot of the rope so it was behind her. She saw the great sheet of ice spreading out before her.

As she picked her way down the slope toward the river, she looked for the safest path across. The wind was blowing, as always, and she found it disconcerting. It would make things a little trickier. Finally, she spotted a way across that seemed sturdy, a broad place just to her right.

"Take it slow," Duke called from behind her. "You can do this."

Yes, he was really trying now. She found it strangely touching. *I guess I should have talked to him about it sooner*, she thought. *Well, at least I'm learning how to interact with human beings.*

Easing down onto her hands and knees, she pulled herself onto the great sheet of ice. It felt slick beneath her hands and knees, far slicker than she'd anticipated. Her hands wanted to slide out from beneath her. This forced her to make small movements, which she knew must've looked ridiculous. In this way, she inched forward.

"You've got it," Duke said. "Keep going!"

Okay, Duke, don't overdo it, she thought. *I need to concentrate here.*

The ice felt sturdy, at least. It didn't move or buckle. It seemed to accept her weight with no problem. She'd reached the halfway point. On the far side of the river, another gradual slope led up to a broad, hilly landscape. She could see the great hill that was their destination. That gave her a little renewed enthusiasm, and she dared to pick up her pace.

Finally, the far bank closed in. She'd adjusted her movements to compensate for the slippery ground, and it seemed to work. She pulled herself off the ice, sliding into the snowbank. Her snowshoes were balanced across her back, and she grabbed them now as she sank into the snow on the far slope. Rising, she slipped them back over her boots and turned to face the others.

Larry, Lana, and Hope stood together between the goats at the water's edge. Duke and Myra watched from beside the small sled.

"It feels sturdy," Fiona shouted, "but it's slippery. Take your time. I'll tie off the rope. You do the same on the other side."

She hunted around for something to tie the rope to, but there were no trees near the water's edge. Finally, she fastened the rope around a large rock that had tumbled down the shallow slope toward the river. Larry did the same thing on the far side. It wasn't as stable as Fiona would have hoped for, but it was better than nothing.

She sat on the rock, as if her weight might somehow make it a little more stable. Larry and Lana exchanged a brief hug. Then he grabbed the lead line of the foremost goat and guided her into the ice. Four goats were harnessed to the big sled. As soon as they stepped onto the ice, they began to slip and slide. This caused the goats to panic, and they tried to rush forward. However, that just made them slide even worse. Larry had the lead line in his right hand, the safety rope in his left, but the wild scrabbling of the goats caused him to lose hold of both. He went down on his knees.

"Careful," Lana shouted from the far bank.

"I've got it," Larry replied sourly.

He reached up and grabbed the safety rope, then fumbled for the nearest goat. Finally, he snagged the harness and pulled himself to his feet. The goats were still struggling on the ice, but they seemed to be regaining their balance. Larry gave a gentle tug on the harness and got them moving forward. They dragged the sled onto the ice.

Fiona held her breath, straining to hear any cracking or popping. Mostly, she heard only the roar of water and the howling of the wind. Fortunately, due mostly to the insistence of the goats, Larry made his way across much faster than Fiona, and the safety rope helped him stay on his feet. Roughly halfway across, however, Fiona heard a distinctive pop, and Larry froze, eyes wide.

"It's fine. It's fine," he said, after a moment.

The goats didn't want to stop, so they forced him to keep moving forward. As they drew near, Fiona rose and stepped down to meet them. She beckoned the lead goat, who seemed to recognize her and went to her. Reaching out, Fiona grabbed the harness and guided the goat onto the snowy riverbank. Larry let go, put both hands on the safety rope, and stepped off the ice.

"That's it," he said, calling back over his shoulder. "I'm safe."

Lana breathed a visible sigh of relief and shook her head, even as the goats dragged the big sled off the ice and up the slope. Lana was to go next with the small sled, but Fiona held up a hand to stop her. She took a minute to inspect the ice. The sled runners had left visible marks on the ice, but she didn't see any obvious damage to the ice. No cracks or gaps.

"We have to get this done," Fiona muttered. She waved both hands at Lana. "Come on, Lana! If you hear any breaking or cracking noises, immediately rush to the nearest riverbank. Got it?"

"Got it," Lana called back. She reached back and grabbed the lead line of the second set of goats and guided them onto the ice.

The small sled was less weight, at least, but Fiona still found herself wringing her hands. The goats scrabbled on the ice, hooves slipping, and Lana was forced to let go of the harness and grab the safety rope with both hands. Hope, Duke, and Myra waited now on the far side, standing together. Fiona could see Duke anxiously massaging the lump of his arm again.

Even without Lana holding their line, the goats kept moving forward, dragging the smaller sled across the ice. Fiona heard another distinct pop. Lana went to her knees, pulling herself forward by the safety rope. Larry went down to meet her, stepped out onto the ice, and grabbed her arms as soon as she was close enough. Fiona met the lead goat and led her up beside the other sled.

"That was the hard part," Larry said, holding his wife. "If the ice can handle the weight of the sleds, then it shouldn't be a problem for the rest of the people."

"Yeah, it was a little nerve-wracking though," Fiona replied. She came back down to the river's edge and beckoned the others.

Hope glanced at Myra, who made a little shooing gesture at her. Nodding, Hope stepped onto the ice and began picking her way forward. When she slipped, she tried to slide over the ice like ice skating. That just made her fall on her butt with a huff. Fiona heard another loud pop, and she traded an anxious look with Larry.

"It's fine," Larry said. Then louder, to Hope, "Hold onto the line, kiddo. Stay low so you don't fall!"

Hope crawled over to the safety rope, grabbed it with both hands, and began dragging herself forward on her knees, as Lana had. The ice seemed to groan then. Still, Fiona saw no obvious signs of damage, no cracks or gaps appearing. She beckoned Hope, trying to gently encourage her to hurry.

"I'm coming," Hope replied. "Give me a minute here."

"Hope, does the ground feel unstable at all?" Fiona asked. "Can you feel it shifting or cracking or anything?"

"No, no, and please don't say that," Hope said with a whimper. "It's a little scary to think about."

As she neared the riverbank, Fiona stepped out to meet her, taking her hand and helping her to her feet. Then they stepped off the ice together and backed up the slope toward Larry and Lana.

"Turns out this was a pretty good idea, after all," Larry said. "You made the right decision, Fiona. We'll get the Coopers across, and then we're on our way."

"Yeah, I think so," Fiona replied.

She beckoned the Coopers then. They were standing together at the river's edge. Myra turned and looked at Duke, but he laid a hand on her shoulder and said something to her, probably telling her she had to go first. Myra nodded and stepped onto the ice. Just then, a gust of wind hit, sweeping down the frozen river. Fiona had to widen her stance to brace herself against it, but Myra was unprepared.

She fell over, grabbing the safety rope on the way down. She landed on her hip, then rolled onto her belly. Duke bent down to help her, but she brushed his hand away. Then, moving on her hands and knees, she proceeded to crawl across the frozen river, using the rope as a kind of awkward, and ill-suited, handrail to pull herself along.

"Just hold on, Myra," Duke called. "Don't let go of that rope. You can do it."

Duke was bent over, grimacing, clutching the lump of his arm. It looked like he wanted to run after Myra and help her, but he stayed put. As for Myra, she slowly dragged herself across the ice. Fiona could see that she was panting, out of breath, but she kept moving forward relentlessly. When she finally drew near, Fiona stepped out on the ice to meet her.

"You made it, Myra," she said, grabbing her under the arm and helping her up. "Good job. It's a lot harder than it looks, isn't it?"

Myra dramatically exhaled and fell against Fiona. "My knees are killing me. I need to sit down."

"Okay, come on."

Fiona guided her off the ice and toward the rock where they'd tied the rope, but she was struggling. Myra was wincing with every step, clearly in pain. Larry let go of Lana long enough to help, and together, they got Myra seated. She sighed, grabbed her knees, and bent over. Lana approached and sat down beside her in the snow.

"That wind really catches you off guard, doesn't it?" Lana said.

"Oh my, yes," Myra replied, still struggling to catch her breath.

That left Duke standing on the far side of the river. He seemed smaller somehow, diminished by the vastness behind him. Fiona stepped to the river's edge again and waved at him. He returned the wave.

"Untie the rope from your end," Fiona shouted. "Hold it tightly, and I'll pull you across!"

He nodded and turned to the rock behind him. Stooping down, he worked at the knot for a minute and finally got it undone. Then he wound it around his good hand one time and held it tightly. Fiona grabbed the rope on her end in both hands and braced herself for the pull.

"Do you need help, Fiona?" Larry asked.

"No, I think I've got it," she replied. And then, to Duke, she said, "Maybe get on your knees. You'll slide better than way."

He nodded and carefully stepped onto the ice. Then he eased himself down, one leg at a time, until he was on his knees. When he seemed settled in place, Fiona began pulling at the rope. He was heavier than he looked, but she managed to get him moving, sliding him along the frozen river.

"That's it," she said. "I've got you. Just hold on."

"I'm holding," he replied. She could see the other arm moving beneath his coat, as if he were tempted to reach out and grab the rope with it.

Fiona leaned back, putting her weight into it, and that got him moving a little faster. The ice gave another loud crack then, which startled her. Myra uttered a fearful squeak.

"Duke, did you feel that?" Fiona called.

"Felt something," he replied. "A little vibration beneath me."

At this, Fiona traded an anxious look with Larry.

"I'll help you pull," Larry said, approaching the rope.

Duke was close to halfway now. As Larry reached down to grab the rope just behind Fiona, another fierce gust of wind swept through, kicking up curtain of snow, which rolled over the people on the bank and temporarily obscured things. Fiona stepped out onto the ice to get out of it, and when she did, she saw Duke slide to one side. The wind drove him upstream, and then knocked him off balance.

As he fell forward, he let go of the rope and thrust his hand down to catch himself.

"Don't let go," Fiona cried.

But it was too late. The wind pulled the rope away from him, even as Duke managed to stop his fall and stay in place. Duke finally thrust his other arm out of the coat, reaching through the front zipper.

"Keep moving forward," Fiona said, but now she had to steady herself to keep from being blown over by the wind.

"Let me...let me grab the rope," Duke said.

The end of the rope had been pushed a few feet away from him, and it was still dancing and skittering along. Duke began crawling to one side, trying to reach out with the bad hand to get it.

"Don't bother," Fiona said. "Forget the rope."

"It's close," Duke said.

Fiona glanced over her shoulder. Myra had a desperate look on her face.

"I'll go out and get him," Fiona said. "You guys stay here. I don't want any more weight on the ice than we absolutely need."

"Please, be careful," Hope said in a whimper, anxiously tapping her hands together. "I think it's breaking under the surface."

"Okay, I'll go fast," Fiona said.

She turned back around to see Duke still crawling upstream. His bad arm was fully exposed now, revealing blackened fingertips, a red hand, as he reached for the rope, which remained just out of reach.

"Duke, hold still," she cried. "I'm coming to get you. Put your hand back in your coat!"

He looked at her then, a grimace on his face. She thought he was going to refuse, to keep striving toward the rope out of sheer stubbornness. Instead, he nodded, rose up onto his knees, and drew his frostbitten hand back inside his coat.

"It's okay," Fiona said, taking another step onto the ice. "I'm on my way."

He nodded again, breathing heavily. "I trust you," he replied.

Fiona took another step. When the ice popped loudly this time, she felt it. The entire shelf beneath her shuddered, and she froze, thrusting her arms wide to maintain her balance. Her gaze was fixed on Duke, their eyes locked. He gave her another nod then, small, faint, as if acknowledging something in his own mind.

"So be it," he said, so softly she almost didn't hear him over the wind.

And then the ice beneath him gave way. A big shelf maybe ten feet across snapped loose, and Duke was kneeling right in the middle of it. The ice beneath Fiona seemed to shift as well, dipping downward. She saw raging water rushing through strange channels that had been carved in the ice, and she knew she was going down into it. There was nothing to grab, nothing to arrest her fall.

Even so, her eyes remained locked onto Duke's as he fell. And then he hit the dark water. It swept over him, large chunks of ice crashing down all around him as his head disappeared into the swift, angry current.

Fiona felt herself going as well, but suddenly strong hands took hold of her. Her coat was grabbed from behind, twisted and pulled, and suddenly she was moving backward. She fell, landing on her back against Larry's chest, snow puffing up around them.

"I've got you," Larry cried. "I've got you, Fiona."

And somewhere, people began to scream in horror and grief.

69

Larry worked his way out from under her, but that left Fiona lying deep in the snow, on her back, staring up at a great billowing cloud. The wind continued to howl, the river roaring even louder now—like a fierce breathless beast that had been roused from a long, hateful slumber. However, behind all other sounds, she heard the cacophony of people screaming, and she recognized each voice. Hope's was a kind of warbling cry, full of fear and despair. Lana was more throaty, terrified, and Myra was a wail of raw anguish.

Fiona didn't want to get up. She didn't want to see the faces behind those voices. In that moment, she wanted the snow to keep rising up until it covered her completely and forever. The ice was still cracking. It sounded like little drumbeats.

"I'll toss the rope," Larry said. He sounded frantic. "He might still be down there, clinging to the rocks or the ice. Maybe he can grab the rope."

She heard his boots crunching on the ice at the water's edge. It was enough to break Fiona out of her stupor. She sat up, swiping the snow off her face. As she did, she saw the grieving shapes off to her right. Myra and Lana were clutching each other. Hope was bent double, her arms wrapped around her head.

But Larry was standing on a shelf of ice that hung out over the water. The river raged at his feet as he pulled the rope up. Fiona rushed toward him. She'd lost her snowshoes, so she dragged her boots through the deep snow.

"Larry, stop that," she cried. "Come away from there."

Now it was her turn to grab the back of his coat. When she did, she leaned back and let her weight drag him away from the river. He fell backward into the snow, and Fiona rolled to one side to keep from being crushed.

"What are you doing?" he said, trying to quickly pick himself up.

"You'll fall in," Fiona said, sitting up. "We can't afford to lose you, too!"

Larry sat up beside her, staring at his gloved hands as if he couldn't figure out how he's lost hold of the rope. The hole in the ice was getting bigger as the edges continued to crumble. Indeed, the spot where Larry had been standing seconds earlier suddenly gave way. The water below was deep and dark, but of Duke there was no sign whatsoever. Even so, she noticed that the edge of the exposed water was changing color already, losing some of the dark blue, as if it were already freezing.

Oh, God, I hope it was quick, she thought, feeling a moment of bitter anguish. *I hope he's not down there somewhere, suffering.*

Despite this, Larry rose and took a step toward the river, but Fiona planted a hand against his chest.

"He's gone," she shouted. "I'm sorry, but he's gone! There's nothing we can do for him."

Larry stared hard at the water for a moment, then blinked, and stumbled backward. "You're right," he muttered. He swallowed hard and nodded. "I just…wanted to try."

The screaming had stopped, but Fiona could still hear those terrible sounds echoing far and wide. She didn't want to turn around. She didn't want to face the others, but she knew they had to keep moving. There was no time to grieve. No time to wrestle with regret or failure.

As Larry turned away from the river, she forced herself to turn with him. They were standing before the rock, Lana and Myra still holding each other

—no longer screaming, but weeping softly. Hope stood to one side, her hands covering most of her face, wide and terrified eyes peering out from under the hood. Fiona couldn't deal with it, not now, not yet. The wind continued to howl, bringing with it a renewed snowfall, and she felt the bitter cold sinking deep into her body.

He said he trusted me, she thought. *And I let him down.*

It wasn't a place she could dwell, so she trudged up to the large stone, knelt down, and began untying the knot on the rope.

"I should have made him go before me," Myra said, miserably. "He insisted on being last. He insisted, but I should have made him go. Why didn't I make him go? It's my fault."

"Now, don't say that, Myra," Lana replied. "It could have happened to any of us."

Fiona began pulling in the rope, trying to get back to that mindless place where she could act without feeling. However, the rope got stuck on something. It seemed to have frozen on something below, but she kept pulling, uttering a string of angry curses. Finally, it seemed to break loose, and she quickly rolled it up into a damp, icy ball and brought it back to the big sled.

"We have to go," she called over her shoulder. "None of us will last long out here. Let's go." And when none of them moved, she added, in a softer voice, "I'm sorry, but we have to hurry."

Larry trudged toward the smaller sled to take Duke's place. As he passed by, Lana fell in behind him. Hope came next, her hands still pressed to her mouth. She moved to the big sled and took a seat in the back, nestled down among the boxes and facing backward.

"Myra, please," Fiona said.

Mrs. Cooper seemed reluctant to leave. She stood beside the rock for a few more seconds, staring at the stream, as if Duke might somehow magically reappear. Then she turned, looked from one sled to the other, and finally approached the big sled. Without a word, she took a seat near Hope.

Duke didn't want to cross the river. Fiona couldn't stop the thought. It came to her unbidden. *He knew the danger, and you didn't listen to him. He trusted you, and now he's gone.*

Fiona took up the reins, nodded at Larry in the other sled, and got the goats moving. Larry soon followed with the small sled. They headed up the slope to a broad snow-covered field, but the hills were very close now, which meant their destination was close. That realization brought no comfort. Rarely had Fiona felt so low. An aching, horrified guilt lay over her, a feeling made all the worse by the fact that Myra continued to sob quietly at the back of the sled.

Finally, she felt compelled to say something. "Myra, this was my fault, not yours," she said, over her shoulder. "I know that. I'm sorry."

Slowly, Myra turned her head to look up at Fiona. Her cheeks were bright red, eyes filled with tears, snow caught in the wisps of her white hair. She gave Fiona a bitter scowl, teeth bared slightly, then turned away. Apology not accepted, apparently, but that seemed more than fair. Fiona didn't feel like she deserved absolution.

Fiona sighed and shook the reins, trying to get a little more speed. She tried to concentrate on the landscape ahead, looking for some sign, any sign, as the river and its terrible consequences faded into the endless white expanse behind them. Eventually, she spotted some strange man-made object off to the right. It rose from the snow between two hills, partially covered in snow.

A road sign, a big one, and the exposed section was brown. A tourist sign of some kind. Now, she could see a flatter place where the road must have been. Some of the words on the sign were covered, but as she drew near, she spotted the one that mattered most: *Cavern*. An arrow beside it pointed straight ahead.

"That's it," Fiona called over her shoulder. She pointed at the sign. "Snowbird Cavern!"

Only Hope roused herself enough to look up. No one else seemed capable of excitement. They passed between the hills approaching a larger hill, and Fiona saw what might have been a small building in a parking lot that had a vast mound of snow on its rooftop. Beyond that building, a path led into the trees and curved toward a steep side of the hill. The parking lot, visitor center, and cavern entrance. That's what it seemed.

"We're here," Fiona said.

As she drew near, she saw what appeared to be footprints and animal tracks moving all over the place. People had been here! People and dogs, perhaps? It was a ray of hope in the pit of despair, and she almost said something. However, she stayed her tongue for the moment. Better to wait. Better to be sure.

She aimed for the open space that might have been the tourist parking lot. The gap between the trees was wide enough for the sleds, so she aimed right for it, scarcely slowing down. However, as she crossed the parking lot, she got a better look at the existing footprints. They were old enough that the snow had almost erased them, and most of them seemed to be centered around the visitor's center. None led to the path or the cave entrance beyond.

Still, it could have been Jarred, Zane, and Smoke, she told herself. *If they got here yesterday, their tracks might look like this.*

She wanted to believe it, though that would have meant that they were moving significantly faster than the sleds while on foot. Unlikely, but not impossible. When they passed into the trees, it blocked the wind, and suddenly things became very quiet. Myra was no longer crying, but Fiona could hear sniffles and hiccoughs.

Looking back, she saw that Hope had repositioned, rising to her knees so she could see forward. The small sled was just entering the tree-lined path, and Larry raised a hand to her. When Fiona turned back around, she saw the gaping entrance to the cavern. It was a broad slash through the rocks, the passage beyond angled downward into a misty darkness.

Fiona reined in the goats and came to a stop just outside. They'd finally made it, and the dark, snowless interior was so inviting, but under the circumstances, she felt no elation. Larry drew the small sled up beside her on the left and came to a stop.

"Are they here?" Lana said. "Larry, are they here? Do you see any sign of Zane?"

He didn't answer but quietly set down the reins. Hope hopped up, tripping over boxes as she climbed off the sled.

"Wait a second, everyone," Fiona said, dropping her reins. "Let's not rush in there. We have to make sure it's safe."

But Lana and Hope ignored her. Larry followed them, but Myra kept her seat, slumped on the back of the sled. Fiona thought to go to her, to encourage her in some way, but she didn't think it would be well received under the circumstances. So, she went to Larry instead and followed him toward the cavern entrance. She petted some of the goats in passing.

Larry leaned in close and said, "No one's been here lately. No tracks outside the cavern."

Hope and Lana entered the cave, their speed checked only by the damp and uneven ground beyond. As soon as Fiona got there, she felt a warm air emanating out of the darkness.

"Do you feel that?" she said, pushing her hood back.

"Yeah, it's like we said before, the cavern maintains an even fifty-five degrees year-round," Larry said.

It'll work, she realized. *This place will work.*

But realizing it brought only another wave of grief and despair. Yes, they'd reached the cavern, but what had it cost them? She looked back and saw Myra following at a distance, almost reluctantly. They'd lost almost half the group to come here. Had it been worth the cost?

"Dad! Dad, are you here? Dad!"

Hope had picked her way down the slope to a broad rocky shelf a few yards inside the cavern where the walls opened up. Though it was very dark ahead, the echo of her voice suggested a vast chamber ahead. Hope had her hands cupped to either side of her mouth as she shouted.

"Dad! If you're here, say something!"

"Zane! We're here," Lana said, joining Hope's voice. "We've made it!"

Fiona and Larry stood just inside the cavern, listening to the cries of the women moving through distant, deep chambers. It was a haunting sound. They went on like that for a good two minutes, and finally stopped. The echo continued for a while, fading only gradually. The silence that followed was almost absolute. Finally, Hope spun around, smacking her gloved hands together, then swooping her hood off her head. Her short hair was drenched with sweat, her face flushed.

"He's not here," she said furiously, glaring up at Fiona. "You said Dad would be here."

"I said they *might*," Fiona replied.

Hope stomped a foot, burst into tears, and sank onto the ground. Lana began crying as well and sat down beside her, face in her hands.

"We came so far." That was Myra, coming up beside them, sounding frail and broken. "Lost Duke, lost Jarred and Zane, lost almost half our supplies, the strongest goat, the dog, and here we are." As she passed by Fiona, she shrugged and shook her head. "Here we are." And then, sarcastically, she added, "At least it's not a drafty barn with a hole in the roof, right? That makes it all worthwhile."

Fiona didn't know what to do. She felt entirely responsible, and the guilt was paralyzing. However, she saw the group sinking into despair, and she knew she had to do something. It wouldn't take much to sink into this bottomless pit and never rise. Acting despite her feelings, she picked her way down the damp rocky slope, deeper into the cave, and sat down beside Hope. The poor girl was weeping.

Though she fully expected to be shoved, pushed away, yelled at, she slipped her arms around Hope. Surprisingly, the girl received the hug and fell against her, burying her face against Fiona's shoulder.

"It's not fair," Hope said, voice muffled, "to make it all this way without him. I need him!"

And thinking of Jarred then, seeing his face in her mind, Fiona felt tears burning in her eyes as well.

I need him, too, she thought.

70

With no moon or stars to guide them, no flashlight, torch, or candle, Jarred and Zane were in a darkness so complete that it almost seemed to be a solid mass. Jarred's vision had adjusted just enough that he could perceive the shapes of objects as they drew near. The shouting of their pursuers chased them, kept them moving through the dark night.

Ramses, at least, seemed to have some clearer sense of the terrain ahead. Whether by smell or some other unknown sense, he managed to adjust their course from time to time, taking them around large objects, such as trees, rocks, and hills. Still, Jarred feared that they might step off a cliff, that he'd find himself tumbling in the open air before he even knew what was happening.

"Are we headed in the right direction?" Zane said. "I can't see anything."

"No idea," Jarred replied. Just then, he kicked through a snow drift and almost fell. "Eventually the sun will come up and show the way." He was out of breath, sore, and shivering from the frigid endless wind. "Until then, we just have to keep moving and stay away from these people."

The snow had let up. Normally, this would have been a small blessing, but it also meant their tracks would not be covered up. Even if they got far ahead of their pursuers, they would be easy to follow. Jarred didn't know what to do about this. It took everything just to keep moving forward.

"Should we lay a trap for them or something?" Zane asked. He was panting hard, hands pressed to his stomach.

"I'm not sure how we would do that," Jarred replied. "Certainly not until the sun is up."

Fortunately, they still had their snowshoes, but even so, the deep powdery snow checked their speed. Ramses would occasionally sink too deep, and when that happened, he would hop and kick his way back to the surface, like some strange swimmer. It was slow going, and with little way to track their progress, he couldn't tell how far they'd come. The night went on and on.

Eventually, they were forced to stop and catch their breath. They'd approached some half-buried trees, and they moved to the leeward side out of the wind. Jarred loosely tied Ramses's short rope to a branch. Then he dared to sit down with his back against the trunk. Zane collapsed beside him with a huff.

"You think there's any chance we'll see them again?" Zane said, softly. "Hope, my parents, the Coopers?"

"I'm holding out that hope," Jarred replied. He eased his hood back to let the cold air against his face. He felt a constant dull ache in his cheek where Tom had punched him. Worse was the pain in his ankle, though he had walked on it anyway. However, what bothered him more than any other ache or pain was the lack of sleep, the sheer exhaustion, which made his mind foggy. "Things will be a lot clearer in the morning."

This answer seemed to satisfy Zane, and he grew quiet. Ramses was nibbling at the nearby tree, as if looking for something to eat. Otherwise, the night seemed very still, and in that moment, Jarred became aware of a new sound. At first, it just seemed like distant white noise. However, as he studied it for a moment, he gradually realized what it was.

"Water," he said. "A stream."

"Are you sure?" Zane replied. "Wouldn't a stream be frozen over?"

"Maybe not completely," Jarred said, picking himself up. "There was a river on the map in the direction of the cavern. I remember seeing it. That could be it. If so, it's still sounds pretty far, but maybe…just maybe…we're headed in the right direction."

He untied Ramses's rope and beckoned the kid. Zane picked himself up, brushing the snow off the seat of his pants.

"Man, I really hope you're right," Zane said. "If the sun comes up and we find out we're back in Glencole, I'm going lose it."

"I think we're on the right track. If we can manage a brisk pace, we might reach the cavern before Jessica and her people catch up to us."

Jarred gave Ramses's rope a gentle tug and headed in what he thought was the direction of the water. Zane seemed to have regained some of his energy, and he broke into a jog. Unfortunately, Jarred just couldn't get there, even with this little glimmer of hope. He was limping badly, but more than that, it was a struggle just to keep his eyes open. It felt like they were moving very slowly. If Jessica was determined, she wouldn't have a problem catching up. But all she had to do was get within shooting range by the time the sun came up.

Somehow, we need to buy more time, Jarred thought.

He fell back into a routine, step after step, with little sense of time or distance. The roar of the river didn't seem to be getting any closer. However, at some point, in a kind of daze, he became aware of light rising to his left. It drew the dark line of the horizon, revealing the distant humps of hills before them.

"It's morning," Zane said. He'd lost his second burst of energy, trudging along with his hands sunk deep into the pockets of his coat. "I don't see Glencole. That's a good sign."

Off to the right, Jarred spotted a row of smaller hills. Jarred had the strange impression that they were walking over a buried neighborhood, where quaint little homes had once sat behind neatly manicured lawns. Now, it was just this blanket, this damned everywhere-blanket of colorless cold nothing. Directly to the left, he saw a line of trees. They must have been towering before the snow half-buried them. Even now, they still rose ten or twenty feet.

Then he looked behind them, and there he saw the stark line of their footprints cutting across the field. It was like a dark dotted line leading right to them. More than that, being out in the open like this made his skin crawl. Although he didn't see anyone behind them, he could imagine a shooter peering through a scope, taking careful aim.

"Maybe we should head to those trees over there," he said, pointing to the line of trees on their left. "It might hide our tracks a little bit."

"I'm not sure there's much we can do to hide our tracks," Zane said.

Despite this, Jarred turned toward the trees, leading Ramses. The goat must've been tired by now, but he came willingly. As they drew near the trees, however, some smaller shape darted through the branches and out into the open. Then another, and another. Soon, they had a small herd of deer bounding out into the open. Jarred froze and held an arm out to stop Zane. The deer leapt across the open field.

As they drew near, Jarred made a loud sound, which seemed to startle them. They turned, heading toward the distant hills, moving fast. They had to constantly leap, bounding almost like rabbits, which left deep grooves in the snow.

"That'll do," Jarred said, thinking out loud.

"What do you mean?" Zane asked.

"We'll follow those deer," he said. "Use their tracks to hide our own. It's not perfect, but it at least muddies things up a little bit."

He adjusted their path enough to meet the deep grooves left by the deer. By then, the deer were long gone, moving far into the distance. Jarred followed their tracks, and they seemed to do a good job of obscuring their own footprints. The deer had also managed to push through the loose, more powdery snow to something firmer, so walking in their tracks made it a little easier for Jarred and Zane. They picked up a bit of speed.

The roar of water was getting louder now, and he became aware of a shadowy line ahead of them. Gradually, it revealed itself as to be a broad icy river flowing through a shallow ravine. The water had mostly frozen, creating a shelf of dark ice, but he could see deep cracks and gaps in some places. Not completely frozen. Or perhaps that was a hollow beneath where the sheer strength of the current had managed to continue flowing somehow.

"Is that river both frozen *and* flowing at the same time?" Zane asked.

"Sounds like it," Jarred replied. "My guess would be that the portion exposed to the winter air turned into ice, but the deeper water was insulated and kept flowing."

The deer had run to the river but then turned and ran along the bank. Apparently, they did not want to cross.

"We don't have to cross that, do we?" Zane asked. "It looks dangerous. Seems like it would collapse beneath us."

Jarred gazed at the large hills beyond the river, one towering above all others. "If I'm right, then those hills are where we're headed, so I'm afraid the answer is yes. We have to cross that river."

It stretched to the left and right as far as he could see, and there were no bridges in either direction. However, the surface of the river had mostly been swept clean of snow, leaving the ice almost entirely exposed.

"The ice will help to cover our tracks," Jarred said, "but it does look fragile in some places. I'm not sure what to do here, kid."

"If the ice breaks, we're dead," Zane said. "Even if the water is only waist deep, we'll freeze to death. We won't survive. And what a horrible way to go. I wouldn't wish that on my worst enemy."

Indeed, Jarred could imagine it. The ice breaking beneath him, plunging him into a raging river that was only a degree or two above freezing, feeling that icy water seep into his clothes. A hellish way to go.

"Okay, maybe you're right," Jarred said with a sigh. "We'd be crazy to risk it. So, let's follow the riverbank for a while, go the way the deer went, and hope that we find some safer way over the ice."

Zane sighed. "Thanks, sir."

Once they reached the slope above the river, he found that the snow was less deep, and it had frozen just enough to be firm without being slippery. This enabled them to pick up even more speed. Jarred stayed close to the deer tracks, which followed the course of the river toward what he thought was probably southeast. The slope also allowed them to get down out of sight, so any distant pursuers might not see them.

Nevertheless, as the day grew brighter, the morning passed slowly, and the broad expanse of ice on their left remained impassible. If anything, it seemed more treacherous, more cracked and broken, as they went.

"I wish there was a way to fly across," Zane said. "Or pole vault or something."

"Just keep your eyes peeled," Jarred said.

Even as he said it, he spotted a strange shape ahead. Scarcely more than a shadow at first, it seemed to stretch out over the water. However, as they continued, it gradually resolved itself into an old single-land truss bridge. The deer were using it to cross the river at the moment, digging their deep grooves through the snow that had piled on the road.

"Well, there you go, kid," Jarred said. "A bridge, and it seems safe enough. If it can bear the weight of those deer, surely it can handle us. And with the big hills on the other side, we must be close to our destination."

"I can't believe it," Zane said, shaking his head. "I didn't think we'd make it out of that rest stop, to be honest, and now we're almost home."

Home. That struck Jarred as odd. He definitely didn't think of the cave as their home. It was just a place they were running to in order to escape the snow. Would it ever feel like home? How could it?

As he was thinking that, he heard a familiar sound coming from somewhere behind him. A dog barking. Paws scrabbling on the snow.

"Zane, could that be…?"

71

They spent a long time just sitting there in the damp chamber, ten or twenty yards from the cavern's entrance. Myra, Lana, and Hope were each facing a different direction, each lost in their own personal grief. Larry had approached them at one point, but now he was just standing there, his hands on his hips, staring into the darkness and doing nothing, saying nothing.

Fiona let them grieve for a while, longer than she should have, if only because she felt responsible for so much of it. How could she command them to stop nursing the wounds that she had inflicted upon them? So she stood by herself in the passageway before the chamber and tried to occupy her mind by making plans.

Okay, it's enough, she thought, after a few minutes. *If we grieve forever, we won't survive.*

Finally, she approached the group and cleared her throat loudly to get their attention. Only Larry and Hope turned to look at her. Lana and Myra scarcely seemed to notice.

"We need to bring our animals and belongings inside the caverns," she said. "It's really cold out there. And we could start building a fire as well. I'm sorry, friends, that's just what we have to do."

"You're right, of course," Larry said. He reached down and poked Lana on the shoulder. "Come on, dear. Help me unharness the goats and bring them inside."

Lana sighed, but she rose, swiping some of the mud off her backside. "Yes, of course." She turned to Fiona and said, "You said we would send out a search party. If we reached the cavern, we would send out a search party to find the others. I remember that."

"Yes, I did say that, and I meant it." The thought of heading back out there, of potentially trying to get across the river again, made her sick to her stomach. Still, she couldn't take back the words. "Let's bring our things inside, get a fire going, and then we'll discuss the search party."

"Good," Lana replied. "Very good."

At that, Hope got up as well. "I don't suppose I can be part of the search party," she said.

"We'll discuss it after we've unloaded," Fiona said.

Only Myra refused to come with them. She drew her knees up and laid her arms across them, as if settling in for a long time. Fiona decided not to push the issue. She headed out with the others. First, they unharnessed the goats, who seemed overjoyed at being set free. They led the animals down into the cave. There really wasn't anywhere to pen them, but they huddled together near a wall anyway. Next, Fiona unloaded a crate of feed and set it in their midst, and they munched happily away.

As she did that, Larry, Lana, and Hope brought all of the other bags and boxes in and created a crude wall near the goats. It was the best they could do at the moment. When Fiona checked the chicken cage, she found more dead animals inside. They'd simply frozen to death, despite the fact that she had covered the cage and tried to insulate it. Only five were left alive. She set them free inside the cavern so they could hunt bugs and spiders.

Once the supplies were all inside the cavern and only the two sleds sat outside, Larry and Lana found a place to sit down again. Hope found one of the largest crates and sat as well, her head in her hands. They were exhausted, but Fiona was too restless to relax. She opened the toolbox and pulled out one of their flashlights.

"I'm going to explore a little deeper into the cavern," she said, clicking on the flashlight. "Anyone want to come with me?"

"I think we'd just like to sit for a while," Larry said.

"Maybe later," Hope added.

"I understand," Fiona said with a sigh.

Fiona shone the light around the chamber and saw the high ceiling above them. Tiny lumps of bats were visible in some places, and a mist or fog hovered near the ceiling. Across the room, she saw another passage leading down, so she headed in that direction. The rocks were slick everywhere, and she heard the occasional drip of water. Guano was piled up in some places. Still, the air temperature was warmer than anything she'd felt since leaving the farmstead. This was nice. She could survive here.

She made her way down the passageway, stepping carefully over uneven rocks. The passage curved to the left and grew narrower, until her shoulders were brushing the damp walls on either side. After perhaps forty or fifty yards, it opened up into another large chamber, where massive stalactites hung down from the ceiling. Fiona heard a trickle of water and began searching for it, swinging the flashlight back and forth.

Other passageways headed off in many directions, and she sensed that this place was larger and more complex than it had seemed from the entrance. She walked in the direction of the water, entering a wide passage to the right. Rounding a bend, the flashlight beam shone across what seemed like a small pond of crystal-clear water in a rocky pit. Larry had said from the beginning that there was water in this cavern. He'd been correct. This water looked so clean and crisp that Fiona couldn't resist tasting it. She pulled off the glove from her left hand with her teeth, knelt at the water's edge, and dipped her cupped hand inside. It was cold, but not freezing.

She dared a sip. Despite a slight mineral aftertaste, it was as good as anything she'd ever tasted out of a tap. There seemed to be an endless supply of it as well. Indeed, the pool before her seemed to be continually fed by a small rivulet streaming out of a gap in the wall, then flowing down a narrow channel on the far side of the pool.

It's not stagnant, she thought, *and the temperature in the cavern will keep it from freezing.*

She couldn't have asked for more. Of course, the surrounding cave was gloomy and foreboding. Strange air noises moved through vast unseen chambers, which was eerie. The stalactites dripped, and the ground was damp and dirty. Still, all things considered, their destination had turned out as good as she'd hoped.

This'll make a fine home, she thought. *It's a sanctuary, a haven. The roof will never collapse because it's made of stone and it has stood for thousands of years. If only everyone had made it here alive.*

She shook the excess water off her hand and rose. Just then, she heard a sharp cry from around the cavern entrance. Because of the strange echoing acoustics of the cave, she couldn't tell who it was, but they seemed to be in pain. Fiona wiped her hand off on her coat and made her way back through the cavern, trying not to slip on the damp rocks.

Did the wolves follow us here? she wondered.

She stooped down and grabbed a fist-sized rock in passing. Other than her pocketknife, it was the only weapon near at hand. By the time she reached the curve in the narrow passage, the shouting voice had become many voices. It sounded like many people speaking over each other.

As soon as she entered the large chamber, she saw what appeared to be bodies crashing together. Larry and Lana tangling with some other people, new people, and she cocked her arm back, ready to throw the rock with all of her strength. Hope was crying loudly. And then she saw another shape running around, whimpering and wagging his tail. Smoke!

"My goodness, boy," she said. "Is that you?"

The moment of panic and confusion passed, and she realized the people weren't fighting. Larry and Lana were hugging someone, laughing and speaking to him. Hope was hugging someone else, and the dog was so excited, he didn't know where to go or what to do. Only Myra stood off to one side, frowning sadly.

When Fiona entered the room, Smoke came running toward her and hopped up, putting his paws against her belly. She petted him, and he barked, then dashed back toward the others, as if beckoning her. She crossed the chamber, stunned.

"Zane, Jarred," she said, her eyes welling with tears. "Where did you come from? How…?" She was too choked up to speak.

Jarred was still hugging his daughter, but he turned to look at her as she approached. And wonder of wonders, Ramses was standing behind him, staring around with those beautiful yellow eyes. He bleated at Fiona, as if in greeting.

"You found him," Fiona said to Jarred, brushing away her tears. "You brought him back safely to us. Jarred, I can't believe it!"

She felt such an urge to hug him that she rushed forward, unable to contain herself. Thankfully, Hope saw her coming and stepped aside, a small smile on her face. Fiona wrapped her arms around Jarred, pulling him into a tight embrace.

"I didn't know if we would ever see you again," she said. "Where did you go? How did you get here?"

He grabbed her shoulders and gently pushed her to arm's length. In that moment, she saw the fear in his eyes.

"Fiona, listen to me," he said softly, gravely. "We've got a big problem."

72

She wanted to keep hugging him, that was the truth. It was something she'd thought she might never get to do. In her heart, she had believed him lost to the endless winter, though she hadn't dared admit it to herself, much less say anything to the others. And now that he was back, she felt so overwhelmed, so warm and happy, that she wanted to wrap him in her arms and never let go.

It was the look in his eyes, the depths of the fear there, that held her back. He stepped to one side and called to Larry and Lana. They, too, seemed reluctant to let go of their son, but Zane finally pulled himself out of their embrace and went to Jarred's side. What in the world had they seen out there? Fiona expected him to say something about wolves, perhaps. What else could it be?

"Someone's missing," Jarred said. "Duke. Where's Duke?"

Fiona desperately wanted someone else to answer, but she knew it was her place to deliver the news. "He…didn't make it," she said, feeling the sting of her own failure all over again. "We tried to cross a frozen river, and it gave way beneath him. He's…he's gone."

Jarred nodded slowly, sadly. "I see."

"It was my decision to cross," Fiona said, "so it's my fault."

"No, we all agreed to it," Larry quickly added. "No single person bears the blame for what happened."

"Well, I'm sorry about Duke, I really am." Jarred looked over to Myra who had been sitting quietly. "But I'm sure…you made the best decision, under the circumstances, Fiona." Jarred said. "It's dangerous out there. We can make all the right decisions and still lose people. Unfortunately, we're not safe yet. Far from it. An attack is coming."

At this, even Myra wandered over, though somewhat reluctantly.

"An attack?" Larry said. It was strange to see him with his coat unzipped, revealing the sweat-soaked sweater beneath. "Who is attacking us?"

"What happened out there?" Lana asked.

"We ran into this group," Jarred said. As he said it, he consciously or unconsciously reached up and brushed the red welt on his cheek with his fingers. "They were camped outside of an old highway rest stop. Initially, they sort of took us captive."

"They were going to kill us and eat Ramses," Zane said, "but then we helped them."

"We escaped the camp in the middle of the night," Jarred said. "They gave chase, and in the struggle, I shot one of their leaders dead. The rest of them are behind us somewhere, and they're out for blood. Believe me when I say these people won't have any problem taking all of our supplies and animals and killing the rest of us."

"They said they were police officers in their former lives, but we don't think it's true," Zane said. "They had bloody clothes and blankets in their supplies, even a blood-soaked *baby blanket*, for God's sake, and they're armed. Very well armed."

"Bloody clothes and baby blankets," Fiona said, trying to envision this. "They're pirates, then, robbing and looting homes?"

"Apparently," Jarred said. "And their targets are set on us now. I'm not sure how they'll come, but they'll come. We'd better be ready to defend this place. Any ideas for how we might do that?"

Fiona glanced around the dim chamber, at the high ceiling, the little shapes of bats in the high corners, the faint mist that hovered in the air. They hadn't been in their new home more than a couple of hours. Were they already going to be forced to defend it at the risk of their own lives? Finally, she crossed the room, went down the short winding passageway, and approached the entrance. It was fairly small, a narrow gap at the top of a narrow slope. Still, it wasn't so small that they could easily stop others from coming in. There were only six of them, plus the animals, after all.

Gradually, Fiona realized the others had followed her. When she turned, she that every eye was fixed upon her. Even Myra. She found it shocking. Did they still want her to make leadership decisions after the disastrous choices she'd made in the last couple of days?

"I'm not sure you want me coordinating the defense," she said. "My recent track record's not so great."

Larry cleared his throat and said, "You helped get us here, most of us. It was a hard road, but we could have *all* easily died out there. Here we stand, in this nice warm place with a roof over our heads. I think your track record's pretty good, actually."

"We trust you," Lana added. "Even if some things didn't go our way."

And then, to Fiona's astonishment, Myra nodded. She didn't say anything, didn't speak, but that nod was perhaps the most profound comment of all.

These people are nuts to trust me, Fiona thought. *But maybe I should trust them* now.

"Okay, if you guys say so," she replied. "Jarred, how many people are in the other group?"

"There were at least ten pursuing us, maybe a few more," Jarred said. "They always have people walking patrols, so I never saw the full group. They're led by a woman named Jessica, a stout woman, kind of rough-looking."

"Scary-looking," Zane added. "Dead gray eyes."

Jarred walked back into the chamber. When he returned, he was lugging a blue duffle bag. He unzipped it and set it at Fiona's feet. She stooped down and pulled it open, revealing weapons. Numerous rifles. Larry whistled in amazement.

"We took this from them on the way out," Jarred said.

"So everyone can be armed, at least," Fiona said. She spotted her own rifle and pulled it out, brushing some mud off the stock. "Of course, that also contributes to the problem, because they have an additional reason to attack—getting their stuff back."

Myra spoke up then, softly, raising a hand to get their attention. "Wouldn't they leave us alone if we gave them back their guns?"

"Oh, no, no," Jarred replied, vigorously shaking his head. "It's far too late for that. Unfortunately, in trying to escape, I did something that they'll never forgive. I killed their leader, Jessica's partner. I had no choice, but still…this is personal to them now."

Myra sighed and nodded. By the look on her face, she seemed disappointed in Jarred, like a kindly grandmother disappointed by a wayward grandson. Once again, he'd gotten up to some shenanigans.

"Well, it sounds like we're outnumbered," Fiona said, "and we don't have much time."

Jarred glanced around the cave and nodded. "Unless they've turned back, which is unlikely, they're probably just a few hours behind us. Maybe closer."

Fiona felt a flutter of fear. This was something she hadn't anticipated and wasn't prepared to deal with. Larry, Lana, and Zane were all holding each other, clearly scared. Hope moved over to her dad and grabbed his arm. Had they really made it all this way only to be killed by some maniac gang of rogue cops?

"Okay, well, this is what we have to deal with, then," Fiona said, speaking to herself as much as the others. She turned to face the group, clearing her throat as she tried to work up the words. She had their undivided attention.

"The first thing we need to do is create more of a bottleneck at the entrance. We're not going to let this group just waltz inside. Let's get to work. This is our home now, and we're going to fight for it."

73

All of their supplies, indeed all of their worldly possessions, were carefully piled against the wall on one side of the central chamber. Fiona had directed them to open every crate and bag, so she could look at everything they'd brought. The additional scrap metal and wood would have come in handy now, it seemed, but there was no use lamenting what they'd left behind.

Once every container was open, and all items were displayed in a rough semicircle before her, she stood and considered their plans. The other people were arrayed behind her. She heard them whispering quietly to each other, nervously.

"The sleds," Fiona said. "They'll do a lot of the hard work for us. Let's pull them up to the entrance. Come on."

She beckoned the others. The sleds had been unloaded and set to one side. The smaller of the two was maybe eight feet long and perhaps five feet wide. Fiona got her hands under it. Jarred grabbed the other side, and together, they lifted it and carried it up the passage toward the cave entrance. Larry, Hope, and Zane did the same with the larger sled, and Lana and Myra brought some of the large pieces of scrap wood and metal.

The cave entrance was a wide angled slash through the rocks, like a crooked open mouth. A natural rock awning thrust out over the top and kept the snow away from the opening, but the approach was direct and easy. As Fiona set the smaller sled down, she gazed out into the white expanse beyond. No sign of their attackers yet.

"Okay, we're going to create a crude wall with the sleds," she said. "We'll connect them and brace them with some of the scraps. The goal is to block as much of the entrance as possible."

They leaned the sleds side by side against the opening. As sleds, they were in poor shape, cracked and battered from the long ride. The scrap wood was in worse shape. Larry retrieved a hammer and nails and did his best to attach all of the pieces together for extra stability. In the end, after perhaps half an hour of work, they'd blocked over half the entrance. Fiona stepped back to admire their handwork. Only a corner of the entrance was open now, though it was still wide enough for at least a couple of people at a time to slip through.

"Well, at least they won't all be able to rush through at once," Fiona said. "Two at a time is better than seven or eight at a time."

"So, what do we do?" Jarred asked, standing at her side. "Do we position ourselves near the door and pick them off as they try to come through?"

"Yeah, maybe if a couple of them get shot, the rest will see the futility and leave," Fiona replied.

Zane made a small scoffing sound. "Unlikely," he said, dabbing his cheeks and forehead with his sleeve. "Not these people. I don't think they give up."

"We'll see," Fiona said.

Jarred and Zane were in rough shape. Filthy, reeking of campfire smoke and some other chemical bitterness, they were bruised and battered, their hair all in damp tangles, their faces glistening with sweat. Jarred still looked fairly handsome, even in his filthiness, but the poor guys needed a bath, a change of clothes, and a nice, long nap. It didn't look like they were going to get any of those things soon.

"If we take out Jessica, the others might stop," Jarred said. "Let's hope she's in the lead."

"Just remember," Larry said, "they'll be returning fire."

It was a troubling possibility. Fiona studied the natural walls and roof around the entrance. There wasn't much cover, except for the shadows.

"We should pile some boxes in the area," Fiona said. "We can use those for cover. They're not bulletproof, of course, but they might at least make it harder to aim."

"The dark will provide cover," Hope said, speaking up suddenly. "It's still light outside, so they won't be able to see when they come inside, not right away. Dark clothes in shadows will be better. If you pile anything, they might see it, but people in dark coats crouching in the shadows will be hard to see."

"Good idea, Hope," Fiona replied.

Her gaze was drawn to the rock ceiling above the entrance. Now that she studied it, she realized that the crooked angle of the entrance was largely caused by an enormous boulder that was thrust out of the wall. It seemed precarious, but an old wooden framework was built in one corner to hold it in place.

What would it take to bring it down? she wondered.

A fleeting thought. They didn't have the tools or resources to move it, and even if they did, it would completely block the cave entrance. And then what? Yes, they wanted to keep the attackers out, but they couldn't afford to trap themselves inside. Their new home might then become a tomb.

"Okay, we know what we have to do," she said. "Let's arm and ready ourselves."

74

Fiona knelt on the rocks within feet of the entrance, choosing a spot near the wall where the shadows seemed especially dark. She chose an AK-47 from the supply of weapons. It had seen better days, but she knew these kinds of weapons were quite sturdy. It also had a full magazine. Jarred crouched beside her with her Weatherby rifle. He'd been through a lot with that gun lately, it seemed, so she'd encouraged him to keep it. Fortunately, he'd found a box of Remington Core-Lokt bullets in the duffle bag that fit the gun. Larry was positioned a little farther back against the opposing wall, positioned on one knee, with his rifle resting on a large rock.

Hope and Zane had wanted to join them, but Fiona had insisted they stay farther back, along with Lana and Myra. She didn't want to create too many targets for their attackers. Now that they were all positioned, it seemed inordinately quiet. What if their attackers didn't arrive after all? What if they'd already turned back?

How long do we sit here? she wondered. *What if they wait hours, then try to attack in the middle of the night?*

Of course, she didn't have an easy answer for that. Clearly, they would have to take turns guarding the entrance. All she heard outside was the soft howling of wind in the trees that lined the path. Tense minutes passed.

"They'll come," Jarred said softly. "Trust me. They won't give up so easily."

"I just hope they don't make this any harder than it has to be," she said. "More people don't have to die."

She was comforted by his presence. Having him back certainly helped. Jarred had a calming effect on her mind, which made it easier to bear the burden of leadership. Fiona glanced over her shoulder and saw Larry in his place. He was staring intently at the entrance, finger by the trigger.

When she turned back around, the saw the sliver of harsh whiteness beyond the cave entrance. And still the wind howled. Suddenly, darkness filled the cave entrance. She heard a single heavy footstep on the damp stones. There were no voices, no sounds of people gathering outside. No warning. One second, she saw only whiteness outside the cave. The next instant, a man was there, pushing his way inside. He was big, broad-shouldered, and he moved almost silently. She saw the fuzzy edge of a knit wool cap, the scruffy edge of a beard, the long shape of a knee-length coat.

Startled, she fumbled with her rifle, but Jarred was ready. He pulled the trigger. The muzzle flash and bang seemed to fill the whole cavern, and in that brief light, she saw a harsh face before her. The bullet hit him in the chest. Fiona saw a little puff as the coat fabric popped open. The man uttered a single brief cry before tumbling face-first and slamming onto the ground just inside the entrance.

As he fell, Fiona saw vague movement behind him. People moving in and around the trees beside the path. She took a shot in that direction, and someone out there cried out. The vague movement disappeared behind the trees.

"Andy," Jarred said, nodding toward the man on the ground before them. "That's his name. He's one of them."

Andy made a brief, soft gurgling sound.

Death rattle, Fiona realized. *Got him right through the heart.*

All went quiet again. She heard nothing except the soft, anxious breathing of Jarred beside her. Sweat trickled down her forehead, ran through her eyebrow and into her eye. She blinked it away, not wanting to look away from the entrance even for a fraction of a second.

A tense minute passed. Suddenly, something moved in the trees again beyond the entrance. Fiona took a shot, but the gunshots were diminishing her hearing. It was just so damned loud inside the cavern.

"Careful now. Careful," Jarred said. "No idea what they'll do next. Expect anything."

"I'm ready," Fiona replied, her finger brushing the edge of the AK's trigger. "No one's getting through that damned entrance."

A voice spoke then from the snowy wasteland outside, cutting through the wind, sharp as a blade's edge.

"You can't stay in there forever," it said.

"Yes, we can," Fiona replied.

Jarred mouthed the name at her: *Jessica*. She had a severe voice, but she sounded young. Young and angry. Fiona couldn't tell how far away the speaker was.

"And what if we seal the cave mouth and bury you inside?" Jessica shouted. "How does that sound?"

"Sounds just fine with me," Fiona replied. Though she tried to put some force behind the words, she was so tired that her voice sounded weak and wimpy. "Just don't try to come inside, and we won't have a problem."

"My business is with your two friends," Jessica said. "Send them out here, and we'll spare the rest of you. We don't want the cave. We don't want anything else."

"I don't believe you," Fiona yelled. "Aren't you the people killing families, killing children, and looting homes? I believe I heard something about baby blankets covered in blood? That doesn't sound like people who can be trusted to keep their word."

There was silence for a moment, and when Jessica spoke again, her voice was sharper, angrier. "You people aren't very smart, are you? If you know what we're capable of, then why would you try to provoke an attack?"

"Maybe we enjoy it," Fiona replied. She couldn't help herself. Exhausted and grieving, she was in no mood to be civil, especially not with people like these. "Maybe it's fun to provoke maniacs. Maybe you deserve it."

She was still speaking when multiple people opened fire from the path outside. She heard bullets cracking against the rocks, against the sleds. She saw sparks on the floor and walls, some of them very close. The barrage of bullets continued. When she heard one of them sizzle over her head, she scrambled backward.

"Back up. Back up," she said, grabbing Jarred's sleeve and pulling at him.

He came, but reluctantly. Chips of rock were flying. One of them bounced off the top of her head. She backed down the passageway until she was almost out of sight of the entrance. Jarred came with her, dropping onto the ground on his belly. Larry took a few shots toward the entrance before a bullet sparked off the wall mere inches from him. Finally, he cursed and backed away as well.

The barrage of shots stopped immediately, altogether, but the sound kept spreading through the vast chambers behind them for almost a full minute. And from outside, she heard Jessica laughing. Clearly amused.

"Stay down," Fiona said to Jarred. "Don't get up, not even to take a shot. As long as we don't do anything rash, we have the advantage."

"They can hold us here a long time," Jarred said. "That's why she's laughing. Jessica knows *they* have the advantage."

75

Fiona still had a view of the entrance, but it was partially obscured now. However, she could lean her shoulder against the curved rock wall on her left and aim the rifle around the corner. It seemed her plan had worked. Blocking the entrance made it practically impossible for their attackers to get inside. Jarred was flat on the ground, his arms resting on a higher step. He had a clearer view than her.

The group outside had grown quiet. Jessica was apparently all talked out.

"Do you suppose there's another entrance into this cave?" Jarred asked.

"If so, I don't know about it," Fiona replied. "Hopefully, neither do they."

"If this is the only entrance and they block it," Larry said, kneeling against the far wall, "we may be in trouble. Surely we'll have to go outside at some point."

"I'm not letting them camp outside of our home," Fiona said.

Shadows appeared in the door. Then she heard boots on the rocks. Two men entered the cave then, brushing the sides as they passed through the opening. They immediately opened fire, spraying bullets in all directions that pinged off the walls and off the floor. Fiona managed to return fire, but then a bullet hit the floor right in front of her. She saw sparks and felt chips of rocks hit her face.

She shuffled backward, moving around the corner out of sight. Jarred managed to take one more shot, but enemy fire was hitting far too close. Finally, he crawled backward to get away from them. Larry had slid back down the passageway as well, where a bend gave him some additional cover, even as the attackers continued to fire wildly. They sounded like large-caliber rifles. The sound was deep, explosive, and the men were shouting at the same time, adding to the noise.

In the wall behind her, there was a shallow alcove, little more than a wide crack in the rocks. Fiona backed into this space and raised the rifle, intending to pick off anyone who came around the corner. Jarred had continued back down the hall, so she could no longer see him. The attackers kept shooting for a few more seconds, then suddenly they stopped. The last of the shots trailed off. Her ears were ringing, her head pounding, and the stench of gun smoke was heavy in the air.

Fiona felt a moment of panic. She was trapped in the alcove with no way out but straight ahead. A strategic blunder. Wanting out, she rose to a crouch, thrust the rifle ahead of her, and stepped forward. As soon as she entered the passageway, she saw a figure coming around the corner. He was dressed in a long gray coat, the lower half of his face hidden by a balaclava. As he came around the corner, he raised a rifle, aiming it down the passageway. Fiona quickly ducked back into the alcove. She didn't know if the man had spotted her or not, but she hunkered down, making herself as small a target as possible, and aimed her rifle toward the passageway.

After a moment, she heard other footsteps. More than one person entering the cavern.

Damn, we let them get inside, she thought.

She heard another shot, then another, sounds of a struggle, men cursing.

"I'm pinned down." It was Jarred. She couldn't tell where it was coming from. Had he ducked behind a rock or found another alcove in the wall to hide behind? Larry shouted something as well, but she couldn't quite make out the words.

We can't let any more of them get inside, she thought. *They'll overrun the place. I have to drive them back.*

If Jarred was pinned down and Larry had been forced back down the corridor, then it was up to her. What was the worst that could happen anyway? If she got shot, so be it. Better to risk her life and save the others, especially after the way she'd failed Duke Cooper.

Just go for it, she told herself.

She was trembling badly, her teeth chattering. The surge of adrenaline made her whole body feel tingly and electric. It was time to go. She couldn't delay any longer. Steeling herself, she rose, tightened her grip on the rifle, and rushed forward.

Whatever happens, happens, she thought.

Stepping out into the passageway, she swung the rifle right to left, but she didn't see anyone. They had gone around the curve. The large rock that Larry had been kneeling behind was across from her, and she headed for it, turning as she ran to aim for the entrance. She saw men standing just inside the entrance, and she fired at them.

She fired repeatedly as she dropped down behind the rock. They returned fire. She saw the flashes of their muzzles, heard the crack of bullets. As she landed on the damp rocks, she couldn't tell if she'd been hit or not. Her whole body seemed to be on fire. Whether it was from bullets piercing her or adrenaline, she couldn't tell. She'd landed on her side, but she rolled onto her back, trying to get the gun into position. The men were now hidden by the rock before her, but she had a partial view of the sleds blocking the entrance, and of the large boulder hanging out over the gap. From this position, she could also see the man-made framework of wooden beams that braced the ceiling above the entrance.

"Stick your head up again, you little weasel," Jessica said. "We'll clip your hair for you."

More gunshots rang out from somewhere down the passageway behind her. Jarred cursed, someone else cried out in pain. Fiona considered her predicament. She'd gone from being trapped in an alcove to being trapped behind a rock. Now, she didn't dare raise her head.

"Come on out, little weasel." Jessica again. Her companion laughed. "Or do we have to come in there and get you?"

More gunshots from down the corridor. Larry cried out, something or someone hit the ground with a thud.

"Alrighty, here we come," Jessica said.

Fiona heard boots on rock. It sounded like at least three people, maybe more. She glanced up at the ceiling above the cave entrance. Her gaze went to the old wooden framework. The attackers were approaching fast. Within seconds, they would be upon her.

Hands shaking, heart hammering against her ribs, she aimed the AK-47 at the top of the wooden framework. She didn't have time to take careful aim, so she just began firing. As fast as she could, she pulled the trigger, the butt of the rifle kicking against her shoulder. Bullets were hitting all over the place. She saw little puffs of dust, fragments of rock, then the wooden beam splitting, breaking, and still she fired. Over and over, until she could feel the heat of the rifle.

Suddenly, the topmost beam split right down the middle in a spray of splinters. And then the weight of the large rock caused the whole framework to shatter. Not just a single large rock, but the entire ceiling above the entrance came down. A fierce wind blasted down the passageway, bringing with it a choking cloud of dust and rocks. Fiona turned her face and shut her eyes, hair whipping in the wind, and somewhere, beneath the terrible earthquake rumble, she heard people screaming in terror and pain.

76

The rumble went on and on as the roar of wind and debris blasted down the passageway, until Fiona feared she'd brought down the whole mountain. She heard shouting now from both directions. Had she just killed all of her own people along with the enemy? The thick cloud of dust and debris prevented her from seeing anything. All she could do was curl up into a little ball behind the rock, wrap her arms around her head, and hope for the best.

Gradually, the rumbling faded, the wind died down, and the cloud of dust began to settle. Fiona still heard a few panicked voices, but most of the shouting was gone. Finally, she dared to sit up, brushing bits of rock off her side. She'd dropped the rifle, but she picked it up now. Beyond the rock, the cavern was utterly dark. The only light seemed to be coming from behind her, an ambient glow coming from around the corner.

"My gosh, what did you do?"

She turned to see Jarred approaching from around the corner, his rifle hanging from one hand. Fiona ran to him and, without really thinking, threw her arms around him. He dropped the rifle and returned the hug.

"I think I just blocked our only way out," she said.

He gently pushed her back at arm's length and looked over her shoulder. Fiona followed his gaze and saw the great pile of rocks and debris filling the passageway around the entrance. The way out was now entirely blocked.

"How in the world did you manage that?" he asked.

"Lucky shot," she said, laughing with relief. "Or two or three or four."

The light grew brighter, and then Larry came around the corner. He had a flashlight in one hand, a rifle in the other, and he was out of breath. When he saw the collapsed cave, he stopped, eyes widening.

"It felt like an earthquake," he said. "How many of our attackers are under the rocks there?"

"At least two," Fiona said. "Not counting the one that was already dead."

Jarred jerked a thumb over his shoulder. "We've got two more of them back there. They must've gotten past you somehow. We exchanged a few shots, but they're dead." He put his arm around her again.

"That's half of the group, then," Fiona said. "I'm pretty sure one of the people that got buried was Jessica. I don't think we'll have to worry about that group any longer, but we're now trapped inside the cave."

"That's better than the alternative," Larry said, shining the light along the pile of rocks that now blocked the passage. "We had all the advantage there, and they still almost took the cave. They *would* have taken it if you hadn't brought down the ceiling."

"I guess we'd better check on the others," Fiona said.

She headed back down the passageway. Jarred and Larry came with her. As they rounded the curve, she saw two bodies sprawled face-down on the cave floor. One had a large pool of blood around his head. The other had a line of bloody bullet holes punched into his coat. They'd dropped their weapons nearby. The walls on either side of them were pockmarked from bullets.

And then she noticed Hope. Jarred's daughter was standing just beyond the bodies, staring down at them with a look of gape-mouthed horror on her face. Jarred rushed past Fiona and went to his daughter, but Fiona stooped to check the bodies and search them. Larry shone the light down so she could see clearly.

"Dad, you killed a bunch of people," Hope said softly, as if she only wanted him to hear.

"We didn't have a choice," he replied.

Fiona found a police badge in one of the pockets, along with a folding knife, a wad of money, and some random jewelry that seemed like it must've been lifted from numerous people.

"But, Dad, didn't you kill one of *their* people first," Hope said. "We made an agreement about hurting people." She sounded like she was on the verge of crying.

"Sweetheart," he replied, hugging her. "In order to get back to you, I had to kill a man who was trying to stop me. I didn't want to, but he chased after us and attacked me. There was no alternative. They would have taken us captive again, probably killed us, and then you never would have seen me again. You never would've known what happened to me and Zane."

At this, Hope nodded sadly. "Well, I'm glad that didn't happen, then. But... do we still live by our code?"

Fiona began searching the pockets of the second man. He had a small leather wallet containing driver's licenses and other cards that had belonged to a bunch of other people. She saw faces staring back at her that were definitely not his face.

"Yes, we still live by our code," Jarred said. "Hurting people is bad, but it's something you have to do sometimes in order to survive. We'll make sure it's the last measure we take. I think that's the best we can do."

Fiona rose and met Jarred's gaze. He smiled and nodded at her, and she realized all over again just how much better she felt having him back. "Hope, I'm really glad your dad did what he had to do in order to get back to us."

"Me, too," Hope said.

Fiona stepped past the bodies and continued down the passage into the first chamber. Here she found the others. Lana, Zane, and Myra were sitting together on boxes, the goats huddled behind them. They were all gazing at her fixedly, as if waiting to hear some kind of official pronouncement.

"We're safe now," she said. "I think the battle is over."

At this, they all visibly relaxed, and Lana put her arm around her son's shoulders. Even Myra seemed to take comfort in the news. Larry, Jarred, and Hope came into the chamber then, and they all gathered together around their supplies. It was the first moment in a long time where Fiona felt the anxiety and burden drop away, and she dared to feel a glimmer of hope. Once again, everyone turned to look at her. Didn't they always?

"How strange that this whole journey began with a ceiling collapsing," she said, "and now it has ended with a ceiling collapsing. This time, it saved us. If I was more superstitious, I might think that was some sort of sign, but it's not." She felt herself rambling, suddenly scatterbrained now that they didn't have an immediate threat to deal with. "I'm sorry the journey wasn't more successful, but I think we're relatively safe for now. That's the best I could do."

"Hey, like I said before, the journey could've been a whole heck of a lot worse," Larry said, setting down his rifle and placing the flashlight on a box so that it was angled toward the ceiling. "Let's just all remember that. Personally, I'm surprised we didn't wind up as wolf food back there in the quarry."

The memory was still too fresh. Fiona didn't want to retrace their terrible steps that had led them to this moment, so she decided to change the subject. Better to think about the work ahead than to dwell on what could have been. "Well, we have a lot of work to do to make this place a real home. I'm sorry to say, we can't rest just yet."

"We're ready," Jarred said, giving her an encouraging nod and smile. "Let's get to work."

Ready, indeed, Fiona thought.

77

It was a strange expedition that set off deeper into the cavern. The goats were all roped together with Ramses in the lead. The big male goat seemed to have developed some kind of bond with Jarred and Zane. Fiona noticed that he always seemed to stick close to one of the two. They packed up most of the gear and supplies and let the goats carry it on their backs.

When it came to the order of the group, Fiona took the lead, with Hope and Jarred beside her. Jarred led Ramses on his leash. Then the Bishops and Myra brought up the rear to ensure the goats kept moving in the right direction. As they entered the narrow passage on the far side of the chamber, Fiona held the flashlight and lighted the way. Just in case, she kept a rifle over her shoulder.

"Now, this is a scene I never could have imagined," Jarred said, glancing over his shoulder. "Exploring a cavern with a bunch of goats. Life is full of surprises."

"I'm ready for fewer surprises, personally," Fiona replied.

The passage narrowed until it was just barely wide enough for the goats to walk single file. Some of the females didn't care for the close quarters and made their displeasure known with loud bleating, but Ramses was determined to stick close to Jarred. He kept the line of them moving forward.

Eventually, they reached the chamber with the large pool of water. Here they allowed the goats to drink. A few of the people did as well. Fiona knelt beside the pool, stripped off her gloves and hat, and washed the dust off her face. The Bishops made their way to the pool and found a spot at the water's edge among the goats. Fiona had just splashed water on her face when she realized someone was standing over her.

Quickly wiping her eyes on her sleeve, she looked up. She fully expected it to be Jarred, but he was sitting with Hope a short distance away. Instead, she found Myra Cooper looming over her. She'd unzipped her coat completely, and she was holding it open with her hands on her hips. She was scowling, and Fiona rose, expecting to be scolded for Duke's death.

I probably deserve it, she thought, flicking excess water off her hands. *If she needs to vent at me, let her vent. It's the least I can do.*

Tears sprang into Myra's eyes, and Fiona braced herself for the verbal assault. However, instead, Myra lunged at her and pulled her into an embrace. As she sobbed against her shoulder, Fiona felt at a loss. Did she want comfort? Did she want Fiona to see and feel the full measure of her grief?

"You were doing your best," Myra said, voice muffled against her shoulder. "I know it, Fiona. I know you were doing your best."

It caught Fiona off guard, so she didn't say anything in return. Finally, Myra pulled back and brushed her tears away.

"I don't blame you," she said. Fiona was aware that others were watching this exchange. "Fiona, I don't blame you for what happened to Duke. You were trying to do the right thing."

"Thanks, Myra," Fiona replied, fighting tears of her own. "It was the wrong call. I just wanted to hurry, but…" She shrugged.

"None of us were prepared for this new world, and every difficult decision has been risky," Myra said. "The truth is, without you and Larry and Jarred, Duke would have died long before now. Take credit for our survival, and blame this awful never-ending blizzard for the misfortune, okay?"

She waited for an answer, so Fiona finally said, "Okay."

That seemed to satisfy her, and she turned away. Fiona stood there awkwardly for a moment. She was touched, but she found it hard to accept the compliment. Needing something to do, she went over and checked on the goats and the gear.

Maybe I'm not doing so bad after all, she thought.

Jarred approached then, taking up Ramses's line. He gave her a big smile. "Shall we get this train moving again?"

She was adjusting some bags balanced on the goat's back, and he reached over and laid his hand upon hers. She grabbed his hand and held on tight. "You'll walk with me, won't you?"

"Always," he replied.

The others were done drinking, washing, and resting, so Fiona got them moving again. They headed past the pool to new passageways and chambers, deeper into their new home.

78

It took about two hours of wandering through twists and turns, seeing beautiful rock formations, crystal-clear pools, and more bats than Fiona had ever gazed upon in her life, but she eventually noticed a change in the air. The mineral-scented mist gave ways to crisp, cold air as they followed a winding passage. Jarred had walked with her through it all, holding her hand most of the time, leading Ramses with the other. Hope walked beside Ramses. She looked fresh-faced and a whole lot less stressed out than before.

"Do you smell that?" Fiona asked.

"Smells like the outside," Hope said. "It's also getting colder." She didn't seem overjoyed at this. Hope, at least, seemed to prefer the muggy darkness of the cave.

"So, maybe there is another exit to the cavern, after all," Jarred said. "We've been walking for a while. We must be approaching the back of the big hill."

Fiona dared to click off the flashlight, checking for any hint of natural light, but the cave was still utterly dark.

"Seems we've got a way to go to reach it," she said, turning the light back on.

"But even if we find a way out, we're not going back into the cold, are we?" Hope asked.

"Not any time soon," Fiona said, "but we'll need access to the outside world if we're going to survive long-term."

"Well, that's true," Hope replied. "We need sunshine. We don't want to deal with low serotonin levels. That'll just make everyone lazy and upset."

"Food, clean water, and plenty of serotonin," Jarred said. "Keys to our survival."

"You joke, Dad, but it's true!" Hope said earnestly.

The passage widened, but it was definitely sloped upward now. After a few more minutes, Fiona dared to turn the flashlight off again. This time, she saw faint light on the rock walls ahead. They'd been walking now for maybe three hours, making pretty good time despite the uneven terrain. The clean outside air was strong now. Yes, they were close to another cavern entrance now for sure.

"It seems bright outside," Hope noted, as if it were a strange thing.

"Must be a big opening," Fiona replied. "Plenty of light getting inside."

"But that's just it," Hope said, moving up beside Fiona to give her a meaningful look. "Shouldn't it be close to evening by now? Even at midday, the sun's not that bright these days, not with all of the clouds, but it definitely should be more of a purple light by now, don't you think?"

As they ascended the passage, the light ahead grew brighter. It was very bright, a sharp white light. Now, she could see the entire passageway before her. She squeezed Jarred's hand, seeking comfort. Behind her, Ramses made a little snort, and further back, the Bishops chatted to each other softly.

"Fiona, what's wrong?" Jarred asked.

She felt a flutter of fear. "That's not sunlight up ahead," she replied. "It's electrical light. Incandescent light. A lot of it. Someone else is in the cavern."

End

PART III

79

They'd been wending their way through endless passageways, past strange rock formations and clear pools of blue-green water, for hours. Jarred had lost track of time after a while. Now, they were at a standstill, indecisive as they gazed at the passageway ahead of them and the strange new light shining on the damp rock walls. Jarred, his daughter Hope, and the group's de facto leader, Fiona, had the lead. The goats were strung together by their harnesses behind them, with the other members of the group bringing up the rear. At the moment, Jarred could hear snatches of conversation from Larry, Lana, Zane, and Myra. Their passage ahead was ascending, weaving back and forth, the light a bright, sharp white that revealed the entire cavern before them. Fiona had taken Jarred's hand, and she held on tightly now. He squeezed back and tried to give her an encouraging smile.

"Are you sure that's incandescent light up there?" Jarred asked. "Not another cave exit?"

"It's definitely artificial light," she replied. "Someone's here. Maybe they had the same idea as us, fleeing to the cavern to enjoy the warmer temperature and protection from the weather."

"Whoever they are, they're being awfully quiet," Hope noted. "Are they hiding from us?"

"Well, to be fair," Fiona said, "they don't know that we're friendly."

Someone else in the cavern. Thus far, their encounters with other people out in the world hadn't turned out great. Jarred was still shaken up over their bloody gunfight with the bandit group of fake cops. Scarcity of resources had made people paranoid and dangerous.

"If you're right, it would be unwise to approach these people openly," Jarred said.

Fiona lowered her flashlight and clicked it off. The light coming from farther down the passage was bright enough now that they didn't need it. She came to a stop and signaled Hope and Jarred to stop as well.

"I don't hear a generator," Hope said. "Must be a battery. Or maybe it only *looks* artificial because its sunlight filtered through some kind of glass."

"It's too bright to be just one light," Fiona said. "Some kind of living space, I'd bet."

"Should we discuss it with the others?" Jarred asked. He turned around. The line of goats stretched out around the passageway. He could see Myra and the Bishops standing together at the back of the line at the edge of the light's reach.

"Probably so," Fiona said. She turned and beckoned them.

The passage was just wide enough that the others were able to squeeze past the goats and approach the front of the line. Larry led the way, taking time to calm each of the goats in passing. Only Ramses didn't receive it. When Larry patted him gently on the side, the big he-goat turned and bleated angrily in his face.

Well, if they didn't already know we're here, they do now, Jarred thought. It wasn't the first time he'd daydreamed about clamping a muzzle on the big goat.

"Is it possible we've found the other end of the cavern?" Larry said, pressing up against the wall so Lana, Zane, and Myra could squeeze past him.

"No, I don't think so," Fiona replied.

The humans huddled together. Jarred beckoned everyone to come in close so they could speak softly. If there was another group in the cavern, it might be best to discuss things without being overheard.

"We've taken so many twists and turns," Fiona said. She'd let go of Jarred's hand so she could grab the strap of her rifle. Did she really think they were in imminent danger? Jarred reached up and felt for the strap of his own rifle. "We've passed countless chambers and passageways. I doubt we could find our way back, and even if we did, I brought the entrance down. It's completely collapsed."

"Without power tools, it would be nigh impossible to dig our way out," Larry added. "There's no getting out the way we came in."

"That's right," Fiona said.

Myra swiped a hand in front of her face, as if shooing away gnats. "Why are we talking about finding our way back?" She was clearly in a bleak mood, still grieving the recent loss of her husband. "We didn't come all this way, walk for hours and hours, just to turn back all of a sudden, did we?"

"We might have another group up ahead," Fiona said.

"We've finally got the chill out of our bones," Myra said. "I'm not ready to return to the bitter cold. It makes my old joints ache. Professionally, I think it's better for us to stay here."

"Professionally?" Fiona said.

"Yes, and personally," Myra replied. "This was a hard-won victory, Fiona. We can't turn back. There are people up ahead, but there were people outside, too. What's the difference?"

Larry leaned to one side to look past Fiona's shoulder at the lit passageway beyond her. "I say let's go say hello. They had the same idea as us. This cavern is certainly large enough to accommodate multiple groups, and heck, maybe we can even trade supplies."

But Jarred saw bloody blankets in his mind's eye, hostile faces around a bright orange campfire, crates and crates full of guns. "I think we should be very careful about how we approach strangers."

"Approaching strangers is a bad idea," Zane said. "Jarred and I already learned that the hard way."

"Should we assume everyone is hostile, though?" Larry said. "Heck, we were all strangers to each other not so long ago."

"Most people are decent at their core," Myra added. "Everyone's a little desperate because of this historic storm, but odds are they'll be polite, as long as we don't threaten them."

"I suppose you've seen a few desperate people in your line of work," Fiona said.

"Well, yes," Myra said. "It's a different context, but yes, as a former nursing assistant I dealt with thousands of patients—and their families—over the course of my career who had their lives uprooted, who were clinging to survival by any means. I'm saying most people are decent if you give them a chance to be."

"Even if you're right, it's still a big gamble," Jarred said. "Approach the wrong people, and it's all over."

Fiona was firmly clutching her rifle strap and tapping the flashlight against her thigh. They were all tired. Jarred certainly felt it, and he could see it on Fiona's face, in her eyes. Tired and discouraged. They'd been through hell, but Fiona bore the heaviest burden. Even now, as the others waited for her decision, it was clear that she was either indecisive or doubting herself.

After a few moments, as Fiona continued to idly tap the flashlight against her thigh, Myra shuffled over to a large shelf of rock and eased herself down. She seemed to be out of breath, panting and dabbing her face on the sleeve of her jacket.

"Myra, are you okay?" Jarred asked.

She waved off the question. "Adjusting to the damp air. No big deal. You know, I had asthma as a child. It was all my treatments over the years that inspired me to enter healthcare, actually. Asthma doesn't usually bother me as an adult, but occasionally some change in the air will set it off. It's very mild. Don't worry about me."

Lana Bishop walked over and sat down beside her. "I know you don't want to go back outside into the cold, but this stuffy cave air can't be good for you, mild or not. We need access to the outside. That's all there is to it."

Fiona finally stopped tapping the flashlight and turned toward the lit passageway. She was still beating herself up over Duke's death. Jarred knew that. He'd tried to comfort her on the long walk through the cavern, but it hadn't much helped. As she took a few steps forward, he moved to join her. Larry and Zane went to stand beside Myra and Lana.

"Look at the situation objectively," Jarred said, speaking softly. "Forget about anything that happened in the last few days. What does your gut tell you?"

"My gut won't stop flip-flopping," Fiona said. "If I'm right and there are other people ahead, it could spell trouble. Jarred, you're right. One hostile group could be the end of us. How sad would that be? To come all this way, make it through so many dangers, only to die in this cave. Who would ever know? Who would ever find out that we'd died here? It would be as if we never really existed."

Her words hit Jarred hard. Indeed, they touched on something he could not have clearly articulated until that moment. The endless freak blizzard had made him feel less solid, less real, as if he didn't fully exist the way he had in his old life. If he had died before the storm, he knew people would have grieved for him, memorialized him, remembered him. Now, it felt as if they were all a breath away from disappearing out of all memory.

It was his turn to reach out and grab her hand, needing comfort. "We didn't come all this way just to die and be forgotten," he said. "If we have to defend ourselves again, we will."

She sighed and nodded, as if answering some question. Then she squeezed his hand and looked at him. "Okay, I've made a decision. I know what we're going to do."

80

Fiona didn't feel entirely comfortable with her decision, but she was convinced it was the only way forward. She let go of Jarred's hand and turned toward the rocky shelf where Myra and Lana were sitting. Ramses stared at her with his fiercely curious yellow eyes. Smoke, Fiona's Australian cattle dog, had reappeared from his latest roaming, and he was standing beside the lead goat, panting contentedly.

These poor animals need food, all of them, she thought. *The goats were eating produce from my garden, but that's all gone now. We have to do something.*

"We continue forward," Fiona said. "First of all, we need to know what's up there…*who's* up there, especially if this place is going to be our home. I know it's a risk, and we may have to confront hostile people. Still, it's our best chance of finding another exit, and since we can smell the outside, it must be close."

Larry and Zane came toward her. Myra and Lana rose as well. Larry was nodding enthusiastically, but she could see that the others weren't quite as excited.

"Maybe we should sneak past these other people to reach the exit," Zane said.

"Or sneak up close and take a peek at them before they know we're here," Jarred said. "We might be able to determine whether they're hostile or friendly."

Larry shook his head. "If they catch us spying on them, they'll assume we're bad guys. A hostile first impression will be hard to overcome."

"And if we approach with a full caravan of goats, people, weapons, and supplies, they'll think they're being overrun," Jarred said. "The intimidation factor alone will kill any friendly reception."

"Plus, they'll want our stuff," Zane added.

"We could simply approach and offer our services," Myra said. "I'll offer to clean and bandage any wounds they might have, treat minor ailments, that sort of thing."

"Not a bad idea," Jarred said, "but we should still take a quiet peek first, I think."

Fiona considered this. "We haven't exactly been quiet," she said. "There's a good chance they've already heard us." As if to emphasize the point, Ramses bleated loudly, and the sound of his voice echoed throughout the cavern. Larry moved to try to calm him. "Even if they haven't, we don't know what the passage ahead looks like," Fiona continued. "Sneaking by might not be an option, and spying on them could provoke a violent response if they have people keeping watch."

"If they see the goats, they're going to want to eat them," Zane said. "That's what happened with the last group of strangers."

"Fresh meat is scarce," Jarred agreed. "We only managed to appease the last group with a vending machine full of junk food."

Fiona nodded. Of course, she'd heard the full story by now. Jarred had shared it all during the long march through the cavern.

"There's no way to eliminate risk entirely," Fiona said. "Judging by the use of artificial light, the group ahead might have access to resources. Still, I don't want to tempt desperate people, so here's what we'll do. A group of us will go on ahead, approach these people, and try to make a friendly first impression. The others will stay here with our animals and supplies."

"You sure that's the best approach?" Larry asked, trading a glance with his wife.

"Not a hundred percent, no," Fiona replied, "but it's what we're doing. Larry and Jarred, you guys are coming with me. We'll attempt to approach this group as friends, but be ready for a hostile response. We won't provoke it ourselves. Hope, Myra, Lana, Zane, you four stay behind with our animals and supplies."

Nobody responded at first. They were all just staring at her, as if unsure how they felt about this plan. Finally, Jarred grunted and said, "Okay, that's the decision, then. Like you said, we can't avoid risk completely. The last time we approached a group of strangers, we lost the gamble. Maybe this time we'll win. Either way, I'm with you, Fiona, so let's go for it."

"You're going armed, at least, aren't you?" Myra said, taking her seat again. "Friendly or not, it would be foolish not to have some way to defend yourselves."

Fiona glanced at the Weatherby rifle strapped across Jarred's shoulder. She was holding the strap of her own gun, the AK-47. Larry had an AR-15. They had plenty more weapons, most of them taken from the bandit group. Currently, they were stuffed in a large duffle bag being carried by Ramses.

"Okay, yes, we'll go armed," Fiona said, "but keep your rifles on your backs, at least initially."

"Hope for the best, be ready for the worst," Myra said. "That's what I think. Don't wait for them to shoot first, because there's not much we can do to treat gunshots wounds."

"Got it," Fiona said. "Myra, Lana, you four should be armed as well, in case this doesn't go well."

Lana traded a look with Myra, who shrugged at her.

"I've never handled a gun," Myra said. "Duke went hunting from time to time, but I never went with him. I know to pull the trigger, but that's about it."

"Zane, you've been hunting with your dad," Fiona said. "Grab a rifle. Be ready to defend this area, if it comes to that."

"Okay," he said. He grimaced but turned and headed to Ramses.

"And someone make sure Smoke stays here," Fiona added. "He might want to follow me, but he'll introduce a bit too much chaos to our first encounter with these people."

"I'll keep an eye on him," Myra said, reaching down to pet the dog on the head. With her other hand, she gently grabbed his collar.

"Okay." Fiona nodded. "Good. Let's do this."

Fiona turned back to the passageway. Beyond where they stood, the path ascended a slight slope and swung to the left, the walls narrowing as it rounded a bend and disappeared. The ground was damp and uneven, the white light from beyond glinting off small puddles and rivulets. She still had the flashlight in one hand, but she tucked it into the pocket of her jacket. Then she beckoned Larry and Jarred and started forward.

"Be careful on the wet rocks," Fiona told Jarred. "This would be a really bad time to reinjure your leg."

"Don't worry," he replied, giving her a smile. "I've been taking it easy. My leg is pretty strong now, but I won't do anything crazy. No rock climbing, no kicking people, just easy steps."

Jarred walked beside her as they entered the passageway, but the close walls forced Larry to walk behind them. Just before they rounded the corner, Fiona glanced back at the others. Myra and Lana were sitting together, looking incredibly anxious. Myra had Smoke at her feet as she gently held his collar. Zane had dug a Remington rifle out of the duffle bag, and he was checking the magazine at the moment.

Then Fiona followed the passageway and lost sight of them. Ahead, the narrow passage continued for about thirty feet before curving back to the right. The artificial light was very bright here, as if it were close. Despite this, Fiona heard no unusual noises. No one talking, breathing, moving around. No sound of equipment. Indeed, it seemed even quieter ahead than behind.

What are we about to step into? She was tempted to pull the rifle off her shoulder and hold it, but she knew that might be a bad idea. *Jarred's right—*

this is a big gamble. I have to be ready to defend us if these people turn out to be hostile.

She touched the strap of her rifle, resting her hand nearby, ready to pull it off at a moment's notice.

"Seems awfully quiet up there," Jarred said in a whisper. He, too, was holding the strap of his rifle. "What if we don't find anyone? What if the owners of that light already left the cavern?"

Fiona pressed a finger to her lips. Slowly, she inched forward, careful on the uneven rocks that made up the ascending floor. As they rounded the next bend, a large chamber came into view. The floor here was mostly flat, a broad shelf of rock with walls that rose up and curved overhead to create a kind of domed ceiling. She estimated it to be about forty feet across, maybe a bit more, and it was brightly lit. Indeed, the electric light was so intense that she had to squint as she stepped out of the narrow passageway.

The light was coming from a large battery-powered lamp with a green plastic shell and numerous white bulbs behind a slightly translucent white globe. It sat on top of a large card table to one side of the chamber. Some camp stools and chairs were set in a rough circle near the center of the room. Fiona came to a stop, studying the room before her.

Jarred pointed at something on the table. Enamelware plates with half-eaten food on them. Shredded chicken, green beans, slices of white bread. Wadded napkins and metal utensils were scattered across the table as well.

"Seems they left in a hurry," he said in a whisper.

"We didn't smell the food cooking," Fiona whispered back. "When did they leave?"

Farther back, she saw blankets and sheets hanging from a rope, creating a curtain that enclosed an area near the back wall. She dared to step into the room, treading lightly on the floor. People had been here not so long ago. That was clear. The food wasn't rotten or desiccated, so it couldn't have been sitting out long.

There were a number of narrow passageways leading out of the room, some ascending, others descending. She saw no one in any direction, nor did she hear them. It was strangely still here. Fiona stepped up to the table and picked up a fork. Residue of chicken on the tines, still glistening. She carefully set it down again.

Jarred came up beside her and touched the edge of one of the plates, as if making sure it was real. Larry went toward the ring of chairs and laid a hand on one of the padded seats.

"Still warm," he said quietly. "Someone was sitting here."

Fiona studied the ground around the other passageways, but she saw no obvious footprints or other indication of which way the cave dwellers had gone.

"They heard us approaching and fled," she said. It was the most likely scenario. They had left food uneaten, dishes uncleaned, and they were wasting battery power by keeping the light on. Clearly, they had left in haste. "Ramses must have given us away with his awful bleating, but he's hungry. He's not going to be quiet."

She couldn't blame these people. If she'd been in their place, she, too, would have been disturbed by that awful sound suddenly echoing out of the dark cavern.

"Should we call out to them?" Jarred said. "Let them know we've come in peace? Or should we just keep going?"

"Well, I don't feel right taking any of their stuff," Fiona replied, "no matter how much we might need it. If they want to hide from us, it's their right. I guess we keep going and leave them in peace."

"That's probably the wisest course of action," Jarred said. "I don't suppose we could take some extra food for the animals and leave behind payment of some kind. What do you think?"

Fiona was about to answer when she heard a soft scrabbling of rocks. Strangely, it seemed to be coming from above her. Gazing up, she realized the domed ceiling overhead was not fully intact. There seemed to be an opening, like a large crack, high above the passage she'd just come out of. She turned and backed up, trying to see who or what was on the other side.

As she did, she caught faint movement deep beyond the opening. The hair on her neck suddenly stood up, a shiver of deep animal fear passing through her body. Acting mostly on instinct, she lunged to one side, hit the table, and went down on one knee. As she did, a small shape whistled out of the darkness above.

Before she could see what it was, it smacked into the rocks near her foot, cracked, and bounced off. Only as it went spinning past her did she realize it was an arrow. An orange plastic shaft, white fletching, a wedge-shaped metal tip that had broken on the rock floor.

"Ambush," she cried.

81

Her sudden cry startled both Jarred and Larry. Neither had seen the arrow, their attention turned elsewhere, but her cry was enough. Larry pushed off the ground and lunged toward the makeshift curtain at the back of the room. Jarred fumbled at the rifle strap and dropped onto the ground beside the table. Fiona started to rise, intending to run back the way they'd come, but a second arrow suddenly embedded itself deep in the tabletop, cracking the edge of a plate.

"Get down," Jarred shouted, crawling under the table. "Find cover!"

Fiona dropped onto her hands and knees and pulled herself in behind him. As she did, she glanced up. Through the gap in the ceiling, she saw a figure standing on the other side. The woman had a rather impressive-looking blue compound bow in her hands, and she was already nocking another arrow. Then Jarred grabbed her arm and pulled her back.

She looked for Larry, but he had disappeared through the curtain.

"They heard us and set up an ambush," she said, heart racing. "So much for making a good first impression."

"I guess that answers the question if they're friendly or not," Jarred replied.

The archer had good form. That was clear even from a momentary glance. She'd also had a clear shot and plenty of time to aim. Had she missed on purpose? Or was Fiona just lucky? She didn't know.

"We should return fire," Jarred said, sliding the rifle off his shoulder. "How many are up there? They have bows, we have rifles. As long as there aren't too many of them, I think we've got this."

"I only saw one," Fiona replied. "But judging by the amount of leftover food, there must be others out there somewhere." She slipped the AK-47 off her shoulder, struggling to get it in position while remaining under the small table. "I'm going to take another quick look."

"Don't stick your head out," Jarred said. "Too risky."

"It's possible our attacker missed on purpose," Fiona said. "I'll be quick, but I have to see who we're dealing with here."

"Let me distract them first." Jarred hunted around beneath the table and found a dropped spoon. He tossed it across the room, so that it clattered loudly on the rock floor. "Go. Now."

Raising the gun, Fiona leaned toward the edge of the table, then quickly peeked out from underneath. The opening in the ceiling was almost directly above the table, but that put it between their current position and the nearest exit. Their attacker was standing at the edge of the opening now, legs apart to stabilize her balance. She had the bow turned slightly sideways so it fit through the gap, the arrow drawn and aimed, but the noise of the tumbling spoon had drawn her attention for the moment.

The attacker wore simple clothing, a long brown shirt, and pants that seemed handmade and well-worn. Her black hair hung down in many long braids, framing a long, lean face. The arrow was aimed right at Fiona, as if their attacker had anticipated exactly where she would reappear. White light reflected off the silver arrowhead, and Fiona ducked back under the table.

She felt a sharp, crawling unease.

"How many?" Jarred said.

"I only see one," Fiona replied. "She's directly above us."

"Surely, we can get past one person. Let's open fire and make a run for it."

Fiona considered their options. They couldn't escape without stepping back out into the open. They could open fire and hope to drive the attacker back before she released the arrow. But that left Larry. He was trapped on the far side of the room. How could they get to him?

There's another option, she told herself. *Try to reason with her.*

"Hi there," she called. "We're not your enemies. We didn't come here to hurt you or steal anything. Will you let us leave in peace?"

She got no response, but she heard a soft scrabbling of rocks, as if the attacker was shifting position.

"There's no reason for us to fight," Fiona said. "The cavern is more than big enough for our two groups. We're just going to leave now."

As she spoke, she eased toward the edge of the table again. The attacker still hadn't responded.

I'll never get a shot off, Fiona thought. *The second I stick my head out, I'm getting killed.*

"Fiona, we just have to open fire and run for it," Jarred said. "We're not getting out of here through diplomacy. She attacked without saying anything. She's already made their intentions clear."

Fiona nodded and tapped a finger to her lips.

"I'll go right, you go left," Jarred said, quieter. "We both open fire at the same time. Either we hit our attacker, or we force her back behind cover long enough to get out of the room."

"What about Larry?' Fiona asked. "He's behind that curtain."

"Larry's smart enough to follow us when we run," Jarred replied. "Let's do this."

"Okay." Fiona got her feet under her and prepared to lunge out into the open, intending to fire wildly toward the ceiling as she raced for the exit. With a little luck, the bullets would drive their attacker back just long enough to get away.

Jarred took a position on the other side of the table, wincing slightly. Clearly, squatting was uncomfortable for his leg, even if it was mostly healed by now.

"Don't bother trying to attack us." The voice came not from the gap in the ceiling but from somewhere behind them. A deep voice, full of gravel and grit. "You'll never get out of the room alive. You might as well lay down your weapons and surrender."

Fiona spun around. A large, looming figure stood in the opening of one of the other passageways. Like the attacker above, he wore simple handmade clothing, and he had a yellow nylon rope in place of a belt. He was an older gentleman, his long gray hair pulled back into a low ponytail. His face was craggy, with deep-set eyes and a broad mouth. Despite his age, he seemed to be in good shape, lean and muscled, and he had a black compound bow in his hand, an arrow nocked and drawn.

Unfortunately, his position gave him a clear shot at Fiona and Jarred under the table.

"You are more thoroughly surrounded than you realize," he said. "Throw down your weapons. We don't want to kill you all, but we will."

As if to prove the point, a third figure appeared in another passageway. An older woman with long gray hair, she wore a simple leather headband, a plain brown dress, and sturdy boots. She, too, had a bow in her hands and a clear shot at the people under the table.

"We heard you coming," the old man said. "We're well prepared, and like I said, we've got you thoroughly surrounded. Even though you have guns and we have bows, you won't win a fight with us."

He stepped into the room, lowering his bow long enough to reach over and snag one end of the hanging curtain. He whipped it aside, exposing Larry, who was huddled among the sleeping bags on the other side.

"Drop your weapons and nobody will get killed," the old man said. "If that's not good enough for you, then do your best. Go for it. Charge left and right, like you said, and try to shoot us before we shoot you while you run away. We know this cave in a way you people never will. We are blessed and favored."

Jarred glanced at Fiona, and she shook her head sadly at him.

"We can't surrender," he said, softly.

"What choice do we have?" she replied. "We don't know how many of them there are. What if they have our other people surrounded, too?"

To this, Jarred had no answer. Finally, he blew his breath out and nodded. "Fine."

"Okay, we're setting down our guns," she called to their attackers. She slowly lowered the AK-47 onto the rocks at her feet. Jarred did the same with the Weatherby. "We don't want to fight. We didn't come here to attack you."

"So prove it," the old man said with a bark of a laugh. "Raise your hands and come out from under the table."

Fiona crawled out, raised her hands above her head, and rose, trying not to make any sudden movements. The old man had the arrow nocked and drawn again. It made her skin crawl. Jarred rose up beside her.

"The third guy, too," the old man said, nodding at Larry. "Get out here. Stand with your friends."

Larry sighed and let his rifle strap slide off his shoulder onto one of the sleeping bags. Then he stood up and stepped toward the center of the room, holding his arms out to either side. Fiona moved toward the center of the room and came to a stop, facing the old man but all too aware of the arrows aimed at her back and side. Jarred stepped up on her left, Larry on her right.

Jarred cleared his voice and spoke. "Okay, we don't have any weapons now. You can see that. Keep your word and don't hurt us."

"We didn't come here to harm you or your people," Fiona said. "And we're not thieves. We only wanted to talk."

"We know *exactly* why you're here," the old man said. "We know what you wanted. I told you, we know this cave far, far better than you people ever could. We are *blessed* and *favored*."

"If you overheard us earlier, then you already know that we're not hostile," Jarred said. "Heck, we didn't even eat the food you left behind or sit in the chairs. In fact, we've not done a single unfriendly thing since we found your camp."

Fiona was grateful that he was doing some of the talking. She was trying to figure out how to get out of here, and talking her way out was definitely not her strong suit. The old man had his steely eyes locked on her. Did he know she was the de facto leader of the group?

"We set our weapons down," Fiona said. "Why don't you lower yours as well, and then maybe we can talk like civilized people? Or are you too 'blessed and favored' to make peace?"

The old man smiled at her, glanced up, nodded at the woman in the gap overhead, and slowly lowered his bow, easing the drawstring. The woman in the other passageway did the same.

"Oh, we are big believers in peace," the old man said. "We know of a deeper peace than you can ever imagine."

82

The old woman came out and gathered up their guns one by one. She handled them delicately, almost tenderly, resting the straps in a row across her forearm. As she did that, the older man came into the room, propping his bow against the rock wall. The woman in the murder hole above disappeared into the shadows and reappeared in one of the lower passageways a moment later. She no longer had her bow.

"The three of you can have a seat," the old man said, gesturing to the various chairs and stools that were scattered around the room. "Take it easy. Rest. We will be joined by the others shortly."

"Where's she taking our guns?" Larry asked.

"Don't worry," the old man said. "We're just putting them out of the way for the time being. We're not stealing them from you. That is not our way."

The old woman carried their guns out of the room. Fiona briefly considered fleeing. Now that there were no weapons pointed at them, it might be possible. Jarred seemed to be considering it as well. He kept glancing over his shoulder at the narrow passageway behind them. However, Fiona didn't think escape would solve anything, especially if these people knew the cavern as well as they claimed. Where would they go? And, anyway, if they'd overcome the initial tension, maybe there was a chance to work toward a mutually beneficial outcome now.

She eased herself down onto a folding camp chair and signaled for Larry and Jarred to do the same. They chose stools near hers and sat down, though Jarred gave the passageway one more longing look. Once they were seated, the old man went to the table and worked the arrow out of its surface. The younger woman, the one with the long black braids, moved into the room.

"Did you miss me on purpose?" Fiona asked her. She had to know. It was really going to determine how she felt about their current situation.

"I *only* miss when it's on purpose," the woman replied, a hint of a smile playing on her face. "I could have put that arrow right into your brain stem the second you entered the room, if I'd wanted to. You'd have been dead before you even knew what hit you."

"Big believers in peace, huh?" Jarred said, sourly. "Sounds like it."

"I said I *could* have," the woman replied, "but I didn't. I *chose* not to."

The old man tossed the arrow across the room. It landed on the floor with a clatter near his bow. Then he picked up the electric lamp and turned down the knob, dimming the whole room.

"Clearly, you people have been living here for a while," Larry said. He had chosen a large plastic stool, and he was sitting up straight with his arms crossed. "Did you come here when the storm started? That would mean you've lived in this place for two months. How many of you are there?"

The old man carried the lantern over to the sleeping area, set it on a shallow rock shelf, and clicked off the light. The only remaining light came from a row of candles on a shelf, which cast a dim orange glow across the room. Nobody bothered to answer Larry's questions. They just went about their work as if he hadn't spoken. The old woman returned and rehung the blanket on its rope, blocking the sleeping area.

"I'm not probing for information," Larry said, finally. "I'm just trying to have a friendly conversation."

"I enjoy a nice conversation sometimes," the old man said. "That seemed more like an interrogation, which you are in no position to conduct."

Fiona had only seen three people, but there were enough seats and enough sleeping bags for three times as many, at least. These people moved about the cavern with confidence. They seemed very comfortable here. She had a hundred questions she wanted to ask, but it didn't seem like they were open to providing answers. Larry, however, hadn't quite given up.

"The air smells nice and clean in here, I notice," he said. "We must be pretty close to the outside. Either that, or you people have got a fantastic air freshener somewhere."

"Not a question," the old man said, "but still somehow an interrogation."

Jarred spoke up then. "You can't blame us for being curious about who you people are. This is an unusual arrangement you've got here."

The young woman crossed the room and picked up the old man's bow. Casually nocking an arrow, she held it at her side pointing downward and turned to face the group. The old man and woman stood together near the curtain. They were almost entirely expressionless. Fiona couldn't tell if they were genuinely bored or just trying hard to hide their feelings.

The old woman finally sniffed and said, "Well, I suppose we can provide a few answers. We might as well let you know now...*I'm* the one in charge here. Not him." She jerked a finger in the direction of the old man. "You can address your questions to me, but let's wait until your group has been happily reunited before we talk."

And at that moment, Fiona heard the clop of hooves in the passageway. Ramses gave a loud snort. She turned in her seat just in time to see Zane enter the room, holding Ramses's leash. Smoke walked beside them, but he ran over and sat at Fiona's feet, curling up contentedly. Hope appeared behind him, walking alongside the big goat. Then Lana and Myra appeared, heads down, as if they were both afraid to look up.

"Hope, are you okay?" Jarred asked. He started to get up, then seemed to reconsider.

"Fine, Dad," she replied glumly.

Two more cave dwellers appeared then. Men dressed in the same simple handmade clothing, they were young, well-muscled, one with a thick black beard and hair, the other with a pale-blond goatee and spiky hair. They had bows in their hands, arrows on the drawstrings. Lana had the lead-line for the other goats, who came last. The whole group of goats and people crowded into the room, filling the space beside the table. Seeing the rest of her group being led into the room by armed men made Fiona furious.

Jarred was right, she thought. *This is another violent group using weapons to get what they want.* She was tempted to lash out, but she restrained herself. Hope, Lana, and Myra joined them at the stools. As they did that, the two armed men left the goats and went to stand beside the older couple.

That put the cave dwellers' group at five. Now that they were standing together, Fiona thought most of them looked related. Except for the blond man, the others had similar skin tones, similar straight hair, lean faces. The strangers were huddled together, three of them still armed with bows, but none of them speaking at the moment. The room grew strangely quiet other than the restless noises of the goats.

Are they waiting for us to say something? Fiona wondered.

She caught movement in one of the passages across the room. Small, furtive shapes emerging from the shadows. A young face with big eyes, a messy mop of hair, a very simple brown dress. Fiona couldn't quite tell her age. Maybe eleven or twelve, judging by her waifish frame, but something in her facial expression made her seem older. A second young person appeared behind her, roughly the same age but stockier, with an unhappy glint in her eyes.

They stared for a second, then started to approach, but a woman's hand reached out of the darkness behind them. She grabbed the older girl by the shoulder and pulled her back. The girl grunted unhappily, but she didn't resist being drawn back into the shadows. The other girl went as well.

The old woman had been standing idly in front of the curtain for a while, but suddenly she cleared her throat loudly to draw the attention of everyone in the room. She stepped forward, her hands on her hips. She wasn't particularly tall, but she seemed strong, well-built, despite her age. Her hands were leathery and callused, as if she knew hard work.

"Well, now that we're all settled and everyone is calm, I suppose we can have a real conversation," she said. She had a strong voice, high but with a rough edge. "My name is Brigid Hobb." She pointed at Fiona with one long, bent finger. Her nails were thick and yellow, jagged on the edge. "Something tells me you're in charge of this group."

"What gave me away?" Fiona asked.

"The way you speak to them," Brigid said. "The way they respond with their eyes. Your demeanor, your bearing. Do I need to elaborate further?"

"No," Fiona said, and shook her head.

"Do you deny it, then?"

"I don't have any *actual* authority over these people," Fiona said.

"We trust and respect her decision-making, that's all," Jarred said.

"So you *are* the leader of this group, then," Brigid said. "I really don't want to play mind games with you. I'd much rather speak plainly to each other."

"I agree," Fiona said.

Fiona had originally thought the old man was the boss. Unfortunately, the old woman gave off a much less pleasant vibe.

Larry started to say something, but Brigid held up her hand. "Not you," she said sharply. She nodded at Fiona. "I'm speaking with *her*. If I want to hear from you, I'll let you know. Thanks. Now, I want to know why you were spying on us."

Fiona glanced at Jarred. She saw no reason to keep secrets from these people, but she needed some kind of reassurance from someone she trusted. Jarred nodded at her, as if to say, *Go for it.*

"We came here from a farmstead out beyond Glencole," Fiona said. "After two months of relentless blizzard, we were running low on supplies, and my goats were eating their way through my produce. My house collapsed from all the snow and ice, so we were living in a drafty barn. We were just looking for a place with a steady, livable temperature, access to clean water, a roof over our heads. Snowbird Caverns seemed like our best bet. That's why we're here. It never occurred to us that someone might already be living inside. Anyway, we made it through the front entrance of the cavern, but unfortunately, it collapsed after we came inside. Finding your camp was a complete surprise."

"The front entrance *collapsed*?" Brigid said tightly. "It seems unlikely that a collapse would happen on its own. Did you bring it down?"

"We were attacked by bandits," Fiona said, "and in the exchange of bullets, I shattered an old wooden support beam."

Brigid gave her a disgusted look. "So you *did* bring it down." She turned and frowned at the old man beside her. He shook his head and scowled, clearly upset.

"We weren't trying to cause problems for you," Fiona said. "Like I said, we didn't even know you were here. We were just trying to survive."

"But now you're trapped in here with us," Brigid said.

"Yes, unless we can find another way out," Fiona replied.

Brigid turned away from Fiona and beckoned the old man close. When he approached, she whispered something in his ear. He nodded and whispered something back. They spoke back and forth for a few minutes. Fiona's own group was restless. Hope kept shifting in her seat, as if fighting an urge to jump up and run. Larry and Lana held hands, and Zane gripped his forehead. Myra was endlessly tapping her left foot, her hands clamped to her knees. Only Jarred sat calmly, arms crossed, eyes occasionally flitting toward Fiona as the old couple continued to talk.

Finally, Brigid turned back to Fiona.

"Well, we've discussed the matter," she said, "and we've concluded that it must have been God's will that our two groups should come together. There's no other explanation for it. At first, I was annoyed to hear you'd collapsed the front entrance, but Josiah here has convinced me that its destruction might actually be a sign from above. And because of that, we will not harm you. In fact, more than that, I would like to extend an invitation for you to join our family."

And with that, she broke into a small smile that didn't look quite right on her face. The old man beside her, Josiah, joined her, his smile fighting against the deep crags in his face.

"Welcome to your new home," Brigid said.

83

The invitation was not received well. Larry and Lana gave each other a queasy look. Hope leaned back in her seat and gripped her forehead. Myra pursed her lips and ceased tapping her knee. Only Jarred didn't change. He kept right on sitting there with his arms crossed, staring coolly at Brigid.

When Fiona turned back to Brigid and Josiah, they both just stared back with little smiles on their faces.

"Are you giving us a choice here?" Jarred said, after a moment. "If we turn down the invitation, will we be allowed to leave in peace?"

"An invitation is not an order," Brigid replied. "If you know of some other way to leave this place, we will not stop you from trying to get there. However, we must know your answer."

Jarred gave Fiona a questioning look. The invitation seemed genuine. Fiona really had no desire to stick around and get to know these people. They'd already struck her as odd and unpleasant, even if they weren't violently hostile. Still, it made sense to accept the invitation for now, then figure out what they really wanted to do later.

"Well, thanks for extending the invitation," she said, trying her best to conjure up a smile for Brigid and Josiah. "After the way this encounter first began, I'm surprise you want us around, but to answer your question, Brigid: Yes, we gratefully accept."

Hope seemed the most surprised by her words, wheeling about in her seat to stare hard at Fiona. Zane lifted his face from his hands to look at her as well. Jarred, at least, seemed to understand what Fiona was doing, and gave her a knowing look before saying, "Of course we do."

"I'm glad to hear that," Brigid said. "Nick, Alex, you're being rude to our new friends."

She made a little gesture with her left hand, and the two young men lowered their bows. They stepped back and stood in one of the open passageways, setting their bows on the ground. The woman with the long black braids approached and stood with them.

"There you go. That's much better," Brigid said. She gave them a sharp, lingering look for a few seconds. Then, seemingly satisfied that they would behave, she turned back to Fiona and held out her hands.

"Let me welcome all of you," she said. "Now, there are just a few rules that our community lives by." She held up one finger. "First and foremost, everyone works. Of course, it depends on individual ability, but we expect every individual to contribute as they are able." She held up two fingers. "Second, everyone shares. We're a community here. No lone rangers, okay? That means we make sure everyone has what they need. No one gets neglected or left behind. No individual hoarding or stockpiling. We keep plenty of food and supplies in the communal storehouses. Do the rules make sense so far?"

Fiona looked at the others. Hope was still shifting restlessly in her seat, and Larry and Lana were staring at each other with clear concern on their faces.

"Does that mean private property and personal possessions are forbidden?" Jarred asked.

"What, you've got sort of a communist thing going on here?" Larry said. Lana visibly clamped down on his arm.

Brigid's smile faltered, and Josiah grunted unhappily.

"I didn't say that," Brigid replied. "I never used that word. I only said everyone *shares*, and we don't hoard things for our own individual well-being. We take care of one another. Is that a problem for you?"

Larry shrugged. "Poor choice of words. Excuse me. I was just trying to understand."

"To answer your question," Brigid said to Jarred, "hoarding and having personal possessions are not the same thing."

"Got it," Jarred replied, giving her a thumbs up.

"Very well," Brigid said. "There's a third rule, and it's very important." She held up a third finger.

Here comes the bad news, Fiona thought.

"Only those who have passed the trial can guide others or walk through the cave alone." She paused again, as if to let these words sink in.

"Wait," Jarred said. "We can't walk through the cave alone? What's the reason for that?"

"You can walk freely through the dwelling places," Brigid corrected, "but nobody walks alone in the darkness beyond until they've proven themselves. As to the reason?" She reached over and laid a hand on Josiah's shoulder. "It is because of God's will."

Yep, there it is, Fiona thought.

"It is only within the darkness that one can find the path to God," Josiah added in his gravelly voice. "And only those who have proven themselves through the trial have earned the right to walk with Him in the darkness."

Fiona traded an anxious look with Jarred. Recognition passed between them. *Uh-oh, these people are flaky.* Hope got so anxious that she actually tried to stand, but her father reached over and gently pushed her back onto her seat.

"Uh, a religion..." Jarred started to speak, an edge of laughter in his voice, but Fiona held up a hand to stop him.

We have to handle this delicately, she thought.

"No walking alone in the cavern beyond the living spaces until we've passed a trial," Fiona said. "It's strange, but I kind of get it. Who am I to argue with the will of God?" She hoped the words didn't come across as sarcasm. "Tell me about this trial, because I think I'd like to prove myself."

Brigid grinned at this and came toward Fiona. "I knew I saw the glint of something in your eye. You might just be one of the select few. Time will tell if you've found favor. You will learn about the trial when you're ready. If you pass, you will be granted the knowledge of how to get from the main camp here to our other areas without an escort."

"And if we don't pass the trial?" Jarred asked. "Does that mean we can never leave the dwelling places? We're just stuck here forever?"

"Those who have not found favor with God must be blindfolded and escorted by one who has," Brigid said.

Myra had been sitting quietly through all of this, her hands clasped together, her gaze mostly fixed on the floor. It was hard to tell by the expression on her face how she felt about these weird cave-dwellers, but she raised a hand now. Brigid gestured at her, and she said, "Is this a safety issue? Are the passageways dangerous? That would make sense to me because injuries must be hard to treat down here."

"It is dangerous, yes, but it's more than that," Brigid said. "Walking the tunnels alone without having passed the trial is sacrilege." She still had a smile plastered on her face. Did she really believe what she was saying? "It's a rejection of God's truth, so it is perhaps the greatest danger of all."

"God's truth," Jarred echoed.

Brigid glared at him hard for a second. Again, the smile faltered, but she quickly recovered it. "That's right. Now, you..." She pointed at Fiona. "What's your name?"

Briefly, Fiona considered lying, but what was the use? Any lies or deceptions ran the risk of being exposed and making the situation a whole lot worse. "My name is Fiona Scarborough."

"Excellent. What a lovely name," Brigid said. "Are you really brave and bold enough to attempt the trial?"

"Well..." She traded another anxious look with Jarred. He seemed to be struggling mightily to govern his tongue. No, he was not a fan of this situation or these strange people. She could see that. "Exactly how hard is the trial? Even if you can't tell me the specifics, I would like to know the odds."

"My husband and I have passed the trial," Brigid replied. She put an arm around Josiah, and he beamed at her proudly. "We have the knowledge to walk the tunnels alone in the utter darkness. Others have passed. Some have not."

"And...how many have attempted the trial and failed?" Fiona asked.

"That I cannot tell you." Brigid wagged a finger at her. "Now, I would not have you commit yourself to the trial recklessly, so we will take you to a private place where you can discuss this among yourselves. Follow Nick and Alex, please."

Nick and Alex picked up their bows and stepped to either side of a passageway. A private place to talk. That, at least, seemed like a good idea. Fiona rose from her seat, and Smoke followed her, wagging his tail. Then the rest of them began to rise, though they seemed somewhat reluctant. Zane and Myra, however, stayed in their seats.

"Come on," Fiona said, beckoning them. "We'll make this decision together."

At that, Myra sighed and stood up. Zane still hesitated, so Larry reached down and hooked a hand under his arm. Then he practically hoisted his son out of the chair and onto his feet. Nick and Alex backed into the passageway, and Fiona followed them. They were led down a dark corridor, around a corner, to a second smaller chamber. The only light here came from a small oil-burning lamp hanging from a hook in the ceiling.

By that light, Fiona saw a row of chair-desks set in the middle of the room, the kind one might find in an elementary school classroom. There was also a blackboard against the wall. She noted that there were no other exits—this chamber was a dead end. As soon as the whole group had entered the room, Nick and Alex left them and disappeared around the corner.

The group was alone. Fiona sat down in one of the desks and gestured for the others to do the same. Jarred wound up sitting on her right, and the others followed suit. Smoke sat down dutifully at Fiona's feet. Of all of them, the dog seemed the least concerned about this place. Fiona wanted to take that as a sign. Would he sense or smell danger?

"Well, that was really quite weird," Lana said, rubbing her cheeks with her gloved hands. "I expected a lot of things from our first encounter with these people, but not all of that God talk."

"This is some kind of religious sect or something, it seems," Larry said. "Possibly a cult with Brigid as the cult leader."

Fiona motioned for him to keep his voice down. "I don't know what to make of the God talk, honestly," she said, "but I do know that we're now unarmed and in a rather desperate situation. We can't afford to make enemies right now, so let's talk quietly and be careful what we say."

"They only have bows and arrows," Jarred pointed out. "And they seem sort of primitive. They got the drop on us before, that's all."

"A compound bow in the hands of a skilled archer is just as deadly as a gun," Fiona said. "Let's not underestimate what they're capable of."

Jarred patted her on the forearm. "We're not allowed to walk in the corridors outside of their living spaces without an escort. That's the rule they've imposed. Sounds like a vague threat to me. What happens if we defy them, reject their invitation, and attempt to leave?"

"I don't know, Jarred," Fiona said. "I assume they would be hostile."

"Right," he said. "Surely you're not okay with that. Surely some part of you wants to fight our way past these people and get out of here! I know you said we would accept their invitation, but I assume that was just buying us time so we didn't get arrowed to death right there around their dinner table."

She held up a hand to stop him. "No, I meant it," she said. "I don't want to fight them. On the contrary, I think it might be a good idea to join this group. At least, for now. Until we figure out our next steps."

She felt a jolt go through the group. Hope's mouth dropped open. Zane rolled his eyes and shook his head. Larry and Lana grabbed hands. Even Jarred couldn't hide his amazement.

"Join them?" he said. "Do you really mean that, Fiona? These people are religious fanatics, and you want to join them?"

She nodded. She didn't expect them to understand, not completely, but she figured she owed them some sort of explanation that made at least a lick of sense. "For the time being, yes. Not permanently. We just spent hours trekking through this cave looking for another exit. Unless we find another way out, we're essentially trapped in here. We're running low on supplies. The goats are basically out of food. We don't have much choice, not if we want to survive."

"I went to church every Sunday until this blizzard started," Myra said, her hands folded in a prayerful gesture. "I never heard anyone talk like that woman. I don't know what religion this is, but it's not a reasonable one. It's certainly not mine. I don't much like it. The vibe is all wrong. I don't think I'd feel comfortable joining their cult."

"These people aren't going to church and singing songs, that's for sure," Lana replied. "This is something a lot weirder and possibly more dangerous."

"Not more dangerous than being trapped inside the cave without food, with no idea where to go or how to get out," Fiona said. "We can put up with a bit of cultish weirdness for a little while if we have to, especially if it's going to help us in the long run."

"That depends on what these trials turn out to be," Jarred said. "What if it's fasting for forty days or ingesting poison or getting flogged?"

"Brigid said she's passed the test," Myra noted. "She doesn't seem debilitated or scarred. Her gaze is clear, and she has plenty of energy. I think if she'd been poisoned or flogged, it would be evident."

"So you want to join these weirdos?" Jarred asked.

Myra shook her head. "No, just sharing an observation. I have no interest in being part of a cult, even if they're not dangerous. I'd rather move on."

"The air is cleaner in this part of the cavern," Fiona said. "Can't you feel the difference, Myra? It'll be better for your asthma."

Myra took a deep breath, coughed, but nodded. "It's better, yes, I'll give you that. I'm not back to my normal self, but I can feel a difference. Still, I'm not comfortable with all of this talk about finding God's path in the darkness."

"These people have been living here successfully for a while," Fiona said. "They clearly understand the cave, and somehow they have access to fresh food, batteries, and raw materials for making clothes. They're better off than we've been since we left the farmstead. Yes, some aspects of this situation might be uncomfortable, but I think the only smart course of action right now is to share our meager resources with them and let them share resources with us. We can learn from them, hopefully gain a bit of knowledge, and when we're ready, we'll work on finding an exit."

"What if they make us participate in creepy rituals and worship?" Jarred said. "Are you comfortable with that?"

"No, not really, but this is still our best chance for survival," she said. "I'd like for us all to be on the same page about this. We'll need everyone to play along for the time being. If even one of you causes problems, insults their beliefs, or tries to break the rules, you'll blow it for the entire group."

Every eye was on her once again. She saw them staring hard. Maybe she'd finally asked too much of them. Maybe they would finally reject her leadership.

84

The group went quiet for a long time. Fiona could see the wheels turning, but no one said anything. They hated her idea, clearly, but maybe they didn't want to tell Fiona that she'd lost her mind.

"Okay, look, I know I've made a string of questionable decisions," she said. "I led us into the quarry. I led us to confront the wolves at the slag pile. I led us to cross the icy river. And now I'm leading us to join a cult. My track record isn't amazing. I get that."

"I don't think any of those things were wrong," Jarred said. "The quarry, the slag pile, the river—all had inherent risks, but that doesn't mean you led us wrong. Joining a cult feels a bit more uncomfortable, though, I will admit."

"You think I'm wrong about this?" Fiona said. "Maybe you're right. Maybe desperation has set in, and my judgment is impaired."

"I didn't say that," Jarred replied. "Actually, I can see how this might work, as much as I'll hate it. We pretend to join, go along with things, listen and learn, gain access to resources including food for the goats. We bide our time, pretend like it's all good, then make a break for it when we can afford to do so."

Larry grunted and shook his head. "It won't work if we all get killed trying to pass the trial. Even if it's not something as harsh as a flogging, it must be difficult. Otherwise, all of these cultists would already have passed it."

"Only one of us has to pass the trial," Fiona replied, "and that'll be me. I'll take on whatever the risk is."

"You assume you can pass it," Larry said. "Brigid didn't say what it entails."

"I can. I must. I will. It's as simple as that. Hey, Brigid passed it, and she must be at least sixty years old. It can't be that hard."

"Okay, well, if that's the case," Larry said, "then I suppose your plan makes a little bit of sense," Larry said. "We can go along with the religion stuff for now if that's what it takes to have full bellies and a place to sleep at night."

"They certainly seem to eat well," Myra said. "They're all fit and healthy looking. I suppose an exchange of resources might be worth it, even if I get a weird vibe from these people."

"If Myra and Larry are in, I'm in," Lana said. "I just hope it won't take too long to gather the knowledge and supplies we need to get out of here. We're in a cave with a cult. I don't like it."

That left Zane and Hope, and they seemed the most reluctant. When they realized people were waiting for their answers, they looked at each other. By the expression on her face, Hope seemed like she was in pain.

"Oh, whatever," she said, finally, with an explosive breath. "It's not like I'm going to go off by myself. Let's just hurry up and do it. These people freak me out, I don't want to join in with their religion, but I'll deal with it."

"Yeah, whatever," Zane said, swiping a hand in the air. "It's not worse that marching through a blizzard for days on end. Let's just do it."

That settled it. Even if they weren't enthusiastic, the group was at least united in their decision. Fiona rose from the desk and went to the door, clearing her throat loudly to try to get someone's attention. After a moment, Nick and Alex appeared in the passage and came into the room.

"We've reached a unanimous decision," Fiona told them.

They said nothing to this, so she walked past them into the corridor beyond. The rest of her group followed as she walked back to the large central chamber. Here, she found Brigid and Josiah sitting on stools, chatting quietly. The woman with the braids was sitting at the table. She'd resumed eating, though she had a particularly aggressive way of going about it, as if the little pieces of chicken and green beans made her angry.

"We're in agreement," Fiona said, sitting down across from Brigid. "We want to join your group."

"Very good," Brigid said. "I expected nothing less."

"To be clear," Fiona continued, "joining your group means that we will all share equally in resources and knowledge. Is that right?"

"Yes, it is," Brigid said. "Of course, the sharing of knowledge, especially knowledge about the dark paths, will depend on passing the trial, as I stated before. However, even if you don't attempt the trial, we will be happy to share our other resources and show you how to survive in this place."

"I believe your first impression of us was a negative one," Josiah said. "As was our impression of you. But you will learn that we are a most reasonable group of people. We will share all of our knowledge with you except for the ways through the darkness. *That* knowledge comes only through the trial."

"You've made that clear," Fiona said. "I intend to pass the trial as soon as I'm able to do so. Is that okay?"

"If and when you attempt the trial is up to you," Brigid said. "But I would encourage you to rest up, gain your strength, and spend some time in self-reflection first. Knowledge of the dark path is only granted to the truly devout because the outside world led to the temptations and corruption of our present age. You understand, don't you?"

It sounds like pure, unfiltered nuttiness to me, Fiona thought. But she fixed a phony smile on her face and nodded. "Yes, we talked about it. I think we get it. Very soon, I want to prove my devotion. As soon as I'm ready."

And then, to her surprise, Jarred sat up straight and said, in a surprisingly sincere voice, "We want to join your group and learn God's true path. I think we've finally found the place where we belong, a place that is blessed and favored, even as the rest of the world suffers just punishment under this never-ending storm. Amen."

The "amen" seemed a bit much to Fiona, but Brigid and Josiah smiled at him. Nick and Alex were standing off to one side, and they smiled as well. Fiona thought even the braided woman began to eat less aggressively. Jarred had said exactly what they wanted to hear.

"Excellent," Brigid said, rising from her chair. "I had my doubts initially, but you do seem like a devout man, after all, don't you? This evening, we will throw a feast for the blessing God has granted us. Allow me to introduce you to the members of our group."

She beckoned them. Nick and Alex came over. The woman at the table approached. Another woman appeared from a passageway they had not seen yet. She was very tall, black-haired, and thin, with sunken cheeks and sharp, probing eyes.

"First, you should know that we call ourselves Dwellers," Brigid said. "Most of these other people are my own children. This is my husband, Josiah, whom you already met." She pointed at the old man sitting beside her. "Nick and Alex are also my children. Nick by birth, Alex by adoption. Blond hair does not run in my family, not by blood." She then pointed to the girl with the long black braids. "This is Henny, my daughter. I believe you met her as well."

Henny acknowledged them with the barest hint of a nod, but she definitely had the most subdued response, and the unfriendliest look. She quickly resumed eating, bent over her plate as if to protect it.

"Finally, this is Seb," Brigid said, gesturing at the tall, skinny woman in the passageway. "Short for Sebrina. She's my oldest daughter. She's usually watching the grandchildren when they're not in school. I have five grandchildren, but they will remain in their rooms for now. When we've become more familiar, they will be allowed to mingle." She waved dismissively at Seb. "You can go back now."

Seb nodded, gave Fiona a weird little wave, then turned and shuffled down the passageway into the shadows. Brigid waited until she was gone, then said, "Okay, that's the family. Please introduce me to your people."

Fiona went down the line and introduced each member of her group in turn. They were each warmly greeted by name. For all of their strange religious talk, the Dwellers were very welcoming. Of course, the reality of the trial lurked in the back of Fiona's mind throughout all of the warm greetings, handshakes, and hearty hellos.

When they were done greeting each other, Brigid rose from her seat and approached the passage that Seb had used. "And now, let me show you to your room. I told you we share everything here, and that will start with a nice meal. Your supplies seem somewhat meager. I'm sure you must be hungry. Your animals, as well. We can feed both."

"We've brought some raw ingredients," Fiona said, gesturing toward the large bags draped over the backs of some of the goats. "Help yourselves to whatever you need. I don't know how many of the vegetables survived. We were running low to begin with."

"We'll take a look when we get a chance."

As she followed Brigid through the passageway, Fiona glanced back beyond her group to the goats. They were standing together on the far side of the chamber, seeming fairly confused by the day's events. Ramses had his yellow eyes fixed upon her. The duffle bag that had contained their weapons was no longer roped around his back.

Of course, they would remove the weapons, she thought. *I'll have to figure out where they're being stored before we make our escape.*

She fully intended to become well acquainted with this part of the cavern before she attempted an escape. She just hoped the rest of the group would be patient while they learned and made their plans. Brigid led them down a dark hall and through a narrow opening in the rock wall. After a moment, there was the snap of a lighter, and a row of candles awoke on a high shelf. This revealed a broad chamber with some large trunks, a row of rolled sleeping bags against the far wall, a few plastic stools, a barrel full of water, and a large plastic bucket with a toilet seat attached in place of a lid.

"This is where your group will sleep, for the time being," Brigid said. "Of course, you'll mingle with the rest of us most of the time, but I figure you might appreciate some alone time. Judging by the look of you all, you endured a long journey to get here, first out in the punished world and then in the cavern. I will summon you later when the feast is prepared. Until then, make yourselves at home. Please don't wander."

She said this in a friendly tone, but she gave Fiona an intense look as she said it. Don't wander. Yes, she'd made the danger of wandering clear enough already. It seemed to be commandment number one among the Dwellers. As soon as the last of Fiona's group entered the room, Brigid turned and left. As she did, she pulled a curtain shut across the door.

Fiona listened to her footsteps moving back down the hall. Then she walked over to a large trunk and sat down. Myra sat down on the nearest plastic stool, but the rest of the people continued to stand. Jarred was looking around the room. Finally, he nodded.

"Well, to be honest," he said softly, "I'm actually relieved that things went so easy. When we first got here, I was afraid we were in for another brutal fight to the death. A bit of kooky religious nonsense, plenty of food, and a safe place to sleep—not a bad deal."

"The bandits at the rest stop seemed okay for a while, too," Zane noted. He walked across the room, turned, and leaned against the cave wall. "They shared their food with us and invited us to stay, but they were maniacs, and you've still got a bruise on your face to prove it."

Hope was right next to the curtain, her hands on her hips. "Dad, I don't understand why you and Fiona were so quick to join these people," she said. "It all happened so fast. I just don't get it. You wouldn't visit a random church one time and then decide to join, so why did we join these Dwellers after a ten-minute conversation?"

Jarred walked over and sat down beside Fiona on the large trunk. "Right now, our survival is the most important thing, honey, so if these people can help us in return for learning about their religion and way of life, so be it. It's a short-term inconvenience for a long-term benefit."

"I guess a little education never hurt anyone," Larry muttered, his arm around his wife.

"They have plenty of food," Myra said. "Most of them look healthy, although the one named Seb could use a higher caloric intake. Still, I must say, I get a weird vibe. Not just because of their faith. I have faith myself, so I don't hold that against them. There's something else. I don't know what it is."

Fiona really didn't want to debate the matter further. They'd made a decision, and there was no undoing it now. Didn't the others see that? They had to make the best of this situation. Still, she felt she owed them at least some final bit of encouragement.

"We made the best possible decision under the circumstances," she said. "Jarred is right. This is about our survival now, so please just go with the flow for the time being. Try not to offend these people. I've got a long-term plan, so we're not here to stay. It starts with me passing that trial. For it to work, I need you guys to play along. Fake it as best you can."

Everyone was staring at her, as they often did when things were confusing, uncomfortable, or dangerous.

"I don't see as we've got much choice," Myra muttered. She seemed even tinier and more bent than usual. "What's done is done. We might as well relax and go along with it. My only advice would be to eat plenty of whatever food they provide. It won't hurt us to pack on a few pounds so we have energy reserves for whatever lies ahead."

Hope grunted unhappily. "I'm so tired. I would unroll one of those sleeping bags and take a nap if I could, but I doubt I'll be able to rest easy in this place. What if they're spying on us? What if they have peep holes in the cave walls?"

"I can't blame them for keeping an eye on things," Lana said, "but she's right. They might be spying."

"You should at least take a seat," Fiona said. "Get off your feet. We spent a long time walking across the wilderness and through the cavern."

Larry and Lana took her advice and sat down. Hope continued to stand near the curtain, and Zane leaned against the wall. The poor kids seemed too anxious to relax. They'd been in worse danger, of course. Fighting wolves in a rock quarry during a snowstorm had been a lot worse. Still, Fiona didn't blame them for being uncomfortable around the Dwellers.

"Oh, fine, I'll sit," Hope said with a sigh, after a moment.

She chose a stool on the far side of the room and dropped down with a huff. Only Zane remained standing.

"I just wish there weren't other people in the world," he muttered. When this earned him a sharp look from both of his parents, he grimaced and said, "Okay, I didn't really mean that. It's just that every group we run into has turned out to be creepy or dangerous, starting with that weirdo park ranger, Benjy Hartman. The only people I trust are the ones in this room."

The unexpected reference to Benjy made Fiona wince, but she didn't allow the memories of him to take over. She had more pressing issues to think about now.

"We have to trust people sooner or later," she said. "Even if just for a little while. Even if we don't *fully* trust them."

Zane seemed to accept this and sank back into sullen silence.

After that, they all sat around and said very little. There were a lot of things to think about, to worry about, including what the Dwellers would do with their animals, supplies, and weapons, but nobody seemed willing to talk about it. Fiona was glad for that.

The chamber was dim, cool, and damp, not especially restful, and there really wasn't anything to do to pass the time. Finally, after what might have been a couple hours or more, the curtain parted and the tall, black-haired girl named Seb appeared. She beckoned them with one finger, then departed without a word. Fiona rose and followed her, as the others fell in line behind her.

"It'll be nice to have a good meal, at least," Jarred said behind her. "I hope they don't serve us cooked cave spiders or fried bat wings or some other disgusting thing."

"They were eating decent food when we first showed up," Fiona reminded him.

As soon as they entered the passageway outside the room, Fiona caught a whiff of cooked fish, and immediately her stomach rumbled. She was far hungrier than she'd realized. Seb shuffled quietly down the hall, her head down, the hem of her long, handspun dress swaying just above her ankles. When they approached the central chamber, Fiona saw that a series of tables had been lined up to create a makeshift banquet table. It was covered in a coarse tablecloth and surrounded by chairs. Nick, Alex, and Henny were already seated in a row on the far side.

"My goodness, that smells amazing," Larry said, and took a big, loud sniff as he entered the room.

The tables had been laid out with large platters of food. Fiona was shocked at the sheer amount of it. Hadn't these people just enjoyed a rather generous lunch a few hours ago? How much stuff did they have stashed away in the cave? Most of the food arrayed before them clearly came from cans, but she saw fresh mushrooms and, most surprisingly, large fillets of what appeared to be trout or some other large river fish.

Seb guided them to the table, and they wound up sitting in a row across from the Dwellers. Fiona had Jarred on her right, Myra on her left, and a huge platter of fish fillets glistening with some butter, paprika, salt, and pepper right in front of her. She could scarcely believe it.

"Where in the world did you folks get the fresh fish?" Jarred asked.

Henny grabbed a large pitcher and began to fill the cups of the visitors with some kind of fruity drink. When she spoke, she had a flat, emotionless way of talking.

"There's a river that passes through part of the cave," she said. "The current is swift enough that it remains unfrozen under a thick shell of ice outside, and where it enters the cave, the warmer water has attracted plenty of fish. Though they might not be plentiful for long, we're grateful for God's blessing when he gives it."

"I would love to do some fishing," Larry said, raising his cup and taking a sip.

Just then, Brigid and Josiah entered the room from another passageway. Distracted by the sight and smell of food, Fiona hadn't realized until that moment that the goats and their supplies were gone. She made a mental note to ask about them later, but for now, she just wanted to enjoy this rare meal.

"In order to fish," Brigid said, taking a chair at the head of the table, "you must first be able to travel alone. You would need to pass the trial. Once that has happened, Seb could lead you to the fishing spot."

Josiah walked to the other end of the long banquet table, sitting across from Brigid. Brigid looked at Josiah, and the two nodded at each other.

"Let us observe a moment of silent reflection," Josiah said, "in recognition that all our provisions have been granted by the true God who dwells in the deep places."

It was a jarring change of subject, and Fiona sat awkwardly while the dwellers bowed their heads. After almost a full minute of incomprehensible muttering, Brigid finally raised her head and gestured for the visitors to serve themselves, and Fiona immediately used a spatula to serve herself a fillet of trout. Josiah pointed at Henny, then at this cup, and she reached for the pitcher again.

Fiona grabbed a fork and took a bite of the fish. It was well-cooked, nicely seasoned, so tasty that it made her swoon. The others were eating now with wild abandon. It felt so good to have a full belly that Fiona felt emboldened. She made it through most of the meal before she just couldn't contain herself. Finally, she set her fork down, cleared her throat loudly to draw the attention of everyone else at the table, and turned to Brigid.

"I've made a decision," she said. "I know you told me to give it time, to gather my strength, but I want to be the first person in my group to attempt the trial. I'm ready to get started."

The Dwellers looked at Brigid, but the one called Henny, the girl with the long braids, gave Fiona a frown.

"If you'll allow it, I'd like to try tomorrow," Fiona added. "As early as possible."

Brigid and Josiah traded a look, clearly impressed, but Henny just scowled more intensely.

"Are you sure about that?" Josiah said. "Have you considered this carefully?"

Fiona nodded.

"She is placing herself in the hands of God," Brigid said. "I respect it. Very well, Fiona Scarborough. Tomorrow you will attempt the trial, and we will learn if you have favor…or not."

85

With full bellies, it would be much easier to rest. Fiona and the group set up the sleeping bags in a semicircle along the back of the chamber. They left a single candle burning in a corner near where they'd set up their toilet bucket and a crude wall of wooden trunks. It was by no means the worst accommodations they'd endured in recent weeks.

Fiona placed her sleeping bag at one end of the semicircle facing the curtained door, just in case they received any visitors in the night. She lay on her back, her hands clasped upon her belly, watching the faint candlelight dance on the uneven rock ceiling above her. Jarred lay beside her.

"That was the best meal I've had since before we lost the house," Jarred said. "These people can cook, I'll give them that."

"And it was so good for us," Myra added. "Trout is high in omega-3 fatty acids, proteins, and calcium."

"I wish they'd let me go fishing," Larry said. "I guess we'll see what this trial is like. If it's easy enough, I'm doing it, just so I can fish."

"Now, now," Lana said, "let's not get too comfortable here. This isn't a vacation, Larry."

"I just want to go fishing," Larry replied. "It would make me feel practically normal, if only for a little while."

"Fiona," Jarred said, "why did you volunteer for the trial so quickly? You said you were going to gather your strength for a while. Shouldn't you wait until we've had a chance to really learn about this group before we get too involved in their secret rituals?"

"We're not going to learn everything we need to know until we've earned the full respect of the leaders," Fiona said. "That means at least one of us has to pass that trial. Plus, I want access to the corridors alone without causing any problems. That might come in handy when we finally figure out what we're doing next." She tried to speak quietly, but the air inside their chamber was so still and stale that even a whisper seemed loud.

"But we don't even know what the trial entails," Jarred said, turning his face toward her and dropping his voice further. "If you wait a few days, maybe we can figure it out. We might be able to gather some clues. Is it a physical trial? Is it a mental exercise or an endurance test? What if it requires some knowledge about their beliefs that we don't possess because we haven't read their secret holy book?"

"I doubt we'll learn anything about the trial without attempting it," Fiona said. "Nothing that will actually help me pass it. And if it turns out to be too risky, then I won't do it. I'll accept that I'm not blessed or favored by their deity, back out of the trial, and I can't roam the corridors. But passing the test sooner will be more advantageous than spending days trying to collect clues."

"Well…" He grunted. "So be it. I guess I can see it both ways, so I'll trust you to do what you think is best. Did you notice how that girl Henny responded when you volunteered? She seemed dubious, like she doesn't think you'll pass. She was maybe even upset or angry."

"That's because she hasn't passed the trial herself," Fiona said.

"Don't you think that's a bit weird?" Jarred said. "She seems young, fit, healthy. Why hasn't she passed the trial? I'm telling you, there's something dangerous in this whole situation."

"You're probably right," Fiona said. "I don't intend to put my life in danger, but I'm still convinced it's the right thing to do. Unless we figure out how to navigate the caverns and access the river, unless we're able to feed ourselves here and stay safe, we will remain purely at the mercy of the Dwellers. They seem like nice enough people, but I don't really want to stay with them indefinitely. I feel, like most of you, that there's just a bit too much talk about God's plans and stuff like that."

"Oh, I think we *all* feel that way," Jarred said with a laugh. "I was never a particularly religious person myself. I went to Sunday school occasionally when I was a kid, and it was okay. I don't resent those experiences. But these people are something else. I get the sense that it wouldn't be hard to offend them, and I don't know if I can keep up the religious talk for long."

"Well, if we're not joining the cult permanently, then at least one of us has to pass the trial," Fiona said.

"Are you sure *you* should be the one to attempt the trial?" Jarred said. "We can't afford to lose you, Fiona. Maybe it should be someone else. I'll do it."

"No, you won't," Fiona replied, "not with your healing leg. This is my decision, and I'll assume the risk. I don't necessarily think I'm the most athletic, but I'm not in bad shape. Anyway, I feel an obligation to assume the biggest risk. Myra needs some fresh air. We have to find a way out of here sooner rather than later for her sake, at least."

"Okay, fine, I know we don't have a lot of other options," he said, "but please, whatever the trial turns out to be, go slow and easy. Don't rush ahead. Keep your eyes peeled and proceed with caution. If it looks too dangerous, back out!"

"I'll be careful," Fiona said. "I'm not going to do anything crazy, but I intend to pass the trial as fast as possible, if I can."

And finally Jarred sighed quietly and said, "I just don't know what we'll do…what *I'll* do…if something happens to you. It's going to be damned hard to pretend like I'm okay with this cult if you get hurt or worse. I'm not sure I could stop myself from lashing out."

At this, she reached over and laid a hand on his chest. He smiled sadly and placed his own hand on top of hers.

"I know my track record's not perfect, Jarred, but I'm asking you to trust me one more time," she said.

"I do," he said. "I trust you more than anyone. But I don't trust *them*."

"Neither do I, but I'm willing to play along because we need their help. I think we can make this work. If we handle it the right way, we can even part ways in peace with them in the end. That's what I want."

"I'll do my best to play along," Jarred said.

There wasn't much more to say than that, and they both drifted into a troubled silence. She kept her hand on his chest, and he kept his hand covering hers, until they both went to sleep. Smoke wedged himself in between their bodies and curled up tightly. Smoke, at least, of the entire group, seemed the most content with their new circumstances. He'd been well-fed and well-treated, and he had a nice, warm place to lie down. What more did he need?

As for Fiona, she felt a low, trembling dread over the upcoming trial, but her sleeping arrangements weren't bad—more comfortable than what they'd had in the last couple of weeks. She fell asleep with Jarred's heartbeat drumming against the palm of her hand. Unfortunately, it was a sleep that didn't last nearly long enough.

She soon awoke to a bright light shining in the doorway, casting a ruthless white glare across the room that made it impossible to fully open her eyes. She raised a hand to her face to shield herself from it, as she rolled toward the doorway. Someone was standing there. Fiona saw a floor-length skirt of plain brown cloth, a rope belt, a hint of leather-soled sandals.

"It's time for the trial." Brigid's voice.

Fiona rubbed her eyes and sat up, pushing back the sleeping bag cover. Stirred by the sudden movement, Smoke rose with her, panting, and looked up into the light. It was the electric lamp. Fiona saw that now. Brigid held it aloft in her left hand. Just behind her, Josiah held the curtain open.

"How early is it?" Fiona said, her voice a sleepy croak.

"Quite early," Brigid replied. "Just after sunrise, by my estimation. Come. It's time. This is what you wanted."

Fiona slipped out of the sleeping bag and pulled on her boots. She started to reach for her coat, but she didn't think she would need it. The cavern's temperature was practically perfect for her long-sleeve denim shirt and jeans.

"Okay, I'm ready," Fiona said, standing up.

"Are we coming, too?" It was Jarred. He had one bleary eye open and peering up at her. "I would like to observe the trial, if that's okay."

Brigid shook her head. "No, under no circumstances are you to follow or observe the trial. Doing so would automatically disqualify Fiona, and we would consider it a profound violation of our faith. Stay here, and we will return when this is done."

Fiona was still so sleepy that she found it difficult to mentally prepare herself. As she headed for the curtain, she heard the others stirring. Looking back, she saw Jarred sitting up, clutching Smoke's collar to keep the dog from following her.

"Good luck, Fiona," Jarred said. "Please, be careful."

"You can do this," Larry said.

"Don't take any crazy risks," Lana added.

"Think before you act," Myra said. "Avoid serious injury."

Fiona passed through the curtain and let it fall shut behind her. Brigid and Josiah led the way, the bright lantern shining on the walls. The rest of the Dwellers were not present. Instead of heading for the big central chamber, they went the other way, down a winding passageway and past numerous small openings, some of them covered in curtains.

"Put your hand on my shoulder," Brigid said, after a moment.

The older woman was right in front of her, so Fiona grabbed her right shoulder. As soon as she did, Brigid clicked off the electric lantern, plunging them into utter darkness. It was a blackness so absolute that Fiona's eyes began to play strange tricks on her, making weird colors swirl in the nothingness. She tightened her grip on Brigid's shoulder as she picked her way along.

"Don't let go," Brigid said.

Fiona was tempted to ask if the utter darkness was necessary, but she decided it would only make her seem like an unwilling participant. She could feel that the uneven floor was gradually sloping downward. She kept stumbling on rocks and bumping into the walls of the narrow passage, but Brigid didn't slow down. The old woman was muttering under her breath something that sounded like a prayer.

What have I gotten myself into? Fiona wondered.

On and on they went, winding this way and that. Finally, Fiona had to twist the coarse fabric of Brigid's dress in her hand to keep from losing her grip. Josiah was whispering as well, but so quietly that it almost sounded like a bit of wind in the passage. Gradually, she became aware of a new smell, something acrid and sharp. She couldn't identify it, but it was distinctly unpleasant.

These people could do anything to me here, she thought. *If they abandoned me now, I doubt I would ever find my way back. If they killed me, they could dump my body somewhere that it would never be found.*

She felt a shudder of unease, something edging toward full-blown panic. The walls seemed to be closing in, smothering her, until it was finally more than she could take. She could keep silent no longer.

"Are we close?" Her voice echoed, and she realized the sense of closeness was an illusion. They were in some kind of large chamber.

The bright lantern light erupted before her, so fierce and white that it blinded her. Fiona squinted. The smell here was very strong, bitter and stinging in her nostrils. She saw the silhouette of Brigid in front of her, but it took a moment for her vision to adjust to the brightness. Slowly, a massive chamber emerged from the veil of light.

"We're here," Brigid said, turning to one side and raising the lantern high.

Fiona lost her grip on the woman's shoulder and stepped back, taking in the cave before her. The ceiling of the chamber was so high above that a slight mist hovered there. The whole ceiling seemed to be moving, as if it were melting. It created such a strong illusion that she had to step to one side and reach out to the wall to steady herself.

"Bats," she noted. "Those are bats."

"This is one of their sleeping chambers," Brigid said. "We call it God's Belfry." For some reason, this comment made her laugh, as if she'd made a clever pun.

Josiah was standing deeper in the room, gazing up with a look of almost childlike wonder, as if he were standing in a beautiful cathedral. "This is the location for the first trial," he said.

Fiona stepped up beside Brigid, and now she saw the source of the bad smell. The rocks of the chamber's floor were piled with bat guano, and quite a lot of it. She could see it falling from time to time, dripping from the moving ceiling of bats like muddy rain.

"What do I need to do?" Fiona asked.

"The bat is a creature who lives in darkness," Brigid said, lowing the lantern to her side. "It makes its home in the womb of the cave and needs no light to travel and survive. Much like those who pass the trial to become closer to God and gain the ability to travel through the caverns."

"Also, their excrement is a gift," Josiah added. He had his arms held out to his sides. "It is used to fertilize our gardens, and it can serve as a fire starter."

"To pass the trial, you must climb and grab a bat with your bare hands," Brigid said. "It is as simple as that."

Fiona had wondered if the trial actually, in some strange way, granted people the physical ability to navigate the cavern, but it didn't seem that way now. The ability was granted by the will of Brigid. The trial was simply a strange physical challenge.

This is about appeasing the cult leader, not learning any useful skills, she thought. Of course, she was committed now, but she filed this realization away for later reflection.

"So I can obtain the bat in any way I see fit?" Fiona asked.

Brigid shook her head dramatically and moved deeper into the vast chamber. "There is a specific path." She pointed across the room to a section of the wall that was speckled with cracks, pits, and mineral deposits. It was angled inward slightly as it ascended toward the domed ceiling. However, just in front of the wall, there appeared to be a big drop into some lower chamber. The higher she climbed, the more the angled wall would take her out over the drop.

Climbing, she thought. *Why did it have to be climbing?*

Fiona just didn't have much experience at it, and the ceiling was a good twenty or thirty feet above the chamber floor. However, the drop-off seemed much deeper. If she made it close to the ceiling and lost her grip, she could easily die from the fall. She slowly approached the drop, her heart racing. The wall could be approached from the sides, but it narrowed as it went higher, which would force her out over the drop. There didn't seem to be any safe way to reach the bats.

Maybe I shouldn't do this, she thought. *I told Jarred I would take any crazy risks.*

Brigid came up beside her and thrust something at her. When Fiona took it, she realized it was a small net made of thin hemp ropes attached to a short flexible rod.

"Use this to grab one of the bats," Brigid said.

Well, at least I don't have to grab it with my bare hand, she thought, slipping the rod under her belt. *The last thing I need is for a bat to bite me and give me rabies.*

"Do your best," Brigid said. "Beyond that, your fate is in God's hands. We will see if you've found favor."

Fiona briefly considered backing out of the trial, but she feared backing out would only compound their problems. She had to at least try.

Take it slow and easy, she told herself. *You can do this. You need to!*

So she approached the climbing wall from the left side, stepping just beyond the big drop and reaching up to grab a large protruding rock. She nodded at Brigid, at Josiah, then fixed her gaze on the imposing wall before her. She pulled herself up.

Just to her right, she saw a notable foothold, and she kicked her leg toward it. She got the side of her right heel hooked over the edge, then pushed herself higher. Scanning the wall, she saw another large handhold a few feet above her. She reached for it and got the fingers of her left hand over it. From there, she was able to pull herself to another foothold.

Okay, this isn't so tough, she thought. *What was I afraid of?*

Above her, she spotted another narrow ledge, and she stepped up with her right boot. It seemed stable, so she planted her left boot on it as well. She was being forced to her right, however, and she was now above the dark drop-off. Behind and below, Brigid and Josiah had become utterly quiet. If not for the bright light, she might have thought they'd left the room.

With both feet on the ledge, she thrust herself up toward another handhold. She managed to get a couple of fingers around the rock, but the soles of both boots slipped off the ledge. Then her hand slipped off the rock as well. At the last second, she was able to get one foot up and push off the rock wall. This sent her flying away from the rock wall, so as she fell, she flew over the gap. She landed hard on her back on the guano-drenched floor at Brigid and Josiah's feet.

The impact knocked the wind out of her, and for a minute, she struggled to catch her breath. They said nothing, just staring down at her, their faces emotionless and unreadable. Finally, taking a deep breath, Fiona rolled onto her side and pushed herself farther from the drop-off. Her shirt and pants were filthy from the floor, and the stench of this place burned in her nostrils.

"It's a bit slippery," Fiona said, picking herself up. Her back hurt, but she seemed uninjured, though it felt like she would develop some impressive bruises.

When she turned to Brigid, she caught a momentary look. A twist to her lips, one eyebrow going up. Was it satisfaction? Whatever feeling it betrayed, Brigid quickly wiped it off her face, nodding at her gravely.

"I'm sorry, but you have failed the trial," she said.

She's glad I failed, Fiona thought. *Though she tried to hide it, her real feelings showed for a second.*

"Let me try again," Fiona said, rubbing her right elbow. Apparently, she'd smacked it against the rocks.

"No, you failed," Brigid said, more firmly. "We must now return to the camp."

"Why? Aren't people allowed to take the test more than once?" Fiona tried to swipe some of the filth off the back of her denim shirt, but the effort felt futile.

"You might be granted the opportunity to try again some other day," Brigid said. "For now, we need to tend to our people. It's morning, and there's a lot of work to do. I'm sorry things didn't go the way you wanted, but it seems God has spoken."

Some other day? Not allowing her to try again immediately seemed like an arbitrary limit. It certainly had nothing to do with God. This was just Brigid playing games with people, and Fiona was angry and ready for a heated argument. Brigid, perhaps seeing this on her face, promptly shut off the lantern.

"Reach out and put your hand on my shoulder," she said. "We're heading back to camp."

With a sigh that barely contained the sheer depths of her frustration, Fiona reached out, fumbling in the dark until she found Brigid's shoulder. She clamped down just a little harder than was necessary and proceeded to follow the woman back across the chamber, her boots squishing on the filthy floor.

86

The absolute darkness was so utterly disorienting that Fiona's irritation collapsed into despair. The climb had been going well initially. A single slip of her feet had put an end to it. She still wanted to argue for another chance. Indeed, she was tempted to climb anyway, but she knew it would be futile. Even if she managed to grab a bat, it wouldn't mean she passed the trial unless she did it on Brigid's terms.

As they crept back through the blackness, she listened to the changing pitch and shape of her own breaths as the size of the passageway changed around her. It felt like a crude form of echolocation. However, unlike a bat, she had no better sense of where she was than before. She tried to make some kind of mental map of the path back, but there were far too many twists and turns. At times, she heard air sighing through vast unseen chambers, but it was all confusion.

She suspected that some of the turns Brigid took were unnecessary, that she was simply trying to complicate the path back. If so, it was effective. Fiona could not have found her way from the Dweller's camp to God's Belfry if she spent years. Even with a light source, she thought it might be close to impossible.

All of this together put her in a very bad mood. She was at the mercy of a fanatical weirdo with arbitrary rules, and she couldn't even climb a damned rock wall. Finally, after what felt like an absurd amount of time, she saw orange light ahead of her.

"We're here," Brigid said. As she said it, she clicked on the electric lantern and flooded the corridor with light.

Fiona saw a familiar dingy curtain covering an opening in the corridor on her left. As they approached, the curtain flew open and Jarred appeared. The others were crowded in behind him, trying to peer over his shoulder.

"She failed the trial," Brigid said, in a tone that Fiona thought was rather cold. "She has not found favor."

"But she's okay?" Jarred replied. "She's not hurt?"

"I'm sure she will tell you all about it," Brigid said. She turned to look at Fiona and gestured toward the curtained doorway. "Rest and recover here for a while. We'll prepare breakfast and summon you when it's ready. As you rest, reflect on what you learned today."

And with that, Brigid and Josiah kept going, walking down the passageway in the direction of the central chamber and taking the bright light with them. Jarred had a sympathetic look on his face, but it did nothing to dent the anger and disgust Fiona felt. She forced herself to give him a nod as she flung the curtain out of her way and entered the room.

The others parted to let her pass. Myra was sitting on a stool. Smoke was curled up at her feet, but he came running toward Fiona now. Not even petting the dog appealed to her, but she stooped down and scratched him behind the ear anyway. The sleeping bags had all been rolled and put away, the stools arrayed across the room. She chose the nearest stool and plopped down with a huff.

For a moment, no one said anything, and she was grateful for it. Then Jarred pulled the curtain back in place and came toward her.

"How...how did it go?" he asked. "What was the trial like?"

He hesitated to ask, she thought. *I guess my foul mood is obvious.*

"You heard what the old cult leader said," Fiona replied. She could smell the filth coating the back of her shirt. She considered changing, but she didn't feel like getting up. "I failed the test. I failed it fast, too. Maybe in record time."

"Really?" He started to reach for her, then seemed to reconsider and squatted in front of her instead. "I'm surprised. You're generally pretty good at accomplishing whatever you put your mind to, especially if it's something you really want."

She appreciated his encouragement, even if she didn't agree with it, and even if it didn't bring her out of her bad mood.

"Would you mind telling us about the trial?" Larry asked, sitting on a stool nearby. "What did it entail? You look rather filthy and smell like guano, so I'm guessing it was a physical challenge."

Fiona could think of nothing she wanted less at that moment than to describe her failure. The whole situation was embarrassing, and her back and elbow still hurt from slamming down onto the rocks. She hated the way they were all looking at her, so she bent over and sank her face into her hands.

"It was just a stupid climbing test," she said, speaking through the gap between her hands. "There's a big chamber in the cavern that they call God's Belfry. It's a sleeping chamber for bats. They're all over the ceiling, and the ground is thick with guano. Brigid told me to climb up and grab one of the bats."

"And that was it?" Zane said. "That was the whole trial?" And then, apparently realizing it might offend her, he added, "I mean, it wasn't something more…religious?"

"That was it," Fiona said. "Climb a wall and grab a bat."

"I'm surprised by that," Jarred said. "It's not really safe to grab a bat. They often carry diseases like rabies. It's not safe to be around them."

"Also," Hope added, "I read that if they're hibernating and you wake them up by messing with them, it could ruin their season and possibly kill them."

"I know all of that," Fiona said. "Take it up with Brigid. The trial was her idea."

"Do we really have to pass this trial just to walk through the cavern on our own?" Lana said.

"As dumb as the trial sounds," Fiona replied, "Brigid and Josiah clearly know the cavern well enough to navigate it with ease in complete darkness. If we want to learn how to find our way around, we'll have to give them what they want. They have the knowledge we need to survive long term, so, yes, we have to pass the damned trial no matter..." Her voice was getting louder and sharper, so she caught herself. "No matter how dumb or dangerous it is," she finished quietly.

The room got quiet, and she was grateful for it. She would have loved to be alone at that moment. If she could have found some kind of private chamber somewhere without distressing the rest of the group, she would have done so.

"Hey, Fiona," Jarred said softly, after a moment. "I used to do a bit of rock climbing when I was a younger man. It's been a few years, but I remember it well enough. I know you're worried about my leg, but it's getting stronger every day. If someone needs to pass this trial, couldn't I try it? You went first, so you can advise me on what to expect. It doesn't matter who passes the trial first, really. We'll get the knowledge we need either way."

It was tempting, but she couldn't do it.

"No, Jarred," she said with a weary sigh. "You might be better suited for this trial than I am, but I have to pass it. It has to be me."

"Why?" he replied softly.

"Because..." Oh, how she didn't want to get into it at that moment. "Brigid sees me as the de facto leader of this group, and she lost respect for me this morning. I need to gain it back. Plus, it's my fault we're in this cavern in the first place, so I feel like the risk is mine to take."

"Actually, I'm the one who first mentioned Snowbird Caverns," Larry said sheepishly. "You're not responsible for bringing us here."

"Yeah, but I made the decision," Fiona said. "I made us leave the homestead. And I kept pushing us until we got here. I'm the reason we marched and marched through the cavern. I'm the reason we approached the Dwellers. We've gotten to this point because of me. The climb is more dangerous than I made it sound. The wall is slick and angled out over a drop. I don't want anyone else getting hurt. I *need* to overcome this myself, and I won't feel right until I do."

"You seem to think you owe us penance for what's happened since we left your home," Jarred said. "The problems we've had, the losses we've experienced, none of them are your fault. We've worked together and struggled together along the way. I don't think we would have made it this far without you. You didn't force us to leave the farmstead. The roof collapsed, and we made a group decision to leave. We all agreed to it. You're the biggest reason why most of us are still alive. If you're going to take the blame, take the credit, too. And let someone else take the risk."

Fiona finally raised her head. Jarred was right in front of her, and he had such a genuinely compassionate look on his face, it almost melted the ice inside her. Fiona looked over his shoulder to Hope, his daughter, who was sitting cross-legged on the floor behind him. She seemed distressed—no doubt troubled by her father trying to volunteer for a dangerous trial.

"You have a daughter," Fiona said. "You can't risk your life when you still have someone to take care of. No, Jarred. You might be better at climbing, but it's better if I'm the one who keeps attempting the trial."

Jarred started to say something else, but then he glanced back at his daughter. "Okay, I get it," he said. "I don't like it, but I get it."

"Great," she said with a sigh. "Let's leave it at that, please. I don't want to keep debating this issue."

Jarred gave her a sympathetic look. "Fiona, you need to rest. Would you like to be alone for a while?"

Shocked that he'd read her mood so well, she just stared at him for a few seconds before saying, "Yes, I would. No offense. I just need some time to myself."

"All right," Jarred said. He rose from the stool and turned to the others. "Folks, why don't we head to the main room and give Fiona some time alone here. I think she's had a frustrating morning."

He gestured at the others and headed for the curtained doorway.

"Do you have any cuts or scrapes I should take a look at?" Myra asked as she rose. "Bat guano could give you a nasty infection."

"I'm sure I've got a big bruise developing across my back," Fiona said, "but I don't think I broke anything. Let's deal with it later, Myra. I'm fine for now."

Myra nodded and followed Jarred to the door. Zane and Hope went with her. Larry and Lana went last. Once they were all gone, Fiona breathed a sigh of relief and slid from the stool down to the floor. Smoke laid his head in her lap. Now at least she didn't have to hold back, hide how she really felt, or coddle their feelings.

"All I had to do was climb that damned wall and grab a bat," she muttered, petting Smoke between his muddy ears. "That's all I had to do. Instead, I almost got myself killed, and now I've got Jarred talking about trying this stupid trial so he can break his leg all over again."

She lay down on her back, feeling the cold of the rock floor seep through the denim shirt. The stench of bat droppings still lingered.

I've done more to hinder this group than help them, no matter what Jarred says, she thought. *They're in a safe place now. They could stay here, share the work, share the food with these people, and it would be fine. They'd probably be better off without me.*

"No," she whispered, shaking her fist at the candlelit darkness. "No despair, Fiona. I'm going to pass the trial. I don't care how many times I have to try; I don't care what risks are, I'm going to pass the damned trial and find a way out of this cave. That's all there is to it. If I have to play Brigid's stupid game, so be it."

87

Breakfast was scrambled eggs, pan-baked biscuits, and hash browns. When Jarred inquired about the eggs, he learned that the Dwellers kept chickens in one of their dwelling chambers. Fiona's own chickens had already joined their little feathered community. They also clearly had gardens somewhere and storehouses of grains and dry goods. Despite the impressive array of food, however, breakfast wasn't a wholly pleasant affair. Brigid and Josiah seemed to be in a great mood, chatting and laughing even more than usual. Their kids were the same as always, rather quiet and disconnected.

Brigid's grandchildren had joined them this morning as well. The five youngsters sat together, but they were also unusually quiet, somber children in plain clothes and simple rope sandals. Two of the girls appeared to be young teens to Jarred's eyes, either twins or very close in age. The other three were much younger, two girls and a boy, and they kept glancing at the newcomers with wide, anxious eyes.

Jarred was troubled by Fiona's failure that morning. Actually, more than that, Jarred was disturbed by her bleak mood. He'd never seen her like this. She'd been frustrated before, upset, sad, but this was something else. Something darker, and he wasn't sure what to do about it.

"You're growing potatoes around here somewhere?" Larry said, spooning up some hash browns.

"We have a big garden with a variety of vegetables in a higher chamber," Brigid replied. "We brought plenty of soil with us and made beds for planting in a special place. Maybe someday you will see the garden, if you find favor. Maybe not. We shall see. But I'm telling you, we have a *very* good arrangement here, we're stocked to the gills, and I look forward to your contributions to our thriving community."

"These hash browns are perfectly cooked," Larry said. "I can't believe they were prepared in a cave."

"You can thank Henny for that," Brigid said. "She went to culinary school, and she has made the most of our current situation."

The daughter with the long braids gave Larry a weird little salute, then went right back to eating. The chamber was nicely lit by candles set in a row down the center of the table. It seemed the group sometimes used electric light, and sometimes didn't. Jarred wondered how many fresh batteries they had in their supplies.

"Eat well this morning," Brigid said. "We have plenty of work for everyone to do today. No idle hands, that's our way."

"What sort of work will we be doing?" Larry asked.

"Nothing strange or strenuous," Brigid replied. "Just regular chores, but we will appreciate the extra hands. Surely that doesn't bother you. We share resources here, including food and light, but we also share work. We prefer to spend most of our days doing useful tasks. I believe I explained that on your first day.

"You did," Jarred replied, "and we're fine with it. I'd rather have something productive to do than sit around all day."

Jarred was struggling to think kindly about these people. They'd offered a place to sleep, they'd offered their food, but they'd also taken all of the supplies and animals. More than that, they had poor Fiona caught up in some ridiculous religious game that was clearly discouraging her. She had enough self-doubt without some pointless trial adding to it.

We might have to live with these people for a while, especially if the storm continues for a long time, he reminded himself as he chewed his eggs. *And if we're going to live with them, then we need to try to understand them and their ways, even if they're extremely odd. The more we know about the Dwellers, the more we can avoid problems and take care of ourselves.*

At that moment, Fiona showed up. She walked quietly into the room and sat down beside Jarred without comment, adjusting her chair. It had been an entire day since her failure, but she was still in a sullen mood. She'd attempted to clean her clothes, but the back of her denim shirt was still stained from collar to belt. The grandchildren all paused in their eating to look at her, as if she were some strange animal they'd never seen before.

"Help yourself," Brigid said to her. "You'll feel better after a nice breakfast."

"Right. Thanks," Fiona muttered, reaching for the serving spoon in the hash brown pan.

Jarred smiled at her. She noticed and even gave him a little nod, but she couldn't apparently muster up a smile in return. Instead, she began eating in an almost mechanical fashion. Her failure that morning had clearly hit her hard. Jarred could understand feeling disappointed, but why had it taken root in her so deeply? Why was she sinking into despair over this? The group was doing okay, for the most part. They had food and shelter. Yes, it was weird living in a cave with no sunlight, but all things considered, it could be a lot worse. She'd failed a silly religious trial, but there would be other chances in the future.

"There's enough food for a second helping, if you want," Brigid said, waving an arm over the table. "We can feed the leftovers to the goats. I'm sure they'll love it."

"Don't give them too much human food," Fiona said sullenly. "All of the added sugars and salt are not good for them." Then she seemed to reconsider her words and glanced up at Brigid. "Thanks for feeding them, by the way."

"No problem. They'll get other food," Brigid replied. "Never fear. Have you never considered butchering them for the meat?"

"Oh, I have," Fiona replied. "Especially the male. But I've resisted the urge, possibly for sentimental reasons. But they pulled our sleds all the way here, so they've earned a reprieve, I think. Plus, the females can be milked, so they have some utility."

"I'll set someone to the task of milking them, then," Brigid said. "We have a small bit of powdered cow's milk left, but the goat milk can be used for many things."

A few took Brigid up on the offer of a second helping, but Jarred had had his fill. He excused himself and went to use the restroom. He then used a bucket of fresh water from the cavern streams to wash his face and hands. It had been a long time since he'd had a real bath, and he missed it terribly. By the time he returned, breakfast was over, the table had been cleared, and people were scattering to various assigned tasks.

Jarred needed to get busy. Otherwise, he was going to spend too much time worrying about Fiona, so he walked from chamber to chamber looking for some way to help. Finally, he came to a small room and found Brigid working at a long table. The room had a rough carpet on the ground, a big bucket of soapy water in the corner, and a row of chairs behind the table. It appeared that Brigid was currently fixing a tear on a pair of crude pants. More clothes covered the table.

Well, here's your chance to get to know these people, he thought, stepping into the room. *A forced friendly conversation with a few careful questions.*

"Hey there, Brigid," he said.

She looked up and gave him a friendly smile. At that moment, she seemed very grandmotherly. Jarred approached the table, pulled a chair back, and sat down.

"I don't suppose you could use a little help, could you?" he asked. "You didn't assign me a task."

She paused in her work, a needle and thread in one hand, the handmade pair of pants in the other. She gave him a long look, as if appraising him, and finally said, "Do you know how to use a needle and thread?"

"Well…" He considered fibbing, but he knew he would only reveal the truth eventually anyway. "No, not really. I understand the basic concept, but I've never attempted it, actually. I'm always willing to learn a new skill, though."

Brigid grunted and set her stuff down. She reached into a small wicker basket beside her and produced another long needle and a roll of black thread. She set them in front of Jarred, then grabbed another pair of pants off the pile and tossed it in his lap.

"These pants have a hole in the knee," she said. "They belong to one of my grandchildren. I'll show you how to fix them. Come on. Let's go."

He picked up the needle and thread and set the pants on the table. He could see a big hole in the right knee.

How hard can it be? he wondered.

Brigid proceeded to show him how to thread the needle in the dim light of the cave by rubbing the thread in his palm. It took him a few tries to get it right. Then she helped him knot the thread and took him step-by-step through the process of stitching. It was trickier than he'd imagined, but once he got started, he found it strangely soothing to mend clothes. Something about closing the rips and tears and making things whole again was deeply satisfying.

"You're getting the hang of it," Brigid said. "Just take your time. We're not in a hurry, and it's better to take your time and do it right. We want these clothes to last as long as possible."

"Got it," he replied. "Actually, there's something kind of familiar about this. The attention to micro-detail, pushing and pulling the needle through the fabric, reminds me of soldering circuit boards when I was in college."

Just then, he accidentally jabbed himself in the fingertip with the needle, and he gasped in pain.

"Here, use this," Brigid said. She reached into her basket and produced a small brass thimble. "Can't have you bleeding all over the clothes."

He grinned sheepishly and set the thimble on the forefinger of his left hand. As he resumed stitching the pants, he felt the needle stabbing against the pitted thimble repeatedly.

"My aim with this needle could use some improvement," he said.

"It just takes practice," Brigid said. "You'll get plenty if you're amenable to this kind of work."

After a while, he felt like he was starting to get the hang of it. However, he hadn't come here because he liked repairing worn clothing. His goal was to get to know Brigid and maybe learn more about her and the other Dwellers. She didn't seem particularly interested in talking about anything other than the work at hand. Still, he had to try.

"You've really developed this part of the cavern," he said, after a while. "It's impressive what you've achieved. Kitchen, bedrooms, gardens, storehouses, dining room, and who knows what else? You must have moved in here right after the snowstorm started to get all of this set up."

She gave him a wry smile, as if she knew he was probing for information. He expected her to deflect his attempt at conversation and turn his focus back to the work. However, she hesitated only a few seconds before responding. Perhaps she had weighed him in the balance and found him worthy of an honest and open response.

"My family was already quite familiar with Snowbird Caverns," Brigid said, talking without missing a beat on her mending. "We'd spent a lot of time in here over the years, especially here in the main cave. When the snow began to fall early and we heard the reports, we knew it was a sign from God. What else could it be? Yes, I'm sure there is some scientific explanation for it. Climate change or some such thing. But there's often Providence behind acts of nature, whether we allow ourselves to see it or not. We'd always believed that God would wipe the slate clean, just as he did with Noah's flood—the world had become so evil—and sooner rather than later. Using a never-ending snowstorm to do it this time just seemed like pure poetry. Make the world as white as a blank page, and then the faithful few can begin to write a brand new story on that page."

Jarred grunted and nodded, hoping she would take it as some sort of agreement that would encourage her to keep going.

"So while everyone else began to immediately panic and do stupid things, we, Josiah and I and the children, rounded up all the supplies we could get our hands on and headed to the cave," she said. "A lot of people assumed the storm was temporary—freak weather that would eventually go back to normal—but we knew better thanks to our faith. This snow is never going to stop falling. The bitter wind will never stop blowing. It's not a seasonal storm but a whole new ice age."

"New ice age," Jarred echoed. The words were ironically chilling, and he recalled a long-ago conversation with his friend Atul who had first warned him about the enduring nature of this change in the weather.

"I use that term loosely, of course," Brigid said. "I don't know if there ever *was* an ice age in the past. Maybe. Maybe not. But we're in one now, and that's what matters."

"There have been numerous glacial periods throughout earth's history, actually," Jarred said. "We're currently supposed to be in an epoch between ice ages called the Holocene. Supposed to be."

Brigid gave him a funny look, half-smiling, eyes narrowed. "You read that in books. Silly books. I get it, Jarred, but I only trust my faith, nothing else. I'd advise you to do the same. All of those books couldn't save the world from this storm."

"Got it."

Brigid had finished the pair of pants she was working on, so she carefully folded them and pushed them to the other end of the table. "Fortunately, my wise father had already prepared the caves for our eventual habitation. Oh, yes, he was working on this place throughout my childhood, mostly in secret, using the cover of his employment with the state government. Years of shaping rooms, stashing supplies in various places, and getting ready for the end of the wicked world. If regular people had known what he was doing, they would called him crazy, but here we are."

Jarred glanced at her. She grabbed a sock with a hole worn in the ankle and proceeded to darn it. There was an intense light in her eyes as she spoke, a look made even more intense by the dim candlelight glinting on them.

"As a young girl, I spent countless hours sitting alone in the darkness of these caves," she said softly, "listening to my father work and trying to get as close to God as I could."

"Oh, yeah?" Jarred fixed his gaze on the pants and tried his best not to let his real feelings show on his face. The truth was, this lady was really starting to creep him out. Her voice had gotten low and breathy. "How did your family learn that God was going to erase the whole world? Where did you acquire this secret information?"

"When I was very young, my grandmother had a vision," she said. "Maybe you don't believe in visions. Many people only believe what they can touch and taste. In her vision, a voice from Heaven told her that the wrath of God would come down upon the earth one more time. Only it wouldn't be a flood this time." She shuddered, as if the very memory of it almost overwhelmed her. "Well, she never said what form the wrath would take, but as we've all learned, he spared us the rising waters and sent a flood of snow instead to softly bury human civilization until it smothers and dies. I sometime daydream about it, the millions of people slowly being buried alive in their mansions and courtyard gardens and saying, 'How could this happen? Nobody warned us!'"

Jarred found himself getting increasingly uncomfortable with this kind of talk. He came from a world of academia and science, so this was too strange. All he could do was concentrate hard on the work at hand and let her keep going.

"Anyway, I'd moved away from my childhood home, so when the storm hit, we had a long journey to get back here," Brigid continued. Her voice was thick was emotion. "We tried to drive here in our van, but we went off the road after a few miles. Slid into a ditch and broke an axle. Nick's wife was injured badly. Went halfway through the windshield. Broken arm, battered face, damaged eye, injured back. So we had to continue on foot. What choice did we have?"

She glanced at Jarred, as if gauging his response. He returned the glance, gave her his best sympathetic look, and nodded, before quickly returning to his work.

"We walked for three days, dragging our supplies in trunks and suitcases," she said. "Nick's wife died the first night in her sleep. I think she must have had internal bleeding. Blood had run from her mouth and nostrils and pooled around her head in the night. Nick wept and wept. He wanted to stay by her side, but we made him continue." And then, even softer, she added, "He's never been the same."

"I'm sorry to hear that," Jarred said. "We lost someone, too."

"I know," Brigid replied, giving him a knowing nod. "I believe his name was Duke?"

Jarred shuddered. He couldn't remember if anyone had spoken about Duke Cooper since their arrival at the Dwellers' place. "Yes, that's right," he said.

"I wish it had been our only loss," Brigid said. "Seb's baby died on the morning of the third day. We were so close to the cavern, but he developed pneumonia. We did what we could, but he died under the rain canopy of a gas station about a mile from here. Poor thing." She shook her head and sighed. "But it could have been far worse. We might all have died out there if God had not already provided this cave and sent his servant, my father, to prepare the rooms. After we moved in and got settled, we made a couple of trips outside to gather additional supplies, but after a while, traveling outside became impossible. By then, however, we were well-stocked and perfectly comfortable. We have everything we need now to last for years, maybe generations. The remnant of the storm, the penitent few, can stream to us, and we'll begin recreating the earth right here. I can see—"

She stopped talking abruptly and turned in her chair. Jarred had just finished repairing the pants, and she reached over and grabbed the needle from his hand. With her teeth, she bit off the thread, then tied it, and put the needle back in the basket.

"That'll do," she said, picking up the pants and setting them with the other repaired clothing at the end of the table. And then, without another word, she rose and walked across the room.

Are we done? Jarred wondered. *Am I supposed to keep working or follow her?*

When she reached the door, she stopped and looked back at him. She had a strange little smile on her face, but for a few seconds, she just stared at him, as if studying him. Then she nodded and walked out of the room.

Why does it feel like I just passed a test? Jarred wondered. And that sent him down a rabbit trail of wondering if Brigid's story had been wholly true. Had she been testing his response? Had it been one of the trials, a much easier one than Fiona's climb?

"No, no, no," he whispered. "You're letting them get in your head."

As he sat there feeling awkward, staring at the pile of clothes on the table before him, he felt a sudden urge to seek out Fiona. He just wanted to spend time with someone he liked, someone he understood, who didn't say strange things, express intense emotions that he couldn't read, or talk about apocalyptic visions. He even rose from his seat, intending to go looking for her.

But he caught himself before he got to the door. Fiona had been keeping to herself, and her mood at breakfast had made that clear. It wasn't a good time to try to talk her out of her funk, not in the middle of a workday.

Wait for the right time, he told himself. *When you have privacy and can speak freely. When Fiona is ready.*

And for now? He really didn't know where to go or what to do, so he returned to the table and sat back down.

88

Hope had never felt more uncomfortable around a group of people. That was quite an accomplishment on their part, because she was generally uncomfortable, or at least awkward, around most people. At school, she'd been one of the oddballs in the robotics club. But the Dwellers made her feel awkward on a whole other level, and she wasn't even sure why. Plenty of people were religious. She'd had friends who went to church every week, but the way Brigid and Josiah talked was different somehow, more intense.

She dealt with this primarily by trying to keep to herself and ignore what was going on. At least they had protection from the snow in the cave, somewhere relatively comfortable to sleep, and plenty of good food to eat. That made it all worth the strangeness. Didn't it?

As the moment, she was helping Zane and the tall woman named Seb to wash the breakfast dishes. They had one bucket of soapy water, another bucket of clean water, and then a bamboo rack on a rocky shelf as a drying rack. Hope took her time, meticulously scrubbing each utensil. What was the point in hurrying?

They were in a small rocky chamber just off the passageway where their bedroom was located. Hope wondered about all of these rooms the

Dwellers used. They didn't seem entirely natural. A cavern didn't usually form such convenient little rooms with flat floors and rocky shelves on the walls. She suspected work had been done to shape the cave somehow.

"Don't scrape the pan with a fork," Hope told Zane. He was trying to get some charred potato off a cast iron frying pan and having little luck. "You'll scratch it. Just put some soapy water in it and set it aside for a few minutes. The residue will soften. Then you can wipe it out with a rag."

"Washing dishes was never really my forte," he said, with a sheepish grin. "I let the dishwasher do all of the hard work."

He dipped the pan into the soapy water and set it on the shelf. Seb glanced at them but said nothing. She wasn't especially talkative anyway. Mostly, the tall woman went about her business in silence, a blank expression on her face. But sometimes, Hope would catch a few glimpses of something in her eyes, and she was pretty sure it was grief.

Something bad happened to her, she thought. *Probably not very long ago.*

Suddenly, someone cleared their throat loudly from the doorway. It startled Hope, and she dropped the serving spoon she was scrubbing. It fell, hit the side of the water barrel, and went clattering across the rocky floor. Without comment, Seb chased after it and grabbed it.

Hope turned and saw the old woman Brigid standing in the doorway. She wore the same kind of plain brown dress that she wore every day. Was it the same one, or did she have a whole bunch of identical dresses hanging in a closet somewhere? Hope couldn't tell. Her gray hair was in a kerchief, the shadows on her face deep as crevices in the candlelight.

"Hope and Zane," she said. "You must go with the other children and attend your lessons."

"What lessons?" Hope replied.

"All of our children must spend time in class a few days every week," Brigid said. "Yes, we have a school here. All children need to be in school, learning and growing. Please join the others in the classroom. It's the room with the desks. You've been there already."

Hope glanced at Zane, who shrugged. "Does my dad know about this?"

"You may ask him on your way there," Brigid said. "I'll expect you in a few minutes."

And with that, she turned and left. Hope did not like the idea of going to class, not with these people, so at first, she just went back to cleaning. Maybe she could pretend like she'd forgotten about the class. Then she realized Seb was staring at her intently.

"You'd better go," Seb said. "Brigid wasn't joking. School is mandatory for all children who live here. I can finish cleaning."

With a sigh, Hope rose. Zane was already on his way out of the room, and she hurried after him. They went back down the corridor, through the central chamber, and then down another passageway. As she passed a door, she spotted her father sitting behind a table inside. He had a couple piles of clothes in front of him and a small wicker basket, but instead of working, he was just staring blandly at nothing in particular.

Hope stepped into the room and approached the table.

"Dad, do you know what they're making us do?" she said, a little sharper than she'd intended.

He reached for the nearest pile of clothes, as if he wanted to pretend like he was working. But then he crossed his arms over his chest and leaned back in his chair instead. "What is it this time?" he asked.

Hope glanced over her shoulder. Zane had apparently kept going. "That old woman says we have to attend class with the other children," she said, struggling to keep her voice down. "First of all, we're not children. We're teenagers. Second, why do I have to go to their weird school? I'm not a student here. I don't *want* to be a student here. I just want to mind my own business."

"Hope, it's not a big deal," he said. "Remember, we're trying to learn more about these people. Going to class will be a great chance to do that. It's not like they're going to hurt you or anything."

"But what are they going to teach us?" she said. "Flat earth stuff or what?"

He beckoned her closer. She approached the table, and he took her gently by the shoulders. "Hey, you don't have to believe any of it," he said quietly.

"You just have to sit there and play nice. That's what we're all trying to do for the time being. Think of it as a survival technique. If you hear anything notable, store it away and share it with us later."

"Well, it's not like they're going to talk about how to pass the trial during class," Hope said.

"We don't know that," he said. "Even if it's just a bunch of boring math and reading lessons, at least you'll have a chance to get to know the other kids here. Look, we're probably going to be staying here for a little while and spending a lot of time with these people. The more we learn about them, the easier it will be to make sure we leave this situation in the best possible condition."

Hope groaned. She really didn't want to go, but she couldn't argue with her father's logic. "Okay, fine," she said, after a moment. "I'll just grit my teeth and bear it."

"You can do it," he said, patting her on the arm. "We're not here permanently. For now, it is beneficial. Keep reminding yourself of that, okay?"

"I've told myself that, and my own brain isn't quite convinced," she said, "but I'll behave."

She trudged back out into the corridor. The classroom, she knew, was the dead-end chamber where they had first debated whether or not to stay with the Dwellers. The row of student chair-desks in the middle of the room was already familiar to her. A large blackboard stood against one wall with two bright brass oil lamps on tall stands providing light.

Brigid's dark-haired son, Nick, was standing beside the blackboard. He was a striking figure, his muscles straining against the sleeves of his shirt. His hair and beard were short but thick and very black, which made a sharp contrast with his pale skin. Somehow, he managed to be both handsome and a bit creepy at the same time, but Hope found the overall effect intimidating.

"Welcome to class," he said, as Hope entered the room. "Please have a seat."

There were a few other students in the room, Brigid's grandkids, who ranged in age from little kids to teens. Hope hadn't seen much of them. They tended to keep to themselves. Zane had taken a desk at the end of the row, however, which forced Hope to sit on his other side, right beside one of older Dweller girls. She appeared to be ten or eleven, a gangly and gawky thing in a dress that was so loose, it made her seem tube-shaped. She glanced at Hope with darkly circled eyes as she sat down.

She's the child equivalent of a cave lizard, Hope thought, and felt a little shiver of unease.

"Okay, all eyes to the front," Nick said, picking up a piece of chalk. "Let's go over our agenda for today's lesson. As always, no talking, please. If you have a question, raise your hand and wait patiently until I call on you."

Oh, gosh, I'm really back in school, Hope thought. *I never thought I'd see the inside of a classroom ever again. Now that it's happened, it's in a weird cavern full of weirdos.*

"First, we're going to talk a little bit about how visions work," Nathan said, scribbling a list of topics on the blackboard as he spoke.

Hope glanced at Zane, but he was slouched at his desk, staring with obvious boredom at a spot somewhere above the blackboard.

"Then, we'll learn about some of the common wildlife that dwell in God's cavern with us," Nick continued. "After that, we're going to run a very special errand. Since I'm your teacher, I have the right to take you to a secret place in the caves that you've never seen before. Now, doesn't that sound interesting?"

This actually produced some gasps and excited looks from the Dweller kids. A secret place? It made Hope nervous, but maybe this was exactly the opportunity her father had been talking about. If she could just make it through a religious lecture about visions, she might get to see something meaningful. She settled more comfortably in her seat, rested her hands on the undersized desktop, and braced herself for what was to come.

In the end, the religious talk was neither particularly interesting nor disturbing. Mostly, it seemed to be an attempt to comfort the children about the fact that their whole Dweller existence was the result of an apocalyptic vision about the end of the world and God's wrath. Nick actually did an impressive job of spinning it into a message of hope. *The vision is proof that we are being looked after*, seemed to be the theme. *Clearly, the whole human race isn't being wiped out. A privileged few were warned and are now being taken care of.*

Once that lesson was done, Nick went into a long lecture about the different species of animals that lived in the caverns, illustrating his talk with decent hand drawings on the blackboard. They learned about the big brown bats of Ohio, different kinds of cave spiders and lizards, centipedes, salamanders, the fish that lived in the underground stream, and various other bugs and insects. Hope found this a little more interesting and useful than the vision talk.

When the second lesson ended, Nick announced that it was time for their special adventure. The Dweller kids bounded up from their desks, as if they'd just been told Santa Claus was on his way to visit them. Hope and Zane were closer to the door, however, and got to the front of line just behind Nick, as he led them out of the classroom and back down the corridor.

"Uncle Nick passed the trial recently." It was the cave lizard girl. She had a squeaky little voice. She had come up on Hope's left side and was directing this comment at her. During class, she'd learned that the girl's name was Samara. "That means he's now allowed to lead us through the darkness. Isn't that great?"

Hope didn't want to speak openly and honestly with Nick so close, but she nodded at the girl and said, "Sounds great, sure. Do you know anything about the place he's taking us?"

Samara shrugged dramatically, her bony shoulders rising up around her prominent ears. "Maybe. Probably not. I don't know. But isn't it fun?"

"Yeah," Hope replied. "I guess so."

Nick led them silently through the central chamber and down another passageway that descended into absolute darkness. Wind was moaning somewhere ahead of them, and Hope shuddered at the sound.

"Put your hand on the shoulder of the person in front of you," Nick said, "and whatever you do, don't let go. Don't stop walking, and don't be afraid. As long as I'm with you in the darkness, you'll be okay." And then, more quietly, he added, "I have God's favor here. He made that crystal clear."

Hope put her left hand on Zane's shoulder, as he put his hand on Nick's. Then Samara grabbed Hope's right shoulder with her tiny hand. A few of the children farther back in the line whimpered, but Nick kept striding forward. He entered the narrow passageway and was soon swallowed by absolute darkness. Hope felt a brief moment of trembling panic at losing that last bit of residual light. To calm herself, she clamped her eyes shut and focused on breathing slowly.

The rocky floor beneath her was uneven, and the walls pressed in closely so that she occasionally felt them brushing against her on either side. More than once, she heard someone stumble. The children were clearly afraid, but none of them cried out, none of them wept or begged Nick to stop. They just kept going, a single-file line creeping through a lightless void.

Well, this experience is sure to show up in recurring nightmares, Hope thought.

Eventually, she heard the sound of water. It sounded like it was pouring down from the ceiling somewhere. The sound grew louder for a minute. Then, suddenly, light awoke in the darkness. Nick had produced a tiny LED flashlight, and he shined it into the large chamber before them, where a massive pale stalactite hung down from the ceiling. Water ran from cracks in the ceiling down the sides of the stalactite, then poured like a small faucet from the tip onto the rocks below.

Nick turned to the children. He was holding a stack of small plastic buckets in the crook of his right arm that he hadn't had when they'd entered the dark passageway.

He must've had them stashed in the darkness somewhere, Hope thought.

"Okay, children, we're going to collect a bit of water from the stalactites," Nick said. "Everyone, come here and take a bucket."

The single-file line broke apart as the children gathered around Nick. He passed out the plastic buckets. Hope waited until the end and got the last bucket. It looked like something a child would have taken to the beach, except the plastic handle was missing.

"Can we drink the water, sir?" Samara asked, trotting over to the big stalactite.

"It's safe to drink, yes, because it's filtered by the rocks above us," Nick said, ushering the rest of the kids toward the stalactite. "But we're not going to drink it now. We're here to collect the water and bring it back for storage. Go ahead now. Fill your buckets."

Most of the kids crowded around the big stalactite, battling with their buckets to get them under the pouring water. However, Zane found water trickling from a smaller stalactite farther back and went there instead. Hope moved to join him.

"Don't go too far now," Nick told them. "The last thing you want to do is step out of the light. That is strictly forbidden and quite dangerous. You could fall into a deep place and never be seen again."

That sent a little shiver down Hope's spine, as she envisioned bottomless pits all around them. The small flashlight cast an arc of light across the room that didn't quite reach all of the walls or ceiling. However, as Hope positioned herself next to Zane and raised her bucket to catch one of the trickles of water, she noted a dark spot in the wall to her left. She could see just enough to tell that a path ascended into a narrow corridor beyond. More than that, she felt a faint breeze blowing out of the opening, cold against her face and hands.

"The air coming out of that passage there," Hope said quietly to Zane, nodding in the direction of the dark opening. "It feels colder than the cavern air. What do you figure is down that way?"

To her surprise, Nick answered. He had moved close to them without her realizing it. "That knowledge is forbidden to someone who has not passed the trial," he said. "Your curiosity is understandable, Hope, but I encourage you to let it go. Maybe someday you'll be old enough and able enough to pass the trial and find out on your own. Until then, trust the rules and resist curiosity."

He wagged a finger at her, gave her a little half-smile, then walked back over to the other children. Irritated at being scolded, Hope sniffed loudly and turned her attention back to her bucket. However, she couldn't help but glance at the dark opening again. A passage leading up. A passage with cold, fresh air.

"Just don't even think about it," Zane muttered. "If anyone passes the trial, it's not going to be you or me. I doubt they'd even let us try because of our age."

"I know," Hope replied. Her bucket was full now, so she pulled it against her belly and wrapped her arms around it. "It's not against the rules to look and wonder."

Nick went from child to child, inspecting each bucket to make sure they were all full. Satisfied, he nodded and clapped. "Very good," he said. "We'll head back now. Remember to keep one hand on the shoulder of the person in front of you, but wrap your other arm carefully around your bucket. Try not to spill any water."

The children lined up behind Nick again, but this time Hope was the very last in line, and it made her skin crawl. Something about having only the empty utter blackness behind her gave her a sense of vertigo, as if she were teetering on the precipice of a vast drop. However, as they walked back, she tried her best to memorize the steps she took, the various turns. She figured it was only maybe a hundred yards before they came in sight of the entrance to the chamber beyond.

I could probably find my way back if I had to, she thought. *It seemed farther the first time because of the darkness.*

Nick led them to the little supply room where Hope had helped wash dishes earlier. All of those dishes were dried and neatly stacked on shelves against the far wall, and the water buckets had been moved to one side. The barrel of rinse water was half empty now, and Nick directed the children to pour their buckets into it. They did this one at a time. Hope patiently waited her turn.

"Now, children, it's important to remember that we didn't walk through a dark cave simply to fetch some water," Nick said. "This cavern that we live in is a sacred space. It was given to us long before the endless snow began to fall. The task we just performed, small as it was, helps to preserve what has been given to us, and that makes it a meritorious act."

Hope noticed that some of the Dweller kids stared at Nick with wide-eyed wonder whenever he veered into religious talk. She had only gone to church a few times in her life, and that had been just fine—normal. Some singing, usually a sermon full of gentle encouragement. This was something else, something weirder.

"It was our very own ancestor, Mama Brigid's grandmother, who first had the vision," Nick said, beaming at the kids proudly as he spoke. "Many years ago, she spoke to God directly, something no other human being had ever done, and that's how she learned that all of the manmade religions are wrong, the Bible is wrong, every holy book is wrong, and all of the churches, mosques, and synagogues are wrong."

Nope, that's definitely not something I've heard before, Hope thought. It was her turn to empty her bucket, and she quickly dumped it, sloshing some water over the edge. Nick didn't seem to notice or care.

"Our ancestors listened to God's words, not man's words," he continued, the Dweller kids gathering around him. "They completed their own trials, and from that, they wrote their own truth, the real truth—not in a book, but upon tablets of stone carved by their own hands. The truth about the one true path of God. The only path."

Hope couldn't take it. She turned away from Nick toward the door. Yes, her father had told her to listen and learn, but something about this kind of talk made her squirm. Zane clearly felt the same way. He was near the doorway, his back against the wall, a grimace on his face.

"Uncle Nick, can you tell us again why God sent the snowstorm?" Samara asked, scuffing the sole of her shoe on the damp rock floor.

"This endless winter storm that has afflicted us is a test for his true believers," Nick said, holding up a finger. "Make no mistake, those who pass the test will live on in his glory, while the rest of the world succumbs to his cold wrath. Now, permit *me* to ask the questions."

Some of the children clapped at his little speech.

"Hope, please turn and face the same direction as the other children," Nick said gently.

She winced and turned to face him, sinking her hands into her pockets.

"Sorry," she said. "I got distracted thinking about what you were saying."

"Okay, here's the first question. Who carved the Dwelling?" Nick asked.

"The hand of God!" All of the Dweller kids answered in unison. More than that, they said the answer like they were singers in a choir hitting a perfect note.

"Second question. When will the snowfall end?"

"When every soul has been judged and the whole world is made new," the children chanted. Samara even raised a fist over her head and shook it.

"Third question. Where do we find the path of God?"

"In the darkness! The utter darkness! The absolute darkness!" the children cried. With each answer, they got a little more zealous.

Hope glanced at Zane, who shrugged. Were they going to have to memorize the answers to these questions at some point?

"Fifth question. Where was the one truth written?"

"On tablets of stone with their own hands!" the children squealed. Samara hopped and flapped her arms. Other children laughed and danced.

"That's right," Nick said. "Very good responses." And then he looked right at Hope, let his gaze linger for a second, as if weighing what he would say next. "Okay, Hope, you're new here, so let me ask *you* a question. Feel free to give an honest answer. We understand that your perspective has been largely shaped by the outside world, but that's okay. What would you say is the cause of the winter storm, this blizzard that never ends?"

Hope knew what he wanted her to say, but she just couldn't bring herself to do it. The thought of parroting the answers of the Dweller kids made her sick to her stomach, so she cleared her throat and said, "Well, according to a scientist from the National Oceanic and Atmospheric Administration who is also a friend of my dad, the storm was basically an accidental byproduct of a project that was meant to re-form glaciers and help stop global warming."

Nick laughed, and there was something contemptuous in it. The Dweller kids joined him, and Samara practically cackled, covering her mouth with one hand.

"A scientist from the National Oceanic and…what? That was a mouthful. Good one, Hope," Nick said, shaking his head as he chuckled. All of the laughter made Hope furious, but she bit her tongue. "I'm sorry for laughing, but you're wrong about the storm. Do you really think that mankind is so powerful that we could change the weather pattens for the whole world?"

"Well, I mean…" Hope shrugged. "I guess so, yeah."

Nick shook his head again. "You believe it because that's the craziness they taught you out there. It's not your fault. The storm was God's wrath. There were no natural changes in the world, and man alone does not have the power to affect the weather so drastically. Only God's will can bring such a widespread transformation."

Some of the kids were still giggling, and Samara was staring at Hope with a mocking look on her face. Hope was getting even angrier. How was she supposed to answer the teacher's questions correctly when the answers were mind-melting nonsense? If the mockery hadn't made her so mad, she might have laughed at Nick's words. Did he know how crazy *he* sounded? How could he say something so patently absurd with such sincerity?

I'm sorry, Dad. I have to say something, she thought. *I can't just stand here and take it. Someone has to tell these people they're crazy.*

"Well, there's this thing called science—" she began.

Suddenly, Zane clamped his hand down on her shoulder. She looked back, and he shook his head at her. She was surprised to see an anxious look on his face.

"Oh, uh, sorry, sir," Hope said. "You're…you're right, of course. I'm just repeating things I was told in the outside world." Saying it left a bitter taste in her mouth, but it was all she could do.

"Very good, Hope," Nick said. "I know you're just beginning to let go of the lies you were told in the past, so I'm not upset with you. Keep learning. Keep struggling and striving to be free. You'll be a better person for it. I promise."

Seb stepped into the doorway then and made a little hand motion at Nick. He nodded in return.

"Okay, kids," he said. "I want all of you to head back to the classroom. I'll be there in a few minutes. You can chat quietly, but take your seats and behave, okay? Go on." He brushed his hands at them.

Hope gladly led the way, slipping past Seb and hurrying back to the classroom. Once they got there, she quickly took her seat, slinking back in her chair to brood by lamplight.

"I didn't mean to laugh at you," Samara said, walking past her to take the next desk. "What you said just sounded funny, that's all. I never heard anything like that before."

"You've never heard of a NOAA scientist?" Hope replied.

Samara shook her head. "NOH-uh?" she said, trying to reproduce the way Hope had said the agency's abbreviated name. "I don't even know what that is. But it looked like I hurt your feelings. I wasn't trying to."

"No, my feelings weren't hurt," Hope said. "I just…it just…" No, she couldn't be honest, not about this, not about how she truly felt. It would only alienate her further. "It's fine, Samara. Don't worry about it."

The other older girl walked up then. She bore some similarity to Samara, but she was stockier, with a rounder face and tangled black hair. She also looked at least a couple of years older than Samara.

"It was really funny, that's all," the older girl said. "Funny and a little bit strange. No big deal. Don't get offended."

"I'm not offended," Hope replied. "I didn't say it was a big deal. Heck, I didn't even bring it up. Samara did."

Samara pointed at the stockier girl. "This is my older sister. Her name's Vanya."

Zane had returned and taken his seat. He was leaning way back, with his legs stretched out in front of him. "How old are you two?" he asked. "For some reason, I can't tell."

Samara and Vanya glanced at each other. They seemed confused by Zane's comment.

"I'm fourteen," Samara said, "and Vanya's sixteen."

Hope was shocked. The girls were both quite a bit older than she'd expected. What accounted for that? Maybe it was just the way they dressed and kept themselves. As she considered this, the other kids filed into the room. Samara and Vanya were clearly the oldest of the Dweller kids. The others were tiny, including one little thing who couldn't have been more than four or five.

"It's not weird to be fourteen and sixteen," Vanya said sharply. Apparently, she had read the astonishment on Hope's face.

"It's just fine," Hope replied. "I didn't say it was weird."

"You had a funny look on your face," Vanya said.

She has no idea why I was shocked, Hope thought. *These kids might just be a little bit naïve.*

"Can I ask you a question?" Samara said. As the other children took their seats, she and her sister remained standing in front of Hope's desk. "How did you guys deal with God's punishment when you were outside the cave? I've always sort of wondered about what outsiders go through."

"God's punishment?" Hope replied. She couldn't help being a little obtuse. "You mean the snowstorm?"

"Yes, of course," Samara said.

Hope glanced toward the door to make sure Nick was still nowhere to be seen. Then she sighed and turned back to Samara, "Okay, I'm sorry, but I have to be honest, even if you guys laugh at me again. I can't hold it in. This thing that you call God's punishment is actually just a freakish long-lasting winter storm. At worst, it's a new ice age that will go on for years, but an ice age is something that has happened a few times in our planet's history. Scientists may have accidentally induced this one, but most of the time, they're a perfectly natural phenomenon. God wasn't punishing anybody."

This time, Samara and Vanya didn't laugh. Without Nick to show them how to respond, they seemed mostly confused.

"There have been other ice ages in the past," Hope said. "Heck, humans even survived at least one previous major ice age, back in the day when they were hunting mastodons and tangling with Neanderthals. Have you never heard any of this?"

Vanya shook her head, and Samara shrugged.

"What's a mastodon?" Samara asked.

"An extinct animal that lived about ten thousand years ago," Hope replied. "They looked a bit like an elephant, but they were covered in fur."

"If they're extinct, how does anyone know they existed?" Vanya said, planting her hands on her hips.

"Because people have found whole skeletons of them," Hope said. "They've found cave paintings that humans made of them. If you had the internet in your cave—assuming the internet still exists—you could look this up for yourself and see the pictures. Everyone knows about mastodons!"

Vanya and Samara traded another look. The younger sister, in particular, seemed utterly baffled by this conversation.

"Well, it sounds to me like you're making things up," Vanya said, finally. "I put mastodons alongside pixies and goblins and other fairy tale creatures."

Zane sat up. "What would be the point of making it up? Hope has nothing to gain from it. A basic education would have taught you about the previous ice ages, people living in caves, hunting mastodons and mammoths and stuff, and surviving. That's the thing. Humans survived past ice ages! Even if the storm never ends, it doesn't have to be the end of the world."

"It just sounds way too weird," Samara said. "Nick never told us about any of that, and he's the smartest man I know."

"No, and he's not going to tell you," Hope replied.

"He's not?" Samara said.

Samara and Vanya both looked suddenly toward the door, eyes going wide. Hope followed their gaze and saw Nick strolling down the corridor. The sisters quickly took their seats.

Maybe I said too much, Hope thought, *but I couldn't help it. I hate how poorly educated these kids are.*

"Sorry about that, kids," Nick said as he entered the classroom. "I had to help Seb and one of the newcomers with a little project, but I'm back."

As the teacher moved to the blackboard, Hope dared another glance at Samara and Vanya. The two sisters seemed to be deep in thought. Samara, in particular, had her head down, her lower lip thrust out.

They believe me, Hope thought. *Or, at least, they're not able to dismiss what I said completely.*

"All right, let's pick up where we stopped," Nick said. "Who would like to recap our previous lesson?"

By sheer instinct, and because she was already in a talkative mood, Hope opened her mouth to say something. Oh, she could recap the conversation all right. However, Samara reached over and lightly brushed her arm. Hope looked at her, and when they locked eyes, Samara shook her head slightly.

Is she worried about what I'll say? Does she want to keep me from provoking him?

Either way, Hope nodded and clamped her mouth shut.

89

At times, Fiona was troubled by just how easy it was to stay in the hopeless and lonely place she'd sunk into. To make matters worse, she was pretty sure she could talk herself out of it if she wanted to. Was it really such a big deal that she'd failed the trial on her first attempt? Yet somehow it felt like the end of the world, like all hope and light had fled her. She knew it was about more than just the trial. Falling from that damned wall had caused a lot of things to finally catch up to her, and she was feeling the weight of it all.

For a couple of days, she just went from room to room, trying to stay out of everyone's way. She didn't feel like talking, and fortunately, she didn't have any pressing leadership decisions to make. Her people had plenty of food, plenty of work to occupy their time, and a seemingly safe place to lay their heads at night. All told, it was a pretty good arrangement.

That gave Fiona the luxury of stewing in her negative emotions, contemplating all that she'd lost, all the unfortunate decisions that had made things worse, the bleak future that lay before them. Despite the despair, however, she still had a singular goal in mind. She was furiously determined to pass the trial, if for no other reason than that they would eventually need to find a way out of the cavern. The Dwellers were too strange to be a permanent solution.

The few times Fiona dared to bring up the possibility of attempting the trial again, she was quickly, but politely, rebuffed by Brigid. Until one morning when Fiona was helping Henny wash clothes. This particular task was done in a damp room beyond the sleeping chambers. The Dwellers had installed a long trough against the back wall, mounting some washboards along one side. It was an old, crude way of washing clothes that required a lot of vigorous physical activity, but Fiona was grateful to finally be able to clean her own filthy garments.

Henny wasn't especially talkative, for which she was also thankful. Indeed, Henny seemed like a fellow brooder. The moment that Brigid walked into the room and cleared her throat, Fiona was in the middle of grinding one of Jarred's only other shirts against a soapy washboard.

"Are we almost done here?" Brigid said. "I need both of you to help with the animals next."

Fiona flicked the excess water off her hands. She had a bunch of clothes strung on a line already, a few more items on a pile beside her.

"We're almost done," she replied, spinning on her stool to face the old woman. She decided to go for it. "When are you going to let me attempt the trial again?"

Brigid sighed and shook her head. "Must you bring this up every single time I speak in your vicinity?"

"Until you give me another chance, yes," Fiona said.

"Fiona, dear, maybe it isn't in God's wishes for you to pass the trial," Brigid said, taking a step into the room. "Has that occurred to you?"

"We won't know for sure unless I try again," Fiona said, and then, because she thought it might win Brigid over, she forced herself to add, "I want to get closer to God. I want to be as close to him as you are, and how else can I do it?"

Brigid made a little clucking sound and stared hard at Fiona's face, her eyes narrowed. Fiona heard Henny breathing extra loudly beside her. There was some kind of emotion behind it, but she wasn't sure what it was. Did Henny see through the lie? Was she just annoyed at Fiona's insistence?

"You want to get closer to God?" Brigid said, one eyebrow going up.

Fiona decided to double down. "Isn't that the way forward in life? Isn't that what you're teaching us here? Do I only get one chance to follow your way?"

Brigid started to smile, then she seemed to catch herself and settled her expression again.

She likes what I said. It's exactly the kind of thing she wants to hear.

"Very well," Brigid said after a moment. "Come with me. You can attempt it *right now*. Why put it off a moment longer if it means so much to you?"

Fiona pulled the wet clothes out of the trough and folded them over the edge.

"How many times will she be allowed to attempt the trial?" Henny asked, clearly annoyed.

"Once more," Brigid replied sharply. "Henny, finish washing her clothes and add them to the line. She can collect them when she comes back."

"*If* she comes back," Henny corrected.

"That's correct. As always. Finish washing her clothes."

Fiona didn't look at Henny. She could feel the woman glaring at her back as she left the room, walking past the small lanterns that lit the place. Brigid moved briskly, leading her down the corridor back toward the central chamber. When they arrived, they found Josiah and the blond son, Alex, sitting together at a table. As they drew near, Fiona realized they were fixing the fletching on some arrows. Were they preparing for a battle? For a hunt?

She was tempted to ask, but she didn't want to derail her opportunity to attempt the trial again.

"Come with us," Brigid said to Josiah, grabbing the electric lantern off the table. "Bring the net."

She didn't need to say more than this. Josiah nodded once, set down the arrow he was working on, and promptly stood up.

"Alex, you finish up here," he said. "I'm taking Fiona to God's Belfry."

"Got it," Alex said, glancing at Fiona. At least he didn't seem annoyed like Henny.

"Fiona, you remember how this works," Brigid said. "Put your hand on my shoulder and don't let go."

Josiah led the way, marching back down the corridor past their sleeping chamber. Fiona put her hand on Brigid's shoulder, grabbing the coarse cloth and holding tightly, as she walked behind them. Though Brigid had the lantern in her right hand, she didn't turn it on, so as soon as they passed all of the Dweller's chambers, they entered the impenetrable darkness.

Just as they stepped around a corner and left the last faint glow, Fiona heard a voice call out from somewhere behind her. "Good luck, Fiona!" It was Jarred. They must have passed him at some point, but she'd been oblivious, too focused on the path ahead. She felt a pang of regret at how she had neglected him the past few days.

I'll make it up to him once I've passed the trial, she thought.

Then again, it wasn't going to be good luck that got her through the trial. Fiona knew it was going to take her own willpower and relentlessness. As they followed the twisting path through the dark, she tried not to let it get to her. At least she knew what to expect this time. That helped, and in a more focused state of mind, the path to the first trial didn't seem as long or as winding.

Finally, the electric lamp awoke and cast out the darkness. Brigid held it aloft, revealing the vast, domed chamber called God's Belfry. The vast multitude of bats writhed against the ceiling, and directly across from them, the climbing wall rose, angling out over the drop.

"Well, here we are," Brigid said, turning to Fiona. "Shall we see if you find favor this time?"

Josiah stepped toward her and held up his hand, thrusting the net at her. Fiona took it from him and tucked the short handle under her belt in the back, well out of the way where it couldn't interfere with her climbing. Both Brigid and Josiah had what appeared to be mocking smiles on their faces.

They expect me to fail, Fiona thought. *Why does that amuse them? Don't they want people to follow their path?*

Maybe not.

"You remember the goal," Brigid said. "Climb the wall, grab a bat in the net, and bring it back down. Try not to fall. It's a long way down if you hit the drop-off."

"Yeah, I get the idea," Fiona replied.

She took a deep breath and let it out in a rush. Then, shaking out her hands to limber them up, she approached the far side of the climbing wall, where it was most accessible. She tried to psych herself up, but the memory of her last attempt was still too fresh in her mind. She could see the small ledge where her feet had slipped before.

She grabbed a low handhold and pulled herself up, mapping out a different path, one that would take her well away from the slippery ledge. Angling slightly to the left, she picked out the sturdiest handholds and footholds, trying to concentrate on her grip each time. It felt less damp, and therefore less slippery, along the left edge of the rock wall, and there were a number of deep pockmarks in the rocks that made the ascent easier.

In short order, she had sailed past the place where she'd fallen during her first attempt, but now she was angled over the drop, forced to shift to her right to follow the wall. She felt far more confident this time.

The first failure was a fluke, she thought, kicking her right leg up and working the toe of her boot into a deep depression. *If that old woman down there can pass this trial, so can I.*

Pushing herself higher, Fiona looked up and saw the bats high above her. However, as she scanned the wall, she noted that a few bats were clinging to some of the outcroppings of rocks well beneath the ceiling. They were much closer. One bat in particular was directly above her, nestled on the underside of a fist-sized pale rock.

You're the one, she thought.

Aiming for the bat, she grabbed another pockmark with her left hand and pulled herself toward it. However, the bat suddenly spread its wings and took off, as if it had sensed her intention. It flew to the right, then swung around and came back. Fiona realized it would pass directly above her, but she didn't have the net in her hand. And she didn't think she could grab for it. Her hold wasn't strong enough at the moment to risk letting go with her right hand.

The bat passed within inches of her face, and she could do nothing but track its movement. She watched as it flew along the face of the rock wall and suddenly disappeared into the shadows where the climbing wall ended. Not a shadow, but a large crack in the rock. A moment later, another bat flew out of a shadow to her right. Another crack. Fiona was pretty sure it was the same bat. Apparently, there were many small hollow spaces within the wall here.

That was disconcerting. It made the whole wall seem fragile. Fiona put her left boot against another ridge and pushed herself higher, working the fingers of her left hand into what appeared to be a deep pockmark. However, as she reached inside, she realized it was another small tunnel that went deep into the wall. She could have thrust her whole arm into it, if she'd wanted to.

Maybe there are bats inside, she thought. *If I felt around in there, I might be able to grab one, assuming I don't get bit.*

She reached with her right hand and got her fingers into the same opening. Then she scrabbled against the rocks with her right boot. She'd just managed to get the edge of her heel against a rock when she felt a shifting beneath her hands. The rocks at the mouth of the tunnel crumbled. As they did, another bat flew out of the hole, flapping its wings in her face. This caused her to flinch, which made her feet slip.

Suddenly, she was falling, crying out. She twisted around in midair and saw the ground rushing up, the great black drop-off like an open mouth. Brigid's and Josiah's faces shone bright and pale in the lamplight. Directly beneath her, Fiona saw both the ledge and the drop. She was going to hit either on her belly or her chest.

She tried to grab at the rocky floor so she wouldn't slip off the edge. However, the fall lasted only a second. She didn't have time to adjust. Fiona slammed into the rocks at the edge of the drop, her left arm curled under her at an awkward angle. Sharp pain stabbed into her elbow, and her breath was knocked out of her. But with her right hand she managed to fumble along the ground and grab hold of a shallow fold in the floor.

That left her dangling over the drop, her hips, legs, and feet hanging. It was a struggle to draw breath, however, and she couldn't concentrate on climbing. As she hung there, panicking, Brigid and Josiah watched calmly from a few feet away, unmoved. Finally, Fiona managed to gasp and fill her lungs with air again. Then she swung her right leg up, got it onto the ledge, and she dragged herself up onto the floor of the chamber.

As she rolled onto her back, she felt another sharp pain in her left elbow. She cupped it with her right hand as she sat up. Furious, disgusted with herself, she tried to move the arm. Though she could move it, the pain was so intense that she swooned. Brigid and Josiah continued to watch calmly as she unbuttoned the sleeve of her denim shirt and rolled it up past her elbow. When she did, she uncovered a rather hideous bloody scrape.

Brigid made a *tsk-tsk* sound, as if Fiona were a child who had done something she wasn't supposed to.

"That will need to be cleaned and bandaged," Brigid said coldly. "But, anyway, you failed the trial again. I hope this has finally made things clear to you. It's time to return to camp."

Fiona rose on unsteady legs, still struggling to breathe. She scarcely had time to reach out and grab Brigid's shoulder before the old woman clicked off the electric lantern.

"Don't let go," Brigid said, as she moved off into the utter darkness.

90

She thought she'd hit rock bottom before, but this was a deeper and angrier place. One mistaken handhold had cost her the whole stupid trial, and she'd almost broken her arm in the process. Instead, she had a deep gash, and the blood ran freely down her arm. She felt it pooling in the palm of her hand, and when she got back into the lighted passageway, she looked down to see it drying on her forearm, on her knuckles, between her fingers.

Brigid and Josiah were quiet, leading her back without a word. They offered neither comfort nor condemnation, not even a single "I told you so." She was grateful for that. However, as she passed the doorway of one of the working rooms, Jarred stepped out into the corridor and fell in beside her.

"You're hurt," he said.

"I am," she replied tightly.

"Myra should take a look at that," he said. "What happened?"

"I can't talk about it right now, Jarred. I'm sorry. Please, no questions right now. No comfort. Nothing."

He took the hint, ducking his head sadly and falling back. She felt bad about that, but in her current bleak mood, it was as polite as she could be.

Brigid and Josiah seemed headed for the central chamber, possibly to obtain bandages for her arm, but Fiona slipped into her own room as soon as she could.

Flinging the curtain out of her way, she strode into the dimly lit space. It was empty except for Smoke, who was curled up on one of the sleeping bags. He lifted his head and looked at her as she entered.

"Make room, buddy," she said, approaching the sleeping bag and lowering herself beside him.

He panted contentedly and tried to lick her face, but she gently deflected his tongue. Then she sat beside him, and he curled up against her.

"Sometimes, I miss the days when it was just you and me," she said, petting him. "I had a whole lot less to worry about, that's for sure, and I didn't have a bunch of people counting on me."

She sighed and cradled her injured arm across her lap. Her shirt and pants were already bloodstained. It didn't seem to matter now.

It's just a stupid rock wall, she thought. *Why can't I climb it? Twenty feet, that's all. It shouldn't be this hard.*

Somehow, she was losing the mind game. That was it.

I don't have to put up with these trials, she thought. *Why am I allowing the Dwellers to set the agenda?*

And then she answered her own question. *Because they have all of your guns, animals, and people now. They have a seemingly endless supply of food and clean water, and they know this cave.*

Smoke raised his head suddenly and looked behind her. She turned and saw Jarred standing in the doorway. He had a small wicker basket in his hands and a sheepish grin on his face.

"Brigid said you might need this," he said, holding up the basket. "First aid supplies. I can go and find Myra if you'd like. She'll probably know better how to clean and bandage your arm, make a sling, and stuff like that."

Fiona turned away. She couldn't do it. She just couldn't handle people right now, not anyone, not even Jarred. Couldn't he see that? Couldn't he give her this one thing and let her brood alone until she passed the trial?

But he either didn't or wouldn't take the hint. She heard him crossing the room, and suddenly he was standing over her. He held out the basket.

"Here, I'll just leave it with you, if you prefer," he said. "Maybe you want to bandage up the arm by yourself."

Instinctively, she started to reach with her left hand, but that was the wounded arm. Sucking in her breath, she let the arm fall back onto her lap. It hurt so badly now, she could barely lift it, and she didn't think she could grip anything with that hand.

"Just leave it here," she said. "I'll get to it eventually. Sorry, I just need to think, and I do that best on my own."

But he squatted down in front of her instead and set the basket between his feet. "We need to treat that wound so it doesn't get infected. Sorry. I don't have Myra's training and experience, but I'll do my best. I'll work fast, and I won't say much."

He produced a sealed disinfectant wipe and ripped off the corner with his teeth. Fiona knew he was right, of course. *Someone* had to clean and bandage the wound. She felt dumb for failing the trial twice, but she was going to feel a whole lot dumber if she got an infected wound. As he pulled the wipe out of the package, she raised one leg and propped the wounded arm on her knee, putting it in easy reach.

"I'll be quick," he said, gently turning the arm so he could access the wound. When he saw the ugly gash near her elbow, he grimaced briefly before he began cleaning the area.

He deserves an explanation, she scolded herself.

"I made it about twice as high this time," she said. God, she hated talking right now. She hated it so much. "Handhold crumbled."

"Well, that's progress, at least," he replied. He was working his way around the edges of the wound with the wipe, but it still stung.

"I can't afford to fall from much higher," she said. "Anyway, this time I noticed that there are bats nestled lower on the wall. I saw one fly into a crack and come out another crack higher up."

"Does it count if you grab a bat off the wall instead of the ceiling?" he asked. He bent down and blew on the wound.

"I don't know," she replied, "but I might have an idea how I can get higher next time. If Brigid gives me another chance. She might not. Whatever. I just…best not to discuss it right now. My mind is in a bad place, Jarred. It's not just the trial. A lot of bad emotion seems to have caught up to me."

"It's okay," he said. "Let me just clean and bandage the wound. You don't have to say anything else if you don't want to."

She shut her eyes and bit the inside of her cheek. "Do we really have to be so meticulous with the cleaning? Just slap a bandage on it. That'll keep the dirt out."

"Fiona, this wound is deep," he replied. "You're going to need stitches at the very least to keep this wound closed so it can heal."

"Stitches?" she replied. "Are you sure about that?"

"Have you seen how deep this is?" he replied.

Fiona shook her head. "I didn't probe the depths."

"I know you probably don't want to hear this, but it's particularly unsafe that you cut yourself in a room full of bats and guano," he said. "You can be mad at me. That's fine. I'll take it. But for your sake, we really need to stitch up this wound. Let me go and find Myra."

"No, I don't want more people around me right now," she said. "I can't handle it. And I don't want word getting out about how badly I'm injured."

"Then I'll stitch it myself," Jarred said.

"Do you even know how?"

He pulled a wound-sewing kit out of the basket. "As it turns out, I recently received some training on stitching up torn things."

"Stitching a wound is different from repairing clothes," she said.

He pulled a long, curved needle out of the kit. "I get that," he said, "but I'm pretty sure I can figure it out. I'm afraid you'll have to trust me, Fiona. Sorry. Let me get this done, and then I'll leave you alone."

"It's fine," she replied. "Do what you have to do."

He threaded the needle, and Fiona averted her gaze as he went to work. The wound already hurt so bad that she scarcely noticed when he pierced the edge with the curved needle. Jarred worked meticulously, intensely focused. Helping her even though she'd been rude and dismissive to him. Taking care of her even when she didn't take care of herself. And asking nothing in return.

She could feel the hard shell cracking, the sense of isolation and despair leaking out. Finally, he used small scissors to cut the thread and tie it off.

"Two stitches," he said. "That should be enough to hold it shut. Now, let me bandage it, and we'll be done."

She looked at the wound. His work wasn't perfect. She could see that. A bit sloppy, actually, but the wound was shut. It hurt less as well.

"Not too bad, eh?" he asked, opening a fresh bandage.

"Not too bad," she agreed.

He gingerly applied the bandage, pushing down the edges. "There you go. Hopefully, I won't get scolded by Myra for the low-quality medical care, but that should keep the wound safe from infection. You'll want to wash all of that blood off the rest of your arm at some point, but I'll leave that to you." He put everything back in the basket, closed the lid, and rose. For a moment, he just stood there biting his lip, as if he wanted to say something else. However, he finally turned to leave.

"What is it?" she asked. "What is it you want to say?"

"This might not be the best time to bring it up," he replied, "but I really think I should be the one to attempt the trial next time, especially now that you're injured. I have climbing experience. Yes, I know my leg only recently healed, but I think it'll be okay. Plus, I'm taller than you, which means I can reach the goal faster. It just makes sense, doesn't it?"

Fiona bowed her head. No, this was probably not a good time to have this conversation. It took her a moment to collect her thoughts so she didn't inadvertently respond rudely. Even so, what came out was, "It only makes sense if you don't think I can do it. If you think I'll fail again and hurt myself worse."

He hesitated a moment before responding. "That's not what I said." Still, his hesitation betrayed his real feelings.

Maybe he's right, she thought, and felt a surge of despair. *Maybe I can't complete the trial. Maybe the next time will be my last time.*

"No, I have to do it," she said. "Jarred, I have to complete the trial myself."

"Why?" he said, rounding on her. "Why do you insist on taking all of the risk upon yourself?"

The answer was there, of course. The despair had been pushing her toward it. It was right on the tip of her tongue, but she couldn't say it.

Instead, she said, "Do you remember how upset Hope was when you were hurt before? Do you really want to risk putting her through that again? And if you died, you would leave that poor girl alone and fatherless."

She expected his resolve to crumble at this, but he held his ground. "She wouldn't be alone. If I died, Hope would have you, she would have the others. That's her family. But what about if *you* died during the trial? Don't you realize it would be just as much of a loss to Hope and the others?"

Fiona shook her head. As much as it warmed her heart to hear him say it, she knew it wasn't true. She had not fully earned the trust or devotion of the rest of the group, not after the mistakes she'd made. If Jarred couldn't see that, it was because he didn't want to see it.

"Can we talk about this another time?" she said. "I'd prefer to be alone right now."

He pursed his lips and sighed. Clearly, he was frustrated at leaving this point unresolved. "I'll go now. Just please think about what I said."

"My feelings about this won't change," she said. "I'm sorry, Jarred. Thanks for helping with my wound."

He stood there for a second, frowning deeply. Then he nodded and quietly walked out of the room, leaving her in peace.

91

Jarred left the room so deeply troubled that he couldn't think about going back to work. He couldn't figure out what was going on in Fiona's mind. How had she become so obsessed with passing the trial herself? He walked a short distance down the corridor, heading for the central chamber, then came to a stop and just leaned against the wall.

Is she trying to prove her leadership to us? he wondered. *Does she still feel responsible for the bad things that happened to the group before we got to the cave? She helped us make the best decisions we could make with available information. Risks were unavoidable. Accidents happen.*

It seemed the most likely cause of her dark mood, but what could he do about it? He'd tried repeatedly to encourage her in the past, and somehow it didn't seem to take. He was frustrated with her, far more frustrated than he'd ever been. He stood there in the corridor, feeling the cold rock wall against his shoulder, his upper arm, his hip, and he seethed.

"I could do it," he muttered. "That's the thing. I could pass the trial. I have the experience, and I know I could do it. I feel it in my gut." He made a fist and smacked the wall. The wall didn't seem to notice. "And anyway, if I passed and learned how to get around this cavern on my own, isn't that a good outcome for the whole group, including Fiona?"

With no answers and no obvious solution, he pushed off the wall and resumed walking. When he reached the central chamber, he found Brigid and Josiah sitting at the table. She seemed to be repairing one of her many handwoven baskets, and he was fixing the broken handle of a cooking pot. Jarred walked over to the curtained area that hid the family's sleeping place. The first aid kit was kept on a shelf just on the other side, and he reached through to put it back in place.

We can both attempt the trials. The thought came to him like a whispered suggestion. *Just because I make an attempt doesn't mean Fiona can't try again.*

Would she be angry about it? Maybe, but why? His attempt had nothing to do with hers. And surely Hope would understand. He turned toward the table. Josiah glanced up at him then quickly back down at his work, but Brigid gave him a fixed look, as if she sensed something was wrong.

If you pass the trial, maybe Fiona wouldn't be in such a rush to try it again, Jarred told himself.

That decided the matter. In a fit of boldness, he approached the table.

"I want to attempt the trial," he said. "Right now."

Brigid continued to stare at him for a few seconds, a slow smile creeping up her face. She was going to say no. Of course she was. He could see the denial etched on her face, and it pleased her. Fiona had just tried, so why would she allow another member of the group to immediately attempt it?

Brigid pushed her chair back and rose, dumping her work materials on the table.

"You want to attempt the trial right now, do you?" she said, grinning. She turned to him. "Very well. Josiah, bring me the lantern. Quickly, now. This man is in a hurry."

Josiah set the half-repaired pot on the table and rose. He, too, was smiling for some damn reason. Were they mocking him? As Josiah trotted over to the shelf that contained the lantern, Brigid took a step toward Jarred and gave him an intense, appraising look.

"I'm glad you volunteered," she said. "I have a feeling about you, Jarred. I think it's in God's plan for you to pass the trial. I really do."

Josiah approached with the lantern, and she took it from his hand. Jarred wasn't sure what to make of her confidence in him. She had never expressed anything like it before, and she certainly hadn't said anything like that to Fiona, that he knew of.

"Josiah, stay here," she said. "Jarred and I will proceed to the belfry alone."

"Are…you sure about that?" he replied. He seemed wounded by this, but she turned and pointed at him. He nodded and went back to the table.

And then Brigid promptly marched out of the room, setting a brisk pace down the corridor, and Jarred hurried to catch up. Sometimes, he still felt a bit of a twinge in his leg, though it was mostly fine. Still, he knew if he fell from a distance and landed on it, he could easily break it again. That was a hellish experience he greatly wanted to avoid.

So don't fall, he told himself. *Remember your old rock-climbing skills and get it right the first time. Remember what Fiona told you about the cracks in the wall and the bats that are hanging beneath the ceiling.*

As he passed the plain brown curtain that covered the opening to their bedroom, he was tempted to call out to Fiona. She wouldn't receive it well, he knew, but he still wanted to reach her somehow, to let her know that he was going to do what he could to make things better for her. However, he hesitated, and the opportunity was soon gone.

"Grab on to my shoulder," Brigid said. "Do not let go. Our path will be very dark."

Though she was holding the lantern in her right hand, she did not turn it on, which meant they were quickly walking into the deepening dark. He placed his hand on her shoulder and clamped down as tightly as he dared.

Once they were in the dark, the old woman seemed to be turning frequently, as if trying to complicate their route unnecessarily. It didn't take long for him to feel completely turned around and disoriented. Brigid moved fast, as if she knew the path very well, but Jarred kept stumbling on the uneven ground. Still, he held fast to her shoulder and refused to let go.

Suddenly, she stopped, and he almost ran into her. Then she turned on the light, flooding the vast chamber before them with the brilliant glow. Jarred saw a great domed chamber before them, countless brown bats clinging to the ceiling. The air here reeked, and the ground was muddy from all of the bat guano. The stench turned his stomach. More than that, he knew that the fumes of guano could be deadly if they were strong enough, so it was probably a good thing that only people who had passed the trial knew how to get here. Limited exposure would prevent sickness.

"This is God's Belfry," Brigid said, with a grand sweep of her arm. "The location of the great trial. Your task is straightforward enough. Climb to the ceiling and grab one of the bats in this." She pulled a small net made of thin hempen rope out from under her belt. It was attached to a short wooden rod.

"Is there anywhere in particular I should be climbing?" he asked, taking the net from her and tucking it under his belt.

"The wall across from us," she said, pointing to the broad multicolored wall on the far side of the room. It was angled inward slightly, the surface pitted and spotted with various mineral deposits. He noted a dark gap between the floor of the room and the rock wall. "There are many paths to the top, so I recommend that you listen to God. If you find favor, he will show the way."

"I can do that," he replied, stepping past her.

"You can begin the climb whenever you're ready," she said, raising the lantern above her head.

He approached the drop and stopped, gazing up at the wall for a moment. Though he didn't listen for a voice of anything, he did take a few minutes to study the ascent. There were a few ways up the wall that looked obvious upon first glance, but as he studied them, he realized that the wall was brittle and soft in some place. He could see pockmarks where mineral deposits had broken loose, other places that were damp with seeping water and muck. Oh, yeah, it was far more treacherous than it seemed.

This damned wall is a death trap for anyone who doesn't know what to look for, he thought. *Fiona did a fine job just returning to us alive. At least she warned me about the crumbling handhold.*

Because of the drop, the wall had to be approached from the edges. He moved to the far side of the chamber, to the edge of the wall that seemed to be less used. He could see what appeared to be a few sturdy handholds just above him here.

"Okay, here goes nothing," he muttered. *Should I have said goodbye to Hope before I did this? I didn't even tell her I was going. It was an impulsive decision. The poor kid is in class right now. What if I don't come back?*

There was no sense regretting it now. He wasn't going to back out. That left only one option: complete the trial and get back alive. He grabbed a small lip of rock just above his head and began the climb. As he ascended, he moved to his left, avoiding some of the small handholds that he thought might be loose rocks. The pockmarks were safer, but even so, he had to be careful.

The rock-climbing instincts came back to him, though his weary body didn't move as confidently or as strongly as it once had. He reached up to a large outcropping of rock, tugged on it briefly to test it, then pulled himself higher. Though he was tempted to get the trial done quickly, he forced himself to go very slowly, measuring his breathing, selecting each handhold and foothold very carefully.

He found a small crack and wedged the toe of his right boot inside, then grabbed another pockmark in the wall to pull himself up. Thanks to Fiona's information, he knew to look for bats on the wall beneath the ceiling, and he spotted a small brown shape nestled in the shadow beneath a large rock just a bit higher and to his left.

He thrust his hand into another crack, tested it for a second, and felt some of the rock crumble. Not that way. So, he reached a little higher and grabbed a small lip of rock instead. He planted the edge of his right boot into a pockmark and hoisted himself to within reach of the bat. However, it squeaked suddenly and flapped its wings.

Jarred fumbled with his right hand, trying to get the net out from under his belt, but the bat took off. It flew in a tight circle around his head, then sailed into a dark crack. After a moment, it reappeared a little higher, fluttering out of another larger crack near the ceiling. It was just as Fiona had said. And suddenly he had an idea. He climbed toward what appeared to be the largest crack on the wall, which was a short distance to his left above another small outcropping of pale rock. He grabbed the pale rock and pulled at it, testing its sturdiness. When it didn't give way, he dared to put his weight on it, pulling himself up toward the crack in the wall.

Once he was right in front of it, he realized the crack was quite large, a horizontal split that somewhat resembled an open, toothless mouth. It was easily large enough for him, so he thrust his arms one at a time deep inside, wedged his hands into the narrow ends, and pulled himself inside. It seemed big enough that at least two people could have lain side by side inside and still had a bit of room leftover.

Jarred pulled himself forward until everything but his feet was inside the crack, and then he rested his cheek on his arms. His healed leg was throbbing from the climb, still not back to its full strength, if it ever would be.

Thanks, Fiona, he thought. *You gave me the key to making this climb. This is what teamwork looks like. We're going to do this.*

He scanned the end of the crack and realized there were smaller holes in the floor and ceiling. It seemed there was a whole network of cracks and tunnels within the climbing wall that the bats could use to get around. Jarred reached down and worked the net out from under his belt. Then, holding the rod in his right hand, he positioned the net over one of the holes in the floor.

"That should do it," he muttered.

He rested another minute, then began the arduous process of twisting himself around and pulling himself partway out of the crack. There were numerous bats on the ceiling and wall directly above him. In fact, he was kind of nervous about getting guano on his face. With his hands, he felt along the wall right outside the crack. Finally, his fingers gripped onto a small protruding rock, and he could tell it was loose. He worked at it, twisting and pulling until a fist-sized chunk broke loose.

He was lying on his back, which made the angle awkward, but he cocked his arm back and threw the rock as hard as he could toward the ceiling. On the way up, it angled toward the wall and finally hit it, making a loud *crack*.

This startled about a dozen bats, and they all scattered, flying in different directions. He was pretty sure a few went into the wall at various points.

Suddenly, he heard the wooden pole of the catch-net dancing against the rock floor beyond his feet. He twisted his upper body back inside the crack. Though the light of Brigid's lantern was greatly diminished here, he could see some small, dark shape flailing about inside the net.

"I got one," he whispered, his heart racing.

He worked his way back toward the net and grabbed the pole. Keeping the circular framework pressed against the ground, he pulled the net toward him. The big brown bat was thoroughly entangled in the thin ropes, but it fought mightily. Working carefully to avoid being bitten, Jarred twisted the net between the bat and the framework. Then he worked his pocketknife out of his pants pocket and cut one of the ropes. Pulling the cut end of the rope to the far side of the framework, he tied it in place. This closed off the net effectively enough that the bat would have a very hard time escaping.

"I got one," he said again, much louder. He heard his voice echoing in the large chamber behind him.

From there, he backed out of the crack and made his descent. He had to clutch the pole between his teeth, which made his jaw ache, but he used the same handholds and followed his own path back down. The bat was squeaking and flailing about far too close to his face, but he tried not to let that distract him. Inch by inch, he made his way back down to his starting point. Then he took a final hop and landed on the floor of the chamber with a cry of relief.

"The trial is passed," Brigid shouted, following it with an uncharacteristic whoop of excitement.

When he turned to her, he saw her big, toothy grin in the lamplight. She approached, shaking a fist over her head. The old woman seemed incredibly happy, a gesture which Jarred found strangely touching. She reached out and grabbed the pole, taking the net from him.

"This bat will be used as bait for fishing," she said.

"Well, at least I didn't disturb its sleep for nothing," he replied.

Brigid laughed and said, "I knew you had God's favor when we spoke the other day. I just knew it. I'm never wrong about these kinds of things. Follow me, Jarred. This time, you will get to see the sacred path with your own eyes."

She turned, the net in one hand, the lantern in the other, and started back across the room. This time, she left the light on as she entered the corridor. Jarred followed her, out of breath, his right leg sore, but feeling exhilarated. He'd done it! He'd passed the trial! Wouldn't Fiona be excited? Now he could tell her all that he'd learned, and then she could pass the test as well. After that, they could find a way out of here together.

The cavern between God's Belfry and the Dwellers' place was honeycombed with passages of all shapes and sizes, as well as countless rock formations in a wild variety of colors. However, Jarred discovered that the path Brigid took was clearly marked. Arrows had been chiseled into the rock at many places, pointing the way. The ones that Brigid followed were painted a bright yellow, but he noted other arrows in a variety of different colors: pink, blue, green.

"Every color marks the way to a different destination," Brigid said over her shoulder. "You see that now. Yellow leads to the belfry."

"That's rather ingenious," he replied. "You guys did a lot of work in here marking various paths."

She stopped and turned then, raising the lantern so it was right in his face. "Jarred, you are not to share this knowledge with anyone else. What you have seen here in the passageways must not be spoken about in the presence of anyone who has not passed the trial. To do that would be the worst of blasphemies. Are we clear about that?"

For a second, she had a steely look on her face and a deep, cold light in her eyes. Though she was smaller than him, something in that look made him shudder. She didn't outright say it, but he got the feeling that if he shared anything about the colored arrows with Fiona and the others, the consequences would be violent.

I could take her, he thought. But could he? Did she have secret methods of protecting and punishing people? And if he overpowered Brigid, what about the rest of her group? What would the outcome be if things turned violent between them? After all, Jarred's group had surrendered their guns and supplies.

"I won't breathe a word of it," he said, crossing a finger over his heart. *For now*, he added in his mind.

Brigid stared hard at him for a second, then smiled again and turned. "Very good. I knew there was something about you. Come on."

She resumed walking. The path back seemed so much faster now, shorter, less complicated. How had the darkness ever confused him so much?

"You've found favor, Jarred," Brigid said. "I hope you understand the magnitude of this. I hope you never take it for granted."

"I don't know how I found favor," he replied, "but I certainly won't take it for granted."

92

Fiona couldn't sit still. She was in a foul mood, and her mind simply wouldn't rest. After a long, futile attempt, she finally rose from her sleeping bag and decided to go find some kind of work to occupy her time. Caring for the goats and chickens would be right up her alley—an old task from her former days that would take her back to more peaceful times.

When she stepped into the central chamber, she found the old man, Josiah, working on a broken pot. He seemed to be carving new screw holes to reattach a plastic handle that had broken off. On the table across from him, the materials for basket-weaving had been left in a pile. The old man glanced at Fiona as she entered, then quickly resumed his work.

"I was thinking about tending to the animals," Fiona said. "I haven't spent any time with my goats lately. Do you know if they need care today? The male goat, Ramses, can be a handful."

"I believe they've been fed and watered, their stalls cleaned, not long ago," Josiah replied. "Your friends Larry and Lana went with my Alex. Henny is preparing the ingredients for dinner, if you'd like to help her."

"If you don't mind, I'd like to just check on the animals anyway," Fiona said. "I won't waste a lot of time in there, but I know them best. They're practically pets to me. I miss them."

Josiah shrugged. "If you insist. Henny really could use the help, though, so maybe when you're done, you could head to the kitchen." He nodded in the direction of the narrow opening that led into their kitchen area.

Fiona nodded and started across the room, headed for the passageway that went down to the animal pens. However, she heard footsteps in the corridor behind her and the distinct voice of Brigid. Suddenly, white light danced on the walls around her. She wheeled about in time to see Brigid enter the room and click off the lantern. As she set the lantern on the table, Jarred entered the room. He was sweating and mud-spattered, with just a hint of a limp. He looked at her with a big grin on his face.

"He passed the trial," Brigid said. "The bat has already been given to Seb. Jarred may now access the corridors. God has shown him favor."

She said it loudly, and soon Fiona heard people approaching from other directions. As Jarred stood there beaming, she tried to keep her facial expression from collapsing. She felt utterly defeated. He hadn't even told her he was attempting the trial, and now he'd passed it on his first attempt. He had no visible injuries. He didn't even seem winded or sore.

I'm a failure, she thought. Those words echoed in her head over and over. *I can't do anything for this group. I'm useless and I'm a failure. Jarred, a man who broke his leg just a few months ago, passed the trial on his first attempt.*

He must have read some of this on her face, as his smile faltered for a second. "It's a good thing, isn't it?" he said. "It'll be good for the group. It's good for everyone!"

Alex and the Bishops entered the room from one direction, Nick and the children from another. Seb and Henny from a third. All had been drawn by Brigid's announcement. Fiona saw looks of amazement, joy, surprise. Hope was standing among the schoolchildren, but she broke away, ran past Zane and Nick, and went to her father.

"You passed the trial?" she said, throwing her arms around him. "Wow, Dad, that's amazing."

He hugged her back as Brigid beamed proudly at his shoulder. It was as if the old cult leader's dearest son has passed the trial. And maybe that's what Jarred had become to her.

"That's impressive, my friend," Larry Bishop said. He had a bucket of water dangling from his right hand for some reason. "I didn't even know you were attempting the trial."

"I suppose if anyone was going to pass, it would be Jarred," Lana added.

They were all crowding around him now, leaving Fiona to stand alone. She was sinking fast into utter despair, and she hated herself for it. Jarred deserved her congratulations. She had no right to be angry at him for this. Every member of the group had the right to attempt the trials. Still, that thought didn't save her from the bottomless black hole into which she was sinking.

I'm useless, she thought. *I've never done right by the group. They don't need me.*

She had to flee before she started crying in front of the others. Since everyone was crowding around Jarred, she slipped past them and headed down the corridor to their bedroom. Shoving the curtain out of the way, she stepped inside, chased by the cheers and congratulations. Smoke had been lapping water from a bowl in the corner, but when she entered, he came padding toward her. Fiona headed to her bedroll and collapsed on her side, and Smoke curled up against her belly.

She could still hear the others. The central chamber wasn't all that far away. Everyone sounded so happy, and here she was falling into a bottomless pit. Fiona wrapped an arm around Smoke and shut her eyes.

"I'm never going to pass the trial," she said to him. "I don't know what's wrong with me. I'm just not good enough, I guess."

Feeling sorry for herself didn't help. Nothing seemed to help. All of her mistakes had finally caught up with her, all of her regrets were smothering her, and there was no light. Smoke, at least, didn't judge her, nor pester her, nor try to drag her out of her despair.

"Brigid is never going to tell me how to traverse the cave if I don't pass the trial," she said, "and I'm never going to pass the trial. She probably won't even let me attempt it again. So what am I going to do, Smoke? The group doesn't need me. I still have Duke's blood on my hands. I didn't want to be in charge to begin with. I didn't want guests at my homestead. I didn't want any of this. And now I just want to get out of here. I just want to be alone again."

As if sensing her despair, Smoke turned and licked her arm. There was another solution, of course. It had been nagging at Fiona's thoughts for days. Instead of trying to pass some pointless religious trial, she could simply search for the exit herself. Brigid had to sleep at some point. All of the Dwellers did. And when they were asleep, Fiona could simply slip into the corridors and look for the exit.

I can smell fresh air, she thought. *The exit can't be far from here. And once I find it, I can tell Jarred and the others where it is. Then they can come and go as needed. And as for me?*

As for her, Fiona knew what she really wanted to do. And maybe it was what she *had* to do. The group was better off without her. They had defaulted to her decision-making along the way, but she had never asked for it. Once she was gone, they would stop doing that and start trusting someone else's leadership. Heck, maybe they could just stay with the Dwellers and settle in. She would give them the option of staying or going. It was the least she could do for them before she left.

"I'm going to find the exit on my own," she whispered to Smoke. "At night, when they don't even realize I'm doing it. Then I'm going to tell Jarred where the exit is. And then my obligation toward this group will be satisfied, and I can go off alone and quit bothering people."

She felt Smoke's chest rising and falling. And what about him? What about her beloved pet? The answer seemed obvious. He was safer here with the group, where he would be fed regularly.

Don't think about it right now, she told herself. *Concentrate on finding the exit and deal with the difficult departure later.*

Of course, searching the cave and making her way through the tunnels without someone who had passed the trials was forbidden. Fiona wasn't naive. She knew damn well the risk she was taking, and she knew the punishment for violating this particular rule would be severe if she got caught. Still, she could see no other way forward. If she tried the trial again, if Brigid even let her, she might wind up killing herself. She had to find the exit.

Tonight, then, she thought. *I'm going to make my way into the corridors tonight.*

Of course, that meant covering for herself. If she acted like a broken person, they would expect broken decision-making. Fiona rose and walked over to the water barrel in the corner. Scooping up some cold water, she splashed it on her face, rubbing it in. Then she dried her face on a scrap of a rag nearby, combed her hair back with her fingers, and tried her best to settle the expression on her face.

I have to act like I'm okay, no matter how hard it is, she thought. *No matter how fake it feels. I just have to do it.*

She made her way back across the room, trying to find some safe corner in her mind where the despair and frustration wouldn't affect her behavior. She found no such place. The darkness had seeped into every corner. Still, as she walked down the corridor toward the central chamber, she thought she did a fairly decent job of stilling the emotions on her face.

Jarred was seated at the table, with the others crowded around him. Hope, Larry, and Lana were sitting with him. Hope had her arm around his shoulders, and she was leaning against him. Nick stood with the other children off to one side, and they were all staring with wide-eyed wonderment as Brigid spoke.

"I sensed the favor of God upon him," Brigid was saying. "Only a select few are truly chosen for the trial. When you have that favor, when his countenance has alighted upon you, then the path becomes clear. You can stare at the road ahead and see the way revealed before you, as if a divine hand had marked it out."

"Well, I think there was a lot of luck involved, to be honest," Jarred replied, "and perhaps a bit of good, solid advice."

"In my experience, there is no such thing as luck," Brigid said, wagging a finger at him. "Now, we do not speak openly of the trial in front of those who have not yet attempted it, but trust me when I say that there was more than luck and good advice involved in your success."

Crossing the room felt like dragging her legs through molasses, but Fiona forced herself to do it. One painful footstep at a time, she approached the table, trying her damnedest to put something approximating a smile on her face. Brigid glanced at her, then Larry and Lana, then Myra Cooper, who was sitting on a box in the corner with her hands in her lap.

Myra's broken too, Fiona thought. *Her grief is entirely my fault, whether she forgives me or not.*

No, no, she couldn't think about that right now. She came up behind Jarred and clapped him on the back. He looked up, realized it was her, and his smile faltered. Clearly, he was worried about how she would respond. Did he expect her to lash out at him for attempting the trial? More so for passing it? Somehow, this made Fiona feel even worse about the whole situation.

"Good job," she managed to say. The words tasted bitter in her mouth. "Despite what I said earlier, it's good you took the trial. I was just…worried you might get hurt."

"It wasn't easy," he replied, the smile coming back full force. "Like I said, there was some luck involved."

Brigid wagged at finger at him again. "Okay, let's not discuss the trial further. For now, let us bask in the glow of Providence. Jarred, did I not say you had favor before we set off?"

"You did," he replied.

"I knew. You see there, children. I knew!"

Enduring the celebration, the long dinner that followed, and the tireless religious talk was just about the most difficult thing Fiona had ever done. A thousand times, she had to swallow the despair and her own feeling of defeat. A thousand times, she had to work hard to put some reasonable expression on her face. The Dwellers served a big meal of hearty vegetable stew and crusty bread, and everyone lingered over it. Everyone smiled and laughed. Her own group didn't even seem bothered by Brigid's religious talk, not now. All was right with the world.

Fiona stayed as quiet as she could get away with, eating her food, speaking only when she had to, offering the blandest pleasantries, and just counting the minutes. Fortunately, she was in a corner away from Jarred, because he was the center of attention. When Fiona looked around the table, she saw smiling faces everywhere.

Except for one. Myra. Duke's widow was the only person who wasn't joining in on the celebration. Instead, she sat quietly at a corner of the table and ate her meal mostly without comment. At one point, she locked eyes with Fiona and nodded.

Does she see through my façade? Fiona wondered. *Does she sense how I really feel?*

After dinner, they spent some time in various work teams, cleaning and putting things away. Then, at long last, everyone was dismissed for bedtime. The effort of trying to act like everything was fine had worn on Fiona. She was mentally exhausted. As she entered the bedroom with the others, Jarred came up beside her.

"I thought you'd be upset that I attempted the trial," he said, "especially after what you said beforehand. I know you wanted to try again, and you'll still have that chance, I'm sure. Give Brigid a little time before you ask again. That's all. Heck, I think you'll probably pass it the next time, and then we'll be able to walk the corridors together."

"Jarred, just…you don't have to…" She struggled greatly to keep the emotion out of her voice. "Let's concentrate on your success for now, not my failure."

"Oh, of course," he said with a sheepish grin. "Sorry. I was just trying to be encouraging."

"I know," she said. "It was a long day. My arm still hurts. Yes, I was surprised to find out that you attempted the trial, but at least you passed it. That's what matters. Now, let's get to sleep, shall we?"

He nodded and set off across the room to help unroll the sleeping bags. Larry and Lana helped him, and they set up the sleeping area against the back wall. As they did that, Fiona fed Smoke a few scraps from dinner, which he devoured ravenously. By the time the dog was done eating, most of the group was already lying down.

Fiona's sleeping bag was set at the end of the row beside Jarred's, as usual. When she approached, she reached down and pretended to adjust it a little, but as she did, she slid it away from his a couple of inches. She needed to be able to rise in the night without bumping into him. She looked down the line of sleepers. Myra was already curled on her side with her eyes closed. Larry and Lana were chatting quietly. Zane and Hope were also talking.

Fiona lay on her back, her hands tucked behind her head. At one point, she sensed Jarred looking at her, but she didn't respond. She couldn't let anything distract her now.

"You should sleep, Jarred," she said. "It's been a long day."

"Are you sure you're not upset with me?" he said. "I know you wanted to pass the trial first. I went ahead without consulting you. It doesn't feel right."

"Stop it. I'm not your boss or your commanding officer. We're just friends, okay? You had every right to attempt the trial. Forget about what I said before. It's good that you passed. Now, go to sleep. Please."

He grunted, as if unsure. "Okay. Good night." And finally, he rolled away from her.

The room was lit by two candles flickering away on a nearby shelf. Fiona was tempted to make some excuse for blowing them out. Absolute darkness would make her escape easier, but she knew people would be uncomfortable without some small bit of light. More than that, it would rouse suspicion.

Just bide your time, she thought. *People will be asleep soon enough. They've all worked hard today, and they have full bellies.*

As she waited, she tried to recall her previous journeys to the belfry. There had been so many twists and turns, she couldn't work it out in her head, no matter how hard she tried. After a few minutes, she heard Jarred's breathing slow, and she knew he was asleep. Then Larry began snoring softly. Still, she waited a few more minutes.

Finally, when she could stand it no longer, she sat up, trying to make as little noise as possible. She looked down the line of sleeping bags and saw only the shapes of people curled up within. Smoke was twitching in his sleep, as he sometimes did. It was time to go.

Slowly, painstakingly, Fiona pulled herself out of her sleeping bag and put her boots back on. Though she had surrendered all of her supplies to the Dwellers, she hadn't emptied her pockets. That meant she still had a couple of important items in her immediate possession. Indeed, as she stood up, she felt the bulges: a tiny battery-operated penlight and her trusty old pocketknife.

Both would come in handy, not just now but in the future. She crept across the room, concentrating on each step so she would make as little noise as possible. When she reached the curtain, she glanced back. To her surprise, she found Smoke standing right behind her, panting and ready to go. She motioned for him to go back, but he either ignored or didn't understand the gesture.

Well, this isn't a fight I'm going to win, she thought. *Not unless I shout at him, which I can't do right now, and wouldn't want to do anyway.*

Still, she tried a couple more times to shoo him back to bed, but he ignored her gestures.

Okay, old pal, I guess we're in this together, she thought.

Beckoning him, she passed through the curtain into the hall. This gesture he fully understood, and he followed her out of the room. The corridor was dark and empty at the moment, though she saw some faint light coming from around the corner—candles in the central chamber where the Dwellers slept.

Fiona turned the other direction, to the long, twisted way that led past the working rooms and eventually into the forbidden places. A figure was standing there, little more than a vague shape in the dim light. Fiona felt a jolt and took a stutter-step backward. Then she spotted the shape of long braids trailing down either side of the figure and realized who it was.

No backing out now, she thought. *Make your excuse.*

She approached Henny, clearing her throat.

"What are you doing out here?" Henny asked in an angry whisper.

"I could ask you the same thing," Fiona replied. A bold and confident approach seemed best. "You're pretty far from your sleeping area."

Henny sniffed. "Well, if you must know, I was using the bathroom. I couldn't use the chamber pot because I'm a little sick to my stomach. Do I need to go into gory detail?"

"Well, join the club, then," Fiona replied. "I've got a terrible case of diarrhea coming on, and I'm not going to sit on that bucket where all of my friends can hear and smell me. I intend to use the bucket in the corner of the washroom."

"So we had the same idea, then," Henny said, tipping her head back so she was looking at Fiona down her nose.

"Seems like it." When Henny lingered, Fiona added, "I guess you can go back to bed now. We'll discuss our individual bathroom experiences in the morning."

"Yeah, sounds good to me," Henny said.

She continued staring at Fiona for a few seconds. Fiona realized then that the girl had her hands behind her back. She brought one of them forward now and revealed that she was clutching a bulging cloth bag.

"Here, take this with you," Henny said, thrusting the bag at her.

Fiona grabbed it, and was surprised to find that it was full and quite heavy. Almost too much to hold in one hand.

"It's wood ash," Henny explained. "If you're going to use the latrine in the washroom, sprinkle this around it when you're done. It'll reduce the smell."

And with that, Henny sniffed again, brushed past her, and headed toward the central chamber. Fiona waited a few seconds, her heart still pounding. Had Henny bought the lie? Maybe. Just maybe. Fiona glanced down at Smoke, who was standing dutifully by her side. Then she set off down the corridor, lugging the heavy cloth bag in her left hand. As she passed the washroom, where the farthest portable latrine was located, she noted that there was no smell emanating from the room, not even the scent of wood ash.

She kept going, slowly being swallowed by the darkness. Smoke whimpered a bit, but he stayed at her side.

Don't worry, boy. We'll have light soon. I just want to get farther from the rooms before I turn it on.

She crept through the dark, brushing the wall on her right side with her shoulder. Once the last faint reflection of candlelight was gone, she stopped and dug into her pocket. Pulling out the little metal flashlight, she had a moment of anxiety. What if the battery was dead? She hadn't used it in quite a while. She hadn't changed the battery since she was on the farmstead.

She pressed the button, and bright light awoke in the corridor, revealing the damp, twisting rocks ahead. It seemed too bright, even with her distance from the Dwellers' room, so she tucked the flashlight into her sleeve and let it shine through the cotton fabric. It was greatly diminished but still plenty to reveal her surroundings.

Unfortunately, what it revealed was a complicated set of passageways heading in various directions. Fiona studied the ground at her feet, looking for some indication of regular footsteps. There was nothing obvious, however, so she just kept moving forward as best she could, choosing the path that seemed to make sense.

And then, rounding a bend, she spotted a bit of color on a wall. From a distance, it looked like someone had swiped a red paintbrush across the rocks. She drew nearer and realized that there was actually an arrow chiseled into the rock, and someone had crudely painted the indentation. It was pointing straight ahead. She turned to follow it and spotted another small splash of color, blue this time, on the wall in front of her, but it was pointing off to her right.

The paths are marked, she realized. *Multiple paths.*

So this was the mysterious language of the Dwellers' deity? Colored arrows etched into stone. Fiona hunted around a bit and discovered a set of yellow arrows as well. At least three paths, then, but where did they lead? She considered the possibility that the colors might mean something, but if so, the meaning was unknown to her.

As she was standing there considering which path to follow, Smoke suddenly growled and stepped in front of her. She couldn't see what had drawn his attention, so she bent down and petted him on the side.

"Stay calm, boy. We don't need any noise, okay? Let's be stealthy and quiet."

But he barked and took off running down one of many passageways. Fiona hurried after him, but as she ran, she occasionally flung small amounts of wood ash on the ground to mark her path.

This is what I get for letting him come with me, she thought.

She wanted to shout his name. Sometimes, if she used a sharp voice, he would respond even if he was worked up about something. But she was afraid her voice would carry.

"Quiet, Smoke, quiet," she said in a little hiss. "Get back here."

She followed him around a bend in the passage, and here he came to a stop. He hunkered down in the middle of the passage, eyeing something high on the wall and growling deep in his voice. Fiona aimed the tiny light upward and spotted a cluster of bats hanging from a large rock. They were making the softest little sounds, scarcely audible to her, but perhaps those sounds were a lot louder to a dog.

Suddenly, one of the bats launched itself off the wall and swooped low over Smoke. At first, he seemed surprised, and he backed away. But then the bat turned and flew off down a side passage, and the dog gave chase. Fiona hurried after him.

Smoke's angry charge through the corridor woke other bats, and as they flew away, Fiona noticed that most of them headed in the same direction. There were no colored arrows in this passage, but she decided to stick with it anyway.

Smoke seemed to have a lot of pent-up energy. Perhaps his time in the cave had made him restless. Though he stopped from time to time and looked back, waiting for Fiona to catch up, he managed to keep going for a long time.

A steady stream of bats went before them, new ones constantly added to their number as the relentless dog passed beneath their resting places. The passageway was a wild, twisting maze, with many smaller passages branching off in various directions, but the bats kept to one particular path, as if headed somewhere specific.

There are so many bats in this cave, she thought. *They must be getting in and out somehow. Maybe they'll lead us to an exit.*

The chase went on and on until Smoke finally lost steam. Even then, he kept moving forward, though at a slow trot now. Fiona lost track of time. On and on the passage continued to twist and turn. Finally, Smoke stopped and sat down, panting. The bats flew on and soon disappeared into the darkness.

Fiona squatted down beside the dog and put a hand on his back. "Really? That's it? We chased them for an hour, and what did we get for all of our trouble?"

Smoke looked up at her and tried to lick her face, but he missed and resumed panting. Fiona dared to pull the small flashlight out of her sleeve and aimed the full brightness at the passage ahead. She could see more bats along the ceiling, but the passage made a tight turn to the left just after a few more yards. As she watched, a bat took flight from the ceiling and flew around the corner.

Fiona rose and approached the corner. Smoke followed her, but he was exhausted now. He paused for a moment and lapped water from a small pool. As she approached the tight turn, Fiona felt a sudden chill against her face, soft as a breath but frigid as ice cubes. She had grown so used to the steady temperature of the cavern that this sudden cold sent a shiver through her body. It dredged up days and weeks of memories of trudging through a nightmare wasteland of snow and ice. Still, she pushed ahead. As she rounded the corner, a bat flew over her shoulder from behind. This time, Smoke didn't even have the energy to bark at it.

Around the bend, the passage came to a sudden end against a rough rock wall. However, there was no sign of the bat. It was as if the animal had flown straight at the rocks and somehow passed through them. As she studied the wall, however, she spotted a notable crack on the left side. It was maybe two inches wide at its thickest, two feet from end to end, and running at roughly a ninety-degree angle from the floor.

As she leaned in close, she felt a blast of cold air on her face, as if the crack were some kind of primitive air-conditioning vent. She breathed it in through her nostrils. Yes, it was definitely crisp outside air. Fiona clicked off the flashlight and sensed a faint light shining somewhere on the other side of the crack.

"Well, I think I found my exit," she muttered, turning the flashlight back on.

She looked down at Smoke. He was standing at her side, panting and waiting, as if he expected her to open the wall like a door so they could proceed.

"If we were two inches wide, we could go through," she told him, giving him a quick pat on the head.

Still, it wasn't a total loss, was it? This was definitely an exit. She had seen the gray light on the other side and felt the outside air. She had smelled the winter storm. This was the way out. It would just take some work to widen it. And since it was not on one of the Dwellers' marked paths, they were unlikely to stumble upon this place. She'd marked the way with handfuls of wood ash, but she would have to make these marks very subtle on her way back. She couldn't afford to let anyone else find the exit until her work was done.

93

School days were only about four hours long, definitely shorter than a real school day, but Hope was always mind-numbingly bored by the time they got dismissed. A small amount of what they learned was practical and interesting, stuff about local flora and fauna or cavern survival skills, but most of it was just lecture after lecture about the Dwellers' faith and history.

By the fifth day of school, Hope sat at her desk in a stupor, struggling mightily to pay attention to what Nick was saying. On her left, Zane was slouching so far back in his seat that she was surprised he didn't just slide out. Zane and Hope set a marked contrast to the rest of the children, who remained alert and attentive throughout Nick's many lectures.

On this particular day, as they reached roughly the midpoint of the school day, Nick was in the middle of another lecture about visions and destiny or something along those lines, and Hope was struggling to find something to keep her awake. Her father had said education never hurt anyone, but she felt emotionally damaged by the endless stream of nonsense. She glanced at Samara in the desk to her right. Although the waifish girl had her attention fixed on the teacher, she was frowning. Her mood seemed to have darkened since her conversation with Hope and Nick a few days earlier.

I didn't mean to ruin anyone's life, Hope thought, *but I just had to say something. This whole setup here is weird, and these kids deserve to know it.*

"Now, children," Nick said finally. The change of tone in his voice roused Hope's attention. "We have another fun and important task today. It's been a few days since we gathered water, but Brigid has asked us to go again."

This caused some murmurs of excitement. Indeed, most of the Dwellers had been amped up ever since Hope's father returned from completing the trial the day before. Hope herself had been more relieved than anything, but to these kids, it was like God had appeared in their midst and blessed them personally.

Dad just climbed a wall and caught a bat in a net, Hope thought. *That's all he did. Why do they act like he just descended from Mount Olympus with a shining face?*

"I'm going to get our buckets," Nick said. "We accidentally left them in the dishwashing room last time. Please behave until I get back."

He wagged a finger at the children before walking out of the classroom, the lantern lights flickering at his sudden passing. The Dweller kids immediately began to whisper to each other. Vanya and Samara began speaking intently. Hope used the opportunity to lean over to Zane.

"You know what's been on my mind ever since the last time we gathered water?" she said quietly.

"Probably the same thing that's been on my mind," he replied. "That dark hall at the back."

"Exactly," she said, then glanced over her shoulder to make sure none of the other kids were listening. Samara and Vanya were deep in conversation with each other. "Where do you think it leads?"

"I don't know," Zane said. "Maybe your dad can check it out some time now that he has permission to go into the darkness alone. It's not for us to worry about." He turned and gave her a stern look. "We just need to keep our heads down and not rock the boat anymore."

She was disappointed to hear him talk this way. After all, he had gladly participated in the scandalous talk during class. Apparently, he was willing to prod their religious views a little bit, but unwilling to flaunt their rules. Hope realized she had to cover for herself.

"Yeah, keep our heads down, of course," she replied. "I was just curious what you thought. It's not against any rules to talk about where the passage goes and speculate. Maybe I'll ask my dad to look at it, assuming Brigid lets him, but we can at least guess." She couldn't help but let the littlest bit of bitterness into her voice.

"It's not hard to figure it out," he said. "It leads to more of the cave."

"But didn't you feel the air coming out of there?" she said. "It was crisp and cold. What if it leads outside?"

"Then it leads outside," he replied with a shrug. "Where there's no food or shelter or hope for long-term survival. Where there are hungry, desperate people and hungry, desperate wild animals trying to eat each other."

"Right. Who would want to go out there again?" She laughed awkwardly. "Well, anyway, at least we get out of class for a while."

"Yeah, anything to spare us another sermon," Zane grumbled. "I know more about divine visions and divine wrath and how every other religious sect in the world is dumb than I ever wanted to know."

"It might be fascinating to watch the inner workings of a cult," Hope said softly, "if not for the fact that we also have to be active participants."

"Yeah, but we *do* have to participate," Zane said, "if we want to eat good food and sleep in safety and warmth. We can hate it and go along with it at the same time. That's what I'm trying to do."

"Me, too." And then, under her breath, she added, "Well, half of me. The other half wants to know the way out of here." Zane didn't seem to hear and didn't respond.

Nick returned then with the same stack of plastic buckets. This time, he passed them out to the students before they left class. Then he had them line up again, as before, and led them back into the central chamber and the dark passage that led to the water source. Hope wound up in the front of the line, but she didn't want to be the one holding Nick's shoulder, so she stepped behind Zane.

Nick is fine, she thought. *But I need at least a one-person buffer.*

Fortunately, Zane didn't balk at this. She wound up with her right hand on Zane's shoulder, and Samara's hand on hers. Nick marched them into the darkness. Since it was her second time making the journey to the water room, Hope tried to sense if the twists and turns were familiar. At first, she did fine. She anticipated the first few turns, but then she quickly became disoriented. It was just too much to keep up with, so she gave up trying.

Finally, Nick flicked on his flashlight and revealed the massive stalactite that dominated the room, water running down the sides and pouring into the pool below. Hope looked at the smaller stalactites deeper in the chamber, and from there, her gaze went in the direction of the strange, dark opening. She thought she could feel the cold wind, just barely—or maybe she was imagining it.

All I'd have to do is step a little way into the corridor, she thought. *Then I could be sure if it's outside air or not.*

"Okay, children, fill your buckets," Nick said, gesturing with the flashlight beam at the big stalactite. "Don't go too far. Hurry, now."

The Dweller kids circled around the big stalactite, but Zane headed back to the smaller stalactite that he'd used during their last trip. Hope started to follow him, but her curiosity had taken hold of her. In fact, Zane had only inflamed it by chiding her. How could he not want to see what lay in the dark hall? Even if they found an exit, it didn't mean they had to leave the cavern. It was still good to know, wasn't it?

All of the kids were collecting water now except for her. Nick noticed and turned to her.

"Hope, are you not going to join the rest of the class?" he asked. "We need to fill every bucket."

And in a fit of impulsive curiosity, she made a weird little whimpering sound and said, "Sir, I really, really, *really* have to pee, like, right now. I don't suppose there's a bathroom around here?"

He gave her a pitying look, as if he thought she were simple. "Of course not. Can you wait a few minutes?"

"I don't think so," she said, and tried to stand awkwardly like she meant it. "I really have to go, sir. Don't think I can hold it much longer, and all the running water is making it so much worse. I'm sorry. I don't want to disrupt class, but I'm not sure what to do."

He looked around, clearly frustrated. "Okay, I'll tell you what, you're not supposed to leave the lighted area, but if just step off just a little bit into the darkness, no one will be able to see you. Then you can squat and do your business, but do it really fast. That's the only real option, I'm afraid. Here, I'll point the flashlight at the ground so the light doesn't carry as far."

"Thank you, sir," she said. "I'm not breaking any rules, am I?"

"No, because I've passed the trial, and I'm here with you," he said. "But don't leave our immediate area."

"Does it matter which direction I go?"

"Nope, just stay close," he replied. "Don't go down any passages or through any openings. Got it?"

"Got it," she said. "Thank you again, sir."

He aimed the flashlight at the ground, which created a bright circle of light in the area around the big stalactite but let the darkness encroach. Hope shuffled off in the general direction of the mysterious doorway, trying to look like she wasn't heading straight for it. On the way, she glanced at Zane, but he was busy filling his bucket.

Hope avoided the temptation to look back at Nick. She knew that might arouse suspicion. Fixing her gaze on the darkening floor at her feet, she hurried off into the darkness. Once she was outside of the circle of light, she quickly curved to the right toward where she thought the mysterious entrance was. This was confirmed when she caught a gentle whisper of cold air on her face.

She felt a twinge of guilt, but it wasn't strong enough to stop her. Anyway, she wasn't planning to run off. She just wanted to see what was down the dark hall. Maybe the information would help her father and the others when they made their eventual escape. At the very least, it would satisfy her own curiosity, which had been smothered by the tiresome, friendly ignorance of the Dwellers.

The cold air was strong now. It smelled like the outside. Hope reached out with her hands and found the opening before her, tracing the edges. Then she slipped inside. As she did, she reached into the inner pocket of her coat. Even with the steady temperatures in the cavern, she kept her hooded coat on at all times, and she had exactly two things on her at all times: a pocketknife and a small flashlight.

Move fast, she told herself. *Get in there. Turn on the flashlight for a second. Take a look. Then get back. Hurry!*

She moved low, stepping carefully so she wouldn't trip or fall and make a bunch of noise. The passage beyond the opening was narrow and ascending. That seemed like a good sign that it led out. As she stumbled ahead, she found that the path curved to the right.

Around the corner, I can dare a little light, she thought, *but I have to hurry. This is taking too long.*

She pulled the flashlight out and raised in front of her, but she hesitated to turn it on, unsure if she really wanted to do this.

You got carried away, she scolded herself. *Just like the time you drove off to see Benjy, that creep. For all you know, it's dangerous down this way. Go back.*

Still, her curiosity raged within her, and she didn't immediately turn back. When someone grabbed her shoulder, silently seizing her in the dark, her heart leapt into her throat, and she came very close to shrieking at the top of her lungs. Only her natural quiet turned a scream of surprise into a gasp, as she was forcibly turned around. She assumed it was Nick. He had come looking for her because she'd wasted so much time.

"What are you doing here?" It was Zane's voice. "Are you *trying* to get in trouble? Do you *want* Nick to be mad at you?"

"I went to pee, and I just thought I'd take a quick look," she replied, shaking off his hand. "Nobody has to know."

"Well, you weren't all that secretive about it, because I saw you," he said. He grabbed the flashlight and plucked it out of her hand. "I could tell exactly where you were going, so I followed you."

Hope didn't appreciate having the flashlight ripped out of her grasp. She wasn't a child, after all, and Zane was only a couple of years older than her. He had no right to act like her father. Still, she knew if she snapped at him, her opportunity to see this strange passage would be lost, so she tried a different approach.

"Come on," she said. "Aren't you at least a little curious to know what's down here? There's cold air blowing through this place."

"No, I'm not curious," he said. "I'm cautious, and you should be, too. People who speak about God the way these Dwellers do aren't generally the kind of people who forgive disobedience, especially when you're breaking one of their religious rules."

He grabbed her shoulder again, but Hope looked back over her shoulder. She stared down the passageway, trying to get some glimpse of what was down there. It was very dark here, but she thought she could just barely make out a darker area on the ground a few feet in front of her, and she definitely felt a cold breeze against her face.

"Don't we need to know if there's a way out?" Hope said. "Myra Cooper is in poor shape. Her breathing's not good. She just sort of mopes around all the time. Fiona thinks the outside air would be better for her lungs. Don't we owe it to Myra to check out this hallway? I think the exit might be just a few feet in front of us."

Zane was quiet for a few seconds, then he let go of her shoulder. "Okay, fine. Fine! We'll take a quick peek, but we have to do it fast. We've wasted a lot of time. The other kids are probably done by now, and if we don't come back, Nick is going to know we snuck off."

"I see a darker spot just ahead," Hope said. "I think it's a hole. Let's shine a light down there. That won't take more than a few seconds. Then we'll go right back."

"I said okay," Zane said. "Go on, then. I'm right behind you. Let's get it over with."

Emboldened by his support, she snatched the flashlight back from him and moved down the dark hall, stepping carefully. She clicked on the light, pressing her other hand over the bulb so only a tiny bit seeped out. As she drew close to the dark spot on the floor, she held her breath, tense but excited, and raised the light. As expected, the dark spot was a hole in the stone floor. It seemed a bit too round and smooth to be entirely natural.

Here, the cold air was even stronger, and she shivered. Slowly, she leaned out over the edge, moving the flashlight down along the sheer side of the pit as she looked for the bottom. Zane grabbed the back of her shirt.

"Don't get too close," he said. "You'll fall in. What do you see down there?"

She saw a damp rock floor about ten feet down, and then the light revealed some strange pale shape lying there. It took Hope's brain a second to register the gaping mouth, the hollow eye pits, the desiccated skin, the arms and legs all akimbo. As the realization hit her, she felt a stab of deep, trembling fear. A dead body. Gasping, she stumbled backward into Zane's arms, her hands wobbling so that the flashlight beam danced.

"Did…did you see it?" she asked, struggling to get the words out.

"Yeah, I'm afraid so," Zane replied in a little whisper.

And then a third voice spoke from behind them, and Hope almost leaped out of her own skin. Zane managed to wrap both arms around her, which probably saved her from toppling into the pit and joining the corpse at the bottom.

"What are you two doing in here?" Samara's soft, squeaky little voice was unmistakable.

Hope broke out of Zane's embrace and turned to her. The girl was standing a few feet back, her shadow flailing out behind her as the flashlight beam moved around. She looked frail and colorless in the white light, practically a ghost. Hope was breathing so fast now, it made her dizzy. She couldn't answer Samara's question, and Zane didn't say anything either.

"All of the buckets are full," Samara said. "It's time to go back. Nick said Hope went to use the bathroom and probably got lost. What are you doing in here? Where did you get that flashlight? This place is off-limits."

Hope swallowed the lump of terror in her throat and lowered the flashlight beam. "Come here," she said, beckoning Samara with her head. "Look in this pit. See what's down there."

Samara approached, though she didn't seem particularly concerned. Hope shone the flashlight down in the pit again as the waifish girl leaned over and looked at the bottom.

"Oh, yeah, you're talking about that corpse down there," she said. It didn't seem to surprise her at all.

"Uh, yeah, the corpse," Hope replied.

Samara turned to her and shrugged. "It's my aunt," she replied somberly. "I recognize her. She died of an illness a few weeks ago. When people die, we don't have any choice but to put the body in some dark place. I guess this is the pit they chose for her."

"They couldn't bury or burn the body?" Zane said.

Samara scowled at this. "Why would we do that? This is a very dark place, which means her soul can be close to God here. Don't you remember that God dwells in the deepest dark places? Also, that fresh air will purify her as she decays. It was perfect...until you snuck in here and started shining that light around everywhere. I sure hope you didn't go to the bathroom in here."

"No, no, of course we didn't," Hope replied. Her fear was leaving her quickly now. Samara's explanation, though tinged with religious weirdness, was fairly reasonable. Where else would they put the dead? And now Hope felt dumb and bad that she'd disturbed the place. It was a bit like kicking through a cemetery. "Sorry, I had no idea."

From somewhere outside of the passageway, they heard Nick shouting. "Hope. Zane. Samara. Come out here right now." The kindly tone of the friendly teacher was gone. He sounded angry. "It's time to join the rest of the class!"

Samara gasped and covered her mouth with her hands. "He can't find us in here or we'll be punished," she said, backing away from the pit. "All of us! Oh, no, what have you guys done?"

Zane sighed and grabbed the flashlight out of Hope's hand again. "Nah, neither of you are going to be caught. I'll take the fall. Wait here until it's safe." And with that, he clicked off the flashlight.

Hope froze, unsure of what to do. What sort of punishment awaited them if they were caught? Samara seemed genuinely frightened, but how bad could it be? Even now, in the darkness, the Dweller girl was breathing fast and loud. Hope heard Zane's footsteps as he hurried back down the hall.

What do I do? What do I do? Her mind was racing, but she was frozen in place. The fear had come back full force, but it had shifted from the corpse in the pit to the strange zealous adults who ran this place.

"You there," Nick shouted. He was louder and closer. "Zane! Did you go in that hallway? What were you thinking? I told you all such places are strictly off-limits. You are not allowed to enter the dark places! You haven't passed the trial. This is sacrilege, don't you realize that?"

"Yeah, I realize it," Zane replied, turning the flashlight back on. Hope saw light shining just beyond the opening to the forbidden hallway.

"Turn that light off," Nick said, practically screaming. "Where did you get that flashlight? Are you trying to corrupt the other children?"

"I wasn't trying to break any rules," Zane said. "I was afraid my friend got lost going to the bathroom, but she's not in there."

"You shouldn't be making light of this situation," Nick said. "How dare you!"

"Making *light* of the situation?" Zane said. "That's an ironic thing to say, sir."

Hope glanced at Samara. The girl, wide-eyed and terrified, frantically pressed a finger to her lips. Then the flashlight went off again, plunging them back into the darkness. Samara moved closer, brushing up against Hope, then grabbed her arm with both hands. Heart pounding fiercely, Hope reached up and grabbed one of Samara's hands and clamped down.

"You're coming with me, Zane," Nick said. "Don't you dare try to run off."

"I'm not running off," Zane replied. How could he sound so calm? "I'm right here. I didn't do anything wrong. If I did, it was an accident, which makes me less, uh, culpable."

"That's not for you to decide!"

Hope heard them both walking away. It sounded like some of the other children were murmuring, but Nick shushed them loudly. Then the footsteps faded and left them in a dreadful silence. Samara's fast breathing echoed in Hope's ears. The poor girl sounded like she was hyperventilating.

"Why…why did Zane do that?" Samara said, after a few seconds of silence. "Why would he protect us and turn himself in like that? He's going to get punished for our disobedience."

"He did it because he's my friend," Hope replied. "He looks out for me." But, oh, the guilt was like a twisting knife in her belly.

"It's crazy," Samara said. "It makes no sense. He just handed himself over to Nick. He didn't deny the sacrilege or anything. I don't understand why anyone would do that for someone, even a friend."

"I don't know how to explain it to you," Hope said. "That's what friends do for each other sometimes."

"Not anyone I've ever known," Samara said. "You have to be nuts to admit to sacrilege for any reason at all."

"Well, it happened," Hope replied. "Come on. Let's sneak back to the rest of the group. If we hurry, we can join the back of the line and just make up some excuse when we get back to camp. I'll him I was sick to my stomach or something."

"Zane shouldn't have done that," Samara said. "He should not have admitted to sacrilege. You people don't realize what you've done!"

"He's a newcomer," Hope said. "We've only been here a few days. And it's his first offense. Surely they'll give him another chance."

"That's not how it works," Samara said. "You don't understand. We have to get back right away."

Hope disentangled herself from Samara and hurried back down the hall. Despite the dark, she was able to feel her way back into the big room with the stalactites. From there, the sounds of pouring water oriented her, and she turned in the direction that she thought would take them back to camp. She caught a faint sound of footsteps ahead of her and moved toward them, Samara breathing loudly at her back.

94

Jarred heard the angry voice coming from some other room and knew immediately that things had just gone south. He couldn't even make out the words, but the tone said enough. This was some kind of righteous anger, the sharp and unreasonable sound of someone who had been deeply offended. He had been tending to the goats in the long, low room where all of the animals were kept when he first heard it. He left the roped off pens and set the feed back on a high shelf.

As he pushed through the heavy burlap curtain in the doorway, he realized the voice was coming from the central chamber. It sounded like either Alex or Nick, one of the young men, but others were responding now. Anxious, he made his way down the passage. Along the way, he passed Myra Cooper, who was standing in the doorway to their bedroom, leaning heavily against the rocks. She was wheezing, clearly having a bit of trouble breathing.

"Are you okay?" he asked as he approached.

"Don't worry about me," Myra said, waving him off. "Sounds like someone else needs your attention right now."

"Any idea what's going on?"

"Well, he's ranting about sacrilege, so it can't be good," Myra said with a roll of her eyes. "Honestly, these people…" She shook her head and left the sentence hanging.

"I'll check it out," Jarred said. "Myra, you need to take care of yourself. Isn't there something you can do? Your breathing sounds rough."

"Yes, yes." She waved him off. "A CPAP machine would be very helpful right now, but I'll make do. Slow, easy breaths combined with slow, easy work. Just go."

Jarred moved past her and continued around the bend. When he came in sight of the central chamber, he saw Larry and Lana standing just inside the doorway, clearly arguing with someone. Jarred drew closer and spotted a line of Dwellers on the other side of the room. Nick, the darkly bearded school teacher, stood in the center, his arms spread out to either side. His blond brother stood on his left, scowling, and Henny stood on his right, regarding the Bishops with clear contempt.

"You are deliberately *refusing* to understand the gravity of what your son did today," Nick said. "This was a willful, intentional act of sacrilege. He did it knowingly and consciously, and he admitted it with no sense of guilt. This strikes at the very heart of who we are and what we believe! If this doesn't matter then *nothing* matters!"

As he entered the chamber, stepping to one side of Larry and Lana, Jarred spotted their son, Zane. He was behind the line of Dwellers, standing with his head bowed and his hands in his pockets. Off to one side, the rest of the Dweller kids were all clustered together beside one of many dark doorways, looking wide-eyed and fearful.

"There's no way he understood the gravity of what he was doing," Larry said. "You know we've only been here a short while. You know this whole religion and way of life are new to us. We're still learning all the rules. An accidental offense is bound to happen, but eventually, we'll have it all figured out. Can't you cut us some slack?"

"We have explained to you *many* times that the dark passageways are off-limits to people who haven't passed the trial," Nick said. "We have been *very clear* about this from the very first conversation we ever had, and the kids have even less excuse, because they've heard my teaching at school. Your son knew exactly what he was doing! This was no accident. You can't cover for him."

"Give him back to us," Lana said, stepping past her husband. The breakfast table stood between her and the Dwellers, but she looked like she wanted to charge right through it. She had a wild look on her face. "Give us back our son, and we'll leave your cave. You can kick us out into the cold, and so be it! We'll take our chances outside."

"No, your son is going to face punishment," Nick said. "It is vital for the whole community to see justice done. Otherwise, you undermine all I've tried to instill in the children."

Lana rushed at them, trying to come around the table. Henny and Alex immediately stepped in the way, getting into fighting poses. At first, it seemed like Lana was going to keep coming. She clenched her fists and raised them, but then she stumbled to a stop. Larry reached out and snagged her wrist, pulling her back to his side.

"Surely we can work something out," Larry said. "My son is not the type to cause problems. I just can't imagine he would do this on purpose. Someone must've put him up to it. Or he was covering for someone else."

Zane lifted his gaze then and cleared his throat loudly. "Everything Nick said is true, Dad. Stop trying to make excuses for me. I will accept whatever punishment is given to me."

Movement caught Jarred's eye. Two figures eased out of the shadows beyond the narrow doorway and quickly took their places behind the group of Dweller kids. Hope and Samara. Nick couldn't see them from where he stood, and Larry and Lana didn't seem to notice either. However, to Jarred, the situation suddenly became clear. He knew that look on his daughter's face all too well. Larry was right—Zane was covering for someone: Hope. Her guilt was obvious.

"Where are Brigid and Josiah?" Jarred asked. "Surely the leaders of this community need to be involved in any decision about punishment."

"We will be." Brigid's voice arose from behind him, sharp and determined.

Jarred turned just as the old couple entered the room. Brigid was striding with purpose, her fists clenched at her sides. Josiah trotted along behind her, as if struggling to keep up. Jarred was forced to move aside to avoid them.

"Isn't there room for leniency with a first-time infraction," Larry said. "You can still see justice done, just go easy on my son."

"He's only a child," Lana added insistently, tears in her eyes.

"Oh, can we stop all of this pleading and whining and begging?" Brigid said, swiping both hands over her head. She reached the line of Dwellers and turned to face the Bishops, giving them a look of bitter disappointment. "I told you people the rules of this place from the very beginning, and you agreed to abide by them. You know our beliefs, you know our practices, and you know our story. You've eaten our food, enjoyed the safety and security of our home, and your children have been sitting in that classroom day after day. Did you think the rules wouldn't apply to you? Did you think we were kidding?"

"We never said the rules don't apply to us," Larry said. "We just asked for leniency since we've never done anything to offend you before this. I don't think that's an unreasonable request."

"Where's Fiona?" Jarred asked. "Shouldn't she be present for this? She will certainly want to know what's going on."

"Fiona is working elsewhere with Seb," Brigid said. "And moping as she considers her many failures. It doesn't matter if she's here. She has no role to play in this." She clapped her hands and turned to Nick. "Come on. Let's get this over with. Bring the boy."

Nick and Alex turned and grabbed Zane by the arms. Larry and Lana both moved toward them, but the rest of the Dwellers moved in the way.

"You're not going to stop this from happening, not with all the pleading in the world," Josiah said. "Accept it and let's get on with our lives."

"I accept my punishment," Zane said sharply. "Mom, Dad, stop trying to get in the way!"

Nick and Alex promptly bore him away, Brigid and Josiah falling in behind as they entered one of the unused passageways. There was a soft click and light appeared, showing the way. Henny said something to the children and snapped her fingers, and they all fell in line behind her as she followed the others.

That left Larry, Lana, and Jarred standing awkwardly in the central chamber.

"Shouldn't we go and find Fiona?" Lana asked. "She could put a stop to this!"

"I don't think we have time," Larry said. "Come on."

"I'm not sure she *could* stop it," Jarred added, "not without making the situation much worse. Surely, the punishment won't be too severe."

He said it, but he didn't feel it. These people with their strange beliefs and fanaticism seemed capable of almost anything. He hurried after the group, catching up to the kids at the back so he could walk beside Hope. When she realized he was there, she looked up at him with a sad, guilt-ridden expression. She started to say something, but he shook his head and pressed a finger to his lips.

We'll get to the bottom of this later, he thought. *For now, she needs to stay out of it completely.*

They were led down a passageway past various curtained rooms and finally into a large, round chamber with a high roof. In the center of the floor, there was a pit that had clearly been shaped with tools. It was round, with smooth, sheer sides, and some kind of rope and pulley system installed at the edge. The Dwellers, including the children, proceeded to encircle the pit. Larry, Lana, and Jarred moved up as close to the edge as they could get, though no one made room for them.

"What are they going to do?" Hope said from behind Jarred's shoulder.

"Something bad," Samara replied. The skinny Dweller girl stayed by Hope's side. "Very bad."

Jarred leaned over the child in front of him to see down into the pit. It was about twelve feet deep, with a flat and slimy bottom. As Alex shone the flashlight down there, Jarred saw many small moving things writhing like worms or snakes.

"Oh, God, what is it?" Lana said as Larry held her back from the edge.

"Centipedes," Samara answered. "And slime."

Brigid and Josiah mounted a wooden platform behind the big rope pulley system. Alex and Nick pulled Zane up onto the platform behind them.

"The purpose here is not to harm this wayward boy," Brigid said, gazing across the pit at the others gathered around the rim. Her voice echoed in the high-ceilinged room. "This cavern where we dwell is the one means of salvation from the outside world and the wrath of God, which is wreaking havoc on the old civilization of corruption. By placing this young man deeper into the cavern, he will come even closer to the salvation of God. It will exact a price, but if he can survive in the pit for two days, he will be fully cleansed of his sin."

"Two *days*?" Lana whispered, clutching her husband tighter. "Are you people crazy? You can't keep him in here for two days!"

This is sick, Jarred thought. *Should we be allowing this to happen? And where the hell is Fiona?*

"With no food or water?" Jarred said.

"That's right," Brigid replied. "At least, none that will be supplied by us. Whatever else happens to him in the pit will be between him and God."

"This is our way," Nick said. "It is sacred to us. It *must* be like this."

Jarred watched helplessly as Zane was led to the pulley. He grabbed the rope, and then a pivoting arm was swung out over the pit. As he held on tight, Nick turned a handle on a winch and slowly lowered him. The boy seemed remarkably calm considering the circumstances. He made not a single complaint.

"Needless to say, no one is allowed to approach this pit until the punishment is over," Brigid said. "That would be a transgression even worse than what this boy has already committed. Greater transgression, worse punishment."

Once he was at the bottom, Zane let go of the rope and moved to the center of the pit. He stood there calmly, surrounded by writhing shapes and slimy rocks, with his hands in his pockets.

I have to find Fiona, Jarred thought. *She has to know about this. We can't afford to have her isolating herself any longer. Some evil crap is going down, and we need her input.*

The rope was reeled back in, the pulley arm rotated away from the pit. Then, without another word, Brigid and Josiah descended the platform and headed back to the passage. The Dwellers fell in line behind her. Nick made a point to approach the newcomers, pointing at Larry, at Lana, at Jarred.

"Head back now," he said. "The boy is in God's hands, and there's nothing more you can do for him except to make his situation worse. Consider this a test for you, too—a chance to embrace faith and hope during a difficult time."

"A difficult time that wasn't necessary," Lana said. "You didn't have to do this."

"The boy already learned his lesson," Larry said.

"No, the lesson begins now." Nick waved the couple on.

Larry and Lana turned and walked away. It must have taken a monumental effort. Jarred was impressed with their restraint. Indeed, lashing out or causing trouble now wouldn't help Zane. They clearly knew that. He decided to follow their lead, giving his daughter a gentle nudge to get her moving, then following the others out of the room. As the light left, the pit was plunged into darkness, but Zane made not a sound. No whimper, no cry, no pleading.

It was a somber group that arrived back at the central chamber. Even the Dwellers were hushed and grave. Brigid waited until they were all gathered again. Then she turned to address them.

"Don't grieve for the boy, nor fear for him," she said, looking pointedly at Larry and Lana. "This is a test of faith, for he is in God's hands now. Return to your work. Put it out of mind. In two days, he will be back among us, and he will be clean."

People began to scatter. Larry and Lana, still clutching at each other, headed down a passageway where some of the working rooms were located. Most of the children headed back to the classroom. Nick followed the children. Other adults scattered in different direction, but Henny lingered, standing guard in the doorway to Zane's pit. When Jarred turned to leave, intending to go and find Fiona, he realized his daughter was standing behind him.

"I'm not going back to class," she said, tears in her eyes. "I don't care what they want me to do."

Jarred considered making her go anyway. Instead, he hugged her and said, "Okay, I won't make you go. Come with me. Let's talk."

"Dad…"

She clearly didn't like that idea, but he put a hand against her back and guided her to their room. He hoped to find Fiona there, but when he pushed through the curtain, the only occupant was Smoke. The dog was lying near the back of the room, and for some reason, he was quite muddy, as if he'd gone rooting around in places he didn't belong.

When Jarred and Hope entered the room, the dog rose and came padding toward them. Jarred gave him a brief pat on the head, then motioned for his daughter to sit on one of the stools. She was crying now, wringing her heads.

"He was covering for you, wasn't he?" Jarred asked. "You did something bad, and Zane took credit for it."

Hope dropped onto a stool and covered her face with her hands. "Yes, it's true. I'm sorry! It's all my fault he's down in that pit."

"Why? What in the world were you thinking?"

"It's getting harder to put up with these weird people, especially now that I'm going to class," Hope said. "Something is really, really abnormal here, Dad. They've got all of these off-limits places. I saw one of them, a weird hallway in this room where we collect the water, and I just wanted to find out what was in there. I thought maybe it led outside. It was just an impulse, but I didn't ask Zane to cover for me. I never wanted him to do that."

She was crying uncontrollably now. Though he was upset with her, Jarred was more concerned about her well-being, so he went to her. Kneeling down, he put an arm around her shoulders and patted her.

"Well, what did you find in there?" he asked.

"A dead body at the bottom of a deep pit, with no eyes and a gaping mouth."

At this, Jarred's blood ran cold. Of course, he couldn't help thinking about poor Zane down in a pit of his own.

"It was Samara's aunt," Hope continued, rubbing her eyes. "Another one of Brigid's daughters, I guess. She died of a disease, and these weirdos bury their dead by putting them in dark places like that. Samara said they think it moves them closer to God. I guess their deity lives down in the deep places of the cavern."

That, at least, made Jarred feel a tiny bit better about it. A strange burial ritual for the dead, not something more sinister. He breathed a sigh of relief. "She died of disease. Are you sure about that?"

"Yeah, Samara said she was sick for a long time and then died," Hope replied. "The corpse was all discolored, the skin was shriveled, and the eyes had rotted out. It was disgusting. Maybe they put it there so the fresh air would take the stench away. I don't know."

"Okay, okay, I get it," Jarred replied, his stomach doing a little flip-flop. "No need for a graphic description. People's grieving rituals are varied and personal, and sometimes pretty weird, but it doesn't mean there was anything nefarious about it."

"Why do we have to put up with these people?" Hope said. "They dumped Zane in a pit of centipedes because of their weird beliefs, and we're just letting it happen. They make us listen to lectures about nonsense all day long. Why are we going along with this?"

Jarred hugged her tightly. "I know it's frustrating, and I know it's a little bit scary at times, but believe it or not, we're doing the best thing we can do for our own survival. It's not going to last forever. Now that I've passed the trial, I can go where I want in the cave, so we can start making other plans soon."

"What about Zane?" Hope said. "Will he even survive being in that pit for two days with no food or water?"

"He's a tough kid," Jarred replied. "Believe me. He and I survived out in that storm together. We escaped from that bandit camp. I know what that kid's capable of. He'll be okay. And, hey, maybe we'll be able to get him out a little early. Just wait and see."

Hope pulled away from him so she could look at his face, and he brushed her hair back from her eyes.

"We're going to be fine, Hope," he said. "I promise. Try not to think about it. Everything's going to sort itself out soon."

He tried to believe what he was saying. *What the heck are we supposed to do about Zane?* he wondered. *The poor kid is down in that pit right now. What is this crazy world we've fallen into, and how do we get out?*

95

It was a long, unhappy afternoon and evening, and by the time Jarred lay down to sleep, he was mentally exhausted. Unfortunately, it felt like he had only been asleep a few minutes when he was jerked awake by someone grabbing his arm and pulling on it. His brain was far from ready to return to the land of the conscious. He cracked one eye open and vaguely made out the figures looming over him in the candlelight. At first, he thought if he ignored them, they would let him go back to sleep, but they kept shaking him.

Finally, with a groan, he flung his cover back and sat up. He looked left and right and saw the row of sleeping people. Hope, Myra, Fiona, and Smoke were all there. He hadn't seen much of Fiona that day. She'd spent most of her time working and ignoring everyone else. She clearly hadn't been the one shaking him awake. It wasn't something she would have done in her current state, but he was disappointed anyway.

When he looked over his shoulder, he saw Larry and Lana standing there. Jarred started to say something, but they both motioned for him to be quiet. Then Larry beckoned him.

Do they want to walk, or are they planning to do something stupid? he wondered.

Either way, he had to deal with it. Stifling a yawn, he rose. Smoke looked up at him and seemed like he was going to follow. However, when Jarred stepped toward Larry and Lana, the dog laid his head down again. They led him back across the room, and he tried to prepare himself to stop them from enacting some ill-advised rescue plan. However, instead of pushing through the curtain, they went to the far side of the room behind the water barrel and sat down on stools there. A stool had been placed there for Jarred, but he found it better for his murky mind to remain standing.

"I'm sorry about what happened to Zane," he said, speaking just above a whisper. "Tell me you haven't tried to go back down there and visit him."

Larry shook his head, but Lana began to cry. "We thought about it," she said. "They've got someone guarding the door, but she has to sleep eventually, right?"

"So, you're going to try and free your son in the middle of the night?" Jarred said. "Is that what we're doing here now?"

Larry and Lana looked at each other, both crying now, and embraced. "I saw how to operate the pulley system," he said. "I think I could get him out of there, but…" He shook his head.

"No, we're not going to try to rescue him," Lana said, dabbing her eyes on her sleeve. "Maybe we should, but it's just too big of a risk. And who knows what would happen if we got caught? Something worse maybe."

"If Zane doesn't purge his sins, they'll probably hurt him worse," Larry said. "As much as it pains us, we decided it's best to leave him down there for now while we try to figure out what to do."

Jarred scrubbed his face with his hands, trying to wake himself up completely. "Okay, so no rescue. Then what are we doing here that's more important than sleep? What are we here to discuss?"

Larry and Lana looked at each other, as if in some silent debate about which of them would say it.

"We don't want to stay here with the Dwellers anymore," Lana finally said.

"We can't live with people who use child abuse as punishment," Larry added. "Especially when it's for an imagined slight, for a sin that's not real. Zane didn't blaspheme. Looking down a cave passage doesn't offend God. It doesn't hurt anyone or do anything. It's a made-up rule with an over-the-top punishment."

"You don't have to convince me," Jarred said. Finally, his sleepy legs wobbled, and he sat down. "It's a ridiculous situation, but we've stayed here because these people have plenty of food, they've created a livable space, and we have access to clean water. It's a trade-off, and leaving will put us in a worse situation, even with their weird belief system, even if being here takes a toll on our mental health."

"We'd rather take our chances elsewhere," Lana said. "Especially if that means we won't have to endure people torturing our son. We have to leave."

"We intend to leave as soon as its feasible," Larry added. "We can't pretend to go along with this anymore."

Even in his sleep-addled state, Jarred felt a sinking in the pit of his stomach. They were right to feel this way, of course. Still, it wasn't as easy as packing up and saying goodbye. "I wonder how Brigid and the others will react when we tell them we're leaving," he said. "They might not be open to it. They might refuse to give us our guns, animals, and supplies."

"I don't care how they react," Larry said. "We're still going to leave. If that means we have to fight our way free of the Dwellers, then so be it. We'll fight them tooth and nail."

"Except I'm not sure we would win," Jarred said. "We surrendered our guns, remember? We'd have to sneak into the storage room behind the kitchen to retrieve them, and that would signal trouble."

To this, Larry and Lana had no response. They looked at each other. Suddenly, someone cleared her throat. Startled, Jarred whipped around and saw Myra Cooper standing beside the water barrel.

"People keep sneaking up on me tonight," Jarred grumbled. "How long have you been there, Myra?"

"Long enough," she replied. Then she began coughing. They were deep and throaty coughs, full of phlegm. Finally, she turned and spat. "I'm not getting any better," she said, "as you can hear. It's all of this moist air. I didn't have the healthiest lungs anyway."

"What can we do to help you, Myra?" Jarred asked. "Should we ask for some medicine?"

She waved off his suggestion. Myra definitely looked unwell. Her white hair was wilted in the moist cave, which revealed just how thin it was. Her scalp showed in many spots. She was hunched, too thin, with a sallow complexion.

"I just want to know how we plan to get Zane free," she said. "If I had been there when they dragged him into the pit, there would have been a fight. I don't care if they put me in the pit with him, I never would have gone along with it, I swear to God."

"Well, then, it's good you weren't there," Jarred said, "because that wouldn't have made the situation any better."

We're going to free the boy," Myra said. "Of course we are. It's the only reasonable course of action, and we're still reasonable people, aren't we?" She gave Jarred a bold look, as if daring him to argue with her. "Well, aren't we?"

Lana rose then and approached her. She hugged Myra fiercely. Jarred could see things were getting out of hand fast. Technically, Fiona was still the leader of this group, as far as he was concerned, even if she'd been distant lately. She needed to be part of this conversation, especially if people were making plans.

They came to me instead of her, he thought. *When did our team dynamic change? Is it because I passed the trial?*

He didn't know, but he didn't like it. Jarred had no intention of usurping Fiona's place. Even if she asked him to assume leadership of the group, he was sure he would turn it down.

The pendulum has swung in the wrong direction, he thought, *but I'm not sure I can push it back the other way.*

"Larry and Lana already told me they think it's better to let Zane serve out his punishment," Jarred said to Myra. "I think it's the right decision, so I support them."

Myra broke out of Lana's embrace and studied her face for a moment. "Is that true? That's what you told him?"

"We did," Lana replied, hanging her head, "but as soon as he's out of that pit, we're leaving the Dwellers."

"You said the pit was full of centipedes," Myra said. "Do you realize many species of centipedes are poisonous?"

"How deadly is the venom?" Lana asked.

"They looked like large forest centipedes to me," Myra said, "which means they were brought down into the cave by the Dwellers. They can bite, but I'd say it's no worse than a bee sting. Still, a bite like that can get infected. I'd hate for Zane to get a case of cellulitis while he's stuck in a slimy pit."

Larry and Lana traded a look. Finally, Larry said, "I'm afraid it's a risk we have to take. For now. He'll have to stomp the bugs and keep them away. There's no other choice. If we try to break him out early, there's liable to be a real fight, and someone could get killed. We don't want that to happen. But we are determined to leave this place—and these people—the second his punishment is over."

At this, Myra's expression softened. "Well, that's good to hear, at least."

"Listen," Jarred said. "While we're waiting for Zane's time in the pit to be over, I'm going to try to think of some way to break free of the Dwellers and go our own way without provoking a fight."

Lana gasped and came to his side. "Really? Then you agree with us that we need to leave this place? You'll help us leave?"

"Yeah, it seems like most of our group doesn't want to be here anymore," Jarred said with a sigh. "I don't know how Fiona feels about it, so I'd better talk to her about it before we make any move. We'll try to find a safe way to break free of the Dwellers and go our own way, but just wait a little longer, folks. Hang in there!"

Larry and Lana seemed comforted by his words and nodded at him.

"Okay, I think for now we should…"

He trailed off as he heard footsteps in the room, muffled voices, strange breathing. He couldn't see most of the room because he was sitting behind the big water barrel. He grabbed the top edge of the barrel and rose, as Myra turned around. Behind him, Larry and Lana rose as well.

He saw figures standing near the curtained doorway. At first, just a tangle of bodies, and his sleepy mind couldn't quite make sense of it. Then he stepped past the barrel and realized who it was. Alex, Brigid's blond, well-muscled adult child, was standing there, and he was clutching a smaller, hunched figure by her arm.

Hope. When she lifted her gaze, he could tell she'd been crying. Even in the low light, she had a red, blotchy face.

"What are you doing with my daughter?" Jarred asked Alex. "Let her go."

Hope was clutching something in her hands, pressing it up against her belly, as if to protect it. Jarred glanced toward the sleeping bags. They were all empty, even Smoke was missing. Where was Fiona? Where was Smoke? What the hell was going on here?

"I just caught your daughter trying to sneak into the punishment room," Alex said. "She didn't deny it!"

"I was just trying to bring Zane a sweater, so he wouldn't get cold," Hope said. She held up her hands to reveal the big brown sweater in her hands. It belonged to Zane, one of the extra pieces of clothing he'd packed for the trip.

Jarred smacked his forehead. Was Hope trying to get everyone tossed into pits? She wasn't doing anyone any favors by constantly getting in trouble. "When did you manage to sneak away?" Jarred said.

"While you were talking behind the barrel," she replied. "I was only going to give him this sweater, I promise. Brigid didn't say we couldn't."

By the tight look on Alex's face, Jarred could see that they were very close to an escalation. Somehow, he had to defuse this situation. He approached and snagged the sweater from Hope's hands. When she tried to hold on, he yanked more insistently. She finally let go with a gasp, no doubt surprised by her father's ferocity. He was usually so gentle with her.

"Hope is still young," Jarred said to Alex. "She means well, but I think she needs to be corrected. Let me handle it. I will punish her. You can go back to your post."

Alex stared at him flatly for a second, then nodded. "Okay, fine," he said. "She didn't actually get into the punishment room. I stopped her just as she stepped into the doorway. I guess that's not as bad. As long as you can promise me you'll punish her with appropriate severity, I won't rouse Brigid. It'll make it easier on all of us."

"Trust me," Jarred said with a snarl. He reached out and snagged Hope by the wrist, pulling her free from Alex's grasp. "She's in big trouble. I don't care if she meant well or not, I'm tired of the rules being broken around here." Hope looked at him with big eyes as he drew her close.

"But…Dad…" she said.

"Shut up," he snapped. "Not a word from you until I say you can talk."

Alex nodded. "Okay, good. That'll do."

He turned and walked out of the room, flinging the curtain out of his way as if it annoyed him. Jarred waited a moment, listening to the sound of his retreating footsteps. Once it was quiet again, he softened his grip on Hope.

"What are you going to do?" she asked. "How am I going to be punished?"

Jarred was aware of Myra, Lana, and Larry standing beside him. "I'm *not* going to punish you. That was just for show. Come on. You're going back to bed." He turned her around and guided her back toward the sleeping bags. "For God's sake, Hope, what were you thinking? It's bad enough that you got Zane in trouble, but now you're trying to make it worse."

"I had a bad dream about Zane," she said. "He was shivering down there in the cold, so when I woke up, I just had to help. You were over there talking to Larry, so I went for it. I thought if I hurried, it wouldn't cause any problems. How could I know they'd watch the door all night long? Dwellers have to sleep too, don't they?"

"I'm sure they're taking turns," he replied. "Hope, I need you to listen to me. Zane is very strong. He has been through worse than this. I know this for a fact, okay? He's going to be just fine. In the meantime, I really need you to be on your best behavior, or more of us are going to wind up in those pits. Got it?"

Hope sighed. "Yes, I got it."

"Good." He walked her to her sleeping bag and gestured for her to lie down. "Ignore the bad dreams. Sleep. Zane's two days will be over before you know it."

Hope took the sweater from him, folded it up, and set it on the cave floor beside her sleeping bag. Then she lay down on her bed, clasping her hands on her belly. "I just want to get out of here. Can we get out of here?"

"The adults in our group are trying to figure that out," he replied. "We intend to leave in a way that won't cause hostility because we don't need more enemies. But we're working on it. In the meantime, please trust me and behave."

"I will," she said.

When he turned, he found Larry, Lana, and Myra approaching slowly. Clearly, they had kept their distance, and for that, he was grateful. He looked down the line of sleeping bags. Where the heck were Fiona and Smoke?

This is ridiculous. I have to pull her out of her sadness, he thought. *We really need her to be present now. The disappearing act has to end.*

96

The bag of wood ash turned out to be a perfect excuse for getting away anytime she wanted to work in the alcove. On this particular evening, she ran into Alex, who was coming down the passageway as if he were a security guard making the rounds. And, indeed, that's essentially what it was.

"Why are you out of your bed this late?" Alex asked.

He had a small brass lantern in his right hand, and he held it up as he stepped in her way.

"Just headed for the latrine," she replied. "I've had an upset stomach for the past couple of days, and I don't want to use the bucket in our room…for obvious reasons." She showed him the bag. "Don't worry. I'll sprinkle ash around the latrine. Henny showed me the trick."

Alex grimaced, clearly disgusted by this particular topic. "Well, that's fine, then," he said. "Just don't wander."

"Of course," she replied. "I know the rules, and I abide by them."

This seemed to please him, and he gave her a brief smile. "Very good, then. Do…do what you have to do." He left it at that and stepped past her, moving down the passage in the direction of the central chamber.

Fiona waited until he was around the bend before she got moving again. It was a big risk. She knew that. If one of the Dwellers decided to check the latrine and didn't find her there, it would be the end of her little project. More than that, it would cause a lot more tension with Brigid and her crew, especially given what just happened to Zane, but if anything, that made it even more imperative that she get the work done.

Hopefully, Jarred and the others haven't been too bothered by my absence and distraction, she thought. *It'll be better for them, in the end. I hope they can see that. I hope someday they will understand.*

She kept going past the workrooms, past the latrine, and out of the final faint light in the passageway. She had just entered the darkness when she heard a familiar sound from behind her. It seemed that no matter how quietly she snuck away, Smoke always sensed her absence eventually and came after her. Fiona clicked on her flashlight in time to see her loyal dog run up beside her.

"Well, I guess there's no getting away from you, is there?" she said. "All right, you're my oldest friend anyway. How could I possibly turn you away?"

He looked up at her, panting contentedly. The flashlight now had a bit of cloth affixed over the lens with some thread that Fiona had nicked from the supplies. It gave just enough light to reveal the passage ahead, and she followed the now familiar path to her secret alcove, denying every arrow she passed. After a few trips, Smoke had grown used to the bats. He no longer chased them.

That made it a quiet walk, and since she didn't have to worry about the noise or a running dog, Fiona found herself sinking into troubled thoughts. Now she had something new to wrestle with, something other than her failed leadership, and that was Brigid's unexplained devotion to Jarred. Why had she been so confident about him passing the first trial? What was the motivation behind it? It seemed the old woman didn't particularly want Fiona to pass.

Does she think Jarred will be easier to control? Less trouble? Or does she just like him because he's handsome?

Fiona's only real source of peace now was chipping away at the exit and daydreaming about her own departure. She could tell Larry and Lana were more upset than they let on. Even so, her group would be reluctant to leave a place that had a seemingly unlimited supply of food and fresh water, even with the recent development. Despite the local religious mumbo jumbo, they were safer here. That was undeniable.

Maybe they don't need me. Maybe it's better if I let them stay and head off alone. Zane will be fine. He gets out of the pit tomorrow. He'll come out chastened, upset, and tired, but then there will still be plenty of food for every meal, a roof over their heads, and a safe place to sleep.

She wanted to believe it. She almost did. Fortunately, she reached the alcove then, so she didn't have to think about it long. The narrow crack in the rock wall had been expanded a bit. Instead of two inches wide, it was now about four inches wide. Fiona's progress had been hampered by her lack of a hammer. The Dwellers had plenty of tools in storage, but she hadn't managed to snag a large tool.

Instead, she'd been forced to use the blade of her pocketknife, scraping and scraping for hours on end. She had dulled and chipped the blade almost to a nub, but she still had a long way to go until the exit was wide enough for a person to pass through.

She set the flashlight on a familiar notch in the wall, took her position in front of the exit, and resumed her work. In the last few days, she had banged her knuckles dozens of times until they were all bruised and covered in scabs. She hoped no one had taken notice. She'd also practically rubbed through her gloves and had a nice red mark on the side of her hand. Still, she went to work and tried her best to ignore the pain.

Work consisted of scraping the dull blade up and down along the edge of the rocks. As she did that, Smoke usually sat quietly near her feet. Occasionally, he rose and lapped water from a puddle or found some place to pee.

After an hour of work, Fiona paused to give her hands a rest. She had torn off a scab on her knuckle, and she removed her glove to check on it. A bright bead of blood welled up on the knuckle of her middle finger. She sat on a large rock and tended to the wound, dabbing it with a scrap of cloth from her pocket and rinsing it with some water dripping from the ceiling.

"I don't know what I'll scrape through first," she said to Smoke, who was watching her intently from his spot nearby. "That wall or my right hand. But I don't have much choice. Brigid will never tell me what I want to know unless I pass the trial, and she won't let me attempt the trial again. Keeps saying I'm not ready." Fiona sighed and pulled her glove back on. "Maybe she's right. I came very close to killing myself the last time I attempted the climb. Next time, I might succeed."

As if he sensed her despair, Smoke rose and set his chin on her leg. She petted him, gently stroking the top of his head and scratching behind his ear.

"They'll notice I'm gone," she said. "Sooner or later, someone will notice. Jarred will wake up in the middle of the night and see the empty sleeping bag, and he'll come looking for me. I have to get this done before I'm forced to stop."

She sighed and stood up, gently moving Smoke out of the way. Another hour of work seemed safe. No more than that. She couldn't spend all night out of the sleeping chamber. But one more hour shouldn't be a problem. Flicking open the pocketknife, she approached the wall and went back to work, scraping the dull edge against the rocks, as sparks and tiny bits of rocks flew off.

And then what? she asked herself. *When you finally widen it enough that you can get through, assuming you really do find an exit on the other side, then what? Are you just going to leave? No warning, no goodbye?*

She wasn't sure. She was comforted by the idea of having a way out of the cave, but when it became a reality, what would she do next?

You don't have to answer that right now, she told herself.

Up and down, up and down she dragged the dull blade against the rocks, occasionally slipping and smashing her hand against a hard edge. The cold air on her face felt nice, the crisp smell of outside air. The irony of this didn't escape her. Most of her experiences out there in the snowfall had been brutal.

Just keep working, she told herself.

It was an obsession, and she had enough self-awareness to realize this. Fiona had never been one for deep self-reflection, but she couldn't avoid it this time. Still, realizing it didn't stop her, even as she continued grinding away with her bloody knuckles.

When she took another short break, she heard Smoke making a strange sound in the back of his throat. It was the very front edge of a growl, as if he were just starting to get worked up. She picked up the flashlight and turned it toward the dog. He rose and turned toward the curved passageway behind her. Fiona flipped her pocketknife shut and shoved it in her pocket, lowering the flashlight. Hackles raised, Smoke advanced slowly down the hall with a full-throated growl.

Fiona was tired and hurting, so she felt more angry than scared at the thought of someone or something approaching. She reached down and grabbed Smoke's collar so he wouldn't rush ahead, then crept toward the corner. She couldn't hear anyone or anything. The bats were quiet and still, the narrow passage dampening all sound, even her own breathing. She felt the cold air at her back as she stepped around the corner.

She saw only the narrow dark passage winding off before her, but for some reason, Smoke stopped growling suddenly and began panting. It was something he did when he realized the person he was growling at was someone he knew.

"Who's there?" Fiona asked, shining the flashlight down the passage. "The dog already gave you away, so you might as well show yourself."

Slowly, a figure stepped into the light. A young woman in a simple brown shirt and pants with black hair hanging down in many long braids, framing a long, lean face. She had a bow in her hands, an arrow nocked to the drawstring.

"I can explain this," Fiona said. But could she? What excuse could she possibly give for her presence in the forbidden corridors.

"Don't bother," Henny replied. "I heard you scraping away at the rocks. It's pretty damn clear what you were doing." She shook her head and gave Fiona a look of withering contempt. "I knew it was a mistake to bring you people into our community—*you* most of all. We've all had a bad feeling about you in particular from the moment you first walked into our home and interrupted dinner. What you've done here is a grave sin, worse than what that boy did by far, and you will face punishment for it, by God."

Fiona was caught, and she knew it. Unless she was willing and able to violently attack Henny right here and now, she was not getting out of this. She briefly considered it, if only out of desperation. Could she somehow get her hands around this girl's throat before the girl could fire an arrow at her? Doubtful. Henny was in very good shape, and she held the compound bow with confidence.

Even if I could, attacking Henny might make things a whole hell of a lot worse for the rest of the group, she realized. *I can't do that. I've put them in enough danger.*

"All right, fine," she said. Smoke was calm now, just standing at her side. For his sake, Fiona was glad he didn't sense the tension. "You caught me. There's no excuse for what I've done here. I'll go back to the camp peacefully and confess my sin."

"A very wise decision," Henny said. "Brigid will decide your fate."

97

Jarred had just washed his face and hands, changed his socks and shirt, and was headed for the curtained doorway. Today was the day that Zane would get released from the pit, and he was ready for this horrible event to be over. Larry and Lana had already gone to breakfast. Hope and Myra were still washing up, but Jarred decided to go ahead.

"I'll be right there," Hope said, cupping clean water in her hands. "I can't wait to see Zane again. I hope he's okay. Do you think they'll feed him right away?"

"I'm sure there will be food *and* water," Jarred replied. "If he comes through this unscathed, maybe they'll think he found favor with their little cave deity."

"They better," Hope said. And then she splashed the water vigorously on her face.

Jarred was standing in the doorway now, the curtain hanging over his right shoulder, when he heard two sets of footsteps coming from beyond the workrooms. People returning from the latrines, perhaps? Or maybe Brigid and Josiah had found some reason to wander the forbidden paths.

Maybe Fiona attempted the trial again, he thought. *If so, I hope she passed this time. She really needs the encouragement.*

As he considered this possibility, Fiona appeared, walking with Smoke at her side. She did not look victorious. If anything, she seemed troubled, scowling at the ground in front of her. So perhaps she'd failed the trial again. Jarred was about to say something, to offer some words of comfort or encouragement, when she noticed him and gave him an anxious look and shook her head. He read it loud and clear: *This isn't what it appears to be.*

A moment later, Henny appeared, the scowliest of the Dwellers, following Fiona closely. Jarred hadn't traded more than maybe a dozen words with this particular Dweller since they'd first met. She had her bow in her hands, an arrow nocked but held loosely.

"What's going on here?" Jarred asked. "Where have you come from? Did Fiona attempt the trial again?"

His questions were ignored. As Fiona passed him, he reached out and briefly touched her shoulder, but she kept going in the direction of the central chamber.

"Stay out of this," Henny told him, motioning him back into the room with a nod. "We have another heathen in our midst who doesn't give the slightest damn about our beliefs or rules. Brigid is going to deal with this one."

"Fiona, what happened?" he asked. "What did you do?"

But she kept marching down the passageway, and Henny followed close at her heels. Jarred turned back into the room to check on Hope. She was sitting on a stool, pulling on a clean pair of socks. Myra was hunkered over the water bucket.

"Dad, did Fiona get in trouble?" Hope asked. "Is she going into the pit like Zane?"

"Looks like it," he replied. "I'd better get down there and see if I can help. You might want to wait here in case things go bad."

"No, I'm coming," Hope said, reaching for her boots. "I'll meet you there."

Jarred nodded and left the room, hurrying after Henny. When he reached the central chamber, he found Fiona sitting at a table, Henny standing behind her. Larry and Lana were sitting at a separate table, a breakfast of eggs and oatmeal before them. Brigid and Josiah were just coming in from the kitchen, carrying plates of their own, and Alex and Nick were standing in the doorway to the punishment room.

"What's the meaning of this?" Brigid said sharply, approaching Fiona's table.

Henny waited a second, as if she expected Fiona to confess her crimes. When she didn't, the young Dweller cleared her throat and spoke. "I caught this woman walking in the tunnels alone. Not just *walking* but actually scraping at the rocks, like she was trying to create her own exit. She admitted it. She denied nothing."

Jarred's heart sank. Trying to create her own exit! Is that what Fiona had been up to at night? It was far worse than he'd feared.

"She never even passed the trials," Henny added, practically shouting it, as if everyone needed the reminder. "She tried twice and failed both times. She almost lost an arm the second time! Look at the bloody bandage. And now she thinks she can do whatever she wants to the sacred places."

Brigid dumped her breakfast plate on the table so roughly that she lost about half of her eggs. Josiah set his down beside hers and sloshed some too-wet oatmeal onto the tabletop. As they scowled down at Fiona, Jarred made his way around the edge of the room, trying to get eye contact with Fiona. But Fiona wouldn't look at him. She wouldn't look at anyone. Her gaze was locked on her own hands, which were folded on the tabletop before her.

This is bad, Jarred thought. *Really bad. Worse than Zane.*

For a few seconds, a quiet and terrible tension filled the air. Josiah and Brigid stood across from Fiona, staring across the wasteland of their breakfast at her. Henny loomed over her shoulder, the bow still in her hands. Larry and Lana sat with their heads bowed, as if cowering. Only Smoke seemed undisturbed, sitting calmly beside Fiona's chair, his head resting on his paws. Jarred could see the truth of the accusation. Fiona was wearing her long coat and heavy winter pants, as if she'd been on her way outside. Clearly, she hadn't just been carving an exit, she'd been planning to leave.

What in the heck was she thinking? Was she going to leave on her own?

Were you going to abandon the rest of us? Even me?

That turned a sinking feeling into a bitter sadness. He just didn't understand. Had he done something to push her away?

"I don't have to tell you that you've committed a terrible sin," Brigid said, in a soft but dangerous voice. A quiet Brigid sounded more dangerous than a shouting Brigid. "One of the worst sins. You know full well what you've done, which means you understand the consequences."

"You were right about her, Brigid," Josiah said. "You said she was an unsavory character, not to be trusted."

"Yes, I recognized her as the weak link from the second I met her," Brigid said. "God showed favor to Jarred and not to her, as I knew he would. An aimless, ill-tempered girl without discipline or humility. Against my better judgment, I put up with her, and now I've paid a price for it. Who knows what damage she's done to our sacred places?"

Fiona's lips were pressed tightly together, her half-lidded eyes unmoving. Clearly, she was struggling not to say what she wanted to say.

Lana sat up suddenly, setting her spoon down. "What…what are you going to do to her?"

"She's to be punished, of course," Brigid replied. "If we let this crime go unanswered, our community might never recover."

"A punishment like Zane's?" Larry asked.

Brigid pursed her lips and said, "Worse, I think."

Jarred wanted to say something to Fiona. He wanted to yell at her, plead with her, shake her, but he couldn't bring himself to do it. He was hurt and angry at her. Still, he couldn't just toss her to the wolves. He stepped forward, drawing Brigid's attention.

"Pardon me, ma'am," he said. Politeness seemed important right now. Politeness and respect for these weirdos. "Could I speak to you for a moment?"

"Go right ahead," Brigid said.

"No, I mean, privately," Jarred said. At this, he got the briefest glance from Fiona. For a second, he thought he saw a glimmer of sadness in her eyes, but it quickly passed.

"Jarred, if you're going to try to talk me out of punishing her, forget it," Brigid said sharply, swiping a hand in his direction. "Not even you, crowned with favor though you might be, can ignore the magnitude of what this girl has done."

"No, of course not," he said. "You know I respect our ways here. Would God have shown me favor if I didn't? I just want to discuss the situation with you privately before you make a public pronouncement."

Brigid regarded him for a second, then finally blew her breath out and made a little spinning gesture over her head, "Oh, very well." She pointed at Henny. "Take Fiona down to the cage. Alex, go with her. The rest of you stay here."

Jarred had no idea what she meant by "the cage." He had seen no cages in any of the rooms. It was probably something horrible, and he had to do what he could to save her. Alex and Henny hoisted Fiona to her feet and led her back toward the main passageway. In the process, Henny grabbed her bandaged arm, and she let out a gasp of pain. At that moment, Hope and Myra arrived, but they were forced to step aside as the Dwellers bore their prisoner toward the doorway.

"Jarred, follow me," Brigid said, stepping past Jarred into the passageway that led down to the classroom.

He motioned for Hope to stay put then hurried after the old woman. She strode all the way to the classroom, walked to the center of the room, then turned to face him. As soon as he passed through the door into the room, she held up both hands.

"That's close enough," she said. "Speak, favored one."

Unfortunately, he didn't know what he was going to say. This had all happened so suddenly. He certainly hadn't had time to plan a speech.

Sympathy. Create sympathy, he thought. *That's Fiona's only hope.*

"I'm not trying to get her out of punishment," Jarred said. "I know there has to be an appropriate response to this level of disobedience. I just want to help you understand Fiona a little bit so you can make the wisest and most appropriate decision about what to do with her."

"I think I understand her well enough already," Brigid said. "She was the leader of your group, so she's used to getting her way. The rules here are not her rules, so she chafes under them. I have seen her becoming more isolated over the weeks, especially after she failed the trial twice. I assumed she would eventually act out, and she has not disappointed me. What more do I need to understand about her?"

"Fiona never wanted to be the leader of our group," Jarred replied. "Leadership was thrust upon her by circumstances and the neediness of other people. Will you at least allow me to share her story? It will help you come up with the most suitable punishment."

Brigid rolled her eyes but flicked a finger at him. "I'm here. I'm listening. Speak."

Why are you pleading for leniency when Fiona was going to abandon you? Yes, some angrier part of him resisted this effort. The betrayal hurt. But he pressed on. She needed his help now.

"When I first met Fiona, she was living alone on a homestead miles outside the nearest town," he said. "She lived alone by choice. Just her, the animals, a garden, and that's the way she liked it. She had deep emotional scars from an abusive marriage, and she didn't trust people anymore. But I was injured, I'd broken my leg, and my daughter came to her front door seeking help. Fiona helped me. She pulled me out of the snow and brought me into her home. Hope and I were a huge inconvenience to her lifestyle, a drain on her resources, but she made a splint for my leg, gave me medicine, gave us food, and a place to sleep, and she never complained. She never once complained!"

"That's all very admirable," Brigid said. Had her expression softened just a little? Maybe. He couldn't tell. "What does any of that have to do with her transgression?"

"I just want you to know what kind of person she is," Jarred continued. "All she ever wanted was space, peace, and quiet so she could heal from her past. She feels anxious around people. After years of manipulation and cruelty from her ex, she still gets anxious when she's trapped, enclosed, unable to move about on her own. Yet after she brought me and my daughter into her home, she also brought the others: Larry, Lana, Zane, Myra, and another man who died in the cold. She did this willingly, even though it was a terrible hardship for her. The anxiety, the stress, must have been agony, but she showed kindness to us every day."

Brigid held up a hand. "Okay, Jarred, I see what you're trying to do."

"I can't imagine how hard it is for her in this cavern," Jarred continued. "I can't imagine how trapped she feels, how it must crawl all over her skin. She craves wide-open spaces. She doesn't speak much about the trauma of her past, but I've seen the pain in her eyes. When you have deeply rooted trauma like that, sometimes you react without thinking clearly."

Why had Fiona wanted to pass the trial so badly? Why had she insisted that *she* had to pass it? Because she'd been planning to leave the group. To get away from them. From him. *Why? What did I do wrong?*

"Jarred, I can tell that you are sincere," Brigid said, giving him a sad little smile. "I can tell that you care very much for this person. Yes, she has done some noble things. I do not deny that. But if you're pleading for leniency, then you're wasting your time. It's not up to me. These are God's laws. Do you understand? Fiona didn't break *my* rule. She didn't offend *me*. She broke the immutable law of the god who dwells in the deep places, and she must face punishment for it. If I fail to carry out just punishment, then I will be a transgressor as well, not worthy to lead these people."

She approached him then, and he inadvertently tensed up. However, she simply laid a hand on his shoulder.

"Instead of fretting over her punishment," Brigid said, "concentrate on the fact that Zane's punishment has been met. As soon as we get back to the group, I will send Nick to retrieve the boy from his pit, so he can be reunited with his parents. Won't that be a happy reunion? Think on good things like that. As for Fiona, what will be, will be, as is God's will."

98

Fiona found herself swinging like a pendulum between two extremes. One the one end, she wanted desperately to get out of this situation by any means at her disposal, and she ran through unlikely scenarios in her head. On the end other, she felt only the hopeless and seemingly inevitable ruin, and she accepted it. Some part of her had known and expected that things would end badly for her once she left her homestead, and now that it was upon her, that part was resigned to her fate.

Seb had joined them from the laundry room, and she now led the way with a bright lantern. Fiona walked directly behind her, with Henny at one shoulder and Alex at the other. They were heading back down the passageway past the workrooms, as if they intended to return Fiona to the place of her crime. However, once they passed the latrine, the Dwellers came to a stop, and Henny reached around Fiona's face to tie a blindfold around her eyes.

"Is this really necessary?" Fiona asked.

"Yes," Henny replied, pulling the blindfold knot just a little tighter than it needed to be. "Stop talking. You'll only make things worse for yourself."

Henny gave her a little push to get her moving again. This time, as she walked forward, they held fast to her shoulders. She could just barely make out the lantern light seeping through the rough cloth of her blindfold, but she couldn't tell where they were going. They walked for a few minutes, then she was pulled to a stop.

"We're here," Seb said. She had such a gentle voice compared to the other Dwellers.

Henny removed the blindfold, and Seb stepped to one side, raising her lantern to illuminate the chamber. Before them, a great wall of what appeared to be massive stone teeth rose up. They were red and wet, pointed like the fangs of predators, and the lantern light cast long shadows up to the ceiling. It took Fiona a second to realize she was seeing a row of enormous stalactites and stalagmites that grew together, leaving only narrow gaps in between.

"What is this place?" she asked.

"This is your cage," Henny replied, pushing her shoulder. "Squeeze through."

Fiona stepped past Seb and approached the wall. Most of the gaps were no more than a few inches wide, but a couple of places were closer to a foot or a foot and a half. She chose the widest of these, knowing it was still going to be a tight fit. Removing her thick winter coat, she tossed it onto the floor behind her.

"Take care of that for me," she said.

"Don't worry about your coat," Alex said. "There's never a need for a coat that thick and padded down here in God's cavern."

Turning sideways, Fiona squeezed herself into the gap. The rocks scraped against her, and she felt some hard edge digging into her back. The irony of this didn't escape her. She had spent multiple nights trying to widen a crack so she could squeeze through and get out of the cavern, and now she was squeezing through a comparable gap into a prison cell.

She popped out of other end of the gap, falling to her knees on a smooth surface. The space beyond the stalactite wall was small, with a flat wall on the other side. There was a small metal bucket at one end, but no stool for sitting and nothing to lie down on. She turned and put her back against the wall. Her view of the room beyond the crude cage was severely limited, but she saw Henny standing on the other side, still as a statue, with a bow in her hand and an arrow against the string. Seb's shadow was visible on the floor as well.

This cage can't actually hold me, Fiona thought. *I got in. I can just as easily get out. All I need is for these people to use the restroom or something.*

That desire to escape—not just this crude cage but the cave—had become an unshakable compulsion she didn't even fully understand. It was joined now, however, by a feeling of guilt, and perhaps a little embarrassment. Jarred now knew what she'd been planning. Would he hate her for it? Would he understand?

He will be upset, she thought. *And he will be hurt.*

Of course, Jarred would see it as an attempt on her part to abandon him, a kind of rejection. It had nothing to do with that. If she was rejecting anything, Fiona was rejecting herself. She was rejecting herself as leader and leaving the group in better hands. But Jarred wouldn't see that. Even if he realized it, she doubted he would admit it to himself.

If I'd only worked just a little longer, she thought. *An extra hour here and there. I'd be outside by now, setting off with Smoke at my side. Brigid loves Jarred. She speaks of him so highly. He's practically a son to her. Given time, he might be running this place, and then he could change the rules and make it a more reasonable place to live.*

And he wouldn't see any of that either. She knew him too well. She'd hurt him deeply, and for that, she felt guilty and restless. However, her cage didn't give her enough room to do much more than fidget, take a step to her left, a couple steps to her right.

After what felt like a couple of hours, but could have been much longer—almost a full day, even—she heard boots in the corridor beyond the door. Maybe her time in the cage had been her punishment, and they'd come now to set her free. She wanted to believe it, but it seemed unlikely.

Henny stepped to one side, the lantern light shifted, and then Brigid appeared. Fiona half-expected Jarred to enter with her, to plead for Fiona's life, but Brigid was alone. Fiona didn't deserve it, of course. She didn't deserve to have him pleading for her. Still, when he didn't appear, she felt a sinking feeling.

I'm in worse trouble than I thought.

Brigid approached the stalactite wall, positioning herself so she could gaze at Fiona through one of the larger gaps. The old woman had a steely look on her face, a furious glint in her eyes.

"You have no idea what you've done," she said, hands on her hips.

"I went into a forbidden part of the cave and caused a minor bit of damage to a wall," Fiona said.

Brigid shook her head. "No, that doesn't even *begin* to touch it. You broke the greatest and most serious law that we have in our Dwelling. Carving the walls with unclean hands! You blasphemed in a way that cannot be forgiven."

"And what does that mean?" Fiona asked.

"It means you must face God's Wrath," Brigid said.

Beyond her shoulder, Henny was still standing near the far wall, the big compound bow in her hands. She had a smug smile on her face. It infuriated Fiona, even as she felt rising dread.

"Face God's wrath," Fiona echoed. "Does that mean an execution? I suppose I should have known. Religious fanatics and cultists all end up spilling blood eventually, don't they?"

Brigid gave her a contemptuous look. "We don't execute people here, and a cheap, easy insult isn't going to improve your situation. We leave things to the will of God. God's Wrath is a tunnel in the cavern, and there we will see how he feels about your blasphemy."

Not an execution. Fiona dared to hope. Better not to antagonize her captors. "Okay, sorry about the insult. Is this going to be like another trial?"

Brigid paused, tipping her head back so she was looking down her nose at Fiona. "Everything in life is a trial in God's eyes." Then she turned to someone just out of sight—Fiona assumed it was Alex. "Blindfold her and escort her to God's Wrath."

Fiona was tempted to argue about the blindfold, but she decided to let it go. When Brigid beckoned her out of the cage, she also considered refusing to leave, but she figured that would only make things worse.

"Where's my dog?" she asked.

"I believe he's with Hope," Brigid said. "It's irrelevant. We don't blame the dog for your sins. He will continue to be well cared for. Quit stalling, sinner. Come out of there and face your inevitability."

Fiona sighed and pushed herself through the largest gap again, squeezing between the stalactites and stalagmites, feeling unyielding rock scraping against her front and back. As soon as she popped out the other side, Alex walked up to her and grabbed her good arm. Then Seb approached, holding the lantern close to her face, as Henny pulled the blindfold around her eyes again.

"Seb, lead the way," Brigid said. "Get this done, so we can move past this terrible time of disobedience. Let's just hope my grandchildren learn the right lessons from this whole unsavory ordeal."

Fiona was pushed forward, and she started walking, if only to keep from falling over. Alex kept a hand on her shoulder, guiding her. Through the cloth of the blindfold, Fiona saw a hint of lantern light, but she couldn't make out much of the cave as they resumed their march through the tunnels. Nevertheless, she tried to memorize every twist and turn they took. She felt remarkably calm in the moment. Somehow, the fear and dread had passed, and she was resigned to her fate.

I've alienated everyone. No one came to my defense. It's my own fault. So be it. I was alone in the beginning; I'll be alone in the end.

She considered trying to reason with the Dwellers. Brigid didn't seem to be with them now, so it was Alex, Henny, and Seb. Of the three, Henny had always been the least friendly, constantly scowling at her, but Seb had never been particularly hostile. She seemed shy, an introvert, but never angry. Could she be reasoned with?

Even if I get out of this, I'd have to make it back to camp so I can grab my stuff before I escape. Not likely. Then again, Zane's punishment was being stuck in a pit. If they do something similar to me, I might be able to climb out.

Their footsteps seemed especially loud in the passageway. They were in a narrow place, but the floor seemed to have been shaped and smoothed. Another punishment room, perhaps? Suddenly, she was pulled to a stop. Bodies shifted around her, and then the blindfold was yanked off her head.

She saw some kind of vast, dark space in front of her, the flat floor giving way to a steep, descending slope and a sudden drop. Before she had a chance to consider this, Alex grabbed her by both shoulders and turned her around. She saw a high, smooth wall rising up behind her, a narrow gap cutting through the rock where they'd come from. Seb and Alex were standing close to her. Henny was a few feet to one side, the arrow nocked and partially drawn, as if Henny expected or hoped for an escape attempt.

Alex and Henny both looked so angry, but Seb was calm, almost expressionless.

"Don't move," Alex said, in a low, breathy voice full of threat.

He stepped back and drew a long knife from a leather sheath at his belt. It was a hunting knife with an impressive eight-inch blade that shone in the lantern light. That left Seb as the lone figure standing right in front of her. Fiona made eye contact with the woman, trying to read her. Seb was tall, gaunt, slightly hunched, with sunken cheeks and sharp, probing eyes.

"Now what, Seb?" Fiona said. "Are you really going along with this?"

Suddenly, Seb stepped back and kicked her. She moved so fast that Fiona didn't even register what had happened until she was falling backward. She felt pain where the thick sole of Seb's boot hit her stomach. Then she slammed into the ground and slid backward. It was a steep slope covered in loose rocks, so she soon found herself sliding uncontrollably.

Fiona clawed at the ground, trying to find some handhold to stop herself, but her fingers only dug through the loose rocks. Above her, Seb stood in a circle of lantern light, quickly fading into the distance. Her blank expression never changed—like a mask.

As she picked up speed, Fiona managed to roll onto her belly, but this did nothing to slow her. She was sliding fast now, her shirt pushed up above her belly, which made the rocks scrape at her exposed stomach. She beat at the ground, but it was futile, as futile as everything else she'd tried to do since the snowfall began. Because of the kick, she was struggling to catch her breath, which made her even more helpless. On top of that, the bandaged wound on her arm still throbbed constantly, adding to her pain.

When she reached the drop, she felt her legs sail out into the void. Then her whole body, ejected like a parasite, fell away from the slope, over a cliff, and into a lightless pit that seemed infinite in size. She couldn't even scream as she fell, only gasp and flail.

Don't land on your head. This thought raced through her mind, and she tried to twist around. Landing on her feet seemed the safest course of action. She might break both legs, but that seemed better than a shattered skull. However, it was useless. She had no control over her trajectory.

When she finally slammed into the ground, she landed on her back. The violent jolt went through her body, a painful surge that rushed to the tips of her fingers. She tasted blood as the last of her breath left her lungs, and then she felt the world spinning away from her as she sank into some unconscious place deep beneath dreams.

99

Jarred couldn't stop pacing, and his restlessness clearly bothered the others. Hope and Myra had gone back to the bedroom, taking Smoke with them. Nick had disappeared into the dark punishment room, and Larry and Lana stood anxiously near the door, holding each other. A lot of breakfast food had been left uneaten on the table. Jarred smelled eggs and oatmeal, and it turned his stomach. He had absolutely no appetite.

Brigid didn't really listen to a word I said, he thought, fuming. *Her damned immutable laws made her tune out every single thing.*

His path took him from the kitchen door to the curtain that hid the Dwellers' sleeping place. He was tempted to fling the curtain aside and just start tossing their sleeping bags and supplies about. Jarred was in the rare mood to do some damage, but he knew that would only lead to more trouble.

"Jarred, it won't be worse than what Zane went through," Larry said.

Jarred was facing the curtain, and he whipped around to see Larry and Lana staring at him. Despite their excitement at getting their son back, they were clearly troubled by Jarred's restless behavior.

"We don't know that," Jarred said. "We don't know what they'll do to her, because we don't know what they're really capable of."

Lana put a finger to her lips. "Not so loud. The grandchildren are in the classroom, but they might hear you."

"What I said doesn't break any of their precious rules," Jarred grumbled, as he started back across the room.

He passed the table in the middle of the room. Brigid and Josiah had left their breakfast plates sitting there, and Jarred intentionally bumped the table in passing. That caused Josiah's small enamelware bowl of oatmeal to fall from the edge and land upside down on a chair. The oatmeal had congealed enough that it didn't immediately run out onto the chair, for which Jarred was disappointed.

"I just don't understand why she did it," Lana said. "Sneaking off at night to carve her own exit into the cave? I never would have thought Fiona was capable of such foolish behavior. She always seemed so reasonable, which is why I trusted her judgement."

This irritated Jarred, but he couldn't chastise Lana for it. She was dead right. Fiona's behavior was inexcusably dangerous. Why hadn't she talked to him first? Why hadn't she discussed this with anyone?

I'll have a very uncomfortable conversation with her when she gets back, he thought. *She might not want to talk to me, but she'll have to. Fiona owes us an explanation for her recent behavior.*

"She'll be down in her pit a whole lot longer than Zane," Jarred said, stopping at the kitchen door and turning around again.

"Perhaps, but eventually they'll pull her out," Larry said. "That's the thing."

"And, heck, maybe she'll be more cautious with her behavior in the future," Lana added. "I sure hope Zane has learned from *his* punishment."

Just then, they heard footsteps coming from the corridor. Larry and Lana turned to face the doorway, anxious and clutching each other. Jarred stopped his pacing.

If the kid is gravely injured in some way, I'll wring Brigid's neck, he thought.

Lantern light appeared in the doorway, a warm orange glow revealing the narrow corridor with its carefully shaped walls. Then Nick and Zane appeared, walking side by side. Zane looked haggard, with bloodshot eyes full of sleepless misery. His complexion was worse than usual, and his clothes were spattered and smeared with slime. He seemed to have aged quite a bit down there in the dark. This was not the face of a sixteen-year-old.

Larry and Lana started to rush toward them, but Nick held up a hand, keeping them at bay until they passed through the opening into the central chamber. Then they grabbed their son and pulled him into an embrace. All three cried as Nick stepped calmly to one side, arms crossed over his chest. The Dweller seemed a bit too self-satisfied. Jarred didn't like the little hint of a smile bisecting the thick, black beard.

"And that's it?" Jarred asked. "His punishment is over, and he can come back now?"

"That's right," Nick replied, as the Bishops continued to weep and hug each other. "He received his chastisement well, and he is a better man for it."

"Right," Jarred said, struggling mightily to keep all of the bitterness out of his voice. "Well, he seems to be okay. Unhurt. That's a good thing, at least."

Nick said nothing to this. No one even looked at Jarred. Finally, he decided to leave the Bishops to their happy, tearful reunion and head back to the bedroom. However, when he turned away, he spotted Hope in the doorway. She had heard the commotion and come running.

"Is he back?" she said. "Is he okay?"

"Yeah, he'll be fine," Jarred replied.

Hope started to run to him, but she caught herself against the rocks. A glimmer of something crossed her face—guilt, Jarred thought. Then she stepped back and said, "Well, they're busy now. I'll…I'll talk to him later." Then, tears glistening in her eyes, she fled back down the corridor.

Not quite ready to see him after she got him in trouble, Jarred thought. *I don't blame her.*

He followed his daughter, leaving the central chamber and the tearful reunion. Jarred had always seen himself as a practical person, able to make rational decisions even under trying times. The Dwellers were cultish nutjobs. He'd known that from day one, yet he'd gone along with their nonsense because it had been the more reasonable course of action. However, he was finding it harder and harder to hold on to that notion.

Stay calm, he told himself. *Don't do anything rash. Work it out with Fiona when she gets back.*

He rounded the bend just in time to see Hope fling the bedroom curtain out of her way as she stormed inside. As he approached the doorway, he saw shifting lantern light moving down the passageway beyond their bedroom, and he heard purposeful footsteps on the rocky floor. Finally, Seb appeared, coming around the corner with a small brass lantern in her hand. She was a gangly figure, almost inhuman with her blank expression. Had he ever seen this woman express an emotion?

Henny came next, a clear counterpoint to her sister, with a fixed scowl on her face. Her long black braids swayed as she walked. Jarred watched them approach, expecting some comment or explanation. However, they continued down the corridor, passing him without saying a word, pointedly not looking at him. After a moment, Jarred pushed through the curtain. Hope and Myra were sitting together on stools, and they seemed to be chatting. Smoke was standing between them. The dog seemed anxious.

"Is Zane doing okay?" Hope asked. "Is he...I mean, did he get hurt or anything? Did the centipedes bite him?"

"He appears to be fine," Jarred said, "as you just saw a minute ago, Hope. He's tired, sore, might have a few bug bites, but there doesn't seem to be any serious consequences from his stay in the pit."

"I'll clean treat the bug bites as soon as I can so they don't get infected," Myra said. She made a disgusted face and shook her head. "What I can't stand is the public humiliation. Shaming the boy in front of the entire community—that was always the real punishment. That's why they marched him in there with everyone watching. They wanted him to feel ashamed in front of everyone."

"Yeah, I think you're right," Jarred said. "Shame was a deterrent meant to keep him from misbehaving in the future."

"Is that what they're going to do to Fiona?" Hope asked. "Are they going to publicly humiliate her, too?"

"I'm not sure. They didn't bring us along to witness her punishment."

"That seems like a bad sign," Myra muttered.

Jarred crossed the room to the water bucket and, for no particular reason, washed his face again. Then, instead of sitting on a stool, he took a spot on the cave floor near the barrel, leaning his back against the wall.

There'd been no public humiliation of Fiona. They had marched her off privately. And now the Dwellers had returned quietly, as if they'd been carrying out some ordinary task.

After a moment, a long shadow moved in front of him. When he looked up, he saw Hope standing there, Smoke at her side.

"Dad…did they say how long Fiona's going to be in her pit?" she asked.

"No, they did not," he replied. "They never mentioned a pit at all. I have no idea what sort of punishment they had in mind for her."

"Should we be worried about her?" Hope said, barely above a whisper.

He nodded. "Leave the worry to me for the time being, okay?"

He heard people entering the room, and he leaned to one side to see past his daughter. Larry, Lana, and Zane walked into the room together. As Jarred watched, they led Zane toward the water barrel. Larry grabbed a rag from one of the shelves and handed it to Zane.

"Wash up as best you can, son," he said. "You have clean clothes in a trunk over by the beds."

"I'll never get all of this slime off me," Zane replied.

Hope finally seemed to gather up her courage, and she rushed to his side. "Zane! Did you get any centipede bites?"

"Yeah, a few," he replied, stepping around her. "I stomped a bunch of them, though. At least, I think it did. It was sort of hard to tell in the pitch darkness. I could hear them moving around. It was so gross."

Zane dropped to his knees in front of the barrel. The kid smelled pretty bad. Jarred rose and moved away to give him some room, as his father used a pitcher to scoop water out of the barrel. As Zane proceeded to wash his face, Hope watched him intently. After a minute, Myra walked over and began cleaning a few visible bug bites on his arms.

Jarred was standing a few feet back when Lana turned to him.

"Where is she?" Lana asked quietly. "Where's Fiona?"

Jarred shook his head.

"They didn't tell you? They didn't say *anything*?"

He shook his head again. This caused Larry to look at him as well. Even Zane and Myra stopped cleaning his bites for a moment, as if waiting to hear the answer.

"Are they going to tell us at some point?" Lana asked. "Or are we just supposed to wait until she shows up again?"

Jarred shook his head a third time. "Folks, I don't know any more than you do, but I'll go figure out where she is," he said. "The rest of you stay here. Tend to Zane. Let me deal with the Dwellers."

As he started toward the curtain, it looked like Hope might follow him. But she frowned and remained by Zane's side instead.

"Be careful," Myra said, just before he left the room. "They won't want you getting in the way."

"I'm just going to talk to the boss again," Jarred said. "Don't worry. I'll try not to make things worse. Don't forget—I've got favor. That has to count for something."

He flung the curtain aside and left the room. At first, he feared he might have to hunt around for Brigid, but then he heard her voice coming from the central chamber, punctuated by the click and clack of dishes. Jarred headed in that direction, debating with himself what tone and approach he should take with Brigid. She seemed to like him, though he still wasn't sure why. He intended to leverage his favor to acquire some information.

When he entered room, he found Brigid and Josiah cleaning up the uneaten breakfast food. Henny sat at one of the tables, stitching the shoulder strap on a leather quiver. As for the other Dwellers, they were nowhere to be seen at the moment. Josiah was carrying some dishes away, and Brigid was wiping down the table. Jarred moved up behind her. She sensed his approach and turned to him.

"Jarred," she said, giving him a big friendly smile. Something about it troubled him. It didn't seem natural. "Favor still rests on you."

"Where's Fiona?" he asked. Better to get straight to the point, though he tried his best to say it in a way that didn't sound angry or upset. He didn't quite succeed. "I'm just curious."

Brigid's smile evaporated and she resumed wiping the table. "Fiona is being punished for breaking the most sacred of our laws. You know that."

"I understand," Jarred replied. "I know *why* she was punished. The rules are clear to me, but when Zane broke the law, we all saw what happened to him. It wasn't a secret. I just wondered how Fiona was punished, and where she's at."

Brigid stopped working again and turned to him. A hint of her smile had returned, but it seemed less friendly and a bit smug now. Josiah returned from the kitchen, and he stood still now, observing this exchange. Even Henny paused in her work to watch.

"Well, if you really must know," Brigid said with a sigh, "Fiona was given to God's Wrath."

Vague religious terminology. Did she really think that was an acceptable answer? Jarred felt a swell of anger and fought mightily to keep from acting on it. Was the old cult leader toying with him? Taunting him?

"Given to God's wrath," he said. "What does that mean?"

Brigid was staring at him now, her cold eyes locked onto his. She hesitated a moment before saying, "Fiona is dead." So quietly, so calmly. "Her soul was given to God in the deepest place for final judgment."

Jarred felt like the whole world had just dropped out from beneath his feet. The room around him seemed to recede, and he heard only a faint, high-pitched buzzing in his ears. Dead. She'd said it like the word meant nothing.

They killed her. They killed Fiona. For breaking some imaginary rule of their cult.

"You said she wouldn't be executed," he said numbly.

"We didn't execute her," Brigid replied. "We sent her to God and let a greater authority deal with her. It's not the same thing, even if it ends in the same place. She is dead. God has taken her. It is justice, and I hope you will be able to see that."

What he felt rising up in him at that moment was like nothing he'd ever felt before. It started somewhere low in the pit of his stomach and slowly spread out to his extremities, a fierce, almost painful electricity. And Brigid was just standing there with that smile on her face, the words pounding against Jarred's skull.

He moved without thinking. Something had taken control of him, and when it did, it gave him a strength and speed he did not know he possessed. Lunging forward, he grabbed Brigid, wrapped both of his hands around her neck, and shoved her against the edge of the table. Her eyes went wide, and she made a loud gurgling sound. His hands were clenching, tightening, and he couldn't seem to stop them, even when the whites of Brigid's eyes turned pink.

They killed her. They killed Fiona.

Brigid struggled against him, but he'd tipped her off balance and pinned her against the table. All she could do was bat at his forearms.

"You're an animal," he snarled. "You're not human, and you deserve to choke on your own blood! Do you hear me, you maniac? Do you hear me?"

But then he felt some violent impact against the back of his head. He rocked forward, tackling Brigid onto the tabletop. Then he rebounded backward, losing his grip on her throat. As he fell back, he saw Seb standing over him, a short wooden club clutched in the long fingers of her right hand. Jarred stumbled, trying to keep his feet, but Seb swung the club at him again. It slammed into the side of his head, and the impact seemed to break the whole world loose. It fell spinning away from him, and only the senseless dark remained as he landed on his back on the floor.

100

They heard the shouting all the way down in the bedroom, but Hope was the first to realize what it meant. She'd been standing beside Zane at the water barrel when the sounds arose in the distance. Turning, she recognized her father's voice, Henny, Josiah, and some other terrible sound like a small animal being crushed.

"You're an animal!" Yes, that was her father for sure.

She traded an anxious look with Myra Cooper, then rushed across the room to the door.

"Wait, Hope," Myra said. "You don't know what's happening out there."

But Hope couldn't stop now. Her father had sounded so angry, so furious. She pushed through the curtain and headed down the hall. He'd only gone to talk to Brigid. Had something gone wrong? Had he said some forbidden thing? What had he learned?

As she came around the corner, she saw a scene of sheer chaos ahead of her. Josiah and Henny were dashing back and forth, frantic. Hope's father was towering over Brigid, making a terrible angry sound deep in his throat, and Brigid was forced back against the table. She was gurgling, thrashing, batting at him with her hands.

Dad's strangling her, Hope realized, a white-hot terror sweeping through her. *He's trying to kill Brigid!*

But Seb appeared in the doorway then, coming from the direction of the curtained sleeping area. The tall, lanky Dweller had a black wooden club in her right hand, and Hope watched in trembling terror as she swung it at Jarred. The first blow hit him on top of the head. He grunted loudly, slammed Brigid onto the tabletop, and stumbled backward. The old woman gasped and grabbed at the edge of the table as she slid down onto the floor.

How did this happen? Why is Dad trying to kill her?

The confusion intensified the shock. As Jarred fell backward, he tried to grab at something, his hands opening and closing on the air. Then Seb hit him again. She had practically no emotion as she did it, and Hope's father fell onto his back on the floor. At some point, Hope realized she was screaming. The Dwellers were standing still now, gathered loosely behind Seb, as the gangly woman loomed over Jarred. However, their heads swiveled to look at Hope.

At some point, Larry, Lana, and Zane had come up beside her. She was aware of their presence, but her gaze went to her father. He was on his back, moaning softly, eyes half-lidded.

"What did you do?" Hope cried, her scream taking shape. "What did you do to my father?"

"My God," Larry said.

For some reason, Larry's shocked voice was like a jolt. Like a gunshot at the beginning of a race. Hope bolted forward, rushing toward her dad. She didn't know what she intended to do. Grab him and drag him away from danger, perhaps. Seb turned at her approach and seemed to be bracing herself for the charge, as if she thought Hope was going to try to tackle her. Brigid's face was flushed, her eyes bloodshot, and she was lightly massaging her throat.

"No, no, kiddo." The voice came from behind Hope, as two arms wrapped around her and swept her off the ground. "Let's stay calm. Come on." It was Larry. He picked her up, turned her around, and set her down in the corridor. "It's okay. We'll sort this out." He was speaking soothingly.

It helped, but Hope was still frantic. As soon as Larry let go of her, she spun around, intending to run back to her father. However, Zane came up beside her. He looked frail, unwell, and he still reeked of the pit, though he'd changed his shirt and pants. But he took her by the hand.

"Wait," he said to her. "Just wait. Don't give them any excuse to do worse."

Hope stepped to one side to see past Larry, but she did not rush forward again. For a few seconds, there was a tense standoff between the two groups, with Jarred lying on his back in the middle. Then Brigid took a deep, raspy breath and raised her arms.

"Everyone just calm down," she said. Her voice sounded rough, and her eyes looked bloodshot. "We're not enemies here."

"Not enemies?" Henny cried, stepping forward. "That man tried to strangle you!"

"He *did* strangle you," Josiah added. "He would've killed you if not for Seb."

Brigid swept her arms out and motioned both of them back. Josiah complied, but Henny moved around the table to stand beside Seb. It looked like she might keep coming, so Brigid motioned at her more forcefully and made an angry clucking sound. Bowing her head, Henny stopped.

"Everyone is overreacting here," Brigid said. She coughed, then snapped at Josiah. "Bring me a glass of water. Promptly!"

Josiah sighed and trotted off to the kitchen.

"Now, Hope, your father is going to be okay," Brigid said. "He lost himself for a moment, and Seb was forced to take drastic action to stop him from doing something he would surely regret."

Hope looked at her father. He was still lying on his back, his eyes half-open. He appeared to be breathing, at least. Josiah returned with a glass of water, and Brigid snatched it out of his hand. She took a long drink and handed the cup back to him. When she spoke again, her voice was not quite as rough.

"These kinds of overreactions are not uncommon," Brigid continued. "When you spend so much time in the womb of the cave, occasional bursts of high emotion are inevitable. We've all felt it." Brigid made eye contact with Hope then and gave her a sad little smile. "The adjustment is hard. Believe me, I know. You've all struggled. I get it. I'm sympathetic."

She was speaking so kindly now, Hope found it disorienting. Hadn't her father just tried to choke her to death? Hadn't her weird, tall daughter bashed him in the head? But she was speaking now like some sweet old granny.

And she was right. Hope had indeed felt bursts of high emotion, some that she didn't even fully understand, since coming to the cave. No sunlight, no fresh air, rock on all sides, flickering candles and lanterns, and damp air. There were times when she wanted to scream, to run as fast as she could.

Zane had his hand on one shoulder, Larry had his hand on the other. They were both patting her gently. The combination of gentle words, comforting touches, and the truth of what Brigid was saying took the fight out of her. Still, she noted that Larry seemed tense and still. He wasn't calmed, but he *was* controlling himself.

"I'm sorry your father was injured," Brigid said. "I think he'll be okay, and once he recovers, we'll put this unfortunate episode behind us. I don't hold it against him." She turned and glared hard at Henny, and her daughter seemed to wilt. "I don't hold it against him! I hope that's clear to everyone." Then she turned back to Hope. "Let him rest a while, and he will be just fine."

Seb stepped back and set her club on the shelf with the candles. As soon as she did, Larry and Zane both let go of Hope's shoulders. She took that as her signal and rushed forward, dropping to her knees beside her father. He looked at her with glassy eyes and reached for her, moaning softly.

"Seb, you can at least help me carry him to his bed," Larry said.

Hope grabbed her father's hand. "Can you talk? Can you think?"

He took a deep breath and let it out slowly. "I don't know," he said in a breathy voice. "Yeah, I think so. I just…" His voice trailed off.

Larry and Seb came up on either side. Hope backed away as they picked him up.

"We're all going to calm down now," Brigid said. "We're going to collect ourselves, rest, and then everything will be fine."

Hope followed Larry and Seb back down the hall. As she did, she looked over her shoulder at the Dwellers. Brigid was still flushed, with notable deep red marks on her throat. She seemed shaken. Henny stood at her shoulder, scowling darkly, her hands clenched into tight fists. Nick and Alex had appeared at some point, standing in the passageway to the punishment room. They looked angry too.

Hope lost sight of them all as she rounded the corner. She followed Larry and Seb back to the bedroom. In the room, she found Myra standing close to the curtain, as if she'd been listening. Hope caught her giving Seb a hateful sneer as they carried Jarred to the far wall.

"Oh, what did they do to him?" Myra said.

"He took a couple of blows to the head," Lana said.

"Oh, gosh," Myra said. "He needs to lie down. Someone get his sleeping bag ready. Let me take a look at him."

Hope rushed ahead and unrolled her father's sleeping bag on the floor. Larry and Seb lowered him onto it. Then Seb left without a word, as Hope sat beside her father. He had fallen unconscious, his eyes closed, but he was breathing. Still alive. Myra eased herself down beside the sleeping bag and began to examine him. She pried open his eyes one at a time, then gingerly felt the places where he'd been hit.

"He may have a concussion," she said, then spent a few seconds coughing and wheezing. "I'll need to stick close and keep an eye on him."

What do we do now? Hope thought, despairing. *How do we get out of here?*

101

Jarred was aware of his splitting headache long before he regained full consciousness. The throbbing pain chased him through dim half-dreams where he was flying down winding passageways. When he finally opened his eyes, he saw orange candlelight dancing on a domed ceiling above him, and it took a moment to remember where he was. The room was still and stale, and he heard the sound of people sleeping uncomfortably.

An image came back to him then, Brigid's wide eyes, bared teeth, his hands clamped around her throat. Had that really happened? Had he tried to kill the leader of this cult? That realization brought him fully awake, cast off the last vestiges of darkness, and caused a cold shudder to go through him. He'd tried to kill Brigid in front of her family. Why the hell was he still alive?

He rolled to one side and saw Hope. She was sitting with her back against the rock wall, her hands clasped on her belly. She was dozing.

"Hope." He whispered her name, then reached over and gently shook her.

She awoke with a start, snorting loudly. Then she rubbed her eyes and looked around. When she saw him, she gasped and grabbed his hand.

"Dad, you've alive," she said.

He shushed her. Alive? Did she think he'd died? He struggled for a moment and finally managed to sit up. As soon as he did, his daughter hugged him fiercely.

"What happened?" he asked in a whisper. "I remember lunging at Brigid, grabbing her, then something hit me."

"It was Seb," Hope replied. "She bashed you in the head twice with a wooden club. You've been mostly unconscious ever since, and it's been at least a few hours. Myra said you have a concussion, and there was a chance you might never wake up again."

Hope's words brought the entire encounter back to him. Brigid's cold statement—*Fiona is dead*—and the surge of violent anger filling his body. The feel of her tiny neck in his hands, loose skin shifting beneath his fingers. The inability to stop himself.

He probed his head, working his fingers through his sweaty hair, and found two lumps where he'd been hit.

"I'm supposed to tell Larry as soon as you wake up," Hope said.

"Okay," Jarred replied. He rose, though it caused a rush of pain. Gripping his forehead, he stumbled away from his sleeping bag. "Wake him. Tell him."

"Dad, should you be getting up like that?" Hope asked.

"Yeah, just wake Larry and the others. Hurry."

He heard her moving as he made his way across the room. Approaching the water barrel, he caught himself against the rim. He scooped up a handful and splashed it on his face. Then he scooped up another handful and drank it. When he turned around, he saw Hope going from bed to bed, waking people. Zane and Larry were already sitting up.

Water still running down his face, dripping from his beard, Jarred made his way back to them. By the time he got there, everyone was awake, and Hope was on a stool, petting Smoke. The rage that had driven Jarred to strangle

Brigid was very close to the surface. He could feel it trying to take over every thought.

"It's good to see you up and moving again," Larry said.

"I was worried about long-term damage," Myra said.

Jarred waved off their concerns. "Brigid told me Fiona is dead. What do you guys know about it?"

The whole room seemed to freeze at this. For a few seconds, there was no movement, no comment, just fearful eyes staring up at him.

"They admitted to killing her," Myra said bitterly. "Brigid was very open about it, seemed proud. And for what? Breaking some imaginary law that means nothing? Sick. Absolutely sick."

Jarred motioned for her to keep her voice down and moved closer to the group. "For Zane's crime, they threw him into a pit for two days," he said. "For Fiona's crime, they murdered her. In both instances, it was a grotesque overreaction to imagined offenses. It's only a matter of time before they hurt or kill someone else."

Zane cracked his knuckles. "We should make them pay for what they've done to us. You don't know how many times I daydreamed about getting revenge while I was down in that pit. You almost choked Brigid to death. I wish you'd succeeded."

Larry reached over and patted Zane on the back, then pressed a finger to his lips. "Now is not the time to get worked up. We must speak very quietly. Stay calm."

"Fine, but I meant what I said," Zane grumbled.

"We're not going to win an open fight with these people, not without casualties," Jarred said. "Even if I'd killed Brigid, it would've only gotten more of us—maybe all of us—killed. They know the cavern better than we do. They have the weapons. And they're more ruthless than we are."

"But we can't just keep living here," Lana said. "We can't pretend like everything's okay. I'll never forgive them for what they did to my boy, much less for killing Fiona."

Jarred felt restless. If Brigid had been in the room at that moment, he thought there was a very good chance he would wrap his hands around her throat again. To work off some of this angry energy, he began to pace, but it scarcely helped.

"Dad, we can't stay here any longer," Hope said.

"No, we can't," he replied. "We can't stay with the Dwellers. We should have left sooner, to be honest, but it was hard to walk away from the food and water supply, the warm air and comfortable sleeping arrangement."

"We were never safe here to begin with," Myra said. "Safety with these people was always an illusion, and the threat of violence was hovering over us from the moment we arrived."

Every eye was on Jarred. In the absence of Fiona, it seemed they were looking to him for leadership. He found it entirely uncomfortable. The absence of Fiona felt like a vast cavity in the foundation of their group.

He stopped pacing and turned to face the group.

"We're going to leave as soon as possible," he said.

"But don't we want to get some kind of revenge?" Zane asked. The tips of his fingers danced down his forearms, sliding over the numerous bandages covering centipede bites. "Don't they need to pay for what they've done to us? We didn't hurt any of their people. We just broke some made-up rules. But they've hurt us, killed one of us. What are we going to do about it?"

"A confrontation could very well get more of us killed," Jarred replied. "I'd much rather get everyone away from here safely, and if we can take our stuff, too, that would be great. I would consider that a victory."

"Do we know *how* they killed Fiona?" Myra asked. "Do we know for sure that she's dead?"

"No, we don't know what happened," Jarred replied. "Brigid said her soul was given to God in the deepest place for final judgment. Since they believe God lives down in the darkness, I assume that means they tossed her into a deep pit somewhere, and I assume they confirmed the death. I don't really want the gory details. Do you?"

Myra pulled a face, as if his question had offended her. "No, I don't want gore, but I think it's fair to wonder what they did. Maybe there's a chance she survived."

"Brigid seemed confident she's dead," Jarred said. "All I know for sure is that we're getting out of here. In order to do that, we're going to need to get our guns back. I don't intend to shoot our way to freedom, but we need at least the *threat* of firepower. Just in case. It'll be better if we're armed, no matter how this plays out. Now, that means getting into the supply room and somehow acquiring a few of our guns."

"I can do it," Larry said. He started to rise, but Lana grabbed his hand, as if to restrain him. "Lana, I work in the supply room every day. They won't think anything of it. Trust me. I can do this." And then, when she still held on, he said it more forcefully. "Trust me."

She let go.

"Can you do it now?" Jarred asked. "Can you get in there safely right now? Maybe you should wait until later."

"It's morning anyway," Larry replied. "It'll look like the normal start of my workday. I've got this. Give me a few minutes."

As he headed across the room, Jarred stooped down and began rolling up his sleeping bag. Mostly, he was just buying a few seconds to gather his thoughts. He didn't have much of a plan beyond gathering up their weapons and heading off into the dark. Surely, they needed something more coordinated than that.

"Which way do we go to get out of this cave?" Hope asked. "There have to be other exits somewhere."

"There's a river that the Dwellers use to catch fish," Zane said. "I'm not sure where it is, but we should be able to find it. Couldn't we swim to freedom?"

"The temperature of that water is liable to be close to freezing," Jarred said. "Even if we managed to swim out of the cave, the cold outside would turn us to human popsicles in a matter of minutes."

"Then maybe the pit with the dead lady in it," Hope said. "I felt colder air there. We'd have to climb down somehow, but—"

Zane shushed her suddenly and made a sharp gesture. Jarred had finished rolling up the sleeping bag, and he turned to see what Zane was gesturing at. It was Brigid. He couldn't help rising suddenly and adopting a casual post, like a kid caught with his hand in the cookie jar. But why should he feel any guilt whatsoever for this woman who had killed Fiona?

As she drew near, he could see red marks on her neck. Despite this, she had a smile on her face, and her hands were sunk into the front pockets of her plain brown dress. Just before the curtain swung shut in the doorway, Jarred saw black-bearded Nick lurking in the hallway. Despite the old woman's smile, the tension in the room was thick. As she drew near, Brigid's smile grew brighter, and Jarred forced himself to return it, even though he'd never felt less like smiling in his life.

Say what you have to say, he told himself. Yet it took a fierce act of will.

"I owe you an apology for yesterday," he said. Oh, it made him sick to say it, but somehow, he kept the smile plastered to his face. "I don't know what came over me, but I deserved that smack on the head for it. I never meant to hurt you, ma'am. You've been good to us."

He just hoped that the others wouldn't react badly to this lie. However, he dared not look at them to gauge their reactions. Brigid nodded and kept right on smiling. Her gaze went down the line, taking in each face in turn.

"It pleases me to see the way you've cared for Jarred," she said to the others. "He has recovered well." She paused a moment, and her smile faltered. Bowing her head, she continued. "I am very sorry about what happened to Fiona. Perhaps you can eventually come to terms with the fact that it was God's will."

At this, the tension in the room became so thick that Jarred could practically taste it on his tongue. He felt it emanating from the others. If Brigid sensed it, she gave no indication. Zane had risen to one knee, and Jarred spotted him clenching a fist. Best to stop this before someone else lost control.

"We're sad," he said. "We're going to be sad for a while, but we understand the reason. We all knew the rules. Fiona knew the rules. I think it'll be better for all of us if we just get to work. Larry's already off on his daily tasks. We should join him and get on with life."

Brigid studied his face for a second, then the smile returned. "Yes, very good. Everything is going to be fine. God will see to it, my friends. Let's get to work. There's a new day dawning."

And with that, she turned and walked back across the room. She went right through the curtain and was gone. Jarred heaved a sigh and turned to the others.

"Well, that was an encouraging little speech, wasn't it?" Myra muttered, rolling her eyes.

"I can't stand listening to her," Zane said. "I hate the sound of her voice."

Again, Jarred signaled for them to keep their voices down. "We're going to act calmly. We're going to say all the right things. And then we're going to get out of here."

Lana and Hope nodded. Myra gave him a sad look, and Zane just scowled at the curtained doorway, as if he could stab Brigid in the back with the sheer hatred of his gaze.

"Everyone get up and start getting ready," Jarred said. "We're going to act like it's a normal day. We're all going to work and school, and we're going to act like everything is fine. Okay?"

Frowning deeply, Hope headed to the water barrel as Lana, Zane, and Myra rolled up their sleeping bags. Once their beds were put away, they took turns washing. Some changed clothes. Lana took a moment to brush out her hair. Then they all headed for the doorway. Jarred was trying to psych himself up to face the Dwellers and put on the phony attitude, but before he could push through the curtain, Larry appeared.

He entered the room with his head down, lips pressed tightly together, and he almost walked right into Jarred. At the last second, he stumbled to a stop and looked up. He wasn't carrying anything, certainly no containers or bags that might hold weapons.

"You made it to the supply room?" Jarred asked.

"Oh, yeah, I walked right in with no problem," Larry said. "Alex saw me and didn't say a word. Just like any other day of work."

"And the guns?" Zane asked, rather forcefully. "Dad, did you get the guns?"

Larry shook his head. "I know where they were stored before, but all the guns and ammunition are missing."

102

As Larry's words sank in, Jarred felt a sense of despair eating at the edges of his angry determination. He stepped back from the door and motioned Larry to follow him back toward the water barrel. Once they were in the alcove behind the barrel, the others gathering around them, Jarred dared to speak.

"What do you mean the guns are missing?" he asked.

"I mean, they're all gone," Larry said. "They were stored in a big wooden box at the back of the supply room behind crates of dry goods and canned shelves of canned vegetables. The box is still there, but the guns are gone. All of the ammo too. Even some of our tools, like the hatchet, knives, things like that. I looked around the storage room a bit, thinking maybe they'd been moved, but there's no sign of them in that room. They're gone."

"When's the last time you saw them in there?" Jarred asked.

"A couple of days ago, I think," Larry said, "when I went about my daily routine."

Stunned, Jarred turned to the others, but they were all looking at him expectantly. Hope had tears in her eyes. Yes, the meaning of this development was clear to her. Or maybe she was still grieving the loss of Fiona. Either way, he put his arm around her.

If the Dwellers moved the guns, then they considered the possibility that we would go looking for them, he thought. *Maybe Brigid came in here earlier to test our mood, trying to determine whether we're hostile. Was my friendly act convincing enough?*

"Without those guns, we're at a dangerous disadvantage," he said. He reached up and touched the knot on the side of his head.

"We could grab some knives from the kitchen," Zane said. "And there are loose rocks all over the cave. Those make decent weapons, too."

"I'm just not sure knives and rocks will be enough," Jarred said. "Yeah, maybe we could get the drop on them if we're really lucky, but there's a better chance that we'll get clubbed to death or filled full of arrows. It's a risk we just can't take."

"I wonder what Fiona would tell us to do in a situation like this," Lana said sadly.

You and me both, sister, Jarred thought. *Why am I the one having to make this damned decision?*

"Maybe we're just trapped here with the Dwellers forever," Hope said, wiping her cheeks. "Maybe we can't stop them or escape, and we'll just have to follow their rules from now on for the rest of our lives."

"No way," Zane said.

"This is largely my fault," Jarred said. "I encouraged you all to assimilate. I told Hope to sit and pay attention in class. I thought it was worth putting up with some cultish nonsense to have a reliable source of food and water and secure shelter for a while. That's why we're in this situation now. It's why we've lost Fiona."

"No, you were right. It made sense at the time to play along," Larry said with a shrug. "We were hungry and tired, and we'd collapsed the only exit to the cavern that we knew of."

"That's not what I mean," Jarred said.

"Dad, since you found favor with their deity," Hope said, "couldn't you just escort us into the cavern? Nick was able to take the whole class into a dark place because he passed the trial. If you led us, the Dwellers wouldn't get upset, and we could all search for the exit together."

"I'm afraid if I led all of us at the same time, they would be suspicious of our purpose," Jarred replied. "I don't know how they'll react to us leaving together, especially if we try to take some of our stuff with us. Our possessions are supposed to be communal now, but we can't leave here with nothing. We won't last long out in the world. No, we need to be able to take some of our stuff with us, and we need to buy time to get far away before they suspect anything's wrong."

"Losing the guns and the goats would be a huge blow," Larry said. "Then again, we'd also need to take enough food to feed the goats. I don't know how we do that, not if we want to leave without being noticed. It's a big mess. We're all bound up with these people now. Leaving is not so easy, and if they'll kill Fiona for a stupid transgression, they'll kill any of us."

Jarred pushed past Larry and the others and went back to the corner where they kept some of their supplies. Mostly, this consisted of extra clothes, but he'd kept a few knick-knacks as well. He rooted through the pile until he found his small pocketknife. He unfolded it, held up the blade into the light, then folded it again and put it in his jacket pocket.

When he turned around, he found the rest of the group gathered behind him, standing in a row like troops awaiting their orders. As Jarred wracked his brain, he began to sense the most rudimentary shape of an escape plan, but he couldn't see all of the steps.

I passed the trial, he thought. *Maybe I should spend some time on my own looking for a way out. I won't be breaking the rules. That way, when it's time to go, we can head straight to the exit.*

That felt like it would take far too long, and the more time they spent here among the Dwellers, the more likely that someone else would be punished. No, that wasn't an option, not anymore. As the group continued to stare at him intently, Jarred began adjusting the plan in his mind.

"Okay, so maybe we can't fight them with guns or weapons," he said, "but we can trick them somehow. Brigid trusts me. Well, she used to before I tried to strangle her, at least. But I think I can win back her trust. I'll never understand why that old woman took a shine to me, but she did. I saw the moment it happened. We were sewing together, oddly enough. Anyway, there has to be a way to use that to our advantage."

"Lead her off into the dark cave somewhere and kill her," Zane said. "Choke her when no one's around to stop it."

"Too risky," Jarred said. "Some of the others might be suspicious if I lead her off somewhere by herself, especially after what I did to her. And anyway, just getting rid of Brigid doesn't save us from the others. If anything, Brigid keeps them at bay."

"Something tells me you have another idea," Larry said.

"Yeah," Jarred replied. "Do any of you happen to know how to use a bow and arrow? Not just *know* but have some actual experience or training?"

Zane and Hope glanced at each other and shrugged. Larry and Lana just stared.

"None of you ever went bow hunting?" Jarred asked. "Or maybe took an archery class in school or something?"

"Went boar hunting with a spear once when I was young," Larry said. "Didn't much enjoy it. The dogs did most of the work. Didn't seem fair. But I've never had cause to shoot a bow and arrow."

"I'd be willing to learn," Zane said.

Jarred shook his head. "No, they would definitely suspect something then."

And then a hand went up. Myra was standing at the end of the line. Her breathing sounded rough, and she coughed a bit, even as she lifted her hand.

"Myra?" he asked.

"I know how to use a bow and arrow," she said, then had a coughing fit. Lana patted her on the back, and the coughing gradually faded. "Duke used to do a bit of bow hunting in the fall when we were younger. He taught me how to use a bow, thinking I'd hunt with him. I never did, but sometimes,

I'd shoot at the hay bale targets with him in the backyard. He always told me I was a decent shot, but I didn't have much to compare myself to."

"Do you think you could still do it?" Jarred asked.

She pulled a sour face and shrugged. "I can probably still pull the string. My aim was decent, and may still be, as long as I don't start coughing right before I release the arrow. How are we getting a bow, and what am I shooting at?"

Myra looked bent, frail, unwell, but if she could still pull a bowstring, then she was their best choice.

"Okay," Jarred said. "Here's the plan."

103

Fiona found herself lying on a steep slope, struggling to get her breath but alive. She heard the low moan of a deeper chamber in the darkness behind her, and she realized she had fallen on a ledge. There was another drop nearby. When she tried to move, the steepness of the slope made her slide a bit in the direction of the drop.

Her whole torso hurt, and when she breathed deeply, she felt a sharp pain deep in her chest. Had she broken a rib? For a while, she lay there on her back, waiting for the pain to subside. No sound came from above. Had the Dwellers left her here, or were they waiting to see if she would try to climb out? Either way, she had to do something.

How am I still alive? That thought kept running through her head. Of course, if she'd landed just a little bit differently, it would have been the end of her. She might have broken her neck. As it was, no limbs seemed to be broken. At worst, she had a cracked rib, but she was aware of the very real possibility of internal bleeding. She'd lived for now, but there was enough pain in her body that she knew it might only be temporary.

Fiona rolled onto her belly, though even that movement sent bolts of pain through her. Once she got there, she was out of breath. Worse than that, she felt her body very slowly sliding down the slope, grinding against tiny bits of rocks and debris. She scrabbled along the ground, trying to find something to grab hold of, but everything she grabbed was loose.

Her feet slid out over a drop. The ledge was quite narrow, maybe six feet at most, and judging by the dull roar of air below, it was a much farther fall from here.

Seb didn't expect me to land on this ledge. That's why she kicked so hard. She intended for me to keep falling. This was definitely intended to kill me. Those damned disgusting weirdos!

She felt a murderous rage, but she couldn't do anything about it right now. She had a far more pressing problem. Already, her legs were thrust out over the drop all the way to her knees. She swiped her hands out to the left and right, feeling for something solid to grab onto. As more of her slipped over the edge, she picked up speed. It seemed a cruel joke that she should survive the initial fall only to die a few minutes later from a second fall.

Seb, you'd better hope this kills me, she thought. *Otherwise, I swear to God, you and I are going to meet again.*

By now, she'd slid over the edge all the way to her hips, but her right hand finally found a small ledge or lip of rock a few inches from the drop. She hooked her fingers around it. Then she brought her left hand over, rolling slightly onto her side. From there, she was able to grab the small ledge with both hands, just as the rest of her body dropped over the ledge. Suddenly, she was hanging by her fingers.

Her grip wasn't strong, and her strength was fading fast. Also, the stitched wound on her arm was throbbing like crazy. Fiona slid the toes of her boots against the sheer side of the rock wall, even as her fingers slowly slipped off their meager handhold. Finally, she found some kind of crack or crevice, and she managed to wedge the edge of her right boot into it. This gave her just enough of a boost to strengthen her grip. But it didn't solve her problem. She was stable enough to hold on for a few more minutes, but then what? Where was she to go next?

Fiona looked around, but it was futile. There wasn't the least hint of light anywhere in this place. It was utterly dark, and her vision played strange tricks on her, creating surreal, shifting color patterns before her eyes. That made the experience incredibly disorienting.

Maybe somebody is up there, she thought. *Maybe if you call out, they'll drop you a rope.*

But would they? If the Dwellers had intended to kill her, what would they do when they discovered she was still alive? She saw two possibilities. Either they would see it as some sign of God's favor, and they would rescue her. Or they would see it as a failure on their part to carry out God's judgment, and they would finish the job—maybe firing a few arrows down at her.

Brigid doesn't like me, she thought. *I don't know why, but she's unlikely to see my survival as God's favor. Like most cultists, her version of God just happens to share her own personal prejudices.*

She finally found a tiny protruding rock where she could place the inner side of her left bootheel. This relieved the weight on her hands even more, and she was able to slowly pull herself back onto the ledge, inch by agonizing inch. She felt constantly out of breath, and the pain in her chest and belly were sharp and unrelenting. Nevertheless, through sheer furious will, she dragged herself back onto the ledge. Kicking her right leg up, she hooked her heel over the thin ledge that also served as her handhold, and from there she was able to get her whole body onto the ledge again.

When she pushed herself forward, the ledge served as a stable place for the tips of both boots, so she was no longer sliding toward the drop. She began cautiously moving to the right, sliding her boots along the ledge. As she did, she stretched out her hands in front of her, reaching up the slope to the wall, hoping that she might feel some way up. However, all she found was flat, wet rock in that direction.

I suppose their faith worked to my advantage, she thought. *Instead of slitting my throat or filling me full of arrows like a pincushion, they cast me to their strange cave god who dwells in the darkness. That's the only reason I'm alive. Apparently, their god likes me more than they do.*

This made her chuckle, despite her circumstances. She was still inching to her right, sliding along the ledge. Gradually, she felt the ledge changing, becoming rougher, more uneven, turning from a flat ledge into what felt like a pile of large rocks. With her right hand, she reached out and felt along the rocks, and she realized the pile went down. Was it a way to the bottom? And if so, would climbing down to the bottom of this pit do her any good?

She couldn't tell, but it seemed better than staying here on the ledge, where she would eventually grow tired and lose her grip. Twisting to one side, she worked her legs over a large round edge, then lowered herself onto what felt like stack of boulders. They seemed stable enough. She was perpendicular to the ledge now, slowly backing down the massive pile of rocks, carefully feeling around before putting her weight on anything. In the darkness, she couldn't tell how far she'd come, and she had no idea what lay below.

It felt interminable, and she was in pain and discomfort the whole way. It still hurt to take a deep breath, and her hands began to feel raw from constantly grabbing and dragging at the rocks. Still, she was driven by anger. She hadn't thought the Dwellers were capable of murder, especially for a crime that was really no crime at all.

How delusional was I to think it was a good idea to leave the others in this place? she thought. *Brigid and her stupid trial got in my head, and I nearly abandoned my only friends and family.*

She would rectify the situation. Oh, yes, she saw everything clearly now, including the only real solution.

"I lived, you old hag," she muttered, seeing Brigid's hard, leathery face in her head. "Guess what? Your god showed me favor, and I lived to get revenge. I'll relish the look on your face when I lunge out of the shadows."

She laughed again, but it was almost crazed this time. Just then, her right foot came down on a rock, and the rock crumbled beneath her. As she shifted, sliding down, she heard rubble tumbling down in an echoing cascade. Listening to the sound, she was able to gauge that the bottom of the pit was maybe another twenty feet below. She stabilized herself against a large boulder and resumed her descent.

And then, after what felt like hours—though time was a blur—she reached down with her left foot and felt a flat bottom. She had reached the floor of the pit. She put her other foot down and let go with her hands.

"You failed, Seb," she said, panting. "You didn't kick hard enough."

Despite a massive surge of relief, she realized just how exhausted she was. She crept forward a bit until she found a nice open spot on the ground, then she sat down to rest. Though she still couldn't see anything, she estimated that the total distance from the top of the pit to the bottom was somewhere between forty and fifty feet, easily far enough to kill someone.

As she rested, she stretched her legs out. Her right boot kicked something, and she felt it spin away from her foot in a strange but familiar way. It seemed weighted at one end. She got on her hands and knees and felt around for it. Finally, her right hand closed on a long, slender object with a shape she knew. The worn wooden handle of an old hatchet. She felt for the head of the hatchet, and it was instantly familiar to her.

By God, this is my *hatchet, she thought. This is the one I brought from the homestead.*

Tossing her personal possessions into the pit along with her body. It seemed strangely cruel, an additional insult. When she felt around, however, she didn't find any of her other possessions. Then again, the bottom of the pit was remarkably large and strewn with countless small rocks and pebbles. Her items could be scattered fire and wide. She might never find them in this impenetrable darkness.

Even so, she wasn't going to waste this gift. She tucked the handle of the hatchet under her belt at her hip. Somehow, finding a familiar object strengthened her resolve to get out of here, so she rose and felt her way to the rock wall. She stumbled on something strange along the way. It felt like another tool handle. She reached down and grabbed it and quickly realized it was a bone. Possibly a femur. She dropped it, felt around, and found another bone. And another. And then a skull.

Others have died here, she realized. How many people have these people killed? The bodies are reduced to bones, so they've been here a very long time. Certainly, before the storm started. How long has this cult been operating inside Snowbird Caverns?

She tossed the leg bone aside and kept going. There had to be some other way up, some way that would take her all the way to the top. She moved past the tumble of large rocks and began feeling the wall. As she continued along the wall, she felt a change in the air, a kind of closing in that told her the pit was narrowing the farther she went. Eventually, she felt the other wall brushing against her back. The pit had turned into little more than a crack. More than that, the walls became less smooth, more pitted and rougher.

I think I could climb this, she said, feeling the rough, uneven surface of the wall before her. Plenty of handholds. She could do it. *This time I'm going to pass the trial.*

First, she felt along the bandage on her arm. It was wet with blood. Pulling back a corner of the bandage, she probed the wound. The stitches were still intact, but the wound was seeping blood. Still, it wasn't too bad. She could ignore the pain.

Okay, go for it, she told herself. *A forty or fifty-foot climb. You can do it, as long as you're careful and take it slow.*

She found a deep horizontal crack and used it as a handhold, hoisting herself up. Her hands were scratched and bruised, but her yearning to get out of here was enough to power through the pain. She found a sturdy protruding rock for her right foot. From there, the climb went fairly smoothly. She chose her handholds and footholds carefully, but there were plenty of them to choose from. More than that, the far wall had moved in close enough that she could lean her back against it for additional support.

Her body was soon screaming at her for relief. Everything hurt. Breathing hurt. Her fingers felt slick with blood, and her back was killing her. However, she eventually reached out for another handhold and found her hand sliding along a smooth rocky floor. She had reached the top of the pit. Not just a ledge along the way but the actual top.

With a great sigh of relief, Fiona dragged herself out of the pit, crawled forward a few feet, and collapsed on her side.

"I did it," she whispered. "I got out of there. You couldn't kill me, Brigid. You failed, Seb. I'm alive. The god of the deep places gave you a big middle finger, didn't he? I can't wait to see your faces when you find out."

She laughed, but even that hurt. Finally, she just lay there on her side, seeing nothing before her, and felt the waves of pain and discomfort washing over her endlessly. Of course, climbing out of the pit hadn't done much to free her. They'd led her here with a blindfold over her eyes, following many twists and turns. How in the heck was she ever going to get out of these endless passages without light or arrow marks to guide her?

I remember a few of the turns, she thought. *I might be able to find my way back. If I can just get close, maybe I'll see candlelight shining somewhere faintly.*

She hoped it was enough. Though she still wanted to lie there—though she would have slept for days—she made herself get up. This was her first test. Could she remember the way across this room to the passage entrance? Sliding her feet along the floor so she wouldn't accidentally fall into a pit, she slowly made her way in the direction that she thought would lead out of the room. Her hands were thrust out in front of her, grabbing wildly at the empty air.

The room was much bigger than she'd remembered, but eventually her fingers found a rock wall in front of her. Feeling around, she came across an opening, and she sensed a change in the air before her. It was an opening to a narrow passage. The way out of this execution chamber.

She started down the passageway. The endless, impenetrable darkness was beginning to feel oppressive, smothering, but she tried not to let that feeling take over. Creeping forward, she did her best to remember the twists and turns that had brought her from the stalactite cell.

Some of the turns seemed familiar when she took them, but others felt utterly alien. Still, she pressed on, until minutes began to bleed into hours. She was thirsty now, and all of the pain in her body was giving way to exhaustion. Her limbs were becoming weak so that just continuing to move forward became a desperate struggle. To make matters worse, she kept stumbling and tripping on things, and she had the constant fear that she would step into another pit or hole. A broken leg would be the end of her.

I'm in no condition to get revenge on anyone, she thought. But even as she thought it, her hand went down to the handle of the hatchet hanging from her belt. *Then again, maybe not. We'll see.*

She became so fixated on this thought—on what she would do when she saw one of the Dwellers again—that it took a minute to realize she could just barely make out the wall in front of her. The barest shape of the rocks was discernible somehow, though they were little more than a hint of shapes. Light on the walls. Light on the floor. It was such a surprise that she felt a rush of elation sweep over her whole body. It drove out some of the pain, much of the exhaustion, and propelled her forward at a quicker pace.

I did it, she thought. *Somehow, by God, I found my way back to the camp!*

Had she really remembered the twists and turns so clearly? It was remarkable but undeniable. The light was growing brighter as she continued down the passageway. She could see the walls, the low ceiling where the shapes of bats were visible like a vague, writhing mass. The floor here was sloped upward slightly, scattered with loose rocks and that potent mix of guano and mud that burned in her nostrils.

How should I approach the camp? she wondered. *I can't just tromp in there like nothing's wrong. If I could get to our bedroom, I might be able to reveal myself to my friends first. That way we could confront the Dwellers together.*

Then again, she considered the possibility of lurking and striking from the shadows like an assassin. It would be safer for the others if she dealt with the Dwellers before they could stop her or retaliate.

The cave before her curved sharply to the left and ascended a series of crude steps. Something was wrong with the quality of the light. This realization cut through all of her daydreams about revenge. No, the light was all wrong. It was slate gray and steady. Not flickering firelight or candlelight. Not the brilliant white of battery-powered LEDs. No, this was some other kind of light. It shone brilliantly from just around the curve ahead, and it brought with it a sudden chill wind.

It's daylight, she thought. *I found a way out.*

104

As much as she hated it, as much as it made her sick to her stomach, Hope had no choice but to return to her old routine. Her father said they had to act like everything was okay for a little while longer. That meant the adults were going back to work, as if they'd shrugged off Fiona's death and the fight that had followed. That also meant Hope and Zane had to return to class like good little girls and boys.

As she made her way to the classroom, the anxiety burned so sharply in her stomach that she thought her stomach might be melting. How could she possibly act normal around these people who had murdered Fiona? How would she possibly keep from bursting into tears? As she entered the central chamber, she caught a glimpse of Alex and Henny heading into the kitchen, and even though they didn't look in her direction, her heart leapt into her throat.

Zane put a gentle hand against her back. "Just don't think about it. Don't think about anything at all. Let Jarred work things out, okay? Your dad knows what he's doing."

"I know. I trust him," Hope replied. "It just sucks." Yet his words comforted her, helped her get into a better state of mind.

They made their way down the familiar lantern-lit hallway to the classroom. The other kids were already there. Some were sitting down, but the sisters, Samara and Vanya, were standing in front of their desks and talking to each other intently about something. When Hope and Zane entered the room, the talking stopped and every other student turned to look at them.

Whatever Dad's plans are, we'll be a whole lot safer with a few weapons in our possession, Hope reminded herself. *I can't do anything about that, but I can help buy a little more time by acting like everything's okay.*

As she approached her desk, she looked pointedly at Samara and made herself smile. Oh, it felt disgusting to look happy. "Hey there," she said. "Is something wrong? What were you two talking about?"

Samara and Vanya glanced at each other, as if silently debating which of them would respond. Finally, Vanya took her seat, leaving her sister to stand alone.

"Well, no, it's just…" Samara cleared her throat. "We all heard what happened. Someone died, and then your father almost killed Grandma."

"Don't talk about it, Samara," her sister said sharply. Some of the younger schoolkids looked like they were on the verge of tears.

"Well? It's not like it's a secret," Samara said. "Why can't I bring it up?"

"You just can't," Vanya said. "Grandma told you everything's fine. It doesn't matter what happened. Sit down."

Samara scowled at her sister but sat down at her desk. As Hope sat beside her, she leaned over and spoke to the waifish girl. "It's all true, Samara. I don't mind that you mentioned it. It's good to talk about things, but maybe not right now."

Just then, Vanya shushed her, and Samara's gaze went to the door. Hope turned to see Nick striding into the room. Zane was bent over his desk, idly picking at the edge with a thumbnail. He didn't bother to look up when the teacher entered. Of course, Zane had said they should act normal, and this was his normal classroom behavior.

"Good morning, children," Nick said.

As he passed in front of her desk, Hope caught the distinct whiff of fish. The teacher was wiping his hands on a rag. Though Nick hadn't been directly involved in Fiona's death or the attack on her father, he was still one of them. He'd helped put Zane into the pit. Hope felt her stomach twist at his proximity.

Instead of going to the chalkboard, Nick stopped in front of the row of desks and looked down the line of students. His gazed lingered just a little longer on Hope and Zane, but she refused to look away. Could he feel her disgust and hatred for him beneath the plastered-on smile? Part of her hoped so.

"So, we won't be having normal class today," the teacher said. He stopped wiping his hands and stuffed the rag into a pocket of his plain brown pants. As the children began to mutter excitedly, he held up a hand. "Now, now, we're not going to goof off, children. Instead, we'll all be working hard, okay?"

That put an immediate stop to the excited murmuring, but Hope was relieved. A day of work sounded so much better than a day of listening to uninteresting lessons and cult propaganda.

"Samara, Vanya, Zane, and Hope," Nick continued, "as the oldest of the kids, you get to scale and clean fish today. I had a prosperous morning with my fishing pole down in the stream."

Hope had never scaled a fish in her life, but she would have volunteered to clean toilets if it would get her out of class. She nodded happily and drummed her fingers on the desktop. Nick gestured at Vanya.

"You know the way to the prep room behind the kitchen," he said. "Lead Zane and Hope there, would you? The fish are in buckets beside a work-table. Go on."

He snapped his fingers, and Vanya rose. As she headed to the door, Hope bounded up and went after her. Samara and Zane came more reluctantly.

"Now, as to the rest of you," Nick said. "You get to clean rooms. Mops, brooms, scrub brushes, soap. It's going to be fun!"

Hope heard the little ones groaning as she left the classroom and followed Vanya back down the hall. Samara had wanted to talk about Fiona's death and the fight. Even when her sister had resisted, she'd insisted on bringing it up. Hope found that interesting. She'd tried her best to reach Samara in the past. Had she planted any seeds? Had they taken root in the girl's mind? Maybe.

I wonder how far I could push things with Samara, she thought, following Vanya back into the central chamber. *I wonder if I could get her to help us.*

As they walked into the kitchen, dodging the big firepit that took up much of the space, walking past a row of barrels, the crude shelves stacked with cooking utensils, Hope began to formulate a plan, but it made her nervous. Indeed, she was practically shaking. The last time she'd formulated a plan, it had put Zane in a dark, bug-infested pit for two days. But this time was different, wasn't it? They were actively planning an escape now.

The prep room was a small, damp chamber between the kitchen and storage room, dominated by a table that was little more than a slab of wood with a row of stools behind it. The room reeked of fish, and indeed, Hope spotted four large buckets full of water and the silvery glint of freshly caught fish. Various kinds of knives had been dumped on one end of the table, and a few large metal trays were set on the other end.

"Do you guys know how to scale and gut fish?" Vanya asked.

"Yes, of course I do," Zane replied. "I went fishing a lot with my dad back in the old world."

"What about you?" Vanya asked, gesturing at Hope. She claimed the stool closest to the pile of knives and began separating the pile, creating neat rows of matching knives.

"I think I can get the hang of it," Hope said. "I'm a quick learner."

She waited until Samara chose a stool, then sat down beside her. That put Zane on the other end of the table beside the trays. As they took their seats, Vanya leaned over and rooted through the buckets.

"Smallmouth bass," she said. "Walleye. A couple of flatheads. Nick really did have a good day of fishing. We'll have a nice lunch, I guess."

"Not me," Samara said. She grabbed one of the knives and pulled it toward her. It had a black plastic handle and a slightly curved blade. "I'm sick of fish. I only want to eat chicken and corned beef."

"Well, you're weird, then," Vanya said. "Everyone, grab a knife. Hope, just follow my example. You'll get the hang of it. I'll give you one of the smallest bass to start with."

Hope bided her time, waiting until they were all hard at work. Vanya showed her how to scale and gut the fish, but it wasn't all that hard. Just a little gross. Still, she waited until they were all in the routine. Zane was a natural; he'd clearly done this before, as had Samara and Vanya.

Finally, Hope decided to go for it. She glanced toward the kitchen, but it appeared to be empty at the moment. Then she turned to Samara, who noticed and gave her a nervous smile in return.

I planted seeds of doubt, she thought. *Let's see if they bore any fruit at all. Otherwise, I'm going in the pit. But I don't care anymore. The adults killed Fiona, and I don't respect them.*

"Hey, can I ask you girls a question?" Hope said, speaking softly. "It's not a bad question, but it's still kind of a secret."

Samara and Vanya glanced at each other, and Vanya gave the barest hint of a nod to her sister.

"Yeah, just don't talk too loud," Samara said, lowering her head. "What's your question?"

Zane paused in his work, but he didn't say anything. He didn't even look at Hope.

"If I wanted to hide something or dispose of something," Hope said, "what would be a good place to do it? It would have to be someplace that it would never be found again."

The question hung in the air for a second. Hope's heart was racing. Was this it? Was this the moment that her punishment began? No one at the table was working. They all sat with knives in hand, fish arrayed before them, scales and guts scattered across the tabletop.

"Well..." Samara spoke. The tip of her knife was shaking, and she set it down. "When we really want to dispose of unwanted things, or things that are...are...what's the word?"

"Anathema," Vanya replied.

"Yeah, that's it," Samara said. "When we really want to get rid of it forever, we take it to God's Wrath and cast it into the bottomless pit."

"Oh, okay," Hope said. "I don't know where that is. I don't suppose you'd be willing to show me where it is. I have something I really need to throw away."

Before Samara could answer, Vanya shook her head vigorously and said, "We don't know where it is. We haven't passed the trial, and no one with favor has ever taken us there, so there's no way for us to find it."

And with that, Vanya went back to work, as if the issue had been resolved. But Samara just kept sitting there. Before his punishment, Zane would almost certainly have opposed this idea, but he was angry now. He neither opposed Hope nor tried to talk her out of it. Still, if neither of the sisters knew the way, then it wasn't going to work.

It was worth a try, Hope thought. *Get back to work.*

But Samara was still just sitting there. Finally, she turned to Hope. She was breathing fast, the tip of her tongue flicking against her top lip. Clearly nervous.

"Yes, I know the way," she said. "I can show you where it is."

Vanya gasped and dumped her fish and knife onto the table. "Samara, you do *not* know the way! How could you? They would never allow you into the dark places."

Samara shushed her sister. "I *do* know the way. Are you going to tell on me so they can put me in a pit, too?"

Vanya grunted unhappily and leaned back in her chair. "No. No, I'm not. Why would you do it? You know what Grandma would do to you if she found out. It's dangerous. It's *wrong*."

"Wrong?" Samara said softly. "Is it? I don't know anymore. I don't know anything."

Vanya grabbed her arm. "Of course it's wrong. It's against the rules. I didn't make the rules. It's not up to me. The rules were in place before we were even born."

"Well...whatever." Samara yanked her arm out of her sister's grasp. "Sometimes I just...wonder about a lot of things. So do you, Vanya. So do you and you know it."

"Whatever yourself," Vanya replied, waving off the comment. But Hope noted that she didn't deny Samara's accusation. "How do you know where God's Wrath is?"

"I've spent more time exploring than you realize," Samara told her sister. "Like when you were working alone, or bathing, or mad at me about something. I've looked at a lot of places. So what? Who cares anymore?" She gave her sister a bold look, and Vanya only gaped in astonishment. "So, guess what? A few days ago, I followed Henny when she went to throw something down in the pit. She never even heard me or sensed me."

As Vanya continued to stare in shock, Samara turned to Hope. "It was a big blue bag with a bunch of stuff in it. I saw her carrying it by the light of her own lamp. I watched her pull items out of the bag and toss them into this big pit one by one. She seemed to enjoy it."

Big blue bag. Hope knew exactly what that was. Their duffle bag, the one that has held their guns. She looked toward the kitchen again to make sure it was still empty. She didn't see any of the adults. Could they be listening from some place just out of sight? The Dwellers' home was full of secret places.

You already took the risk, she thought. *No sense backing out now.*

"Would you be willing to show me where God's Wrath is?" Hope asked.

"When?" Samara asked.

"Right now," Hope replied.

This finally roused Zane. He stopped working and sighed. "Are you sure about this, Hope? You don't want to wind up in a pit, trust me. And anyway, it'd be a shame to mess up your father's plans."

"Yeah, right now," Hope said. She felt bold, and her anger about Fiona had created a willful boldness in her. It seemed best to take advantage of it while it lasted. "Will you take me there, Samara?"

Samara nodded and set her knife down again. She grabbed a rag and began wiping her hands. Vanya looked like she really wanted to protest. Her mouth opened and closed a few times. Finally, she went back to work.

"I'll stay here," she said. "If an adult comes along, I'll cover for you somehow. Just don't be gone too long!"

Zane sighed and jabbed his knife into the head of a fish. "Okay, well, I guess I'm coming too."

"Zane, I don't want you to cover for me again," Hope said. "If we get caught, I'll take my punishment."

"I'm coming to make sure we *don't* get caught," he said. "No one's going in a pit for this. Trust me." He looked at her intently. "No one's going in a pit. I'll make sure of that."

Samara pushed back her chair. Despite her initial discomfort with the conversation, she now seemed raring to go. She had shared her secret with Hope, and now she had a chance to prove it.

"Come on," Samara said. "I know a way to get there that should avoid any trouble."

She reached for her fish, as if she intended to put it away, but Vanya stretched out her arm to block it.

"Leave the fish," Vanya said. "I need proof that you were working so they'll believe me when I say you're coming back soon."

And with that, Samara headed off toward the kitchen. Hope had to scramble to chase after her, tipping her stool over in the process and making a bit too much noise. As she raced out the room, Zane at her heels, Vanya shushed them.

"Keep it down," she said. "And hurry back. I can't cover for you all day. If you get caught, it's on you."

"I know," Hope said over her shoulder.

"We're not getting caught," Samara said.

"No one's going in a pit," Zane said again.

The kitchen was a long room with shelves and barrels lined against one wall, and a stone fire pit and counter against the other. Smoke was funneled into a small hole near the ceiling, though Hope often wondered where that smoke went. Did it lead all the way out of the cavern? Behind the firepit, a makeshift curtain of some kind of shiny material had been hung against the wall. Nick had explained that it was fireproofing material to keep the walls from getting scorched when they were cooking. However, Samara headed straight for it, stepping over a corner of the firepit. She swept the curtain aside, revealing a crack in the wall behind it. Hope gasped, and Samara put a finger to her lips.

"Very quiet now," she whispered. "I told you, there are many secrets ways. Hurry."

She motioned them through. Hope stepped past Samara, slipped through the gap behind the firepit, and found herself in a dark and very narrow passageway. The walls on either side were so close that they brushed against her shoulders. Zane and Samara followed her into the passage. Then the strange silver curtain swung back into place and plunged them into darkness.

"I can't see a thing," Hope said, sliding forward.

"I can fix that," Samara replied.

Hope heard a click, and light flooded the passageway, revealing an ascending floor and a gradual curve ahead of them.

"A flashlight," Hope said. "Where did you get that?"

"It's a really small one," Samara said. "I took it from the supplies a few days ago, on the day after we talked about mastodons and stuff. Actually, I think it used to belong to you guys. Just keep going."

Hope followed the gradual curve of the passage. Eventually, it opened up, and Samara was able to take the lead. From there, she led them through a confusing series of twists and turns. She seemed to know exactly where she was going, and occasionally, Hope spotted colored arrows carved into the walls.

Finally, they entered a low chamber with multiple exits, where water trickled down a great wavy sheet of pale rock. As they did, some low shape lunged out of the darkness, skirting the edge of Samara's flashlight beam as it came straight for Hope. She almost screamed, but managed to get both hands clamped over her mouth before the sound came out. Then she stumbled backward and bumped into Zane.

As Samara turned, the shape resolved itself into the form of a friendly black-and-white Australian cattle dog. Somehow, Smoke had found them, and he stood now at Hope's feet, staring up at her and panting. She stooped down and petted his head.

"Where in the world did you come from?" Hope asked. "You're supposed to be with Myra. Did you get restless and go for a walk?"

He came looking for Fiona, Hope thought. That was the most reasonable explanation.

"Can he come with us?" Hope said.

"I guess so," Samara said. "He seems friendly."

Samara turned and resumed walking. As Hope followed her, Smoke stayed at her side, but he was constantly sniffing the ground. Occasionally, he whimpered. Hope tried to comfort him, but it didn't seem to help. Something had gotten Smoke worked up.

"Fiona went this way," Zane said from behind her. "That's what he smells."

A disconcerting thought. Finally, Samara led them through another doorway into a big chamber with a high ceiling. The flashlight revealed a deep pit in front of them. As they approached the edge, Hope saw a steep drop, and her heart sank. There were a few narrow ledges on the way down, but no easy way to climb down. She could see a lot of debris down at the bottom, fifty feet or so below, including a little blue glint that was almost certainly the duffle bag. It seemed the Dwellers had tossed quite a bit into God's Wrath.

"Well, there it is," Hope muttered, standing beside Samara as the Dweller girl moved the beam from side to side.

"That's it," Samara replied. "If you toss something down there, you'll never be able to get it back."

Hope studied the walls of the pit. The biggest ledge was about twenty feet down, but it was narrow and sloped downward. She could see no way to get to it. This pit was a deathtrap, which meant she had no way to retrieve the duffle bag with their guns.

"Is this where they took Fiona?" Hope asked. "I don't see her down there."

"Her body could be under all of that debris," Samara said. "They throw more than just people down there. They throw lots of stuff. Anything they want to get rid of."

"But isn't this the deepest place?" Vanya wondered aloud. "If so, isn't God supposed to be down there, too?"

"I don't know." Samara sounded hushed, awed, possibly frightened. "I guess so, yeah. Nick has talked about this place a little bit, but not much. And he doesn't answer questions about it. All I know is God's Wrath has existed since long before we ever got here, and the faithful have been putting bad people down there for a long time."

"And you're both okay with this?" Hope said. "It doesn't bother you?"

Samara grunted softly, but Vanya said, "It doesn't matter what we think. Some things you have to accept no matter what."

"I don't like it," Samara added, finally, "but Nick says we have to do this kind of stuff. We don't want to lose favor."

They all stood there for a few minutes gazing down at the vast debris field at the bottom of the pit. Hope could see countless small shapes of various colors, but she couldn't tell what they were.

"Well, have you seen enough?" Zane asked.

Hope sighed. "Yeah, I guess so. We're not getting down in that pit anyway. Let's get Smoke and head back."

But when she turned to the dog, she realized he was gone. She gazed back across the room and saw no sign of him. Somehow, he had disappeared.

105

For a few minutes, Fiona thrust her head through the gap and just let the cold, crisp air wash over her. Strange that she should find it so comforting. The cold outside was a domain of hungry animals and bandits. Yet she couldn't deny that she had an almost primal desire to get back to it. To flee the cult? Perhaps. To flee her own sense of failure? Certainly.

The hole in the rock wall before her was just big enough to stick her head through, but she couldn't do more than that. However, the view beyond the gap was incredible. It appeared to be late evening; a full moon was hovering just above a line of hills far across a broad valley. Moonlight shone upon the undisturbed snow, creating a faint sparkling glow. There were a few old buildings in the field, but they seemed to be sinking into the snow. To the right and left, she saw numerous rock hills rising up, creating walls on either side of the valley.

How long had they been in the cave? Weeks, but it felt like years. How long had they been under the thumb of Brigid's cult? It felt even longer. And there was the world, the free world, arrayed before her. Yet she still couldn't get to it.

My homestead is out there somewhere, she thought. *I never should have left it. I could have lived in the greenhouse, if necessary. But how was I to know we'd find these crazy Dwellers down here?*

A sudden desperation seized her, and she began pushing against the hole, trying to force her shoulders through. She got the heels of her boots against the wall behind her and pushed. Her shoulders slammed against the rim of the hole, and she even thought she felt the rocks shifting, bowing against her weight. But it was no use. Eventually, her shoulders hurt too much, and she was forced to relent.

Fiona backed away from the hole and sank down onto the cave floor, massaging her collarbone. Of course, she had just enough self-awareness to realize that something was wrong with her. This strange all-consuming need to *get away* was not normal. She knew that, but it didn't stop her.

I'm getting through that damned opening, she thought.

Fiona rose, feeling sick and sore all over. She'd scraped up her hands, and her ribs really hurt. Nevertheless, she braced her back against the wall and began kicking at the rocks around the small opening. The first kick was futile. She might as well have been kicking a concrete wall, and the effort sent a little spike up pain up her leg and into her torso, where it seemed to stick in her ribs. She kicked again, but the pain was too much.

She considering giving up then. After all, if she was only going to break her body trying to get out, then she wouldn't have much chance of survival on the other side. However, then she remembered the hatchet at her belt. Pulling it out, she held it up into the early evening light. It probably wouldn't last long against the rocks, but if she could get a few good whacks before it broke, she might be able to finish the rest by hand.

Turning to one side, she spread her feet slightly to steady herself, then raised the hatchet above her head. She swung the blunt end at the rocks beside the gap. Metal against rock sent another spike of pain through her body, but a chunk of rock broke off and crumbled. As it did, she realized the rocks around the opening weren't solid. On the contrary, they seemed to be an amalgam of stones and ice, possibly a human-made construction, as if someone had been attempting to shut off the exit while leaving just enough of a hole to see outside.

She took another swung with the blunt side of the hatchet, breaking off an even larger chunk of the composite wall. With a third swing, she shattered so much of it that she was pretty sure she could now force herself through the hole. Fiona tucked the hatchet back under her belt and massaged the bicep of her right arm. Out of breath, sweating, and in much pain, she took a moment to recover. As she did, she gazed through the larger opening, seeing the shimmering field of snow outside the cave. It looked like a sheen of silver in the moonlight. It almost seemed a shame to mess it up by walking across it.

I could leave right now, she thought. *I'm resourceful. I'll find my way home.*

The possibility was so present, so immediate, that she couldn't say no. Fiona rose and approached the opening. She didn't have much in the way of supplies. A hatchet, a pocket knife, a small flashlight. Cold air on her face, she thrust her hands through the opening and grabbed the outer edge.

"Well, get it over with," she muttered. "You know it's the right thing to do, so don't overthink it."

But just then, a familiar sound intruded into her self-talk. A dog barking. She knew the sound of Smoke's voice well, but he only barked when he was upset or anxious. Fiona stepped back and turned just in time to see her loyal dog come running around the corner. She was so surprised to see him that she just stood frozen as he approached. And then he jumped up, put his front paws against her denim shirt, and his barking became whimpering.

"How in the world did you find me?" she said.

She dropped to her knees, embracing Smoke, as he settled in her lap. Whimpering became contented panting, but he made sure to reach up and lick her a face a few times. Somehow, his sudden appearance and his frantic attitude broke through the wall in her mind.

"What am I doing?" she muttered, tears springing into her eyes. "I'm hardly prepared to go outside. I don't have my gloves or my heavy coat. I have no way to start a fire, no sleeping bag. Oh, Smoke, what am I doing?"

I just want to go to home again, she thought.

She cried, as Smoke kept trying to lick her face and clean up the tears.

"You're a good boy," she said, petting him. "You're such a good boy. You ran through that dark cave all by yourself until you found me."

Finally, he settled down, Fiona's crying tapered off, and they sat together for a while.

"You should be with the others," Fiona said. "If you're here with me, then who's protecting them?"

That, in turn, brought her surging back to reality. The Dwellers were murderous people. They'd intended to kill Fiona. She couldn't leave her friends now. She'd wanted to leave before because she'd been convinced they were well taken care of. However, she'd seen the other side of this cult. Her friends weren't safe here.

"They need me," she said

Smoke hopped up from her lap, tail wagging, anxious to go. Somehow, her beloved pet had pulled her out of the dark place in her mind just by showing up at the right time. Fiona marveled at this. How in the world had she been so willing to abandon her friends, her family, to these cave-dwelling maniacs? How had she been so willing to rush out into the deadly cold so ill-prepared?

I lost my way, she thought.

Beckoning the dog, she headed back the way she'd come in, leaving the cave exit.

"Come on, Smoke," she said. "Let's find our way back to the camp and help our people."

106

Jarred had volunteered to repair clothing again. He didn't particularly like it, and he wasn't very good at it. However, the task put him fairly close to the central chamber, and he knew the Dwellers kept some of their bows and arrows in a recessed place behind the curtain—within easy reach while they were sleeping.

Currently, he had a big pile of clothes arrayed on the table before him. Some belonged to his group, but most belonged to the Dwellers. Their clothes were all plain, homemade, and rather ugly. He picked up a pair of pants that had a tear in the knee. The rough cloth had already been patched in a few places, and the tear in the knee was fairly big. Still, it didn't have to look good. He wasn't at all concerned about the quality of his work, not when he was planning their escape.

I have to get the bows away from them, he thought. *That's priority one. Our weapons are either hidden or destroyed, so as long as the Dwellers have access to their weapons, they have all the power in a fight.*

His plan depended in large part on Larry and Lana. At the moment, everyone was working. Nick had spent the morning fishing. Alex and Henny were working in the laundry room. Seb was making cloth on a loom. Brigid was the tricky part. She'd sent Josiah off on some task, but Brigid was lounging about today—possibly still recovering from her near-death experience. Getting behind that curtain, grabbing the bows, and escaping was going to be a huge risk. Somehow, Jarred had to get Brigid away from the central chamber so Larry and Lana could play their part.

After a few minutes of trying to concentrate on his work, he heard Nick and some of the younger kids headed down the nearby passageway. Their footsteps were accompanied by much clank and clatter. When they passed by the door, Jarred saw that they were lugging mops, brooms, and buckets.

"We'll start in the guest bedroom, kids," Nick said. "We're going to deep clean. Oh, yes, it's fun to clean! It makes everything look and smell brand new."

The little kids didn't look like they agreed. Jarred waited until they'd all passed by, then he listened to their retreating footsteps in the passageway. His heart was racing. Too much was at stake. He couldn't afford to mess this up, and he was afraid that some kind of physical confrontation with the Dwellers was inevitable.

He dumped the pants onto the table and jabbed the sewing needle into a small pincushion that looked like a tomato. Then he carefully pushed his chair back and rose. Fortunately, his workroom was quite dark at the moment, with only a couple of candles providing light. Neither Nick nor the children had looked in his direction.

A fight may be coming, he thought, *but at least I can give my people an advantage.*

Jarred headed for the door. He'd wasted as much time as he dared. As he headed down the corridor toward the central chamber, he tried to work out his conversation with Brigid in his mind. It was going to be tricky. Would she trust him enough to talk to him after the last time?

He stepped into the central chamber and found no one. Light flickered from somewhere deep in the kitchen, and he thought he heard someone moving around in there, possibly working. A chair was pushed back from one of the tables in front of him, as if someone had just gotten up and left. Jarred glanced toward the curtain that led into the sleeping area. It was so close.

If I knew I'd have a couple of minutes alone in here, I'd go for it, he thought.

He reached out and let his fingers brush the coarse cloth. Larry and Lana were waiting for his signal in the washroom, but maybe he didn't need to involve them yet.

Well, do it quickly, then, he told himself.

He grabbed the edge of the curtain and started to pull it aside, but then he heard footsteps coming from the passageway across from him. Jarred quickly let go of the curtain and stepped toward the nearest table. As he did, Brigid entered the room, a bolt of cloth in her arms. She saw him and froze, giving him a look of uncertainty.

"Shouldn't you be working?" she asked.

Unthreatening body language was key. He knew that, but he wasn't sure how to pull it off. He slouched a bit, tried to fix a friendly look on his face, but he couldn't figure out what to do with his hands.

"Yeah, I'm working," he said, "but I just…well, the thing is, I'd really like to talk to you for a minute."

Brigid gave him a questioning look, one eyebrow going up, then she glanced over her shoulder. "Oh, I suppose so. Go ahead, then. Talk."

"No, I mean…somewhere sort of private," he replied. "I understand if you still don't trust me, so feel free to bring someone else along to stand guard. I'm trying to understand the faith better, and I figure you're the one who can explain things to me the best." He was speaking louder than was necessary so Larry and Lana would hear. Did it sound unnatural? Would it give him away?

Brigid approached the table and dumped the bolt of cloth. "You want to have a private conversation of a religious nature with me," she said. "Is that it?"

She doesn't trust me, Jarred thought. *This isn't going to work.*

"Well, it doesn't *have* to be private," he replied. "I just don't want to say something, or ask something, in front of others that might be inappropriate.

I'm trying to work out a few faith issues so I can put my mind at ease. If I can do that, I'll finally be able to let go of any lingering reservations."

Brigid gave him that same little smile. He could never tell whether it was sincere or not. She glanced toward the corridor behind her again, then stepped around the table and approached. "Yes, I can spare a few minutes. Let's use the classroom, since the children are busy with other work."

As she came toward him, Jarred heard other footsteps in the corridor. Were Larry and Lana already on the move? No, too soon. But it was Alex who appeared, entering the room while wiping his hands on a towel, as if he'd come straight from work.

"Alex, why don't you come with us?" Brigid asked.

"Of course," Alex replied, giving Jarred an unfriendly look. "What's happening?"

"A conversation," Brigid said. "Jarred, you don't mind if Alex stands guard, do you?"

Jarred forced himself to keep smiling at the old woman. "That's perfectly fine. I won't take up too much time."

He turned and led them down the passageway toward the classroom. His heart was racing, his whole body tingling with nerves. This was it. Everything hinged on this moment, and he had no way to verify that Larry and Lana were doing their part. He went to the classroom, where the desks were still set in a line in front of the blackboard.

Wanting to seem as unthreatening as possible, Jarred sat down in one of the student desks. He hoped Brigid and Alex would do the same, if only so it would buy a little more time. However, Alex stayed in the doorway, while Brigid stood in front of Jarred's desk with her hands on her hips.

"Okay, Jarred, here we are," Brigid said. "Let's hear it. How can I help you overcome your final reservations?"

"I'm just trying to work out my faith as best I can," he replied. He couldn't look at her, afraid his nerves would give him away, so he fixed his gaze on the desktop. Someone had been picking at the edge of the desk. He could see damage to the old wood. "If I can understand a few aspects of the faith just a little better, I think I'll finally be fully at peace with everything."

Larry, Lana, this is on you now, he thought. *Don't let me down.*

"I'm more than willing to discuss the faith," Brigid said. "Always. There's nothing I love more. Let's hear it, then."

"Well, first of all, I'm having trouble understanding God's purpose in killing Fiona," he said. He did his best to keep the real emotion out of his voice. There was a deep well of anger in him, but he couldn't let the Dwellers see it, not again. "Please help me come to terms with her death. If I can do that, I can move on."

Religious talk would keep Brigid busy for a while. At least, he hoped so.

"Jarred, you have to understand that the rules here exist for a reason," Brigid said. "God does not make demands of us arbitrarily, even if we struggle to make sense of them. The rules have been handed down to us from the time of my grandparents, and as long as we've followed them, we have enjoyed peace and prosperity. It is a sin to walk the dark paths without first passing the trials, because one must be proved worthy. If Fiona had been proved worthy, she could have gone anywhere."

"Yes, but she was frustrated at not passing the trials," he said. He just needed to buy time. Enough time. "That's why she acted the way she did. Surely she might have been redeemed."

"She was carving the walls to create an exit for herself," Brigid said. "There is nothing worse she could have done. Nothing more offensive to our faith. Creating an exit puts our whole community at risk. Not just because it could allow dangerous people into the cave, but because it is an insult to our god in the deepest place, an insult that could jeopardize the favor placed upon all of us, upon our home. There is no undoing that damage either. Our home will now bear the scars of Fiona's disobedience forever. Until the end of time."

It was insufferable nonsense, and Jarred found it incredibly difficult to sit and listen to it. This old woman had murdered Fiona over nothing, and she didn't even have a rational explanation for it. Her conception of God was as deficient as her own mental and emotional stability. But he made himself sit there and stare at that rough carving in the desktop's edge and listen to a voice he'd come to despise deeply.

"Jarred, the only currency that matters anymore is *favor*," Brigid continued. "You must understand this. How can we possibly—"

She stopped suddenly as a commotion arose from elsewhere. Jarred heard a wordless shout, a clatter of something being dropped, and his heart leapt into his throat. Alex spun around to face the corridor.

"What are you doing?" someone shouted from the direction of the central chamber. It sounded like Nick. "How dare you!"

At that, Alex charged down the hall. Brigid gave Jarred a sharp look, then chased after Alex. Jarred rose from the desk and hurried down the hallway. There were now two voices speaking heatedly over each other. Larry and Nick.

"I'm not doing anything," Larry said. "Working."

"That doesn't look like working," Nick replied. "What are you doing in *there*?"

Jarred reached the central chamber just behind Brigid to find himself in the midst of a tense standoff. Larry was standing in front of the curtain in front of the Dwellers' sleeping place, still holding it with his left hand. In his right hand, he had a bow and a leather quiver of arrows. A few feet away, Nick stood facing him, his face flushed and furious. The younger schoolkids were clustered in a doorway behind him, still holding their mops, brooms, and buckets.

Henny had come into the room from the direction of the bedroom, which put her closest to Larry. Her hands were clenched into fists, her body tense, as if she were about to charge him.

"What do you have there in your hand?" Nick shouted. "Who told you to take that?"

Larry glanced toward Brigid and Alex as they came into the room, but Jarred caught movement behind him—someone else on the other side of the curtain. Lana?

How do we get out of this one? Jarred thought.

"I'm working," Larry said. "Nothing more." As he did, he casually hooked the strap of the quiver over his shoulder.

Henny, teeth bared, rushed him then. Brigid shouted her name, as if to stop her, but she lunged at Larry, raising a clenched fist. But Larry saw her coming. Taking the bow in both hands, he spun toward her. And with a cry of rage, he swung the bow like a club right at her head.

107

The upper limb of the bow connected solidly with Henny's forehead, a blow made all the harder by her forward momentum. It was a compound bow, a hefty piece of magnesium alloy. Jarred not only heard the loud crack, he practically felt it. Henny's head rocked back, even as her feet continued to carry her forward. This caused her to flip backward, her legs flying up in the air. She landed on the rock floor with an explosive breath. Then the back of her head bounced, and she came to a sliding stop beside Larry.

He killed her, Jarred thought. *So much for leaving here peacefully.*

Indeed, Henny wasn't moving. She lay on her back, arms and legs askew. Her head was tipped to one side, her mouth hanging open, her eyes half-closed. The bow had left a large red mark on her forehead that would no doubt soon turn into a massive welt, assuming the girl was still alive.

For at least a full second, everyone just gaped in shock. Even Larry stood there, still clutching the bow like a club. Then the room exploded into furious chaos. Nick and Alex rushed at Larry, coming at him from two different directions. The little kids ran screaming toward the kitchen, and Larry backed partway through the gap in the curtain, swinging the bow back and forth in front of him in an attempt to ward off his attackers.

"You scum," Nick snarled. "I knew you people were no good! I *told* Mother we should toss you all into God's Wrath."

Panicked, Jarred ran toward Larry's attackers. Brigid was first in his way, moving just behind Alex.

"Grab him," she cried. "It's God's Wrath for him, right away!"

She didn't realize Jarred was coming for her. Consequently, when he slammed her with his shoulder and sent her flying into the nearby table, it caught her completely off guard. She hit the table with a cry, folded over the top of it, then rolled onto the ground.

"You're a dead man, you filthy sinner," Nick said to Larry.

Larry took another swing at him, but Nick snagged the bow and pulled it out of his hands, casting it aside. Jarred reached for Nick, but just then, he felt something pass in front of his face. It brushed the back of his arm, then hit the rock wall to his left. Only then did he realize it was an arrow. It had come from somewhere high in the room. When he turned to look for the source, he saw a figure standing in one of the murder holes in the domed ceiling.

Josiah. The old man was standing in the gap, a bow in his hands. His hateful eyes shone in the lantern light as he reached back to the quiver over his shoulder for another arrow. It was all chaos and madness. Jarred didn't know what to do or which threat to deal with. Nick and Alex were both grappling with Larry. Henny lay on the ground, unmoving, and Brigid moaned and rolled around on the floor.

"We just want to leave," Jarred shouted. "We don't want to hurt anyone."

"No one leaves!" Josiah shouted from above. "You submit or you fall!"

Jarred froze. Nick and Alex were quickly overpowering Larry. Josiah was nocking another arrow. What in the world was Jarred supposed to do? He looked for cover. The nearest possibility was the table, so he rushed toward it, but as he stepped past Brigid, she grabbed his leg. He stumbled and fell, landing, much as *she* had, on the tabletop. He rolled onto his side and looked up to see Josiah drawing the bowstring and aiming it at him.

Oh, I'm dead, he thought.

Suddenly, the old man cried out, shuddered, and stumbled back a step. It took Jarred a second to see the shaft of an arrow sticking out of his chest, bright yellow fletching catching the lantern light. It was a dead-clean shot, hitting just beneath and to one side of his sternum but aimed upward. The old man fumbled at the arrow weakly, dropping his own bow.

"Kill them all," he said, his voice gurgling wetly. "Nick, kill them all!"

And then he fell forward, dropping out of the murder hole. He landed on the ground just in front of Jarred, smashing onto the floor on his shoulder and face. This drove the arrow all the way through his body so that the bloody arrowhead protruded from his back.

Who fired that arrow?

He turned to look and spotted a small figure standing in a gap at the other end of the curtain. She had a bow in her hands. At first, he assumed it was Lana. He'd glimpsed her behind the curtain at the beginning. But this was a smaller figure, pale and thin, unhealthy, with a shock of thinning white hair. Myra! She was already nocking another arrow, struggling with her frail, trembling hands.

Damn, she's a good shot! Duke taught her well.

Brigid was making an awful sound, practically an animal growl, though she was still on the ground. Nick and Alex had overpowered Larry. Alex had his arms pulled behind his back, and Nick was holding his shoulder and pushing him down. Light shone on a blade, and Jarred realized Nick was holding a long knife.

"Kill them all," Nick said, echoing the old man's words. "It's about time!"

Jarred rushed at the knot of men. Nick was directly in front of him, so he put his head down, leading with his left shoulder, intending to knock him to one side. And hopefully not get stabbed doing it.

He slammed into the Dweller just as he swung the knife. His shoulder hit Nick in the back and shoved him forward. This made him fly past Larry, which turned the knife strike into a wild swing at nothing. Then Nick fell to the ground on his hands and knees, and Jarred landed on top of him.

"You're not killing anybody," Jarred said, grabbing at the man's arm, hoping the get the knife away from him.

Jarred was tall and lanky, Nick was shorter but more muscled. He began to stand, and Jarred couldn't do anything to stop him. On top of that, he was trying desperately to hold on to the man's arm so he wouldn't get stabbed.

"Get off me, you outsider," Nick snarled.

He swung his arm back, and his elbow slammed into Jarred's face, hitting him high on the right cheek near his eye. Jarred felt an explosion of pain and saw stars. The impact seemed to awaken the pain from the welts Seb had left on his head, and suddenly he found himself struggling to stay conscious. Nick rose and, at the same time, shoved him. Jarred was sent crashing to the ground.

Get up! Get up! He's going to kill you.

He landed on his back, flailing his arms. All of his limbs felt rubbery, as sharp waves of eye-watering pain went through his skull. Nick loomed above him, the shiny blade in his right hand. Behind him, Larry and Alex were still locked in a struggle, but Lana was there now as well, batting at the Dweller and pulling at his hair.

"I'm going to cut your throat," Nick said, advancing on Jarred. "You made a mockery of everything we hold dear."

"I didn't mock anything," Jarred replied. "I just wanted to leave with my family."

Nick lunged at him, driving the knife down, as if he intended to dive on top of Jarred and stab him with the full force of his weight behind it. The fist came in from Nick's right, catching him just as he began to drop onto Jarred. It hit him on the side of the face, smashing his cheek against his teeth and turning his head.

The sound was incredibly loud and deep. Nick dropped the knife as he slammed against the rock floor. Jarred blinked tears of pain out of his eyes and saw Nick's attacker. It was Zane, a crazed light in his eyes. Before Nick could recover, Zane punched again, swinging the other fist up and around and hitting the Dweller on the mouth.

Nick collapsed onto his side, and Zane fell upon him, throwing punch after punch. The Dweller raised his hands to block them, but a few got through. Over and over and over again, Zane punched him. The fact that he was so quiet as he did it made it far more intense and disturbing. Nick tried to speak a few times, but each time he got a mouthful of knuckles.

As the attack continued, Jarred rolled onto his belly and reached up to grab a corner of the tabletop. He pulled himself to his feet, his head pounding so hard he thought he might vomit. When he turned, he saw Larry pulling his son off Nick. The Dweller was on the ground, covering his face with his hands and moaning, blood seeping through his fingers.

"It's enough, son. It's enough," Larry said, wrapping both arms around Zane's chest and pulling him backward.

Zane struggled for a bit, his teeth bared and fists flying. But Nick finally went unconscious, his hands sliding off his face to reveal numerous cuts and welts. That seemed to settle the boy, and he finally stop resisting his father's pull.

Where was Alex? Had Larry successfully fended him off? Jarred looked around the room, though he had to do this somewhat slowly because of his fierce headache. Brigid was gone. He saw shadowy figures in the passageway that led to their bedroom. One of them looked like Hope. Myra and Lana were standing together in front of the curtain, and the older woman still had a bow in her hands, an arrow on the string.

Nick and Henny lay on the ground. Henny had blood running from her nostrils and mouth, pooling around her head, and Nick's face was absolutely mangled. Henny didn't appear to be breathing, and Nick had stopped moaning. His hands had slid off his face onto the ground, revealing half-lidded, glassy eyes. If the two Dwellers weren't dead yet, they were very close. Jarred turned around. A group was standing in the dark passageway that led to the water source. Alex stood there with his mother, his hands clasping her upper arms, possibly to keep her from falling. The old woman looked dazed. Seb stood beside them. She had returned from wherever she'd been. She had a bow in her hands, an arrow drawn and aimed at Jarred.

"We're leaving," Jarred said. "That's all there is to it. Fire that bow, and Myra will return fire. We have two of your people right here at our feet. Don't tempt us to hurt them further. Just let us go."

But Brigid, Seb, and Alex just stared back at them. Jarred sensed movement in the kitchen. One of the children peeked around a corner, then quickly ducked out of sight. He thought it was the one named Vanya.

"Where do we go?" Larry said. "Jarred, where do we go now?"

Jarred only knew one place that he could get to in the caves, but he didn't quite remember how to get there. Still, it would have to do. He backed away from the Dwellers, stepping over the bodies on the ground. Larry and Zane moved with him. Then Lana and Myra. They headed into the passageway past their bedroom door and into the dark corridors beyond.

"Stay together," Jarred said. "We're leaving this damned place and these damned weird people."

"Gosh, it's about time," Hope muttered.

108

Jarred was tempted to grab some of their stuff from the bedroom, but he didn't know how long the Dwellers would wait to attack again.

"Dad, don't we need our clothes, our supplies?" Hope asked.

"No, we can't spare the time," he replied. "We're very lucky none of our people got killed just now, but that could change very quickly. I'm not going to lose anyone if I can manage it. Come on!"

"But we can't leave the cave with only the clothes on our backs," she cried.

"If we get out of this alive, I'll consider it a win," Jarred said. "We'll worry about 'stuff' later."

He kept going past the bedroom curtain and down the corridor, glancing over his shoulder occasionally to make sure the rest of the group was with him.

Myra and Lana were directly behind him. Myra still had the bow in the crook of her right arm, a quiver of arrows over her shoulder. It was a strange sight, this grandmotherly figure with her white hair clutching a weapon more than half as tall as her. Hope was running behind them. Larry and Zane brought up the rear, half-turned so they could keep an eye on their retreat. Zane still had a hateful glint in his eye. The kid was raring for another fight.

Just before turning a corner, Jarred spotted another figure farther back. He thought it was one of the Dweller kids, a scrawny little thing lurking well behind the group. Samara. Was she following them? Surely not. He lost sight of her as he moved past the workrooms and headed into the darkness.

"Stick together," Jarred said. "I think I can find the way. Anyone have a flashlight?"

"I do," Hope replied.

There was a click as she turned on a small flashlight and aimed it ahead of them. Jarred beckoned her, and she squeezed past Lana and Myra. They were moving into the forbidden passageways now, and he saw the arrows of various colors carved into the walls.

"Hope, what's your favorite color again?" he asked.

"Blue," she replied.

"That's right, and we're following the blue arrows. We have to get somewhere safe, somewhere where these people don't have a bunch of murder holes to fire on us."

He followed the blue arrows along many twists and turns, slowing down occasionally to let the rest of the group catch up. Myra, in particular, was struggling. Jarred might have offered to carry her if he wasn't already in so much pain himself.

Brigid knows these halls like the back of her hand, he thought. *She can follow us wherever we go. We'll never get away from here like this.*

A troubling thought. All he could do was keep going and hope she wasn't vengeful enough to keep pursuing them. The blue arrows seemed to follow no discernible pattern, taking strange turns, sometimes ascending, other times descending. Jarred couldn't quite tell if this way was familiar or not. It all looked the same.

"Where are we going?" Lana asked. "Where does this lead?"

"Away," Jarred replied. "For now, that'll have to do."

But then he picked up a familiar pungent smell. Bat guano. Lots of it, and it was getting stronger as they moved forward. Finally, they stepped through a narrow opening and found themselves in a room that was familiar to Jarred. A high domed ceiling covered in bats like a living tapestry, a large wedge-shaped climbing wall covered in holes and cracks that had a deep pit in front of it.

He took a few steps forward and came to a stop facing the climbing wall. As the others entered the room, they gathered around him.

"What is this place?" Larry asked. "It appears to be a dead end."

"This, my friends, is the trial," Jarred replied. "God's Belfry. Believe it or not, the god of the Dwellers really likes for people to climb that wall there and manhandle the bats."

"So that's the trial they made such a big deal about?" Myra said, before having a small coughing fit.

"That's it," Jarred said. He took a few more steps forward. "There are some large openings in the wall leading to a series of tunnels. They'd make a good place to hide for the time being. A safe place."

"So we're just going to hide in some tunnels," Zane said. "That doesn't solve anything. It just delays the inevitable. I say we fight them head-on."

"I don't want anyone else to get killed," Jarred said. "We'll be safe from arrows in the tunnels. The Dwellers will look for us for a while, but eventually, they'll have to go back to their living spaces. Once this part of the cave is safe again, we can send someone to scout for an exit. It's not ideal, but it's the only solution I've got."

"If this is what we're doing, then let's do it," Larry said.

Hope raised her flashlight beam, shining it along the ceiling. The brightness of the LEDs disturbed some of the bats, and they took flight, some circling the room, others diving into the cracks in the wall. Jarred approached the wall, beckoning the others to follow. He could still trace the path he'd taken when passing the trial. The large tunnel he'd climbed into was visible, but how was he going to get all of these people up there?

"That's where we're headed," he said, pointing at a dark spot about twelve feet up on the right side of the climbing wall. "The question is, how can we get everyone up the wall? It's not the easiest climb in the world."

"I don't think I can make it," Myra said, suppressing another coughing fit. "Leave me down here, and I'll cover the door with the bow and arrow."

"I'll get you up there," Larry said. "Just climb on my back. I think I can bear your weight."

Jarred walked to the far-right side of the climbing wall, where they had easiest access. As he gazed up at their destination, he had a strong moment of doubt. Maybe Zane was right. Maybe a straight-on fight was the better option.

No, the climb is dangerous, but a fight is even more dangerous, he told himself. *You were about two inches from getting an arrow in the face back there.*

Myra set the bow down and hopped up on Larry's back, wrapping her arms around his neck and hooking her feet around his thighs. Then he began the ascent, picking his way carefully. Jarred called out the best handholds and footholds as he went.

"Mom, I'll go ahead of you," Zane said to Lana. "If you get into trouble, let me know, and I can help you."

Lana nodded, and Zane began his climb, following his father's path toward the tunnel opening. Hope kept the flashlight beam trained on the wall to give them as much light as possible. Zane stayed close to his mother, and they verbally coordinated their handholds as they went.

"Hope, can you make this climb?" Jarred asked.

"I think so," she replied with a shrug.

"You'll go right in front of me," he said. "Give me the flashlight. You'll need both hands."

He took the flashlight from her and trained it on the wall as she approached and pulled herself up. By now, Larry was almost to the tunnel, Myra clinging to his back and burying her face against his shoulder. He appeared to be struggling. Jarred's gaze went to the pit.

This was a rash decision, he thought. *Maybe we should have picked a different colored arrow to follow.*

Too late to back out now. As Hope started up the tunnel, Jarred set the flashlight between his teeth and followed her. This cast long shadows and made the climb a bit more challenging, and it also prevented him from pointing out the best handholds to Hope. His head was still pounding fiercely, and his recently healed leg still felt weak. He had to take it easy when using that leg.

As he gazed upward, he saw Larry pulling himself into the tunnel, Myra climbing off his back to squeeze in beside him. Lana wasn't far behind. At one point, the toe of her boot slipped off a ledge, and Zane reached over to grab her sleeve. Fortunately, she didn't fall.

Concentrate on your own climb, fool, he told himself. *You're not in the best condition right now.*

Right above him, Hope turned her head and looked behind her, as if something in the room had caught her attention. She cried out in alarm, pressing herself flat against the wall. Jarred had about a second to consider what this might mean before something slammed into him. It felt like he'd been punched hard in the side just beneath his ribs, but the blunt impact was soon followed by a sharp, burning pain.

The pain was so intense that his grip on the rocks immediately weakened, and he would have fallen then and there if not for the fact that both boots were planted firmly on a thin ledge. He glanced down and saw the shaft of an arrow protruding from his side just a couple of inches above his kidney.

"Dad! Dad!" Hope was shouting from above him, but the pain was growing. He couldn't tell how deep it was, but the intense heat radiated through his entire torso. His right boot slipped off then. Jarred tried to tighten his grip, but he couldn't quite manage it. The strength seemed to be leaving him fast.

His left hand let go then, sliding off the small rock to hang at his side. His right hand was wedged into a shallow pit, but his fingers were slipping. He could do nothing about it. His position on the climbing wall put him right at the edge of the pit, which meant if he fell, he had about a fifty-fifty chance of falling into the darkness.

Hope was still calling out to him, but he couldn't reply because the small flashlight was still clutched between his teeth. However, he sensed her moving. When he lifted his gaze, he saw Hope right above him. Somehow, she had turned herself almost horizontal on the wall. Her right hand was jammed deep into a crack, her left hand reaching down to him. She managed to grab his left hand, which strengthened his grip on the rock.

"Don't let go," she shouted. "I'll help you."

He looked back behind him, which pointed the flashlight back across the room toward the narrow entryway. He saw three figures standing there. In the center was Seb, the tall, gangly woman. She stood slightly turned, in a bowhunter's stance, with the bow in her right hand, and she was already pulling another arrow out of her quiver. Brigid stood to her left, her hands on her hips. Even from this distance, he could see the smug smile on her face. Alex stood on Seb's right side, arms crossed over his chest.

Jarred couldn't have been an easier target. He was spread out against the rock wall with a flashlight in his mouth, unable to move, already wounded, with no possible cover. If he let go, he would probably topple into the pit, maybe taking Hope with him.

"Hope, let go of me and keep climbing," he said. By speaking, he lost the flashlight, which fell and landed on the edge of the pit among some rocks. But this angled it upward, so that it shone toward the ceiling, illuminating most of the room.

"No, I won't let you fall," she cried.

He couldn't shake off her hand without dislodging both of them. He couldn't do much of anything. As he watched, Seb nocked her arrow and raised the bow.

Killed by a bunch of damned, delusional cultists, he thought bitterly. *What a miserable way to go.*

"Dad, I'm not going to leave you," Hope wailed, her voice echoing in the high-ceilinged room.

His gaze was fixed on Seb as she drew the bowstring. Alex and Brigid were both grinning. From somewhere above him, he heard the others shouting, pleading for his life. All futile.

"I love you, kiddo," he said to Hope, as she wailed in despair.

He watched as Seb took careful aim, Brigid nodding her approval.

A fourth figure lunged out of the darkness then, stepping from the beyond the doorway. She had a small object raised above her head, and as she ran at Seb, she brought it down.

Jarred caught a glimpse of what appeared to be a hatchet before the attacker buried it in the back of Seb's head. A dull *thunk* carried all the way across the room, followed quickly by a brief startled cry from Seb as she fell forward. The Dweller lost her hold on the bowstring as she fell, and the arrow was fired low, sailing right into the pit and disappearing below. Then Seb hit the ground face first, blood spattering the rocks in front of her.

Confused, Jarred looked up into the face of the attacker, and the sudden shock almost made him let go. Fortunately, Hope was still clamped down tightly on his hand. Fiona. Smeared with mud and grime, her hair in wild disarray, she was almost unrecognizable, but he knew that face too well. It was Fiona.

She's alive, he thought. *My God, somehow, she's alive!*

She still had the hatchet in her hand, only now it was shiny with blood. Alex and Brigid turned to face her, and of all things, Fiona grinned at them. The Dwellers tried to circle around her, as if to attack from both sides, but then Smoke came racing out of the dark. Barking madly, he leapt at Alex. Caught between an attacking dog and a madwoman with a bloody hatchet, Alex froze, as if he couldn't decide which was the bigger threat. Then, mid-leap, Smoke bit down on his forearm, twisting Alex around and dragging him to the ground.

Fiona didn't hesitate a second. As soon as Alex was down, she dropped to one knee and brought the hatchet down, driving it deep, deep into the side of his head. Despite his almost breathless elation at her sudden appearance, Jarred had to shut his eyes at the moment of impact. He heard Alex make a brief huffing sound, and when Jarred opened his eyes, the man was already dying.

Brigid took a step back, raising both of her hands.

"You tried to kill me, but you failed," Fiona said. The blade of the hatchet was still buried deep in Alex's skull. Smoke took his place at Fiona's side, growling at Brigid. "You failed, Brigid. It seems I found favor with God. I found favor down in the deep darkness. What do you think about that?"

Brigid stood there a moment longer. Then she turned suddenly, wailed, and dashed across the room. Smoke barked, but he didn't leave Fiona's side. As for Fiona, she was struggling to get the hatchet free. It was a gruesome scene as she worked it back and forth, and Jarred's stomach lurched.

"She's coming after us," Hope said.

Brigid ran for the left side of the climbing wall. Instead of skipping the pit or trying to come from the far edge, she leapt over the gap and hit the wall. Her hands and feet seemed to find familiar places and latched on tightly, catching her. It was an impressive display. Jarred heard gasps from higher up the wall as the others reacted to this.

No wonder she passed the trials, Jarred thought. *She's amazing.*

Brigid began nimbly climbing the wall, moving fast, never pausing to consider her next move, as if she knew this wall like the back of her own hand. Like she'd climbed it a thousand times. The flashlight beam shining straight up was rousing more and more of the bats now, and they began to fly back and forth along the wall. A few of them swooped so close to Jarred that he felt the air against his skin from their flapping wings.

"Dad, she's coming this way," Hope said.

Indeed, Brigid was not climbing straight up. Instead, she was moving at a low angle out over the pit, a path that would take her directly to Jarred. Her fear had turned to anger, and she bared her teeth at him as she quickly closed in.

This vindictive old hag, he thought.

"Hope, keep climbing," he said. "Get away from her."

"If I do that, she'll throw you off the wall," Hope replied.

"If you don't, she'll throw us both off the wall!"

He looked up at the others. Larry, Lana, Zane, and Myra were all wedged into the tunnel now, watching helplessly. Even if Myra had had the bow, there was simply no way she could have fired it from that cramped space. Jarred looked toward Fiona, but she had just now managed to get the hatchet free. Brigid was coming toward him fast.

"You had favor, Jarred, and you threw it away," Brigid said, practically growling at him.

"Seems like Fiona had the most favor," Jarred replied. "You killed her, but there she is. Maybe she rose from the dead. If that's so then it might be time for you to reconsider your theology."

"How dare you blaspheme," Brigid snarled. "After your betrayal, you have the gall to mock my faith? You'll die for it!"

She was within reach now. A bat buzzed by her face, and she smacked it with her hand. The poor animal went spinning down into the pit below. She grabbed for Jarred next, trying to get hold of the arrow protruding from his side. He twisted away from her as best he could, but the pain was so intense, it made him swoon for a second.

"You're going down into the pit, I swear it," Brigid said. "And you won't be rising from the dead. Not you!"

Another bat passed so close to Jarred's face that he felt it brush against his cheek. He flinched, and the bat changed course slightly, heading right at Brigid. She swiped at it, but as she did, Jarred dared to take his left foot off the ledge. He kicked at her. Brigid leaned to one side to avoid the kick, but another bat came sailing out of a crack in the wall near her face just then.

To avoid it, she leaned back, and for one precarious moment, both hands were flailing in the air. Only the toes of her shoes remained stuck to the wall, both planted on small protruding rocks. Then a fourth bat dove down from above, passing right between Brigid and the wall. Brigid flinched, and it was just a little too much. She began to pivot away from the wall, spinning her arms wildly.

"No, no, not like this," she whimpered. Her face was twisted in shock, horrified at this betrayal by the bats. "I found favor! I passed the trial! I kept the faith!"

But her weight and momentum took her backward, and she fell from the rock wall, screaming all the way down. She disappeared into the dark pit, but a moment later, Jarred heard the deep thud of her body hitting some solid surface below. It put an end to her screaming for all time.

109

The adrenaline was wearing off now, and Fiona felt the horror of the whole situation washing over her. In her right hand, she clutched the smooth handle of her old hatchet, the head of which was soaked in gore and dripping onto the rock floor. Seb and Alex were both dead at her feet, pools of blood spreading fast around them, the blood following the gradual slope of the room toward the pit. She'd never thought herself capable of such violence, and despite the justice of it, she didn't like the way it made her feel. Had it been necessary? Yes, she had almost certainly saved Jarred's life, maybe Hope's as well. Nevertheless, she felt a deep, skin-crawling unease as she stepped past the bodies and approached the climbing wall.

The echo of Brigid's death scream lingered in the room as Fiona approached the right edge of the rock wall. Jarred was just barely hanging on, and Hope was poised above him, almost sideways as she clung to the rocks. Fiona dumped the hatchet on the ground. The clattering sound was sharp and annoying. Then she stepped up to the bottom of the wall.

"Okay, we have to get you all down from there safely," she said. Her right hand was bloody. She felt it sticking between her fingers.

Jarred looked down at her, pain in his eyes. "I guess I have to try," he said in a breathless voice. "Fiona, how in the world are you alive? Brigid said they killed you."

"I told you," she replied. "I found favor. Turns out, God didn't like these people." Her own sarcasm made her chuckle, despite the lingering horror that still crawled all over her. "Seriously, though, I was kicked into a deep pit, but instead of falling all the way to the bottom, I landed on a tiny ledge and survived. If Seb had kicked just a little harder, I'd be dead. What are the odds? Now, climb down. You're less than ten feet up. Take it slow and easy. I'll catch you if you fall."

Hope dared to release her hold on his hand, and he began to slowly, very slowly and cautiously, pick his way down the wall. When he was still a few feet off the ground, he finally lost his grip. Fiona thrust her arms out, and he fell into them. Jarred's weight immediately shoved Fiona backward, and she sat down hard on the rock floor. Jarred landed on his side on her lap, crying out in pain.

"I've got you," Fiona said, pulling herself out from under him. "Hang in there, Jarred. You made it down."

Her ribs still ached fiercely, and she'd ripped one of the stitches on her arm. These things hardly mattered to her at the moment. She crawled around in front of Jarred and pulled the hem of his shirt up to inspect the wound. The arrow wasn't deep. It looked like maybe it had impacted his bottom rib. Blood was already oozing out of the wound, so she didn't dare try to remove the arrow.

Jarred raised a trembling hand and beckoned her closer. Fiona leaned in closely, and he looked up at her with pain-filled eyes.

"I thought I'd lost you," he said weakly. "It was such a horrible feeling."

He moved toward her. She didn't realize what was going to happen, but somehow instinct took over. Fiona leaned down and met his lips. It was a lingering kiss, warm and gentle. Broken only when another shudder of pain forced him away.

"Why did you try to leave me?" he asked.

Even as she replied, Fiona pulled a handkerchief out of her pocket and used it to staunch the blood from his wound. "I thought you and the others might be better without me."

"How in the world could you think such a thing?" he replied.

She pressed the handkerchief against the wound, but moving the arrow even a tiny bit made him groan in pain. "I got into a bad headspace. Somehow, failing the trial twice triggered it. I started thinking that everything bad that's happened since we met was my fault, Jarred. If I think about it too much, it does seem like my decisions are consistently bad."

Jarred reached up again and grabbed her wrist. "But that's simply not true. You helped Hope and me when we first crossed paths. I'm able to walk on my leg again because of your care. You helped me get Hope back from Benjy when she ran away. You got almost everyone to Snowbird Caverns when we had plenty of opportunities to die out there in the storm. Without you, we'd all be casualties of the cold by now. Don't you realize that? We're a stronger, happier family with you in the lead."

"Well, if you put it that way…" Tears blurred her vision, but she was aware of people gathering around her. Hope, then Zane, then Larry and Myra, then Lana.

"He's right, of course," Larry said. "We started looking to you as a leader for good reason, Fiona, because whether you realize it or not, you're a natural at it. It seems right, and we'd like to keep it that way."

"It's the way things are supposed to be," Myra said, though she seemed out of breath and clearly struggling. "We discuss problems together, you listen to our input, and then you make the final decision. That's how it's been since we moved into your homestead, and it has gotten us through some awful situations. We lost Duke in the river, but I could have lost him many times before that if not for your help and hospitality. Give yourself some credit, Fiona."

Fiona wiped her eyes on her sleeves, but she could tell this smeared blood on her cheeks. "Okay, I get it. I'm sorry. I just lost my way down here in the darkness. All these shadows got into my mind somehow. Trust me, I'll never try to leave you guys again."

She caught movement across the room. Glancing up, she spotted two figures at the edge of the shadows beyond the doorway. They were small, teens or children, one skinny and frail, the other stockier. She knew them, of course, but they seemed reluctant to enter the room.

"Samara and Vanya," Hope said. "What do we do about them? What do we do about the kids?"

"We just killed all of their caretakers," Lana noted. "My God, how awful for these little ones. None of this is their fault."

Fiona knew the answer. She rubbed her eyes and said, "We'll have to become their caretakers now. We can't leave them down here alone. But first, we have to tend to Jarred. He's hurt badly. Come on."

She gestured at the group, and they began to move at her signal.

110

The snow on this side of the hill was practically untouched, except for rare animals tracks in a few places. No humans had come this way in a long time, so the snow that blanketed the land in every direction was pristine, shiny in the early morning sunlight. Tree branches sagged against the weight of the snow, though the snowfall had ceased for the time being. Above the landscape, a few breaks in the clouds created spots of stunning blue against the slate-gray that had dominated the last few months.

If one had looked carefully near the base of the hill, a slight depression in the smooth blanket of snow might have given indication of the old gravel path that lay deep below the blanket of snow. It cut across a glittering field, wound through the trees, and approached a low place on the hill. Here, it came to an abrupt end.

It had sat like this for months, the memory of a path leading to nothing. If there had ever been human tracks in the snow, they'd long since disappeared. A few rocks were visible at the end of the path, poking out of the snow on the steep side of the hill. And on that particular morning, one of these rocks began to move, as if it had a will of its own.

First, it wobbled, then it tipped outward, and finally it rolled down the side of the hill. Other rocks followed it, crumbling away from the hill and heading for the shallow path below, as if making a break for it. This trickle of rocks became a sudden cascade, as a section of the hill broke loose, revealed itself to be all rocks and ice, and tumbled away.

Now, a large opening into the heart of the hill itself was revealed. A hand and arm thrust out of the hole, a hatchet clutched tightly in fingers that were still smeared with dried blood. When the arm drew back, a woman appeared in the opening, her breath puffing out before her. She had shoulder-length auburn hair that was damp and muddy, hazel eyes, and a freckled face. Her coat was unzipped, revealing a denim shirt that was absolutely filthy with mud, guano, and blood. When she stepped outside, she made an imposing figure. If anyone had been there to see her leave the cave, they almost surely would have drawn back in disquiet.

A dog leapt past her then, dancing in the deep snow. A black-and-white Australian cattle dog, he seemed overjoyed to be outside, despite the cold and the snow, and he bounded this way and that, barking at nothing in particular.

The woman lowered her hand, the darkly stained hatchet still clutched in her fist. Other people appeared in the opening behind her then. A tall, gaunt man with a ragged mustache and beard appeared. He was clasping the hand of a woman in a long red coat. Behind them, a boy of about seventeen followed, squinting at the sunlight. By their proximity to each other, it was obvious that these three were family. They moved up beside the woman, gazing out across the silver-white landscape at the rising sun.

Next, a girl appeared in the opening. A teenager with brown eyes, frizzy hair that had gone wild with the cave dampness, and prominent cheekbones. There were other figures behind her, smaller shapes, but they lingered in the shadows inside the cave.

"It doesn't look as uninviting as I recall," the man with the ragged mustache said. "Hurts my eyes to stare at all of the shiny snow, though. We'll need to make some snow goggles if we're going to be out here much."

"It's colder than I remember," the woman beside him said. "Seems sort of lifeless out here. At least the snow's not falling."

"The cloud cover is broken," the woman with the hatchet said. "No snow falling. It hasn't been this calm since the storm began. It's a lot easier to appreciate the beauty when you're not struggling to stay alive."

"What do we do now?" It was the teen girl standing in the cave opening. She sounded exhausted, and she reached out to touch the cave wall beside her. "Is the snowstorm over?"

The woman with the hatchet turned slowly to face the girl. She tucked the handle of the hatchet under her belt. "I don't know if the storm is over. It's at least taking a short break. As for what we do now…we live, Hope. We live."

111

Jarred and Fiona had done most of the work of shaping and building the new cave entrance. From a crude opening hacked into the rocks, it had been transformed into a sturdy door, hinges set deep into the rocks. Thick deadbolts on the inside kept it locked except when the cave dwellers chose to go outside for hunting, fresh air, or other activities.

Just inside the opening, a well-lit and well-marked path led to new dwelling chambers nearby. Small openings had been carved into the ceiling of each room, giving access to plenty of natural light. The Dwellers here had no interest in lurking in the candlelit shadows. They did not worship deities who lived in deep, dark places.

From the doorway, the first chamber was a broad open room filled with goats and chickens. The animals had plenty of space to move around, sunlight from above, and generous troughs for food and water. They were from the large store of grains left by the Dwellers. The chickens lived in a large wooden coop at the back. Each day, one of the Dwellers took the goats outside for exercise and fresh air.

The next room was a large workspace, with numerous benches, tables, shelves, and boxes holding raw materials. Most of the equipment had been relocated from Dweller chambers deeper in the cave. At the moment, Fiona

Scarborough was using her hatchet to chop wood for the many fireplaces which had been installed in the dwelling places. Nearby, Jarred White sat at a table with his toolbox, creating a simple brass hinge for another door.

"It's going to look like an actual house in here when we're done," he said.

"That's the idea," Fiona replied, mopping her forehead with a handkerchief. "By the time we're done, this cave will be more comfortable than any place we lived in before the ice age began. Even my homestead. You just wait and see!"

"After I get all of the doors installed," Jarred said, "I think my next project will be building some actual beds, with frames and mattresses and everything." He winced a bit as he worked. The wound in his side still hurt.

Fiona set her hatchet down and came toward him. "One of these days, we'll have actual plumbing, too. Hope sketched some ideas for how we could make it work."

"Of course she did," Jarred said. He set the hinge down and looked up at her. "I'm sure she'll eventually figure out how to generate electricity, too. I never thought life could be so good living in a cave. The Neanderthals never had it so good."

Fiona bent down and kissed him, grabbed his hand, and kissed that, too.

Across the hall, a small garden grew in a room that got the most sunlight. The Dwellers had kept some gardens near the surface and had a few bags of soil in storage. All of this had been relocated to the new garden, which was brighter and got better air. The new cave dwellers had laid the soil down in deep rock-lined beds along a row of neatly shaped light-holes. It was a setup that could last them at least a couple of seasons before they would have to venture out and find more soil and supplies.

At the moment, an older woman with white hair was tending a patch of potatoes. Myra's cough was much better these days, though she was still stooped and frail. Working in the garden was perfect for her. Not too strenuous.

As she cleared some weeds, she heard Smoke racing down the corridor outside. Soon he passed by, chased by the younger children. It hadn't been easy for the new children to adjust to this way of life, but they were doing well now, judging by their squeals of excitement. As they ran with Smoke to the deeper rooms, they passed the older kids' classroom, where Zane, Hope, Samara, and Vanya were currently seated in comfortable chairs as Larry taught them algebra. Lana sat at a desk in the back, waiting her turn to teach world history.

The four teens were practically inseparable these days, and they made good students. Of course, Samara and Vanya had grieved. Indeed, they still grieved, but those moments of grief were becoming few and far between. They'd discovered a world without death pits and deities in the darkness, and they'd taken to it well. They were also quite a bit behind in their education, but Hope and Zane were patient as the adults tried to help them catch up.

"Okay, next we're going to talk about quadratic equations," Larry said, "and I think Hope is going to help me explain them. Come on up here, Hope."

What each of these cave dwellers, old and new, didn't realize was how often they individually had the same thought. It was a singular thought, and it came to each of them many times throughout the day, unbidden, sometimes unexpected, always the same:

I'm finally home.

END OF ENDLESS WINTER

PS: Do you love post-apocalyptic disaster fiction? Then keep reading for exclusive extracts from *Escaping Anarchy* and *Endless Storm.*

THANK YOU!

Loved this book? Share it with a friend!

To be notified of the next book release please sign up for Riley's mailing list, at
www.gracehamiltonbooks.com/riley-miller-sign-up

Get prepared and sign-up to Grace's mailing list
to be notified of my next release at www.GraceHamiltonBooks.com.

ABOUT RILEY

Riley Miller lives in Alaska, so you might understand why she dreams of natural disasters whilst living on the edge of the world. In fact, she thinks it is her upbringing in Alaska that has really shaped who she is. Overly aware of our inextricable connection to the environment, she felt she should always be ready for the inevitable shift. This was something instilled in her by her parents, who taught her how to live off the land, and she particularly loved learning about plants and their medicinal qualities. She, in turn, passed on these lessons to her own children, along with some light prepping for any potential disasters like the snow storms that frequent their state.

The Covid crisis really opened her eyes to the true possibility of a massive crisis hitting home, and it sparked her creative imagination. She wanted to explore further how different people react in crises and she found that writing allowed her to do this. Inspired by some of her favourite authors like Grace Hamilton, Stephen King, and Kyla Stone, Riley uses her Alaskan upbringing along with her personal prepper knowledge to dive headfirst into a disaster story and figure out how to survive.

It's not all about survival for Riley though! She also loves to cook and do crafts like sewing and quilting. She spends her weekends gardening with her husband and enjoys reading and the occasional binge watching of a great new series. She's especially excited about her soon-to-be role as Grandmother.

ABOUT GRACE HAMILTON

Grace Hamilton is the prepper pen-name for a bad-ass, survivalist momma-bear of four kids, and wife to a wonderful husband. After being stuck in a mountain cabin for six days following a flash flood, she decided she never wanted to feel so powerless or have to send her kids to bed hungry again. Now she lives the prepper lifestyle and knows that if SHTF or TEOTWAWKI happens, she'll be ready to help protect and provide for her family.

Combine this survivalist mentality with a vivid imagination (as well as a slightly unhealthy day dreaming habit) and you get a prepper fiction author. Grace spends her days thinking about the worst possible survival situations that a person could be thrown into, then throwing her characters into these nightmares while trying to figure out "What SHOULD you do in this situation?"

You will find Grace on:

BLURB

They're trapped inside a prison when the power goes out...

Molly is determined to get the troubled teens she teaches back on the right path and is convinced a trip to a local prison will show them the consequences of bad behavior. But when an EMP blast knocks out all power across the country, Molly and her five students, along with their former-Marine bus driver, Colton, are locked in with the prisoners with no safe exit.

The guards are little help against clever convicts, and when a riot throws everything into chaos, Molly and Colton must find a way to get to freedom with their charges, even if it means trusting a prisoner who is using them for his own gains.

Prisoners aren't the only danger in the suddenly powerless world. Escaping the prison may be more dangerous than staying inside as it becomes clear to everyone that the power isn't coming back, and society is about to crumble.

Get your copy of *Escaping Anarchy*
Available February 9, 2022
www.GraceHamiltonBooks.com

EXCERPT

Chapter One

MOLLY

Molly O'Neil swept a flyaway strand of strawberry-blonde hair from her face and stifled a yawn. She'd been up since before sunrise and was already flagging. Behind her, the busload of school kids she was in charge of for the day was becoming restless, but she couldn't bring herself to confront them. Not yet.

"How much longer?" She bent forward and put her hand on the back of the bus driver's seat.

Colton shrugged his thick shoulders at her and pointed to the ugly red line on the satnav that indicated heavy traffic. "Who knows?" he replied, drumming his large fingers impatiently on the steering wheel. "Could be an hour or more."

Molly looked at her watch and sighed. It was unseasonably warm, and the musty smell of the school bus was making her feel a little car sick. Taking a long sip from the flask of lukewarm coffee she was holding, she wondered

—not for the first time that day—why she, as an English teacher, had been roped into this.

The school's annual "Scared Straight" trip was usually handled by their brash and bulky gym teacher, Mr. Jones. However, this year, the principal had wanted to switch things up. She'd volunteered, not actually expecting to be picked. Now here she was, stuck on the highway on the way to Fairfield Prison with five disgruntled teenagers. The only saving grace was that they weren't all *bad* kids.

"You'd better give them a call," Colton said loudly, breaking her concentration. "We're gonna be late."

Putting down her coffee, Molly bit back a sigh, then started to scroll through her phone; she knew she had the number somewhere. Probably hidden in her emails along with the permission forms and risk assessment she'd had to organize.

She found it, and was about to dial the number, when she stopped and strained her ears. Through the dull chatter toward the back of the bus, she could hear the unmistakable flick of a lighter. She bit her lower lip. What if she pretended she hadn't heard it? What if she just hunkered down at the front of the bus, stared out of the window at the slow-moving landscape, and imagined the scrawny trees at the side of the highway were actually a vast and glorious forest that she could escape to? A place where she could hide herself away and not have to deal with any of this anymore.

Flick. Flick. Flick.

Molly placed her palm on the armrest and steadied herself as she stood up. Slipping her phone into her jeans pocket, she cast her eyes over each seat in turn until she came to the obvious culprit: Lucky.

"Hand it over."

Lucky had been so busy staring at his phone that he didn't notice Molly standing over him until she spoke. "The phone?" he said, slipping his phone-free hand down into the space between his hip and the side of the bus.

"The lighter." Molly held out her hand and wriggled her fingers. "Now, please, Lucky."

For a moment, she thought that Lucky might protest. But he was only fourteen, younger than the others, and essentially a decent kid. So, after looking around to see whether the others were watching, he did as he was told. "I wasn't going to do anything," he said. "And I don't think you've got a right to take my personal property from me."

Trying not to smile at the fake bravado, Molly folded her arms. "Well, you haven't exactly got a good track record, have you?" she said, even though she knew that she shouldn't really be getting into it with him.

Rolling his eyes, Lucky leaned a gangly arm on the rim of the window and waved his hand at her. "It was an accident," he said. "How come no one believes me?"

From the back of the bus, Jenna, who had been in more fist fights than Molly cared to count, shouted, "Because you're a pyro freak, that's why!"

Ignoring her, Molly put the lighter into her pocket and said, "Whether it was an accident or not, you set fire to your uncle's barn. You're on this trip for a reason. Plus, you and I both know that if you're caught in possession of a lighter, you'll be in a whole world of trouble—*especially* if you're caught trying to take a lighter into a prison. So, consider me confiscating this a little taste of what it's like in jail. No luxuries. No control. Someone else deciding what you can and can't do—"

"All right," Lucky whined. "Can we wait till we get there before starting the lectures?"

Molly opened her mouth to reply but thought better of it; she'd been teaching long enough to know that the worst possible thing you could do was allow yourself to be sucked into an argument. Especially if you were trapped in an airless bus on the longest school trip in history.

"If you want it back, you can collect it from the principal's office at the end of the day." Ignoring Lucky's grumbles, she continued her walk down the bus; now that she was up, she might as well check on the others.

At the back, the Banks twins, Erik and Scarlett, were leaning into the aisle and bickering with Jenna. *Seriously?* Molly muttered, *There's only five of them—how can they be this much hard work?*

"Right," she said, positioning herself between the twins and Jenna. "What's going on with you three?"

"Nothing," Scarlett replied, narrowing her eyes at Jenna, and sinking back into her seat to look at her phone.

"Yeah," Erik agreed. "Nothing."

Molly looked from Jenna to the twins, then shook her head. "Okay, well, keep it down. Mr. King is trying to concentrate up there." She had turned and started to head back to her seat, when she unmistakably heard Erik mutter loudly to his sister, "No wonder she gets in so many fights—she's got arms like a freakin' dude."

Scarlett sniggered loudly. There was a millisecond of silence before Jenna yelled, "Yeah, so what if I have!"

Molly spun around, waving her hands calmly in front of her, ready to de-escalate the situation, but Jenna had clearly had enough of Erik's jibes and, ignoring Molly completely, she lunged for him. Erik had already started to scrabble backwards, almost right into his sister's lap, but Molly dashed forward and positioned herself in front of him. Placing her hands on Jenna's shoulders, she met her eyes. Jenna was breathing quickly, her eyes were wide and furious, and her cheeks were flushed.

"It's not worth it," Molly said, willing Jenna to listen to her. "Really, it's not."

Jenna was trembling, but she'd been in too many fights. One more, and she'd be kicked out of school and sent straight to Juvie.

"Jenna—it's not worth it," Molly repeated. Slowly, she saw Jenna's shoulders drop. "Good. Right. Now why don't you go sit up front?"

Jenna nodded. Molly let out a long slow breath as she watched her release her clenched fists, pick up her backpack and move several seats away from Scarlett and Erik. Jenna could easily have taken Erik; he was mouthy when he was with his sister, but he was skinny too, and had never so much as thrown a punch as far as Molly knew. Thank God she'd managed to calm Jenna down and hadn't had to return the kids to their parents with black eyes and bloodied noses. Although, at least if she had, it might have assured she was never selected to chaperone a trip like this again in the future.

Sitting down opposite the twins, in the seat Jenna had just vacated, Molly leaned forward and put her hands on her knees. "Come on, you two. You need to behave and not instigate anything. Out of everyone, I thought the two of you were the ones who probably didn't deserve to be here. Maybe I was wrong."

Scarlett wasn't looking at her; she was buried in her phone. But Erik looked sheepish and almost apologetic as he said, "Yeah. Whatever."

"Well, not 'whatever', Erik—"

Ahead, Colton swore under his breath and it caused Molly to look up. Standing up and stepping away from the twins, she saw that he was shaking his head and gesticulating at something out of the window.

"What the hell is this?" he said loudly.

Molly dipped her head and narrowed her eyes. Ahead, a couple of yards away, the road sign which had—a few seconds ago—announced a detour due to a traffic accident, was flickering. It continued to flicker. The orange lights flashed on and off and on again. Then they disappeared completely. Molly frowned.

At the front of the bus, Lucky let out a clap of laughter. Jenna was sniggering too.

"What the..." Colton turned to look at Molly and she felt her cheeks begin to flush, because the sign now read: SHEEPLE MAKE GOOD VENISON. It was accompanied by a crude drawing of what she could only assume was supposed to depict cannibalism. And Molly knew exactly who was responsible.

"Scarlett...." She whirled around and snatched the girl's phone from her hands.

"Hey!" Scarlett and Erik yelled at the same time.

Molly didn't give in. She put her hands on her hips and shook her head. "You're on this trip because of exactly this kind of behavior."

Scarlett opened her mouth to speak but Molly interrupted her.

"And don't even bother trying to tell me it wasn't you. Change it back." She handed Scarlett her phone. "Now."

Get your copy of *Escaping Anarchy*
Available February 9, 2022
www.GraceHamiltonBooks.com

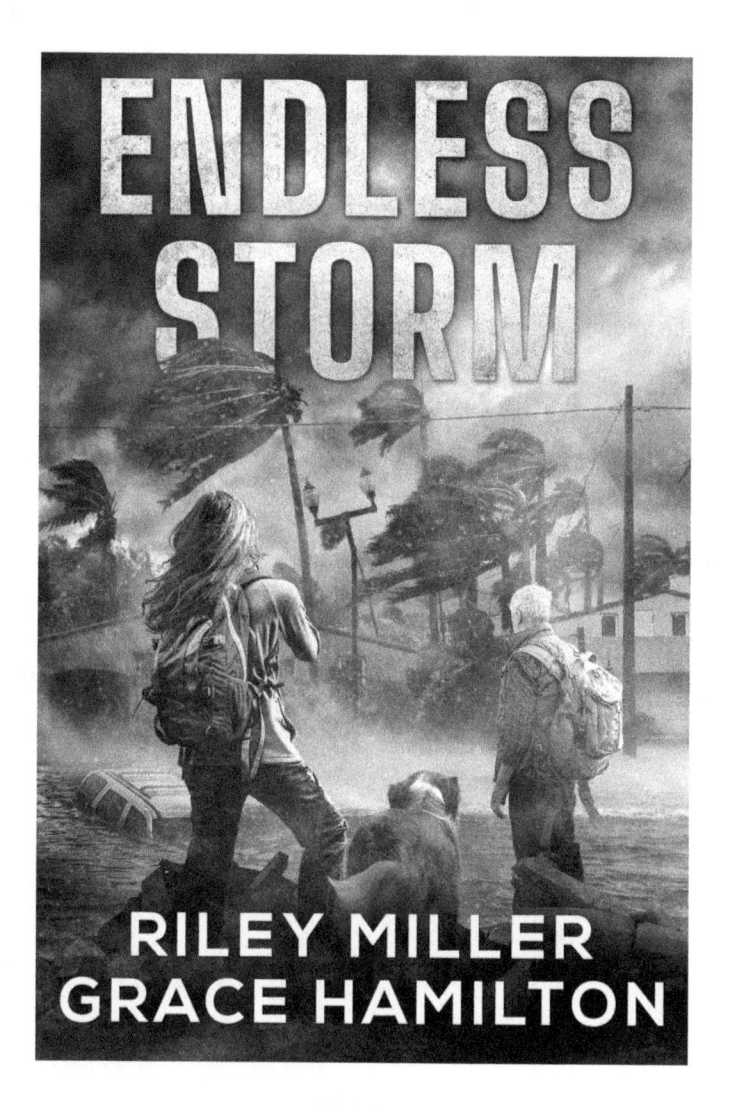

BLURB

A storm like no other plunges the world into chaos…

When an egotistical billionaire's plan to solve climate change goes horribly wrong, it unleashes a catastrophe with devastating consequences. Waters are rising. People are dying. Widowed librarian, Kelly Walker, is determined to escape from Florida with her family before the flood waters rise and life as she knows it disappears.

But when disaster strikes, Kelly's son, Jackson, is missing. She'll do anything to find him. But as brutal winds and power failures accompany the floodwaters, she fears she may already be too late.

Her landscaper brother-in-law, Eddie, must also brave the maelstrom to find his daughter—promising to meet back up with Kelly at a bug-out location. But the rising water is not the only danger. Vicious gangs revel in the chaos, ready to take advantage of anyone unfortunate enough to cross their path.

Kelly's dreams of a haven high up at her parents' retired service dog sanctuary in the Smoky Mountains are dashed, as a deadly plague sweeps the world. And she quickly realizes that their ordeal is only just beginning. A new storm is coming.

Can the two of them reunite their family, as the world descends into madness?

Grab your copy of *Endless Storm* from www.GraceHamiltonBooks.com